Alex Ever Crest Collection Two

<u>Books and Stories by Ron Mueller</u>
<u>Fiction Series</u>
The Alex Evercrest Series
> The River Front
> The Girl on The Grill
> Missing
> Maggot
> Racist
> Votive Candles
> Windy City
> Country Road
> Pool of Blood
> Sins of the Daughter
> Body Parts
> The Skull Collector
> The Vanishing
> The Shadow Fighter
> Moonshine
> Grief's Trajectory
> The Magic Touch
> Nine Towers of Ku
> Abandoned
> Northern Lights
> New Direction
> A Family Affair
> Disruption
> The Saint Lebuinnus Church Murder
> Evercrest Collection One
> Evercrest Collection Two

<u>The Taelo Series</u>
Taelo: The Early Years
Taelo: The Golden Feather
Taelo: Journey of Discovery
Taelo: Dangerous Passage
Taelo: Condor Clan Slingers
Taelo: Circumvention
Taelo: The Journey of Sages
Taelo: Future Leaders Journey
Taelo: Collection

<u>A Taelo Story</u>
White Swan and Quiet Pheasant
The Child's Name
Floating Cloud
Quiet Rabbit
Busy Bee
Little Otter & Talking Wren
Broken Spear
Burley Bear & Meadow Flower

Science Fiction

The Savitar Series:
Journey's End
Savitar
Confluence
The Savitar Collection

Bram Nielson Series
The Fold
The Message
Fold Wormhole
Negative Fold
Ripples in Time
The Nielson Collection

Single Science Fiction Books

Current Past and Future
The Event
The Door
Viajante 7

A Brian Oneil Novel
Hawaiian Phoenix
Moon Curser
Death Broker
Brian O'Neil Collection

The Problem Solver Series
Solutions
Drug Lords
Border Crosser
The Problem Solver Collection

Imagination by Courtney Huynh and Chloe Parker

Ron Mueller

Alex Evercrest Collection Two
By: *Ron Mueller*

Around the World Publishing LLC
Cincinnati, Ohio

This story is a work of fiction. Names, characters, places, and incidents either are products of the author's imagination or are used fictitiously. Any resemblance to actual events or locales or persons, living or dead, is entirely coincidental.

Alex Evercrest Collection Two ©

ISBN 13: 978-1-68223-956-8

Distributed by Ingram
Alex Evercrest Model By: Pi03@ShutterStock
Cover Picture by:
Cover by: Ron Mueller

Ron Mueller

Table of Content

Ron Mueller

Body Parts

1 Business Success

Reston stood in front of the almost live sized human poster of a man with his hands out to its sides. He was surrounded by similar posters of both genders. He was learning the details of the new human body parts business he had been instructed to establish by his bosses in Italy. The poster graphics were detailed and captioned for both the exterior and internal body parts. He felt like a medical student. He was not going to do any memorization, but he knew he would be referring to the posters as the body parts orders came in.

He was use to trafficking in a wide variety of drugs and had never imagined that he would be getting into the business of trafficking in human body parts.

The posters had what each body part was worth. The arrow pointing to the skin indicated that it was worth thirty thousand dollars. The scalp was worth one thousand dollars.

He walked around the room, and it became clear that one body was worth more than a half a million dollars if all the parts could be sold.

He wondered about the people that were willing to pay for the body parts. He knew that he would be making more than the half a million per body. The black market would be many times more.

He had been informed that the legitimate body parts market was a billion-dollar industry. He figured that the black market would be worth to one hundred times more if properly managed

Adding the body parts business to the distribution of drugs had been a path that Reston had not envisioned getting into. He was surprised to find that the company had selected Cincinnati to be the central point of both production, acquisition, and distribution. Many of the body parts were stolen from various legal body parts distributors. The rest would be collected from the appropriate local people.

The posters covered eyes, liver, heart, pancreas, stomach, a large and small intestines, penises, the list went on to cover almost every organ in the body.

He had spent a great deal of time in setting up his own body part production operation. He knew that many of the bodies that he would be asked for would need to be harvested from individuals that he would need to identify that had the right match to some person willing to put up the money to obtain the body part they needed. He knew that speed and maintaining a supply of the most desired parts would be important.

He had spent a fair amount of time designing the layout of his parts production, inventory holding room, and distribution supply chain.

His "factory" was located in a warehouse that had all the legal licensing and had passed the required warehouse inspections so that he had a five-year window before the next inspection. He of course had set it up as a regular warehouse and later added the special features that turned it into a human parts production center.

The interior construction had been done by a special group out of the New York area that were all partners of the mafia. They had come in and used the drawings he and a new York architect had made. The work was quickly done in a quiet low-key way.

His few permanent employees were trusted mafia members who had been recruited, trained, and then sent to him.

Recruiting the right person to do the dissecting of the bodies was not as difficult as he had expected. He had forged papers that he presented to the surgeon that he recruited. This surgeon had been on a list of a dozen potentials that had been identified from their participation in a conference on human body parts. The surgeon was a resident at one of the local hospitals and deep in debt.

He activated his various connections in all the major cities along the East Coast and soon he had a list asking for almost every human body part.

The body parts business was significantly more lucrative than the drug business and distribution was relatively easy since the drug business had an established distribution network.

He kept an eye on the books and soon realized that the money being taken in warranted an expansion.

He was always short of some organ or another. He looked at the back orders and knew that he would need to enlist another surgeon to harvest more parts.

He would also need to be more aggressive in getting the right "donors' on the dissection table.

He had his acquisition leader get more referring doctors enlisted. He was ready to throw the net more broadly so that he could fulfill the surging parts requests.

He spent many an hour watching the harvesting process through an observation window. He had designed a business office that had a window that allowed him to see the dissection table.

He also participated in the inventory inspections of the parts stored in the cold room. Many of the body parts could be held for days and still be used by someone needing it and willing to pay to get around the various waiting lists that prevented them from getting the parts legally.

Those parts that aged beyond their viable period were processed and disposed of in a furnace that operated only at night.

He was making a small fortune running the business.

His surgeon was making one as well.

Reston had set up an offshore account for this surgeon but kept himself on record as a co-account owner. This ensured that the doctor could be kept in check if the working relationship went south. He also tracked much of the doctor's personal life and contacts. He did not want the good doctor to stray from the agreement that had him spending about two hours a day harvesting body parts.

He was currently watching one of the harvesting sessions being performed on specifically ordered body. The good doctor had already removed the eyes. This was an organ that was always in demand somewhere in the country. He was currently carefully sawing the rib cage open so that the heart, liver, and other organs could be carefully removed.

A series of containers were ready to receive each of the organs as they were removed. The process was handled very efficiently, and a body could be harvested in the allotted two hours unless some unique part had been requested.

He always stopped watching when it came time to skin the remains and harvest the skin tissue, the scalp, and any miscellaneous organ. It was the only time he got grossed out.

The young man that was on the table had been identified, tracked, and then brought to the warehouse and kept in a cell. He had been killed just prior to the harvesting session. This was one step that the doctor did know about.

He wondered if the good doctor recognized how fresh most of the bodies he dissected happened to be.

A few weeks later Reston received word that a second surgeon had been recruited. He informed the good doctor that he would be training the second surgeon on the harvesting procedures.

That was when he first got the word that the good doctor wanted to quit. Reston reminded the good doctor that he had made a small fortune, and that quitting was not an option.

The good doctor made the mistake of arguing with the position he was taking and threatened to expose the operation if necessary.

Reston knew immediately that he needed to take drastic and dramatic action to put the doctor back into his place.

Reston had his bodyguard do a little checking and learned that the good doctor had entered into a relationship with a surgical nurse at the hospital where he practiced. He figured that the relationship between the good doctor and the nurse was the reason for the good doctors change of heart. He came to an immediate solution.

The fact that the good doctor had more than ten million in the offshore account was probably an additional incentive to quit.

The nurse was very attractive. Reston obtained records and made note of the key DNA, blood type and other key attributes.

He waited until the right parts request came in. He was going to snuff out the superior attitude of the good doctor. He was going to emotionally destroy him.

A few weeks later after a couple more discussions about the desire to quit, Reston took the action he knew would totally change the good doctors attitude and ensure he had control of the situation.

He had the nurse, that the good doctor was having an affair with, snatched, and brought to the warehouse.

He waited until the good doctor was ready for the next body and walked in and handed him the extensive list of parts to be harvested. The list had every organ, a knee joint, an entire right leg, eyes, and the breast nipples on it.

He wanted to be in the room when the good doctor realized who his next harvest victim happened to be.

He stepped to the far end of the room with a direct view of the operating table. He had Dennis his bodyguard standing next to him in case he needed protection.

Sara was scared as she sat in the cage and watched the two men who had snatched her from the parking lot the day before as she got ready to go home. They had not replied to any of her questions or explained why they had snatched her.

Zack and Brent had exchanged a few quiet comments about their next victim. They agreed she was too pretty to be processed but they had their orders.

Zack got the call to prepare her for the next harvest. He opened the door to the cage and let her know that she could leave the cage.

As she stepped out of the cage, Brent hit her with the knuckles of his thumb on her two temples. She went out like a light when the switch was flipped.

They lifted her and put her face down on the processing table. Brent then slit each of her arteries in her neck and then focused on undressing her as her blood pumped out and ran down into the collection bag. The blood would be filtered and sold to a blood bank.

He admired her beautiful body and was sorry that she had been selected but that was the bosses decision not his.

When the call came to wheel the body into the harvesting room they opened the door and pushed the table in.

James asked why Reston was in the room instead of behind the observation window. He was surprised to hear that Reston say that he had a surprise for him.

James watched as the table with the harvest body was pushed into the room and put next to the dissection table. He walked over to help in rolling the body over onto the table.

There was something familiar about the body, but he could not quite place the feeling.

As the body was turned over, his brain exploded, his life was shattered. It was Sara, the woman that he had fallen in love with.

He heard Reston call out, "surprise" as he picked up his scalpel.

He took the only action that flashed into his mind.

6

2 The Nurse

The large panoramic screen in the living room zoomed out to the mountains, then slowly panned along the river and finally on the campsite where her father was putting up the large tent that they had all shared. Her mother had just transferred all her family videos to the cloud and wanted to view a few. The family had traveled extensively around the country and had camped in many of the national or state parks. The clip that was on the screen had been taken in a campground near the Tetons. She remembered the cold stream water where she swam briefly in a clear pool where she could see the fish swimming below her. She also remembered catching some of those fish and watching her father clean and fry them over the open campfire. At that time, she was probably fourteen. It had been one of many bright memories of growing up.

The other memory of that trip was the drive through Yellow Stone, seeing the buffalo and Old Faithful. She was sure her mother would have extensive footage of that drive as well.

She took a sip of her wine and had to admit that she had grown up in a loving family as a spoiled young girl.

Her early school years were a blur, and she had little recall about specific events.

She considered her high school years to be rather busy and exciting. She had been on the school paper, a cheer leader, and was a lettered field hockey player. Her senior year was especially fun because of all the parties she had attended. The only thing that she regretted about that time was that she had not been very serious about what she was going to do after high school.

As graduation loomed, she decided to go into nursing and was admitted to the University of Cincinnati. That made her parents happy because she would stay near home. She was excited because she felt that she had found her way into a field that felt right for her. She realized that she enjoyed helping people and thought that nursing would satisfy her desires. Her mother had suggested becoming a doctor, but Sara knew she did not have the desire nor the grade point average that would get her accepted in most US schools.

She graduated and was pleased when she was hired by the UC hospital as a practicing nurse. She was first assigned to be a floor nurse. She worked hard and received excellent feedback on her performance.

A year later she applied for and got a position as a surgical assistant. This assignment at first was a little overwhelming and watching surgery took getting used to. She at first had a quesy stomach but slowly got over it.

Then she had assisted Dr. Westin during one of his surgeries. He was fast, accurate, and seemed to have a good sense of humor.

He seemed to like her and requested her by name for several subsequent surgeries.

Their relationship seemed to take a natural turn toward intimacy.

Sara had dated James for more than a year when he asked if she would go on a vacation trip with him. She had accepted and he had asked her to pick the vacation trip that she wanted to go on. She had thought about going to Yellowstone but was not sure that camping out would be that romantic. She decided that an Alaskan cruise sponsored by one of the famous magazines on one of the smaller ships would be just the thing.

They had a main deck cabin that had an outside view. The cruise departed Seattle and for fourteen days they spent their time together. They dined each evening with a number of the guests. Sara noted that there were thirty couples on the cruise and another handful of single people for about sixty people in total. The small number of people was what had attracted her to this particular cruise.

She knew that it was rather expensive, but James had let her know that the cost was no issue.

They had enjoyed hiking, biking, kayaking at various moments, and strolling through Petersburg and learning about its fishing industry. She had followed in her mother's footsteps and used her phone to capture most of what she saw. She of course took many selfies that she sent to her parents.

The tour ended in Sitka Alaska where they caught a flight back to Cincinnati.

Sara felt that it had turned out to be fourteen of the best days of her life.

On the way back to Cincinnati, James suggested that she move in with him. She accepted on the condition that they each had their own bedroom.

He had accepted and said that he currently rented a three-bedroom apartment a few blocks from the University hospital.

They agreed that she would move in as soon as her own apartment contract ended in two months.

Her mother asked her to come to dinner and share the highlights of the vacation. Sara knew that what her mother wanted was the inside scoop on the romance.

She was eager to share that news, but she also had a great video of the highlights of the vacation that she had purchased as part of the tour. It was professionally done, and she knew her mother and dad would love it.

Sara floated along in sort of a haze as she waited for her lease to end. She went to James apartment and was amazed at how spacious and comfortable it felt. She was ready to make the move.

After work, she was walking out to her car when suddenly she was grabbed and felt a cloth going over her mouth and nose. She identified the smell of chloroform before she passed out.

When she came to she was lying in a barred cell. She sat up and tried to get her bearings. She realized that she had been kidnapped and wondered what was happening. She spent the night awake and scared.

Then the next day a person that she did not know approached the cell and told her she was going to be just fine if she did as she was told.

She asked what was going on.

The reply that everything was going to be alright did not satisfy her.

Alright meant to not have been kidnapped.

A short time later, the first person returned with a second one. He said it was time for a surprise and opened the cell door and told her to come out.

She was warry but figured that getting out of the cell was better than resisting and staying in the cell. As she stepped beyond the door, suddenly she was hit on her two temples, and everything went dark.

Zack picked up the young woman and put her on the dissection transport table. They had been instructed to undress her, bleed her, and then turn her face down before pushing the gurney into the dissection room.

He nodded when Brent commented that it was pity to have to kill such a beautiful young woman. The two of them knew better than to question the bosses direction and they did as they were told.

A few moments later they had everything ready.

3 The Doctor

*A*ll he could remember about his father were the beatings that he regularly received and the smell of alcohol as his father yelled at him for doing something wrong or being so stupid. He also remembered the beatings that his mother endured and the purple bruises on her face.

Then his father abandoned the family and things actually got better.

His mother struggled as she tried to raise five children and work to get food on the table. The food stamp program started and that at least ensured that there was food to eat but having a place to live was a struggle. They ended up living in a two-bedroom basement apartment with no windows. The saving grace was it was within three blocks of a park that had slides, swings, and a ball field.

He was the oldest and often had to take his brothers and sisters to the park and watch them. He actually enjoyed this responsibility.

He remembered his father calling him stupid, which made him focus on his schoolwork and focus on getting the best grades possible. He excelled in school and as he went through high school he targeted being the top of his class. He wanted to go to college and was hoping to get a scholarship to do so.

He was also sensitive to the fact that there was little for anything extra. He got a job at a Wendy's and was soon the lead supervisor and made a whopping nine fifty an hour. He worked twenty hours a week, mostly on weekends.

He was a loner that had few friends and in his senior year his extracurricular activity was to work in the refreshment stand which gave him a good view of the football game being played.

He hit his goal of being top in his class and accepted a full scholarship to Case Western Reserve University in Cleveland. He was excited but realized that once again he needed to be at the top of his class to enable his entry to some medical school.

The four years there was far more intense than his high school years, but he ended up as the student with the third highest grade in his class.

He had filled out requests to more than twenty medical schools. He was blown away when he received an offer from the University of Pittsburgh Medical Center (Pittsburgh, PA). He knew they were ranked # 3 in the plastic surgery field. His only concern was paying for the program and again rejoiced at receiving a stipend that went a long way to helping pay for the program.

He knew he would end up in debt but figured he would make it up when he graduated. He had researched and found out that the average salary of a plastic surgeon was three hundred fifty with a high of five hundred fifty thousand dollars a year.

The intensity of his studies increased by several multiples. He often slept at the hospital so that he would not have to go to the apartment he rented. The whirl wind seemed to last for a lifetime but then it was time to get into a residency program. He was very happy to be offered one at the University of Cincinnati hospital. This brought him back to his hometown and to his family. He however had an income issue in that his residency pay though at the top end was only seventy thousand dollars a year and with only a five thousand dollar per year increase.

Almost immediately he began looking for a moonlight job where he could leverage his degree.

He was having a night out and sitting alone at the bar talking to the bartender about his predicament. The bartender nodded and said he might have the answer to his problem. The bartender left and a few minutes later a person, who looked exactly like an Italian mafia actor from the movies came and sat next to him.

He introduced himself as Reston Sanclemente and asked him about his experience as a plastic surgeon.

James shared his scholastic and medical experience and the fact that he was almost a half a million dollars of debt and that his current pay was only seventy thousand a year.

He listened as Reston let him know that he ran a legitimate body parts business and that he was looking for a surgeon that could harvest body parts from fresh cadavers. He pointed out that it was a gory business but very lucrative.

Reston then said that if James could begin immediately he would pay fifty thousand for every cadaver that was processed and that he estimated that each harvest would only take about two hours. He needed someone willing to work six hours a week.

James was surprised and a quick calculation let him know that it was worth about four million a year. He said that he was definitely interested. He was already thinking about what that kind of money would mean for him.

Reston stipulated that James needed to finish his residency and get licensed.

James agreed and before leaving Reston took out a contract that specified everything that had been discussed and James read and signed it.

He focused on his residency, processed bodies at the facility that Reston operated and watched his bank account slowly reach twelve million.

Never in his life had he dreamt of having the kind of money that he was making. He set up a college fund for each of his brothers and sisters and moved his mother into her own home.

Over the first year he came to the realization that something about the operation seemed fishy. He began to pay attention and suspected that Reston was in fact running a body parts black market business.

He knew that he was in too deep to say anything.

Reston approached him to let him know that a second surgeon was being added to the business and that he expected him to bring him on board rapidly so that the new guy could begin contributing immediately.

James decided that it was the time to see if he could get out of the body parts business. He had a blossoming love affair going and he was coming to the end of his residency and had received his license. It was time to move on and get his personal life organized.

He mentioned that it seemed that this was a good time for him to go into his own practice and stop harvesting body parts.

He was surprised by Reston's response that leaving was not an option.

James pointed out that he had fulfilled his contract and that he intended to go into practice on his own. That was when he learned that the millions he had in an offshore account was not going to be available if he left the parts business. He then realized that Reston was a second person on the account and could block his withdrawals.

He thought that a way out was to transfer most of the money to a separate account and then quit. He had no idea what Reston had in mind. His account was blocked when he went to transfer money to another bank. He knew that he was boxed in.

He focused on his work and his new love affair. He was able to pay for the vacation that he and Sara planned. They went together on an Alaskan cruise. Each day he knew he had found the person of his dreams. It was the best time of his life. He came back eager to have Sara with him every day.

Everything seemed to be going right.

He went to his moonlight job where Reston said he had a surprise for him. He wondered what in the world Reston had in mind.

When the next body came in and he turned it over, his world ended. He could hear Reston shouting out surprise and looked down at Sara. He took his scalpel and swiftly pulled across his throat.

The world that he had dreamt about had ended for him.

14

4 A day at the Waterpark

*T*he day was hot and a day at the water park seemed to be the best way to enjoy it. Alex and Matt had joined Trey, Lindsey, and Nolan for the day. They were all in the shallow end of the pool enjoying staying cool. The talk was about their last case, the fun they had in Montreal and the fact that it had been a quiet month since they had returned.

Nolan was having a great time swimming and jumping into the pool. He was content to play alone.

Then Annie arrived with Linda and Lorie, and the swimming action went into full gear.

Alex teased Annie about having increased the noise level three-fold.

Annie pointed to the table that had several bags on it and countered that she could leave but she would have to take the picnic lunch with her.

Alex laughed and said that she was ready for lunch and would set the table. Lindsey said that she would help, and they got out of the water, took a quick clean water rinse, and toweled off.

Lindsey asked what the next work assignment might be.

Alex said that the Chief had purposely not assigned them to a case and had promised that he would try to assign an easy one that might come up. She then laughed and said that was a line he had now used multiple times, but it seemed that easy cases didn't exist.

Lindsey nodded and agreed. She said that she always asked Trey about the cases that were assigned, and he always told her to relax because he had the best partner he could possibly have, and she always took care of him.

Alex smiled and replied that she felt the same about her partner.

The picnic consisted of spareribs, broccoli, asparagus, a half a corn cob and a baked potato. It was a robust meal.

Annie called everyone to get their lunch.

Alex commented that everyone must have been hungry because no one was talking.

Nolan asked who the next bad guy was.

Alex smiled and said that as soon as she knew she would make sure to tell him.

He laughed and said that the last bad guy turned out to be a woman.

Alex replied that the bad woman was one of the worst bad person that she had so far experienced.

It was at this point that her phone rang. She knew not to ignore it because it was the Chiefs' "Hail to the Chief" ring.

He began by asking how she was and what she was doing.

It was Sunday but it was clear that he was about to assign the next case. He apologized about interrupting her picnic but said that the fire department had called him with a situation that he felt she needed to address. He said that it was a gruesome situation and that she and Trey needed to get to the scene and see what to do about it. He said he would join them at the scene and then gave her the address and asked how soon she could get there.

Alex hung up and then she looked at Nolan and asked if he had called the Chief on her. He shook his head and said he didn't have his number. She then looked at Trey and said they had to go. She asked Matt to take her personal stuff back to the apartment and that she and Trey would take the car.

On the way she brought Trey up to speed about what the Chief had shared about the situation. He was meeting them at the site and would go into the warehouse with them.

When they arrived, Alex pointed out the Chief's car and pulled in behind him.

The Chief got out of his car and as he approached them apologized for ruining their weekend but said he had little choice. He explained that the fire chief had called him and said there was a locked cooler that they opened that was full of human body parts.

The fire chief called the owner of the building who claimed to run a legitimate human body parts distribution center. The fire chief then found a surgical room and what appeared to be a preparation room. This was not on the license that his staff found on file, so he had called me, and I called you because I have a bad feeling about this operation. I also called Bill and found out that he and Trevor were boating out on Lake Cumberland. I told them that they should enjoy their time and that on Monday he would bring them on board.

Alex nodded pointed to where the fire chief was standing and led the way.

The fire chief greeted her and said that he was glad to see that the Chief had called in his star detective. He warned that what he was going to show them was gory, disgusting and alarming. The owner claimed to have all the necessary paperwork but had not shown up to present it as promised.

Alex thanked him for the warning. She looked at the Chief and asked him if he had the phone number for Dr. Rogers the police coroner.

The chief replied that he did.

Alex said that even before entering the locker she already knew that she would want every body part to get verified as to its authenticity via a DNA analysis. She pointed out that in the last case that his analysis had been the key clue that had helped to solve the case.

She then said she was ready to enter the warehouse. She looked around the section of the warehouse that had been renovated. It was clear to her that one room was a holding and preparation room and a materials storage room.

She said she would wait until Dr. Rogers arrived before going into the cooler.

During this time Alex examined each of the other rooms.

When she entered the preparation room she stopped dead in her tracks. The room was clear where bodies to get dissected were prepared.

The cage that looked like a barred prison cell sent shivers down her back. The cell that looked like a prison cell clearly indicated that live people were put there.

She pointed to it and said that she thought they had uncovered a criminal operation that was killing people to get the parts that they were selling.

Across from it in the corner was what Alex surmised was a gas-powered furnace. The odor was nauseating to her.

She spotted a door to the side of the furnace and led the way in. She was surprised to find that it was an office area. She was more surprised to find a viewing window into the surgical room. She noted that it gave the viewer a direct view across the operating table.

She pointed out that whoever sat at the comfortable chair in front of the window must be a mentally sick person.

The surgical room looked like any well-equipped hospital surgery room, but it did not have any of the equipment associated with helping keep someone alive.

Dr. Rogers arrived after about an hour.

She was in the surgical room looking at the observation window that from the surgical room looked like a mirror when Dr. Rogers approached her.

Alex greeted him and said that she was asking him to take the lead in examining the body parts in the freezer.

He nodded and replied that every case that he worked for her seemed to get weirder. He asked how much weirder this one might be.

Alex said that she had no clue.

She followed Dr. Rogers in and realized that it was not a freezer or as cold as she expected. Many of the body parts were each sealed in what looked like evacuated plastic bags and there were a number of cooler like containers that she figured held specific body parts.

It was a gruesome site.

Alex took a quick look around and was amazed at all the body parts. She did not take a count but was sure there were hundreds.

She shook her head and said she had seen enough and walked out.

She recalled seeing the body parts of what had appeared to be that of a child. Now her heart stopped as she looked at the cell with a vision of a kidnapped child sitting there.

She shook her head and said that she wanted an arrest warrant put out for the owner of the warehouse and for anyone on record that worked at the facility. She was going to grill them on what might have transpired at the facility.

The Chief nodded and said that he agreed with her and that the next step would be to identify the people she had mentioned and bring them in for questioning.

He took out his phone and made several calls asking that warrants be issued for everyone listed on the warehouse records.

Alex turned to Trey and asked him about his feelings about what they had seen.

Trey shook his head and said that the case seemed to be taking a tack into a very weird world that he had never envisioned. He agreed that they might have uncovered a situation that was more than a nightmare and in a way worse than their last case.

Alex agreed. She said that she was ready to leave. She asked what he planned to do.

Trey made a call and found out that Lesley, Noland, Annie and her two were at his house. He hung up and replied that he was going home, have a beer and watch the kids play and try to forget what they had just witnessed.

Alex asked him to drop her off. She said that Matt had the rest of the day off. She was going to see if he would go out on a bike ride with her otherwise she would have to get on the treadmill and run for the rest of the day to help her release the tension that had built up.

The following Monday Alex and Johnnie arrived at the office and found Bob and Travis sitting at their desks and a box of donuts on her desk.

Travis greeted her and said that he had been warned by Bob not to open the box and let the Boss take her roll first.

Bob piped up and said that he had not issued any warning and that it was Travis's idea to wait for the boss. They both chuckled and said that they were eager to hear about the new assignment that they were all on. They commented that they had each received a call from the Chief and had been brought on board and that they would all be on the quest to solve the mystery of the fire at the warehouses and determine the legitimacy of the human body parts business.

Alex opened the box and took out a bear claw, cut it in half and put half on Trey's desk. She was aware that Trey was later than normal and was about to call when he walked in with his cup of coffee.

Trey greeted everyone and then said that he was late because he had stopped to interview for a door greeters job at the lumber yard.

Alex smiled and told him he would be a failure in that role because he would scare away the customers. His comment worried her, but she would make sure Trey was OK later.. The two of them would be attending the AA meeting together the next evening. She was sure she would know if he was doing alright.

She was about to suggest that they go into a huddle room to discuss the case when the Chief walked in and said that he would like to talk to all of them in his office.

Alex noted that the rest of the people in the bullpen were all watching them closely.

The Chief sat behind his desk holding a cup of coffee. He made the comment that it seemed that lately each case got weirder than the previous one. He then added that he was once again putting two teams on the case because they seemed to work well together, and they solved cases. He asked if that suited everyone.

Travis smiled and commented that they didn't have a choice but to work well together because he just couldn't stand to see Alex cry.

Alex smiled and replied that she would make sure that he got the best assignment for being so sensitive to her feelings. She knew full well that Travis had become one of her supporters.

The Chief nodded, said that he was sure they could work it out and then explained the details of the case as he understood it.

The fire chief had called him and let him know that the fire had been purposely set. A loose connection had been found on the cremation furnace and a short time later they had found the charred remains of a stick with the wick that most likely contained gas or some other flammable. The fire chief has the evidence secured and he said that the crime scene was taped off and was under twenty-four-hour watch.

He then shared the fact that Dr. Rogers had his teamwork working around the clock to move all the body parts into the morgue and he had worked over the weekend to get started in processing the body parts.

He looked at Alex and asked how she was thinking to approach the case.

Alex nodded her head and said that she wanted to get the team to discuss the case in a little more detail before deciding on the approach. She made the point that the proprietor seemed to have skipped, other members such as the person doing the dissection, and any helpers were unknowns and now an arsonist had been added to the list. This meant that there were multiple scenarios that needed to be addressed.

She suggested going to the morgue and getting Dr. Rogers to take on what the case. She added that he would have the best take on the body parts. Then they might talk to the Fire Chief to see if he had an ideas who the arsonist might be.

She added that when they found him they might need to give that person a metal.

The Chief nodded and picked up the phone and made a call. He asked if his team could come to the morgue and get an update on what the doctor had found out.

He stood up and said they should all go down to the lab.

Alex did not like the smell of the morgue. It made her nauseous. When they entered there was a full leg on the table that was obviously a woman's leg. It sent a shiver down her back.

The doctor pointed it out and said that he had started with the largest of the body parts, was running the analysis and was about ready to put the sample back in the bag that it had come in.

Alex asked how long it would take to process all the body parts.

Dr. Rogers replied that it would most likely take the rest of the week.

Alex nodded and then asked what type of information would each analysis give them.

The reply was that they would get DNA, blood type, approximate age of the individual, and that he would add any additional information that he had from the observation of each part. He made the point that they had already concluded that the person doing the body part harvesting was a skilled surgeon.

Alex thanked him and asked him to send up each report individually so that the team could begin to use the information to hunt down who the person might be.

She then turned and said it was time to go to their huddle room and discuss the case.

5 New Digs, New Staff, New Business

*T*he night was dark, and the Cheshire moon seemed to be mocking him as he lay on his sleeping bag looking up at the sky. He had abandoned his apartment and planned to leave the area, but he was thinking through how he could slow down the hunt for him that he was sure to follow. He had learned from one of his informants that the top detective and from the press she received that she did a very thorough investigation and always seemed to catch the person she was after.

He made up his mind that she needed to be killed. He figured that then there would be a lengthy delay, and he would be able to disappear and reappear as a different individual.

He decided to have Dennis, his eager bodyguard, take a shot at taking her out. He knew that Dennis was always wanting to shoot someone, and this opportunity would attract him. He would ask Zack and Brent to back Dennis up. He figured the three of them had a good chance a getting the job done. If they were successful he felt he had a chance to relocate his operation somewhere outside of Cincinnati but still along the main path to the East coast body distribution thoroughfare.

He knew that he had to do so rapidly or face the ire of his bosses in Italy.

He knew that the paperwork he had that normally was sufficient to make the operation look legitimate would not stand close scrutiny. He hoped that most of the body parts would be impossible to trace but he worried about how good the coroner might be. He was sure most of the body parts would be impossible to trace. He had the records of who the persons were. These were records he had matched to the customer needs.

He kept wondering how the fire had started. It seemed that when he drove by that the fire was in the area where the preparation and surgery room was located. He thought about what supplies were stored in that area, and he went through the list of the chemicals stored there. There were cleaning supplies that were flammable, but he had his people store them in a separate area. He thought about the gas lines that came to a small cremation oven where the discarded body parts were cut up and cremated. He felt that it must have been a gas leak of some kind. He would watch the news to see if the fire department made their findings public.

The next morning, he used one his burner phones and called Dennis and asked him to meet him at the Hamilton County Park so they could plan on what to do.

Dennis was excited about the job of taking out "Cincinnati's Black Annie Oakley." He said she didn't stand a chance.

Reston reminded him that she was a dead shot and that several other folks had tried unsuccessfully to kill her.

Dennis smiled and said he did not intend to play fair and that he would shoot her in the back.

Reston asked him to contact Zack and Brent and get them to help him and said there was a ten-thousand-dollar bonus for each of them.

He personally and desperately hoped that Dennis would be successful.

He gave Dennis the building address where the black detective lived and let Dennis know that she rode a bicycle into work early every morning and suggested that he observe her for a couple of days so he could decide when and how to shoot her.

Dennis said that his three fifty-seven would blow a hole the size of a basketball as it left her body. He commented that she would be dead before she hit the ground.

Reston worried about Dennis's self-confidence, but he knew that Dennis was a dead shot and would probably not miss.

He suggested that Dennis buy a getaway car and gave him the name of the dealer he knew had a bunch of cars that were in relatively good condition.

He went to that used car lot, purchased an older Hyundai, and drove slowly toward Cleveland. It was a long drive and on the way he contemplated how he would set up the business in Cleveland.

He took a room at a Motel for the week. He was going to move slowly and keep his ears to the ground to see what would happen.

He transferred some of the money from the Jamaican bank account that he had set up with James his use-to-be plastic surgeon that was now in the body parts cooler. The twelve million was down to a little under eight million because James had set up a series of trust accounts for his brothers, sisters, and his mother. Reston had been aware of the setting up of the trust accounts and had actually thought that was the right thing for James to do.

As it turned out, when James had turned over the body of his fiancé on the parts table and had then slit his own throat it had startled him, but it turned out it was good that he had done so.

He had the new surgeon do the dissection and a few days later the fire had ended the business.

He could not sit in his room, so he spent the next couple of days going to a local pub and nursing drinks and listening to the news broadcasts. He was a little disappointed about the lack of information about the fire in the warehouse. The only thing that had been reported was that the fire seemed to have been purposely set. That just didn't make sense. He wished he could take a walk through the warehouse to get a firsthand look. He wondered who would have wanted to set the place on fire.

He wondered how Dennis was doing and decided to give him a call.

His call gave him hope that things would improve.

Dennis said that he had watched the black detective leave her place for the last three days and knew exactly how he would take her out. He said that she was a dead woman walking but just didn't know it.

It was uplifting to hear the enthusiasm and the certainty that Dennis was exuding. He reminded Dennis to be careful and have his getaway planned. He suggested he call when the job was done, and he had made his getaway.

Dennis took his two helpers on a walk to show them where they would wait the next morning and that they both should plan to wait for him to shoot but then shoot away to make sure that both she and her partner bike rider were dead. He said that he had the getaway car parked so that they would drive and get on US Highway Seventy-One north and drive north to Cleveland. He let them know about the thirty-thousand-dollar reward.

Zack said that it seemed easy enough and that he was sure they would be enjoying the reward.

The next morning the three were standing in the dark leaning against the apartment wall when Dennis heard the apartment door slide open. He had his three fifty-seven in his hand and as the detective was getting ready to mount her bike he fired three shots. He smiled as she was hurled forward but was stunned as she seemed to turn in midair and fire. Then the world ended.

Reston was stunned by the breaking news report that highlighted the fact that Cincinnati's most famous detective was in the hospital where she was being treated for a non-life-threatening gunshot wound. The reporter went on to say that she had killed two shooters and that her partner had killed a third. An apparent getaway car was found parked in the garage across from the apartment, which was the home of the detective.

The camera scene then showed three body bags that were getting ready to be loaded into the coroner's van.

Reston knew that he would need to find a long-term hiding place and sent word to his bosses that the body parts business in Cincinnati had been disrupted.

His bosses told him he was to hide in plain sight and open up a new body parts factory in either Columbus or in Cleveland. They suggested Cleveland because they had a better network there and they had informants in the police department and several of the political offices.

Reston didn't like it, but he knew he was toast if he declined. He changed his identity to Preston Clemente. This was a passport that he had obtain a few years prior. Then he found an apartment that had a view of the lake in a relatively prestigious area. Once he had set himself up in the apartment he went about finding an appropriate warehouse or building to use.

He went out personally and drove around various areas and found a shuttered three-story home that sat on the corner of a sleepy street not far from the lake. He took the time to visit the place several times under different weather conditions to ensure that there was always a good lake breeze. He wanted to make sure that his cremation furnace would not draw any attention. He then looked up the owner of the property and negotiated the sale. It was an easy one because the house had been unused for almost a year.

He then contacted his associates and asked them to recruit the harvesting surgeon and to provide him with three capable associates. He specified that one needed to be a bodyguard that was good with his weapon and had experience.

He also asked to be referred to the appropriate contractor that could come in and prepare the house for use.

He had the operating room on the second floor, the holding room, and the parts cooler on the first floor and the cremation oven in the basement. He put his observation room on the third floor with the viewing port through the floor. An elevator made the multilevel operation a convenient one.

One side of the house had an empty lot that he bought, and he made an enticing offer for the small home on the other side so that he had a buffer all the way around the building.

It was less than a month later that he was ready to begin his new body harvesting business.

His bosses congratulated him on getting back into business and gave him the names of the three persons that would be working for him. They would drive in from New York.

He hoped that the three would work out.

It turned out that the three were fresh from the home country and eager do what he asked. He offered to house them gratis at the small house next door and worked with them to get the house ready for their occupancy.

He went with all of them to a local gun range and was impressed with their shooting skill. He discussed how the body parts business was run and learned that all three were comfortable with how it operated and how the people that might become parts were selected.

He took them all out to celebrate.

He liked all three.

Luca was the bodyguard, but he said that he was willing to do whatever he might be asked to do.

Angelo and Dario were both darker individuals that said the they had no qualms at getting the bodies ready for dissection.

They all asked whether they could trust the surgeon that would be doing the dissecting.

Reston replied that he had not met the surgeon, but he was counting on the family to provide the surgeon that they had vetted, and the surgeon would also be coming from Italy via New York.

6 The Magician

*J*ohnnie was disturbed by the new case. It seemed unreal. He had never imagined a business focused on making a profit from human body parts. When the team had gone to the morgue where Dr. Rogers was working his way through the body parts and getting the DNA signature and other metrics from each part. The doctor had joked about starting with the best-looking body part which was an entire female right leg. He pointed to a row of refrigerated drawers and said that his team had moved all the parts from the warehouse cooler shelves and put them in the top row. He had only gotten everything organized and had the result of only the leg.

He listened to Alex thank the doctor and asked that the information be sent to her so that the team could begin trying to verify whether it was a legitimate body part.

When the team was back in the huddle room he admitted that he was not sure what databases he would need to access to verify a body part.

They had all agreed with Alex that they would work together to get organized and get ideas on how they were going to verify all the parts. She pointed out that the listed business owner had not delivered the paperwork as he had promised and when she checked his given address it was a fake. She figured that the business was probably a black market one.

They discussed the assignment for a short time and then Alex had suggested they call it a day and go relieve the tensions of the day.

The next morning, he greeted Alex as she got off the elevator with her bike. He could tell by her looks that she had not gotten the best sleep. He led the way out of the building. He was just getting ready to get on his bike when the roar of gunfire cause him to drop his bike, pull his pistol and drop prone on the ground. He watched as Alex flew over her bike, spun in the air, and fired her gun four times and then hit the pavement. She had hit two of the three attackers, and he took out the third and put an insurance shot in the second shooter. It was clear to him that Alex had nailed the person who had done the shooting. All three of the shooters were down.

He jumped up ran to make sure that all three were dead and kicked their guns to their feet. He then spun and ran to where Alex was lying face up, but it was clear to him that she was out. He check for a pulse and was ecstatic to find a strong one. He quickly dialed the dispatch center and declare that there was an officer down and gave the address.

It seemed that he heard the sirens immediately after that. He was focused on trying to see what condition Alex was in. He rolled her to her side and saw that she had indeed been hit and was bleeding. He jumped over to his bike and got his first aid kit. With his pocketknife he cut the straps on the backpack that Alex had on and cut open the back of her blouse to expose the wound. He was surprised to see the exposed back of a bullet.

He wiped the blood away and put his largest band aid over it. There was another wound along her right shoulder on which he sprayed a sealing adhesive with pain killer.

Suddenly it seemed that he was surrounded by police and an EMT pulled him away from Alex and said that they would take her to the hospital. He sat back on the curb and watched Alex being loaded onto the stretcher and then into the ambulance. He watched it pull away and then turned to look at the scene.

His bike was OK, but Alex's bike had a bent back wheel that would need to be replaced. He was about to pick up his first aid kit when one of the police officers said that he should leave everything alone and asked him what had happened.

Johnnie stood up and pointed to the three bodies and said that he and Alex had come out of the building with their bikes and were just getting ready to take off when the roar of gunfire started. He described what Alex had done and then what he had done. He pointed to the weapons that the three attackers were using and said that it was a wonder that Alex was alive because all three were using three-fifty-sevens.

He said that he thought the only one that had gotten any shots off was the one that was in the lead position. Alex had nailed him, and the second person and he had taken out the third shooter and he had also put a shot into the second shooter for insurance.

The coroner's van arrived a few moments later and a couple of his people took pictures, asked almost the same questions that Johnnie had already answered and then put the bodies into bags and put them in the van. The van drove off but Dr. Stevens and one of his team continued to work the crime scene.

The Chief arrived and rescued him. The Chief let the officer in charge know that he was taking Johnnie to the station. Trey stopped them and asked about Alex.

The Chief said he had been told that she was still out and that she was being kept that way until she got out of surgery. She had a flattened three-fifty-seven bullet that had lodged in her right back muscle and a graze wound across her shoulder. It seems that the two computers and a one-inch-thick spiral binder that had been in the backpack had saved her.

The Chief shared the fact that both computers and the binder had an almost one-inch hole through them, and the top computer had a groove across it that was most likely made by another bullet that caused her shoulder wound. The surgeon said that he had never treated a patient that had survived getting shot by such a weapon.

The Chief went on to share that the field team was still looking for the third bullet. He figured they would continue looking until they found it.

Trey said that he was going to the hospital to be there when Alex woke up.

The Chief nodded and said that they would all go there together.

They were not surprised to see Matt waiting outside of Alex's intensive care room. He let them know that she was still in the resuscitation area recovering from surgery but would soon be moved into the room where he was standing.

She was going to be kept out for most of the rest of the day because she had hit her head on the pavement and had a slight concussion.

Trey suggested that they go back to the station and let Matt contact them when Alex was awake. They could begin to try and figure out who the three shooters were, and who they might be working for. He also wanted to get a better understanding of how Alex had survived being shot by such a powerful weapon. He said he believed in miracles because he had experienced several in his work with Alex. He was just very happy about the current miracle that had saved Alex.

When they returned to the station, the Chief called down to the coroner's lab and learned that the backpack that Alex had on when she was shot was on his table and he was about to examine in. He said that the three bodies were in the cooler and would be processed in due time. He figured that they were not as important a figuring out how Alex had survived being shot by a three-fifty-seven.

He added that they had found the third bullet buried just past where Alex had landed. He speculated that the third shot was fired as the shooter died.

They all took the elevator down to the morgue where they were greeted by Dr. Rogers. He said that he had gotten word that Alex was going to recover but would have a couple of scars on her back. He pointed to the table where he had systematically unpacked the backpack she had on when she had been shot.

He said that the backpack buckle, the two computers and the one-inch-thick spiral binder had all partnered to slow the bullet enough so that it flattened and then only had enough power left to lodge a half an inch into her back muscle.

He then pointed to the grove that went lengthwise along the first computer and said that the second shot must have occurred as she was being flung forward and the bullet hit the computer and was deflected. He said that three shots had been fired by the shooter, and his team had found it in the blacktop pavement.

He pointed at the notebook and asked when she had started to use it because it had Johnnie's name on it and had only some cryptic notes on the first few pages.

Johnnies smiled and shared that he had given Alex the notebook the evening before because she wanted to make a few notes for the next day. The two of them had been discussing what databases he should be looking in to verify the legitimacy of all the body parts.

Dr. Rogers nodded and said that the notebook was probably the key in sapping the bullets energy because the computers were light laptops that did not have much structural resistance.

Johnnie asked permission to take a picture of the page that had the notes that Alex had written.

Trey commented that Alex had switched from having her cars blown up and burned to having computers destroyed.

The Chief nodded and agreed and then added that it was much easier on his budget to replace the computers than to replace the police cars that she had gone through.

Trey suggested that he and Johnnie join Bob and Travis, enjoy a cup of coffee, and then dig into the case and see if they could make some headway that they could share with Alex when she came out of her sedation.

Bob and Travis were sitting at their desks and the fact that they each had two donuts that they were munching on at the same time showed that both were nervous or upset.

Travis looked at Johnnie and asked how he could have let her get shot.

Johnnie smiled and used the reply that he had heard Alex often give Travis of, "I love you too."

Bill simply said, "touche."

Trey took out a bear claw and said he was going to eat Alex's half for her, and he was going to insist they all go into the huddle room and work together to see if they could take the next few steps without her.

7 The Evil Place

Joshua had taken the job because it offered good pay, and he could do the cleaning and sweeping at night. This allowed him to hold two jobs. He needed both jobs to take care of his family and his ailing mother. He went about his new job with enthusiasm and a desire to do a great job.

He had agreed to take cash for the work and was very happy about the pay that was twice as much as what he made during the day.

He felt that his angels were looking out for him.

But after a few days he began to take notice of the place. Most of the warehouse was empty and did not need cleaning. The part cleaned put him on edge. It had seemed too good to be true and as he looked at the area he was cleaning he became alarmed. He wondered about the cage like a jail cell. The room that the cage was in also had a small furnace in the other corner that had a weird odor to it, and there were two tables on wheels that had trough like edges with a drainpipe on one side. The room gave him goose bumps and literally spooked him.

The next room alarmed him. He was sure that the stainless-steel table was an operating table but there was not equipment to keep people alive.

He saw the mirror that seemed to provide a way to look into the room. He searched out the entrance to what he was sure would be an observation room and found it. He went in and knew he had taken a job that was involved in evil.

He looked around at the room and concluded that whoever sat there was probably in charge of the place because the room was set up to be comfortable. It had a small refrigerator, a small countertop oven and a shelf with a variety of liquor bottles. The small sink had two glasses that were open side down on a towel.

He returned to the room with the operating table and saw a locked door that had a small glass window across the room. He went over and looked through it and almost fainted. He had to hold on to the handle to keep from passing out. He knew he could pick the lock but was afraid to step into the room where he saw a variety of body parts. He figured he had found the door to hell and immediately let go as if the handle had burned his hands.

He finished his cleaning and got out of the warehouse. He vowed to that he would never come back.

What he had seen kept nagging him. He knew he should go to the police, but he was afraid of being exposed. He knew that the person running the place was the devil incarnate and would have him killed and he might end up in the room on the other side of the little window.

He remembered the various items in the place and figured that a gas explosion and fire might end the operation.

The thought would not leave him. He thought through how he could carry out what came to mind and prepared to do it. He figure he needed a couple of vise grips, and he needed an ignition source.

He got everything together and returned the following evening. He had no plan to do any cleaning. He was there to destroy the place.

He went to the window in the room located just behind the holding cell that opened to the ground above and pushed it open a few inches. Then he went to the gas line that went to the oven and loosened the connection until he could smell the gas coming out. He left the area, went outside, and went to the window that he had opened.

When he smelled the gas, he lit the small gas-soaked torch that he had made and threw it in through the window. As soon as he had thrown in the torch the explosion blew out the window. He had expected that and had located himself off to the side. He got up and quickly walked to his car that was parked two blocks away. He could hear the sirens blaring as he slowly left the area. He hoped that the fire crew would not be able to save the place.

He knew that he would need to look for another job, but his soul was lifted by the fact that he had taken out the macabre and evil business.

Now all he had to do was to find another job. He would have to see if one of the fast-food places needed help. It would not pay what he had made for the last few weeks, but he could rest easy and have a clear conscience.

He followed the news and learned that the fire department had determined that the fire had been deliberately set and they were looking for the arsonist that had set it. They had no clue who had set the fire, but they were asking if anyone had information that might help the investigation that was getting underway.

Trey got the news from the fire chief, and the team discussed the fact that there was some unknown person who had something against human body parts trafficking. They put finding him or her on their list of things that needed investigation but they all agreed that they had little energy in trying to track the person down.

He asked if Bob and Travis would take on the search for the person setting the fire and that if they found him they should treat him to a steak dinner at Johnnies favorite restaurant. He figure that person should be treated like a hero.

Travis smiled and said that it was one of the few times he agreed about how a suspect should be treated.

Bob added his normal brief, "Ditto."

Johnnie agreed and said he would personally pay for the dinner, and they should all focus on identifying the body parts and in catching the person that ran the body parts business.

34

8 Return

*A*lex was lying face down with her head turned to the side. She could hear the surgeon's comments about the bullet he was removing from her back. He kept mumbling how amazing that she had been shot twice by a three-fifty-seven and she had only a flesh wound and a grazed shoulder wound.

His assistant replied that it was a miracle but that she had also suffered a concussion from hitting her head on the pavement.

Alex wondered if they knew that she was awake and listening. Then the world seemed to become fuzzy, and she could not make out what was being said. She felt herself being lifted and moved onto a surface that seemed softer and warmer than the operation table.

She kept going between being able to hear and then going back to dreams. She replayed rescuing Annie and the two girls and there seemed to snippets from almost every case that she and the team had been on.

There seemed to be someone holding her hand, but she could not respond.

She decided to relax.

Matt had gone to the recovery room and held Alex's hand. When he felt Alex fall asleep he let go.

Not long after the nurse let him know that the doctor had given the order to move Alex to the intensive care room where she would be for the next couple of days.

Matt was relieved that the Dr. planned to keep her for a few days. He called and let Trey know that it would most likely be the next day before she would be awake and ready for any visitors.

Once Alex had been moved, he realized how exhausted he was and decided to go back to the apartment and get a good night's sleep.

As he walked out, he was pleased to see that the room had two police standing guard at Alex's door.

He had moved in with Alex and when he arrived at the apartment building he was surprised that it was still cordoned off and that there were two police officers watching the scene. All the physical evidence was gone but yellow outlines of everything was still at the scene. One of the officers recognized him and asked how Alex was doing.

He let them know that the operation to remove the bullet had gone well and that she was in an intensive care room and that some of their buddies were guarding it.

He went in and stopped by Johnnie's room and knocked on the door.

Johnnie had just hung up from talking to Mary and letting her know about the shooting and explaining that Alex had survived being shot because of what was in her backpack and how glad he had given her his biggest spiral bound notebook that was being identified as the object that most likely saved her.

Then he heard the knock and went to see who was stopping by.

He let Matt in and told him he looked like shit.

Matt said that he felt that way too.

Johnnie asked if he wanted something to drink.

Matt said he would love a shot of whiskey, but he had given up drinking and said he had just dropped by to let him know that Alex was still sleeping it off but that she was in an intensive care room and would probably be there for a couple of days.

Johnnie thanked him for the update and suggested that he go take a shower and get to bed.

Matt left and went up to the apartment.

Johnnie returned to the table where he had his computer linked up with the local hospital databases. He had no problem in hacking into any of the hospital systems. He was following the notes that Alex had put in the notebook. She had suggested comparing any report they got from Dr. Rogers to the DNA in the hospital databases.

He had gone through several of the hospital databases when he got a hit. It turned out to be that of a nurse who was a surgery assistant. He switched over to the departments missing persons reports and found her listed as missing by her worried parents. He had a hunch and tried to see if there were any missing doctors. He got another hit.

He decided that the next day he would see if Trey would follow up on the two missing persons reports and he would see if Dr. Rogers could process some of the male body parts.

He realized that the day had sapped his energy, and he went to bed earlier than usual.

The rattle of the alarm seemed to come only moments after he had fallen asleep.

He got up and decided to skip breakfast and go for a couple of donuts and a strong cup of coffee at the station. He was going to get his bike off the porch when he remembered that it was currently being held as evidence. He walked out of his apartment with the thought of having to walk to work.

The two police who had the night shift were just getting ready to leave and asked him if he wanted a ride to the station.

He replied that he would love a ride.

Once at the station he walked into the bullpen with his cup of coffee in hand and realized that he was the very first person to show and there were no donuts at hand.

He went to one of the vending machines and purchased an egg mac muffin and bacon sandwich. He threw it in the microwave for two minutes and then went back to his desk and relaxed as he ate the sandwich and sipped on his coffee.

He had just turned on his computer when Trey walked in with a cup of coffee in hand and sat down at his desk. Trey asked how the night had gone and gave a small laugh when Johnnie just grunted.

He commented that his night also deserved only a grunt.

Bob and Travis came in carrying their morning offering of assorted donuts.

Johnnie thanked them for saving his day as he took out two heavily sugar-coated cake donuts.

He shared that he had learned that the female legs and arms were that of a missing surgical nurse who had been reported missing by her parents. He said that Trey needed to get Dr. Steves to process the male parts because he had also found that one of the hospital surgeons was also listed as missing.

Trey said that as soon as the team was in the huddle room he would call down and see if Dr. Rogers would concentrate on the male body parts.

Johnnie nodded and said that he was ready for any additional reports that were available.

The Chief came in and walked over to them and commented that they all looked like he felt. He looked into the box of donuts and took a blue berry muffin and took a big bite out of it. Then he asked if there was anything that he could do.

Trey thanked him and said the team was going to go to a huddle room and figure out what they needed to do next.

The Chief turned to this office and said that he was going to get a few winks to make up for a sleepless night and they should do whatever they needed to do and order in lunch if that would be of any help.

Johnnie spoke up and said that by noon he thought he would want to eat at their favorite Asian restaurant and have Manchurian beef on a bed of rice with a mixed vegetable.

Trey said that he was in and was joined by Travis and Bill.

After lunch, the four of them decided to go and see how Alex was doing.

Trey led the way to the room and was not surprised to see Matt sitting and holding Alex's hand.

Earlier the nurse had come in to check Alex vitals when she was surprised by being asked the time.

Alex came awake as someone approached the bed. She quickly realized she was in a hospital bed and was laying on her right side. She immediately remembered the shooting and the operation on her back. She knew that she had killed two of the three shooters.

She wondered who had shot the third person. She realized that it had to be Johnnie, but she had not realized that he carried a gun. She hoped that he was OK.

When the nurse let her know it was five in the morning. She decided to get some more sleep and closed her eyes.

She opened them when breakfast was delivered but the strawberry Jell-o tasted weak, and the buttered bread and the blueberry desert did not taste good either. She decided to see what the lunch menu might offer.

She wondered how long she was going to be in the hospital.

She smiled and waved Matt over when he walked in. She gave him a kiss and said that she hoped he had not been the one to bring her to the hospital.

Matt handed her a small bag and said that it was her favorite morning treat.

Alex looked in and smiled when she saw that it was a bear claw. It smelled great. She had not poured her coffee that was on her breakfast tray but did so now and then took a healthy bite of the bear claw. She thanked Matt and said that he had helped start her day.

She then asked again if his team had brought her to the hospital.

Matt smiled at the question and shook his head. He said when the call came in about an officer down and the apartment building address was given he almost lost it, but his team was transporting an injured minor whose two parents had just been killed to Children's Hospital. He told her that the team that took her to the hospital was at the station taking a break and were on the scene in less than two minutes and they had her in the ER in less than five minutes.

That team said that Johnnie had cut off her backpack and had applied a huge band aid over the bullet and had sprayed the area that had been grazed by one of the bullets with a sealant. Their team only did the transport.

My team and I showed up about ten minutes later. I stayed and the team went out and worked the rest of the shift one person short.

Alex asked whether he had held her hand during that time.

He smiled and said that he held her hand until she fell asleep after surgery and then for a short time in the room until the nurse on duty suggested he go home and get some sleep.

Alex asked about the shooters and learned that she had killed two of three shooters and that Johnnie had killed the third one.

She smiled and said that Johnnie was fearless and once again he had helped take out the bad guys. She commented that she had not known that he was carrying a weapon.

Matt shook his head and said that was a question that she would have to ask Johnnie and Trey because he had no knowledge of most of the details of what had happened at the site of the shootout.

The two of them chatted the morning away and the lunch tray arrived, and they both commented about the bland selection.

Then a very serious looking Trey followed by a tired looking Johnnie then Bob and Travis entered the room. Johnnie moved most of the things off her tray and arranged her favorite Mongolian beef with brown rice and sweet and sour vegetables on the side.

The smell immediately made her hungry.

Johnnie then handed Matt several small containers that he said was a similar mix but with scallops.

Matt thanked him and said that Alex had all sorts of questions about what had happened that he had no clue how to answer.

Trey looked a Alex and told her to ask away.

Trevor smiled and said that he was pleased to be working with a woman who could take a three-fifty-seven bullet in the back and still kill the shooters.

Alex smiled and replied that, "she loved him too." Then she looked at Johnnie and asked when he had started carrying a weapon.

Johnnie smiled and said that his hover craft, Gunjfor, was not using her weapon, so he had qualified at the firing range and had a legal license to carry her weapon for her.

Alex asked him if he had taken out the third shooter.

Johnnie said that he had, and he had put a shot through the heart of the second shooter. He then said that only the first shooter had gotten any shots off and he had hit her with two shots and the third shot miss completely. He figured that her first shot had killed him, and his third shot was a dying reaction.

Alex smiled and asked if Johnnie thought that a band aid was all that she needed for a bullet in the back.

Johnnie chuckled and said that, and a little sealing spray on the minor bullet graze seemed to be the right thing to do and it was all he had in his emergency kit. He said that he had started carrying the emergency kit after their bike ride along the Loveland bike trail where she had been shot and kept on running toward the shooter with blood running down her arm.

Alex laughed and said that the only reason that she had run toward the shooter was because she saw a crazy old, unarmed Vietnam vet running toward the same shooter crazily shouting insults and waving his hands in the air.

Johnnie nodded and replied that being around her always seemed to draw out the most amazing events. He said that the roar of a three-fifty-seven being fired not more than twenty feet away and watching her fly with bicycle in hand and then spinning around and firing two kill shots was about as amazing as it could get. To then find her alive was for him just a plain miracle.

Alex shook her head and agreed that it was a miracle. Then she added that she had learned that it was that huge almost two-inch-thick spiral bound notebook that he had given her when she asked for a piece of paper that saved her life. She added that the surgeon had wondered where the paper that he had found in the wound had come from. He had commented that the paper seemed to have acted as a cushioning agent.

Johnnie smiled and said that he had just decided not to charge her for the notebook.

The attending doctor had been standing and listening to the banter and said that he wanted to interrupt for just a moment and ask how Alex was feeling.

Alex replied that after eating a decent lunch she was feeling great.

The doctor looked at the tray table and said that he was glad that the Chinese lunch that he had ordered had satisfied her.

Alex smiled and thanked him for being so considerate.

He nodded and said that he would order her dismissal for the coming morning. He wanted just one more day of detailed monitoring and he wanted the psychologist to come in and talk with her to make sure there was not any brain damage.

Trevor spoke up and said that there could not be any more damage because that had already happened and there was little hope of it getting any better.

The Dr. shook his head and said that he wished everyone a good day as he walked out.

Trey spoke up and said let Alex know that the team seemed to be making progress, but the case was taking a weird turn. Bob and Trevor were trying to locate an arsonist who had set the fire. They were not sure of the motive.

Johnnie was on the trail of the female body parts and had determined she had been a surgical nurse who had been reported as missing and that her fiancé surgeon was also missing. This was a twist that he had not expected. He went on and let her know that Dr. Rogers was currently processing the male body parts that fit the surgeon's size.

Alex shook her head and said that everything about the case was weird. She asked that the profit picture for such a venture and the money that all the body parts represented needed to be calculated. She figured if the profit was big enough, then the operation would be set up again and it would be somewhere nearby.

Johnnie said he could put that information together that afternoon. He would also start to gather the missing person reports for nearby cities like Louisville, Indianapolis, Dayton, Columbus, Cleveland, and Pittsburg.

He figured that every body part that they had in their possession needed to be replaced and delivered to a buyer. This meant that the missing persons would have the same makeup of the current body parts.

Alex shook her head in agreement and added that the person or persons perpetrating such a ghoulish crime had no idea about the old hound that was on their trail.

Trey laughed and added that it was good to have Alex back in the mix, but she should take it easy because they all had her back.

42

9 New Operation

Reston, now going by the name of Preston Clemente, walked through his new operation and was proud of having re-established an operation in less than two months.

He went through his previous parts list and confirmed the body parts that were still wanted. He used his previous list to get the DNA and other vital metrics of the parts that remained on order. About eighty percent of his list remained on order. His contacts with a variety of local doctors soon had him zeroing in on the potential donors.

His new helpers had no qualms about the gathering of the right "donors" and bringing them in for processing.

He had several satellite helpers such as a realtor, a used car lot owner and a person in the county records office that would help in disappearing those individuals that lived alone.

The realtor helped in getting any home either on the market to generate cash or off the market.

The used car owner was great at processing and selling a vehicle that the "donor" might possess.

The person in the records office provided an avenue to get a deed changed over to new ownership of a property.

The surgeon was sufficiently skilled to do the dissection, but he had lost his license for his sloppy surgical performance that had killed several of his patients. He was over a million dollars in debt to several families because he had lost the cases that had been brought against him.

Reston actually preferred him to either of his previous surgeons because dissection was his only job and he had been willing to work for a lot less and was only making as much as each of his other employees. Even so he was still making close to three hundred thousand a year and his debt was being reduced by one hundred thousand a year as a bonus. This seemed to currently satisfy him.

Reston was sure that greed would soon cause him to ask for more. He figured he had a lot of room to keep satisfying the doctor for years to come.

The operation started slowly but seemed to be ramping up smoothly.

He had heard nothing from the Cincinnati end since his henchmen had failed and had been killed. He was sure that the trail would cool, and he would be in the clear.

He was surprised when he went to Big Boys Bar and Grill and got into line dancing. He met a lady about his age that he enjoyed dancing with and soon the two of them were making the rounds of the clubs and not only line dancing but also enjoying conga and tango dancing. It turned out she was a dance instructor and soon she had him feeling comfortable trying any dance.

He knew better than allow his relationship to interfere with business and he slowed things down. He was disappointed when she let him know that she was moving on. He knew that was actually the right thing and he used his new dance skills to wine and dine women that were willing to engage in one-night stands.

He spent less time watching the dissection process and more time on optimizing the business. Having a full-time surgeon that was willing to work all seven days of the week let him think about expanding the business. He put out the word to his bosses and received congratulation for improving the business.

He was asked to first help set up a West Coast operation and then consider doing the same for the European, Russian, and Asian arenas. This was very attractive to him because it let him travel and see more of the world then just one city.

He promoted Luca into the role of manager of the Cleveland Operation.

He began to study the West Coast to understand the various communities to determine where an operation would best fit.

Los Angelos and San Francisco seemed to surface as the best location where harvesting would be the easiest. There seemed to be an endless supply of homeless people that would provide the raw materials, and the distributions network highway would provide coverage along the west coast and into the larger towns lying eastward.

He decided to travel to the two cities and get a firsthand look at the situation.

He had made his travel plans when he received word that the Cincinnati investigation was on the verge of solving the case.

He decided that instead of a trip west he would first take a trip to Cincinnati and get a firsthand look there.

He drove down and took a room at a Best Western at the north end of the 275-highway loop.

He took an Uber downtown to meet with his informant. They took a walk around the downtown and then had lunch down by the river front.

The news was that the body parts of a surgical nurse and the body parts of her surgeon fiancé had been identified. Additionally, a local surgeon was in custody and apparently co-operating with authorities.

He contacted a local mafia operative and asked him whether the surgeon could have a fatal car accident or fall out of a balcony during a party or meet with some other fatal accident.

The answer was "Yes" for the right price. The right price turned out to be one hundred thousand dollars.

Reston was actually relieved about the cost and said he would leave the type of accident up to the operative.

He decided that he would return to Cleveland and wait to see how the elimination of the surgeon took place.

A week later he learned that the surgeon had taken an evening walk and had stepped in front of a bus and been killed.

He sent the second part of the money as he had promised to do.

He felt a sense of relief and once again focused his energy on getting the West Coast operation set up.

46

10 The Surgeon

*A*lex was glad to get out of the hospital. Her back ached where the bullet had been removed but it was the graze wound that was the most sensitive. A large pad had been put over it. She planned to keep it in place as long as possible. One of the nurses had fashioned a cover that could be used in the shower to keep the area dry while it healed.

Matt was there to drive her home, but she asked him to drop her off at the station because she wanted to get back to the case.

Matt shook his head but knew it was useless to argue. He knew she would be restless and bored in the apartment.

Alex walked into the bullpen area and realized that the team was in the huddle room. She got her usual cup of coffee and went in.

The bull pen area went silent as she crossed to the huddle room. She waved and said that there was nothing to see, and they should get back to work. She then went into the huddle room.

Trey was sitting back and talking to the team. Johnnie was working the keyboard of his computer. Bill and Trevor were both on the phone.

The room went silent as they all looked at Alex.

Alex smiled put her hand in front of her and said, "still black, not a ghost, why is everyone staring."

The huddle room door opened behind her, and the Chief walked in and asked what she was doing being at work.

Alex shook her head and said that she wanted to make sure the team got the bastard that had someone try to shoot her in the back.

Trey commented that he and Johnnie were hot on the trail and had determined the identity of a second surgeon that was most likely involved. He commented that Dr. Rogers had found a fingerprint on one of the legs. Johnnie ran the fingerprint through and had the name and address of a surgeon. We are about to go out and bring him in for questioning.

Alex nodded and said that talking to this surgeon might give them a break in the case. She added that they needed to make sure that he understood the consequences of not cooperating.

The Chief thanked Alex for coming in but said that she should take it easy and let the rest of the team do all the hard work. He turned to go back to his office.

Travis said he was disappointed that the big Boss had not sent the other boss home.

Alex smiled and pointed at Travis and said that as soon as she thought of the worst job on the case she would be sure to get him assigned to it.

The Chief shook his head and said that it sounded like the team was once again functioning as normal.

Alex smiled and blew a kiss at Trevor. She had to agree with the Chief, it felt like she was back in the groove.

Trey said that the surgeon in question was at the hospital, and they could go and bring him in for questioning.

Alex nodded and said that if he drove, she would go with him. She looked at Johnnie and asked him if that was OK with him.

Johnnie smiled and said that it was and that he would continue to identity the body parts that Dr. Rogers had processed.

Once in the car, Alex thanked Trey for having kept the investigation on track.

Trey thanked her and said it was easy because all of the guys wanted to make sure that we solved the case and nailed the guy that would have someone shoot you in the back. If there is a shootout, I want to be doing the shooting.

Alex remembered how she had reacted when Trey had been victimized and almost beaten to death. She had shot and killed four of the perpetrators and had shot the fifth one to get him to tell her who the boss of the operation was. She had no remorse and in the end she nailed the boss doing the ordering.

She nodded and said she understood the feeling and would step aside and give him the first shots.

They arrived at the hospital and inquired where they might find the doctor.

They went to the nurses station on the floor where they had been sent and asked for the doctor.

They watched him come down the hallway. It seemed he hesitated but then continued coming toward them.

He introduced himself as Dr. Leyton Riley. He then said that he recognized Alex and figured he was being approached about his moonlighting that he had briefly done.

Alex nodded and introduced Trey as her partner and that the two of them were there to interview him and to learn what they could about the moonlight operation. She asked if he was willing to come down to the station with them.

He asked if he was under arrest.

Alex smiled and replied that as long as he willing came along, no arrest was necessary.

He nodded and walked back to the nurses station and checked out for the rest of the day.

As they walked out, Alex suggested that they go and have lunch where they could have their discussion in a more pleasant environment.

Dr. Riley said that would be great and again thanked Alex for getting him out of the hospital in such a low-key manner.

Alex replied that she had no intention of being too public about the case and hoped that he would willing cooperate.

Dr. Riley asked if the body parts business was a legal one as he had been told it was.

Alex shook her head and said that it appeared that it was not a legal operation.

Dr. Riley said that he was shown a license that had a state seal on it and thought it legal, but he later suspected that it might not be.

Alex said that she had obtained the paperwork for the operation that was on file and on investigation the signature of the State Auditor had been found to be forged.

Dr. Riley asked if that made his actions illegal and was his medical licenses in jeopardy.

Alex replied that she had no desire to ruin his life, but she needed his cooperation to arrest the guy that was running such an operation.

She led the way into lunch and was greeted by the proprietor who welcomed her and smiled when she said she would take her usual table.

The proprietor nodded and took three menus to the table where Alex had shot and killed the huge brute that had come to shoot Johnnie.

The proprietor asked if he should expect any action.

Alex shook her head and said that everything would remain calm.

The proprietor smiled and said that the last advertisement that he had made that featured her had his lunch and dinner number up some thirty percent.

Alex said that she was glad and hoped it would stay up.

Dr. Riley asked if Alex was in business with the restaurant.

Alex shook her head and told him that she had shot and killed an attacker from the table that they were seated and since then she had made several advertisements for the restaurant. It seemed that macabre curiosity attracted diners and the business benefited by those curious to dine in the area where the action had taken place.

Dr. Riley shared that he had followed many of the news reports about her cases and was fascinated by the fact that she seemed to survive the gun battles she had been in.

He asked her if the current case would have any gun battles in it.

Alex said that if he was seen as a threat he would most likely be terminated. She shared the fact that this was her first day out of the hospital after being shot in the back by one of the persons associated with the body parts operation.

Dr. Riley frowned and asked if she thought that he was in imminent danger.

Alex replied that she thought that he indeed was in imminent danger.

Dr. Riley said that he was very willing to cooperate with Alex, but he did not have much information. He had only done two operating sessions when a fire had occurred.

The waiter came for the order, and they took a minute to put that in.

Then Alex explained that she thought that he could act as a decoy to attract the person sent to kill him. She wanted to capture that person alive so that her team could track who would have hired him. She wanted the location of the person who had run the body parts business.

Dr. Riley asked whether he had a choice.

Trey spoke up and said that the choice was between having protection or being alone when the killer sought him out.

"Ouch," Dr. Riley said. He shook his head and added that it was worse than being between a rock and a hard place.

Alex said she agreed and that she would see how he could appear to die so that the threat could be removed until the case was solved.

Dr. Riley asked what he would be doing while he was dead.

Trey suggested a vacation to some remote area.

Lunch was brought to the table and the three began to eat.

Alex suggested going to the station afterwards so that anyone watching them would see the Dr. being taken in.

Dr. Riley looked at her and asked if she was serious.

She replied that she was almost ninety per cent sure that they were being watched and that his presence with her was his death sentence.

Dr. Riley again shook his head and commented that she did not pull punches.

Trey smiled and said that working with Alex required that the punches were thrown otherwise you would get hit by a swarm of bullets.

The doctor smiled and asked if he had time for desert.

Alex nodded and said that was one thing there was always time for.

Trey drove to the station and Alex asked the Dr. to wear handcuffs into the station so that it appeared he was under arrest.

Once in the station Alex removed the handcuffs and led the way to the Chief's office.

She introduced the Chief to Dr. Riley and then explained that Dr. Riley had agreed to help in solving the body parts case.

The Chief asked how the Dr. would help.

Alex said that he had agreed to die.

The Chief gave a laugh and said that he knew that she had more in mind than killing a potential witness.

Dr. Riley said that he hoped so.

Alex said that she would like to take Dr. Riley to the morgue to work with Dr. Rogers. She wanted to identify the body parts that Dr. Riley had prepared.

After that she needed the doctor given police protection because she anticipated that the person who had run the body parts business would try to have the doctor killed.

The Chief asked who he should assign to protection duty.

Alex suggested that her team become his protection, but she and Trey would stay in the shadows because they had been on too many news casts.

The Chief nodded and said he trusted that she would set up the right protection duty.

Alex thanked him and suggested they go down to the morgue where all the body parts were currently located. She led the way and made the introductions.

Dr. Rogers immediately took over and asked if Dr. Riley would be able to identify the body parts that he was responsible for.

Dr. Riley replied that would be no problem.

Alex asked that when the two of them were through that she be called, and she would set up the surveillance coverage.

Once back in the huddle room she asked Trey to share that the two of them had done since they had left.

He surfaced the need to provide protection for the doctor and that the three of them had been volunteered to provide it.

Trevor laughed and said he would apologize for his earlier insult if that would relieve him of protection duty and asked why Trey got off so easy.

Bill said that he shouldn't suffer because he had a rude partner.

Johnnie said that next time he would check around the corner for shooters.

Alex shook her head and said that it was too late for all of them and let them know that her partner got special treatment.

She took in how good it felt to be back and interacting with the team. She knew that she had been right in coming in to work.

It was only a short time later when Dr. Rogers and Dr. Riley knocked on the huddle room door. Dr. Rogers said that he wanted Alex to know how helpful Dr. Riley had been and how shocked Dr. Riley had been when he found out that one of the first bodies he had dissected was that of a doctor who had been doing the same thing that he had had done.

Dr. Riley said that he was much more inclined to help in capturing this guy that had claimed to be running a legitimate business but had the previous Dr. and his fiancé killed.

Alex pointed at a chair and commented that if that didn't convince him of the jeopardy he was in then nothing could.

Dr. Riley sat down and asked what was to happened next.

Dr. Rogers excused himself and said he was going back to the morgue.

Alex said that she wanted to know where he lived and about his house or apartment. She added that she wanted the doctor to tell the team in detail what he did each workday and also what he did on weekends.

The doctor was silent for a moment then he began by describing where he lived.

He said that he lived in a second floor two-bedroom apartment on Burnett Avenue about three blocks from the hospital.

His life was rather dull and the routine he followed was to get up around six, have a quick coffee and muffin and then go out for a run for several blocks. He would return to his apartment take a quick shower and then walk to the hospital. He then spent the day at the hospital and usually would stop at one of the fast-food places to get a takeout and go back to his apartment and watch the evening news while he had his dinner.

Alex asked if anyone had any questions. The room was quiet. She then asked if he owned a car.

Dr. Riley said that he did not. He always took a cab or one of the other publicly available rides.

Alex asked what the most dangerous street crossing that he had to face each morning.

The doctor said that the Martin Luther King and Burnet corner was always the one that seemed the most dangerous.

Trey commented that he had driven by there several times when going to the VA facility and he agreed that particular crossing seemed to be the one that was one of the more dangerous places.

He figured it would be the best places to push someone in front of a bus.

Dr. Riley asked how they would be able to keep that from happening.

Alex pointed to Bill, Trevor and Johnnie and said that one of the three would be sitting at the corner dressed as a homeless outcast waiting for him each of the next few mornings until they caught the person that was going to push him in front of a moving bus. She said that she figured the person sent to kill him would be waiting to have a bus moving along at speed coming into the intersection to push him in front of.

Dr. Riley shook his head and said that being a decoy was becoming a little scary.

Alex said that it was, but the alternative choice left him totally unguarded. She made the point that he had a very poor alternative.

She added that she would have a police car parked at the apartment with observation duty to make sure that no one came to just shoot him while he was in his apartment.

Dr. Riley asked if she had any other kill scenarios in mind.

Alex gave a little laugh and said she could think of several others, but they entailed a much more elaborate approach that she did not think the killer would be able to carry out.

She said that she and Trey would be in the comfort of the hospital cafeteria and stay there throughout the day until they captured the killer.

Trevor shook his head and said that being on her team meant smelling like a homeless person, sitting out in the sun while she was comfortably sipping on coffee and eating a sweet roll.

Alex smiled and said that she was looking forward to his glorious morning in the sun.

54

11 The Break

Johnnie let everyone know that he was going to play his ukulele and put out his hat and collect donations as he sat on the corner pretending to be a beggar. He asked Alex to make sure the department knew that she was setting up a decoy at the corner so he would not get arrested.

Trevor said that he would bring his old tuba and do something similar, but he would use an old shoe to collect donations.

Alex laughed and suggested that he leave his tuba at home because she was sure he could not play it quiet enough to keep from getting a huge number of complaints.

Bob smiled and said he had considered bringing his accordion, but he doubted he could still play it.

Johnnie then said that he would split his take among the three of them and they might all be able to buy one cup of coffee to share.

Dr. Riley commented that their banter scared him. He wanted to make sure that they would have their eye out for his killer.

Alex smiled and agree that the three of them always scared her, but they always came through. She made the point that his killer would actually be easy to catch but they had to catch him just before he pushed him in front of the bus. She made the point that if the same person showed up two times in a row they would arrest him and bring him in for questioning. If he was the one then there needed to be a news release showing the doctor in front of the bus with blood running down the street.

She said that she would work with the Metro leadership to set up that scene and with the department film crew to get it filmed.

Dr. Riley said that sounded very elaborate. He asked when that would take place.

Alex suggested that evening and she would have the person editing it put in the early morning sun into the picture.

Dr. Riley nodded and said that things seemed to be moving along at a fast pace.

Trey replied that it was either fast or slow in the detective business and that a moderate pace was not known.

Alex made a call and explained to the person at the other end that she needed the help of the Metro in solving the case she was working. After reaching the President she explained what she needed. He said he would make a call and have one of the spare busses ready for the filming. After that they agreed on the location.

Alex called the police film department and arranged for someone to shoot the scene. She asked that some fake blood be brought to the scene.

She then asked Dr. Riley if he was ready to die.

He smiled and said that he was ready if it was just fake.

A few moments later a person knocked at the door and said that the camera crew was ready to go.

Alex stood up and asked who wanted to go and direct the movie scene.

Everyone stood up and followed. Bob and Trevor got into the camera van and the rest got into Alex's car. Trey was behind the wheel and asked where they were going.

Alex gave him the address, and they all left. She had picked out a street that went downhill like the one on Martin Luther King Drive where she expected the attempted killing to take place.

The camera crew set up and the Metro bus driver positioned the bus as instructed. The camera man asked the doctor to lay face down in the street with his left ear to the street and his arms splayed out. His sports jacket was to be open. His mouth needed to be slightly open so that the blood looked like it was coming out from both his mouth and his head.

He then pulled one of the doctor's shoes off and tossed it down just below the pool of blood.

He asked the bus driver to look astonished or have a disbelieving look on his face.

Alex looked at the scene and commented that she wished she had thought about asking for some extra people to be onlookers.

The camera man said that he could make that happen and asked his two helpers to put on their more casual outfits on. He then set up the camera on a timer and positioned everyone and pushed the remote he had in his hand and took his first shot. He set up several scenes and took shots of each from several angles.

Alex was not sure which scene was best, but she liked the one that had a police officer checking for a pulse best.

She thanked everyone and asked who wanted to be treated to Johnnie's favorite place to eat.

The filming crew asked if they were invited. And the bus driver did the same.

Alex nodded and said the treat was on her. She asked Johnnie were he wanted to go. He suggested where the logs could be seen floating down the river. Alex knew which restaurant that was and gave them a call and asked for reservations for nine.

Dr. Riley asked if they would all allow him to pay.

Alex smiled and thanked him for the offer but said it would look awkward if later they had to arrest him. She said she would have to decline but if Trevor wanted to step up she would be glad to let him pay.

Trevor shook his head and said that he had just spent the last of his saving to pay his son's college tuition to Harvard.

Everyone on the team laughed since they knew that his son was president of his own company and had been out of college for at least ten years and had not attended Harvard.

Alex nodded and said that then it was settled, and they should all head to the restaurant and watch the logs float by and Johnnie could tell them about having learned to play the ukelele and she would pay.

During dinner Dr. Riley asked if he could let his family know that he would really not be dead.

Alex replied that he could, but he would need to make sure his family did not share it with anyone and after the news announcing his death they would put out a statement that they would like to be given the space to mourn.

Dinner ended and the team decided to go their separate ways.

Alex had Trey drop Johnnie and her at the apartment. The crime scene tapes at the apartment were down but the yellow sketch marks on the sidewalk and on the street were still visible. The outline of the bikes made her think about the fact that they would need to walk to work unless they got their bikes back.

She asked if Johnnie wanted to come with her to her favorite bike shop to see if they could replace their bikes.

Johnnie asked why he couldn't just get his from the station.

Alex replied that it would most likely be months before they got their bikes back and she knew for sure she would need to have hers go through a major overhaul. She added that they could probably get a good deal if the shop had any good used bikes.

Johnnie said that it would be fun to shop for a new bike and asked when she thought they could get to the shop.

Alex replied that it would be right after he got off his first day of killer patrol.

Johnnie shook his head and said, "wow yes that begins in the morning. A better question is how will I get in place at the corner."

Alex said that Trey would pick them up at six in the morning and by seven he would be on station. She and Trey would park nearby until it was time for the Dr. to get to the corner.

Once the Dr. made it to the hospital the three of them would return to the station review the death scenes and pick their favorite for release to the news.

Johnnie said it sounded like a good plan.

Alex said good night and took the elevator to the top floor and walked down toward her apartment. She was surprised to see Sandra sitting on a chair in front of her apartment.

Sandra greeted her and said that the Chief had asked her if she was willing to be one of the guards that he was posting. She and her husband had volunteered to be on coverage duty. She said that there was a third volunteer who said he had been the guard outside of Trey's room when he was in the VA hospital.

Alex thanked her and asked whether a glass of milk and some cookies would help.

Sandra smiled and said that she was hoping for just such an offer.

When Alex walked into the apartment she was surprised to see Matt sitting on the couch reading.

He said that his boss told him to take one more day off and make sure that she got a good night's sleep.

Alex smiled and said she had no doubt about being ready for a good night's sleep but wondered if she would be able to do so with the bandages that she had on.

Matt said he would look at the bandages and see if he could make them less bulky so that she could be comfortable in bed.

She gave him a kiss and then said she had to deliver some milk and cookies to her guard at the door and then she would be ready for him to see about making her bandages less bulky.

Trey let her know that he would be leaving about five in the morning. His team was swinging by to pick him up.

Alex said that would work for her because she and Johnnie would be picked up by Trey a few minutes later. She shared that Johnnie had promised her a pancake breakfast with two poached eggs on the pancakes.

Matt smiled and said that his team was arriving with a breakfast sandwich and coffee for him.

Alex said that made the coming morning convenient for both of them.

The next morning Trey showed up and Bill and Trevor were following in their car. Trevor said that Bill had not let him buy donuts and insisted they would follow and make sure that things went down as expected.

Alex thanked them for coming along. She said they should all get on the same chat group so they could communicate with each other at the scene.

Trey then led the way to the corner were they expected the attempted killing to take place.

Alex watched as Johnnie walked to the corner and sat down and placed his hat at his feet. She had asked Bill and Travis to park a few cars behind them. She adjusted her mirror so she could see the Dr. approaching the corner.

She looked along the sidewalk and saw no one but the doctor approaching the corner. Then a person stepped out from between two of the houses and began following the doctor.

She said that she thought the pusher was now behind the doctor.

She heard Johnnie asking for money for breakfast.

The doctor ignored him, but she was surprised to see the pusher take a roll of money from is pocket and put a bill into Johnnie's hat.

The walk light turned green, and the doctor walked across. The pusher turned to his right and walked down the sidewalk.

Alex told the doctor to go to work and for Johnnie to walk across the street and come back to the car and they would all go back to the station.

Once back at the station Bill suggested that they should arrange for a bus to come by at the right time.

Alex agreed and said she would arrange it for the coming morning.

Johnnie said that he had taken a picture of the suspected killer and would see if he could identify who that person was.

The film crew leader came in with his computer and said that he had several options to pick from that could be used as a news announcement.

Alex asked Johnnie to help get the computer hooked to the large screen. She was pleased that all the scenes seemed real. She said she thought the best one was with a police officer checking out the doctor to see if he was dead.

The entire team agreed. The film crew leader said that he liked that one as well and that he would put more people into the scene and arrange for its release when Alex gave him the order.

Alex thanked him and after he had left she said she was going shopping for a bike.

She then let the team know that Johnnie would be the person at the corner on the following morning and if the same guy showed up they would take him into custody and check him out. She made the point that if either Bill or Trevor were to be at that corner they would likely spook the potential killer.

Trevor whined and said that he had wasted the entire previous evening polishing his tuba so that he could play his part.

Alex shook her head and told him that he should then take it to his high school and donated it to the band.

Trey said that he would stay with Bill and Trevor to see if they could figure out who had set fire to the warehouse.

Alex asked Johnnie to drive to the bike shop.

Once there she was greeted by her name as she walked in. She liked the fact that the owner was always polite and cordial. She asked if he had any specials on some high-end bikes.

He asked whether she wanted brand new or was she interested in some good used ones.

Alex replied that a bargain in a good used one would be nice.

He showed her one that had a belt drive that he was offering at half the price of a new one.

Alex liked it immediately and asked if a carrier rack could be put on the back. She asked to take if for a ride around the lot. She came back and let him know that she would take it.

She then pointed to Johnnie and said he needed a bargain too.

The shop owner pointed to a bike that had a sign advertising it as a limited-edition Amsterdam bike that was also belt driven. It was a little less expensive but did not have as big a discount as the one she had chosen.

Johnnie said that he liked the blue color and the front trey that it had and asked if he could take a quick spin.

When he finished he said that he would take it.

Alex took the bike rack out from the trunk and set it up. She and Johnnie wheeled their bikes out and put them in the rack. Her bike was white and his was a lustrous blue. She commented that they looked great.

Johnnie agreed and said they should celebrate getting new bikes.

Alex agreed and asked what he had in mind.

Johnnie suggested a picnic on the weekend along the Loveland bike trail.

Alex said that sounded great and she should be healed enough to enjoy the ride.

They left the car in the police lot in its normal parking spot so that Trey could find it the next morning.

Alex led off and the two rode their new bikes back to the apartment.

Sandra saw Alex pushing her bike up the hall and let out a whistle and commented that her new bike was a beauty.

Alex chuckled and said that the compliment would get Sandra an extra cookie and that today it would be warm because she was baking a new batch of oatmeal raisin cookies.

She went into the apartment and put her new bike in the rack where her old bike was usually placed. It was then she remembered leaving her new rack in the trunk of the car.

The next morning when Trey picked them up Johnnie volunteered to take both his and her bike rack and put them in his apartment.

Alex thanked him.

As they were driving to where Johnnie would be sitting she told him that if the same guy showed up that he should arrest him.

Johnnie said it would be no problem.

Alex pointed out Bill and Trevor's car as they approached. They paused for a moment to let Johnnie out and then drove on and parked a short distance from the corner. Alex checked out the teams connection and was pleased that everyone including the doctor was on.

It seemed like a repeat of the morning before but this time the bus that Alex had arranged would make its approach and the would-be killer would be apprehended as he was about to push the doctor out in front of it.

Alex watched the scene unfold as if it had been rehearsed. The bus was starting across the intersection, the perpetrator stepped forward to push the doctor and as he placed his hand on the doctors back, Johnnie put the point of his revolver to the pushers head and said that he was under arrest and to step back.

Both Bill and Travis rushed up and put the perpetrator in hand cuffs, read him his rights, and led him back toward their car.

Alex got out and walked up to the doctor and told him to go to the hotel in Blue Ash and enjoy the next week or so until the case could be resolved. She said that the news release would be in the morning reporting and would most likely make all the channels.

62

12 Order Fulfilment

Reston was relieved when he watched the morning news. The report focused on the death of Dr. Leyton Riley. It showed the doctor splayed out in the street with blood running out of his head. Things seemed to be looking up. He had been able to fulfill eighty percent of the orders that he had brought with him from the Cincinnati operation with new body parts garnered in his new location. His bosses were pleased, and he was on the road to focusing on the expansion of the business to the west coast, Asia, and Europe.

He was fairly certain that the case would go cold at the Cincinnati end.

He felt very good about how his new crew operated. They were much better at bringing in the people he identified, and they were very good at making sure the personal possessions such as the vehicles or bicycles were disposed of in an effective manner. He had arranged for the cars to be sold and sent out of state, and he liked the fact that his workers filed off any serial numbers, painted the bikes and sold them to a local bike shop. He let them keep the money they made from that endeavor.

He felt that things couldn't be going much better.

He had also learned about a new technique to get rid of the unused body parts that was referred to as liquification. This provided a way to process those parts and did not require the use of the oven. It eliminated any smoke or odor associated with that process. He studied the process and decided on getting a model designed for large pets. The model was large enough for his needs and it kept the seller from linking his operation with human bodies. He got good feedback about how well it worked from his two workers. They commented that all the waste was an odorless white powder.

Things were going well enough and smoothly enough that he gave his three workers a significant bonus for their good work.

Had he known what was happening in Cincinnati he would have arranged for a new hiding place versus setting up travel arrangements.

Back in Cincinnati, the person hired to push the doctor in front of the bus was sitting in a cell.

Alex and the team were sitting in the Chief's office updating him on the situation. Alex highlighted the fact that they had arrested the potential killer as he was about to push the doctor in front of the bus and the fact that the doctors, "death" was making the morning's news. She shared that the doctor was planning to take a fishing trip to the Tetons for the next several weeks or until he got word he could come back to life.

She had questioned the perp and had learned he was to earn five thousand dollars for pushing the doctor. He was a legal immigrant that did small jobs for a local drug dealer. She said they would need to spend more time with him to see if he could identify someone that was connected with the human body parts business.

She turned to Bill and Travis and asked them to update the Chief on how they were doing on finding out who had set the fire.

Bill said that they figured that the fire had been set by the person hired to clean the facility. They had been waiting to get Johnnies help in zeroing in on who the cleaning person might be. They had a list of people offering that service and need to somehow narrow the list down so they could get in the field and question these cleaners.

Alex suggested they look for any cleaners doing advertising in the help pages versus the larger operations. She figured that it would be an individual that was on their own.

Johnnie said he would be glad to get on it immediately.

The Chief thanked them for the update and said that Dr. Rogers had finished processing all the body parts and had put all the reports online.

Alex suggested they go to the huddle room and get organized. She wanted to make some sort of breakthrough that led to the location of the person who had set up the operation in Cincinnati because she was fairly sure he would be setting up a similar operation somewhere nearby.

Johnnie reminded the team that he had already done an initial search of the most probable cities. Three were in Ohio, one in Indiana, one in Pennsylvania and one in New York.

Alex said she was betting on Ohio, but she would go wherever Johnnie pointed. She asked him what his search parameters were. He said that he would look for buildings or houses that had sold since the fire. He hoped that it was not too lengthy of a list, but he figured he had ways of speeding up the search.

Alex asked him to focus on getting her a list of potential new sites before focusing on who set the local fire.

Travis gave a moan and said that once again he was being put on the back burner and that he would be happy to bring in an extra bear claw for her to enjoy so that he could get equal treatment.

The Chief shook his head and told the team to work out their problems outside of his office or he would assign them all to ground clean up duty.

Bill put his arm over Travis's shoulder and as he led him out of the office he said that he felt his pain.

Alex smiled saluted the Chief and said that everything was good.

Once in the huddle room she asked if Bill and Trevor would question the perp they had locked up and see if they could get some sort of information that would help in determining who had set up the hit and where the kill order came from. She added that some names and locations would be useful.

They badly needed to find the new location because she was sure that harvesting of human body parts was profitable enough that it was the drug war equivalent that they now faced.

Bill and Travis left the huddle room and said that they would be back before lunch. Travis smiled and said that he was going to let Bill be the good cop and he was going to be the bad one.

Alex smiled and said that they would both be playing their natural role.

Bill nodded and added that he agree wholeheartedly with her.

Alex turned her attention back to Johnnie and suggested they focus first on the three locations in Ohio.

Trey suggested starting with the most industrial area and the area with the most homeless people.

Johnnie ran that and got the order of the cities with the highest populations and the highest homeless people. He put them up on the screen in one two three order. They were Cleveland, Columbus, and Cincinnati.

Trey said that he would definitely start with Cleveland because it also had a sprawling population down towards Akron.

Johnnie said he would tap into the latest filings of sales registered in the courthouse.

There was only one warehouse that had changed hands and that was between two large freight companies. There was a large number of homes but only about a dozen of larger homes.

Alex suggested they take a look at the larger homes and decide by location and by the arial look which ones they felt were the most likely.

It did not take long before they had shortened the list to the three most likely.

They used the internet and several realty services to look over the three.

Alex picked the two most likely and then said that it was time for the team to take a road trip.

Johnny volunteered to get the team a nice conversion van or something like it so they could all drive up together.

Trey volunteered to make reservations at an Embassy suites.

Alex called Trevor and asked how they were doing with getting information.

He responded that they were sitting at his desk having their perp looking through pictures to see who he could identify associated with his order to push the doctor in front of the bus.

He picked out the three dead shooters and Reston Sanclemente who was the person he saw with his boss.

It turns out his boss has a warrant out for not having paid over twelve speeding tickets so we will be able to pick him up to get more information.

Alex said they should put their perp back in the holding cell and get together for a team road trip discussion.

A short time later, Bill and Trevor came into the team room and asked where they were going.

Trey explained that they had narrowed their guess as to where the new body part processing operation had relocated to two places in Cleveland.

He pointed at Alex and said she was ready to leave and see if they could find the new operation and close it down.

Bill commented that would be great but what were the chances that one of the two places was the new operation site.

Alex replied that Trey and Johnnie had picked the city together. Then Johnnie had identified the sales that were registered since the fire closed the operation in Cincy and then they had worked together and narrowed it to two places. She said that only footwork would now resolve the situation.

Trevor nodded and said that so far Johnnie was batting a thousand and he was ready to get the footwork done.

Alex said she was going to clear the trip with the Boss and that they should all plan on meeting in the station parking lot early in the morning and they would drive to Cleveland and check out the two places.

The Chief listened to Alex's request to take a field trip to Cleveland. He said he supported the trip and that he would call the Cleveland Chief of Police in to let him know that the five of them would be up.

Alex thanked him and suggested that if they found the operation they would get the local police involved in shutting down the operation. She pointed out that they might need to get a speedy search warrant so they could enter the operation.

The Chief agreed and said he would put in the call as soon as she left.

Alex thanked him and said that she planned to leave early the next day but would stay in contact as they drove up to Cleveland.

Early the next morning the stars were still twinkling in the sky as Alex and the team got into their Mercedes luxury van that Johnnie had rented from his car rental friend at a great price

Meanwhile in Cleveland Reston was driving to the Cleveland airport to get on a flight to Los Angelos. He was going out to meet with the local mafia head to see about setting up a body parts operation. He had no idea how close he was to being shut down in Cleveland nor how detrimental the closure would be to his wellbeing.

Alex contacted the Chief and got the number to the Police Chief in Cleveland and after introduction and a rather lengthy discussion she got assurances that she would have search warrants for the two addresses and two police cars backing the team up at each locations. The Cleveland police would bring the warrants for each site with them.

She shared with the team that they would meet the Cleveland team at each site and then together they would surround the buildings and proceed to go in.

She reminded everyone to be ready but not to shoot unless they were shot at or saw someone about to shoot.

Trevor shook his head and said the case that had them coming down from the attic and walking into a hail of bullets was waking him up at nights. He hoped that the group they faced was less gun happy. He commented that he had his entire body Kevlar body suit with him.

Alex said that she was not expecting gunfire, but they should all wear their bullet proof vests and that if they had no vests they would be left in the van. She was pleased to hear everyone say they had brought theirs along.

They arrived at the first house at eleven and were met their by the two Cleveland Patrol cars.

Alex made sure the correctness of the paperwork and of the address. The house looked as isolated as it had looked from the Google Maps view, but it was clear that whoever lived there was taking great care of the place and the flowers around the perimeter of the house and the thriving back garden reduced the likelihood that this was a body process site to nearly zero.

Alex asked everyone to stay back but asked Bill and Trevor to step far enough into the yard to be able make sure no one left by the back door.

She and Trey walked up the steps and walked slowly along the porch and rang the doorbell. Trey took the front and was greeted by an elderly gentleman who asked what he was selling. Trey showed his badge, gave a brief explanation, and asked if he and his partner could come in.

The door opened wider, and an elderly gentleman stepped out and saw the two police cars and the black van. He commented that it seemed that they had expected trouble.

Alex replied that they were pleased to not have any and wondered if they could get a quick look inside.

The wife came to the door and said that they should come in and reassure themselves that whatever they were looking for in the house they would find only the old furniture and things that she and her husband had accumulated for over the past fifty years. They had just moved in during the spring and where still trying to get their things unpacked.

Alex followed her in, and Trey and the husband came in. Alex thanked the wife for the offer of coffee or tea but the two of them had another address to check out. She apologized for disturbing them.

The wife said that no apology was necessary, and they should be careful at the next place.

Alex nodded and said she would be very careful there.

She went out to the two police cars and spent a few minutes talking to the four officers. She introduced everyone and then asked if they knew a good lunch place and added that the Cincinnati detective unit would pay for lunch.

Lunch was at a Mexican restaurant that had a lunch special for only twelve dollars a plate. There was a wide variety of lunch plates that went from twelve to twenty dollars. Everyone selected a different item.

Alex selected Polynesian Pork tacos and an order of onion straws for the table. Trey ordered West coast shrimp tacos and Johnnie ordered smoked brisket tacos. Bill and Trevor both ordered Nashville Hot chicken tacos. They all knew that everyone would be trying a little of everyone else's orders.

The four police officers were sitting at tables at each end of the long table that the five members of the Cincinnati team was sitting.

One of them asked how long the five of them had worked together.

Trevor laughed and said that it had been a lifetime, and they were all still talking to each other.

The lunch took over an hour and after everyone had finished they got up and walked out to their cars.

Alex gave the next address and one of the Cleveland group commented that he knew the neighborhood and it was not as nice as the one they had just left. He figured that this time they should all take positions around the house.

The two police cars led the way.

Alex asked everyone to put on their Kevlar jackets and check their weapons. She commented that she had a bad feeling about the next address.

As they drove into the neighborhood she became almost certain that they were at the new human processing center. She let the team know that she was having one of her Déjà vu moments.

Trevor nodded and said that he was then sure they were at the new human body parts processing center.

Alex asked the four police officers to put on their body armor.

One of the officers asked what made her think there would be shooting.

Alex shook her head and said that she was not sure, but it was better to be safe.

Bob and Trevor took the back of the house. She and Trey took the front.

She asked the four policemen to take the sides. She looked at Johnnie and told him to go wherever he liked but to keep his head down.

She walked up to the front door and announced that the house was surrounded and anyone inside should come out with their hands up.

A few seconds afterwards there was a shot fired from a second story window and one of the police officers went down.

Alex watched as Johnnie rushed over to the officer and as he knelt in front of him he pointed his gun up at some target and fired three times. A moment later she heard what she was sure was a body hit the ground.

She knew that whomever it was would be dead.

She heard Bill shout out telling someone to stop and that they were under arrest and then several gunshots.

Then she could hear a third person shout out that he was surrendering and that he was coming out with his hands up.

She looked at her watch and realized that the entire episode had taken less than four minutes.

Trevor kicked in the front door and the two of them rushed in. Two police officers came in the back and the four of them checked out the entire place to make sure there was no one else.

Alex noted the cooler locker that was on the same level as what looked like a surgery room. She had no desire to look in.

Alex walked back outside as an EMT unit arrived. She walked over to where the downed officer was sitting. He had been hit in the chest area; his body shield had cracked but had held. The EMT team checked him out and Bill said that he had been shot as well and just wanted to have them take a quick look.

Alex walked over to him and asked to see where he had been hit. There was a flattened bullet on the Kevlar jacket. She gave him a hug and said that she hoped the bruise would not be too bad.

Neither of the two had anything worse than what would be a bruise the next day.

A swarm of police cars with their lights flashing arrived. The coroner and his team began processing the two dead shooters.

Alex watched as one of the officers that she was sure he would be the Police Chief approached.

He walked up to her and introduced himself and then smiled and said he had been warned about the Cincinnati Black Annie Oakley and asked which of the two she had shot.

Alex smiled and said that she had not fired her weapon, but Wild Bill Johnnie Hancock had shot and killed the shooter that had shot one of his officers and Wild Bill Danson had survived getting shot in the chest as he shot and killed the second.

She then suggested that the coroner not worry too much about processing the two dead shooters and that he go inside and begin to examine the body parts that he would find in the cooler on the first floor.

The Police Chief walked over to the coroner and after a moment came back and asked about the body parts. He asked how they would be identified.

Alex said that they were still in the process of identifying the body parts that had been in the cooler at the Cincinnati operation and that Dr. Rogers the coroner there would be a good person to contact, and she pointed at Johnnie and said that he would be the resource for one of the Cleveland IT guys. He was the one that was identifying most of the body parts. She added that the surgeon that was doing the work in Cleveland needed to be identified and arrested. He most probably believed he was working for a legitimate company, but he was most likely aware that something was not quite right. She suggested stationing a police squad at the house and that on Monday during the day or early evening they should expect the arrival of the surgeon. They should also expect the arrival of the person running the operation.

She followed the coroner into the house and led him to the cooler door. She said she preferred to remain outside of the cooler.

The coroner and his team went in but two of his team almost immediately came out and said that the scene was horrible, and they needed to get outside.

Alex said she had the same reaction, and she still had nightmares about it.

The Police Chief walked in and looked through the door and shook his head. He asked if the parts came from cadavers.

Alex shook her head. She said that the ones in Cincinnati had been linked with homeless people, and a few had been identified from missing person's reports. They were missing persons who had gone to work and not returned home that evening.

The Chief said that he was going to keep this as quiet as possible and that it would scare the entire region if it got out.

Alex agreed and pointed out that the organizer had not been on location and was somewhere around and needed to be apprehended.

"Damn" was the Chief's last words.

13 Return

*R*eston looked out the window and watched the horizon sink as the plane turned and got into the position to make a landing. It was the end to what he saw as a very successful and productive trip. He had made contact with the LA branch of the mafia and had started the process of getting the parts business established. He would return in a few weeks and help them take the next steps in getting the business going. He knew the details and timing to establish the harvesting, processing, and distribution network. The distribution system was the first thing that was needed then the harvesting network needed to be put in place. The processing entailed the brick-and-mortar elements and were actually the easiest to put in place.

The plane landed but it seemed to take forever to get to the gate and then to unload. He waited impatiently for his bag to slide down onto the rotating carrier. He got his bags and went out and had to stand in line to catch a cab.

During the ride to the house, he made a call to his bodyguard, but Luca did not answer. He called Angello and Dario and none of them answered.

Alarm bells went off in his head. He then saw a police car parked about a block from the house. He told the cab driver to keep going and that he wanted to go to a hotel. They drove past the house and then he asked the cab driver to turn and come back up on the next block. He asked the cab to wait for him while he checked to see if anyone was home at his friend's house. He then got out and slowly walked back to the house on the side that was out of view to the police car. He got to the alley way behind the house and opened the side door. He knew immediately something was wrong. He quietly went through the house. He carefully looked out the window and saw the yellow outline markings of a body on the gravel drive on that side of the house. He looked out the back and saw a similar outline near the garage. Both areas were taped off with yellow tape.

He opened his safe and took out the cash and put it in a large briefcase. He then closed the safe and took his briefcase.

He walked back out the side door and walked back to the cab and asked to be taken to the Sheraton.

He was in a stunned state. He wondered how the police had found his operation. The only thing that made sense was that the Cincinnati Detective group had somehow been able to trace him.

He knew that he was in trouble and that he would have to contact his leader that was in New York and get instructions in how to proceed.

Trey sat in the breakfast area waiting for his pancakes and eggs to get prepared. He was nursing his cup of coffee and had a piece of buttered toast with strawberry jam that he was nibbling on. He watched as Alex made her way to his table. She stopped and got a glass of orange juice and a cup of coffee and put in her request at the grill window.

Alex was not surprised to see Trey sitting at the table. The two of them seemed to trade morning breakfast arrivals. Once she had had her breakfast order in she went to the table and asked how his night had been.

Her phone rang just as she sat down. She answered and listened to the Police Chief as he told her that all three of the confiscated phones had received a call a few moments earlier. Alex thanked him for letting her know and suggested the call came from their boss. She asked if his police squad had seen anyone arrive at the house. The chief replied that the only action had been a taxi that drove by but did not stop at the house.

Alex thanked him for the call and let him know that the team would be in to interrogate the person that they had captured at the house.

Johnnie walked into the breakfast area carrying his computer and came over to the table. He said that he had continued to process the information about the current operation and had realized that the little house across the alley was owned by the same person that owned the house they had raided.

Alex asked what name was on both of the deeds.

Johnnie looked that up and said that a Preston Clemente was the person listed.

Alex smiled and said that their perp must like his name because he had added and deleted a few letters and had almost the same name. She asked Johnnie to check to see if someone of that name had checked into any hotel close to the houses.

She suggested he put in his breakfast order in before doing any more digging.

About the same time Bob and Trevor walked in and came over to the table.

She asked Bob how he was feeling.

Bob replied that he was fine but did have a hand sized bruise on his chest.

A few moments later Johnnie said he had three hits but none of the names were the one that they had discussed.

Alex asked where the hotels were located. She then asked Bill, Trevor, and Trey if they were willing to go to the hotels and show the desk personnel a picture of Reston to determine if he had checked into one of the three.

They all agreed to do so. Trevor asked what she would be up to.

Alex said that she was going to question the one person who had survived to learn what she could about the operation. She figured that Johnnie would be instrumental in checking out what they learned.

Johnnie was at the wheel as they arrived at the Central station. He drove to the entrance to the underground car park.

Alex showed her badge and the guard said he was expecting them. She handed him a bag of chocolate and told him to enjoy himself.

She led the way up the stairs and then checked in at a desk at the entrance to the building. She had been expected and was shown the way to the Chief's office.

He greeted her and Johnnie and asked if she would like a coffee or something else to drink.

Both she and Johnnie said coffee would be fine.

The Chief then said he was going to call a couple of the policemen in that had been with her the previous day because they wanted to say thanks.

Alex and Johnnie sat down and a few moments later the Chief returned with the two. One of them was the officer that had been shot.

He came over and shook Alex's hand and said that his wife insisted that he invite her over for dinner if she had time.

Alex smiled and said that the offer warmed her heart but that it was not necessary. Alex took out a bag of Godiva chocolates and said that he should give it to his wife.

She gave one to his partner and one to the Chief.

His partner commented that her insistence that they wear their protective gear had at first irritated them but as it turned out the situation warranted it and that in the future they would be more cautious.

Alex nodded. She related the fact that her team members had at first struggled with her insistence of wearing their Kevlar outfits but after a few shootouts they had all become believers.

She suggested that the Kevlar outfits made it less bulky and more comfortable to be protected and maybe the Cleveland Police could make it part of the official gear.

The Chief asked what Alex planned to do next.

She shared that her three other members were checking three hotels to see if they could apprehend the leader of the operation and that if one of them located this person she would like the Cleveland police to back her up and then make the arrest.

Both officers immediately spoke up that they and the other two who had been at the house would all volunteer to make the arrest.

The Chief said that he supported the four being the ones that would take the lead, but he would probably have some other units ready to respond as well. He said that he would like the arrest to take place without any shooting. He also reiterated the fact that he did not want any word to get out on the type of operation that was going on.

Alex smiled and said he sounded just like her Chief, and she agreed with the sentiment. The fact that the mafia was getting into the body parts business scared the daylights out of her.

The Chief led the way down to the holding area and talked briefly to the sergeant that was in charge.

After the Chief left, the sergeant looked at her and asked what she had done for the Chief that had him giving her the green light to do whatever she wanted.

Alex smiled and handed the sergeant a bag of chocolate and said that a little sweetness always made things easier.

She said that he looked like he could scare a person if he felt like it and that she wanted the person that she was about to question to be scared. She asked if he would threaten the person, tell him that he would most likely get the gas chamber or spend the rest of his life in a top security prison where he would most likely be the girl.

The sergeant shook his head, smiled, and said that the chocolates did make it easier. He showed her to the room where the questioning was to take place and he explained that a monitor would be recording the session, and he took her to the monitoring room and introduced the monitor who it turned out was a new policewoman on her first assignment.

She and Johnnie were handed headsets and the policewoman explained how the system worked and then adjusted everything so that she would have a good recording.

Alex thanked her and handed her a bag of chocolate, and they went into the questioning room.

Johnnie asked her how many bags of candy she had left.

Alex smiled and asked what he had in mind.

Johnnie said that he wanted to be the kind, generous, good guy and be able to offer the perp a candy.

Alex nodded and asked whether she had to be the bad cop.

Johnnie shook his head and said that her just being herself would probably scare the perp.

There was a knock on the room door and then the hand cuffed perp was brought in and chained to a ring on the table.

Alex greeted him by name and introduced herself and Johnnie. She asked Dario to explain his role in the body parts business.

Dario's hands were shaking, and he had trouble answering her.

Alex asked why his hands were shaking.

Dario replied that he did not want to be put to death.

Alex asked if he had put anyone to death to get their body parts.

Dario shook his head in the negative but did not speak.

Johnnie pushed a chocolate to him and suggested he eat it and asked whether a bottle of water would help.

Dario said that a bottle of water would be nice.

Alex looked at Johnnie and told him that he shouldn't be so nice to a person that was probably a killer of innocent people.

There was a knock on the door, and an officer came in with three bottles of water.

Alex paused and took a long drink.

She then leaned in and put her face about a foot from Dario's and looked him in the eyes and asked if he had watched innocent people being killed.

Tears came into Dario's eyes, and he shook his head in the affirmative. He then whispered out the fact that Luca and Angelo were the ones who either shot or slit the person's throat. He said they made fun of him because he often had to go and throw up.

"So, you were queasy, but you went along," Alex asked.

Dario said that he didn't have a choice.

Alex slammed her hand on the table as if angry. And said that he was a person too weak to make a choice to save innocent people.

Johnnie quietly said that it was not appropriate for her to lose her temper.

Dario said that his entire family was part of the mafia, and he had no place to go if he were to quit. He would be ostracized but more likely he would be killed.

Tell me how many people you have so far participated in killing.

Dario was silent for a few moments and then said there were probably fourteen.

The number caught Alex by surprise, and she went silent. She had spotted the parts of someone that was either small or very young. It made her feel sick. She wished she would have been faster at stopping the operation.

Johnnie pushed another chocolate to Dario and asked what the age range was of the people he watched being killed.

Dario began to sob openly. He finally was able to say nine years old to forty-five.

Alex asked how the target people were identified.

Dario said that he was not sure of the details, but the boss had access to several participating doctors, and he also had access to the hospital databases.

Alex then asked the name of the doctor that did the dissections.

Dario said that he only knew him as Dr. Riley.

Alex let Dario know that the current questioning session was over and that his continued cooperation would make it likely that he could keep from getting a death penalty, but his involvement was deep, and she said he would most likely spent much of the rest of his life in prison.

Alex took the candy bag from Johnnie and gave it to Dario and said she was sure that there would be several more questioning sessions so that he could clarify in detail what had transpired at the house.

Two officers came in and took Dario out of the room.

Alex stood for a moment and asked Johnnie to give her a hug. She was surprised at how empty she felt. She knew that she and the team worked as fast as possible to catch the killers, but to have an operation that in the two months since the Cincinnati operation had been closed kill fourteen people including a child overwhelmed her.

The Chief walked in and said that he was overwhelmed by what he had heard and that in his entire thirty-five-year career he had not handled a case like this one.

Alex nodded and agreed that it was mind boggling, but she had just closed two cases that were horrible. One had a nationwide organization that killed almost two hundred women after abusing them and the other had one individual killing and burying her victims along the US, Canadian border.

The Chief shook his head and said that he didn't know how she could handle it.

Alex agreed and shared the fact that her team had both team and individual sessions with the department phycologist every month.

They also spent many weekends doing picnics and going on outings together.

She pointed at Johnnie and said he took them to the best restaurants for lunch and made sure she ended up paying.

She said that she would be scheduling several additional sessions with the phycologist as soon as she was back in Cincinnati because she knew this case was having a huge impact on her.

The Chief said that he would check to see when the phycologist in his department was available.

The policewoman in the booth asked if he would support her getting an appointment.

The Chief replied that he supported her.

He then shared that one of her members had called in to let the department know that the person they were looking for had checked in at the hotel where they were, and they were standing by to wait for backups.

Alex looked at the texts on her phone. She had Bill texting a no hit and Trey with a negative face and the red circle with a line through it. Trevor had an explosion emoji and simple said hit.

She asked if she could ride along to the hotel to be part of the arrest.

The Chief said she could ride in his car.

Alex stopped by the recording booth and asked that the recording be handled as evidence. She told the policewoman to follow through on getting some counseling because the nightmare would only get better by talking it out.

78

14 Capture

*A*s she, the Chief and Johnnie walked in Alex saw that Bill, Trey were with Trevor, and they were speaking to a woman that was probably the manager.

The Chief walked over and asked where the other guests might be and learned that a few were in the restaurant. He sent two of his men over with orders to keep the guests there.

Trevor shared the floor and room number and the Chief asked where the stairwells were located and sent two men to each location with instructions to keep people out of the stairwell or detain them if any came out.

He then suggested that he, Alex, and her team and two additional officers take the elevator up to the tenth floor.

On the way up, Alex learned from Trevor that Reston had rented the Grand Suite because it was the last available room. He had surprised the desk clerk by paying cash for the six hundred dollar per night rate and had paid for three days.

Alex let everyone in the elevator know that she wanted Reston alive and that she would take the lead in his arrest. Once he was subdued the Cleveland police should take over and make the official arrest.

The elevator door opened, and the gunfire started.

As she stepped out, she felt a bullet hit her in the right side. She shouted out to the people in the elevator not to shoot and then she shot Reston in the arm in which he was holding his gun. She followed with a shot to his left thigh. As he went down, she shouted for the team to subdue him.

Trey was the first to get to Reston and he kicked him in midsection as Reston tried to pick up his gun with his left hand.

The kick launched Reston against the wall. He was trying to breath and seemed to be mouthing curses.

Alex sat down against the wall. She knew she was going to have a huge bruise on her right side.

Bill knelt next to her and asked if she was alright. He said he knew exactly how she was feeling at the moment because he had felt that way on the previous day.

Alex gave him a weak smile and said that she was going to see if she could sit in the hot tub for the rest of the day, but she wanted to tell Reston that she was going to make sure he would get a fair trial and that she hoped he would be sent to the gas chamber or at least get life.

Bill helped her up and they walked around to where two deputies had hand cuffed Reston and read him his rights.

She looked at Reston and told him what an SOB he was. She surprised him by asking who at the front desk had let him know that they were on the way up. Alex suspected that someone at the front desk had informed Reston.

Reston smiled and said that she would need to determine on her own who the greedy person at the desk was.

He had given her confirmation about someone at the desk having called him. She looked at the Chief and asked him to detain all the office personnel.

She watched as the EMT personnel came out of the elevator. She walked over to them and said that she had been shot in the side, but the bullet had been stopped by her Kevlar jacket. She showed them the flattened bullet and asked if they carried Tylenol. She took two and thanked them when the lead EMT told her to keep the bottle.

She looked at the Chief and said that the rest of the action was all his, but she wanted to question the desk personnel before she left.

The Chief made several calls, and he then said that all the people in the hotel office were being detained.

Alex thanked him and signaled the team to the elevator.

When they got on the elevator, she thanked Trey for kicking Reston in the ribs for her.

Trey replied that if she had not let them know she wanted him alive, he would have kicked him harder.

Alex nodded and said that she knew how it felt to just want to kill someone and that she had put that urge to action when they had been kidnapped. Every person who aimed a gun at her had died.

Trevor smiled and said that was the time when he decided to only joke with her when they were in the office. He said he was afraid that on that day she would shoot anyone that made her mad.

Alex nodded and said that day was one of the lowest ones she had experienced in her life. She had watched Trey, who was on the verge of dying being helicoptered out by the EMT's.

Bill gave her a hug and said that he remembered that day and he still wondered how she had been able to subdue the entire group with only a broken piece of an armchair.

Alex smiled and said that she was sure that some frustrated angel was constantly trying to figure out how to keep her alive.

She led the way out of the elevator and went to the desk and addressed the five people that were behind it.

She showed them the hole in her jacket and the flattened bullet stuck to her Kevlar vest. She let them know that whoever had called up and given the person in the Royal Sweet warning that the police were on the way up should step forward voluntarily. She went on and let them know that not admitting it made them an accessory to attempted murder which carried a seven-to-fifteen-year prison sentence. Admitting it would let them face a misdemeanor and they might face some community service as punishment.

There was a moment of silence and then one of the younger desk clerks said that he had made the call. He had just gotten the job and was short on cash. The two one-hundred-dollar bills had been too tempting to turn down. He had not expected the call to lead to her getting shot.

Alex asked if anyone else knew of the deal.

The other two clerks raised their hands.

Alex looked at the other two and asked the manager what she intended to do.

The manager said that she planned to fire all three.

Alex asked that she do her a favor and give them two weeks to go elsewhere.

She gave the three clerks her card that gave her Open Hands Foundation for young women address. She told the person who had taken the bribe that he should show up as well because she would have a job for him.

The manager shook her head and said that she admired her for being so generous to people that had caused her to be shot.

Alex replied that she lived her life with a simple guiding saying her mother had taught her, "Treat others the way you wish to be treated."

Alex then turned to the team and let them know that she wanted to question Reston once he got treated at the hospital and she again wanted to question the perp they had captured the day before.

She said she was going to sit in the hotel hot tub for most of the day and make it an early evening.

She let everyone know that they were free to go back to Cincinnati because the exciting action was over.

Trey let her know he was staying with her.

Trevor nodded and joked that he needed to get back to Cincy and spend some time with his kids.

Johnnie nodded and said the he needed to do the same.

Bill just shook his head and added, "ditto."

Alex led the way out to the curb and asked to be dropped off at the hotel.

When they got to the hotel, Trey said he would meet her by the hot tub and asked if there was anything he could do to make her feel better.

She smiled and replied that maybe the two of them should fall off their AA bandwagon and have a few shots of Jack Daniel.

Trey smiled and said that he knew the feeling, but they had worked too hard at staying sober to blow it.

Alex said that she agreed so maybe he could order in their favorite mix of Thai food to share for dinner.

Trey agreed to do it and then asked what more she hoped to learn from Reston and the other perp.

Alex replied that she wanted to know where Reston had been and what he had been doing. She added that she did not expect to get much from him but hoped that he had been lax about what he had in his hotel room.

She added that the person they had arrested the day before could most likely be flipped to provide some additional information but did not expect much other than general information about what had transpired at the processing site.

Trey arrived at the hot tub about an hour after returning to the hotel. He thought Alex was asleep in the hot tub.

Alex had called Matt and talked with him briefly and let him know what had happened. She then relaxed and closed her eyes.

She had her eyes closed but watched Trey enter. He was talking on his phone. She figured he was talking to Lindsey and maybe Nolan.

Trey said goodbye and sat on the edge of the hot tub and put his feet in.

Alex smiled and asked how everyone at home was.

Trey let her know that Lyndsey had wished her a quick recovery and Nolan had asked if she had shot the bad guy.

Alex shook her head and said she was getting a bad reputation with Nolan.

Trey smiled and let her know that she was Nolan's heroine and that he wanted to be just like her.

Alex replied that she would have to make sure he knew that she had graduated with a law degree. She figured he might like to become a judge.

Trey said he figured he would worry about that in a few years but for now he was just fine with who Nolan saw as a heroine.

15 Adjudication

*F*or Alex, the next morning seemed to come immediately after she put her head on her pillow. She got up took a hot shower and then went down to breakfast where she met with Trey. She called and talked with the Cleveland Chief of police and asked what they had found in the hotel room.

The Chief said that he would send her pictures of the paperwork they had found and that they had also found a briefcase with one hundred and fifty-six thousand dollars of cash.

Alex asked the Chief to send the paperwork information to the Cincinnati Police computer. She thanked him for the information and asked where Reston happened to be. The Chief let her know that Reston would be brought to the Police station around noon and put in a holding cell.

Alex asked that he be kept away from the perp that they had arrested the day before.

She let him know that she would review the information that he had sent her and then be in to question the perp around nine.

She sent the information to Trey so the two of them could review what had been found. She sent the same information to Johnnie and asked him review it and see what more could be learned.

The fact that Reston had traveled to LA under the name of Preston Clemente and that a passport with that name had been found in his room indicated that Reston had been prepared with at least one fake ID. He had traveled first class, so his ego still needed to be fed.

She sent a note to Johnnie and ask him to see who had been seated next to Reston on the way out and on the way back from LA and let him know that she wanted to interview those persons. She also mentioned that the rental car information would most likely provide information about where in LA Reston had been.

Trey suggested that they should share the information with Reston so that he would know how detailed the investigation was going and that they would be questioning the people he had met with. He said that it might get him to inadvertently give them more information.

Trey's comments made Alex think about the fact that Johnnie could probably find the locations of the Mafia leaders in LA and with the rental car mileage information recreate the route that Reston might have driven.

Alex agreed and took a last sip of her coffee and said it was time to get to the station.

They caught a cab and were soon there. Alex was greeted by the same Seargent who greeted her by name but added, "the Candy Lady."

Alex nodded and after reclaiming her weapon led the way back to the Chief's office.

She declined the Chief's offer of coffee then shared her plans for the day. She let him know that she planned to either go back to Cincinnati or to fly to LA and contact the people that Reston had worked with. She Shared that she wanted to close down any operation that Reston might have been out there to help set up.

The Chief nodded and said he was impressed by the speed by which she worked and that if his office could be of any help it was at her disposal.

Alex thanked him and said she was ready to get going.

The Chief called in his support and asked her to show Alex to the holding cell area.

On the way Alex asked the support to check on the availability of flights to LA with a return to two or three days later back to Cincinnati and added that direct flights were preferred.

The officer in charge of the holding cell greeted her and validated her and Trey's identity and then led the way to an interview room. He let her know that the perp would sit at the table across from the two of them but be chained to a holding ring and two officers would stay in the room with them.

Alex thanked him for the information and smiled as she asked whether the two officers were older and mean looking.

The officer in charge gave a small laugh and told her that the two were younger but he would ask them to scowl while in the questioning room.

Alex replied that she would have to work with that.

When Dario was led in and secured to the holding ring on the table he looked like he had not slept well.

Alex greeted him by name and let him know that he had two options. He could cooperate with her and willingly answer questions about the operation and get a much lighter jail sentence or he could plead the fifth but would most likely get the maximum sentence. She let him know that everything he said was being recorded and would be used in a court of law and asked him if he agreed to continue.

She asked him for his choice and his agreement.

Dario replied that he had not killed anyone.

Alex asked whether he had witnessed anyone being killed.

Dario was silent.

She looked up at the police officers and asked what the silence meant to them.

One of them replied that it made him believe that Dario had watched more than one killing.

Alex nodded and said that is what she thought as well. She looked at Trey and asked if he had any questions for Dario.

Trey nodded and asked who had done the killing.

Dario replied that Angelo had been the person who did most of the killing, but Luca had periodically come in and requested to be the one to do it.

Trey followed up by asking how many killings had occurred.

Dario was once again silent.

Trey looked at the police officers and asked how many killing might have taken place.

The other officer replied that he figured there must have been quite a few.

Alex asked Dario how he felt as he watched the killing.

Dario bowed his head and said that in made him sick and usually he closed his eyes. A few times he had to rush out of the room because he got sick. He said that Luca and Angelo teased him about his queasiness.

So, the killings bothered you. Why did you continued working there?

Dario shook his head and replied because he did not want to be one of the bodies delivered to the dissection table.

Alex nodded but said that he could have come to the police.

Dario nodded and replied that had he done so he would not have ended up on the table but would have been dead anyway.

Alex asked him if he believed there was a mole in the Cleveland police force.

Dario nodded and said that he was sure because he had heard Reston talking with that person. He did not know who it was but there was someone.

Alex said that she had experience with moles because she had found one in the Cincinnati police department that had almost ended her life. He was now dead and if she figured out who the mole was in the Cleveland police department he would at the least end up in prison.

She knew that the two police officers would spread the word, and she hoped the informant would be found out.

She then asked Dario why Reston had gone to LA.

Dario said that Reston had boasted about being asked to set up similar operations in LA, Asia, and Europe. He boasted that soon he would be promoted to be the leader of a global body parts organization.

Alex asked if Reston had gone to any place other than LA.

Dario shook his head and said that LA was the first place.

Alex asked if there was anything else that Dario wanted to share.

Dario nodded and said that Reston often sat in a viewing room watching the dissection and that once he had been present to watch the killing and preparation of a child.

Alex shook her head and asked how many children had they killed.

Dario replied that there was only one.

Alex asked how that had made him feel.

Dario shook his head and replied that it had made him sick, and he had rushed out of the room.

Alex leaned across the table and again asked why he had not gone to the police.

Dario nodded and said that he had thought about it, but the next day was when the shooting started, and he was arrested.

Alex sat down. She was shaking because she knew that if she had worked faster the child might still be alive.

Trey knew what was going through Alex's mind.

He announced that the questioning was over and that a formal arrest warrant needed to be filed and that Dario should be held without bail until trial.

Alex nodded and agreed. She looked at Dario and let him know that she would let the prosecutor know that he had voluntarily participated.

Dario thanked her as he was led out of the room.

Alex thanked Trey for taking over. She added that the questioning session had made the decision that they were going to LA.

She did not want the operation there to start up.

Trey said he agreed and that after they got done questioning Reston he was ready to go.

She led the way to the recording room and asked the technician there to send a copy to the Cincinnati police department.

When she and Trey entered his office, the police Chief asked whether they wanted to go out for a quick lunch or eat in the station cafeteria.

Alex replied that she trusted him to make the better choice.

He replied that he had a favorite Cuban restaurant where his favorite meal was a pig knuckle on a bed of yellow rice piled on top of black beans.

Alex smiled and asked Trey if he was ready for a pig knuckle.

Trey shook his head and said that he hoped that they had more on the menu than just pig knuckles.

The Chief laughed and said they had a great menu and even featured vegan meals.

He led the way out of his office and let his support know where they were going for lunch and that she should call him when Reston was brought over from the hospital.

On the way to the restaurant, Alex informed the Chief that he had a mole in his department.

The Chief asked her how she knew that.

Alex let him know that Reston had been overheard talking to that person.

The Chief replied that he would need to figure out how to find that person.

They arrive at the Cuban restaurant where the Chief was greeted at the door and led to his favorite table.

Alex liked the atmosphere of the place and felt like she had been there before.

The menu did not feature the pig knuckles, so Alex asked about it.

The Chief said that he had asked for that when he first came in and the chef had come out and asked him where he had learned about that dish.

The Chief had first experienced that dish when he was a student and the University of South Florida, in Tampa. He had shared that with the Chef who said that his grandfather had been the owner of the restaurant where he had first eaten pig knuckles.

Alex asked Trey if he was willing to share a plate with her.

Trey replied he had never eaten pig knuckle before but was willing to try.

The Chief ordered two pig knuckles and they all agreed to an iced tea.

They chatted about life along Lake Erie and learned that the Chief had his own fishing boat and spent many a weekend out on the lake fishing.

Alex shared that she grew up along Lake Michigan and spent many a weekend with her father fishing. They owned a boat that he kept at a marina.

She showed him a picture of her prize catch.

He said he wished he had such a trophy but so far he had only caught regular sized fish.

The order for the table came.

Alex looked at the size of the serving and said she was glad she was sharing, and that Trey was a big eater.

She took the empty plate and scooped out the rice and beans and cut a piece of meat from the knuckle.

She ask Trey if he thought the two of them would be able to finish it.

Trey replied that he was going to see how the Chief handled it, but he was going to stop when he was full.

Alex said that she thought that what she had helped herself to was more than enough.

She checked to see if there were similar restaurants in Cincinnati and found several that had similar menus and that none had pig knuckles on the menu.

She was just commenting on that when the Chief got a call.

The Chief answered and exclaimed, "you have got to be kidding! Did they catch the shooter? How in the world would the mafia know that? I will be at the scene in fifteen."

He hung up and looked at Alex and said she was not going to believe what had just happened.

Alex replied that she figured that Reston had been killed.

The Chief looked at her and asked how she could have possibly guessed that.

Alex replied that she figured that the mafia did not want Reston to be alive. He had left Cincinnati because of the loss of the business there. He had just lost the Cleveland business and had been captured by the police.

The Chief nodded and said that he had to go to the scene but if they wanted to they could stay and casually finish lunch.

Alex replied that they would go with him.

On the way she asked who he had told about bringing Reston to the station.

The Chief was quiet for a few moments and then replied that he had only told the transport team and their boss about bring Reston to the station.

Alex replied that it could be one of them, but she wondered if his support knew about the transport.

He looked over at her and asked if she was suggesting that his support was the informant.

Alex said that she would ask her magician to check out his support's bank account and her spending habits.

She asked the Chief for his supports name and her home address.

He replied that he would give it to her when they arrived at the hospital.

When Alex had the information she called Johnnie and informed him about what had happened and asked him to dig into the supports finances and spending habits.

Johnnie replied that, "he would have what she was asking for in a few."

Alex walked over to where Reston was slumped in the wheelchair, being examined by the coroner, and getting his picture taken by the coroners team.

She looked at the scene and commented that the mafia had just saved the state a lot of money by killing the person that she figured would potentially spend life in prison.

The coroner looked at her and commented that she was being a little cold hearted.

Alex replied that when he found out what the person in the wheelchair had done he would agree with her sentiment.

The Chief walked the scene and then came over to where Alex and Trey were and suggested they go back to his office. He wanted to follow up on Alex's identification of the potential mole.

Alex suggested they stop for an ice cream so that her magician had time to discover the information that would give the Chief the winning hand.

16 West Coast

*T*he Chief was silent as he drove to Melanies Ice Cream Shop. He led the way in and commented that he was going down the list of ice cream flavors. He said he was about a third of the way down the list. He added that so far he like every flavor.

Alex replied she was going with one scoop of raspberry and one scoop of strawberry.

Trey ordered a dark chocolate and a scoop of coffee ice cream.

They found a table and sat down.

The Chief commented that the coroner had shared Alex's comment, and he had let the coroner know that he agreed with her and that the comment was an appropriate one. The coroner said he needed to find out what the person he was taking to the morgue had done.

Alex took another spoon of her ice cream then added that the incident had helped her decide that she and Trey were going to go to LA to see if they could prevent a body parts business from opening up there. She asked if she and Trey could use the facilities at the station to freshen up prior to going to the airport.

The Chief replied that would be an easy request to fill. He then volunteered to personally drive them to the Airport.

Alex thanked him and as she was finishing the last spoon of ice cream her phone buzzed.

She smiled as she listened to Johnnie as he commented that her last request had been easy to fulfill.

She asked him to hold for a moment and that she Twas going to walk out of the ice cream shop with the Chief to his car where she would put him on speaker phone.

She led the way out to the car and then asked Johnnie to share his findings.

Johnnie said that the support had not tried to hide her new financial gain, or she was not aware that her spending was out stripping her earnings. She was consistently withdrawing cash from her US bank, and her account always had a new deposit from a bank in Jamaica. Johnnie was able to confirm that the Jamaican bank was getting a thirty thousand a month deposit. It was as if she had a straight hose to a cash machine and she was spending freely. He wondered what she was buying.

The Chief spoke up and said he believed it might be clothes, shoes and purses and other personal items. He had recently complemented her on one of her black pants suits.

Alex asked Johnnie to hold for a moment so she could give him the correct connection to the Cleveland computer center where he could send what he had found. She asked the Chief to have his IT send the connection information to Johnnie. Once that was settled she thanked Johnnie for having worked one of his miracles and let him know she was headed for LA.

Johnnie asked whether he could share what he had found with the rest of the team.

Alex replied that was a good next step.

The Chief shook his head and said that he could not believe his office was the direct source of the leak. He wondered how long that arrangement had gone on.

Alex said that he would be able to get that information from what Johnnie sent him. Alex added he would need to have his support volunteer most of the information to be used in court. She let him know Johnnie was her magician not her court information provider.

The Chief smiled and said that he understood and that he would keep the information he got from Johnnie to the side and use it as a guide to get what he needed to nail his support.

Alex said she understood his anger and that he would benefit from a call from her Chief.

She followed the Chief into the building as he seemed to be rushing to his office. Along the way he asked two officers to accompany him.

The Chief stopped in front of the receptionist and asked her to stand up. He then addressed her by name, "Connie Francis Mandolin, you are under arrest."

He pointed to one of the officers and asked him to read her the Miranda rights. He asked the other to handcuff her and take her to a holding cell.

He told her that he was going to charge her for leaking sensitive information to the mafia and she should be thinking about how to save her own hide.

Connie began by saying she was sorry.

The Chief put up his hand and told the two to take her away.

Alex nodded, and said, "sorry to be caught but not yet truly sorry for my sins."

She and Trey followed the Chief into his office.

The Chief looked at some papers on his desk and hand them to Alex. It was the plane reservations to LA. He commented that his folks did not get to ride first class.

Alex smiled and said that she personally paid for the first-class upgrade cost differential because she had a phobia about getting caught somewhere in the middle or back of the plane.

She said that he would understand if he came to Chicago, met her family, and went out with her fishing that she had personal wealth to be able to do so. She did not say anything about the fact that much of the money she had come from a personal friend that was the wife of the leader of a Mexican drug cartel that she had killed.

She looked at the tickets reservation information and said that this information was most likely in the hands of the Mafia. She asked if there was another support who could make similar reservations on another airline that might arrive to LA close to the same time.

The Chief nodded, made a call and a few moments later a Black male support entered the room.

He looked at her and smiled as he listened to the Chief's instruction.

He said he understood the request and he was honored to be making reservations for, "Cincinnati's Black Annie Oakley." "I am Samual Jefferson, and I have recorded every news article that has been presented about your various cases, and I am going to find you the best seats available he went on," as he gave her a little bow.

Alex thanked him and asked him to do the best he could in getting her out of Cleveland and to call her Alex.

The Chief looked at her and said he wondered about the attitude of his police force and said that the word must be out about her. He was sure her action at the hotel had made the rounds. He had caught many of them stopping to look at us as we went past them.

Trey smiled and replied that it was really hard to be a backup for a super heroine and though he had much longer legs he found it hard to keep up with her.

Alex shook her head and said that the Chief should not listen to Trey and that he was a decorated Marine who had been awarded a purple heart and had a metal of honor for his service in Iraq.

The Chief said that both of them were heroes in his eyes.

Alex asked about the locker room and was soon standing under a hot shower, letting the days tension drain away as she thought about how to handle what she might find in LA. Her bruise from the bullet hit made its presence known.

She got dressed in fresh comfortable clothes in which to travel. She always included a suit jacket so she could conceal her weapon. She was first to the cafeteria and bought a bottle of water and sat down. A few moments later Trey walked in. He was wearing the same jacket he had which let her know that he had not brought any extra ones.

She waited until he sat down and let him know that if he needed any clothing they could stop at some shop at the airport, and she would buy them and later expense them.

Trey thanked her but said that he had everything he needed.

Alex pointed out the support approaching them.

Samuel sat down next to her and said that he had found a flight earlier then the pervious reservation. It had a connection in Atlanta and then a non-stop to LA. It only got in an hour before the one from Cleveland. He said he was shocked by the price and had called up the airlines special services and let them know that it was two police agents making the flight but was only able to get a couple of hundred dollars trimmed off.

Alex thanked him for the help, put her ticket into her vest pocket, and handed the other ticket to Trey.

She thanked Samuel for getting the reservation changed so quickly and for his effort at getting the price reduced.

She led the way out of the cafeteria and found her way to the Chief's office. She said that she and Trey were ready to go to the airport. She asked for a plain white envelope.

On the way out of the building she asked the Chief if there was a money machine available. She stopped and took out several hundred dollars. She put a one-hundred-dollar bill into the envelope, put Samuels full name on the front, and put a message on the flap, "Your share of the trimmings."

She handed it to the building receptionist and asked that the envelope be given to the Samuel.

The Chief asked if she were bribing his office help.

Alex smiled and said it all balanced out. She was helping send one office help to hell and the other momentarily to heaven.

The Chief thanked her and led the way to his car. He let her know that he had talked to her Chief and had brought him up to date. He got the impression that she got to do pretty much what she decided to do.

She replied that she always made sure to make her Chief be the face of her cases. He had become one of the most supported detective unit Chiefs and was on the way to getting promoted. She added that she followed her mother's advice of always making the boss happy.

The Chief smiled and said that he was very interested in meeting her mother so he could personally get some advice from a very smart woman.

Alex smiled and said that he should send her the recipe for the Cuban dish he liked so much because her mother was also a renowned Chef.

"Wow, a wise woman and a Chef, your father is a lucky man," the Chief commented as he pulled the car into the drop off area.

He got out and shook both Trey and her hand.

Alex reached up and gave him a hug. She thanked him for making the stay in Cleveland enjoyable.

She then turned and pulled her bag and headed to the check-in area.

Once they checked in Alex led the way to the Airline lounge. Once they were inside and seated with a snack and a drink she said they should exit their plane in LA in their full Kevlar body suit. She did not expect anything to happen in the airport, but she wanted them to each buy a hat with a large brim and to put on their Kevlar head gear when they exited to get to their cab. She added that she would see if she could arrange to be picked up away from where everyone gathered to catch a cab. She was afraid if they were in the crowd the people around them were at risk.

Trey said if she had a premonition of trouble he was all in on being prepared. He commented that the Kevlar outfit was a bit warm and hoped the airplane would be kept on the cool side.

Alex said that she was carrying on her Kevlar top, head gear and socks but would wear the pants. She would put on the rest once they were in the airport in LA.

The wait in Atlanta was short and the Flight to LA was long but comfortable. They both caught some sleep and were ready when they landed. After a stop in the restroom to put on the rest of the Kevlar protection, they were ready to head for the exit.

Alex stopped at a shop that featured hats in its display window. She led the way in and after a brief search she picked the hat with the biggest brim. It completed covered her face. She then helped Trey select his hat. It was a straw hat that had a huge droopy brim. She laughed and said if he sat down people would think he was taking a siesta.

Trey asked her to take a picture so he could send it home.

Alex called for an Uber and asked to be picked up out front where the luggage was delivered to the passengers.

She stopped and pulled on her head gear and put on her hat. She looked at Trey and said he looked like he was starring in the invisible man movie.

Trey responded that she had completely disappeared.

Alex waited until the large SUV with an Uber designation got to the curb before exiting to the curb. It seemed to her that almost immediately Trey pushed her forward, and she hit the side of the SUV. He then pulled her to the ground and pushed her to the back wheel. They each got behind a wheel as several bullets penetrated the SUV roof and hit the sidewalk behind them.

Trey shouted out that a sniper was on some rooftop where he had clear site of them and told Alex to stay down.

Just as Alex thought it was over a van came racing by and a shooter laying on top sprayed the SUV with machine gun fire. Alex kept her head down as she felt the bullets impacts hitting the SUV

Alex heard a host of police sirens and as she stood up carefully to look around a policeman behind her shouted for her to turn around with her hands in the air.

She did as instructed but suddenly the officer was hit. She took off her hat and headgear and quickly ran to him to stop the bleeding that was near his neck.

The officer looked up at her and asked whether she was the good guy.

She nodded in the affirmative.

Trey had taken off his head gear and was holing up his badge shouting for everyone to stay back.

Alex told the officer that she was on his side.

She put compression on the wound and got the bleeding to stop. She asked the officer how he was feeling and that she could see the EMT van approaching, and they would soon have him on the way to the hospital.

As the EMT team took over, she and Trey were both asked for their ID's.

Alex let the officer in charge know that she and Trey were armed but had not used their weapons.

They were both asked for their weapons.

After a brief discussion Alex suggested that they all go to the nearest police station where they would be safe from any additional shooting.

The officer in charge of the scene made a call and then instructed them to get into one of the police cars.

The driver of the SUV rushed up and asked about the damage to his SUV.

Alex said that she would make sure he was compensated but that for the near future it would be states evidence. She added that she would make sure he had another SUV so that he could make a living.

The driver said that there were so many bullet holes in the van that he was not sure he would ever be able to use it again.

The officer let her know that the SUV would later be taken to the station. He said that the driver would be questioned to see what he knew or had observed.

Alex and Trey got into the police car. She commented that she was glad they had slept on the way because the rest of the day was going be hectic.

At the station she was taken to an office with a sign identifying it as the Commandant of the LA airport police.

Alex and Trey were seated in front of the Commandant's desk, and they were asked for their identification.

Alex introduced Trey and then herself and said they were on the way to disrupt a hideous business the Mafia was setting up in LA and that speed was critical. She pointed out that the shooting highlighted how the Mafia felt about the two of them arriving in LA.

The Commandant asked what type of business she was trying to stop.

Alex handed him a phone number and asked him to call her boss, the Chief of Detectives in Cincinnati, and let him determine what she was allowed to share.

The commandant made the call. After some introductions and sharing the situation in LA he asked what type of assignment the two detectives he had sitting in the office were on. He shook his head and said that he was not aware of such a business and that it was a horrible one to contemplate.

He said he understood and would make sure they had all the support they needed.

After hanging up he said he was going to make a couple of calls so that they would have some backup if they needed it.

Alex nodded. Her phone buzzed. She knew that it was the Chief. She excused herself and went just outside of the office.

The Chief asked how she was feeling and then added that he wanted to make sure that she was getting the support he asked for.

Alex let him know that the attitude had changed from one of challenge to support.

The Chief told her to be extra careful because the mafia must see her as a potent threat that needed to be eliminated.

Alex thanked him for his help and let him know that she was making sure he was being kept in the loop.

She re-entered the room and sat back down in her chair.

The Commandant said that her Boss made the request that the LA police provide all the support that they could afford, and that Alex was trying to stop the Mafia from setting up a human body parts processing and distribution center. He said that seemed like a horrible business.

He shook his head and said that he would make sure she had the support she needed and that two units were on the way and would be at her disposal. She could determine how close to keep them but suggested that they always were only a couple of blocks away.

He let her know that the two units would be out at the curb in a few moments.

He asked what they planned to be driving.

Alex let him know that she had rented one of the larger model cars but did not know what she would drive out of the lot. She would make sure her two units knew what she was driving and the license plate number.

She thanked the Commandant and asked if they could get a ride to the rental car lot with one of their support units.

The Chief nodded and said that would be no problem and walked with them out to the curb.

He asked the four officers to get out of their cars and made introductions. He instructed them to give close support to Alex and Trey but to stay about two blocks away.

One of the officers said that he had learned of Alex's reputation for action from a friend he had on the Cincinnati police department and was pleased to have been asked to back her up.

Alex let them know that the morning's event was enough for her, but she would do what was necessary and appreciated their help.

The Chief held the back door of one of the units and wished her good luck.

A few moments later they arrived to the car rental facility. Alex asked the two units to stay put and she would drive around and let them get a good look at the car she rented. She followed the signs and took the elevator to the floor where the car rental was located. She asked Trey which car he preferred.

He picked a converted Chevy Suburban.

Alex nodded and said she liked being in a big car.

After getting their car out of the parking lot Trey drove around to where the two police cruisers were parked.

He got out and went over to where the four officers were standing.

Alex said she would make a call to Johnnie to find out if he had found out where Reston had gone while he was in LA.

Johnnie gave her the route that he had figured out from the mileage on the car and studying the map and the buildings in several warehouse areas. He commented that Reston had gone to several warehouse locations. He figured that Reston had been looking at the different locations so he could pick the most suitable one.

He gave Alex the address of the three and suggested the address that seemed most likely. Two of the locations were new warehouse construction that Johnnie termed prefabricated warehouses, but the third address was one of an old brick and mortar warehouse, it was on the small side as compared to the much larger ones and it was on sale at a reduced price.

Alex thanked Johnnie and let him know she was going to drive by the first two and planned to stop at the third.

17 Los Angelos

*A*lex walked over to where Trey was chatting with the four policemen. She said that she had three warehouse addresses that she wanted to go to. She let them know that the first two addresses would be drive by and the last would be an actual stop. She shared that all three warehouses were either listed to sell or to lease and that the last address was for the oldest and smallest warehouse and the only one to be built out of brick.

She and Trey would see if they could gain entrance to it so they could inspect the interior.

She said that they should stay within sight of the SUV until they approached the third warehouse. Then they should drop back and stay out sight.

Trey led the way to the SUV. Once they were underway he asked how sure she was about the third warehouse.

Alex said that they should wear their full body armor.

Trey nodded and said that he would be ready for action.

The drive-by of the first two warehouses visually confirmed what Johnnie had shared with her.

As they approached the third warehouse Alex noted that there were several cars in the parking lot. One them was a black stretch a limousine.

Alex called back to the police squads following and said that they were driving by but would turn around and park in the street and approach the warehouse on foot. She suggested that the two squad cars park immediately behind the SUV and the four get out and get ready for action because there were cars in the parking lot and one of them was a limousine. She stated that it most likely meant that the mob boss was in the building.

She asked them to put on their body armor.

She planned to surprise the folks inside and added that she doubted they would be welcomed. She said she would leave her phone on so they could hear what was going on and if any shooting started they should enter immediately.

Trey led the way. He pointed to the black limo and said that the driver was most likely sitting in the car waiting.

Alex approached from one side and Trey the other. She knocked on the driver's window and when he rolled it down she put a gun in his face and instructed him to get out.

She called for the officers to come and arrest the driver.

Once he was being taken back to the police cruiser, Alex continued the approach to the warehouse.

Trey was in front as they approached a door, and he slowly opened the it.

He waved and then stepped in and to the side.

She did the same and stepped to the other side.

They were in a large empty part of the warehouse that had two truck doors at the back right side. There was a regular door and a truck door at the other end of the room. The brick wall seemed to be new.

Alex signaled for Trey to go around the truck entrance side, and she would go around the other side toward the regular door that was on her side.

She got to the door and waited for Trey to get to where she was standing.

She slowly opened the door and stepped in with Trey immediately at her heals.

The scene in front of them stopped them cold.

Alex counted seven people in the room. Two were pulling a young Black woman who was struggling, toward a stainless-steel table. There was one person at the table with a knife and there were two men who were apparently bodyguards to the third person who fit the stereotype of a mob boss. There was a person standing with the mob boss with his hands crossed at his back that seemed to be a spectator.

Alex shouted out that they were all under arrest and to put up their hands.

For a moment everything seemed to freeze in place.

Then the two bodyguards turned to shoot.

Alex knew that she had only one shot per person, so she shot the two gunmen in the forehead then she dropped to the floor as the rest of the group except the spectator pulled out a weapon and began to fire.

Alex took out the two closest to the young woman.

Trey took out the person who had been holding the knife.

Alex shouted out for Trey not to kill the leader, and she shot him in the gun arm and once in his thigh.

The two of them rushed forward.

Alex gave the young woman a hug and let her know she was safe.

Trey had hand cuffed the leader.

The four officers came rushing in looked around and made a call for an ambulance and for the coroner. One of the other officers called in for a search warrant to be brought out to the site. The other asked the young woman about what had happened.

He recorded the fact that she had gone shopping for groceries and was loading her car when she was pulled into a van and had a hood pulled over her head. When the hood was removed she was in the cell. She had spent the night sitting in the cell and this morning the guy who had been standing at the table had let her know that she was to be the first person that would inaugurate the new West Coast human body parts business.

She broke down and said that she had refused to come out of the cell and had fought the two guys pulling her toward the table.

The mafia boss sat on the floor holding one hand on the bullet hole in his thigh and the other over the bullet hole through his arm. He cursed her and asked how she had found out where the operation was being set up.

Alex waited to reply while one of the officers arrested him and read him his rights.

Alex shook her head and said that she had a magician working for her but what he should be worried about was which prison or gas chamber he would be visiting. She told him that her magician would find out about all the wrongdoing he had been involved in, and he would either spend the rest of his life in prison, visit the gas chamber or have one of his bosses send word to eliminate him when they found he had been flipped and was for the law.

Alex and Trey each put their guns into evidence bags and then gave each other a hug.

Alex complemented Trey, who in turn complemented her and said he was glad she left a couple of shots for him.

The mafia boss sneered at her and said neither she nor anyone else would get him to flip.

Alex smiled and replied that she wasn't going to try to get him to flip she would just make sure the media got the message that he had.

He cursed her as he was being put into the ambulance.

Alex walked over to where the young lady was being questioned by one of the officers. She checked to make sure that she was alright and had someone who would be meeting her. She then introduced herself and then gave her one of her Helping Hands cards and told her it was a foundation that helped young women through tough times and that she was welcome to stay for a few months at no charge. She should call the number on the card to make all arrangements, and it would all be a free service.

The woman introduced herself as Daniela Brickly and replied that at the moment getting out of LA was the one thing she wanted to do.

Alex gave her a hug and told her she would be welcome in Ohio.

She walked over to the officer that seemed to be in charge and asked him if she and Trey could leave.

He replied that his instructions were to secure the site and when the search warrant was granted to search the entire facility and secure the warehouse. He had been informed that she and her partner could do whatever they wanted except search the site.

Alex nodded and said she had no desire to go anywhere in the warehouse, but she was going to see about getting a flight home.

She led the way out to the SUV where she leaned against it and asked Trey if he was ready to go back to the waterpark and finish the picnic that they had been called away from.

<u>The End of Body Parts</u>

Skull Collector

1 Skull Collector

Levi lay on the lawn enjoying the concert and playing visual games with the clouds passing overhead. Once in a while one would trigger a memory. He was slowly thinking through and visualizing the first time. He remembered his fascination with Heather. He was always standing just down from her locker so he could get a look at her when she was getting ready for the next class. It was during the late summer football practice when the cheerleaders came out for their practice that he finally went over the edge. Heather was thrown in the air and then landed on the shoulders of the guy that had thrown her up. Her hair had flown back, and her perfect features had been exposed. Her smile that he was sure was meant for him had closed the deal.

It was the moment that his mind seemed to clear, and he knew what he wanted. He wanted Heather to be with him forever.

He spent the next few weeks figuring out how that could happen.

He found a place in the forest that was at one end of the farm. He prepared the grave. He made sure it was dug neatly and to the proper depth. He wanted it to be a perfect place.

He then waited patiently. The school session started, and he kept watch as he waited for the right time. Then one day Heather came to her locker alone to put her books away. She had just locket it and was going toward the gym with her gym bag.

He walked up and said hello. She stopped, smiled, and asked what he wanted. He replied that he wanted to take her out on a date. Her smile caused his heart to beat twice as fast.

He knew she was going to turn him down, so he took the next step. He pulled out his hunting knife and pressed it against her side and told her to walk out the door and guided her to where he had his old pickup parked.

She said he was hurting her.

He told her to be quiet and walk. He put his arm over her shoulder, and they walked slowly to the pickup. He told her to get in and he slammed the door shut. She tried to open it, but he had removed the inside handles for both the door and the window. He hurried to his side and got in, started the engine, and drove slowly away and headed toward the farm.

Heather reached for the steering wheel trying to make him go off the road.

He pulled the chloroform-soaked cloth from the plastic bag and clamped it over her mouth.

Heather went out as she tried to pull his hand away.

He drove down the lane toward the house and then took the small gravel road that led to the lake and pulled in next to the grave. He looked to make sure his dad was not fishing. He heard the tractor and knew that his dad was most likely out pulling the John Deer multiple row hoe that cleared five corn rows at a time. He knew that he had all the time in the world, and he should enjoy what he planned to do next.

He pulled on his hip high fishing waders to make sure he didn't get any blood on his clothes. He then lay Heather face down and with his hunting knife he cut her throat. He was amazed at the amount of blood that kept pumping out. Every year his dad butchered at least one large pig, and he always hung the pig up and then cut its throat to bleed it. He had not expected so much blood from such a petite body as Heather's.

Once the pulse bleeding stopped, he reached down and cut off her head and rolled the body into the grave. He threw her gym bag down after her. He kneeled down and skinned her head and threw all the fleshy parts down into the grave. He rolled the skull around so he could get a good view from the front.

He threw it into the plastic five-gallon bucket that was half full of diluted lye water. He put on the lid and made sure it was against the back corner by the tailgate.

He walked to the lake to wash the blood that was on his waders until he was sure that it was all off. He then took them off and put on his sneakers.

He then filled in the grave and put a layer of leaves and several limbs over it to camouflage it. He stood back and admired his work. It looked like the rest of the forest floor. He figured that by spring it would be unnoticeable.

He drove back to the small barn and looked around to make sure no one was looking and carried the bucket in and took it up to the loft and put it behind some old hardware that had been untouched for years. He would come back in a few days to see how Heather's skull looked.

He went into the house where his mother asked him how school had been. He replied that it had been a great day and sat down for his afternoon snack that she always had ready.

He realized he had been daydreaming when the concert music he was listening to ended and the crowd gave a thunderous applause.

He sat back up and once again looked at the two women he had scoped out.

He gave up on his first selection when it was clear that she had someone with her.

He kept his focus on his second choice. He followed her out of the park and watched the direction she was walking in.

Lisa was walking home after the free concert in the field and didn't realize the mistake she had made until it was too late. It was a long walk home and it was getting dark when she accepted a ride. The driver of the black pickup seemed friendly and as she got in; he asked her where she needed to go.

She put on the seat belt as he requested and gave him her address. She was about to thank him when he sprayed something at her. It was the last thing she saw as the world slowly went dark.

Levi smiled and opened the window on the passenger's side to let the fresh air in. He had perfected using the spray bottle to deliver the chloroform. It sometimes made him woozy, but he had learned to hold his breath while he was spraying his prize with it.

He reached over and pulled the young woman's hair back so he could get a good look at her profile. He liked what he saw and imagined what her skull would look like once he processed and mounted it.

He headed straight to the processing center where he would sell her body for a cool fifty thousand dollars. He would keep the head. This was a deal he had set up with the Body Parts manager that would have her chopped up and sell her body parts. He was sure the he was only getting about ten percent of what her body was worth but for years he had to do the hard work of burying the bodies. Now he was getting paid a nice sum and he walked away with a clean skull.

He had called and let them know he was at the door. The warehouse door opened, and he drove in.

He followed as they took her to the next room, put her on the table and undressed her and cut off her hair and bagged it. They said that he was in luck and the doctor that did the dissecting was expecting her in the next room. He would take the scalp, the ears, eyes and tongue and facial skin and they would bring back the head for him. They said the boss would bring out the money.

This was his third delivery. He was now doing about one delivery every other week. He knew that it was risky to be harvesting so many skulls, but he was strategic about it and made sure he picked up his targets in different county jurisdictions and from quite different venues.

He had picked up one guy by mistake but decided to collect him anyway. Most of his skulls were of women but he had accumulated three of young men. He actually thought the three male skulls were appealing because they were noticeably larger than the rest of his trophies.

Delivery to this local facility was very convenient, and the money was more icing on the cake then he had ever dreamt of.

He had made what he had at first thought was accidental contact at a nearby bar with the person running the operation. He learned later that he had actually been targeted to be a victim to become some of the body parts but somehow during the conversation he had connected with the person who ran the operation he had asked if the body parts business needed any bodies. He had been invited to bring in a body.

He had been surprised by the change in the conversation but the person making the invitation promised that it was a legitimate offer, and the money was substantial.

He had taken his next prize in and had gotten a tour of the operation and an offer of fifty thousand per body. The arrangement was not only financially attractive, but it was even more alluring because he did not have to go through the effort of digging a grave and preparing the skull. It saved him time and a tremendous amount of work.

His father had died a couple of years before, and his mother had passed away the previous year. He missed them both. They had been good parents. He had fond memories of the many family outings and vacations that they had taken him on during his early teen years. But their passing made it much easier to pursue his main interest of collecting skulls.

He moved from the family farm to an old mansion that he had renovated with the money he got from his parents. He thought it was remarkable that they had saved three million dollars to pass on to him. He smiled as he thought about the fact that they were not only good parents but amazingly frugal.

He hired a professional farming group to run his farm, and he had the farmhouse refurbished and then had a rental agency manage it. This provided him with a steady cash stream that allowed him to invest all of his inheritance with a local investment firm.

He figured he would not have to work for the rest of his life and could focus on his fishing trips to Lake Cumberland, hunting in the fall and going to concerts, plays and sports events as he hunted out his next victim.

He felt that he had been rewarded for being good in his early youth.

Hunting for the next victim was the sport that he liked the best because it was done in different venues and the selection varied significantly. He always kept his eye out for that exceptional looker that had great hair and was gullible enough to accept a ride from him.

He knew that his good looks and a reassuring smile were key in getting them to accept a ride.

He was now at the Cincinnati River front attending a concert in the park. He was hoping to get his next prize that evening.

He had an eye on a young Black woman sitting out on the lawn and a young blond sitting almost to the top back of the inclined lawn. They both had the look that he wanted. He liked the Black woman the best and figured he would make a move on her when the concert ended.

Alex was sitting next to Matt and enjoying the concert that had been sponsored by one of the large Cincinnati companies. She let him know that she felt that someone was watching her.

Matt asked her if she wanted another iced tea and that he would see if he could spot anyone that seemed to be watching her.

She thanked him and said she would love a refill.

Matt got up and walked slowly to where the portable refreshment stand was parked.

Levi took note of the tall rather handsome Black man standing up and walking toward him. He remained seated but made sure not to look at him or the young woman who he had been sitting with. He wondered if he had been made.

Matt walked by and went over to the refreshment stand and purchased two iced teas and two chocolate ice cream cones. He casually scanned the crowd on the way back.

When he sat down, he let Alex know that he had spotted three potential guys that were alone and looking over the crowd.

Alex thanked him, took a sip of the iced tea, and said that the ice cream cone was just what she needed.

Levi decided that the blond sitting by herself would be the one he would try to intercept. He would invite her to a treat and if she accepted would then invite her to one of the local clubs for a drink.

He made sure not to look at the Black lady again.

It was his lucky night. The young woman took him up on his offer of an ice cream cone and afterwards a drink. She said that she had a club in mind.

He knew he had scored when she selected the place to get a drink. He needed to play it low key and to be as invisible as possible at the club.

Alex had a feeling that something was wrong. She walked out scanning the crowd trying to see if anyone seemed distressed. She saw several young people mingling and talking. Everything seemed to be OK.

Levi seemed to sense that he was being looked at and made sure to keep his back to the departing crowd. He focused on getting the young lady to accept him as someone she wanted to have a few drinks with.

Alex asked Matt if he would later be able to identify the three guys that he had observed.

Matt replied that he thought so. One had red hair and lots of freckles. One had blond hair and was rather young looking and the other had dark brown eyes and he thought brown hair, but that person had his sweatshirt hood on, so it was hard to tell hair color.

Alex nodded and took his hand, and they walked back to their apartment.

Levi and the lady that had identified herself as Elsy walked to a local night spot that had a small dance floor where they drank and danced until close to closing time. Levi did not want to be the last to leave the bar, so he offered to drive her home.

She accepted saying that it would save her a walk up to Mount Adams.

Levi was thrilled. Once in the truck he sprayed Elsy with his chloroform spray. She went out like a light.

It was three in the morning. He had been drinking iced tea in a whiskey glass, so he was ready for the drive up to Cleveland. He would get there early in the morning and be home to have a late lunch. He had been disappointed when the Body Parts operation moved to Cleveland, but the drive was a minor inconvenience relative to doing everything himself to collect the skull.

He figured when he got back to Cincinnati, he would do Chinese carryout for a late afternoon meal and then spend the rest of the evening preparing her skull.

He drove a little over the speed limit but made sure there were other cars driving faster.

The timing of the delivery went off as planned.

He parked in the alley on the side of the house opposite the main street. Two new guys came out and took her in.

He had a short wait, but he soon left the operation with the money and his head that he put in the large toolbox in the back of the truck.

He was just getting back to Cincinnati when a cop turned on the red lights and pulled him over.

He briefly entertained making a run for it and if he had been out by his farm he would have because he figured he knew how to out fox any cop on the roads there. But he pulled over and kept his hands on the steering wheel.

One cop shouted for him to get out and stand behind the pickup. The other walked up to the passenger window and looked in. He then went around to the driver's side and examined the inside more closely.

Levi hoped that he would not get inspected too closely.

He presented his driver's license and listened to the officer that said he had been doing sixty-five in fifty-five-mile zone. He was asked if he had any alcohol in the pickup.

Levi was glad that he had not stopped to stock up on beer. He only had an iced tea from the big Mac in the pickup.

The officer looking inside of the pickup said it was clear.

He was asked to close his eyes and touch his nose with both index fingers.

He did that with no problem.

The officer nodded and said OK and wrote out the speeding ticket and advised him that he should stick to the speed limit.

The two cops got back into their unit and waited for him to go on his way.

He was so glad that he had no outstanding tickets. He had only one ticket in his life that he had gotten when he was sixteen.

Levi got back into his pickup and drove away doing fifty-five and being passed by every car on the highway. He figured that the cops were getting in their quota of speeding tickets. He knew that the ticket would cost him somewhere around three-hundred dollars, but he was so relieved that no detailed search had been done that he smiled and thanked the lord for small favors.

He then focused his thoughts on the upcoming processing of the head. This was the part he especially enjoyed. He was pleased that the body processing group always wanted the eyes, the tongue, the ears, and the scalp. That made his cleaning of the skull easy, and he did not have to deal with a bunch of waste to dispose of. The disposal had been reduced to scraping the flesh off the skull, boiling that residue, and then putting it down the sink through the garbage disposal.

The rest of the processing involved bleaching the skull and the mounting it. He enjoyed making the small plaque that had the young lady's picture a brief description of his time with her and the date of her beheading.

When he moved into his current home, he had converted the entire third floor into his display floor. It had a beautiful wood floor that had star patterns positioned strategically around the rooms. He had display pedestals made that were then positioned on each star. He had organized all the skulls in order of the date and had put each skull on its own separate pedestal. He was proud of the way he had arranged the layout and the spot lighting for each pedestal.

He wished he could give tours of his collection. He thought of the collection as a show of high art.

Many of his evening hours were spent walking the third floor and recalling the events leading to him getting each of his trophies.

The first floor had an entry area that he had arranged using the same pedestals as on the third floor but instead of heads he had put fake statues of Greek and Roman nude women.

The morning after the conference at breakfast, Alex shared the fact that she had a nightmare about the feeling of being watched the day before. She shared that she had one of her premonitions about the situation and was going to be extra careful for a few days until she could sort out what was going on.

Matt said he would be sure to keep a watch to make sure none of the three guys were around.

She took her bike down as usual and met Johnnie at the elevator. She asked him to pick a route to work that they usually did not take.

Johnnie asked what was going on.

Alex briefly shared what had happened.

Johnnie nodded and said he would pick a different route.

Once in the office, as they all sat down for their morning coffee and rolls Johnnie asked Alex to go into more detail about the concert in the park.

Alex described the situation and said that she had a dream about it and woke up in the morning with a premonition of trouble.

Trevor shook his head and said he hated it when she got her premonitions because so far, every time, she had one the team was faced with a major gun battle.

Trey said that he agreed but that every time they had all been prepared for the resulting gun battle and they, working together, had weathered every one of them.

He added that in every one of those situations Alex had taken the point and led them to victory. He also highlighted the number of times when she had been attacked while by herself and she had taken out her attacker.

Alex shook her head and said that this premonition was different, and the difference was what was bothering her.

The Chief came out of his office and joined them. He shared that he had just gotten off the phone with their friend, the Chief of Police of Loveland, who wanted to see if Alex and Trey would be able to stop by around lunch time. He wanted the two to meet a friend that was dealing with three missing young women each who had gone riding or hiking alone in different parts of the county and had never returned home.

Alex shook her head as she wondered if the lunch meeting would lead to what was bothering her. She said that she and Trey would go to Loveland for lunch.

She looked at Johnnie and asked if he was willing to come along to hear the story because she had a bad feeling about the meeting. She said that she wanted him to look for any missing women who had not returned from the concert in the park.

2 A Nagging Feeling

*A*lex sat in the passenger seat of her car as Trey drove to Loveland. She went through each of the previous cases where she and the team had intervened in situations where young women were about to get abused before being killed. It haunted her that during the time it took to break each of those cases young women had faced the situation by themselves, had been brutalized and then killed. This fact always came up when she engaged in a new case and the desire to solve the case as rapidly as possible became a key consideration. She had that feeling now. She was sure that in some way she was going to be presented with some situation that would have her driving the team to move fast.

She smiled as she realized that Trey had detoured to her favorite store and said that he would go in and buy the bags of candy and that he only wanted to know how many bags to buy. She asked for at least a dozen bags, but she insisted that she pay.

She looked back at Johnnie and let him know that one was for him. She wanted him to scan the missing person reports for Hamilton County and every county that bordered it and gather all the ones about missing women. She asked him to keep an eye out for one that had happened in the last couple of days.

Johnnie nodded and said that he would do it, but he wondered if he could negotiate for a tray of her cookies instead of a bag of candy.

Alex smiled and nodded but stipulated that a tray of cookies would mean he would need to set up breakfast each morning for the two of them for the rest of the week.

Johnnie nodded and replied that was an easy ask.

She enjoyed their close relationship and thought of Johnnie as her second father. Johnnie was a few years older than her father. Older but she knew Johnnie was in great condition and was exceptionally strong.

He had demonstrated his physical strength when he had lowered a reel of wire cable from the bed of a maintenance truck. He had backed her up when

Trey had been in the hospital recovering from near death after being brutally beaten. He had demonstrated his strength by lowering a roll of wire cabling from the back of a maintenance truck and then his bravery by pulling the wire cable off that reel through the legs of the helicopter and tying it to a fire hydrant. When the copter went to take off to shoot at her it crashed to the ground as it tried to take off.

Trey returned with the bags of candy, and they drove on into Loveland.

They arrived at the police station where they were cordially greeted like a part of the Loveland unit.

Alex looked at Trey and commented that a few bags of candy went a long way in making friends.

Sheriff Williams greeted them, thanked Alex for the bag of chocolate, introduced his Friend Arthur Milster, Sheriff of Missteer and asked whether they were ready for lunch. He said that he preferred to have them listen to Sheriff Milster after lunch.

Alex handed Arthur a bag of chocolate candy and introduced Trey and Johnnie.

She then said that she was not sure that ready was the condition she would find herself in, but she was willing to have lunch first and then return to hear the details afterwards.

Johnnie spoke up and said that it sounded like a good plan. He wanted to enjoy the lunch and watch the Little Miami to see if there would be any logs floating downstream.

Alex smiled at the reference to logs floating downstream because this was a Johnnie euphemism for thinking deeply about a case. She knew that he was probably already figuring out how to get the information she had requested.

A short time later they arrived at the restaurant, and they sat at an outside table that indeed had a great view of the Little Miami. It had not rained for a few days, so the river was running calmly by. She figured no actual logs would be floating by.

Alex made sure that Johnnie had a view of the river. She was sure the only floating logs would be in Johnnie's mind.

Sheriff Williams volunteered to order for all of them, and everyone agreed to let him do it. He put in an order for three of his favorite tacos and made sure the waiter knew that he wanted one for each person. He also ordered one tostada for each person. The final order was for three orders of donut holes with chocolate and caramel sauce drizzled over them. He reassured Alex that donut holes would be more than enough for all of them.

Alex joked with him that he would need to let them sleep in his van after lunch to recover from all the food he had ordered.

He nodded and replied that he wasn't worried about any of them falling asleep when they listened to what Sheriff Milster shared with them.

Johnnie nodded and said that he already had a premonition of the story, and he planned to enjoy lunch.

Alex agreed and added that she was especially looking forward to the dessert.

Sheriff Williams made sure that the conversation remained light. He asked each person to share a highlight about themselves. He knew that his friend was feeling down and concerned about the fact that he had come up empty handed in trying to solve the cases of three missing women. His friend had worked for almost three years and had come up empty handed. All three cases were now cold, and they hung heavy on his friend's mind.

He knew how that felt because he had carried a similar weight for more than fifteen years when Annie, a young teenager, had gone missing, and the case went cold. He also knew how he felt when Alex, against all odds, had solved the case and had rescued Annie and her two kids from the forests of Pennsylvania. Alex had become a person who he thought about often as he followed the cases, she took on that had stumped other agencies and then marveled when she solved them.

He was an ultimate Alex supporter.

Alex enjoyed the lunch, but she would have liked not to be anticipating some horrific case from Sheriff Milster.

After lunch they all rode back to the Loveland police station, to a conference room and sat around a large meeting table. Sheriff Williams had iced tea and lemonade brought in and when everyone was seated, he asked Sheriff Milster to share the situation he faced.

Alex asked Johnnie to connect his computer to the Cincinnati police computer and see if there would be anything like what Sheriff Milster was about to share.

Sheriff Milster said that he liked how fast Alex was planning to try to help. He added that he hoped she would be successful where he had failed.

Alex nodded and replied that she figured he had only bad news to share and that every case in the past that she had taken on had a sad or horrible beginning and she was only trying to be prepared.

Sheriff Milster then described having three missing persons reports about three young women that seemed to have no connection to each other. Each had occurred several years ago but almost exactly one month apart in his jurisdiction.

Each young lady was reported missing, but each had a very different disappearance scenario, and the three did not know each other. The only similarity was that each had gone out alone and had never returned.

He then described the first situation where the young lady had gone by herself to an outdoor concert and had never returned home. She was last seen by some of her friends talking to a young man that was described as dark haired and rather handsome. They had interviewed several additional people that had been at the concert but did not come up with anything.

The second young lady had gone out hiking along the country roads that were around her farm but never returned home. He had his men follow several hiking routes her mother described but again there was no additional evidence. He had driven each potential road that the young woman might have hiked and had not seen anything.

The third had gone to a night club where she often went, and she was last seen leaving as she chatted with a person that one of the waitresses said was a slender dark haired rather good-looking guy. She had looked out the window as the two got into a black pickup truck.

When she was asked about a license plate number, she said that she had no clue, but she did comment about the license plate holder. She described it as bright silver with red devil horns on each corner. He had his men look for black trucks, but none had that type of license plate holder.

Alex felt a shiver go down her back. She asked if the sheriff had the names of the friends and of the waitress. She also asked if he knew the hiking path that the other young woman had taken.

He said that he had the names, but he had no knowledge of the exact hiking path that the young lady had taken. He had walked out to the first country road with that young lady's mother but even the mother was not sure which way she would have gone because there were several more crossroads that she may have chosen to go down.

He added that he had one of his units travel every road looking for any clues but after a week they had come up empty.

Alex nodded and added that it was most likely that she had been whisked away and was not to be found.

She looked at Johnnie and asked if he had any additional questions or information.

Johnnie nodded and said that he had only enough time to search Hamilton County and Warren County records. He said that he had two more counties in Ohio and then counties in Indiana and Kentucky to search. He said that so far, he had six additional missing person reports that met her search criteria. He speculated that the number could double.

Alex nodded and let everyone know that she would go back and see if her boss would let her take on the case. She added that it appeared to her that a serial killer was at work.

Sheriff Milster asked why she thought it was a serial killer.

She shook her head and said that it was just a premonition.

She then asked Johnnie to shut down his search and they would go back to the office and once the case was officially agreed to, they would dig deeper and see if they could find who was doing the killing.

Both Sheriffs thanked her for coming out and listening to them and asked that they be contacted if the case was going to be taken up.

Alex said that she would of course do that. She then suggested that they give her Chief a call and request that he support making this an official case.

Sheriff Milster shook her hand and said that he was already feeling better and hoped that she would take on the case.

Once they were in the car Alex asked Johnnie how far back in time he had gone in his search.

Johnnie responded with the fact he had only searched back one year.

Alex asked him to do what he had done in the Pool of Blood case and determine when the serial killer had started his journey. She was not sure how long he had been at work but most likely his early years of his killing habit would have been at a low level.

Recent events may have triggered an increase in his activities. She asked Johnnie to identify the first victim and to chart out the hockey stick pattern she was expecting to see.

When they arrived at the station, Alex led the way to the Chief's office.

The Chief's door was open, and he waved her in. He asked whether he should call Bill and Trevor in.

Alex nodded and said that if he accepted the case she was about to describe, the case might cover the tri-state area and that would require a significant amount of coordination that would require their help.

The call from Loveland from the two sheriffs had prepared him and he had already alerted Bill and Trevor. He stepped to the door and signaled for them to come to his office.

Once everyone was in, he closed the door and asked Alex to fill them in on what she had learned over lunch with the two sheriffs. He shared the fact that both of them had talked to him and asked that he take up the case.

Alex positioned her chair so she could face the rest. She then took them through the details of the case and made the point that Johnnie had already surfaced six additional missing person reports that fit the description of the three missing person reports that Sheriff Milster had given them.

She was relatively sure they were dealing with a serial killer who lived somewhere in the area and had recently increased his kill rate.

Bill asked why she thought the killing rate had gone up.

Alex replied that Johnnie had only gone back one year in his initial search and the number seemed high not to have been noticed earlier. She had asked

Johnnie to go back as far as possible to determine what the killing hockey stick data looked like. She commented that this was the approach that had helped her solve the case where she had dealt with a serial killer in Hawaii.

She added that she had promised Johnnie a tray of oatmeal raisin cookies for him to define the hockey stick for this case.

Trevor asked what he had to do to get a tray of her cookies.

Alex smiled and replied that Johnnie was checking the missing person reports in Hamilton County and all the surrounding counties and that they would need to interface with the seven counties that surrounded Cincinnati. She would like him and Bill to be the face of the team to each of the organizations involved and get them to give the team legal access to their missing persons reports.

Trevor gave a groan and asked why Johnnie got the easy work and he and Bill got the hard stuff.

Alex smiled and said that to make the deal a little sweeter she would add a tray of brownies to the deal. She added that this case gave him a chance to be in the news, and she was doing this because she wanted to flaunt his superior capabilities.

Bill smiled and added that he knew that it was because, "she loved them too."

Alex smiled and said that the only person not getting any cookies promised to him was Trey, but she planned to bring a batch over to his house as soon as she received his next invitation to a back yard cook out.

The Chief spoke up and said that he was officially launching the investigation into a potential serial killer, and he would let the hierarchy know. He wanted it all kept low key until they were close to capturing the killer.

He did not want the news speculating on a potential serial killer operating in the Cincinnati area.

Alex said that she agreed to keep it low key and that the only other person in the department that she wanted to read in was Dr. Rogers. She figured his help would be critical if they found any bodies.

The Chief called the meeting to an end and suggested that the five of them figure out how to attack the case.

Alex led the way out of the office. She suggested that they spend the rest of the afternoon outlining how they would handle the case and what each of them would do. Then they could reconvene in the morning and set up a detailed plan.

Johnnie said that would give him some time to decide how to best reapply his Hawaii data search technique. He shared that he had learned a ton about programing in both the legal side and on the hacking side since then and thought he might be able to speed up the search.

Alex said that she was counting on him being able to give the team a way to identify this mysterious young man who drove a black pickup with red horns on the rear license plate holder.

3 Reconnection

*L*evi looked out of the windows of the third floor and took in the view of downtown Cincinnati and the Kentucky hills beyond. The river was mostly hidden but the tops of the bridges all were visible. The purple people's bridge reminded him of the walks he enjoyed taking across to the shopping center on the other side where he often took in a movie and afterwards, he would stop for a drink and then walk back to his house.

He really enjoyed working in his preparation room. It had been one of the major reasons he had purchased the house. The view had been one reason, but he also liked the way the third floor was arranged. He had recognized how the floor could be laid out like a cultural museum. He had spent a great deal of time thinking through the layout, the lighting, the floor details and even what would go on the fireplace mantles that each room had. He had no plans in using any of the fireplaces, he figured he would put some of his mother's nick knacks on the mantles.

He had all the carpeting ripped out and had the hardwood floor redone. On the third floor he had decorative stars put into the floor on which he would put his display stands that he had designed.

He also had the spot lighting installed. He was able to turn each light on and off separately at a control board at the entrance to each room. This let him stand at the entrance and highlight each skull independently. He often enjoyed going light by light slowly around the room. He would leave the room dark and turn on one light on the selected skull and then walk over and stand and admire it.

He had found a woodworking shop that made the pedestals that now was on each star. He had enough pedestals and stars to hold fifty heads. He figured he had enough space to double the size of his collection in the near future. He figured that might happen if he lived beyond eighty.

He had just finished putting the latest head on her pedestal. He felt that he was getting to be a top-level professional skull preparer. It took him a week of concentrated work to get the skull a nice white color. He had worked on perfecting the way he would slowly get the skull to be a translucent white color.

He would then carefully mount the skull on its brass holder. The brass holder was a bracket that he had designed and then had a small local company produce it. He had fifty of them, but he figured when he used all of them, he could go back and get more made.

He had thought through on how to increase his skull collection without alerting the police. He had decided to expand his search area across the tri-states and potentially randomly go even farther out. He identified all the state parks in the tristate area and researched when they had crowd gathering events.

The house was much too large for him, but he spent much of his time on the third floor with his collection, so it really did not matter to him. He had hired a house cleaning team that took care of the two first floors.

He enjoyed sitting on the couch near the window of the third-floor workshop as he spent time finding out about other events that gathered large crowds.

Outdoor venues like concerts were the best ones and when it got cold then there were outdoor venues like ice skating and skiing that were also quite good.

The indoor venues were a little more difficult to get to meet and lure one of his prizes, but he found that standing outdoors and observing the young women coming alone also yielded potential skulls.

He hung up a huge calendar in the third-floor work room that had all the events across the three states and then he prioritized which ones he planned to attend. He thought about the twenty five percent success rate that a hunting lion experienced when it hunted and figured that he didn't need to be that successful to keep his plate full.

He studied his calendar and figured that he had a solid ten days per month of event attendance. If he had a lion's success, he should easily be able to garner two heads a month. This represented a perfect fit with the time to properly process and put a head on display. He hoped it would also be low enough that the various agencies would not recognize what he was doing.

He smiled as he thought about the fun, he had with each of his conquests. He always treated them to as good a time as he could get them to accept. It was like giving the condemned their last meal before walking them to the gas chamber. He grinned and shook his head as he thought that the only difference was that he used chloroform as the gas that took them out.

He thought about how hard it had been to keep his personal hobby from his parents. They had both died one after the other. His dad went first and was followed by his mother less than a year later. He missed both of them, but his life had become much easier since they had passed away. He now had a home that his inheritance from them had made possible, where an entire floor was dedicated to what he considered his purpose in life.

It was so much more relaxing since he did not have to sneak around as he went about adding to his collection and he had been able to make his collection into a showcase that he could enjoy on a daily basis.

Levi had several restaurants in the Cincinnati area that he frequented fairly often. He was always on the lookout for his next head, but he made a point of only looking when he dined out while he focused himself in enjoying some unique dinner. But as his father use to say, "he looked at good looking women because he was not blind."

He was now very selective about where he was hunting because he had to drive to Cleveland to deliver his prizes. Because of that drive he had decided to extent the search area from Cincinnati to the Cleveland area. This would add new territory and distribute his take across additional different jurisdictions.

Columbus was the home of The Ohio State University. He bought football tickets offered by the scalpers and started to attend the games. Hunting there was relatively easy. There seemed to be an overabundance of beautiful young skulls. He was hesitant to harvest at the University but there was also a minor league ball club, many other events in downtown Columbus and a significant bicycle path that offered good hunting.

Cleveland had a professional football team that offered a hunting ground, but most single desirable heads could not afford to go to the games, but the surrounding nightclubs teamed with younger women interested in meeting someone and he was quite willing to be met.

He researched the events in both cities and added them to his calendar. He decided to try to get a head from each city every other month.

He set things up so that his next collection would be after a baseball game in Cleveland. He figured that the watering holes would provide the prey. He made the point of doing the rounds before the game to scope out the different bars and decided on the one he would go to during the next game.

He would focus on the game and on scoping out the potential new head. He felt good about his hunting ability. He would watch the single women and figure out which ones seemed to be on the hunt and who were not professionals. The professionals gave themselves away by being more aggressive in their hunt whereas the women that he was seeking were often more hesitant and sat at a table versus the bar.

When he approached the one, he had selected, he was lucky. She had a great smile and said she would love to dance when he asked. After the dance he asked if he could join her at her table. He learned her name was Madeline and she was attending nursing school. He and Madeline spent the evening talking and dancing. He invited her to dinner and again she accepted. He asked her to choose the restaurant and made sure she understood that a top end restaurant was fine with him.

She asked if it was alright to try Luigi's Steak Restaurant that had a five-star rating and was rather expensive.

He smiled as he said it seemed like a great choice and at the same time, he was thinking about it being her last meal and he wanted her to enjoy that.

The service and the dinner were superb. It was clear that Madeline was enjoying her meal.

Levi figured she would not have been so jubilant had she known it was to be her last meal.

He smiled to himself when later she accepted coming up to his room. He figured if she ate breakfast, she had one more meal coming. He would try to make sure it was one that she loved.

Once in his hotel room, he opened a bottle of his favorite wine that they shared. Madeline was enjoyable to talk to and to listen to the stories she shared about her younger years.

A short time later they went to the bedroom where he enjoyed a wonderful session of love making. He decided he would need to put this approach into use more often.

The next morning before breakfast he made a call to the processing center to let them know that he had a delivery on the way. He was assured that they would be ready.

Early the next morning he and Madeline went to Luke's breakfast place where Madeline ordered two eggs over easy, hush puppies, bacon, and a cup of coffee. She was in a jubilant mood and smiled and chatted away as she ate.

They got back to the truck and Levi asked for instructions to take her home.

Madeline never knew what hit her when he reached over and sprayed her with his chloroform spray. She went out like a light. He then opened both windows and let out the breath he was holding.

The chloroform spray was something that he had perfected and that made it so easy to overpower his victim.

He drove slowly to the body parts house and drove down the alley between the house on the corner and the smaller house across from it.

Three attendants came out and took Madeline in. The youngest of the three escorted him to the room on the second floor. He entered and was greeted by the person he only knew as Reston. He declined an alcoholic drink but accepted an iced tea.

He and Reston exchanged small talk. Reston periodically looked at a large screen that displayed the action taking place on the dissection table.

Reston said that it was a good body and placed fifty thousand dollars of cash out in bundles on his desk.

Levi thanked him and put the fifty bundles into the cloth bag that he had brought with him.

Reston stood up and let him know that the head was in the cooler by the door and said he looked forward to his next delivery.

Levi held up his bag, thanked Reston, and made his way out of the office. He was not sure he trusted Reston but the money he was getting for the bodies covered his worries. He was able to live a great life with the money that the bodies provided, and he was slowly accumulating a huge nest egg.

He carried the cooler out to his truck and put it into his truck's built in toolbox. He dropped the bag of cash next to it and locked the toolbox.

He remembered the speeding ticket he had received recently and drove carefully to the highway and took his time driving just below the speed limit back to his house in Cincinnati.

He kept thinking about what a good time he and Madeline had shared and knew that she would be one of the special skulls in his collection. He would put a little gold star on her plaque.

4 On the Hunt

*T*he following morning, Alex asked Johnnie to set up his computer so he could share the information he was getting from the counties around Cincinnati.

She asked Bill and Travis to put in a request for the names of each County's missing persons list and ask them for access to their computers and for the names of the persons who handled missing person reports.

She looked back to Johnnie and asked him to continue to hack his way through all the systems, but they would use his information only as a guide. She wanted to move with as much speed as possible but to collect all the formal information in a way that would stand up in court.

She reminded the team that speed against the SLATE groups had in each situation saved a young woman's life and she felt that speed in this case would save some women's lives.

Trevor nodded in agreement and said that it made him recall the fact in every battle she had been the first one in and the last one out. Her preparation had saved all of them. He was all in on executing with speed. He just hoped that he would not end up with all the bullet hits he had taken in the last few cases.

Alex commented that she did not think this case would be one of gun battles but one that tested the speed of their thinking. She said that the Hawaiian serial killer was a loner, the Canadian was a loner and she figured that the one they were now after would be a loner.

Trey spoke up and said that he thought they were dealing with a persuasive loner but one that had a very troubled mind and was most likely capable of any action. He commented that serial killers were killers and when cornered they would react violently.

Johnnie displayed the telephone numbers for each surrounding county. He said that he had sent the numbers to each of the team's phones.

Bill took out his phone and confirmed that he had the numbers. He asked if it made more sense for him and Trevor to go to another room and begin the calling and arranging for the one-on-one visits for the two of them.

Alex nodded and said that was a good idea.

She looked at Johnnie and asked if he had the records of the bodies that had been found in Cleveland.

Johnnie said that he did.

She asked him to send them down to Dr. Rogers. She said that she was going down to the morgue and enroll him in the case.

Johnnie let her know the Dr. Rogers already had the paperwork from Cleveland. He would send him the missing person reports.

She asked Trey if he wanted to go with her to the morgue.

He smiled and said that he couldn't decline since she had just invited him to one of his favorite places to visit. Then he added, "not."

Dr. Slivers looked up from his desk as Alex walked in and commented that she looked like she was bringing work with her.

Alex smiled and said that indeed she was coming to ask for his help on a new case.

She briefly explained that there was an uptick on reports of missing young women, and she wanted to see if any of these missing women might be in the body parts collection that had been amassed in his morgue or in the Cleveland police morgue. She added that all the missing person reports had been sent to him and wondered if he could use that information to check against the female body parts.

Dr. Silvers replied that he indeed could as long as the missing person reports had DNA information.

Alex said she was not sure, but she would make sure that for every report, her team would obtain a DNA sample to go with it. She added that his work needed to be kept out of the general police information system and should not be made public.

Dr. Silvers smiled and replied that only she was the only person who spoke to him on a regular basis so it would be no problem.

Alex nodded and said that she only visited because he was her favorite department coroner.

"Ok, I am on the case and will make sure I keep you updated as I learn something," he finished and added that he was the only coroner in the department.

Alex smiled, nodded, and thanked him and walked out to the elevator.

Trey commented that he thought she had made the doctors day.

Alex said that he was the one that would most likely provide the material they would need to nail the person who was kidnapping and most likely killing young women.

If this person was delivering bodies to the body parts production system, then perhaps they might get a clue from when and where the bodies were being delivered.

Trey looked at her and said that he was getting the vibe that they would be talking to Dario once again.

Ale smiled and nodded that she had been wondering whether there might be a way to get Dario to shed some light on the case.

She wondered what Lindsey would think about the two of them taking a road trip to Cleveland or where Dario was now being incarcerated.

Trey suggested that she and Matt come over on Sunday around twelve for some grilled dogs and she could ask Lindsey that question.

Alex smiled and said that she had worked all morning to get an invite. She was not sure about Matt, but she would be over. She said that if Matt did not have duty he would also love to come. He always enjoyed playing with Nolan.

He said that it was almost quitting time, and he figured he would go, change, go home and start the weekend. He wished her a safe ride back to her apartment.

He walked back with her to the team room and extended the invitation of a grill out in his back yard to the other team members.

He got a yes from Johnnie and declines from Bill and Trevor because they had fishing reservations down at Lake Cumberland. They said they would be glad to share part of their catch since they each planned to catch the limit which would be more than they could possibly handle.

Both Johnnie and Trey said they would love to get a fish or two.

Alex said that she would love to get a fish and then declared an end to the day and said she was going to change and ride back to her apartment.

Johnnie said he was ready.

On the way he asked what her plans were for the evening and for Saturday.

Alex said that she had none for the evening because Matt was on the second shift. The two of them were on for an early morning ride at sunrise and then Matt and she would have lunch but then he was once again off to work.

When they got to the apartment, Johnnie asked whether she was up for an early dinner that evening at their favorite Thai restaurant.

Alex said that sounded great, but she was going to do a few miles on the treadmill, take a quick shower and then she was ready for the walk over to the restaurant.

Johnnie replied that it sounded like a plan. He went into his apartment and got his computer online and then went and took a quick shower. A short time later, he walked down the hallway to the gym and looked in. Alex was still running full speed on an inclined treadmill. He shook his head and went back to his apartment and sat down and continued processing missing person reports.

He had been able to hack into all the counties that surrounded Hamilton County and had set up an automated search program that flagged the reports that Alex had specified.

He then set up a search going back ten years. He set up an algorithm to flag when a specific set of missing person reports took a hockey stick turn upwards.

He planned to leave his computer running the algorithms while he and Alex went to dinner. He figured when he got back, he would have the data from all the counties and then he could determine if there was a hockey curve set of data.

He spent the last few moments before he expected Alex to knock on his door setting up an integration routine that would combine all the missing person reports and again look for the hockey stick pattern in the combined data.

As he was finishing coding the routine, Alex's the familiar shave and a haircut knock was at his door.

He smiled and went to the door. He was looking forward to dinner and he hoped that afterward he could surprise Alex with the information that he hoped to have.

Alex sensed Johnnie's upbeat mood and asked what he had cooking.

Johnnie smiled and said that he had an after-dinner surprise for her that would be worth multiple trays of her cookies.

Alex knew better than to press for more, but she said that she wanted to have dessert at his place.

After what they both agreed had been a superb dinner, Johnnie set a brisk pace back to the apartment. He was eager to see what his database withdrawal routines had come up with. He knew that the hockey stick routine would define if the missing person pattern was limited to one county. He had set up the integration routine because he did not expect the missing person pattern to be limited to one county.

He was betting on it being a multicounty situation because three of the initial missing person reports were from Warren County and several seemed to be from Hamilton County.

He was expecting to fire off his integration engine against all the counties missing person reports to learn if a multicounty hockey stick curve would occur.

Alex was eager to get to Johnnie's apartment to learn what he was up to.

When Johnnie walked into his apartment, he took a quick look at his computer and smiled. He had the data from all the counties. He had the ingredients that with a little tweaking would present a breakthrough in the case. He set off his multi-county integration routine but left the graphing routine off because he wanted to have Alex launch it.

He went about leisurely serving dessert.

It was hard for Alex to relax as Johnnie made a production of getting out the ice cream and warming up some of the cookies she had brought down to him the day before.

It was clear to her that Johnnie was planning some sort of surprise for her. She took her first bite of ice cream and asked what he was so secretive about.

Johnnie replied that he had automated his search and now had all the missing person reports from all the surrounding counties.

He then explained that his routine had ruled out a hockey shaped curve for any one county but while they enjoyed desert, the routine was pulling all the information together and he was going to have her launch the graphing routine.

Alex complimented Johnnie on his ever-increasing programing expertise.

Johnnie nodded and said he had been working hard at improving not only his hacking capabilities but all his other coding skills. He commented that he had learned more about databases, their creation and management than he had ever dreamed about. He had investigated and reviewed the attributes of all the newer databases.

He smiled and added that the hacking field had also exploded and that both arenas seemed to be competing against each other.

He added with what he had learned, he had put many of his own twists to and then modified his hacking routines and had spent a great deal of time perfecting his ability to hack into a database and quickly set it up to voluntarily send out the information to an external non shielded program that he then collected and erased. This let him get the data and never be apprehended and made the trail to his hack virtually invisible.

Alex laughed at his explanation, said that she had a top-class pickpocket as her magician analyst and that she figured it was going to cost her many a cookie.

Johnnie checked to see if the integrating routine to was done. He made sure that the data was loaded into his hockey stick analyzer.

He turned the computer so Alex could see it and sat down next to her. He instructed her to hit the enter button.

Alex asked what she should expect when she hit enter.

Johnnie replied that she would see a hockey stick curve, the date of the first missing person report, and the counties that were involved with each subsequent missing person report.

Alex looked at him and asked if he was serious.

Johnnie nodded and reached over and pushed her finger down on the return button.

Alex smiled as the figure of a steel ball hitting a vertical one and to send it swinging up and returning to do the same to the ball that had hit it as the two marked time. She had a similar physical one on her desk at work and often spent time watching it when she was thinking. She figured Johnnie had used it on purpose.

Johnnie commented that this was his first time at using the data integration program and he was beginning to worry that there was a problem.

Then he let out a loud Marine "Hurrah" as the graph popped up and Hamilton and the three surrounding counties were on the list.

He pointed to the initial date and groaned.

Alex shook her head and asked if the hockey stick could possibly reach back twenty years.

Johnnie called up the missing person report for that date and the six subsequent ones. He said that even if the program was fifty percent off it would still reach back ten years.

Alex nodded as she silently went through what the team needed to do to verify what Johnnie had just presented. They would need to interview the people that had put in the missing person reports and if possible, get a DNA sample for each person. They would need to do that for every report that made up the curve.

It was monumental. She thought about her Pool of Blood case where they had concentrated on high schools and colleges around the location where the first missing person lived. She hoped that this first person would have been someone that was in the same school as the serial killer.

She looked at the detail of the first person and saw that she went to high school at a school in Warren County. This was the same county where Sheriff Milster had three recent missing person reports.

She gave Johnnie a hug.

He said that over the weekend he should do any additional tweaking he thought was necessary and that by Monday he would have every report available to share with the team.

She added that on Sunday they would share this with Trey when they went to the grill out at his place. On Monday they would bring the rest of the team on board.

She gave him another hug and said that he could pick any restaurant he desired to have lunch the next day, and it would be her treat.

Johnny sat back in his chair with what he knew was a huge smile. He felt great about the speed at which he had been able to come up with the information that he was certain would solve the case. He was personally proud of how far he had come since being saved by Alex.

He replied that he wanted to go to his favorite Brazilian churrascaria. He suggested they walk so he could have a few of his favorite Caipirinha drinks.

Alex nodded and said that she hoped they could do that drink without alcohol so that she could join him.

She looked at the time and said that it was time for her to get to bed so she could get up in the morning and get a bike ride in with Matt.

5 Closing In

Johnnie could not put down the top of his laptop. He kept processing and analyzing. He spent all of Saturday morning getting information on the first five victims. He identified their school and the years they had gone there. He needed some additional information to get things to fit together.

He hit upon it when the fourth missing person report was in a high school in the same area that was in Sheriff Milster's jurisdiction. He got into the school's computer but was disappointed that they had not transferred their old records into it but had chosen to only put the information in since the installation of the new computer system.

He was at least pleased that Bill and Travis would be able to go to the school and get the yearbooks so they could search through them for their serial killer. He knew that Alex would work her way through all the likely young men in the yearbook. Like her previous case she would be like a coon dog on the trail and would not stop until she had the rascal treed and was baying at the moon.

He gave a small laugh thinking about his comparing her to an old coon dog. He thought about it again and decided she was more like an attacking Rottweiler or a ferocious Doberman, a force to be reckoned with and deadly.

He closed his laptop and looked at the time. It was just twelve and he had a great lunch to look forward to.

He decided to wait for Alex by the elevator. He had no more gotten there than Alex walked out with a great smile on her face.

She let him know that she had called ahead, they had a reservation, and she had been assured that the bar tender would make her a caipirinha with no alcohol.

The two of them set a leisurely pace and a short time later arrived at the restaurant and were shown to their table. They put in their drink order and were just toasting with their first drink when a young girl came to the table and asked for her autograph.

Alex looked around and was waved to from a table across the room. She asked the girl's name and then signed her name and put in one of her favorite sayings, "dream your dream, then act to make it real."

Johnnie watched the interaction, and he modified his previous description to a Doberman with a loving heart.

He had joined Alex in ordering an alcoholic free caipirinha and commented that he would most likely just get a sugar high, but he liked it better than the alcoholic version.

Alex said that she liked the fact that the bartender had so easily matched the flavor of a real one. She said that she was going to help herself to the palm heart, caviar, and olives from the salad bar before all the meat began to arrive.

Johnnie joined her but focused on the deviled eggs and the smoked fish that was also at the salad bar. He walked around it and decided a complete meal could be had just at the salad bar.

Alex returned to the table, enjoyed the palm hearts and the variety of meat that was piling up on her plate. She finally turned up the red side of her card to indicate she was done taking any more meat. She looked at what was on her plate and wondered if she would be able to eat it all.

The family with the young girl that had asked for her autograph came over and the mother thanked her for giving her autograph and for the inspirational message. She added that the family had followed her many cases and thought of her as a Cincinnati heroine.

Alex nodded and thanked her for her kind comments, and she wished her daughter great success in school and college beyond high school.

After the family left Alex looked at Johnnie and commented that she would like the incident kept out of the office.

Johnnie looked at her and replied that she was just a shy Doberman with a warm heart.

Alex had no idea what he was referring to and she focused on the various pieces of meat still on her plate.

After they had finished, she said she was going to walk to the river and then along the river front wall to the symphony in the park greens and then back to the apartment. She asked if he wanted to walk along with her.

Johnnie readily agreed.

As they walked, he shared what he had learned where it had all started and that he thought he had the high school where the first victim had attended but verification would require old-fashioned footwork because the records were in paper form.

Alex responded that he had been holding back on her.

Johnnie gave a small laugh and said that he had done so because he wanted to enjoy lunch without talking about work related stuff.

Alex said that she would have him share his breakthrough with Trey and with the Chief if he was at the picnic.

Johnnie agreed and said that they should make sure that they did not scare the kids.

Alex nodded and said she would make sure the kids were either across the yard or playing inside.

The walk was just what she needed. When she was back in the apartment, she let Johnnie know that she was going to put as much time as possible in the gym, take a shower, read a good book, and then get to bed early.

Johnnie asked what time Matt got off his EMT shift.

Alex said that it would be something like three in the morning.

Johnnie let out a groan and commented that he didn't know how Matt kept the pace that he did.

Sunday morning Alex focused on baking cookies and making chocolate fudge with her mix of nuts, wedges of figs and diced marshmallow.

Matt came out from the bedroom and complained it was impossible to sleep when she baked. He poured himself a cup of coffee and volunteered to be a taste tester.

Alex apologized for disturbing his sleep and gave him a square of fudge and an oatmeal cookie. She asked him if he wanted something more substantial.

Matt shook his head and said that he was going to save his stomach for whatever Lindsay and Trey had for their grill out.

He asked her how her lunch with Johnnie had gone.

Alex shared that lunch was great but even better was the breakthrough that Johnnie had made on the case. She said that she would save that for Johnnie to share during the grill out.

Matt went to the couch and stretched out.

Alex smiled when she saw that he was sleeping.

She prepared a tray of cookies and fudge and took it down to Johnnie's apartment.

She had a cup of coffee with him and asked what he had been up to.

Johnnie replied that he had been able to process all the missing persons reports and had gotten all the addresses listed so that they could be assigned to anyone doing the investigation.

He had wondered if the two sheriffs would be willing to assign resources to make initial contact with the families of the missing women.

Alex said that she thought that was a great idea since they would be closer to the area and more likely to be known to the people then someone from Cincinnati.

She let Johnnie know that she was planning to leave for Trey's house around eleven because she wanted to get there early.

When she returned to the apartment, she saw that Matt was still asleep on the couch. She decided to change into her gym outfit and go work out at the gym.

Matt woke up and saw the sticky note on the edge of the couch cushion. It said, "at the gym." He looked at the time and decided to take a hot shower.

Alex came in from the gym and heard the shower. She smiled and walked into the bathroom stripped, opened the shower door, and asked if she could join in.

Matt smiled and pulled her in. He made sure the shower stall became even steamier.

After the shower he dried Alex off and luxuriated as she returned the favor.

A short time later Alex led the way to her car.

Johnnie met the two as they exited the elevator. He commented that he did not want to know why the two were smiling like Cheshire cats.

They all got into her car and drove to Trey's house. The entrance to the highway took her under the bridge where she, Trey and her assigned bodyguard had been attacked. She was hit several times, but her Kevlar vest had saved her. Her bodyguard had taken three hits to the chest but had also survived because she was wearing the vest that Alex had insisted, she wore. The shooters were not so lucky. Alex shot both in the neck just below their protective helmets and above the body armor they were wearing.

She shook her head as the thought went through her head.

A few moments later they arrived at Trey's home.

Lindsey greeted them at the door and Nolan ran out to Alex and gave her a hug as he shouted out, "it's Aunt Alex and her gang." He shook Johnnie's hand and then he gave Matt a hug and took his hand and said he had the Chess board set up and ready to go.

Alex smiled and followed Lindsey into the kitchen. She watched as Johnnie went out through the enclosed porch and out to where Trey stood at the grill.

Lindsey looked at Alex and asked what she was supposed to ask her about.

Alex smiled and said that originally, she was going to ask when the best time to go to Cleveland would be in the coming week but that had changed because the person she was planning to question had been transferred to the Mansfield Correctional Institute and that would be a day trip with an early departure and a late return if the questioning took more time than expected.

Lindsey smiled and replied that she didn't need to approve trips even if they took longer than expected. She knew that the team was always trying to get ahead of some killer before another person fell victim.

Alex nodded and replied that it haunted her when she realized that a day often meant the loss of another life.

Lindsey nodded and said that Trey also shared that view and praised the team at its willingness to put in the extra time and effort. He made the point that she had brought Bill and Trevor into the fold and had created an unbeatable team association.

Alex smiled and said that Trey was the rock that held the them together by the example he had displayed during the gun battles they had faced. She showed the picture of the gun Trey had been using that had a bullet in the barrel and had been shot out of his hand.

Lindsey smiled and said that was a picture she had on her nightstand that she often looked at before saying her nightly prayer. She was sure it represented a miracle.

Alex nodded and said that she would have too many pictures of what she called miracles if she tried to put them on a nightstand. She added that each picture was embedded in her mind, and she prayed all day long.

Lindsey suggested they go out to the porch and sit down with a glass of iced tea and wait for Trey to bring in his grilled prizes. She added that Trey had decided to focus on steak and was grilling Filet mignon, New York strip, Top sirloin, Ribeye and Steak tips and a variety of grilled veggies.

She had made a sliced tomato, cucumber salad with only olive oil drizzled over it. She figured that each person could salt and pepper it to their taste.

Alex commented that it all sounded great.

Lindsey replied that it was an easy way to make a filling lunch for a large group.

Alex asked who would be coming.

Lindsey replied that Annie and the girls were on the way and that the Chief, and his wife were on the way as well. They had received, "a have a good time from both Bill and Trevor" saying that the fishing was really great, and they would bring some of their catch back to share.

Alex said she looked forward to having Annie come over because she always enjoyed watching Laurie and Linda playing with Nolan.

Lindsey nodded and said the three were the best of friends and they were always talking about the highlights of the cases that Trey had with the team.

Alex smiled and said that she would need to emphasize the need to go to college to be able to do what one loved doing.

Lindsey smile and commented that Trey had shared that she was worried about being thought of as a gunslinger. She went on to say that she should not worry because she had listened as the three kids talked about all the skills that their, "Cincinnati Black Annie Oakley" had beyond just being the best shot in the world she was the smartest, the best at flying a hover craft, the best in hand-to-hand combat, the best at throwing a knife or a hatched. She laughed and said the list went on as each tried to outdo the other at what their favorite "Aunt" was best at.

Alex smiled and said that she should be thankful that she had the reputation of being the best.

Just then the front doorbell rang, and Alex jumped up and reached for the weapon that was not on her but locked in the car glove compartment.

Lindsey noticed and put her hand on Alex's and said she knew it was Annie and got up as Annie walked onto the porch carrying a foil covered tray that she put on the serving table.

She came over and gave both Lindsey and Alex a hug.

Alex got down on her knees to hug Linda and Laurie and laughed when she realized that the two were now taller than she was if she kneeled. She got up and finished the hug and asked when they had grown so much and that it was only a couple of weeks ago that they had been at the pool and were little.

Annie replied that it was a little over a month ago, but she agreed that the two had shot up dramatically during that month.

The doorbell rang again, and Lindsey went out and let the Chief and his wife in.

Trey and Johnnie each carrying a foil covered tray came in and put the grilled meat down and came over and joined in welcoming everyone.

Lindsey called down into the basement for everyone to come up and get their food. She then asked for some help in bringing out the salad and the drinks.

As she walked by the end of the table, she flipped open the cooler that had a variety of soft drinks and several visible bottles of Pelligrino.

Alex took in the gathering and knew that she was lucky to be in a job that had a great boss and such great and loyal friends.

Matt looked at the time and commented that his team had exchanged positions with another EMT team and had the north part of the county as coverage. This gave him a couple more hours but then he would have to leave.

Nolan said that would be enough time for them to finish their Chess game.

Matt smiled and said it was clear he was on the way to losing so they should play a game where Linda and Lauri could join in and the three of them could figure out how to beat him.

Alex was always surprised at how well Matt interfaced with the three kids. She figured he was going to be a good father.

She decided to take a couple of bites of each meat, several pieces of grilled vegies and the salad with a bottle of Pelligrino and when she looked at her plate, she knew that it was all that she could possibly eat.

She noted that everyone had dug in and was busy eating and talk fell almost to silence except for the praise for how good the food was.

Matt and the kids were the first to get done and they headed for the basement.

When Lindsey, Annie and Rose-Anne went to the kitchen to clean things up Alex went to the top of the basement stairs and let Matt know it was time for him to join everyone on the porch.

Lindsey went down to play with the kids.

Once Matt was seated Alex asked Johnnie to share what he had learned and the additional focus he was able to provide that would accelerate the team in solving the case.

The Chief shook his head and asked if any of the information could be used in court.

Alex shook her head in the negative and said that Bill, Trevor, she, and Trey would use the breakthrough that Johnnie was providing to gather the evidence needed in court to send whoever the serial killer happened to be to jail and that he should stand by to announce the success of the case to the public.

The Chief nodded and said that sounded like a good plan, but they should figure out what the public message should be. Even if the case was solved, he did not want to go in front of the news with the fact that a twenty-year-old serial killing case had been solved.

Rose-Anne came out and asked whether the three of them in the kitchen had given them enough time because it was time for either tea or coffee and dessert.

Alex nodded and said that Monday was the next time the team would focus on getting on with solving the case and that dessert definitely took precedence over work.

6 Shoe Leather Patrol

Matt had been picked up by his team and when the grill out ended, Alex left with Johnnie, but stayed off the highway. She asked if it was OK to take her time because she wanted to think about the case and how they might speed it along.

Johnnie said he had no need to rush home. He said that they should start with the high school where the first girl had come up missing. He pointed out that it was going to take a very personal tone when they approached the persons who had put in the missing person reports, and they should make sure that Sheriff Milster took the lead but that they go with him to each place.

Alex nodded and she said that Bill and Trevor should go to the high school and get into the yearbook and other paper documents that they identified as pertinent. She added that the Sheriff should do the initial introduction to the high school staff to ensure their cooperation and help.

Johnnie suggested that they bring on board a couple of the Sheriff's deputies to aid in any follow-up that might be needed that the team didn't have time for.

Alex turned into the police station parking lot and parked in the back of the lot farthest from the door. She snickered and commented that no one ever parked in her personal parking spot.

She then locked the car and led the way toward their apartment building. On the way she asked whether Johnnie had been able to retrieve his bicycle from the police evidence lot.

He replied that he had forgotten to follow up but had expected to get notification when it was no longer considered evidence.

Alex nodded and said that she too had forgotten since they both were riding their second set of bikes, but they should follow up the next day.

They arrived at the apartment building and parted ways at the elevator.

Alex had enjoyed the day and decided to take a shower, relax with a cup of tea and a good book.

She figured the week ahead would be a long and tough one. She planned to go and question Dario to see if there was any connection between the body parts factory and the serial killer she was now hunting. She would have Bob and Trevor get the information from the high school and arrange an interview with the parents of the missing persons that she had in mind.

She wanted Trey and her to do the interviews, but she also wanted Sheriff Milster to be present.

She decided that she needed to spend the next morning making sure the team was organized and coordinated. She wanted everything to move rapidly and lead to the capture of the serial killer.

The next morning Johnnie met Alex at the elevator said hello and said she needed to put on her headset so he could get her up to date on what he had been finding out about their serial killer.

Alex could tell that Johnnie had pulled another one of his all-night hunting sessions. She listened as he talked all the way into work. She cringed when he said that the hockey stick that begun some fifteen years ago had a steep slope before reaching the point where it went asymptotic.

She asked how many missing women made up the hockey stick.

Johnnie replied that he estimated that there might be as many as forty.

Alex almost fell off her bike. She exclaimed, "Forty, how could forty missing person reports not raise a red flag."

Johnnie replied that the reports were scattered over time across seven counties and three states. He said that to this date the different organizations did not have a unified database. He had hacked into more than one database per county. He added that getting the official paperwork from each office would keep Bob and Trevor fully occupied for more than a week.

Alex got off her bike and rolled it through the door and told Johnnie that he should set up in the team room and she would get the rest of the team to join him. She went to locker room where she was now keeping her bike. She changed to her work clothes and went to the bullpen area where the only other persons that had arrived were Bill and Travis.

Bill said good morning and pointed to the box of donuts.

Alex smiled and said they should all grab a cup of coffee and go to the huddle room where she hoped Johnnie had already set up his computer.

She was leading the way to the huddle room when Trey came in with his cup of coffee and followed them.

Once in the room she said that they needed to accelerate in what they were doing because Johnnie had spent all night hacking and had determined that the serial killer was possibly killing up to four women a week.

Trevor shook his head. He commented that seemed high and that it would have sent up red flags.

Alex said she agreed with him, but the serial killer had been strategic about his killing by spreading his hunt across more than seven counties. She pointed out that even if Johnnie was fifty percent wrong it would still be twenty-four women per year at the current hockey stick curve rate.

Trey sighed and commented that so far Johnnie had delivered. He was shocked at the number but said that the team should not spend time arguing about the number but get clear what each of them had to do to get the killer ASAP.

Alex nodded. She then asked Bill and Trevor to do three things. First arrange to interview the parents of the first missing person and of the three missing persons that Sheriff Milster had given them.

Second get the high school yearbooks for the time the first missing woman was in high school.

And finally collect all the official missing person reports that Johnnie had identified. She asked that they gather the missing person reports in reverse time order and see if they could also get DNA samples with each of the reports.

Trevor laughed and asked if that was all he and Bob had to do.

Alex smiled and let him know that if he wore out the soles of his shoes, she would buy him a new pair. She then added that she planned to take it easy was going was letting Trey drive her to Mansfield where they would do one easy interview, have a luxurious lunch, and then drive back.

She pointed at Johnnie and said that she was sending him home to get some sleep because she wanted him to be awake when on Wednesday, she would interview the parents of the first missing person.

Then on Thursday she wanted to interview the parents of the three missing persons that Sheriff Milster had brought to them.

Bill spoke up and added that it was going to be a hell of a week and that the way she was pushing them she might solve the case by Friday.

Alex replied that she wished that would happen.

She then said that it was time for the team to split up and get to work. She was going to go to the morgue and enroll Dr. Rogers to check the body parts he had and the body parts in Cleveland to see if any of them matched the DNA of the missing women.

She looked at Trevor and asked him to send any DNA information that he gathered to Dr. Rogers.

Trevor smiled and asked if instead of a pair of new shoe he and Bill could get a tray of cookies.

Alex laughed and said that she would give him a tray of cookies next week for all the good work he did this week.

Bill laughed and asked if she were quoting from a Popeye cartoon.

Alex nodded and added that they should also believe that the cookies were in the mail. Then she said that it was time to get to work.

The Chief had arrived, and he saw Alex and Trevor exchanging a series of comments. He wondered what was up.

He watched as the team left the huddle room. It was clear that Johnnie was leaving. Bob and Trevor each went to their desks and got on their phones.

He waited as he watched Alex heading for his office.

He was shocked when she brought him up to date and what her plans were. He could not believe the number of potential victims that had been identified.

When he was asked to arrange for a late afternoon interview of Dario at the Mansfield Correctional institute he nodded and asked what time he should schedule the interview.

Alex looked at the time and said she had to stop at the morgue then they had about a two-hour drive. So, they would be there by eleven. She added that she wanted the interview to be with only the three of them.

The Chief nodded. He said that it would be against the normal procedure, but he would share the fact that they needed to protect their informant.

Alex thanked him and said that she would be back the same day unless they needed to do some other errand. She then led the way to the morgue.

Dr. Silver looked up from his desk and commented that it looked like more work had just walked in.

Alex nodded and said that the case needed acceleration, and it needed him to deliver a breakthrough. She then brought him up to speed.

Dr. Silver bowed his head and said that if she had come to him with her story before he had gotten involved with processing the body parts in her last case, he would not have believed what she had just shared.

He said that he understood the need for speed. He would check the body parts against DNA from the missing person reports.

Alex thanked him and asked him to just put the information in her team folder.

She then excused herself and led the way out to the car.

Trey asked whether she needed to stop and buy some bags of chocolate.

Alex nodded and said that when they got to Mansfield, she also wanted to stop at a fast-food place and buy a full meal with a Strawberry swirl smoothie.

Trey smiled and said, "chocolate for the guards and a smoothie for Dario."

Alex nodded and said that she was a devoted follower of her mother's advice.

It was clear they were expected when they arrived at the correctional institute. They were guided to a specific parking spot and then led into the main office building where the institute director met them.

He introduced himself and said that he was familiar with her reputation and that her boss had emphasized the need to keep the information she was seeking from having any way to get out. He said that he would go with them to the interview room and make sure that they had total isolation.

He thanked her for the bag of chocolate Alex had given him and smiled. He asked how many more bags she had with her.

Alex replied that she had one bag for every officer that had been asked to step back. She lifted her bag that had a triple cheeseburger, fries, and the strawberry swirl. She said that the bag was her interview equipment.

The director nodded and said that he figured she would prevail and get the information she was after. He then asked her to follow him and led the way to the interrogation room.

Alex saw that Dario had his hands chained to the table. She asked that Dario's hand be freed and that his leg chain be secured to the ring.

When two guards came in to make that change, Alex asked how many of the guards had been asked to step back from their normal duties.

The older of the two said that there were four of them that were asked to do so.

Alex thanked them for their cooperation and handed them four bags of candy that they should share.

Both guards smiled and said that a chocolate reward would make them all enjoy the break from their normal routine.

The director pointed to the call button and said she should press it if they need anything and left with the two guards.

Alex looked at Dario and pushed the bag over to him. She said that she hoped that a triple cheeseburger and fries would help him to answer the questions she would be asking him but first she wanted to hear how he was doing at the institute.

Dario took out the smoothie and took a sip, then the burger and took a bite, he closed his eyes, and then replied that he wanted to thank her for putting his life on a path that he thought of as salvation.

He said that he was taking educational courses that would give him a high school equivalent degree and that since he was going to be in jail for most of his life, he planned to take college courses and get a degree. He added that he was thinking of getting a psychology equivalent degree and see how he could help inmates in the prison system.

He then smiled and said that he had fallen in love with raising and training dogs that then were provided to the community. He laughed and said that he trained them well so they could go out to the community and be free to enjoy their life.

He looked at Alex and thanked her for helping him get transferred to the institute.

Alex smiled and said that she hoped he would be able to find a useful way to spend his life. It would not be the same as being free but if he was lucky, it would be fulfilling.

She then said that she needed his help and that it dealt with the body production system.

She asked how the bodies were procured.

Dario was quiet for a moment. He then said that he was not sure how the specific bodies were procured but there were about a half dozen regular guys that brought the person in either alive or just recently killed. They were on some sort of payment system where they brought the body in and then left immediately after delivery with an impressive amount of cash. He was not sure how much they got for a body, but his two partners said that it was fifty thousand dollars.

Alex asked if there were any other person or persons that were not the normal body parts providers.

Dario was silent for a moment as he took several bites of the burger and a sip of the smoothie. He then nodded and said there was one weird guy. He was rather good looking, and he brought in several women that were still alive but out. He would go up to the boss's office and wait for the only part of the body he wanted.

Dario shook his head and said the guy only wanted the skull.

Alex closed her eyes for a moment as she took in what Dario had said and the impact it had on the case. It added a horrific element that had not entered her mind until Dario shared the part of about the skull.

She then asked if Dario had ever seen the vehicle that this person drove.

Dario nodded. He said that it was a large black Dodge pickup that had a large built-in toolbox where this guy always put the cooler with the skull and a bag that he thought was probably full of money. He added that the guy was always polite and said thanks for the skull as if it was a normal thing.

Alex asked if he had ever seen the license plate number.

Dario closed his eyes for a significant amount of time and then said that what stood out was the shiny license plate holder with a red horn on each corner. He added that he thought it was a vanity plate because it was different than most cars. He could recall the letters LAM and that the numbers were two thousand something.

Alex asked if there was anything else that Dario might recall.

Dario said that the last delivery was different in the fact that the guy was humming a tune that reminded him of someone's song about having done it their way. It seemed that the guy was unusually happy.

Alex thanked Dario for his time. She asked if he had any request.

Dario smiled and said that if there was another interview, he would like to have Spaghetti De Mare with Alfredo sauce.

Alex replied that if his information was used to solve the case she was working on, she would have the meal delivered.

She then asked Trey to push the call button.

She waved to Dario as the four guards came in.

The director met them and walked with them to the car. He said that Dario represented somewhat of a mystery to him because he had been transferred to him with a sealed folder. He was a model prisoner and was thought of highly by the guards.

He asked why he had a life sentence.

Alex replied that he had lost his way in his previous life and had been associated with the worst of the worst. He had been instrumental in getting a very horrible case solved and she had worked to give him a second chance in life but a life behind bars.

The Director nodded and asked if he had provided her with the information she needed.

Alex said that she thought so and if he had she would like to reward him with a dinner he had expressed he would love to have.

The Director smiled and said that he hoped to arrange for that meal, and it would be in his office.

Alex asked him if he liked Spaghetti De Mare with Alfredo sauce.

The director nodded and said he hoped the information would help her solve the case.

Alex shook hands with him and led the way to the car.

Trey looked at her and asked if she thought she had gotten the information she needed.

Alex shook her head and said that she had gotten more than she had bargained for. Their serial killer was a skull collector. He was young, rather good looking and vain. He had vanity plates.

She said that it was going to be hard not to spend the night working with Johnnie to see if they could determine who the guy was.

She shook her head again and quietly added, "a serial killer who collected skulls."

She looked at Trey and said that if that didn't keep one up at night or in being scared to walk alone at night then there was nothing that would affect you.

7 The Body Count

It was hard for Alex to keep herself from calling the entire team together to share what she thought was a huge breakthrough. She decided to go to the gym and run on the treadmill until she was exhausted. Then she would think through how to adjust the team's effort based on what she knew.

As she ran, she came to realize that she really did not have anything concrete. She had no evidence, she had no criminal, she had nothing but some great leads. She was glad that the run had cleared her mind.

She wanted to get Johnnie to do some more digging but decided to wait until morning. As she got off the treadmill her phone gave the Matt ring. He said he was on the way back to the apartment and asked if he should pick up dinner. She told him to surprise her and get whatever he fancied. She said she was going to take a quick shower and would see him soon.

She was under the hot shower thinking about how to accelerate the case when the door to the shower opened and Matt asked if he could join her. Her thoughts about the case evaporated and she pulled him in.

They were both drying off when Matt's phone rang. It was the surprise meal delivery.

Alex asked if he had ordered drinks and got a no. She said she would make some iced tea while he went down to get the dinner.

Alex smiled when Matt let her know that is was Spaghetti Vongole. It was different from what she had promised Dario, but it was Italian. Matt had added Pan Fried Scamorza, Potato Focaccia rolls and a small mixed salad.

She figured that she was getting a message from above and was able to put her case away for the night.

She was up early the next morning and went down and knocked on Johnnie's door.

He let her in and offered a cup of coffee and breakfast if she wanted some.

Alex asked if he had caught up on his sleep.

Johnnie smiled and said that he had indeed. He had slept twelve hours and was eager to go after whatever she wanted.

She smiled and said that once they got to the office, she was going to inundate him with work but now she was going up fix breakfast for her and Matt and then she would be ready for their ride to work.

Johnnie said he could hardly wait.

Once they got to work, Alex called the team into the huddle room. She asked each person to give an update of what they had accomplished the previous day.

Bill highlighted the fact that they had contacted all the missing persons offices in every county of interest and had set up times to visit each to get the desired missing person reports.

Trevor said that he had worked with Sheriff Milster to set up the desired interviews. Two interviews would be on Wednesday and two would be on Thursday.

Alex said that what she was going to share would potentially change some of what the team would do. She then went through the information that Dario had provided.

She looked at Johnnie and asked him to locate the truck and the owner of the truck. Once he had that she wanted to know where he lived and his complete life history.

She looked at Bob and Trevor and said that she was not sure when but as soon as Johnnie identified the serial killer, they would then begin to shadow him. She was not sure for how long, but it would be until Johnnie provided them with what the perp owned and they getting search warrants. She expressed the fact that she wanted the team to put on their after burners and she wanted to capture the serial killer tomorrow.

Trevor shook his head up and down and said that once again Bob and he got the shaft and had to do the hard work.

Alex smiled and reminded him that he was about to get multiple trays of cookies.

"Cookies as the bribe to get me to smile," he said as he put up a fake smile.

Johnnie interrupted and said the he had the killer's name, address, and truck license plate number.

Alex looked at Bob and Trevor and said they would have to begin their tailing work sooner rather than later.

She added that she would get the Chief to assign a police unit to go and collect the missing person information from the various police precincts.

Trevor smiled and said that getting that chore reassigned was almost as good as a tray of cookies.

Bill asked if she cared how he and Trevor tailed the killer.

Alex shook her head and said anyway he wanted to as long as the killer had no clue.

He asked whether they could use her car during work hours. At night they would use their own cars. This would give them four cars to switch around and not be so obvious when they were following him.

Alex put her car keys on the table and said that they were available for them to use.

Johnnie spoke up and said that he had found the name of the person the that the house was registered in, and that this same person owned a farm.

Bob reminded Alex that the interviews were set for the next two days and for her not to miss them. He picked up the keys and walked out of the huddle room with Trevor following behind.

Trevor looked back, smiled, and said he preferred brownies.

Alex smiled. She felt the team kicking into action and the case coming to a thundering close. She could feel them making progress.

She said that it was time for them to update the Chief and get him to have search warrants prepared and the searches scheduled and staffed.

She wanted to proceed as fast as possible, but she wanted to have an airtight case. She wanted one that took the killer off the street permanently and maybe sent him to the gas chamber.

What bothered her was that she did not want a trial to expose the hideous nature of what happened to the missing young women. They were dead but their parents and close friends would be very negatively affected if they learned the details of the deaths of their loved ones.

Trey had been watching Alex and knew that she was up tight as ever. They had an AA meeting that evening and he was trying to figure out how he could help her release some of her tension.

Alex looked at Trey and said that she could read his mind and that no he should not try to question her at the AA meeting about what was bothering her. She said that she thought the killer had been looking for his prey during the concert that she and Matt had attended and that he had scoped her out.

Trey asked what had happened.

Alex said that Matt had gone and purchased an ice cream cone and tried to identify who was watching her. When he came back, he said that there seemed to be three guys toward the top of the lawn that were alone.

Trey nodded and said that was creepy.

Trey then said that maybe if they went to lunch with Johnnie, they could let him relieve their tension.

Alex said that sounded good and that the three of them should share what they had with the Chief. She said that afterwards they would go to the morgue to see if Dr. Rogers had anything for them.

She led the way to the Chief's office.

The Chief kept saying he didn't believe it, but he was glad to get warrants, arrange for the searches and get the missing person reports picked up. He said that the only condition that he was going to ask to be followed was that he, Trey, and she had to be at every location during the searches.

Alex nodded and said she would like to include Johnnie as well. She added that she wanted to keep Bill and Trevor following the killer.

The Chief nodded and said he would have search warrants that day.

Alex thanked him and left and went down to see Dr. Rogers in the morgue.

When she arrived and shared what she had learned about the case, he shook his head and said that he thought the body parts case was an extreme and now she had just taken that to an entirely weirder level.

She let him know that Johnnie would give him the forensic information about the missing women and that she wanted to know which ones were to be found in the body parts that were either in Cincinnati or in Cleveland.

Dr. Rogers nodded and said that he had all the information about the body parts in his computer system and he would identify any matches. He asked how many bodies their might be all together and when Johnnie shared that there might be forty or more women, he stopped for a moment and let the magnitude set in.

He asked how that would even be possible without it having been identified long ago.

Alex said that had been her question as well. She then pointed out that Johnnie had accessed seven different missing persons databases and there were probably some that had never made it into those systems.

She made the point that this serial killer was probably very cognizant of keeping a low profile by spreading a wide net.

She thanked him and then led the way back to her desk.

She got the addresses of both the house and the farm and said that she wanted to drive by the house and then drive out to the farm to get an idea of the logistics associated with the searches.

The drive to Mt. Adams to the house took only a few minutes.

The turret tower that rose one level to the third-floor roof line was the dominant feature of the mud-colored brick mansion looking home. She commented that their serial killer seemed to have all the money he needed. He not only had a huge home but also owned a six-hundred-acre farm in the middle of Ohio.

She suggested having lunch at one of the restaurants on Mt. Adams before driving to the farm.

The restaurant menu had a wide assortment to choose from. Alex decided on a large mixed salad and an iced tea. She took a bite of Trey's roast beef and a bite of Johnnie's T-bone steak.

Johnnie commented that he had brought along Gunjfor because the farmhouse was in the middle of a wooded area and at least a mile into a heavily wooded area at the back of the farm. He said that he could fly her in and allow them to see the area without trespassing.

Alex complimented him for thinking ahead.

She drove about an hour to get to the farm and parked at the side of the road and the three of them sat with their backs to the car.

Johnnie flew Gunjfor across the tall stalks of corn. He commented that there was a great yield of corn. He then crossed a green clover field that was almost ready to be mowed and baled. The arial view provided the perspective that highlighted the isolation of the farmhouse.

Johnnie hovered over the large brick farmhouse that had sometime in the past been modified and expanded more than once. There was a small road over grow with weeds that left the house and went back to a small lake that had a deck jutting out to where a large flatbottomed boat was tied. Johnnie quickly turned Gunjfor back over the trees when he spotted someone sitting on the deck fishing.

He zoomed the camera in and got a close up of the person's back.

Alex suggested they call it a day and leave. She said that she did not want to give their suspect any warning about being on the team's radar.

She asked Trey to drive because she wanted to make a couple of calls.

She called Bill to let him know that Levi Misle was at his farm fishing. She asked them if they could position themselves and begin their surveillance when he left the farm. She smiled when she heard Trevor complain about having to spend the night in the car.

She knew how she felt about such situations and suggested they a get good dinner and load up on snacks in case they did have to spend all night.

Johnnie suggested they bring one of their drones so they could keep track of Levi if he chose to stay on the farm.

Trevor replied that the drone would at least give him an opportunity to have some fun.

Alex wished them good luck and then called the Chief to find out what he had arranged.

The Chief was glad that Alex had called in. He let her know that the search warrants were issued and that he had scheduled the searches for Friday at noon. There would be two backup units at the house, two at the farm where they would work with Sheriff Milster and his team. They all knew to stand by until they got his orders. He said that the Sheriff was surprised by the address of the farm because he was acquainted with the family who had always been cordial to him and his officers.

Alex thanked the Chief and let him know that she and Trey would be with Sheriff Milster to interview the parents of the three victims that he had brought to them. They would meet with the first victim's parents on Wednesday morning.

The Chief said that he did not envy her. He always dreaded having to talk to parents who had lost a child.

As they drove back, she asked if they wanted to eat out or go home.

Trey smiled and said that it was home for him.

Johnnie nodded and said that he was for something simple with the least amount of effort possible.

Alex agreed and suggested they get to work early the next day and prepare for what she thought would be a stressful day and likely a long one.

She figured that she would order in her favorite Thai dinner and make it an early evening.

8 The Parents

*M*att had come home in the wee early morning hours and collapsed into bed. Alex was awake early and quietly got ready for work. She left the coffee on, two hard boiled eggs on the counter and a bowl of oatmeal by the microwave for him and after eating one soft-boiled egg and having coffee she rolled her bike to the elevator.

She and Johnnie rode silently into work. It was clear to her that the nature of the case seemed to suck the energy from a person. She had some dread about the next two days. She knew she would be opening deep wounds with all the parents and knew the impact that would have on them and on her and Trey as well.

The sun was just coming up as they arrived at the station. She thought about Bill and Trevor and wondered how their surveillance had gone. She then realized that she was going to miss not having her half of a bear claw with her coffee because the two of them were the ones that always came in with the box of rolls and donuts.

As she and Johnnie approached her desk, she smiled and wondered how the donut box had arrived at her desk. There was a note on the box that said that it would take two trays of cookies to make up for making him miss his morning donut. It was signed Trevor.

Alex called Trevor and thanked him for being so thoughtful and asked him how the night had been.

She learned that Levi had stayed on the farm for the night and had not yet been spotted. Trevor commented that he and Bill had taken turns flying the drone that they had with them as entertainment and that it was a great refresher.

He commented that they had taken turns sleeping in the back seat.

Alex let him know that she would be out his way to interview the parents of the first victim and she would be glad to bring them lunch.

Trevor said that he hoped that Levi would go back to Cincinnati before then but if they were still parked in the forest across from the farm field, he would let her know.

Alex thanked him for thinking about the donuts and let him know that he had made her day.

He laughed and said that she was easy to satisfy.

After she hung up Johnnie commented that Trevor had really come a long way and was now one of her strongest advocates.

Trey walked in with his cup of coffee and pointed to the half bear claw on his desk. He looked at the message and commented that the long hand of the Trevor was very welcome.

Dr. Rogers walked up to Johnnie and handed him six reports and said that three were associated with the Cincinnati body part operation and three were associated with the Cleveland operation. He added that he had looked at the other missing person reports but most did not have any information that let him do anything more.

He looked in the donut box and asked if he could have a glazed cake donut.

Alex thanked him for bringing up the reports and said that he should take several donuts because two of the team were not going to be coming into the office.

The Chief walked in and came over and helped himself to a jelly filled roll. He looked at Alex and asked her if she was ready for a really tough day.

Alex shook her head and said there was no way to get ready to open the wounds of parents who had lost their daughter, but she would save her crying until she and Trey were back in their car.

The Chief nodded and said that he had visited several parents with the bad news about their child and it had affected him for months. He asked if the team was still holding sessions with the department therapist.

Alex nodded and said that the team considered her an essential part of the work they did.

"Good, see you Friday morning," the Chief said as he headed for his office.

Dr. Rogers said thanks for the donut and left as well.

Alex asked Johnny to stand by during the day and as they finished an interview, she would call him if she had any additional sleuthing requests.

Johnnie said that he was going to go back to the apartment and work from home.

Alex nodded and said that was a good idea. She signaled Trey for them to go and led the way to the car.

Trey confessed that he would rather be in a gun battle then to do the parent interviews. It was really hard for him to watch the pain of their loss resurface. He added that she should not expect any questions from him.

Alex agreed and said that they could cry on each other's shoulders after they left the house.

Sheriff Milster met them when they arrived. He asked whether they wanted him to drive to each place they would be going.

Alex replied that she wanted the meetings with each family to be as low key as possible, and she preferred not to use a marked police car.

Sheriff Milster said that would be no problem and that he would drive an unmarked police car that the unit had just acquired. It would be the first time he would have a chance to try it out.

Alex nodded and said that she was all in for him to drive.

Sheriff Milster made a call to the first couple to verify that they were still agreeable to going through their daughter's disappearance.

The drive took them about twenty minutes and when they arrived, they drove up the lane of a house that was in the center of a large yard that was probably an acre in size.

Alex took in the roses along the front of the house and the evenly trimmed low hedge along the side of the garage. She noted the ten-foot diameter round garden in the middle of the front yard with brown eyed Susan flowers giving it a warm appearance. She hoped when she left the flowers would lift her spirit up after the interview.

Sheriff Milster rang the doorbell and was warmly greeted and invited in.

He introduced Alex and Trey as Cincinnati detectives that he had enrolled to see if they could help with the cold cases that he had not been able to solve.

Alex was surprised when the mother commented that she had seen her on the news and had been impressed with the fact that each time the report was about a case that she had solved. The one she recalled the most and thought about often was when she had solved the case of a young girl missing for fifteen years and had saved her and her two daughters. She admitted it had made her cry for several weeks. She asked if Alex still had contact with that young woman.

Alex smiled and said that she did and that she and her two daughters were doing well.

The father commented that he hoped she could pull off another miracle.

Alex replied that she hoped so too but miracles were few and far between. She added that what she would promise was to capture and if justice played out the way she hoped she would see the perpetrator go to the gas chamber.

The mother smiled and said that would at least let them close a door to a painful section of their minds.

Alex nodded and confessed that the questions she was going to ask would be personal and potentially painful. She said that it was one of the more difficult parts of her work.

The mother held up her hand and asked if they could sit around the kitchen table. She offered to serve cookies, hot or cold tea, coffee, or milk.

Alex thanked her and said that the kitchen would be a great place and that a cup of coffee would be great.

The five of them sat down and after the drinks were poured the mother said she was ready for the questions and that Alex should understand that she and her husband were very appreciative of having someone looking once again into the case. They were not expecting a miracle but were hoping for closure.

Alex nodded and asked if either of them remembered anything about the day their daughter went missing that stood out.

There was silence for a few moments then the mother said that the morning had been like all other school mornings. She had called for her daughter to come down for breakfast multiple times. At the last moment, her daughter had rushed down, drank her glass of milk, took a bite of her egg, grabbed two strips of bacon, ran out of the house with her backpack and ran to the end of the lane as the bus arrived.

She wiped a tear from her eyes and said that she had not been given a hug.

Alex took a bite of the cookie and a sip of coffee. She looked at the cookie, said it was delicious and asked what it was called.

The mother smiled and said that it was a short bread cookie with a twist that she had added. She then added that it had been her daughter's favorite.

Alex nodded, she then looked at the father and asked what he remembered about the day his daughter went missing.

He shook his head and said he remembered rushing to the school because he was running late and was supposed to pick her up after her cheer leading practice. When he got there, he could not locate her and asked the other cheer leaders if they knew where she was. They let him know that she had not been at practice. They all thought that she had gone home early.

He then called the house only to learn she was not home. He walked through the entire school asking about her and one grounds keeper said he had seen her walking out with one of the young men, but he had no clue about who it was.

He had then walked the entire school grounds and then driven home having a feeling of dread.

They had called Sheriff Kagle, now retired, to ask him to have his team keep an eye out for her. He said he would do it and that they should come in the following day if she was still missing and put in a missing person report.

That was now at least twelve years ago.

Alex asked if they had the names of their daughter's friends.

The mother got up and returned with a yearbook and said that all of their daughter's friends had a star on the upper right corner and often a note on the edge of the page. She pointed to the tabs that she had put on each page that had a friend marked.

She said that she had talked to each of her daughter's friends at the time of the disappearance but had never gotten anything that was of any help. She had asked about boyfriends but none of her friends thought she had one.

Alex asked if it was possible for her to borrow the yearbook so she could go through it in detail.

The mother nodded and said that she hoped that Alex would have better luck with it than she had, and she added that of course she wanted it returned.

Alex said that she would indeed return it. She asked if there was a hair sample that she might get so they could check for DNA. She also asked for some hair from each of them so that she could use them to make a positive match if necessary.

The father asked if she was asking because she had a body.

Alex shook her head and said that she did not, but she wanted to be prepared with the DNA so that she would not need to ask for it later.

The mother smiled and said that it made her sad to think what the DNA might uncover but she was pleased with the way Alex was preparing. It was more than anyone else had done to date.

She left the room and came back with three brushes and put them in zip lock bags and used a sharpie to put her name, her daughter's name, and her husband's name on them and put them on the table. She tapped her finger on the yearbook and said that she wanted it back and she wanted her daughter's hairbrush back but the other two did not matter.

Alex thanked her for being willing to provide the materials with which she hoped to solve the case.

She asked Sheriff Milster if he had evidence bags and if he could get them to put in what they were gathering.

She then smiled and said there was only one more very important question. She shared the fact that she used cookies, brownies, and muffins to bribe her co-workers and she handed out bags of chocolate to folks like Sheriff Milster in hopes of getting their cooperation. She would love to add the delicious short bread cookie to the cookie list she currently baked.

The mother smiled and said that she would be the first person that she was going to share her recipe with, and she hoped that it would help Alex solve the case. She got up and walked to the counter, wrote for a few minutes, and returned with a note that had the recipe and the preparation instructions.

She smiled and thanked Alex for the way she had conducted such a personal interview with such a warm touch.

Alex nodded and said that she would see if she could do justice to the cookie recipe. She had a very demanding team who would give her their honest feedback.

The Sheriff returned with the evidence bags. Trey put the two brushes into one evidence bag and the yearbook into the larger evidence bag and then sealed both of them and signed his name.

He asked to have both Alex, and the Sheriff sign it as well.

The Sheriff nodded and said that it was a good idea to treat the evidence in the proper fashion.

Alex stood up and gave the mother a hug and wished her the best and that she would personally contact her when she solved the case.

She then shook the father's hand.

He smiled and asked if he was going to get a hug from her.

Alex reached up and pulled him into a hug.

Trey stood up and got a hug from the mother and a handshake and back slap from the father.

Sheriff Kagle shook hands and said that he would stay in close contact with Alex.

He led the way out to his car.

The yellow brown eyed Susan Garden did make her feel better, but she was really sad because she did not expect to find their daughter, Heather, alive.

Once in the car Alex let out a sigh. She said that the interview had gone much better then she had expected, and the attitude of the parents had made it less stressful then she had thought it would be. It was clear to her that they missed their daughter but had managed to move on with their lives.

Sheriff Kagle looked at her and complimented her with how she had won both parents over and had gotten more than anyone else had ever gotten. He said that he had never seen the yearbook and he had been in the department when their daughter went missing.

Alex said that she was sure the killer had his picture in the yearbook, and she had a firsthand witness that would verify it before morning.

She added that she thought that by the weekend she would have the DNA match that would nail the killer.

Sheriff Kagle shook his head and said that he hoped so because it had been a weight around his neck since he was a young cop.

Alex asked if he had a place in mind for lunch.

He said that he liked to go to a small mom and pop diner which featured a variety of burgers with fries, tater tots or onion rings on the side.

They would be early and hopefully ahead of the crowd because he had never seen the place empty. There was always a huge crowd that always seemed to fill the place.

Alex said that it sounded like they would get a good lunch. They should have lunch and get prepared for their next interview.

After a quick lunch Alex said that she did not think the next interview session was going to be as smooth as the first because the parents would have had less time grieving and would still be looking for information and answers about their missing daughter.

Sheriff Kagle agreed that the next three sessions would be tougher because the parents were still processing the grief and they were in the angry stage where they were looking for someone to blame. He said that he and his folks had been the focus of that anger.

Alex nodded and said she understood their anger and that their daughter's disappearance had happened in the last few months. She hoped that they would cooperate, but she understood their frustration and anger.

The Sheriff said that their next victim had been the one that had come home for the weekend, had gone hiking and had not returned. The parents had driven every country road that they thought she might have hiked along and had even gone up and down a small local creek hoping to find her. They had been angry with his desk help, who told them that they would need to wait twenty-four hours to put in a missing person's report. He was not sure, but he had a suspicion that they were racist.

Alex looked at Trey and asked him if he would take the lead for this interview.

The Sheriff again went first and made the introductions.

Alex came in last and when the introductions were made, Trey got a handshake from the mother and father, and she got a nod from each of them.

They were led into the living room and asked to sit down.

Alex sat down and listened as Trey asked the questions. It was apparent that the attitude was more hostile, and the sheriff was asked repeatedly whether his unit was continuing the search.

Trey got the samples of hair. He had evidence bags that the sheriff had provided and put the hair into them and handed them to the Sheriff.

He asked for the most recent picture that he might get a copy of and received sharp reply that the Sheriff already had a picture.

Trey looked over at Alex and the Sheriff and asked if they had any other questions.

Alex asked what the last word each of them had shared with their daughter.

The father let out an expletive and asked what that had to do with finding his daughter. The mother admonished her husband and said that her last words had been to wish her daughter a good hike and that she would have her favorite dinner ready when she got back and then she had given her a hug.

Alex nodded and said that is what her mother always promised when she went on a hike, and she always took the hike with that thought in mind. She added that she was sure that was the thought her daughter had with her during her hike.

The mother nodded and asked what role Alex had on the case.

Alex smiled and said that she was the lead detective on the case.

The mother nodded and smiled, and she said that the family reputation must have gotten out. She added that personally she was the normal one in the family, but she kept a low profile.

Alex nodded and replied that she was often taken by surprise that after more than a hundred years color was still such a barrier for people to get along.

The husband stood up and declared the meeting was over and walked out.

The wife stood up and apologized and said that the daughter had been his favorite child and he had withdrawn and had refused to go to counseling with the rest of the family.

Alex nodded and apologized for resurfacing the pain, but she added that she needed to understand firsthand what had happened and might be back to personally hike the roads her daughter might have taken.

The mother nodded and said that if she did come out to make the hike, she wanted to accompany her because she was not sure about the reception she might get if she hiked alone.

Alex thanked her and she said she would let her know.

She then asked the Sheriff to lead the way back to the car.

Once in the car the Sheriff again complimented her and said that he was learning a lot about how to manage grieving parents.

Alex nodded and replied that she followed a simple saying, "treat others the way you wish to be treated." She added that she also imagined or visualized how a person might be feeling in the specific situation they found themselves in.

Sheriff Kagle asked if they should follow the same approach for the interview process the next day.

Alex nodded and said she and Trey would meet him in the morning and he could take them to each interview.

Once back to her car she asked Trey to drive.

She made a call to Matt and asked him to schedule a time early Friday morning to be at the station to look through the yearbook to see if he could make an identification of the person he saw at the concert on the green.

She then called the Chief to update him.

After that she called Trevor to see how surveillance was going.

9 The Farm

*T*he interview with the last two parents was better than the second one had been. They learned that one of the young women had gone to an outdoor show that featured the battle between the local Indians and the settlers of the time that used real horses in a large outdoor venue. One couple came forward and said they thought that they had seen the missing young woman talking to a slender man dressed in black jeans wearing a blue T-shirt, but they had not been close enough to see much more.

The second missing young woman had gone to a concert in downtown Columbus and had never come home. The follow-up investigation did not come up with any leads.

Sheriff Milster said that he wished they had come up with more during the interviews.

Alex told him that she thought they had what they needed to solve the case.

Early Friday morning she had Matt sit down in one of the huddle rooms with Trey and go through the yearbook to see if he could identify the person he had seen in the park. She had covered the names so that he would have to pick the picture based on only facial recognition.

She had the process officially captured by the department film crew who were also told they would likely be witnesses in court if Matt was asked about his identification of the perpetrator.

When Matt turned to the M's he stopped and pointed to a picture and said that it was the person sitting on the lawn at the concert.

Alex thanked him and made sure the film crew closed with a close up shot of the yearbook picture with the name covered and then with the cover removed so the name, Levi Aram Misle was clearly visible.

She thanked everyone and emphasized that the film was to be treated and handled as evidence.

She looked at the time and said it was time to get ready for the search of each of the properties.

She called Bill and asked where he was, and he said they were at a downtown grocery store shopping. He commented that he thought that Levi may have made them. He guessed that following him into the store might not have been wise.

Alex said that Levi could be arrested. She said that his properties would be searched and hopefully the case would be closed.

Bill said he had to go and hung up.

Alex walked into the Chief's office and said that it was time to do the searches, and he should have the properties seized.

The Chief nodded and made a call and then led the way to his car.

Alex said that she needed to go to the locker room to get her Kevlar outfit.

Trey said he would do the same.

The Chief picked up his gym bag and said he had his. He would put it on when he got to the farm.

Alex said that Bill had been instructed to make the arrest. She suggested searching the farm first.

She took the seat behind the Chief and Trey took the passenger seat. Johnnie sat behind Trey and put his drone carrier between him and Alex.

The Chief nodded and took the highway north.

Alex's phone buzzed. It was Bill calling to let her know that Levi had escaped.

Alex was silent for a moment and then decided to reassign Bill and Trevor.

Alex suggested that they drive to the farm, and they could assist on the search for bodies. She asked them to bring both of their drones.

Levi had spotted the two that seemed to be following him. He made a bee line to his truck and sped out of the city. He figured he would go to the farm where he had supplies and then head out of the state. He wondered how he had been made. As he drove, he thought about his situation and figured even the farm might not be safe. He decided to go to the far corner of the property where there was a shed where one of the huge tractors was kept. He could get a good view of the house and much of the surroundings from the roof.

He was glad that he kept his rifle and shotgun under the back seat of the truck. He at least had the firepower to defend himself or to take action if he thought it would help him.

Alex commented that she had Levi dead to rights but now she needed bodies. She looked over to Johnnie and said that when they got to the farm, he should take the lead and with Bill and Trevor search the place for grave sites.

Johnnie nodded and said that the Canadian border case had given all of them practice in identifying the very slight depressions on a forest floor that an aged grave made. He would organize the search on each side of the road leading to the little lake where they had spotted Levi fishing. It seemed to be a natural place to bury bodies.

Alex nodded and said that she and Trey would search the outbuildings. She asked the Chief to take the farmhouse with a set of officers.

The Chief smiled and said that it felt good being in on the action and having someone else take the lead.

Alex asked if he wanted the lead.

He replied that he liked it just the way it was coming down.

He was stopped at the end of the driveway to the farm by one of the Sheriff's deputies. The deputy recognized Alex and said that Sheriff Milster was at the house waiting for them.

Alex thanked him for the information.

Alex let him know that she had two of her team coming in behind her.

The Chief parked next to the Sheriff's car.

After a brief handshake Alex said that they should check the place out.

The Chief and the Sheriff headed for the house with four other officers.

Alex asked two officers to accompany her, and she headed for the largest of what she thought of as barns.

It was apparent that the larger barn was set up to be a milking barn and it seemed to still be a functioning one. She walked around until she was sure there was nothing to find.

She asked one of the deputies to call out to the two at the end of the driveway and to hold anyone coming to the farm to do the milking because she did not want anyone in until the search was over.

She then led the way to the second barn and decided it was the storage barn. It held stacks of bags and was filled with hay and bales of straw. An orange forklift was parked with its prongs inserted into a pallet stacked with ground feed for the cows.

She saw the ladder going up and asked one of the deputies to take a look. He called back that it just held old rusty equipment.

Alex did a thorough check. She did not expect to find anything useful and said that the search was over, and they should go outside.

Johnnie walked out to the end of the road leading back to the lake and found a tree that had fallen over. It was in the shade and provided a good place to sit. He took Gunjfor out of her carrying case and took her for an initial warmup spin. He decided that he would search on one side of the road. He would have Trevor search the other side and Bill could search around the lake.

He had just finished mounting Gunjifor's weapon when Bill and Trevor arrived.

Trevor saw the gun in Gunjfor's gun holder. He asked which grave Johnnie planned to shoot.

Johnnie smiled as replied he was just going to be ready to get even with anyone who ticked him off.

He put a quick call in to Alex to let her know that the body search team was soon to be searching the grounds.

Levi drove slowly around to where the road was running along the back corner of his farm. He took out his deer hunting rifle, mounted the scope and made sure he had some extra ammunition with him. He then climbed up on the roof and slowly scanned the house and the two barns. He watched as four people came out of the main barn.

He immediately recognized the Black woman. She had been his first choice when he had been searching for his next victim. Now he realized she was some kind of law. He now recalled seeing her in the news. He shook his head at the bad luck he had stepped into.

He decided to kill her. He moved into a better position, carefully adjusted his rifle, took notice of the wind, and figured the drop for the distance. She would be just like any deer that he shot. It would be one to the heart and then he would hightail it out of the country.

He needed to withdraw as much money as he could from his local bank. He also had a huge sum of money he would need to get transferred to a new account.

Then his mind refocused on the smaller barn. The door had been left partially open and one of the deputies walked out in the lead. Then a tall plain clothed policeman and then the petite Black policeman. She was walking out in perfect position when he slowly squeezed the trigger.

He watched her fly back into the deputy behind her and lay on the ground at his feet. He picked up his ejected casing and quickly made his way down from the shed roof and ran to his truck. He threw everything to the floor behind the driver's seat and jumped in behind the wheel and roared out to the highway. He knew he needed to get away as quickly as possible.

Alex walked out and was about to head for the house when she felt that someone had kicked her hard in the center of her chest. She flew backwards into the person behind her. She stayed down as she tried to get her breath back. It was clear to her that she had been hit hard and had suffered some sort of significant injury. She closed her eyes and focused on getting her breath back.

Trey and the two police officers had their guns drawn and were trying to located the shooter.

Johnnie heard the shot. He immediately took Gunjfor as far above the tree line as he could and spotted the black truck barreling along the road out beyond the other side of the lake.

He flew Gunjfor as fast as he could toward the intersection where the smaller road joined the main state highway. He dove Gunjfor towards the truck at the fastest speed possible and fired a series of shots at the truck. He was sure he had hit it at least five times but it did not stop the truck.

He had to land Gunjfor because her battery was done and there was no more power left to get her back.

He got up and raced over to where Alex was now sitting up against the barn. He could hear that emergency vehicle as it came down the lane.

Alex closed her eyes as she tried to recover her breath.

The Chief and the Sheriff and all the rest were standing around her as the EMT group pushed passed them.

They stopped when they saw Alex sitting by the barn. The lead asked where she had been hit.

Alex put her finger through her suit jacket and then pointed to where the flattened bullet had bonded with her Kevlar vest.

The EMT asked everyone to get back so they could back their unit in as close as possible. He then asked Alex if she could stand and be helped into the unit. He said that the team had one female member who he introduced and then asked her to examine Alex. Once Alex had been helped in, he closed the back doors.

Alex sat down on the side bench and leaned against the side of the unit. She was amazed by the impact that the bullet had delivered.

She was still trying to catch her breath.

The female EMT opened her blouse and commented that Alex was lucky to be alive because the bullet had hit almost directly over her heart. Her heart was probably working hard to recover from being shocked. She would probably need to spend a couple of days in the hospital under observation.

Alex shook her head and said that wasn't going to happen at the moment. She was going to rest for a moment and then she was going to Cincinnati to search through a house where she hoped to get the evidence that would put the person who had shot her in prison.

She buttoned up her blouse and said she would like to get out.

The EMT shook her head and opened the doors.

Alex took Trey's hand as he helped her down. She smiled and asked why he was standing in front of everyone else.

He looked at her and said that he knew she would be wanting to get out and get to Cincinnati.

Alex nodded and asked if anyone had figured out where the shot had come from.

Johnnie said that he had when he took Gunjfor up after the shot. There was a shed at the corner of the property that was the most likely location. He explained that he had gotten five shots at the black truck, but it had gotten away.

He explained that Gunjfor's battery had run low, and he had landed her in the forest at the corner of the property.

Alex complimented him on his quick reaction and asked him to continue the body search after he had Gunjfor back in action.

She looked over to where Bill and Trevor were standing and asked if they had found any possible grave sites.

Bill shook his head in the negative, but Trevor gave a thumbs up. He said he had about a half a dozen potential graves.

Johnnie then added that he had a similar number in the area where he had been searching.

Alex looked at the Chief and asked if Cincinnati could provide additional personnel that could work with Sheriff Milster and his folks and begin to dig up the potential graves.

Sheriff Milster shook his head and said that it was hard to believe they had more than twelve potential grave sites and her team had only looked for less than an hour.

He asked one of the deputies to drive Johnnie out to get his drone.

He then looked at Alex and asked how deep he thought the graves would be.

Alex replied she had no clue and that he should dig one up to determine the depth. She then asked why he wanted to know.

He replied that he wanted to use a backhoe to dig about two thirds of the way down and then proceed by hand shovel until the remains were found then the forensics team could do the rest. That would speed up the recovery and reduce the amount of work and the number of people he would need.

Alex thought that was a good idea. She added that she wanted to keep this out of the news until she at least captured the killer so he would need to use people that he trusted to keep quiet.

Levi knew that he had to get off the road as soon as he could. He remembered an old, abandoned barn not far from the main interstate and close to a couple of used car lots. Because of the three bullet stars on the back window, he knew he had to abandon his truck and get out of the area as soon as possible.

He had five hundred dollars in cash and hoped that the car lot had a car that still ran but would not cost more than that.

He organized everything he planned to take with him and put it in the back of the truck. Then he walked out to the first used car lot.

He spotted two cars that were marked up as fix up deals.

He asked the lot dealer about them and was told that if he paid four hundred in cash, he could drive out with the title in hand but there would be no refunds. The cars would run but they were at the end of life.

Levi asked to listen to both cars running. He could hear a knock in one. The other seemed to run smoothly so he chose it.

The dealer gave him the deed for the car and said the he hoped it was what he wanted.

Levi adjusted the mirrors, put the seat where it seemed about right. The gas gauge was nearly empty. There were several gas stations within sight.

He felt like he was sitting in a bathtub looking over its edge as he drove.

He drove slowly out and in the opposite direction of where his truck was parked. After a few miles he turned back and stopped at a gas station, filled the car up, checked the oil level which he had to top off. He figured that using oil was probably an issue, so he bought two quarts and put them in the trunk.

He then drove back to the barn and put all of the stuff he had in the trunk and drove back to the highway and headed west.

Alex sat in the passenger seat and leaned back and relaxed.

She knew that she had once again been lucky. She took the time to call Matt and let him know that she had been shot but was doing fine.

Matt asked if she had gotten the shooter.

Alex replied that she had not even seen the shooter, but that Johnnie had gotten a few shots at the shooter and that the shooter was very likely the guy he had identified.

Matt asked what she was up to for the rest of the day.

She replied that she was on the way to the house to search for any evidence that it might hold.

He wished her luck and said he would check on her after she was done at the house.

10 The House

*A*lex relaxed and lay back in her seat. She closed her eyes and thought through the upcoming search. She was still wearing her bulletproof vest but was not expecting any more gunfire.

She wondered where Levi would go and how he might be trying to escape. She figured he would try to change vehicles.

She called Johnnie and asked if he had researched Levi's finances.

Johnnie replied that things had moved so fast that he had not had time to do so. He said that as soon as he got to where he could get a Wi-Fi connection he would do so.

Alex told him to finish the body search and then go after the finances.

She looked over to the Chief and commented that Johnnie was one of the team's star members. He was superfast at hacking, had been the only one who had spotted and shot at the shooter and was now leading the effort to recover bodies.

The Chief nodded and said that he had no knowledge of any hacking being done in his organization, but he agreed with everything else.

He maneuvered up the winding Mt Hill road and then turned up a side street and parked behind one of the squad cars.

The senior officer greeted him. He told him that it was time to searched the house.

Eight patrolmen walked up the long walk to the front door. The officer in charge said he had two more officers in back in case anyone tried to leave. Those going in the front were assigned two to a floor.

He led the way up.

When Alex had to stop to catch her breath, she knew that she had most likely been hurt more seriously than she had expected.

She looked over at Trey and told him that as soon as they had any evidence she was going to the hospital.

Trey put her arm over his shoulder and literally picked her up and walked the rest of the way up carrying her.

As they got inside, they heard a shout from the top floor that they needed to come up immediately.

Trey looked around and found a small elevator. He got in and pulled Alex to him and pressed the button for the third floor. When the door opened they were in a room that made both of the stop in shock. The room they were in was full of mounted skulls.

Alex stopped. She heard the Chief loudly curse and say that he had never expected to find such a horror chamber.

The two patrolmen who had come up first were still holding their weapons at the ready.

Alex suggested that they put them away and that the room was off limits to everyone. She led Trey out of the room. Once she was out, she made a call to Dr. Rogers and told him that he needed to bring his team to examine and process more skulls than she could count. She said that she was keeping everyone away until he was at the scene, then she would take a tour with him before leaving.

She found a chair and sat down and took some deep breaths.

A short time later, she was surprised when Matt and his team followed Dr. Rogers and his team up the stairs.

She looked over at Trey who nodded his head in the affirmative.

She stood up and followed Dr. Rogers into the room.

Dr. Rogers asked his team to stay behind, and he led the way in. He kept mumbling, "Oh my god," as he walked through the four rooms.

He pointed to the pictures and the descriptions that each skull had at the base of the stand holding the skull.

When they got to the very back room, the stand in front of the fireplace had a large star on it. When they looked at the picture and the note, Alex knew they had found the young lady that had been taken from her high school. She was the first victim.

She looked at the Dr. and said that she had hair samples of the young lady as well as from her parents. She would have all her evidence delivered to him at the morgue. She said that how he handled the skulls for processing was up to him.

On the way-out Alex pointed to a door at the side of the room. The room led into the turret of the house. It had windows around two thirds of it. The door was on the back side of the turret. The room had a great view of downtown Cincinnati.

Alex walked up to the far side near the windows to a couch. She looked at the cushions and figured that this was a couch where Levi often sat.

The room was set up like a surgical arena with a stainless-steel table at its center and counters all around it.

It was clear to both of them that it was the skull preparation room.

Dr. Rogers said that he would set up his analysis room at the table and first process each skull locally and have samples taken to the morgue for more detail analysis.

Alex said that she had to leave and go to the hospital because she had been shot and was feeling the effects long after she had expected to.

He said that he wondered what Matt and his team were doing following him up all the stairs.

When she got back to the entrance to what she now thought of as "the Skull Museum," Matt pointed to a body board and asked her to lie down.

She nodded and let him help her to do that.

The rest of the EMT team went into action and strapped her to the board and then slowly carried her down three flights of stairs inside of the house and three flights of stairs leading to the street.

Once they were in the EMT unit, they took her vitals and began a conversation with the hospital emergency staff.

Alex decided that closing her eyes and relaxing was the only way to handle the situation.

The attending emergency room Dr. told her he was going to give her a mild sedative to let her body relax and that she would be put into an intensive care unit as soon as it was ready and that she would be staying at least overnight.

She asked if it was really necessary.

Matt said that he had gotten a detailed description of what had happened from Trey and was sure that it was necessary.

He had just finished when Trey walked in.

Matt looked at Trey and thanked him for the call. He said that he and his team needed to get back on duty because it was the beginning of the rush hour when bad things would be happening.

Trey nodded and said he would stay until Alex was in the intensive care unit.

Alex was just about to ask Trey why he had called Matt when the nurse came in with a person pushing a unit that turned out to be an x ray machine.

The technician asked everyone to get out of the room, and he then pushed a plate behind Alex's back and took a series of pictures. He then took the plated and put it on the cart and wheeled the unit out.

Trey came back in and said he had called Matt while she was sitting trying to recover and he didn't want to hear any complaints. She should just think about the time she had almost killed him by hiding him in an ice water puddle.

Alex smiled, nodded, and said that she was glad he had her back.

A few moments later another doctor came in and said that he had just looked at her x rays and said she had a partially collapse lung and that once she was in intensive care they were going to put her on an oxygen assist that would provide extra pressure to the lung as she breathed in to see if after an overnight stay the lung would go back to normal.

He added that she would most likely be in the hospital over the weekend.

Alex let out a groan and said that being in the hospital was not what she had planned for the weekend. She knew that Matt would have the weekend off because they had arranged for a ride along the Loveland trail for his team. They had invited Johnnie to join them.

She called Johnnie and asked him how the finding of graves was going.

Johnnie said that they had found thirty-two graves so far but only one had been dug up.

Bill had found bodies on the far side of the lake back up into the woods which had not been counted or marked. He had only started finding them when the sun was into the late afternoon. Before then he could not see the grave depressions.

He asked her how she was feeling.

Alex replied that she was in the hospital and would soon be in intensive care for the weekend.

There was silence on the phone for a long period.

Alex was about to ask if he was still on the line when he spoke up.

He said that he, Bill, and Trevor would be in to visit and did she want any Thai food for dinner.

Alex smiled and said that she did and anything they got would be good.

Johnnie added that he was about to call her to let her know that he would not be able to go on the bike ride because he, Bill and Trevor had agreed that they needed to be on hand when the digging started in earnest. He had called Dr. Rogers to let him know about the bodies that would need processing and that his team needed to be on site.

Alex was interrupted when the nursing team that was going to move her to the intensive care unit entered.

Alex asked her if visitors would be allowed that evening. When she got a no, she told Johnnie to postpone any visit until the following day.

Johnnie said he understood and wished her a good night.

Alex hung up and lay back and took a deep breath. She felt exhausted.

The nurse came in and said that there were two people outside of the room that she thought were police officers. One was requesting her clothes to take in as evidence and the other told her to say that Sandra had her back.

Alex realized that the Chief had assigned a protection detail for her. She thanked the nurse for the information and said that her clothes should be given to the person seeking it as evidence and to let the other officer know that she appreciated being protected by such a wonderful person.

The nurse suddenly turned and seemed to be trying to shield Alex.

She heard the Chief identify himself.

Alex let the nurse know that it was safe.

The Chief came to the end of the bed and asked how she was doing.

Alex asked what was up and why the protection detail?

The Chief replied that the press had found out about the raid at the house at Mount Healthy and then had found out about the farm.

The officer at the farm had called and let him know that they had shot down a camera drone that belonged to a local independent reporter.

It was almost immediate that the raids made the news and that a Black policewoman had been seen being taken away in an emergency vehicle.

There are other Black police officers, but you are the one that made the news.

The Chief came over to the head of the bed and whispered that it was under her pillow.

Alex knew immediately that he had put a weapon under her pillow.

She thanked him for putting a guard outside her door and said he should make sure her guards used their armor.

The Chief nodded and wished her a good night and that he would be back in the morning.

Alex wondered if she would be able to fall asleep but after making sure her weapon would not be discovered she was almost immediately asleep.

The room was dark when she heard gunfire. She rolled out of the bed and crouched on the floor. The door opened and a rapid volley of bullets hit the bed, and she had to roll to get away from the barrage.

She jumped up and ran to the door and slid out along the floor. That slide almost made her faint. She looked down the hallway but could not find the shooter.

She crawled over to where a police officer was sitting against the wall. It was the officer that had stood guard for Trey when he was in the hospital. She checked his vitals and was relieved to get a pulse. She then went to where the nurse was lying and applied pressure to the shoulder wound that was bleeding.

A hand pulled her away as she was told by a feminine voice that she should get back in bed because her butt was showing.

Alex stood up and almost wanted to laugh but as she looked around, she realized that not only was the shooter a serial killer he was an angry cornered animal seeking revenge and would go after anyone that he felt was a threat.

She watched as a blue wave seemed to roll down the hallway toward her.

She looked at the police officer sitting against the wall, and he gave her a thumbs up. He pulled open his shirt to show her his Kevlar vest.

She smiled and thanked him for guarding her and for buying the vest.

She went back into the ICU and sat down after putting her weapon in the closet under some pillows. She looked at the bed where one of the pillows was full of holes. It had fallen forward when she jumped out and she was sure that in the dark it looked like a body.

About a half an hour later two hospital personnel came in to wheel out the bullet riddled bed. Alex stopped them and asked if there was anyone in the hallway to accept the bed as evidence.

One of them returned and said that the officer in charge had said that he would see that it was handled as evidence.

They then wheeled in a new bed.

Alex retrieved her weapon, turned the bed so she faced the door and then climbed into it. A male nurse came in and hooked her up to the monitoring equipment and the oxygen.

She was asleep almost instantly.

It was five thirty in the morning when a new female nurse came in, introduced herself and took her vitals.

Alex next woke up at eight when the attending physician came in to see how she was doing.

The Chief came in a short time later to let her know that the officer that had been shot was recovering well and said that she should know that many of his buddies had teased him about him buying his own Kevlar suit, but he had just told him that he was eternally grateful that he had.

Alex asked how the Chief's request for the force to buy vests for every officer was going.

He shook his head and said that the budget constraints were keeping it from getting any traction.

Alex asked if she arranged a donation of body armor would he see that every officer received them.

The Chief nodded and said that would be easy.

Alex said that he should set up a group to manage such a donation and she would make sure they got the suits.

She then asked how the digging at the farm was going.

The Chief said that they had dug down to the point where they could confirm it was a grave with a body for ten of the graves. Once they got to that point they stopped, and they covered the graves with plywood. Dr. Rogers had called in FBI resources to help with the forensics work but they would only arrive and get started in the coming week.

Dr. Rogers had retrieved enough DNA from the about twelve of the skulls and had matched them with data he had, but he said that he would need to get DNA samples from the parents for most of the skulls.

Alex thanked him for the update and said he should go home and spent time with Mary-Anne.

She planned to relax and later go for a walk around the hospital hallway with Matt.

Matt walked in about the time that she finished talking.

The Chief said good morning to him and then said she was all his.

Alex gave Matt a kiss and asked what he had in the bag. He opened it and took out a box that had a bear claw and some butter and maple syrup for a pancake.

He said it seemed light but figured it would tide her over to when Johnnie, Bill and Trevor would deliver the Thai lunch they had promised.

She thanked him and said that she needed to rest for a while, but she then wanted to take a walk with him to visit the two that had been shot.

178

11 Bank Account

*L*evi was shocked when he watched the news about the raid on his house. He was really surprised when the person being put into the ambulance was the detective he had shot. He had no clue how she had survived. When he shot her, he had watched as she flew backwards into the deputy behind her. He knew exactly who it was when he saw the camera zoom in and he recognized the tall Black EMT. They had both been in the park where he had zeroed in on her and one other potential skull.

He shook his head and wondered how he could have been so unlucky to be where one of the most successful detectives happened to be.

He knew that he had hit her, but she must have been wearing some sort of very good bulletproof vest. Even then he was amazed that she had survived. He was sure that he had hit her exactly over her heart and the impact alone should have been enough to kill her.

He had gone to the bank and withdrawn nine thousand dollars and had transferred most of the rest to a different bank so he would have access to money.

He figured that his investments would most likely be discovered so he went online and split his account over three other financial institutions, and each time put a different name on the account. He smiled as he used several of the names from his skull collection. He felt good about honoring his first by using her name on the account where he put the majority of the money.

He was staying in a motel and was angry about having to lower his standard to being cooped up in such a small place. He was especially upset to have had to abandon his pickup. He wondered how anyone could have had a weapon and been able to hit his pickup from so far away. The pickup was a favorite of his that he had purchased when he had started taking care of his parents. It had all the comfort features and a great sound system.

He thought about his nemesis and decided that before leaving the area he was going to shoot her at close range and make sure she got what she deserved. His only regret was that he would not be able to process her skull and mount it in his collection. Thinking about that made him even more angry than he was already. He did not know how he could ever replace such a fine collection.

He loaded his .44 magnum and put a refill in his sweatshirt pocket. He figured he would only have time to empty his gun and then hightail it out of the hospital. He planned to fill her with lead and then hightail it. He would reload when he got back to his car so he would be ready in case he was stopped.

He smiled at the thought of her bullet riddled body bleeding out in her hospital bed. He almost laughed when he thought about her going to the hospital only to be killed in her bed.

He drove to the hospital and parked near an exit of the parking garage. He took note of the cameras but figured that at this point it didn't matter.

He walked in and asked what room his friend was in. He learned the intensive care room that she was in and was informed that there was no visitation allowed. He shook his head as if he were disappointed and left by the door he had entered. He walked slowly around to another entrance and made his way to the wing where the room that she was in. The stairs came out about two rooms away from her room.

He spotted a policeman sitting outside of the door. He didn't say a word but shot him in the chest and watched as he was thrown against the wall and slid to the floor.

A nurse rushed toward him. He was impressed by her courage and shot her in the shoulder instead of the chest. He figured she would live but she would most likely think twice next time about rushing a person with a gun.

He opened the door to the room and stood in with one foot holding the door open. It was dark inside, but he could make out the body in the bed. He emptied his gun and then turned, hurried back to the stairs, and ran down. He then walked calmly out of the hospital. He watched as several squad cars rushed in, and the police ran into the hospital.

He then walked to his car and drove slowly back to his hotel room.

He figured it was time to head west to someplace where he could start a new life.

Trey was the first to arrive and come into the intensive care unit. He said he was glad that she had avoided being shot and asked if she had gotten a chance to shoot Levi.

Alex shook her head and said that she had just barely avoided being shot.

A few moments later the Chief walked in and said that she was ruining his weekend.

Alex smiled and said that she was the victim and that he should go easy on her.

He asked if she had fired her weapon.

Alex shook her head in the negative.

The Chief nodded and then said he was doubling the guard at the door, but he figured that Levi would not be back.

Alex agreed and said they would need to find out what kind of car he was driving. She figured he had ditched his truck.

The Chief agreed and said that he would see if Bill and Trevor could check out the used car lots up around the farm.

Alex said that she expected them around lunch time, and she would work with them on that.

The Chief nodded and said that he was going to go to the driving range and try to work out his concern about the situation. He wanted to arrest Levi and lock him up.

Alex agreed and added that she wanted to get him to the gas chamber.

The Chief chuckled and said that it was too bad that for a special case like his there wasn't a torture chamber they could send him to.

Alex smiled and said she agreed.

Matt walked in with a bag and declared that breakfast had arrived. He asked why there were so many police cars and officers around the Hospital.

Alex replied that she was such an attraction that they had all come out to get her autograph.

Matt looked at Trey and asked him the same question and listened as Trey explained.

Matt came over, gave her a hug and kiss, and handed her the breakfast biscuit with sausage and cheese. He said that he had gone light because he knew that Johnnie was bringing in a full Thai offering for lunch.

Alex thanked him and asked him to bring her some of the bags of candy so that when they went for a walk around the hospital, she could give them out.

Matt nodded and said that he would go back to the apartment and bring them back. He asked how many of the bags he should bring.

Alex told him to bring them all.

A police officer came in and excused himself but said that he had to get information for the incident report.

The Chief nodded and said that he was just leaving.

Trey said he was on the way out as well.

Matt said that he was going to go as well and would return for lunch.

The officer looked at Alex and apologized for running her visitors out.

Alex let him know that once she had answered her questions, she was going to take nap.

The officer went through the standard series of questions and within fifteen minutes was done.

She thanked Alex for the information and wished her a speedy recovery.

Alex had no plans on napping. As she ate her sandwich and sipped on her milk, she thought through what she wanted Johnnie, Bill, and Trevor to do. If they had to go back to the farm, she wanted the truck found. She figured it would be close by. When they found the truck, they should look for used car lots where Levi might have purchased a car.

She wanted Johnnie to go after any money that Levi might have. Once it was located, she wanted to strip him of it in a way that would appear to be so legal that no one would challenge it. She wanted him broke. From previous cases, she knew how effective it was to strip someone of their money.

She wondered how much money Levi had. It seemed that he did not work but owned a huge house and a large farm. She figured it had to be in the millions.

She shook her head as she thought about a multimillionaire serial killer that collected the skulls of his victims.

Matt arrived with the bags of candy and Alex got out of bed and pushed her oxygen bottle ahead of her toward the door.

The nurse stopped her and said that she was in intensive care and could not go walking around the hospital.

Alex smiled and replied that she didn't want to arrest her own nurse but would if she obstructed an officer going about her police duty, she would have to make an arrest.

The nurse smiled and said that she had been warned about her and asked that she at least use a walker and let her partner handle the oxygen tank.

Alex handed her a bag of candy and agreed to use the walker.

She then asked for the room numbers of the officer and the nurse that had been shot.

The nurse looked up the room numbers and gave them to her.

The nurse watched as the two police officers guarding the door followed her patient. She looked at the bag and realized it was top quality chocolate and one of her favorites. She knew the ones in the gold covering had a caramel filler.

Alex stopped and handed the two officers a bag each and thanked them for keeping her safe. She had the pistol that the Chief had given out of site in in her gown pocket.

She then went to the room where the police officer, Jack was in.

She knocked at the door and then went in.

She called him by name and thanked him for having been on duty. She handed him a bag of candy and said that the last time she had given him a bag was when he was guarding her partner at the VA hospital.

Jack smiled and said that he would eat all the chocolate by the end of the day. He had been told that he would be released by the end of the day. He planned to go home and stand under a hot shower for hours. He said he would be praying and thanking his maker and her for having inspired him to have purchased the Kevlar outfit.

Alex nodded and said that she knew exactly how a hot steaming shower felt and that she was going to do the same as soon as she could.

Jack then said that he had been ragged because he had purchased his own Kevlar outfit for a substantial part of his monthly income but now, he figured it had been a lifesaving investment.

Alex agreed and said that her vest was currently bagged as evidence and figured his was as well. She asked him his size and told him it would be delivered in the next few days.

He asked what he would owe her for that.

Alex smiled and said that his continued support was all that it would cost.

She told him to enjoy his shower and that it was time for her to see the nurse who had also been shot.

He asked her if she was going after the person who had shot him.

Alex said that she would and that she planned to make sure he would spend the rest of his life in prison.

A few moments later the nurse that had been shot was as surprised as Jack by her visit. She broke down and cried when Alex handed her a bag of candy.

Alex said that she understood the emotion of being shot and realizing how close it was to being killed.

The nurse said that her husband normally worked on Saturdays at Kings Auto Mall but had taken the day off and was bringing in their nine-year-old son and seven-year-old daughter.

Alex handed her two more bags of chocolates and told her it was for the kids.

The nurse smiled and said that she had been told how tough "That Cincinnati's Black Annie Oakley" was but now she would have to add "with a heart of gold," to the moniker.

Alex smiled and thanked her for the compliment and wished her a speedy recovery.

She told Matt that she was ready to get back to her bed.

Shortly after she was back, the intensive care doctor came in and said that she was ahead of him. He had been planning to encourage her to walk the hallways but had heard from the nurse that she was already doing that. He asked her how she felt.

Alex admitted that the walk had tired her out. She shared that she ran three miles at least four times a week and was not used to getting tired so quickly.

The doctor nodded and said that her routine and the strength of her heart was probably what had saved her life. He figured it had put her in intensive care versus the morgue.

Alex smiled and said that statement provided a lot of motivation to get back to her routine.

The doctor nodded and said that she should work back up to it slowly. He suggested that she take two months to work back up to her old routine. He smiled and asked if she sported a six pack.

Alex handed him a bag of candy and said that she would like to show him her six pack, but she was too modest to do so in her current outfit.

The doctor thanked her for the chocolates and said he was going to order an x-ray for later the next day.

Monday morning, he would determine if she was ready for release.

Alex nodded and said that any more time in bed would drive her crazy.

After the doctor left, Matt shared the fact that his EMT team had volunteered to be on duty and had suggested they reschedule their bike ride until she was ready to lead the way.

He planned to be with the team for the evening shift but would come by the following day and then again go on duty for Sunday night.

Alex said that was great because she really was looking forward to the ride with his team.

Lunch was close at hand, and it was not long before Johnnie led the way into the room with Bill and Trevor close behind. Each of them carried a bag of food.

Alex greeted them and thanked them for saving her from the hospital food. She was not going to tell them about the one pot roast meal that she had enjoyed.

Trevor complained how much the price had gone up.

Alex told him to submit an expense report because she was going to talk business over lunch.

After lunch had been dished out, she asked Johnnie to determine where Levi kept his money and to cut him off.

She asked if they would be out at the farm over the weekend.

Bill verified that he was working with the FBI who were sending a dozen people to the site, and he was going to work with them to orient their efforts for the coming week.

Alex asked him to take some time to locate the pickup that she was sure had been abandoned and to see if they could determine what Levi was now driving.

Johnnie excused himself and said he was going to run out to the car and get his computer.

Trevor shouted after him that he should save himself from all the stress and whiz out on a wheelchair.

Alex wondered what had triggered Johnnie.

Bill commented that it seemed that Johnnie was feeling bad about having Levi get away and then the fact that she had been shot at in the hospital had probably been the last straw.

Alex gave a little laugh and commented that Johnnie was the only one on the team who had struck a blow against Levi.

Johnnie returned carrying his computer. He sat down and put his computer on the stool used by the doctor and soon he was smiling. He said he had picked up the trail to Levi's money that he had been moving to a new account. He laughed, then said he had him.

He said that Levi opened up an account for his niece Heather Preston who was seventeen years of age. Levi was listed as the controlling agent.

Alex smiled and asked Johnnie to disappear Levi from the record and put Heather's name in and make everything a part of a trust set up for her and make her parents the ones that the trust would go to incase of her death.

Johnnie hummed away and then he loudly declared, "Done."

Alex then asked if he could transfer the deed for the farm and put it in the trust and do the same for the house.

She asked if Levi had any other assets.

Johnnie was humming away as he kept saying, got it, got it, got it. He said that he had transferred everything into the trust fund under Heather's name. He said that Levi was now penniless, and the trust fund was worth close to ten million dollars.

Alex smiled and said that she figured that she would work with Heather's parents to rename the account The Heather Helping Hands fund and set it up so each parent of one of the victims would get twelve thousand a year for the rest of their lives and when they died and there were no more parents alive the fund would give the money to Charities that each parent had designated into perpetuity in their daughter's name.

Trevor shook his head and commented that it was getting harder and harder for him to come up with a dig at her.

Alex smiled and said that it would not take a very long time for him to recover since she was not going to let up on him.

She suggested that he go home and play with his small kids and spend a few hours with his wife.

Bob smiled and said that it was reassuring to see her getting back into form.

She nodded and said the doctor had asked her to work slowly up to her old self over the next two months and then to get back to her old exercise level. She would do the same with the give and takes.

She asked Johnnie what he was planning to do for the rest of the weekend.

Johnnie smiled and said that he was going to fly Gunjfor and work with Bill and Trevor to find the truck.

12 Escape

Levi was in a funk. He thought through what he needed to do. He figured he needed more than the two quarts of oil he had bought so he stopped at an Auto parts store and bought a case of oil and some bottles of thick goo that claimed to reduce the oil a car burned. He was not sure about the claim, but he figured he might as well try it.

He poured one bottle into the oil fill point as instructed.

There was a cash machine in the parking lot, so he decided to withdraw some additional money. He was surprised to be rejected because of insufficient funds. He had put more than ten thousand dollars into that account. He tried with another card that had the same amount in the bank and was rejected again. He looked at the ATM and wondered if it was damaged or not connected to the same system as his cards. The hair on the back of his neck stood on end.

He stopped at a convenience store where his credit cards were again rejected. He paid in cash as he realized that his money was not available to him. He had just shy of ten thousand dollars with him. His entire world was imploding.

He sat in his car for some time thinking about his situation.

He was glad that he had shot that Black detective in her hospital bed. She and her team had ruined his life. He only wished he would have had time to take her head.

He realized that if he managed to get away, he would need to work for a living. The easy life was over.

He thought about going back and getting his truck. He knew that the police were on his property, but they had no idea where he had put the truck. He figured it would take them a long time to discover where he had parked it. It was where no one would go for a long time.

He changed his mind about his truck and headed towards Indiana. He figured he might stop by a distant cousin's place and then go on toward somewhere in the west.

He thought about the time in Idaho when his parents had gone to the Idaho panhandle to visit friends. They had camped at a place near Coeur d'Alene. He had no intention of trying to find the friends, but he remembered thinking that it was a place he would like to live. He figured since he had nowhere else in mind it was a good place to go.

It was early afternoon as he went past where the distant cousin lived. He really didn't know them, nor did he want to get involved with family, so he decided to keeping going at the thunderous speed of fifty-five miles per hour until the sun went down. He was well into Iowa when he stopped at a motel that had a flashing sign that promised a clean room for sixty-nine dollars. He laughed when he remembered that on his last fishing trip stayed in the Grand Suite of a top-of-the-line hotel. He almost wanted to cry as he was checked by an old guy whose name tag boasted "a clean room at a great price." If the bedroom was ten by ten, he would have been surprised and the sink faucet in the small sink was slowly dripping and there was a rust stripe down to the drain.

He spent part of the evening figuring out which back highways. He wanted to stay off the interstate because he felt they might be looking for him.

Then tuned in to the news to see if there was anything about him being aired on the evening news. He was relieved that there was nothing.

When the best he could then tune in was a show highlighting the capabilities of one of the top tractors on the market he decided to get some sleep

He figured he would be able to make his way west with no problems. He was glad because he had figured out, he was limited to about fifty miles per hour otherwise he generated a large plume of grey smoke.

Johnnie, Bill, and Trevor drove up to the farm early on Sunday. They talked about working together to do one more sweep of the forest to verify that they had found all the graves, and they were going to make sure each grave was clearly marked. They shared the fact that they had been shocked by how many graves there were. They wondered how Levi had kept his activities hidden from his parents. They figured the parents never walked the woods and when they went to the lake, they probably walked down the road.

There were four officers at the farm. Two were at the entrance lane and two were outside of the house and barn. The two at the house said that all of them would be replaced by four additional officers late in the afternoon and then would be back on duty on Monday morning.

One of the officers added that they had been offered help by the FBI and were looking forward to getting back to their normal work hours.

The three walked along the small road to the dock. Johnnie commented that he didn't believe in ghosts but if they existed this would be the place they would haunt.

They sat down and Johnnie put Gunjfor into the air and went slowly through each section of forest verifying the grave sites and searching for any additional ones. Johnnie flew his drone slowly as close to the forest floor as possible and looked for depressions.

They had agreed to use only one drone and since he was the best pilot, he should use Gunjfor.

All three of them were monitoring the video screen.

Johnnie let out a groan as on the far side of the lake, they found one more spot that appeared to be depressed.

Johnnie made another pass and they all agreed that it looked like another grave. Johnnie landed Gunjfor on the suspected grave site and the three walked around the lake to where she was resting. They examined the site and agreed that it was a forty-second grave.

Bill said that since it was in his search area, he would come back with one of the orange stakes to mark it.

Johnnie said that would allow him time to put Gunjfor's battery into the charger so he would have plenty of battery in case they had to use her when they hunted for Levi's pickup truck.

Trevor shook his head and said that he hoped no additional bodies would be found.

Johnnie said he agreed, and he added that he hoped they would be able to close all the cases. He said he cringed every time he thought about being the parent of one of the missing young women.

Bill suggested they finish the day by searching for the truck.

Johnnie said that he had two additional batteries for Gunjfor, and he hoped that they would be able to locate the truck quickly.

He suggested they drive to someplace close that had a used car lot and hopefully a restaurant where they could get lunch.

Trevor got on his phone and found a nearby highway off the interstate that had several fast-food places and two used car lots.

They agreed that seemed to be a logical place to start their search.

As they turned and drove toward the interstate, Johnnie suggested they stop at the gas station that had a large sign advertising a sit-down restaurant and the best chicken in the world. They all agreed that would be preferable to the fast-food places.

Once they were seated Johnnie leaned back in the booth and said that he felt that after getting control of all of Levi's money and putting it into a trust controlled by Heather's parents, he felt great and for the first time in weeks, he had slept like a baby.

He figured that Alex would figure out how to nail Levy and would get him sent to prison.

There was general agreement that Alex would get him.

After lunch they drove over across the highway to the closest used car lot and after identifying themselves inquired about any recent sales to a rather handsome tall black-haired man.

The lot owner said he hadn't made a sale in a week.

Trevor thanked him and they drove to the second lot where they immediately got a hit.

The lot owner pointed to a lone car sitting on the far corner of the lot. He said he sold one that was similar to the red one, but it was blue and in slightly better condition. They were both scheduled to be taken to auction so he could get them off the lot and he had been happy to make a cash deal with a guy that fit the description that they had given him.

He said that he put on a temporary license plate and signed over the car title. The buyer never gave his name and drove toward the interstate. That was all he knew.

He asked what the guy was wanted for.

"Let's just say he is a bad guy with the police looking for him," Johnnie replied.

The lot owner said that he figured they might have a change to get him if they let the highway patrol know about a blue ford that was putting out a plume of smoke. He added that if the car went over fifty it began to put out lots of smoke.

Johnnie thanked him. He looked around and then asked how far it was to the next small highway or road.

The car dealer commented that about a mile to the east there was a small single lane road that traveled for miles toward the north and passed several smaller farms and then came to an end at a point where the fields became immense. Those fields now blocked the highway. Those huge fields were managed by some big agricultural concern.

Trevor asked if all the smaller farmers were still living on their farms.

The car dealer replied he only knew about one farm that no longer had anyone living on it. It was the one closest to the intersection. Those folks had been married for sixty years and died within two months of each other. He had not known them but had been familiar with an older son who had retired to Florida.

Bill thanked him for the information. He left the car lot and drove toward the intersection in question. He turned onto the one lane black top and drove slowly along the road. They came to the first driveway and stopped for a moment and then he turned into the gravel road that was beginning to be overgrown by weeds.

Johnnie pointed out the broken weeds in front of the car. He bet that they would find the pickup either in the garage or in the barn.

As the crested a slight hill the saw a two-story red brick house with two loft windows. When they got closer, they saw that all the windows of the house were boarded over and a do not trespass sign was stapled on the front door.

Trevor wondered how many kids the couple might have had and why the farm had not sold.

Bob said he had no idea, but they should act as if Levy was on the property. He stopped in front of the house. He asked if everyone had their vests on. After getting the yeses he was seeking, he took out his weapon and proceeded to the garage. It was locked and sported a do not trespass sign.

He followed as Trevor led the way to the small barn that was across a small field from the house. It had the same do not trespass sign, but the latch mounts had been pulled out of the wood.

He pointed to it. Bob got to one side Johnnie stood behind Trevor as he slowly slid the door open.

They all stepped in and did a quick search and once they were sure Levi was not there, they approached the pickup.

Bob pointed to where three bullets had hit the back window and complemented Johnnie on his shooting. He pointed to a dent in the large black tool chest.

Trevor laughed and said he had found a fifth hit. He pointed to the dent in the center of the rear license plate.

He asked whether Johnnie had been upset and put the last shot between the devil's horns that were on each side of the plate.

Johnnie thanked them for their complements and said he regretted not having a more powerful weapon and no he had not intended to hit the license plate, but the pickup had picked up speed and that was where the last bullet hit.

Bill called Sheriff Milster to let him know that they had located the truck, and it would need to be towed in and put into a secure location until it could be processed.

The Sheriff asked them to wait until a tow truck could get to the pickup to bring it in.

Trevor took pictures of the truck and sent them to the Chief, Alex, and Trey. On the picture of the license plate, he commented that Johnnie was trying to put one between the devil's eyes but had missed the driver.

The Chief texted back and complimented them on finding the truck. He asked about the make of the car that Levi was driving and whether they had any idea where he might be going.

Trevor said the car was a blue fifteen-year-old Ford sedan that was burning oil and gave him the number of the temporary license plate. But they had no clue where it was headed.

After sending the pictures to the Chief, Trevor put his phone in speaker mode and said he was calling Alex to let her know about finding the truck. Alex said that she had just looked at the pictures he had sent. After talking about the car, he added that they had also found another grave.

He then asked if she had any idea of how to figure out where Levi was going.

Alex thought for a moment and asked if there was any way to find out where the family had taken vacations when Levi was younger. She figured that perhaps he would head to a place that he had enjoyed and where he thought he would be safe and hard to find.

Johnnie said that they would look through the house on the farm to see if there were any family albums with pictures. He reminded her that the house had been renovated, and he thought maybe even rented out for a while so there might not be anything to find.

After the call and after the tow-truck hauled away the truck, they drove back to the farmhouse to see if they could find an album that had pictures of family vacations.

Trevor smiled and commented that the search blew his idea of getting off from work early. He told Johnnie to be thinking about a great place to have dinner.

Johnnie smiled and said he had one restaurant in mind that was halfway to Cincinnati where they could have a great meal.

The search of the house went faster than expected. The family albums were stored in a sequential series on one bookshelf. Bill found the one that seemed to highlight the earlier years of family get togethers and vacations. It seemed that they had often frequented Lake Cumberland and several other nearby parks with lakes. They agreed that those places were too close.

There were three vacations that included the Grand Canyon, Yellow Stone Park, and a ski vacation in Idaho. Bill held up one picture that had the Levi standing with a lake and mountain view behind it. He turned the picture over and read the inscription that said, "Levi said this was a place where he would like to live." It was dated in a year that would have made Levi about fourteen years old.

Johnnie said that he would do a little digging on the internet to see if he could locate such a place and then share what he had learned with Alex to see what she wanted to do.

He suggested that they call it a day and head toward Cincinnati.

Trevor agreed but then said that he preferred dinner at home.

Bill nodded and agreed with him.

Johnnie simply said, "Ditto."

The day had been trying and long enough for all of them.

13 Long Road West

Levi was forced to follow various highways as he made his way west. He now understood why the Interstates had been built. He was traveling through many small towns and along highways that had huge fields either growing corn, soybeans, or alfalfa.

He was nursing his car along and slowly working his way through the case of oil. If he forgot and began to go over sixty a grey burnt oil smelling plum would begin to trail him and let him know. Fifty seemed to be the maximum he could do without burning too much oil.

He figured it would take him a full week to get to where he was going. He thought about his finances and figured he would sleep in his car so that he would have enough money to get a new start when he got to Idaho.

He wished that the radio would work but all he got was a crackling sound from it.

Damn was all that would come to him as he thought about how good his life had been. He was so happy that he had shot and finally killed the Black bitch.

Monday morning the doctor came into Alex's room and said that her lungs were both operating at full capacity, and he was signing the release order. He asked if she had someone to pick her up.

Alex said that she had, and her ride would be at the curb when she got down there.

The doctor wished her a smooth and steady recovery and reminded her to go slow.

A short time after the doctor left the nurse came in and said she was pleased that Alex was recovering. She said she had a message from the nurse that had been shot wishing her all the best and to get the bastard that shot her.

Alex smiled and said that was what she planned to do as soon as possible.

She put in a call to Matt and asked him to meet her at the front of the Hospital. Matt let her know that Johnnie would be driving her car since they had talked and decided not to rent a car or count on the timing of a taxi.

She said that was great and then got dressed in the fresh set of clothes that Matt had brought to her on Sunday. She put the weapon she had been hiding into her shoulder holster she had asked him to bring and then put on her suit jacket. She was ready to go to work.

Johnnie had put on his Ivy Gatsby Newsboy Cabbie Cap and joked with Matt about getting a job being Alex's new chauffer.

Matt laughed and said that he thought his current role as Alex's magician was as high of a position as one could get.

Alex was rolled out in a wheelchair as required by hospital rules but as soon as it stopped rolling, she was up and ready to get in the car. She wished she could go for a long run, but she would be glad to be in at work figuring out how to close the case.

Johnnie tipped his hat as she sat down and in a fake English accent asked where she might be going.

Alex smiled and replied, "please take me home, James."

Johnnie nodded and replied, "as you wish, my fair lass."

Matt shook his head and asked if everyone was having fun.

Alex said that she felt great and that she planned to have a catered lunch at the River Front Park. She wondered if anyone had a specific lunch that they could all enjoy.

Matt called up a menu from a local caterer and they ordered a Greek Salad, a Korean BBQ bowl, a Beef rice bowl, two orders of onion straws and some drinks.

When they arrived, Alex took out the large grey blanket from the trunk and led the way to the area where she had a great view of the river.

After spreading out the blanket, she asked if Johnnie had his computer with him.

Johnnie nodded and said that he did and took it out of a cloth bag that had in it a thick notebook as well. He showed the thick notebook and said that he had decided to carry one after he had realized that a similar one had saved Alex's life.

Alex chuckled and said that she would stand behind him if any shooting started.

Once he had his computer online, she asked if he had figured out where Levi might be going.

Johnnie nodded and said that they had gone through the family photo album and had found one picture of Levi when he was probably about fourteen. The picture was of him with a lake and some mountains behind him. The inscription on the back said that this was a place that he wished he could live.

The other pictures were in a campground somewhere in or near Yellow Stone.

Johnnie said he was betting on the location of the lake. He had run a picture recognition routine and had a hit on a lake that seemed to have the same background.

Alex asked where the lake was located.

Johnnie pulled up a map and showed Alex a view of the mountains near Coeur d'Alene.

Alex said that she was going to put out an APB warrant with instructions to notify her if the car was spotted but to track and not arrest.

She called the Chief and asked him if he would set it up and that she did not want Levi arrested but only tracked she wanted to capture him and bring him back to Ohio so they would not have to go through an extradition process.

The Chief agreed with her adding that he wanted the trial to be quick and to be in Cincinnati.

The lunch arrived and Alex concentrated on getting a taste of each lunch item, sipping on her tea, and enjoying the onion straws. She was thinking about how to get ahead of Levi.

She asked if Johnnie had seen any logs going down the river.

Johnnie shook his head in the negative and said he had been too busy defending his Korean BBQ from her to look for logs.

Alex apologized and handed him her Beef rice bowl and said he could have it.

Johnnie shook his head and said she had already contaminated it, and he would just have to be satisfied with what he had.

Alex studied the shapes of the clouds floating slowly by high in the light blue sky and was almost falling asleep when her phone rang. She answered and listened as the Chief let her know that they had a hit on a secondary highway near Dickinson Montana of an old blue Ford sedan clearly burning oil with an Iowa license plate. It was heading toward the Idaho border at about fifty miles per hour.

Alex commented that the Iowa license plate made sense. Levi had probably replaced the temporary one with one he took off of some car.

The Chief asked what she was thinking about doing.

She replied that she was thinking about a field trip. She would need an arrest warrant, and flight tickets to Idaho.

Alex asked if Trey was in the office.

The Chief said that Trey was in. He added that he would arrange to get the flight tickets for the two of them and he would have the arrest warrant by the time Trey was ready to go to the airport.

Alex thanked him and said that she would likely stop by the office on the way to the airport.

She sat up and said that lunch was over, and she needed to get ready for a field trip.

Matt shook his head and said that she had only one speed and that was full speed ahead. He helped up and said he hoped that she was flying first class so she could rest during the flight.

Alex smiled, gave him a kiss, and agreed but that in each case she always knew that she was getting a bad guy off the street.

Johnnie smiled and said that she should just shoot this guy and get it over with.

Alex agreed that would be appropriate, but she would only do so if he resisted arrest and took another shot at her.

When Johnnie drove into the parking lot, Trey was standing on the curb by the side entrance to the station.

Johnnie dropped Alex off and then parked the car at the very back of the lot where Alex always parked. He walked up to the two and said he was going to walk home.

Johnnie was walking away when the taxi came into the lot. He watched as Trey helped Alex into the car. He figured that Trey would make sure she took it as easy as he could.

Once they were on the way, Trey said that Nolan had wanted her to know that he expected her to get the bad guy but that she should be sure to wear her Kevlar vest.

Alex smiled and said she had her spare along and would follow Nolan's advice.

Trey nodded and then added that Lesley had simply said they should be safe and watch each other's back.

Alex verified they had the right paperwork and were ready to make the arrest.

The flight out was long but the treatment in first class was superb. Alex ate a banana and then went to sleep. She knew that she was not yet in top shape.

Upon landing they went to the car rental and picked up the SUV that had been reserved for them and then drove out of the airport.

They had landed at the airport closest to Coeur d'Alene, but it was actually in Oregon. They drove across the border into Idaho.

It was a short drive back to their destination. It gave them a magnificent view of the Rocky Mountains towering high into the puffy clouds that seemed to be hugging the peaks.

The Chief called them and said that the Idaho police had followed Levi to a campground near the eastern end of Lake Coeur d'Alene. He gave her the location and told her to take care.

He gave her a phone number and said that this was the person who would be with her when she made the arrest and would be a witness at the trial if it was necessary.

Alex thanked him and verified that she had a return ticket for Levi.

The Chief assured her that she did, and it was in first Class next to Trey.

Alex made the call and arranged to meet a Brigham Slayen, Sheriff of Coeur d'Alene. He asked where they should meet. She suggested a lunch spot of his choosing.

She put the address he gave her into maps and settled back as Trey drove. She closed her eyes and relaxed.

He looked over at her and asked if she was going to try and get back to Cincinnati on the same day.

Alex nodded and said that she figured a redeye would have seats available.

They met the Sheriff and after greetings he said that the restaurant was rather new, but it had great food. He suggested they sit outside and enjoy the sun. After they sat down, he said that he often ate at this restaurant and had tried both the fish and the meat, and both were superb. He added that the signature desert was to die for.

Alex smiled and said that she had to be awake when she made the arrest.

After the orders had been put in, the Sheriff asked whether this person was dangerous and what he was being arrested for.

Alex said that the arrest warrant was for the attempted murder of a police officer.

The Sheriff asked how that officer was doing.

Alex smiled and said she was doing fine.

The Sheriff said he was glad to hear that. He would certainly not want this guy in his jurisdiction.

Alex said she agreed with him and hoped to arrest him early in the afternoon.

She asked if he had body armor to use during the arrest.

The Sheriff smiled and said that he wished he did, but the budget had never been big enough for any of his guys to have anything but a bullet proof shield.

Alex nodded and asked him to use his shield.

The Sheriff looked at her and asked if she was serious.

Alex nodded and said she was.

The order came and she sliced through one of the lamb chops and was delighted with how it was done and how the cranberry sauce enhanced its flavor.

She asked Trey to split the desert she had ordered and smiled when he said that he had counted on that and had passed up ordering one for himself.

The Sheriff asked how long they had been partners.

Alex smiled and said that the partnership was not in years, but it was over several lifetimes.

The Sheriff stopped as he took a bite of his desert. He looked at her and then asked if she was known as "Cincinnati's Black Annie Oakley."

Alex nodded and said that was a moniker that would follow her for her lifetime.

The Sheriff let out a "Wow" exclamation and said that his wife and daughter were constantly talking about her and how she was inspiring young women to do what had always been forbidden by society for them to do.

They pointed out the fact that that she had a law degree but had chosen to become a cop instead of a lawyer.

Alex smiled and said that she was honored to be thought of that way. She said that she had simply decided that getting the bad guy to be judged by a jury of his peers was a role that she preferred.

The Sheriff said that he wanted to get a picture with her because his wife and daughter would never believe him when he shared who he was having lunch with.

Alex handed Trey her phone and asked him to take a picture of the Sheriff and her.

After lunch Alex suggested they all drive out to the campground but go in on foot. She said she hoped not to scare any of the people camping.

She verified that the Sheriff had his shield in his trunk.

He said that he did and asked where her shield was.

Alex pulled her jacket back and said she was wearing hers.

The drive out took about twenty minutes. It was about three in the afternoon on a sunny but cool day with a light breeze that was coming across the lake. It was the type of weather anyone that camped cherished and enjoyed.

They parked behind a police car that was already there.

The Sheriff introduced one of his deputies who let them know that the car that they were looking for was parked six campgrounds back into the park.

As she led the way in Alex was impressed. The camps were separated by lush green grass and a bed of lavender stone crop flowers along the front edge of each green area. It made the campground seem like a small paradise by the lake.

She hoped that they could capture Levi without a gun fight.

Had Levi known that he was about to be arrested he might have had his weapons ready instead it was laying by his side, and he was daydreaming about his new life in the west. He had already seen several potential new skulls earlier when he had walked around the campground.

He figured it was too early to harvest but it didn't hurt to look. He figured he would see if he could find a farm that needed help. He was betting on locating an old couple on some out of the way farm. Life would once again be good.

Alex indicated that the Sheriff should stay in the lane, the deputy should go to the lake side of the car and she and Trey would approach the car.

She slowly approached the driver's side and Trey took the other side. She was crouched down by the rear door when she gave the signal and they both opened the back doors at the same time.

Levi looked up and bolted out of the door and knocked Alex down all the time screaming that it was not possible. He had his gun in hand and turned to run away from all of them.

Trey ran around the front and hit Levi from the side and the two of them slid across the grass parallel to the border of the flower bed.

Trey hit him once with the flat of his hand across his mouth, flipped him over, put the handcuffs on and pulled him to his feet and read him his Miranda rights.

The Sheriff's deputy put the gun into the evidence bag.

Levi was still blubbering about the fact that he had killed her and that it was not possible.

Alex walked up to him smiled and let him know that she had a deal with the devil that let her stay alive if she sent guys like him down as a gift.

She looked at the sheriff and asked if there was a holding cell she could borrow and if he could arrange to have the car taken to a secure holding area because she was sure there would be evidence that need to be processed. She said that she was specifically looking for a high-powered rifle.

The Sheriff said that her request would be no problem. He gave instructions to his deputy and then said that they should all head to the station. He would take the perp back in his car.

Levi seemed to have gone over the edge. He kept mumbling and repeating that she had a deal with the devil.

Once back in the station Alex made a call to the Chief and let him know that they had Levi and had been able to do it without a gunfight. She asked to see if the Chief's support would arrange for a redeye special back to Cincinnati.

When the Sheriff heard the request for the flight back, he said that she would have several hours waiting, and would it be possible to ask that his daughter and wife could have dinner with her.

Alex said that dinner would be fine, but she needed a nap before then and asked if there was a cot available.

The Chief asked if she was the one that the perp had shot.

Alex said that he had hit her once and had tried a second time to kill her when she was in the hospital.

The Sheriff said he had just the place for her to take her nap and made a call.

He then told Trey to follow him.

Alex was surprised to enter a neighborhood that bordered a golf course and then have the sheriff pull into a double wide driveway and park.

Trey pulled up beside him and they all got out.

Alex smiled as the Sheriff welcomed her to his humble abode. She knew that he was proud of his abode, and it was far from humble.

His wife and daughter rushed out.

The Sheriff introduced them and stepped back.

Alex was surprised to be pulled into a group hug by his wife and daughter. She gave a small laugh of surprise as she was gushed over as they said it was like a dream come true that they would be able to meet her and have dinner with her.

Then she was pulled in and taken to the guest bedroom for her nap.

14 Body 43

*T*he flight home provided Alex with time to reflect. She had captured one of the most horrific individuals in a small town in Idaho where she was treated as a heroine by a family who admired her. She was going to get back the day after having left and would be able to sleep in her own bed.

She had ended up eating a catered dinner at the Sheriff's house.

She learned that Trey had suggested it, and they had ordered from the same restaurant where they had lunch. He let her know that he had ordered the steak she had mentioned during lunch as her second choice, and he had ordered a lamb roast in case she did not want the steak.

The dinner conversation centered on what the Sheriff's daughter was thinking about majoring in when she went to college. When asked for her suggestion Alex had suggested going for a degree that would allow her to have a good income in a field that seemed to hold the potential for a good life. Once she was into that field, she should see what doors were open for her to make her life fulfilling and go for it.

On the way to the airport the Sheriff stopped at the border and said that his jurisdiction ended at the border and transferred custody of Levi to her. He presented her with a golf bag that he said had the rifle and the gun inside and handed her the paperwork that would allow her to check it in.

He thanked her for the advice she had given to his daughter.

Alex and Trey got to the airport and once at the gate had let Levi know that they would be flying first class, but he would have his ankles chained to the seat and would not be allowed up.

He nodded and agreed to let Trey take him into the men's room before boarding.

Every time Levi looked at her, he would mumble something about the devil, or the witch and he deal she had.

During the flight, Alex thought about the case. She had survived another attack on her life. But what bothered her the most was of the very grotesque nature of the case that would leave forty-two families devastated for the rest of their lives. She would recover and would continue to seek out the bad guys, but she knew there was no end to bad guys whether they were men or women. It gave her the chills sitting next to a person that looked like any other person but had a mind so warped that he had methodically hunted for, killed, and beheaded all those young women.

It was a redeye flight but there was no way she would fall asleep. Earlier she had instructed Levi to be quiet when he kept asking how she had survived. He had finally complied when she asked the flight attendant if she had any duct tape.

Trey was a little cruder and told Levi he would break his jaw.

For the rest of the flight Levi merely mumbled to himself.

Alex was relieved when the pilot announced they would soon land. It had been one of the most uncomfortable flights she had so far taken.

She was more relieved when she got on the up escalator to baggage claim and looked up and saw Bill and Trevor.

The two greeted them and said that they were there to take all of them back to the station. After retrieving the luggage, they took Levi between them and led the way out to the black panel van, and they all got in. There were two policemen in the front two seats and the five of them sat in the back.

Bill let her know that the Chief had told her to go fishing or to do whatever she wished but that she should not come into work.

Alex replied that what she wished was to get some sleep and she was planning to do that as soon as she got to her apartment.

Trey said he was going home and do the same.

Bill volunteered to take him home since he lived close by.

Trey thanked him and said that would be great.

After being dropped off Alex went to her apartment, stood under the hot shower, and let all the tension melt away. As she dried off, she decided to make a call before getting into her bed.

She dialed John Williams and asked him to take the Levi's case when it came time to formally charge him. She asked that he make sure that the judge did not allow bail and would put Levi in prison until his case came before a jury.

She then wrote a quick text to Matt letting him know she was home and getting some sleep.

She did not wake up until some twelve hours later. She felt much better but took a pill to reduce the pain she had in the center of her chest.

A few days later she was sitting in the court room as Levi was arraigned. The judge had been appraised about the horrific nature of the charges. John had

Brian Lexter, the Cincinnati FBI bureau chief, describe the excavation of forty-two graves that was going on at the farm formally owned by Levi.

The lawyer for the defense corrected Brian and said that the defendant still owned the property. John objected and said that he had checked the facts and that a Linda and Arnold Preston now owned the property that the defendant Levi Misle had put into their deceased daughter's trust.

Levi looked over at her and she returned a smile and a nod.

He said something to his lawyer and then looked down at his hands on the table. He knew he was screwed by the witch that made deals with the devil.

The defense withdrew the objection.

The judge ruled that Levi would be held in a high security prison without bail until he was brought back to stand trial.

She banged her gavel and declared the court session was over.

Alex was walking out the door with the Chief when the judge stopped to congratulate the Chief on getting the case closed so quickly. She did not look at Alex but said that she was pleased to have her bring another bad guy before her and looked forward to many more. She added that she was very biased against this latest person and was glad to see that Alex had worked her devil's magic.

It was clear to Alex that the judge was speaking to her but did not want the public to know. The two of them knew each other well.

Alex smiled but remained quiet.

The Chief stood for a minute as the Judge walked away. He looked at Alex and told her he did not want to know anything about the devil's magic.

Alex was about to walk away when John and Hanna walked out of the building and said they were going to their favorite coffee shop to celebrate getting Levi locked up for good.

She accepted and asked the Chief if he wanted to join in.

The Chief said he would be going back to his office and that Alex had the rest of the day off.

Once they were in the coffee shop and had placed their order, John thanked her for giving him the information about the property transfer. He did not want to know how she had gotten the records changed but he let her know that he had his team check out all the paperwork and they had let him know that all signatures on the transfer paperwork were authentic and were Levi's.

She took a sip of her latte and smiled, nodded, and replied that she had a magician working for her.

She thought about her meeting with Linda and Arnold Preston. She had put them in charge of a ten-million-dollar trust named after their daughter that would give each of the forty-two parents twelve thousand dollars a year for the rest of their lives. And then the trust would be available to the future generations of those families.

They had welcomed the opportunity and had accepted the financial institution's offer to manage the account for them.

She looked up from her latte as she realized she was daydreaming and asked John and Hann if the two of them would like to take part in a bike ride that she and Matt were going to take with his team on the following morning.

They thanked her but declined because both of them had cases in full swing and that they needed to keep on track.

Early the next morning, Trey and his team took off along the river front. Alex and Johnnie were at the rear. They were both riding the bikes that had been impounded during their last case when they had been shot at by three would be killers that together they killed. It had taken months to get the bikes released and then Alex's bike needed to have the front wheel replaced and the back wheel straightened.

They had laughed about the fact that the bike took longer than her to get back into shape.

Alex enjoyed the day as she realized what a great team Matt had working with him. They had repeatedly been the team that had either shown up and supported her or had taken her to the hospital and were instrumental several times in saving her. The ride was a resounding success, and she felt great that she was once again back to her normal physical form.

The day after the bike ride the Chief called her into his office. He said he had just gotten off the phone with the head of the high security prison that Levi had been sent to. He asked if she had anything to do with what had happened there.

Alex looked at him and said that she had no idea what he was talking about.

He nodded and let her know that Levi had been killed during an outdoor ball game at the prison. He was the pitcher for the winning team. The players from both teams ran to the pitcher's mound and surrounded Levi as if to celebrate.

When the prisoners moved away, the guards saw that Levi's head had been cut off and his head was being held up on a broken baseball bat planted in the ground and the number forty-three had been scratched into the dirt on the mound.

The Chief said that somehow the prisoners had learned who Levi was and imposed their own justice.

Alex shook her head. She said that she had nothing to do with it, and she was sure that her team would not have done anything like it.

She said that she and her team focused on bringing the bad guy to face the judge and be judged by a jury of his peers.

The Chief nodded and reassured her that he was sure no one in his department would have leaked the information. He added that he was not going to assign any resources to figure out who had because he could think of nothing better than for Levi to have been treated as he had treated so many other innocent women.

Alex walked out of the office knowing that it was someone who had somehow learned of the situation and there was a short list of those "someones" and it would be quite easy to find out who. She planned to have Johnnie make that list hard to find.

She knew that she would sleep much easier knowing that Levi was down with the devil he had served.

The End of the Skull Collector

The Vanishing

1 The Comacho

A red bandana hugged the head of the person handing a small package to the person who in turn was passing a hand full of cash back to his other hand. This was a scene being repeated in numerous dark corners or alleys throughout the city. Business was booming and Comacho controlled a lucrative part of the drug distribution business. He was not the biggest distributor. He was one of the toughest and in control of his distribution area, and he was raking in the money. He purposely kept a low profile and maintained good relations with his competitors by agreeing to the territory in which he distributed, and he gave a small cut of the take to keep the good relations greased. His adversaries also were very aware of his ruthlessness.

He knew he was destined to go to hell. He figured he might be able to pal around with the Devil. He planned to continue to be ruthless and to control those who worked for him. He had grown up as one of the Reds and had learned that strength and ruthlessness were the ingredients that let one survive in the harsh environment that he had been raised in.

He had no patience with those who hesitated to do as he commanded. He had personally shot and killed more than a dozen men and women. Yes women! They demanded equal treatment, and he gladly gave it to them. He had no patience for insubordination. When he ordered something, he expected immediate follow-through, and he usually got it.

There were two ways he handled those he decided to eliminate.

Regular offenders who would not pay out or distributors that encroached on his territory were taken care of by his hirelings.

For those more egregious offenders he had a special ceremony that he personally orchestrated.

He would have a fifty-gallon barrel filled three quarters of the way with a chemical that was heavy on lye, and he would have his nude victim placed feet first into the barrel. Then he would ask the screaming individual to ask him to shoot and kill them. When they asked him to shoot, he would but he would shoot that person in the arm. Then he would ask the screaming individual to tell him where he should shoot. Often the request was in the head, sometimes through the heart.

But he would not do it until he made the person say, "Please shoot me in the ---." Often the legs of the individual would give out and he had to be held in the vertical position.

Once the individual was dead, he left the area after giving instructions to sink the body into the drum and then seal it. The drum was filled to the very brim before sealing it so it would sink like a rock. He had the drum taken out to sea and ensured it would sink by adding additional weight to it.

Only one woman had suffered that fate. She was an assassin hired by a competitor drug dealer. She had been the toughest of the twelve that had stood in the barrel. When he asked her where he should shoot her, she had screamed "put the bullet in your head" and she had then she crouched down into the barrel and put her head under the chemical bath.

He had been amazed by her toughness she had not started to scream when placed into the barrel! He almost regretted that she had tried to kill him. He figured she might have been his soul mate. A vile soul mate from hell. "Oh, well," he laughed as he thought about the Devil sending him a message.

He decided to kill the drug dealer that had hired her, to see if he would be as tough as she had been. He was not. He cried and screamed like a baby.

Ironically, the word got out about his having eliminated the female assassin and the drug dealer and he was charged with murder. He of course pleaded innocent. The problem for the prosecutor was that he did not have a body and was operating on hearsay. His lawyer and the prosecutor reached an agreement that if he left the state the case would be dropped.

He set up his second in command to run the drug distribution business. He wanted thirty per cent of the take to be sent to an offshore account.

He had no plans to stop distributing so he looked around to see where in the country he would set himself up.

He figured he needed to find a low-profile location but one that was well positioned geographically in the drug trade.

He looked north to Seattle and decided that it was not well located.

He looked to Chicago but realized that the battle between the Mafia and the Mexican cartels would put him in the middle between two powerful and deadly groups. That situation eliminated Chicago.

New York City was out because of the state's focus on rooting out drug distributors. It would make it hard to carve out distribution territory.

He went down the list of the large cities in the east and eliminated all of them.

He looked at the US map and realized that one central point in the drug distribution was the city that had been described by one New Yorker as, "the sleepy little city by the Ohio River." He moved the arrow on the screen and made a circle around Cincinnati.

He bought a one-way first-class plane ticket to Cincinnati.

He had his Mercedes-Benz SL Cabriolet driven there so that he would have his favorite car to use.

He spent a few days in Cincinnati in a luxury downtown hotel suite while he explored the city on foot. He walked the Ohio Riverfront Park. He located the police station and walked all around that area.

He found the place he was looking for. It was a bar about three blocks away from the police station. He walked in and asked the current owner what he wanted for the place.

The owner asked why he would want a place that did not do much business. He said that he was ready to sell but didn't want to unload a dying bar. He gave a price of what he thought the building and property was worth and said that he currently was breaking even on the business. He asked again why he would want to buy the business.

Camacho replied that it seemed to be located in a place close to the downtown area but out of the beaten path. He agreed to the asking price but wanted six months' time before he needed to make the payment.

He then asked who the regular customers happened to be and was not surprised to learn that there were several cops that frequented the place. He hoped that one of them would be open to a little extra cash for inside information about what was coming down. He also needed to make sure the regular cops were willing to look the other way to the traffic of distributors that might be entering and leaving the bar.

He made it a point to be friendly with all of the cops that came in and slowly figured out which one was most likely to be susceptible to making a lucrative arrangement and would agree to be an inside informant.

When that policeman's bar bill began to build up, he made his proposal. The policeman thought he was a great bargainer and bargained for free drinks as a part of such an arrangement. Comacho figured that a bottle of booze a week was a very cheap bribe, and he added that if he got the information that he requested he would sweeten the arrangement. He figured that he could keep the monetary honey at a low level.

His early requests were simple and information he could get himself, but it provided a way to get the informant relaxed and willing to share information. The first thing he asked about was the number of high schools inside the two seventy-five loop. He figured the roughly twenty-five that he got an address for would be about the right number to set up a lucrative and low-key drug distribution network.

It was time to set up a small local distribution organization. He reached back to his L.A. network and got the names of three individuals that he could hire. One was located in Cincinnati; one was from L.A. who had worked for him there and one was from the Columbus area. He figured the mix would give him a small group that had the moxie to run the operation. He hired the three and assigned them the role of recruiting drug distributors at each of the high schools and distributing the drugs to them.

He gave them the profile of a good high school drug distributor. The individual had to be a person that demonstrated being a leader but who was either a loner or an individual who bullied others. It could be a female but most often would probably be a male. He or she would stand out during the morning when school started and during the end of the day rush out of the school. He or she could be of any race. The poorer the better. However, they could not be on any drugs to be a distributor.

The individual would be given a starting bonus and initially five percent of the sales income.

He let the three who would be doing the recruiting know that they would each get five percent of the drugs their high school distributors sold so they should make sure to coach them and give them some additional rewards like free meals or rides to social events. In other words, set up a positive relationship with these young distributors. Finally, they should be setting up the next person to take the place of a high schooler that was graduating.

Setting up the distribution network and getting a local drug production facility established took him about six months. He was lucky and found an abandoned fire station just across town that he was able to lease. He imported a druggist from L.A. and set him up in the station. He funded the operation but stayed well away from what he figured was a group of druggies making more drugs.

He was able to buy a large home with several acres on the east side of the city that was only about fifteen minutes from the bar where he would have his operational office.

He felt good about the transition. Cincinnati did not have the nightlife that was available in L.A., but it featured a variety of engaging theatrical plays, orchestra performances, boating on nearby lakes and on the Ohio River. He figured he would enjoy a quieter lifestyle and become more active outdoors.

2 The Vanishing

*T*he hallway was a maze of students weaving around each other, talking in small groups, or yelling to friends. There were also confrontations between some students and consistently three bullies would corner some person but most often some young female that they would harass.

Jesse navigated his way down the crowded hall as he hastened to make it to his next class. He had just escaped another scrimmage with these three bullies who were his nemesis. He was being hounded because he had interceded when the three had cornered a reluctant female student. The three were recognized throughout the school as bullies. He also suspected them of being the school's drug suppliers. He was certain they were connected to the Red Bandana gang that controlled the drug distribution in the area. This worried him because he knew that the gang was violent and would corner a person when they were alone.

It was Saturday morning, and he was on the way to buy a new pair of basketball shoes. He spotted a young woman being harassed. He should have minded his own business, but she was getting attacked by these three mean looking dudes wearing red bandanas. He shouted at them to stop and when they turned to respond to him the lady dashed away.

He took off but they caught up with him. When they caught up with him, he realized they were the three bullies that often pushed him around at school. He knew he was in big trouble.

They began pounding on him and said they were going to beat him to death. He fought as best as he could, but he took a brutal beating. It only stopped when a police car came driving by and turned on its red lights.

He used that moment, like the young woman, to dash away but he heard one of the bully's shout at him that they were not through with him or anyone else in his family.

The Vanishing

The image of his sister came to his mind. His sister, April, was only fifteen and was a freshman. She was excited about beginning high school. She was doing well in her classes, was a junior varsity cheer leader and had a minor role in one of the theatrical school plays.

He adored April. He figured if he vanished from the scene, the three hoods would move on, and she would be alright. This was all he could think of as he ran seemingly in a random direction.

That had been earlier in a grey cloud covered day that deteriorated into a continuous drizzle that had seemed determined to make him cold and miserable. His sweatshirt was soaked and the only reason he kept it on was because even in the wet condition it was keeping him warm.

He pulled his hood tight trying to keep the drizzle out. The day had faded into a night as dark as the thoughts in his mind. He found himself walking eastward but he had no clue where he was going. The blood had stopped running from his nose and the drizzle seemed to be keeping it moistened. His other cuts had all crusted over. He was a mess. He would need to find a place where he could wash up so he would be somewhat presentable. He felt lucky to have escaped alive.

The beating had been almost eight hours ago. The rumble in his stomach gave him a blunt unadulterated reality check about his current situation. He was wet, he was hungry, and he had no place to stop to get some sleep.

He had just made the basketball team and that morning he had emptied his money box so he could buy a new pair of Nike basketball shoes. That money was in his backpack. The idea of buying the Nike shoes was now history. That money had to last until he could get to wherever he was going, and until he got paid for the job, a job that he knew he needed to get.

He wondered if he had enough cash to carry him through until he had a job and a first paycheck. He thought about how his mother stretched her paycheck to make sure she always had food for the family. She always bought fifty-pound bags of rice and beans, large jars of peanut butter, of strawberry jam and grape jelly, and day-old loaves of bread. She made a point of letting him and April know that chicken, ham, and any other meat was a treat and would be cooked sparingly.

He figured that he would have to copy what she did when shopping so he could stretch the money he had in the backpack.

He looked ahead and saw a large honeysuckle bush growing under a railway overpass. He crawled under it and got as close to the trunk of the bush as possible and made himself as comfortable as he could. He would have liked to take off his wet sweatshirt, but the night was already cold to him. He hoped that it would be sunny the next day so he could dry off.

He felt like death warmed over, was miserable but he finally fell asleep.

The morning sun woke him up and the clear blue cloudless sky gave his down feelings a lift. He took off his sweatshirt and hung it from his backpack. His long sleeve shirt was damp to the touch, but it soon dried off as he walked.

He was on one of the smaller highways going east across Ohio. The occasional car or pickup went by, but none stopped to offer him a ride. As a Black man he did not expect to get picked up. He took long strides and kept walking.

Just about the time he was about to give up on getting to somewhere where he could get something to eat, he came up over a hill and saw that down in the valley, there was a small one street village hugging the banks of a small river. Tall old oaks and maples provided a shading canopy for most of the buildings in town. They appeared to be the barrier that kept the weeping willows along the river at bay. As he approached the town, it was as if he had stepped back in time. He half expected to see gunslingers and horses.

He saw only one store that had a sign advertising that they were a hardware and grocery. He entered and was greeted by an older lady sitting on a tall stool who asked him how she could be of help.

He asked if she had any sandwiches or something that he could have for a late breakfast. She led the way to the back of the store where there was a large coffee pot, a microwave and small freezer that had a variety of sandwiches and other microwaveable offerings.

She let him know that a cup of coffee and any one selection from the freezer was five dollars.

After looking over the selection he chose a mac and cheese package because it was the largest amount of food.

After wolfing down the food he walked around the small grocery section and selected a two-pound bag of rice and a large bag of dry black beans. He then found a small metal pan that he figured he would use to cook with. Finally, he picked up a large bottle of water.

He took everything to the counter where, as his selection was being rung up, the lady asked where he was going.

He answered that he was not sure but somewhere along the East Coast.

She smiled and let him know that in the next town he would be able to catch a bus. She then let him know that breakfast was on her and wished him good luck.

He thanked her for being so kind and then paid her with some of his precious cash.

He then went on his way. Now he was thinking about where on the East Coast he would go, and he wondered if he had enough money to buy the ticket and still have enough left over so he could last until he landed a job.

In the next town he located the bus station. He was surprised that he could go to almost anywhere along the East Coast for about one hundred dollars.

He felt a sense of relief that he would have enough money left over for food, but he would need to figure out where to sleep at night. He was sure that he would not be able to stay in any hotel or motel.

After considering the cities along the coast, he chose Virginia Beach as the place that he would try to establish himself. He was not at all sure why he had selected it, but it seemed to be the halfway point between going north or going south.

The bus ride gave him time to get some sleep, think through what he would do so he could feed himself and where he might be able to find a place where he could sleep.

He figured he would have to locate a homeless shelter and hope that he would get the help he needed to find a job and an affordable place to live.

The bus arrived early in the morning. Once again, his stomach was growling. He walked out of the bus station and looked around. He saw an old Black guy pushing a cart filled with bottles and tin cans.

He walked over to him and asked if he knew where a person could get something to eat at no cost.

The old guy looked at him and told him he was too young to become a beggar and should get a job.

Jesse nodded and asked him where he might find a job.

The old guy smiled and said that he should go to the Mayfair Home of Hope where he could get a good meal and while he was there, he should see if they could point him to a job. He added that it would not be a job being the president of some company, but it would let him make enough to let him eat. He pointed at his cart and said that his other option was to collect bottles and cans and take them to the recycling center where he would get about two cents per bottle and a penny a can. He added that he covered the territory for blocks around and would fight him off.

Jesse thanked him for the information and asked for directions to the Home of Hope.

The old man pointed in the direction opposite to the one he was going and said that it was about seven blocks. He said good luck and continued on his way.

Jesse took up a brisk walk and he soon saw the sign outside a building that looked like it might once have been an apartment building.

He read the sign on the outside of the building that said it gave food, comfort, and the opportunity to start anew.

He figured that he qualified and that he was certainly starting new.

He walked up the steps and entered.

He was greeted by a gray bearded person that looked like an anemic Santa Claus. He was asked what he needed.

Jesse let it all flow out, "something to eat, a place to sleep and a job."

The old guy said that he was in luck and would be able to get a tray of food before the breakfast line closed to get ready for the noon meal. He told Jesse to get his tray of food and while he was eating a social worker would come out to ask him a few questions.

Jessi went in, grabbed a tray, and went down the line.

There was only one server who smiled and put huge helpings on the tray. He commented that normally he should not expect so much but it had been a slow morning. The server put two apples and two bananas on the counter and said he should take them as well.

Jessi could hardly carry the tray to the nearest table. He looked around and realized he was one of five people in the cafeteria.

He was famished and dug in. The scrambled eggs, the three patties of sausage, and a large blue berry muffin disappeared. He went over to a large coffee pot and poured himself a cup and put in three creamers and carried it back to his table to finish a sugar covered cake donut. He planned to eat the bananas and apples later.

An older Black woman approached and introduced herself as Renee and let him know that she was a registered nurse and psychologist, and she had a few questions to ask him.

Jesse nodded and waited for the questions.

The first question was about his age, then what level of education he had and then what job experience he had.

She reacted to his age and said that he looked older than eighteen. Then she asked why he had not finished high school.

Jesse said that he had to run because he had crossed wires with the local drug dealer, and they had threatened to kill him and had almost succeed. He opened his shirt to show the bruises that were now turning yellow.

He then listened as Renee said that he was in luck, and she would be able to take him in and get him an interview at a local restaurant as a bus boy. The pay would not be enough to enable him to rent a room somewhere so he might need to get a second job. However, he would have a couple months to get the second job and to find a place to live.

She asked if he wanted to finish getting his high school diploma.

Jesse said getting a high school diploma would be great and would give him the chance to try and go on to college.

Renee smiled and said that she liked his attitude and said that he would be shown to his room, and he should get oriented. She added that there would be no cooking in the room. If he had a hot plate, he should not think about using it.

She told him that he should be ready to go at eight the next morning. She was going to make a couple of calls and get a job interview lined up.

Once in his room, he got oriented. It had a shower, a bar of soap, and some towels. He decided to take a shower and wash his t-shirt, drawers and socks and put them in the sunlight to dry. He wrapped the towel around his waist and lay down on the bed. The mattress was a hard one that he thought was just what he needed.

He went to sleep wondering how he would wake up to get to breakfast and be ready by eight.

A blasting horn in the hallway at six in the morning brough him wide awake. He now knew that he would not have to buy an alarm clock.

He got up and went to the sink, opened the medicine cabinet, and found a comb, a toothbrush, and a tube of toothpaste. He brushed his teeth, spruce up, got dressed in his still damp clothes and went down the stairs to the cafeteria.

By six thirty he had a tray in hand and went down the breakfast line and selected the over easy eggs, some sausage, two pieces of toast and two patties of butter. He added a carton of milk and took a banana. He looked around and realized he was one of the first people in the cafeteria.

Renee came over to his table and gave him a card with the person at the restaurant that would be expecting him, and that the restaurant was a twelve-block walk.

Jesse asked for the directions and Renee handed him a piece of paper with a hand drawn map on it.

He thanked her for getting him an interview so quickly. He added that he hoped to come back and let her know that he had a job.

He left right after breakfast and after a brisk walk arrived thirty minutes early. He let the breakfast host know he had come for a job interview.

He was asked to wait at the entrance. He watched the people arriving and realized he was definitely in a white neighborhood.

The manager came out and led him to a table in the back corner where he offered him something to drink.

He said that the water would be fine.

The grey-haired white manager appeared to him to be in his late forties or maybe early fifties. He was clearly overweight and seemed out of shape.

He asked a few questions and then asked him to sign a paper that would let the restaurant to check his background. He then offered a busboys job, one meal each day, the minimum hourly rate of pay plus a share of the tips.

Jesse accepted and asked when he could begin.

The manager replied that it could be immediately and asked Jesse to follow him.

3 Cincinnati Connection

Rose-Anne sat at her desk pondering whether to call Alex. The last time she had called and asked Alex to help her in a case, Alex had been abducted by the Chicago Mafia and almost killed. Then a crooked cop had tried to kill her, but Alex's shooting skill had saved her. She still felt guilty about having asked her.

She thought that the situation that she was going to ask for Alex's help was very different. During a recent legal seminar about the cost-free services her practice offered, she had been approached by a mother that told a her a story about a missing son. She was going to ask Alex to check into the missing person's report and see what Alex could find out.

She, after thinking it through for the third time, decided to make the call.

Alex had just ordered lunch when the harp tone phone ring let her know that her mother was on the other end. She knew that it would not be a social call at this time of day and wondered what her mother was going to throw her way. She got up and walked out to the sidewalk so that she would not disturb the rest of the team. After their initial greeting, her mother shared her request.

Alex had one of her premonitions and she felt the hair that she knew didn't exist on the back of her neck, standing up. She knew that it seemed too simple. She asked what would happen if she found something suspicious.

Rose-Anne volunteered to call Alex's boss and see if she could convince him to assign her the case and she would arrange for the finances from her end.

Alex agreed to review the missing person's report and see what she could find out, but she reminded her mother that she needed to get permission from her boss to make it an investigative case.

When she returned to the table, Trey smiled at her, said that he recognized the ring and asked if they had just gotten a new case from Chicago.

Alex nodded and said that at the moment it was a request to check into a missing person's report but knowing her mother it most likely would turn into an assignment for the two of them.

Johnnie smiled and commented that he was glad to not be included.

Alex shook her head and said that if it became an assignment, he too would be in the middle of it. She reminded him that he had become indispensable.

Johnnie smiled and said that it was great to have such an important role on her team.

She said they should all enjoy their lunch and then walk back to the station and see what they would be doing.

The Chief was standing in the doorway to his office as they walked in. He crooked his finger and pointed into his office.

Alex, followed by Trey, walked in, and sat down. She commented that her mother must have called.

The Chief smiled and said that indeed she had and added that he had wrangled another fishing trip on the lake for himself. He said that her mother was going to make financial arrangements similar to the last time she had lured you to take a case for her. He said that he had made a deal with her to split the cost of getting a missing person's report investigated.

He added that she had pointed out that she was doing this gratis and there would be no personal gain, and she had enrolled her friend the Illinois Lieutenant governor to get some funds to help.

The Chief asked what Alex knew about the request to look into the missing son of one of her mother's clients.

He then handed out two copies of the missing person's report.

He said that the two of them and of course Johnnie should look into the issue.

Alex smiled and said that his fishing offer was a better one than what she had received. She commented that the Lieutenant governor participated with her mother in providing legal help free of charge to those clients that her mother chose.

Alex replied that at that moment she had no clue about where the missing person's report would lead her.

Alex took a minute to review the missing person's report.

She then asked if Bill and Travis could be included in the investigation.

The Chief asked what she had in mind.

Alex replied that there were three high school individuals that appeared to be connected to the Red Bandana drug distribution gang. She said that she would plan to do an interview with the three and she wanted Bill and Travis to follow them afterwards to see where the three went.

The Chief nodded and said she could get them involved.

After saying, "great," she asked when her mother had invited him to go up and go fishing because she did not have an invite so far.

The Chief chuckled and said that he only needed to give a week's notice, but it could be anytime.

Alex stood up and said that he should give her the same weeks' notice and then walked out toward Bill's and Travis's desk.

She asked if the two of them were willing to get involved in a new case where the first thing she was going to ask of them was to follow three high school tough guys that seemed involved with the Red Bandana gang.

Trevor looked at Bill and commented, "see I told you that she was in convincing the Chief to give us the shit detail."

Bill smiled and replied, "but it's worse than you were thinking, she is asking us to get involved with one of the worst drug gangs in the nation."

She looked over to where Johnnie was sitting, looking at his computer and seemingly ignoring her.

She smiled and asked if he had already solved the case.

He looked at her and replied that he had no clue what he was supposed to do.

Alex gave him the name of the person submitting the missing person's report and the name of the missing person.

Johnnie typed the two names and hit the return button. He had previously set everything up so he would be able to get the missing person's report. He almost immediately had what Alex had asked him for.

He looked at Trey and Alex and said it was in their e-mail.

Alex took a quick look at the report and suggested that there would most likely be two paths in the investigation. One would be the potential drug related implications, and the other would be where the missing person or his body was.

She said that she wanted to find the body and he and Bill could deal with the drug connection.

Trevor shook his head and commented that once again he and Bill got the hard and dangerous part and she and Trey got the safe and easy part.

Alex laughed and said that working with her was never easy or fair because she cherished her safety and kept her risk taking at a minimum by assigning the dangerous part to him and Bill.

Trevor smiled, nodded, and asked how many bullet holes she had in her body.

Alex nodded and replied, "too many."

Bill then added that had it not been for their Kevlar outfits all of them would have had too many as well and she would have had double the bullet hole scars that she now carried.

Johnnie commented that he had followed up on the three young men that had been named in the missing person's report and had discovered the fact that they seemed to be drug distributors for a local gang called the Red Bandanas.

Alex looked over at Trevor and asked if that gang was too dangerous for him and Bill.

Bill spoke up and said that it was becoming one of the strongest and most active gangs in the Cincinnati area and had branches in many cities across the US.

Alex then said that they, as a team, should spend some time laying out a plan on how they could all work closely together so they could watch each other's backs. She added that so far, they had been lucky to survive their interactions with the drug dealing business.

Trevor added that the Red Bandanas were known for their drive by shootings so they should all wear the Kevlar vests as a normal part of their daily attire.

Trey added that when they were on foot out on the street, they should also be alert to anyone approaching them that could draw a gun and fire. He wanted to make sure that one of them would fire first.

Alex explained about the drug connection, three high school senior bullies and the potential involvement of the Red Bandana gang and the missing person. She said that she had little hope for the missing person, but she wanted to address both sides of the issue and take out the gang as part of the case.

The Chief had joined them in the conversation and now he shook his head and said that he figured accepting a bribe to go fishing on the lake by her mother was going to cost him. He had not expected it to lead to a confrontation with some drug gang in Cincinnati.

Alex gave a laugh and said that lately fishing on the lake had been a surprise for her and that she had experienced as much gun battle action as fishing action.

The Chief's returned to his office, and the team went to their favorite huddle room.

Johnnie connected his computer to the big screen and brought up the pictures of the three high school seniors. Their size and expressions seemed to fit their reputation as bullies. They were tough looking, and they each sported tattoos on their fore arms.

Alex picked out the one that was probably the ringleader and bet Trevor a cookie she was right.

Bill shook his head and said that he figured the smallest one of the three was the ringleader and he said he would put up a lunch for a tray of her cookies.

Alex liked the interaction they were having. She agreed to Bill's wager.

She then said that she wanted to arrange interviews with the three at the school. She asked Bill and Travis to wait outside of the school and be ready to tail the three and learn who in the Red Bandana gang they associated with.

Trey, who usually was the quiet one in the group, smiled and asked why Alex was picking the job that got them exposed while Bill and Travis got an easy job that let them remain in the shadows.

His comment caught Alex by surprise, and she raised one of her eyebrows and asked if he was frightened.

Trey put on a face that usually Trevor used when he complained and asked if she had read anything about the Red Bandana group and about the number of drive by shootings attributed to them.

Bill commented that Trey had given a terrible rendition of Trevor's behavior, and he should stick to his shooting and taking down gangsters.

Alex asked Bill to call the high school principal to see if they could get an interview with the three bullies.

Bill said he was going step out and make the call.

A few moments later he returned and said that he had gotten through and that the principal had agreed to arrange to have the three in his office at two.

Alex suggested they go in two cars. She said that she and Trey would go in, but Bill and Travis should stay in their car and then follow the three bullies when they got out of school.

The principal was at his desk when Alex and Trey were led in by his support. He stood up and commented that the person that had made the meeting arrangements had not let him know that the most famous Cincinnati detective was the person who was coming. He then shook hands and said that it was a privilege to be working with her. He said that he hoped she would also take the three bullies out of his school.

He then added that the three would be in his office in fifteen minutes.

He asked what the three had done to get her to come out to talk to them.

Alex replied that she was not sure. They were names in a missing person's report that was submitted for Jesse Maliber.

The principal nodded and said that he had been interviewed by a couple of officers about Jesse. He said that he had been surprised because Jesse was a good student and stayed out of trouble, did well in school and had just made the basketball team when he went missing.

Alex asked what he knew about Jesse's interaction with the three students named in the missing person's report.

The principal shook his head and said that Jesse was known to stand up to the three and had intervened multiple times in their bullying of other students.

Alex asked if he thought the three were capable of doing more than bullying.

The principal shook his head and said he had no idea, but it would not surprise him if they were.

The principal's support interrupted and let them know that the three students were in the office meeting room.

Alex followed the principal into the meeting room.

He introduced she and Trey to the three and then asked each of them to give their name.

Alex sat down across the table from the three and asked them how the day was going.

She noted that the smallest of the three was first to respond. He was the one that Bill had selected as the leader. She mentally smiled as she figured that Bill had just won a tray of her cookies.

The first to respond gave his name, Rick, and said the day was going well until they were called to the office. He pointed to the person next to him and said that he was Eli and that next to him was Sylvester.

Alex responded that the reason she had wanted to talk with them was to see if they had any idea where Jesse Maliber might be.

Rick said that they had been asked that question only a couple of months ago and their answers had not changed. They had no clue where that prick had gone but as far as he was concerned it was good riddance because the ass was always poking his nose into business that he should have stayed out of.

Alex asked what kind of business Jesse had poked his nose into.

Rick replied that Jesse was a pain in the ass and would not leave the three of them alone. He added that Jesse was a relentless bully.

Alex asked if Jesse got in the way of the three of them pushing drugs at school.

Rick put his hands on the table and looked at Alex and commented that he had been trying to be polite to a Black bitch, but he was now ending that and letting her know to mind her own business or trouble would come her way.

Alex smiled and commented that she was minding her own business, and he had just stepped into her cross hairs and trouble would most likely come his way.

Rick smiled and said that he would see her outside of the school and then she would find out what it meant to get him mad.

Alex nodded and asked if that is what had happened to Jesse.

Rick looked back at her and said that he was done talking and stood up. When he stood the other two stood up and they walked out together.

Alex thanked them for their help as they walked out.

The principal said he could get security to bring them back.

Alex shook her head and said that she was quite satisfied with what she had found out.

She asked if the principal could tell where the three were going.

He made the call and let her know that the three were headed for the school's front entrance.

Alex made a quick call to alert Bill that the three were coming his way.

4 The Steep Hill

*L*isa was finding it hard to concentrate on the operation. She needed to stay focused and not miss any requests the surgeon made. She had been lucky to wrangle this position. Her years of experience and the help of her friend had taken her over the job interview finish line, and she had landed this job. Finally, the operation was over, and the last suture was complete. She walked out of the surgery room and changed out of her operating room clothes. She said good night and walked to the central park that was surrounded by the two wings of the huge hospital.

She and April lived in a two-bedroom apartment located just three blocks away.

She sat down on one of the park benches and leaned back, closed her eyes, and went over all the things that had happened in the last few months.

She had listened to her son enthusiastically announce that he had made the basketball team and that he was going to buy himself a pair of Nikes with the money he had saved. She knew that being on the basketball team was Jesse's one goal about which he was always talking. He had spent every moment staying late at school shooting hoops and running the back and forth across the court drills. He had worked hard and had been noticed by one of the coaches.

She wiped tears from her cheeks. She was sure that the three bullies at school had something to do with Jesse's disappearance. She felt sure she had lost her son, but she wished with all her being that he might still be alive. She had so little hope of that, and more tears ran down her face. She felt a hollow in her chest that seemed larger than the Grand Canyon.

She had left Cincinnati to save her daughter who had just started at that same high school.

She knew that she had made a mistake in following the three bullies to a bar near where the police station was located. The mistake was to go into the bar and confronting the drug dealer.

That confrontation had been the catalyst for the move. It had been a hard move. She had sold or abandoned all but her personal things and come to Chicago and spent a week with an old friend who she had gone to nursing school with.

Her friend had gotten her an interview at the hospital. She knew she needed to get a job as soon as possible and felt great when she got the offer before she left the interview. Being a surgical assistance was not her first choice of what she wanted to do but it paid well, and it was the job that was offered. She took it.

She was even more lucky about finding the apartment she was now in. The hospital administrator that had interviewed her was the one that let her know about the apartment. So, on the same day she got the job, she called the realtor handling the apartment and got the apartment. She felt like she had scored two home runs on the same day. It was a great feeling that lifted her spirit.

She stood up and walked in the direction of her apartment.

Her thoughts went to the seminar that she had attended with her friend on Saturday. Because the topic was about being a woman of power and choosing to make your career one you loved, she had also convinced April to come with them.

The speaker was a lawyer named Rose-Anne Evercrest.

Refreshments were served outside of the room where the presentation was to be given. She was impressed by the fact that six round tables, each with a shrimp cocktail bowl surrounded by a variety of fruits and vegetables, was part of a free seminar.

April commented that she was glad she had come as she stood eating shrimp.

Rose-Anne came to the door of the large presentation room and invited everyone in.

She watched as April grabbed more shrimp, put them on a napkin, and carried them in with her.

The presentation was also a surprise. It was not a dry description of the services that was offered by the law office of Evercrest and Holly. Rose-Anne welcomed everyone and then did a quick walk around the room and highlighted the services that were offered.

She then went to the speaker's podium, and asked, "Are you doing what you love to do?" The next line and then the story that followed led to the fact that a person had to follow the call of the road. She made the point that a person might begin their travel in life with the thought of doing a specific thing and then realize that what they had envisioned was not what real life delivered. It was then that one had to have the strength to choose to follow the call of the road. She then highlighted her daughter as an example.

Her daughter had followed her into the practice of law and had graduated at the top of her class from Northwestern University. She had gone on to become a licensed lawyer only to discover that it was not a job that suited her. She had then looked around and chose to become a deputy in a small town just north of Chicago.

She listened as Rose-Anne admitted that at that moment she had been disappointed by her daughter, and she described how when she had asked her daughter how she could give up the great job she had, she had learned that she had a daughter that was stronger than anyone she knew.

Her daughter had replied that she wanted a more hands on life than sitting in an office being bored. She intended to seek out the bad guys and bring them to the prosecutors and a jury of their peers to make sure the bad guys ended up in jail. She planned to be a huntress, and she planned to make it a life that would constantly challenge her.

It was a great story, and it was not until the end that it hit Lisa that the person that Rose-Anne was talking about was the Cincinnati detective that she had seen several times in the news. She was the detective known as "Cincinnati's Black Annie Oakeley."

At the end Rose-Anne invited anyone that had a problem with which they were struggling with to share it with her.

She said she would be available at the refreshment tables.

When Lisa walked out, she was again surprised because the offerings on the table now were comprised of a variety of cake, rolls, punch, and other drinks.

April commented that they were greeted with hors d'oeuvres and now they got desert.

She patiently waited as various people in the audience thanked Rose-Anne for the inspirational speech. She almost gave up hope of getting to talk to her. Finally, she saw an opening, approached Rose-Anne, and shared the fact that her son had gone missing, and she wondered how she might get help in finding him.

Rose-Anne nodded and suggested they go back into the presentation room so she could get the details and see how she could help.

Lisa shared her situation and the fact that she had hurriedly moved out of Cincinnati.

Lisa was surprised when Rose-Anne said that she would get her daughter to look into her situation.

That had been on Saturday and now it was Monday, and she was wondering if anything might be happening.

She went home to her apartment with some hope in her heart and that was more than she had been expecting. She wanted to get a snack ready for when April came home. She had saved her daughter and now she had initiated some action in the search of what had happened to her son.

She did not know what else as a mother she should be doing.

Back in Cincinnati, Alex walked out of the High School thinking about what she should do next. She decided that the next day she would look into the police side of the missing person's process. She would talk to the person who handled the paperwork.

Once back in the office she planned to get Johnnie to find out who had been on the street patrolling the area around where Jesse lived. They might have seen something that was not in the missing person's report.

Bill and Trevor had easily spotted the three high schoolers as they exited the school. They followed the three. They were not surprised when about a block from the school all three of them put on red bandanas. A few moments later a black chevy passed their parked car and then pulled over and picked the three up.

Bill followed them to a small pub just a few blocks away from the police station. The black chevy parked and the three followed the driver into the bar.

Trevor commented that the drug business was right in the station's backyard. They seemed to be operating in plain sight. He wondered who on the force was getting the money to be looking the other way.

Bill said that it was time they found out. He called Alex and let her know about the situation.

Alex listened as Bill shared where he had followed the three. She was not surprised and agreed that someone on the force was looking the other way, but she said that first they were going to focus on their prime objective to find out what happened to Jesse.

Bill said he agreed and said that the three were coming back out, each carrying a backpack and were getting into the car. He would let her know where they ended up.

Alex looked at Trey who had been listening to the exchange with Bill and asked him what he thought of the situation.

Trey replied that it did not look good for Jesse if he somehow crossed wires with the Red Bandana gang. He figured the three had just gotten their next consignment of drugs that they would distribute at their high school and the surrounding area.

Alex agreed and said that at a minimum she intended to bust the three as pushers and she said they should plan to raid the location where they had picked up the drugs and see who they nabbed.

Trey suggested they call it a day and get an early start in the morning.

Alex agreed and said that the next day she wanted to talk to the person who had processed the missing person's report. She also wanted to find out which officers were out on patrol in the area around the high school on the day that Jesse went missing.

She walked in and found Johnnie at his computer.

He smiled and commented that if Matt were on shift, he would fix a quick dinner before she spent several hours on the treadmill.

Alex suggested they call ahead and order takeout at their favorite Mexican restaurant. They could ride back to the apartment where she could get ready for the gym while they waited for the food to be delivered.

She smiled and said that he might even have time to get online and solve the case.

Johnnie nodded and said that he could go along with that and if she told him where to hunt, he might have a clue how he could solve the case.

They rode back to the apartment. Alex took her bike up to the apartment and changed into her gym clothes.

A short time later Alex was at Johnnie's apartment door. She had spent the bike ride back to the apartment and the short time it took her to put her bike on her porch and to get her running shoes on thinking about the case.

More than ever, the interview of the bullies gave her the feeling that this was going to be a case that had a happy ending. She certainly could use a case that once again held a miracle.

She would ask Johnnie to look into the reports from any police units around the high school area about some sort of disturbance. If they got a break, she would have Johnnie search the system to see if he could find where Jesse was now located.

5 The Red Bandanas

Johnnie was at his desk doing more research about the Red Bandana gang. He found out that they were loosely associated with the Bloods crime group that had originated in California in opposition to another gang called the Crips. He determined that the gang in Cincinnati was more interested in distributing their crack cocaine and other drugs then gaining control of the entire city and county.

It seemed the local gang was not as ruthless as the West Coast Bloods. They focused more on setting up profitable networks that distributed the cocaine and other drugs to mostly high school and college customers. They did have competition and periodically gun battles emerged but quickly faded.

He learned the names of several local Red Bandana leaders and found out that they were so successful that they drove luxury cars and that the primary leader lived in an opulent multi-acre fenced in estate on the east side of town.

He located this person's offshore bank accounts that had millions of dollars in them. He was always surprised that these folks thought that their success at accumulating wealth would go on indefinitely and they stayed put instead of leaving the US, stopping their criminal activity, and then setting themselves up and living comfortable, enjoyable lives in another country.

He looked over to the huddle room where Alex and Trey were talking to the officer who had handled Lisa Maliber's missing person report. The three had entered the room some thirty minutes ago and he wondered what if anything more they had been able to learn. He knew that Alex always seemed to find some angle that led to a new investigation path. He was always amazed that her mind worked in such a nonlinear way.

He took the last sip of his now cold coffee and watched as all three walked out of the room.

He recognized the look she had on her face as she approached his desk. He was about to get asked to search out some new information.

Alex had listened carefully to the person who had handled the missing person's report. She had asked if the person had any idea which unit might have been on patrol around the area that she thought Jesse would have been in that Saturday morning.

She now had three things that she wanted Johnnie to do some research on.

First what police units might have been around the area and what they had seen.

Second, identify the most likely highways that left Cincinnati going east that a person on foot might chose to take.

And then try to determine where on the east coast Jesse might have gone.

Johnnie smiled and thanked her for only giving him three needles in a haystack. He said he would identify the police units in the next few minutes. The other two needles would take much more time.

As expected, he was able to identify the two police units that were patrolling around the area where Jesse might have been.

Alex took the information and arranged to meet the two units for lunch. At lunch, after a brief introduction she, Trey and the four officers went into the Tex-Mex restaurant and after ordering she asked if there had been anything unusual that they might have experienced on the date of the disappearance.

There was complete silence at the table. Alex was about to ask another question when one of the officers pulled out a small notebook and flipped through the pages. He held it up and pointed to the date she had given.

He commented that he had forgotten about it, but they had broken up a fight that had been going on. The person that had been getting the beating was black and had run away and the three young white men claimed that they had been attacked. The three wore red bandanas and had been the ones doing the beating. He had written their names down but when he checked there were no outstanding warrants on them.

Alex looked at the names and recognized that the three were the ones she had interviewed. They had lied to her but now she knew that they had not killed Jesse. The knowledge lifted her up like a hot air balloon leaving the ground or an Eagle rising from the surface of a lake with a fish in its claws.

The location of the beating seemed to also identify the most likely route that Jesse was likely to take.

Alex decided that she would drive the most likely route and see if she could help Johnnie find one of the needles in the haystack. She felt that in the next few days she would know where Jesse was.

As they left the restaurant, she asked Trey if he was up to a drive through the Ohio countryside.

Trey gave a laugh and said that he was sure he had no choice and suggested they stop and get a couple of drinks and some snacks to take along.

Alex agreed and suggested they get a smoothy and some pretzels.

She then took the small highway she thought was the most promising.

As they came up over a hill, Trey pointed out the small town ahead and commented that it looked like a quaint old town that was still in the pervious century.

Alex agreed. She slowed down to a crawl as they entered. She stopped in front of the only hardware/grocery store. She looked around the square and after a moment she got out and led the way into the store.

An elderly lady who was sitting on a high stool greeted her and asked how she could be of help.

Alex identified herself and Trey and asked if a few weeks ago a young Black man might have come in.

The woman nodded, gave her name as Maurine, and said that indeed a young Black man had come in. He had been polite and had been very hungry. She hoped that she had not helped a fugitive get away because she had treated him to a breakfast of a large helping of Mac and Cheese and a cup of coffee.

Alex smiled and said that no he was not a fugitive but a young man most likely trying to protect his sister and mother by disappearing. She was now trying to find him so she could link him back up with his family.

She then asked if by chance he had mentioned where he was going.

The Maurine replied that he had not but that she had told him where he might catch a bus. She added that there was a bus station in the next town east along the highway.

Alex thanked her for the information and then asked what kind of treats that she and her partner might buy.

Maurine led them back past the hardware to where there was a row candy and chips.

As they walked out to the car, Trey asked why she had bought so many bags of Godiva chocolates.

Alex replied that she had wanted to reward Maurine for the information, and she was getting ready for when they got to the bus station.

The drive to the next town took another half hour. Alex figured that it would have taken most of the day to walk that far. She estimated that Jessi would not have gotten there until late in the evening.

She led the way into the small corner bus station that was across the street from a small well-manicured maple and oak tree lined central park that had an old-fashioned Gazebo surrounded by rose plants in the center. She noted that a few red roses seem to be trying to hold on before the first of the coming frosts. She decided that this was the town that was always shown when the media wanted to show "a true American town."

Trey commented that the bushes that made a border around the park would have been a good place to spend the night.

She approached the young lady that stood behind a chest high counter at the far end of the room. She introduced both herself and Trey and the reason they were there.

The young lady introduced herself as Judy said that she could look back at the registered ticket sales if she knew the date and time.

Alex said that she could give her the one or two days, but she could not give the time for certain but that it would most likely be the evening of the first day or the morning of the second day.

Judy spent a few moments at the computer keyboard and then said that she thought she remembered selling a ticket for a bus heading for Norfolk, Virginia with a destination of Virginia Beach to a young Black man. She said that the computer let her know that he paid cash. She had put a note in that he had a backpack but no luggage. She added that she was required to put in that information. She then asked if the person was a fugitive or had committed some crime.

Alex replied that it was neither. She thanked her and asked for the best place to get a good meal.

Judy smiled and said that she recommended her aunt's diner that was just across the street and that she had recommended the same place to the person that she was looking for.

Alex handed her a small bag of the cholates and thanked her for the information and then led the way out.

Trey commented that it seemed that they were closing in on their missing person.

Alex smiled and said that she was getting a good feeling about the case and that she might have to walk along Virginia Beach as part of the search.

When they entered the diner, they were greeted by an older version of Judy, who introduced herself as Ruth and let them know that Judy had called her to let her know and had also told her about the young Black man that had eaten there a few months ago.

Alex looked at Trey and commented that news traveled fast.

Ruth gave a small laugh and said that any stranger coming into town was news that spread like a tidal wave. She said that strangers did not stay strangers long but became the focus of the local population.

She waved her hand across the nearly empty dining room and said that she would see if she had an available table or booth.

Alex said she preferred a table and pointed to one that was about in the middle.

She asked what Ruth would recommend.

Ruth replied that she had just finished a brisket pot roast that she had just put under the heat lamps, and she had steak that she had seasoned and was ready for the grill or there was a fresh garden salad waiting to be mixed. She handed Alex and Trey menus and said that she could prepare anything that was on her limited menu.

Alex said that she would go for the brisket and a small mixed salad and an iced tea.

Trey asked what cut of steak was ready for grilling.

Ruth said that it was prime T-bone and said that it came with grilled onions and blue cheese over it and the plate would have mashed potatoes and some grilled asparagus.

Alex said that he should go for the steak, and they could share.

Ruth took the order and said that she would be right out with the two iced teas and some extra plates. She commented that she liked it when her customers shared the food at the table.

She returned with the tea, four hot roll with butter at the side and the plates.

Alex asked if there was a chance that she could ask about the young Black man that had come in a couple of months back.

Ruth said that she would get her cook going and be right back.

Alex asked Trey how he thought they were doing.

Trey responded that he was getting worried that it was all going too smoothly, and he wondered when the gallows trap door was going to open.

Just as he finished, Alex's phone went off. She recognized Johnnie's ring tone called "waterfalls."

She answered and listened as Johnnie updated her on his continued data-based searches for Jesse. He thought he had found him in DC.

Alex gave a small a laugh and said he was too far north and that he should try searching for Jesse in the Virginia Beach area.

Johnnie asked how she managed to out-search his computer.

Alex replied that it was just good old fashioned foot leather detective work.

She asked how Bill and Trevor were doing.

Johnnie said he had not talked to them since she had left.

After the call ended, she put in a quick call in to Trevor.

She learned that that he had taken numerous pictures of the three bullies selling packets of drugs.

Trevor asked whether they should arrest the three and take them in.

Alex looked over to Trey who had been listening. He mouthed arrest.

Alex nodded and told Trevor to take the three in, book them and put them in holding cells. That if the three started to look like liabilities to the drug pusher, getting them off the street would most likely save their lives.

As she ended the call the cook brought out both plates. Trey had the best-looking plate that was crowned by three large onion rings. Alex's plate had the same three large onion rings garnished with cilantro.

Ruth sat down and asked how she might be of help in finding the young man.

Alex asked what Ruth may have learned while she had served him.

Ruth commented that he had ordered the least expensive item on the menu and had chosen to drink water. She knew then that he was running from something, but he was polite and even left her a nice tip. She said that he paid cash.

She said that she had asked what he was going to do when he got to where he was going, and he had said that he would need to get a job as soon as possible.

She said that was all she knew and suggested the two of them eat while the food was still hot.

Alex cut a piece of her pot roast and put it on the clean plate and pushed over to Trey.

Trey did the same with his steak.

The two of them commented how good the food was and dug in and they were both quiet for the rest of the meal.

Alex took the last sip of her iced tea. She asked Trey whether he wanted the rhubarb-cherry pie with ice cream for dessert.

Trey said he would split the desert with her.

Alex put in the order and after dessert when she paid for the dinner, she gave Ruth a bag of chocolates.

As they walked out to the car she asked if he would drive back to the station while she thought through the next steps.

Trey nodded and said that he would enjoy the drive back and asked what she had in mind.

Alex smiled and said she was thinking about going fishing.

6 Bullied Bullies

*A*lex was idly taking in the countryside as Trey drove back to Cincinnati. She looked at the time and realized that she and Trey would be back to the station well after work hours. She asked if she should call Lesley and let her know that they were still on the road back. When she got Trey's yes nod, she dialed Lesley and let her know about the road trip across much of the southern part of Ohio and that Trey was going to be late getting home. Lesley thanked her for the call and said that she would keep dinner warm.

Alex then decided to call her mother to see if she could schedule an interview with Lisa Maliber in the next day or two.

Her mother said that she could arrange for an interview after Lisa got off her shift at the hospital. She added that she thought the shift ended around four.

Alex asked Trey if a trip up on a Thursday, with an invitation for him and family to spend the weekend at her house sounded doable.

Trey smiled and commented that Nolan would be super excited, and he personally would love to go fishing as long as she kept the gun battles to a minimum.

Alex let her mother know about the weekend and listened as her mother said that it was great to have her and Trey's family for the weekend. She asked if Matt would be coming.

Alex replied that she was not sure about Matt and would call later to let her know.

Alex, after getting off the phone, asked Trey how he felt the day had gone.

Trey said that for once it seemed their case was on the good side because it seemed that Jesse was alive. He smiled and said that he was sure that Johnnie would find the exact address in the next few days.

Alex agreed and said that they should wait to celebrate because they were not done with the drug side of the case yet.

She said that she was very interested in what Jesse's mother might know. Separately she wanted to question the three drug pushing bullies that Bill and Trevor had arrested. She added that she was not really interested in them other than to get them off the street, but she was more interested in who they were pushing drugs for and in stopping that operation.

Trey nodded and said that their personal history with drug pushers gave him goose bumps. He said that they both had suffered from both beatings and shootings. He hoped that this time around they would get the upper hand from the start.

Alex smiled and asked whether he regretted being her partner.

He laughed and asked if she was kidding. Then added that she had changed his life for the better and certainly didn't blame her for what the drug kingpins had done.

Alex smiled and said he was the best partner she had ever had.

He chuckled and replied that so far as he knew he was the only partner that she had ever had.

"You're the only one but you are the best," Alex replied.

She then decided to call Matt to see what his weekend schedule would be.

Matt laughed when she asked if he wanted to go fishing and asked if they would also go apple picking for additional excitement.

Alex shook her head and said that she was beginning to think that everyone was getting the impression that she was a magnet for trouble.

Matt joked back and said that he could remind her of the gun battle on the way to the apple orchard, or the one when they had been out on the lake fishing and she had burned up a tugboat and coal barge, or the one she had when they went on vacation in Hawaii, or the one in Toronto, but he said that he wouldn't. He then said that he would trade workdays so that he could go fishing with her.

Alex thanked him for not reminding her about being a magnet for trouble.

When Alex got off the phone, Trey commented that he figured the trip to Chicago was going to be a small bit of business and a lot of family fun.

He dropped Alex off at her apartment and asked what time they would be flying out for Chicago.

Alex let him know that she had reservations for a flight at noon and that they should plan on being in the office at the regular time. She added that she planned to question the three bullies before they left for Chicago.

The next morning Trevor and Bill were sitting at their desks as Alex walked in with Johnnie. Trevor smiled and asked what had taken her so long to get to work.

Bill just shook his head and said good morning.

Alex smiled and replied that she wanted to make sure that her Bear Claw was there when she got to her desk with her coffee.

Bill handed her a Bear Claw as she got to her desk.

Alex was just putting half of it on Trey's desk as he walked in.

Trey said good morning, took a bite of the Bear Claw, a sip of his coffee and asked how they were going to handle the questioning of the three bullies.

Alex smiled and said that she thought that Bill should take the role of the good cop and Trevor should try the role of the mean cop.

Trevor flexed his arms and let out a growl. He smiled and said he was ready to be his true self, and they should head for the questioning room. He suggested that they question the biggest of the three first and their small leader last. He would weave in his meanness and get them to spill all they knew.

Alex nodded and said let's do it.

Johnnie interrupted and said that he had information about the Red Bandana's boss that might make the questioning easier. He shared that it seemed that this boss had come from California where he was suspected of two murders but was not charged because no bodies had been found. He added that street rumor was that the bodies, if they were ever found, would be decomposing in lye filled drum barrels.

Alex asked Trevor if he could use this information during the questioning.

Trevor said he would have the three bullies crying before the questioning session ended.

He asked Johnnie if he could get a picture of a body in a barrel of lye. He said he recalled one being found in Mexico. He said that a picture whether it was one of the bodies in California or Mexico would make a shocking impression on the three high schoolers.

Trevor said they should go to it and get it done so that Alex could go fishing.

Alex thanked him for his support for her getting to Evenston and out on the lake.

She, Trey, and Johnnie entered the viewing room and sat down.

A moment later Johnnie announced that he had found the barrel with the body in it and said that it had a human hand floating on top, but the rest was just a murky white mess.

Bill and Trevor looked at the picture and commented that it was just what they needed.

Bill said that the two of them were ready and they should send in the first bully, and they would see how brave he was.

Alex watched as one after the other the three bullies succumbed to Bill and Trevor. She smiled and quietly said that Trevor had hit the nail on the head in suggesting the use of the visual of the barrel with the human hand floating on top. The picture broke the resistance of the bullies. They gave up the name of the person who they got the drugs from and where they were taken to pick up the drugs. They had little else to share.

They admitted to beating Jesse up, but that Jesse had run away, and they had never seen him again. They all verified that a few days later Jesse's sister had quit coming to school.

Bill let each of the bullies know that if they pushed drugs in the school or on the street he would go to the press and let the press know that the three of them had co-operated and fingered their drug contact as the boss of the Cincinnati Red Bandana drug cartel.

Each of the three said that was not fair because they did not have a choice and they did not want to end up in a barrel.

Bill suggested that they plead guilty to distributing drugs and he would see that they served their sentence in a low security prison facility where they would be out of the reach of the person that was supplying the drugs.

Each separately agreed. The leader was not going to agree until Bill made the point that his two buddies had already agreed.

Bill asked for all three to be brought in together. He wanted to review the paperwork with their admission to pushing drugs at the high school and on the area around the high school.

He read the confession to the three of them at the same time and asked that each sign a copy of the admission paperwork.

After signing the three were led away and taken to holding cells.

Alex entered the questioning room and congratulated Bill and Travis for the great job they had done.

When they were all together, Johnnie laughed and commented that he had super imposed the floating hand because the barrel that had the body in it only had a very decomposed body that was not visible through the white murky haze.

Alex let Johnnie know that she would give him a tray of cookies for his creativity.

Travis asked how many cookies came with the congrats on the good job that he and Bill had done.

Alex smiled and replied that they would each get a tray of her cookies. But for a tray, she wanted to know who came to the hearing for the three bullies. She was sure that the internal leaker would get the word out to the drug boss. She wanted to see if they could figure out who the internal leak might be, and she wanted to know which lawyer might be working with the drug boss.

Bill said that they would make sure to get a picture of everyone that came to the hearing and get Johnnie to find out who they were.

Alex looked at Trey and said that it was time for them to catch a flight to Chicago where they had important work to get done.

Trevor smiled and said that he too always figured putting a worm on a hook was very important work.

Alex turned, waved over her shoulder, and commented that she loved him too.

The Vanishing

7 Regrets

*J*esse looked at the three pictures he had hung up on the wall in front of his work desk. Two were framed certificates that were on either side of the third picture of his mother with her hands over his and his sister's shoulders. One certificate was his High School Diploma that he had earned in a short two months, and the other was his certificate of completion to be an IT programmer. He felt very lucky to land an IT role with a large company that let him work remotely. He was getting paid more than he had thought he would ever earn.

He still held the goal of getting a college education, but he figured that he would save up for it and perhaps do a lot of the work at a local junior college.

He had immediately set up a bank account where his paycheck was being sent.

He was just getting started and hoped that he would soon be able to move to a better place to live and maybe even get a car so he could get around.

He tried to see if he could find out how his mother and sister were doing but had no luck online. He decided to take a trip to Cincinnati to find out in person, but he did not yet want to make contact. He wanted to make sure that he did not trigger some sort of retribution by the three bullies against them.

This time he had enough money for the bus ride and to feed himself.

His trip to Cincinnati was a bust. He found out that his mother and sister had moved. He had no clue where they might have gone. He went to the hospital where his mother worked and asked for her but was informed that she no longer worked there. He tried to get her address but the only thing he learned was that she had moved away from Cincinnati.

He returned to Virginia Beach and tried to think how he might be able to find them.

Little did he know that he was going to be the one to be found.

Johnnie had been scouring the internet for some clues about where on the east coast Jesse had chosen to locate. He succeeded when he found a certificate of completion on a site that claimed to train and get jobs for people who graduated from their program for a Jesse T. Maliber of Viginia Beach. He dug a little deeper and got the address that Jesse had given in his application to the school.

He did additional follow up and found the e-mail sent to Jesse and followed up on all the job applications he had sent out. He was impressed with Jesse's thoroughness and the number of applications he had sent out.

He found the three that had offered him a job and then zeroed in on the acceptance by Jesse. He had accepted the offer that allowed him to work remotely. It was not the highest dollar offer but the feature of being able to work from anywhere in the country must have been what Johnnie figured had made the difference for Jesse.

He sent the information to Alex so that she would have it when she interviewed Jesse's mother.

The plane was just pulling up to the gate when she received Johnnie's message and the information he had collected. She shared this with Trey and asked how they should use the information when they interviewed Jesse's mother and sister.

Trey suggested that they wait until they had concluded the interview and had gathered the information that his mother and sister might have about Jesse's disappearance. He said that the decision to move to Chicago might have been based on more than Jesse's disappearance. Jesse must have left under duress and perhaps to protect his mother and sister.

Alex agreed with Trey and said that they should concentrate on getting to her house and finding out what her mother had planned for dinner. She added that she hoped not to gain too many pounds due to her mother's cooking.

During the ride to the house, where she had grown up, she decided to call Bill to see if they had any additional information.

Bill replied that he had asked Johnnie to continue to dig into the Red Bandana organization to see what else they could learn. He said he was interested in the source of the drugs that were being distributed.

He shared that some of the drugs were being produced locally. He chuckled and said that the location was a small building that had been a firehouse that was close to where the Body Parts group had set up their operation that had subsequently burned down. He commented that it was somewhat ironic that had the fire house been in operation they might have kept the fire from destroying the building housing the body parts operation.

Alex thanked him for continuing to dig into the drug side of the case. She said that the happier side of the case would most likely end on a high note, and afterwards she wanted to shut down the Red Bandana operation.

She asked Bill if he was willing to go to Virginia Beach and verify that the person that Johnnie had found was the Jesse Maliber they were looking for. If it turned out that he was the one, then he should see if he were willing to meet with his mother on a fishing trip out on Lake Michigan.

Bill agreed that he and Trevor would fly out and get a positive identification and asked whether the two of them should escort Jesse on the fishing trip.

Alex gave a laugh and said that the trip would be on her and that their spouses were invited as well.

Alex heard Trevor in the background shout out that he would put the worm on her hook, and he would also bring a case of beer.

She then called Johnnie to invite him to join the fishing trip.

Johnnie thanked her for the invitation but said that he and Mary had plans for the weekend but that she should bring him a fish that he would prepare for her and Matt.

She said goodbye as Trey turned into the driveway to her parents' house.

The trees on either side of the long driveway had continued to grow and had formed a tunnel that framed the center of the house. She noticed immediately the round flower bed at the center of the circle driveway had yellow roses in full bloom.

Rose-Anne had been waiting for Alex and Trey and rushed out when they drove into the circle.

Alex congratulated her mother on the prominent display of yellow roses blooming in the center circle garden. She said that it was the first time she had seen them and asked when they had been planted.

Rose-Anne led her over to the edge of the garden and commented that she, with some help, had planted them the day before especially for her favorite daughter.

Alex looked at Trey and commented that now she knew where she had gotten that phrase, "favorite partner."

Trey chuckled and replied, "like mother, like daughter."

Rose-Anne said she had no clue what they were talking about, but they should all go into the house and after they put their stuff into their rooms, they should all meet out by the pool for a casual dinner.

When she walked out to the pool, Alex could tell that her mother had ordered the food from her Pizzeria. The onion rings were stacked up on a vertical holder, three varieties of pizza were offered on a large platter, and a variety of non-alcoholic drinks were in a large ice filled bucket.

Her father was now home and sitting at the pool side table. He got up and gave her a hug and let her know that her Jaguar was in the garage and ready for her to drive.

Alex took a nonalcoholic beer, opened it, took several onion rings, and sat down next to him.

She asked her mother how business was going at the Pizzeria.

Rose-Anne smiled and said that ex-sheriff, Jason Shephard was personally making it a success. He had introduced the onion rings, cheese sticks and a few additional sides. He listened to his customers, and it resulted in a whopping thirty percent business revenue increase.

She said that it was even better because she, Jason, and his wife all got along, and Jason's wife had taken a full-time position as front cashier and waitress.

Alex nodded and said that it made her feel good that he had found the work that let him enjoy his day. He had been a great first boss when she had decided to get into the field of police work.

Trey had come out to the pool and had listened to the discussion about the sheriff and commented that he had a chance on the last trip to talk to him and had learned about all of Alex's weaknesses from him and that it had made a huge difference in how carefully he treated her.

Alex laughed and said that she loved him too.

Rose-Anne asked Trey how the family was doing and what time they would arrive.

Trey gave her the time on Friday afternoon when they would arrive and commented that Nolan was super excited about coming up and that Lindsey said she was looking forward to taking it easy. He said that Lindsey said hello and thanked her for being so gracious.

Alex asked what boat they would be going out on.

Her father smiled and said that Dexter insisted that they take his Golden Goose and that he would personally skipper her.

Alex said that was great, but she wanted to make sure that she paid for the use of the yacht. She added that she knew that Dexter would not accept payment, but she would give the appropriate amount to his favorite charity.

Her father nodded and said that Dexter had commented about payment and that she would have free rides on the Golden Goose for as long as he ran the marina. He commented that he still felt guilty for aiding his college friend's attack on her.

Alex shook her head and commented that his friend had almost sunk the Golden Goose and that he was not responsible for his friend's actions. He certainly did not "aid" him.

And to boot, the fishing boat that his friend had used was a total loss.

Her father said that made logical sense, but it was not how Dexter took it.

Alex asked Trey if he was OK with her picking Harold Zimmerman's Aunt's restaurant as the location for the lunch the next day. He responded that the location did not matter to him and figured she would pick a good place.

Alex called the restaurant and made reservations for the private room. The receptionist said that the room was usually reserved for larger groups and asked if a booth or table would be acceptable.

Alex replied that she needed the room so she could do a very personal interview. She referenced Harold as a person that could be contacted if there were any additional questions. She made the point that she would pay whatever the price was for the room.

Once the reservation was made, she focused back on the dinner and the conversation at the table.

The evening went well into the night. Alex was in no hurry to go to bed, she figured she would sleep in at least until eight in the morning. The lunch interview on the following day was the only work item.

She wanted to enjoy driving her Jag but she figured that they should take the SUV so they could both host Lisa and her daughter and take them to lunch and then afterwards go to the airport and pick up Lesley and Nolan.

Trey had come down early the next morning and was enjoying a cup of coffee and talking to Rose-Anne. He had enjoyed breakfast with Russel, who left right after so he could get ready for an early morning lecture.

Alex came down the back stairs that entered directly into the kitchen and smiled when she saw her mother and Trey chatting. She knew that her mother was fond of Trey and had a very positive impression of his character.

Her mother asked what she wanted for breakfast.

Alex replied that a soft-boiled egg, a piece of buttered toast and jam and a cup of coffee would be all she wanted.

She asked when her mother needed to get to work.

Rose-Anne smiled and said that she was working from home and that she worked from home almost every Friday and that often she would do a little work on Saturday as well as Sunday. It allowed her to manage her time in a flexible manner. She added that she had made the workday change for all the people in the office.

Alex said that it seemed to be a good way to keep from having Friday be a stressful day.

Rose-Anne asked if she was planning to use the Jag. She added that her father had taken it in and had it serviced, tuned up and had it detailed. She added that he periodically drove it to keep it in shape.

Alex replied that though she would love to drive the Jag, using the rental for the day would provide the room they needed. They would first ferry Lisa and her daughter and go to lunch. Then after that they could go to the Airport and pick up Lesley and Nolan and have plenty of room for the luggage.

Rose-Anne said that the dinner was coming mostly from the Pizzeria, but it would not be pizza. Sylvester was preparing T-bone steaks for everyone, and the sides would be cold slaw, baked potato, and onion rings. Her contribution was to make a cucumber and tomato salad. She asked if that would be enough or should she add something more.

Alex commented that she would eat a light lunch so that she would have room for what sounded like a huge dinner. She asked if Sylvester would eat dinner with them.

Rose-Anne said that he planned to only cater the dinner, but she added that he and his wife would be part of the group going fishing.

Alex nodded and said that she looked forward to chatting with him when they went fishing.

Later, on the drive to downtown Chicago, Trey asked how Alex was going to handle the interview.

Alex replied that she would ask leading questions and then listen carefully to the replies. She said she agreed with him that the move away from Cincinnati might have been triggered by more than just Jesse's disappearance.

Trey nodded and commented that when the drug trade was mixed with family affairs things could be very messy.

When they arrived at the hospital where Lisa worked, they found a parking spot that let them see the front door.

Alex commented on the large size of the park that the Hospital wings surrounded. She added that on a clear day like the one they were enjoying, it felt like she was at the bottom of the pool looking up through the water.

A few moments later, Trey pointed to a person exiting the hospital and asked if it was Lissa Maliber and her daughter.

Alex said she thought so and opened the door and got out. She walked over to where the two were standing, introduced herself and Trey and then verified their identity. She complimented both on their dresses.

Lissa thanked her for the compliment and added that she was so happy that she had lucked out and met her mother and that she was the mother of the most successful detective in Cincinnati.

Alex smiled and replied that her success was due to a partner like Trey and a team of supporting detectives.

She pointed to the SUV and suggested they go to lunch.

A few minutes later they arrived at the restaurant and were escorted into the private room. Harold Zimmerman's aunt came in and apologized for the initial problem Alex had in getting the room. She said that dessert would be on her. She suggested the strawberry rhubarb pie with a scoop of vanilla.

Alex thanked her for such a kind gesture and asked what she recommended for lunch.

The recommendation was a slice of heart of shoulder roast beef with gravy, roast asparagus and mashed potatoes smothered in butter.

Alex smiled and said it sounded very good. She looked around and asked if there were any takers.

Both Lissa and April said that the recommendation sounded great and asked to have iced tea with it.

Alex said that though it sounded delicious she knew that her mother was having a special dinner catered so she was going for a small mixed salad and a lemonade.

Trey said he would have the same since he too would be at the dinner.

Lissa commented that she had learned that Alex's mother was also known to be a chef.

Alex nodded and said that she had chef friends all around the world. She added that the evening dinner would be catered by a family friend and not prepared by her mother.

Once the drinks arrived Alex asked Lissa to share with her what had happened when Jesse had failed to come home.

Lissa thought for a minute and then said that on that first day she had gone out all around the neighborhood trying to find him.

She had then called several of his friends to see if they knew where he might be. She had then tried to put in a missing person's report but was told she would have to wait for twenty-four hours.

The next day, a Saturday, she followed the three bullies that Jesse had told her about. She followed them to a bar only a few blocks away from the downtown police station. The three had gone in and when they came out their backpacks were bulging. She figured they had gotten a supply of drugs.

She admitted that she wanted to scream at them that they were horrible individuals, but she had turned so they could not see her face.

She then went into the police station and put in the missing person's report. She made sure their names were in the report.

She looked over at Alex and said that then she had done something stupid and gone back to the bar. She went in and confronted the person that she suspected was the local drug dealer.

The lunch order was being brought in, and she stopped talking.

Once the food was all on the table, Alex asked Lissa to continue.

Lissa nodded and then said that going into the bar was a huge mistake. She had confronted the person who seemed to be in charge. His response was to threaten to kill her and put her in a barrel of lye. He had smiled and said that he would make sure her daughter would join her in the barrel where they could be together for eternity.

She had almost run out of the bar and had gone home, called her friend in Chicago, and asked if she could come up and stay until she got a job there. The next day she packed up the few things she owned, cancelled her apartment rental agreement, took April out of school, and drove the rental moving truck to Chicago.

She admitted that once she was on the road, she felt a huge weight lift from her shoulder.

She went on to say that things in Chicago had gone very well. She got a job almost immediately. She was able to get April into school and found an apartment that she could afford in the following week.

She focused on getting into her work and getting oriented at the hospital.

Then one day she had attended Alex's mother's conference on legal support and now she was talking to her.

Alex asked April what she knew about the three bullies.

April said they were terrible guys who were always picking on some girl or other. They seemed to get away with doing whatever they wanted.

Her brother was one of the few guys who stood up to them and refused to let them have their way. He had several fights with them in school and always came out on top because he had his own friends who would help him.

It was clear to her that the three bullies only acted when they had a person outnumbered.

The Friday afternoon that he had left to go to buy his shoes he let her know that afterwards he planned to go back to the gym at school and shoot hoops. She had not seen him since that afternoon.

Alex let them know that the three bullies were under arrest for distributing drugs and would end up serving time.

She added that she knew about the leader of the Red Bandanas who was the drug dealer in the bar. He would be arrested and charged once she got done with her investigation of the missing person's report.

She added that he was a person who had left California where he was suspected of killing several people and putting them in a fifty-gallon barrel full of lye.

She looked over to Lissa and said that her decision to leave had most likely been a wise one.

Lissa thanked her for the information. She added that at the time she had thought she was a bit fanatical.

Alex then asked if the two of them liked to fish.

Lissa replied that was one of the things she, Jesse and April had done often because it was one of the least expensive ways to spend a day along the Ohio River. She said she loved to fish.

Alex then invited the two of them to go out with her on Lake Michigan to fish.

Lissa thought for a minute and asked if this meant that there was bad news and taking her fishing was a way to soften the news.

Alex said that on the contrary and that the invitation gave her more time to pursue a much more positive approach.

After lunch Alex took Lissa and April to their apartment and after making sure they understood that a cab would be at the curb at five in the morning to take them to the marina where she would meet them, she and Trevor left for the airport.

The Vanishing

254

8 Maliber Reunion

amacho sipped on his beer and stared into the mirror across the bar from him. He took in the silver streak in his otherwise black hair. He figured it indicated how the past few years weighed heavy. The law in California had forced him to move out and now he was in sleepy, slow moving Cincinnati pushing drugs in the surrounding area. He was trying to be as low key as possible and to avoid conflict with the other drug dealers already established in the area.

The most lucrative areas were the high schools, the university and surprisingly the business district. He also covered all the poorer areas, but they were harder to manage. His high school pushers were the easiest to manage and to collect from. The business professionals needed to be discreet and made the drug transfer a delicate dance.

He shook his head as he thought about the most recent confrontation that he had had with an angry mother who had accused him of hurting her son. He had threatened to eliminate her, and she had bolted out of the bar.

He probably should have kept his threat to himself.

He had sent a couple of his men out to round her up. They came back with the news that she had left town and there was no forwarding address.

He found out from the three high schoolers pushing for him in that area that they had a run in with her son. The three were in the process of beating the hell out of him when a squad car came by and stopped the fight. The person they were beating had run away and escaped. They had not seen him since that afternoon.

He now understood the confrontation he had had with the angry mother. He had little concern about that situation. He just moved on. That family was not a threat to him or his business.

What worried him more was that the three said that they had been interviewed by a Black female detective and her partner about the missing son and about their involvement in pushing drugs. When they gave him her name a cold shiver went down his back.

He knew her reputation. She had made news that had reached him when he was still on the West Coast. Now she was very close to his doorstep. So close in fact, not only because his center of operation was only a few blocks from her office, but also because she had interviewed three of his pushers. He figured he would need to eliminate the three.

He thought through his options. He might not need to do a thing, but he figured he should think through all the options.

He could relocate his operation away from Cincinnati. This, however, would most likely put him in conflict with some other drug distributors and he would have to establish a presence by force. That was always a very risky thing to do.

His other option was to put the Black detective so to say in the barrel. He figured he could skip the barrel and just have one of his guys shoot her.

He contacted his police informant to find out her address. He then scoped out the location and the place where a sniper could be located. He found the place from where he would shoot and figured that one shot would eliminate his main problem.

He returned to his normal bar office location and relaxed. He made a call to a professional sniper and arranged for the kill. He assigned one of his men to be a spotter to watch the apartment entrance and get the timing of when the sniper would need to be in place. He was set and confident that it would soon all be cleaned up and he could continue doing business as usual.

Bill and Trevor flew to Norfolk and then drove out to the address on Virginia Beach. Johnnie had provided them with the address and a picture of the apartment building, so they were confident that they were at the right place. They rang the entrance doorbell and identified themselves to the person answering the bell. They entered and took the elevator to the fifth floor.

They knocked on the apartment door and were greeted by Jesse.

Bill introduced himself and Trevor. He verified that Jesse was from Cincinnati.

Jesse asked how they had found him and was he in trouble.

Trevor chuckled and said that maybe he was in trouble with his mother but not with the law.

Bill explained that his mother had obtained the help of someone in Chicago, who had contacted the Cincinnati Detective department. He was listed as a missing person and through some detailed investigation had been located. They were there to invite him to a fishing family reunion.

Jesse said he had never heard of the police inviting someone to go fishing.

Bill smiled and replied that he would meet a detective and her family that loved to go fishing and who was inviting him to a fishing family reunion.

Trevor then handed Jesse his airplane tickets for that afternoon.

Jesse looked at the first-class tickets to Chicago. He looked at Bill and said that he had never flown first class, in fact he had never flown anywhere. He looked at the ticket again and let out a low whistle and said that he hoped they treated the passengers in first with special kid gloves.

Bill said they were all sitting in first class compliments of Alex Evercrest, the lead detective on the case.

Trevor handed Jesse his hotel reservations in Evanston, Illinois and said they were all staying at the same hotel. He asked if Jesse could be packed and ready to go in the next hour or so because the plane would not wait.

Jesse nodded and asked if they might want a coffee or something else to drink or to snack on. He commented that he felt a little disoriented by the invitation to go fishing as part of a family reunion and flying first class all seemed to be the buzz that came along with a high.

Bill said that he had been disoriented ever since he had started working with the detective, he would meet on the fishing trip.

"She is definitely a unique person," Trevor piped in.

Not long after they were on their way. The flight was only a couple of hours. The trip to the hotel took as long as the flight. They all checked into the hotel just before dinner.

Both Bill and Trevor's wives had already checked in and said they would meet them in the dining area.

Bill extended a dinner invitation to Jesse who accepted.

It was pitch black when Alex looked out her window. The big blue numbers on the clock clicked over to five. She wanted to roll over but instead she sat up.

She pushed on Matt. Leaned over and gave him a kiss on the cheek and said it was time to go fishing.

He got up and walked into the bathroom.

She got up, got ready and went down to the kitchen where she knew a cup of coffee would be waiting for her.

She was finally getting to drive her Jag to the fishing pier.

Lesley led a sleepy-eyed Nolan into the kitchen and joined in having a cup of coffee. Nolan sat down on the floor against the wall and closed his eyes.

Alex suggested that they take off for the marina and get on board the Golden Goose and then enjoy a great breakfast of pancakes drenched in maple syrup, have a side sausage patty and cup of black coffee.

She led the way to the garage. Lesley and Nolan got into the back seat and Matt sat in the front seat. The drive to the marina was one of silence.

She hoped that all the folks would make it on time.

She could see the lights on the Golden Goose as she parked her car. She led the way and boarded. She smiled when she saw that all the ingredients to make breakfast had been put out along the counter.

She asked Nolan if he was ready for some breakfast.

He nodded and laid his head on the table.

She started the breakfast preparation.

A few moments later, Alex watched as Lissa and April got out of a cab. She asked Leslie to handle the pancake and walked out onto the pier. She waved at the two and they walked toward her. A black SUV entered and parked in the parking lot. She saw Trey and the rest of her family got out.

Alex led Lissa and April onto the Golden Goose and asked what they would like for breakfast.

A few moments later Jason and his wife arrived.

Alex was pleased that everything was happening in the sequence that she had hoped.

Bill waited until six thirty as Alex had requested and then he drove to the marina. He knew that Alex was staging his arrival so that it would be a surprise to Jessi's mother.

The sun was just threatening to come over the horizon when he parked next to the black SUV.

He had Trevor lead the way with the two wives and he and Jesse followed. He had asked Trevor to have his camera ready to take pictures of the reunion.

Alex watched as Trevor led the way. She distracted Lissa and April, so they were looking at the sun that was just breaking the horizon.

Jessi was the first to speak and say hello and rush forward as Lissa stood up. The scene was one of hugging, kissing and tears.

Lissa turned to Alex and told her that she would never forget this moment, gave her a hug, and thanked her.

Dexter came on board and asked if it was time to cast off.

Alex nodded and said that they should all enjoy the ride and get ready to fish once they were at her favorite spot on the lake.

The fishing was good. She caught one that she planned to take back for Johnnie and then stopped fishing. Everyone caught at least one and then enjoyed grilled hamburgers, bratwurst, and hot dogs for lunch.

The Maliber reunion was a continuous cycle of tears, hugs, and laughter.

Alex sat with Bill, Trevor, and Trey. She commented that they should all cherish the moment when they could enjoy a happy ending to part of their case.

Trevor nodded and added that he would remember this one for quite a while. He commented that he now knew how Alex felt about finding and saving Annie and her two daughters.

Alex smiled and said that it was a feeling that she always embraced when a case was trying to pull her down.

Trey pointed over to where Matt was playing checkers with Nolan and added that seeing Nolan play with Annie's two daughters always brought back the memory of watching Alex run out ahead of him to get to Annie and her two daughters so that she could save them from a deranged kidnapper. What stood out was that she had stepped in between Annie and the deranged kidnapper and taken a bullet in the arm and in the chest even as she shot and killed him.

Trevor then said that he really loved Alex for who she was.

Alex shook her head and said that she was going to sit with Lesley, and the rest of the women.

Dexter announced that he was shutting down the grill and would soon point the Golden Goose toward the harbor.

Dinner that night was a continuation of the reunion of Jesse and his mother and sister.

Alex was enjoying catching up with her first boss. She learned that he and his wife were having the best time of their lives in running the Pizza shop and in exploring the area that they had lived all their lives but seen so little of.

He asked her how working in Cincinnati was going. He commented that he had kept up with her many cases and talked to her boss frequently.

Alex smiled and said that she thanked him for his original recommendation and that Cincinnati was a wonderful place in which to work and to play. The only issue was that she was often on cases that pulled her away to other cities and locations.

He looked over to where Matt was playing with Nolan and Trey and asked whether she had found her soul mate in Cincinnati.

Alex shook her head and said that they had met in the deep south during one of her cases. He had followed her to Cincinnati and made it clear that he was after her. She added that he was the soul mate she had been looking for.

Jesse came over and thanked her for arranging for him to meet back up with his mother and sister. He let her know that he was planning to move to Chicago as soon as his lease in Virginia ended. He planned to stay in Chicago for another week and asked if the return ticket would still be good and if he could downgrade it and use the money.

Alex nodded and said that it was his ticket, and he should do what he wanted with it.

The next morning after a light breakfast, she, Matt, Trey, Lesley, and Nathan all rode together to the Airport. The flight back to Cincinnati was uneventful.

They parted ways at the luggage area. Lesley had suggested a picnic, and they had agreed to figure out where to go during the week.

She sat quietly on the drive to the apartment. The weekend had been a great success. It was the part of the case that would rate as the number two of getting loved ones together. She had a handful of young women she had saved who stayed connected with her and that as a group was the number three set of positive memories. She figured that saving Annie and her two daughters would remain number one forever.

Matt knew that this case was one that Alex was feeling positive about. He hoped that the second part of the case could be handled quickly and with the success that Alex always seemed to accomplish.

He drove his van into the parking garage that was across the street from the apartment building and parked in his reserved spot. Each apartment had an assigned spot that they paid for, but it made it easier to have a reserved spot, so he thought it was worth it.

He got his luggage out and then followed as Alex walked out and got ready to cross the street.

Suddenly he spotted a red dot on the back of her neck. He lunged forward and knocked her down and felt a burning sting in his left shoulder.

Alex was surprised at Matt's sudden push, but her impulse reaction took over and she rolled, pulled her weapon, located the barrel of a rifle pointing down from the top of the parking garage and fired.

The shooter was surprised at the fast reaction of the person behind his target. He tried to hold his shot, but it was too late. The bullet hit the guy instead of his intended target. He leaned forward to get a second shot.

He felt the bullet hit and suddenly he realized he was falling and then the world went black.

Alex jumped up and checked to make sure the shooter was dead. She kicked his weapon away and then went to Matt.

Matt lay still as he realized he had been shot. He wondered if his EMT team would be the ones that would show up.

He looked up at Alex and asked if she had killed the shooter.

He could hear the sirens and knew that in a few minutes the two of them would be surrounded by police and the EMT's.

He smiled and said that he preferred to pick apples on a warm fall morning.

Alex gave him a kiss on the forehead and said she thanked him for the push, and she was sorry that he had taken the bullet.

Matt looked up and laughed when he realized it was his team that was going to treat him. He said hello as they went into action and strapped him to the board and soon, they had him in the van and were driving off.

Alex verified where they were going and let Matt know she would bring him a treat once he was in his room.

She then held up her shield and walked over to the policeman that seemed to be in charge and identified herself. She pointed to where she had put her weapon down on the ground. She described what had happened and said that she did not know who the shooter was or why she had become his target.

She walked over to where the coroner's team had turned the body over. She asked to take a picture of his face.

It took almost a half an hour for the scene to be processed.

She made sure it was OK to leave the site of the crime and then took the suitcases to her the apartment.

Then she went down to see if Johnnie was in his apartment. When he opened the door, she entered and let him know what had just happened.

Johnnie commented that he had been in the shower and by the time he had gone out to see what had happened the coroner's van was driving away.

Alex asked if he could track the shooter down using the picture that she had taken.

Johnnie opened his computer and said he would give it a try.

He asked if Alex wanted some of her own cookies and a cup of tea or coffee. After having poured two cups of coffee he began his search.

A few minutes passed then his computer gave a drum roll and flashed three times and the on-screen picture had a name and a list of priors. He was a member of the Reds in LA and wanted for murder.

Alex then asked Johnnie to share the information with Bill, Trevor, Trey, and the Chief and let them know that on Monday she planned to arrest and bring in the local Red Bandana leader and charge him with attempted murder.

She then asked if Johnnie had any extra cookies that she could take to Matt at the hospital.

9 Robin Hood

The evening news came through to Camacho like a hundred police sirens wailing in the night. The assassin from LA that he had contracted and had just paid had been killed but his target was unscathed.

He hoped that his connection to the assassin would be untraceable. It was a verbal agreement and a ten thousand dollar up front, and it would have been another ten thousand after the kill.

He felt he was fine, but he had to admit that he was as nervous as a cat in a room full of rocking chairs. He needed to get his tail out of the room.

Not having heard from his three high school distributors who had put him on the trail of eliminating the Black detective made him even more nervous.

He did not like being in the dark and uninformed. He was used to being in control and keeping others in the dark or putting them permanently in the dark.

Johnnie waited for Alex in the hallway across from the elevator. He knew that she had stayed with Matt in the hospital until at least midnight. He hoped she was wide awake and ready to go.

She had sent out a message that she wanted to shut down the Red Bandanas. He was sure that meant some digging on his part. He just needed to know what she wanted so he could focus his effort. He knew Alex as always would want to move fast and he knew when she was attacked, she would move faster than an eagle diving for a trout in a lake.

Alex stepped out of the elevator, greeted Johnnie, and guided her bike toward the door. She was certain that the shooter who she had killed was hired by Comacho Lopez. She was trying to figure out how to prove it. She needed to get something that linked the shooter to him. She had to find some physical evidence. There might be a phone conversation and there might be traceable cash. She was going to see if Johnnie could use his hacking skills to give her the edge. The assassin had failed but he had made the situation very personal. As personal as if he had tried to sleep with her instead of just kill her. She was in a vengeful mood.

The ride to the station was silent. She was trying to think how she was going to get some sort of evidence to connect the shooter to Comacho.

She changed into her work outfit, got a cup of coffee, and walked toward her desk. She saw that Bill and Trevor were at their desks and there was a half of bear claw on her desk and the other half on Trey's desk.

She picked it up, took a bite, and thanked whoever was so kind to as to get her started.

Trey walked in and said hello and asked when he was going to be able to shoot a local drug dealer.

Trevor shook his head and asked what Trey had eaten for breakfast.

Trey just shook his head and said that at this moment he wanted his sniper rifle and a target to take out.

He asked Alex how Matt was doing.

Alex said that he was feeling fine when she left him late the past night. He said that the team should nail whoever had set up an assassin to kill her.

Johnnie took a sip of his coffee and asked how he could help nail the perp to the wall.

Alex said she needed to find the link between Camacho and the shooter. They had the identity of the shooter, but they had yet to find out how he had gotten to Cincinnati. Where he was staying. How he got paid. Where he had obtained his weapon. How he had known where she lived.

Johnnie opened his computer and began typing. A few moments later he said he had the rental car information for a John Smith for a grey sedan, and he had a license plate number. He asked if a car had been found that may have been driven by the assassin.

Bill dialed the dispatcher and asked which units had processed the shooting scene. A few moments later he was talking to someone that had been at the scene. He asked if they had found a car and gave him the license plate number.

He got off the phone and said that a unit was going to drive through the parking garage and all the close-by parking lots to see if they could find the car. They would call if they found the car.

Alex asked if Johnnie had the time when the shooter had landed in Cincinnati.

Johnnie worked for a few more minutes and said that he thought it would have been a red eye special from LA that had landed at five thirty Sunday morning. The car rental was at seven.

Alex nodded and asked if there was any way he could get into the computer system of the bar that Camacho used as his headquarters.

Johnnie said that maybe he could walk past the bar and find out if there was a local area network inside. If there was, he could get the name and then he would be able to hack in.

He said that he would go home and get into his bum's uniform and then take a walk past the bar. If he got the hubs name, he would cross the street and put out his hat and hack in.

Bill said that he and Trevor would follow about a block behind him and then turn around when he crossed the street, and they would walk back toward the police station.

Johnnie nodded and a said that once he was in, he would see if he could link into the bar's hub or hubs to the cloud so he could access them remotely.

Alex then asked what had happened to the weapon that the shooter had used. She made a call and found out it was in the evidence holding area. It had been processed and the fingerprints entered into the database.

Alex asked if the rifle's owner could be identified.

She was told that there were no noticeable serial numbers. She asked for the weapon to be sent to the lab to see if they could get a serial number from it.

Johnnie ran the fingerprints that had been on the weapon and came up with the actual name of the shooter. He was a freelance assassin that worked for anyone willing to pay his fees and expenses. He was formally linked to the Reds gang in LA.

The call came in that the car had been found in a parking lot two blocks from the location where the shooting had taken place.

Alex asked that the car be isolated, and she would be over immediately to field process it. She led the way out to her car and she and Trey went to the parking lot where the rental was located. She asked one of the policemen to unlock the car.

The front and back seats were empty. She popped the trunk and found what she had been looking for.

She unzipped a black sports bag and found it full of money. There was a carrying case for a rifle and extra ammunition. She bagged the sports bag in a large evidence bag and then told the officers to have the car towed to the evidence parking area and have it processed. She told them that it should not be torn up but only processed for fingerprints.

She then drove back to the station and took the evidence bags into the main work area.

Johnnie knew immediately what the sports bag held and what Alex was going to ask him to do. He walked toward their favorite huddle room and set up his computer.

Alex put the rifle holder on her desk and asked Bill to have it processed for fingerprints.

She carried the sports bag with the money to the huddle room. She opened the bag and counted the bundles of banded bills as she laid them out on the table. There were fifty bundles. She counted one bundle and found out that each bundle was two thousand dollars and made up of one-hundred-dollar bills.

She asked Johnnie if he would be able to trace the bills.

Johnnie said that they looked new and fresh and that he should be able to find the bank that had last processed the bills. He took one number and began to check which bank might have issued it.

A few moments later he said he had the bank. He then spent the next few moments poking around the bank's database and found a series of bill numbers that were withdrawn at the same time and the number on the one bill he had started with.

Alex and Trey had been entering the numbers of bills into their shared database so that Johnnie could process them.

He commented that there had to be another bank because the amount withdrawn from the one, he was in was not enough to cover the number of bills on the table.

Johnnie verified that all the bills in the bundle where his first bill had come from were withdrawn at one time.

He then began to run the rest of the numbers. He found three additional local banks.

He also found out that the withdrawal happened on different days of the week and always at some level that would not draw attention because the amount was always below five thousand.

Alex asked if he could hack into the bar's computer and see if there was any accounting information that might link the money withdrawn or any other transaction with the banks. She commented that if there was money to withdraw then there must be money deposited.

She figured that there might also be links to other banks.

She let Johnnie know that once they had the accounts directly controlled by Camacho, she wanted the money to be transferred to a holding account that he had no access to, and she wanted his accounts to look normal but have only a couple of hundred dollars in them.

Johnnie asked what she would do with the money.

She said that she planned to funnel it to various charities.

He laughed and said that she was becoming the Cincinnati Robinhood.

She nodded and replied, "take from the rich crook and give to the poor and needy."

Bill came into the huddle room and said that they had been able to pull the serial number off the rifle and had the name of the last registered owner.

Alex asked Bill to talk to that owner and find out what he knew about the rifle and if he had sold it, she wanted to know who it had been sold to.

She asked about the fingerprints on the carrying case and on any of the ammo.

Bill said that they were being processed and would all end up in the database file that she had set up. There were fingerprints of someone other than the shooter, but they would have to be run to see if they were in the database.

Johnnie looked up from his computer and said he would set up a fingerprint to visual search as soon as he was done with transferring the money into Alex's charity Robin Hood account. He commented that he had the local banks and three offshore banks where Camacho had accounts. He had left only one hundred dollars in each of the local banks, and he was going to zero out the offshore banks so that there would be a very limited amount Camacho could draw on.

Alex suggested that they call it a day and that she and Johnnie would work together at his place.

She commented that she wanted to shut down the Red Bandana operation in the next day or two, but she wanted to have bullet proof evidence against Camacho and as many of his distributors as possible. She looked over at Trevor and asked if he was ready for a dirty work assignment the next day.

Trevor smiled and said he would take the dirty work if she took on the shooting work.

Alex shook her head and said that she was letting Trey take the lead because she wanted to shoot first and then ask questions afterwards.

Bill spoke up and reminded her that Trey had been asking to shoot someone so he was not sure anyone at the bar that pulled a weapon would survive.

Alex said that she was going to update the Chief, and that everyone else should go home.

Alex knocked on the Chief's door and went in when she heard him say, "Come in."

The Chief asked if she had what she needed to close the case.

Alex nodded and said that by the following afternoon she planned to shut down the Red Bandana operation. She said she would want several backup units at the bar and several out at the Meth lab. She added that she and Trey would take the bar and Bill and Trevor would take the meth lab.

The Chief said that he would arrange for the backup units to be ready to move at her command. He said that he wanted to be with Bill and Trevor. He felt that they might face an illogical response at the lab. He smiled and said that he trusted that she would give Comacho a chance to be arrested.

She nodded and said that she would, but she added that if he pulled his weapon he wouldn't live for long because both Trey and she were in a very angry mood.

The Chief nodded and said that in either case he would have her back. He wanted to make sure everyone practiced safety first.

Alex thanked him and said it was time for her to go to her apartment and then see how Matt was doing.

Johnnie talked constantly as the two of them rode their bikes to the apartment. As they got to the elevator, he watched Alex get on and then asked how Matt was doing.

Alex replied that after she showered and cleaned up, she was going to the hospital to find out.

She got to her apartment and opened the door and almost dropped her bike when she saw Matt sitting in the recliner.

Matt smiled and said that he had convinced the Dr. who he knew quite well that his team would escort him to his apartment where he would rest and relax much better than at the hospital.

Alex put her bike on the porch and then came over and gave him a kiss. She asked if there was anything special, he wanted for dinner.

He smiled and said he wanted the Spaghetti Alfredo that he had ordered and then he wanted a hot cup of tea, a scoop of vanilla over some fresh strawberries and a hot oatmeal cookie.

Alex gave a small laugh and said he could have it all. She would go down and pick up the Alfredo when it was delivered. She asked if it was alright to invite Johnnie up because she wanted him to do some work that evening.

Matt replied that it was OK with him because he was going to sit and relax.

He added that she and Johnnie could work as long as they wanted.

10 Laying Low

The news about the shooting and the fact that his assassin was dead had Camacho focused on getting out of town. He packed his most important belongings into his Mercedes. He would leave everything else alone. He figured he could lay low for a time and then return when the heat was off.

Everything seemed to be going fine. He went into his back office to download all his files onto a thumb drive and then he was going to factory reset the computer so it would be clean. He had just withdrawn twenty thousand dollars from his accounts in order to pay the assassin and he wanted to see if he could withdraw some from another account so that he would be able to use cash instead of his credit card. When he got into his account, he was shocked to find only one hundred dollars in the account. He knew it should have had close to one hundred thousand dollars in it. Whenever an account reached one hundred thousand dollars, he would transfer the money to one of his offshore accounts. He had not transferred any money! He wondered who on his team knew about the accounts. He could not think of anyone.

In the office safe he had the money that had come in the previous day, so he had almost twenty thousand dollars, and he had the ten thousand that would have been the payment for a successful hit. He opened the safe and put the money in one of his gym bags.

He factory reset his computer.

He then decided to contact his police informant to see if he could find out what was going on with the investigation into the shooting and decided it was time to leave.

His informant let him know that his Meth lab had been located and that it would be raided the following afternoon, and the bar would also be raided. His contact said that the rifle that the shooter had used was being processed and the fingerprints on the rifle and the rifle carrying case were being processed.

Camacho knew that he had not touched either, so he knew he was in the clear, but he knew that one set of fingerprints would belong to one of his lieutenants that had brought the case in and had handed it to his assassin. He thought about the rifle and knew that the serial numbers had been filed off but figured that some new sophisticated technique might pull the numbers out. That probably meant the same lieutenant whose fingerprints were on the carrying case would get connected to the purchase of the rifle at the flea market.

It was time to leave. He would clear out and figure out how and where he might start over.

Once he got to his car he looked nervously around to see if he was being watched.

He was now spooked. He wanted to go to each of his local banks to check about his accounts but if he did, he would show up on surveillance cameras. He knew that he needed to get out of town.

But driving his car on the highway was an invitation to be stopped by the highway patrol. He decided to go to his trustworthy supplier of cheap cars. This supplier was a used car lot owner that also helped distribute drugs.

He would leave his car at the lot and get a good working used car and use a temporary plate. He would pick up the Mercedes at a later date.

He had been pondering where he might go. He did not want to go to any major city where he might be made by some other drug pusher. He was not so worried about the cops because they hardly communicated within their own departments let alone with other jurisdictions.

He decided to go to a bed and breakfast in the New York State, Finger Lakes area where he had enjoyed fishing a few years ago. He could do some golfing, fishing, and hiking. He figured that by moving from one finger lake to another he could stay hidden for a substantial amount of time.

He could also get money transferred from one of the offshore accounts to a local bank so he would not have to worry about running short.

He was lucky that it was off season at the Finger Lakes. He was able to book a week at the first bed and breakfast he called. The next four went just like the first. He said that he would pay cash when he arrived and got agreement at all four.

He took his time and arrived at the first B&B in the late afternoon. He got the pick of the rooms and chose one on the top floor with a view of the lake. He asked about going fishing and was told that the B&B had a boat at the public pier, and they had the fishing tackle with the boat. It had a small electric motor that would need to be unplugged from the pier's electrical outlet. The bait had to be purchased from the bait store at the head of the pier.

Comacho figured he would do some fishing the next day.

He got the address of a local bank and planned to go there and set himself up before doing any fishing.

He sat outside on the slope of the lush green lawn and enjoyed the sunset as it went down on the other side of the lake. He was now more relaxed and felt that he would be able to survive this bump in what had otherwise been a good road.

The next morning, he drove to the local bank. He was surprised at the diminutive feel of the entrance area, but he was quickly greeted and then ushered into a private room when he said he wanted to set up an account.

He had a fake passport, the account number, and the bank routing number for the offshore account he was planning to get the money. He asked to have four thousand dollars transferred into the account he was setting up.

After setting up the account, the bank manager said that she was ready to transfer the money in. He gave her the account and routing number. After a few moments she looked at him and said that the message from the bank stated that the account had been closed the previous day.

Comacho had to control his facial features. He had no clue how the account could have been closed. He smiled, apologized, and said that his accountant must not have had time to notify him about having closed it.

He looked in his walled and pulled out a card that had the account and routing number for another bank.

The bank manager put the transfer request in and a few moments later shook her head and said that she got the same response as the first bank.

He was now in a state of alarm.

He pulled out another card and gave her the numbers.

The result was the same.

He was now in total shock. He found it hard not to scream.

He asked how much he needed to deposit to open the account.

The manager said that one dollar would open the account, but it would not allow any withdrawal of monies.

He opened his wallet and took out four fifty-dollar bills and put it on the desk. He said he would deposit more in the next couple days as soon as he talked to his accountant.

He shook his head and said that he was going to give his accountant a call and read him the riot act for not letting him know what was going on.

He was in a daze as he walked out of the bank and got into his car and drove away. He drove to the fishing pier, bought some bait, a beer, sandwich, and a cap with the words, "Finger Lakes" over the blue finger lake background.

Camacho went through putting the bait on the hook, casting, and slowly reeling in the line as he sat staring in a mental haze. The three banks had close to seventy-five million dollars each that was his personal nest egg. He kept the operating money in his office safe and was constantly paying out for more drugs and paying each of his distributors with that money. That money flowed smoothly and periodically he could skim some off and put it in his offshore accounts.

He had no open accountants. He had never given any of the offshore information to anyone in his operation. He had always thought that the offshore banks were ultra-safe. He wondered how someone could have zeroed out the accounts.

He looked around and when he knew he was the only one within ear shot he let out a blood curling scream. He wanted to put somebody into a barrel of lye.

Johnnie let Alex know that he had found Camacho's home address and car registration and license number for his Mercedes.

As soon as she had the home address, she asked the Chief to dispatch two units to watch the house and make sure no one left while she was at the bar.

She reminded the Chief about everyone having their protective gear on.

He chuckled and said that Trevor had reminded him to be wearing his Kevlar.

She then asked if Johnnie wanted to have a quick lunch before she had the raids begin.

He shook his head and said that he was running the fingerprints on the rifle carrying case and on the barrel of the rifle. He figured knowing the identity of this person might be useful before the raid.

Alex nodded and said she would have his favorite pizza delivered. She took the information on the Mercedes and put out an APB while she waited for the pizza delivery.

Trey commented that if Comacho had left town he doubted he would drive his personal car.

Alex looked over to Johnnie who was sitting and relaxing. She asked if he had a hit on the search.

Johnnie shook his head and added that he had launched an automated search application that allowed him to relax.

Alex smiled and said that he continued to surprise her. She sat down and tried to relax.

The pizza arrived and as soon as they each had taken a bite the search engine rang a bell.

Johnnie flashed the picture and name of the person that was a match to the fingerprints. He sent the picture to the team.

Alex thanked Johnnie and said that as soon as they were done with lunch, she would trigger the raids.

After lunch, Alex called the Chief and let him know that he should let all units know to it was time for the raids.

He said that he, Bill, and Trevor were in position, but he had arranged for the two units that had led several previous Meth lab raids to take the lead. They had double respirators and goggles and had issued the three of them sets that they were to wear. They had suggested that we stake the exterior in case any of the folks inside jumped out of windows. They had also given each of them thin rubber gloves to wear. He said that he was glad he had let them take the lead.

Alex replied that she was glad that he had put them in charge and wished them luck.

Trey had been listening and commented that he was glad they had taken on the bar.

Alex led the way out of the station and walked toward the bar. She saw the two units parked ahead of them and gave them a call and let them know she was approaching on foot.

The four got out and greeted her.

She verified that they had their armor and head gear with them. She asked that two of them take the rear entrance to the bar and two the front of the bar.

She let them know that she and Trevor would go in. If they heard any shooting, they were to enter with guns drawn ready to fire. She did not want them to shoot her or Trey by mistake.

One of the younger policemen smiled and said that they would make sure not to since he had heard that every person that had taken a shot at her was dead.

Alex smiled and said the dead ones all had hit her or had made the mistake of trying to.

She then pointed to the bar and said they should get into position.

She led the way to the front door and stepped in and to the right as Trevor stepped in behind her and stepped to the left.

The several screens were playing scenes of various sports games but were silent. The lights were bright, and the walls were decorated with pictures of a variety of famous baseball and football players.

She shouted out that it was the police, and no one should move except to put their hands in the air.

The bar tender put his hands up as did the two guys sitting in one of the booths.

Alex watched as the person at the bar reached into his jacket and began to turn his left side toward Trey and her. She shot him in his right arm triceps muscle.

He screamed out that she had shot him in the back.

Alex said that it was the back of his arm, and he was lucky to be alive.

The four officers rushed in, and hand cuffed the other three as Alex and Trey handled the person she had shot.

She addressed the person she had shot by his name and said that he was under arrest as an accomplice to the attempted assassination of a police officer.

Trey read him his Miranda rights as he handcuffed his left arm to the bar foot rail. He stepped away as the EMT team entered with some additional police.

Eli, the person that had been shot said he had nothing to do with the shooting.

Alex told him to save his breath and tell his story to the judge.

She asked one of the older officers who she could leave in charge to handle the situation and after making sure that the person she had arrested was taken care of she said that she was going to leave the scene because she was going to a raid at another site.

She said that the bullet she had fired had hit the bar and skip over and had hit one of the bottles of liquor on the other side somewhere near the last three bottles.

She put her weapon in an evidence bag and handed it to him.

He asked what she wanted to do with the other three.

She told him to check them out and if they had any tickets to arrest them and hold them for as long as was legal.

The officer said he had the crime scene under control and would get the details about the raid of the bar from her when she was back from the other raid.

Alex led the way out and she and Trey walked back to where her car was parked. She asked Trey to drive.

The call she was expecting came in. It was Trevor calling.

Trevor said that Bill had shot some crazy guy wearing double filter breathers and goggles that had jumped out the window shooting at them and yes, the guy was dead.

He said that the people inside were all being escorted out and placed on the ground in the fire station parking lot. He said that the three of them were done and ready to leave.

Alex gave him the address where she and Trey were going and asked if the three of them could join her.

She heard the Chief reply that they were on the way and that she should wait for them and that he had already been informed that she was weaponless.

Alex chuckled and said that she had borrowed Matt's weapon that he had gladly loaned her.

Trey spoke up loudly that it was his turn to do the shooting.

They waited for the Chief and as soon as everyone was ready, Alex, Trey, and the Chief took the front, Bill and Trevor had the back and the four other officers had the two sides of the house.

Trey took the lead and after the house had been cleared and when it was certain that no one was in the house Alex asked that they search the place to see if they could figure out where Camacho might have gone.

Bill said he knew the routine and began looking for picture albums.

Alex got a call from Johnnie who let her know that he was at the bar and was examining the two computers that were part of the internal network. He let her know that the one in the back office had been factory reset but he had located that back up that was always done by the reset routine, and he had downloaded that to his computer. He said that he would soon have all the information about the operation. He chuckled and said that he had done everything in a legal and above way and all his information could be used in court.

Alex told him that he had just earned a special lunch and a tray of cookies.

Johnnie laughed and said that he loved working with her, but she should stop trying to fatten him up.

Trevor spoke up and said he thought he had where Camacho might have gone. He held up a picture that had Camacho holding up a pole with a large fish still on the line and he had the middle finger of his right hand prominently displayed. He said the back of the picture was dated a few years ago and the words "caught on a fly on the middle Finger Lake."

Alex asked Johnnie if he had heard what Trevor had just said.

Johnnie replied that he had, and he was on it. He said he would search the hotels and B&Bs to see if they had any recent single men check in.

Alex suggested that they repeat their work session in her apartment. She would check with Matt about what he wanted for dinner and get that set up. She suggested a seven PM start.

11 Finger Lakes

Rose-Anne was shocked when she heard that Matt had been shot as he saved Alex from getting assassinated. She had been sure that this request for help would not be a threat to either of them. She was about to apologize when Alex told her not to say it.

Alex had called her mother to let her know about the attempted assassination and that the assassin was dead and she was on the trail of the person who she thought had hired him. She assured her mother that both Matt and her would be fine.

Rose-Anne suggested that the two of them come up and relax and go fishing.

Alex said that she would talk it over with Matt and that she would let her know later about going fishing.

That had been a few days ago.

Since then, the raids had taken place, and she was certain that it was only a matter of time before she would have Camacho under arrest.

She and Johnnie set themselves up to work at her kitchen table. They first feasted on some ribs that Matt had ordered in. Johnnie thanked Matt for picking one of his favorite meals and he hoped he would be able to stay awake long enough to figure out where in the Finger Lake area Camacho was staying.

Matt laughed and said he had ordered the ribs because he planned to fall asleep while they worked into the night.

Alex sat on the recliner arm as she ate one of the ribs and then gave Matt a barbecue sauce kiss and thanked him for being so gracious.

Matt laughed and licked his lips and said it was the sweetest kiss that he had gotten from her in a long time.

She suggested that while Johnnie was searching for the needle in the haystack in the Finger Lakes, she would make a batch of cookies and then serve them with vanilla ice cream topped with fresh strawberries and some whipped yogurt.

Johnnie said that he thought she had a great idea. He focused on linking first with the B&Bs and getting into their computer hubs to get to their guest registers. He got the addresses of all he B&Bs on the central Finger Lake.

He hoped that Comacho would return to the place in the picture. That would greatly shorten the search. He put his automated hacking software to work and then sat back and picked on the remains of the dinner.

Alex asked how he was approaching the search and after listening to Johnnie's explanation said that his approach made a lot of sense.

She had made cookies so many times that she could do it blindfolded. As she took out the tray of oatmeal raisin cookies from the oven, Johnnie exclaimed that he thought he might have where Comacho was staying. The reservation had been called in about the time Comacho would have been leaving Cincinnati. The transaction was to have been in cash.

Johnnie commented that now it would take good old fashioned shoe leather to verify that it was actually Camacho.

Alex smiled and asked Matt if he wanted to come along to the Finger Lakes.

She took out three bowls and scooped out some vanilla ice cream, added a half a dozen fresh strawberries to each bowl and then put on a scoop of yogurt and topped off with honey. She put a spoon in each bowl and passed them out.

She sat down facing Matt and asked if he felt good enough to ride to the Finger Lakes. They could rent a room and relax there for several days.

Johnnie said that he could drive Matt up after she and Trey captured Camacho.

Alex shook her head and said that she planned to bring Camacho back to Cincinnati and then return afterwards with Matt if the place met her expectations.

Matt said that a stay in the Finger Lake area would be a great way to use his recovery time.

Alex looked at the time and decided it was still early enough to let Trey know about their drive to the Finger Lakes area. She asked Johnnie how far it was to the middle lake.

Johnnie said that the middle lake and the B&B were about five hundred miles by car.

Alex thought for a minute and then called Trey and let him know about the drive to the Finger Lakes and that he should come prepared to spend the night. They would drive up, arrest Camacho, and then drive back the next day.

After hanging up with Trey she called the Chief to update him. She verified that she would be able to use the department's prisoner transport van. She also asked him to contact the sheriff of Aurora, New York and give him a heads-up about the situation and her intentions of bringing Camacho back to Cincinnati.

The Chief complimented her on finding Camacho and said she could have the van, and he would contact the sheriff.

Alex thanked him and said she would see him in the morning before leaving.

She then asked Johnnie what else they should be doing before she got up there.

Johnnie said that he was not sure that he could think of anything else.

He smiled and said that he would make sure that Matt got a good lunch and dinner the next day.

Alex nodded and said that she felt much better about the fact that Matt would have someone to look after him.

Matt said that if it weren't for the bandages and the sling he would go for a bike ride, but he said that he preferred to eat out for lunch and dinner because it would give him a chance to do some walking.

Johnnie nodded and said he would be glad to walk with him to make sure that if he fell, he would have someone to pick him up.

Matt laughed and said he had been shot in the shoulder, and his legs were just fine.

Alex asked Matt about the need to change the bandages.

Matt said that his team was dropping by the next day in the afternoon to redo the bandages and reduce their size. He was hoping for a big band aid on each side of the wound if it was not oozing. He figured he would have to keep using the arm sling for a couple of more days.

Johnnie cleared the table, closed his laptop, and said that he was going back to his apartment.

Alex said that she would ride in on her own and leave her bike at the station.

Johnnie shook his head and said that he would ride in with her and then she could bring him and the two bikes back to the apartment, get her suitcase and then go on to the Finger Lakes with Trey.

Alex said that was a great plan. She would meet him at the elevators in the morning.

The next morning, she walked into the office to find Bill and Trevor sitting with suitcases by their desk. She asked where they were going.

Trevor handed her half of a bear claw and said that he understood that she was sponsoring an overnight at the Finger Lakes and he and Bill did not want to miss out.

Alex smiled and asked if the Chief had called them.

Bill nodded and said that the Chief had more or less ordered them to go with her. He had said that Comacho might be very angry at being taken down and might get violent.

Alex took a bite of her Bear Claw, a sip of her coffee and walked to the Chief's office and knocked on the door.

The Chief called out for her to come in.

Alex thanked him for inviting Bill and Trevor but asked if he thought it was necessary.

The Chief replied that the last time he had let her, and Trey go alone on a drug case Trey had ended up near death and she had killed four gangsters.

She again thanked him and said she would keep him linked in.

She left and as she stepped out, she saw that Trey had arrived and was eating his half of the bear claw and joking with Johnnie.

She came over and asked who wanted to drive first.

Trevor said he would be glad to.

She pointed to the exit and said that it was time to get going.

They stopped to drop Johnnie off.

She took her bike up to her apartment and got her suitcase.

Matt wished her a good trip and then she left.

She put her suitcase in with the other three and then got into the seat behind Trevor.

After each hour they changed drivers, they stopped for a sit-down lunch and then continued. They stopped at a family restaurant for dinner.

Alex called ahead and made reservations at a B&B near where Camacho was staying. She planned to arrest him the following morning and then drive back to Cincinnati.

She let everyone know that she wanted to be at the B&B where Camacho was staying when he came down for breakfast. So, they would need to be out at his B&B at about five thirty.

The next morning the four of them drove the short distance to the B&B.

Alex asked Bill and Trevor to stake out the back of the house and Trey should take the front. She was going in to speak to whomever was preparing breakfast.

She walked in and made her way to the kitchen where she introduced herself, showed her badge and asked if she had a guest name Comacho.

The proprietress said she had only one guest at the moment, but his name was Hank.

Alex pulled out Camacho's picture and showed it to her.

Yes, that's Hank was the immediate response.

Alex asked if he had come down for breakfast yet.

"He went out early to do some fishing," was the reply. She went on to say that he asked her to hold his breakfast and he might bring in a fish for lunch.

Alex asked her if she could see Hank's room. When she looked in through the open door of the room, she commented that it had a great view of the lake. She walked to the window, and she could see Camacho fishing.

She looked around and saw a duffel bag tucked under the edge of the bed. She wanted to look inside but did not have a search warrant, so she walked out of the room.

She thanked the proprietress and said that she would wait for Hank out by the pier.

She walked out the front and asked Trey to get Bill and Trevor. She walked to the corner of the house and watched as Camacho caught a nice large bass.

She pointed out where Camacho was sitting in his boat then asked Bill and Travis to move the police van out of sight and then come back.

Alex moved behind a large old oak with limbs spread out as if to shield those standing below them. She had Trey stand behind a similar tree on the other side of the dock.

Bill and Trevor had returned and were standing at the corner of the house.

Trevor waved at her and held up his gun.

Camacho figured that one large fish was all he needed for lunch, so he took the boat in, brought it along the pier, and tied it off. He got all the stuff out of the boat and plug the battery in. He held the bass about the size of his forearm with a finger in its gills and carried the rest of his gear with his right arm.

When he got to the end of the pier and as he passed the bait shop and was approaching the tree that Alex was standing behind, she stepped out and declared that he was under arrest and should put everything down and raise his hands in the air.

Camacho dropped everything and drew his gun and got one shot off.

Alex had anticipated the reaction and had stepped to the right as she pulled her weapon and shot him three times.

Three other shots rang out at almost the same time.

Camacho was surprised at the speed of her actions, but he never got to think about anything else because his world went black. It took his body a moment to realize it was dead and fall to the ground.

Alex walked over to his body and moved his gun aside with her toe.

The proprietress came out the back door where Bill stopped her.

She looked at him and said that the Black detective seemed to be such a sweet person.

Bill replied that she was until someone shot at her then she was deadlier than a rattlesnake with babies to defend.

Alex called the Chief and informed him of what had happened and asked him to call the local sheriff and inform him about the situation and that she needed a legal search warrant to go through Camacho's room and personal stuff.

She suggested that the Chief arrange to have Comacho's body sent back to Cincinnati so the coroner could do his job. She asked if the lot of them would need to leave their weapons as part of the evidence. She let him know that if they got done in time they would drive back to Cincinnati.

She then walked back to where Bill was standing with the proprietress and apologized for them having had to shoot Hank, but he had shot at her first and they had all responded.

The proprietress asked what Hank was wanted for.

Alex explained that Hank was a drug dealer known as Camacho. He had hired and assassin to kill an officer of the law. He also operated a drug production operation that had been shut down.

The proprietress shook her head and said that he had seemed to be a nice person. He had talked about setting himself up to live in the area and had even asked about where he could find a trustworthy bank.

Alex asked about what bank that might be. Once she got the name, she sent it to Johnnie and said that she would deposit any money found in the bag that Camacho had in his room into that account and then later Johnnie could transfer it to the Robin Hood account and zero out the one at the at the Finger Lake bank.

Bill let the proprietress know that the sheriff was coming with a search warrant so they could legally search the room that Comacho had rented.

He asked if she would serve them lunch. He assured her that they would pay whatever she decided to charge them.

When Alex heard him making the request she walked over to where the fish was still flopping and picked it up and carried it to where the proprietress was standing and said that a fish for lunch would be great.

The proprietress took the fish and said she would put it in the oven with some small potatoes and cut carrots around it and bake it.

Alex asked if a room with a good view was available for the rest of the week.

The proprietress laughed and said that one had just come open.

Alex said she would take it for at least five days.

12 Middle Finger…Lake

*A*lex's return to Cincinnati was anticlimactic.

The Chief congratulated her and asked what she had planned. She let him know that she was taking vacation and returning to the Finger Lakes with Matt to do some fishing and just relax. She let him know that she would drop off her official case report in the morning.

The Chief suggested that she send it in with Johnnie and save herself a trip.

Later that day, she, and Matt agreed that they would take their time driving to the Lake. They planned on one stop at about the halfway point on the way up. They both had enough vacation, and they had decided to spend a full seven days on the Lake.

She called her mother and let her know that she was going to vacation and fish in the Middle Finger Lake.

He Mother joked about getting the middle finger treatment.

Alex laughed and replied that was not the case, but she and Matt had decided to fish in a new lake.

Alex stayed just at the speed limit, which was uncharacteristic for her. She usually drove a few miles over the limit but for this trip she had decided to relax and that to her meant staying at the speed limit when driving.

During the halfway stop, the two of them ordered room service and watched a movie with a happy story.

When they arrived at the B&B, Evon, the proprietress, greeted them and then said that she needed to apologize but she had advertised that she was hosting a world-famous detective from Cincinnati known as "Cincinnati's Black Annie Oakley" and the B&B was fully booked. She said that she had six guests from Cincinnati and several from around Ohio.

Alex laughed and asked if she could reserve the fishing boat for each morning so she and Matt could get their fishing in.

Evon said that she had arranged to have enough boats for everyone that wanted to go out would have their own boat. She said that this surge was going to keep her business afloat for another year. She asked if what she had done was OK with Alex.

Alex said that it was not and that it would cost Evon a free dinner with the fish she and Matt would bring in.

Evon smiled and said that she would even clean the fish and prepare it any way that Alex wanted.

Alex asked about Mom-and-Pop restaurants that might offer great meals.

Evon said she would make a list of the places that were within walking distance and those that might be a drive but worth it.

Two days into the vacation, Alex got a call from the Chief. He let her know that all of those arrested had court dates during the coming few days. He let her know that he and the rest of the team would cover the arraignments and she did not need to be there. He wondered about the fact that Camacho' business showed a zero balance in the one bank account that was still open.

Alex replied that as one of his last acts Camacho had opened a charity called, "Open Hands to all Needing Help." He had given it close to three hundred million dollars.

The Chief laughed and said that he was sorry that Camacho was no longer around to get the praise he deserved for being so kind and generous.

Alex replied in a serious tone that she had been deeply depressed after she realized that the team had shot and killed such a nice guy.

The Chief told her to get over it and to enjoy the fishing and he would see her when she got back.

The fishing was good and every day the two of them would bring several fish in and give them to Evon.

Evon asked if she could prepare the fish and serve them to her guests.

Alex said that she could do whatever she wanted with the fish. She added that they had eaten all the fish that they had wanted to. She added that she and Matt were planning to enjoy the T-bone that she had on her menu for that evening.

During the week Alex was approached numerous times by the guests and asked for her autograph.

Matt commented that he felt like he was out with a superstar.

She was pleased that Matt had healed well and no longer needed to wear his sling. She helped him rebandage the bullet wound and was pleased that it had only left a small entrance scar and a larger but clean exit scar.

On their last day both of them caught their limit. Alex picked out five of the largest fish and she and Matt cleaned them and put them in a cooler in the ice. She planned to give one to each of the team.

Evon thanked them for their stay and let Alex know that the ads she had placed in several of the B&B magazines and the ones online were all generating additional bookings. She invited both of them back whenever they wanted to enjoy some more fishing.

Alex thanked her and wished her well.

She and Matt left after breakfast and did the drive back in one day. This time Matt insisted that they share the driving.

Alex stopped by Johnnie's apartment and gave him his fish and asked how things had been going.

Johnnie replied that it had been going slow, but he thought he might have a case that she should look into.

Alex put up her hand and told him to enjoy the fish, but she did not want to hear about a potential case because she still had a mark on her chest where she had been shot on the last special case, he had brought up.

Johnnie thanked her for the fish and then reminded her that the kids that she had saved now called her Aunt Alex.

Alex gave Johnnie a hug, said goodnight and then left.

Matt had waited at the elevator and the two rode up together and walked down to their apartment.

Matt let her know that while she was talking to Johnnie, he had gotten a call to verify that he would be at the curb a five in the morning to be picked up.

Alex nodded and said that shortly after that she would be riding in to work with Johnnie.

The following morning Johnnie was at the elevator. He was eager to let Alex know about a potential case that he had run across by accident. He figured she would be the one that would solve such a mystery.

Alex knew immediately that she was going to be listening to Johnnie about his potential case. She told him that she did not want to hear a thing about a new case until everything connected with the current case was complete.

She added that her goal for that day was to hand out the fish that were in the cooler she was strapping to her bike.

Johnnie smiled and replied that she was missing out on a really interesting twist to a case that had gone unsolved for many years and that he was sure she would get hooked as soon as she heard the details of the case.

Alex put on her helmet and said that it would be at least a week before she would be willing to hear what he wanted to tell her.

The End of the Vanishing

The Shadow Fighter

1 Enforcer

*A*driano had researched his new home and learned that Chicago was the third largest city in the US. He was taken by its impressive architecture, and vibrant music history. He experienced firsthand why it was known as the Windy City. He walked the entire waterfront and had a faceoff with Lake Michigan and its cold wind coming directly at him.

He knew that it was equally famous for the Mafia families involved in the distribution of booze and drugs. Mafia families that had often been decimated by the violent battles that transpired. The most famous was the St. Valentines Day massacre.

Gennaro Visentino, his predecessor and his mafia leadership team met their demise in a similar way as the 1929 St. Valentine's Day massacre.

He was sent from Itali to take control of what remained of the Mafia organization.

He had moved the Mafia headquarters to another location farther south but still along the shore of Lake Michigan. The location he selected reminded him of the view along Marsala's Contra da Spagnola and his favorite fishing spot on the Sicilian coast where he had fished in his younger days.

He liked to walk along the lake shore and feel the cool breeze as it blew through his dark black hair, and he had found a place where he could cast his line and catch fish. He recalled and preferred the warmer air, the seaweed, and fish odor of the waters of the salty Tyrrhenian Sea and the fish he caught there. He had only been in Chicago for a few months and was still trying to get use to a much faster and hectic pace of living. His days back in Italy now seemed a luxury as compared to navigating the Chicago competitive drug market. He was taking an aggressive approach and soon hoped to have his organization back to its previous level of drug distribution.

He had reached back to his many loyal Sicilian associates and brought them to Chicago. In a way the ill-fated demise of his predecessor and his entire leadership team had opened the organization at the higher levels, and he was able to establish his loyal followers into those top ranks. This at least provided him a buffer from the struggle the organization faced out in the intense and competitive drug distribution level.

He had moved carefully and slowly to reestablish the Chicago family. It had now been two years since that massacre that was blamed on a black female detective out of Cincinnati. It was hard for him to envision a single person having been able to eliminate the entire Chicago family. He personally believed that the main Mexican drug cartel that competed with his organization had a hand in the massacre, but he did not desire to start a war with them, so he was careful as he pushed against them while he slowly regained control of the protection and drug distribution market that the family had previously controlled.

The involvement of a lowly Cincinnati detective was a matter that personally irritated him, and he felt the need to take some sort of retribution action. He sent one of his trusted men to spend time in Cincinnati to observe and get information on this detective.

For six months the reports coming to him indicated that she was careful, was always active in the community and did not seem to be worried about her exposure. She seemed to be just a normal detective that had been very successful.

As he reviewed the information about the cases that she had resolved he came to believe that she was more lucky than smart. He pondered what he should do. His low opinion of her led him to hire and send a sniper to eliminate her. He would have liked to bring her to Chicago to have her go swimming face down in one of the rivers in the city.

He reached back to Sicily to recruit Lorenzo who was considered one of the best assassins in the business. This was a person that he felt would quickly deal with the assassination in and in and out manner. When Lorenzo arrived, he greeted him, and they agreed on the price. After arranging for him to be provided with a snipers rifle of the design that Lorenzo requested, they agreed that once the assignment was over, a return flight to Sicily out of Cleveland would be paid for.

He knew that it would only be a matter of time until he would get a success report from Lorenzo which then would be followed by a news report on the sad loss of a such a beloved detective in Cincinnati. Not sad for him. He would go out and celebrate the removal of a nuisance.

Alex, that nuisance, had no idea that she had once again become the focus of someone that she had no idea that in some way felt compelled to punish her.

She was busy planning an upcoming fund-raising event with Annie, who she had rescued from fifteen years of chained captivity in the Pennsylvania forest. She was very happy that Annie had made what seemed to be a full recovery from that trauma and now with her two daughters had moved to Maui to live with the person that Annie had met, fallen in love with and whom she called her soulmate.

When Alex received all the paintings that was to be displayed at the Art exhibit, she realized that Annie was now painting prolifically, and her painting reflected a radiance that some of her earlier paintings lacked.

Together they were planning a fund-raising event that was scheduled for mid-July.

She was fund raising for her Helping Hands charity and her Helping Hands retreat.

Annie was holding an art exhibit with Scapes as the theme with forty percent of the sales promised to Helping Hands.

They planned an event at the Cincinnati water front that would feature a band or orchestra that Annie's two daughters, Linda and Lorie were setting up.

She and Matt were celebrating having moved into their new home that they had purchased at an extremely low price. A price that together they had been able to pay off in less than a year. It was the house in Mt Adams where the "Skull Collector" had made the third floor into a skull museum. Alex was converting the museum into one of Art and Rewards. The Art would be many of Annie's paintings, but she planned to also feature paintings of area artists. The featured accomplishments of the young ladies that had gone on from her Helping Hands retreat to make significant improvements in their lives was the other feature of the museum.

She planned to give the first award out as part of the River Front fund raising event.

Back in Maui, Annie, sitting out by the pool was able to see Kekoa and Brian busily discussing their current upcoming trial of Remi Frensby who they had captured out on the Gulf of Mexico. They had been able to influence the trial to begin in the middle of July. This had allowed her and Alex to set their exhibition and fund-raising event at that time.

She was focused on finishing one more painting before focusing solely on the upcoming exhibition in Cincinnati.

Alex was in a great state of mind. She and her detective partners had been enjoying a lull in their usual very busy days.

The Chief was also enjoying the fact that the lull allowed him to give his top two detective teams a rest. He had no idea that the lull was about to end.

Lorenzo flew in from Chicago and registered in one of the top downtown hotels. He was impressed with the downtown area. He spent the next few days checking out the water front. He walked by the area that was being set up for the upcoming art exhibition and concert. He made it a point of going by it several times so he could get the lay of the land.

He located the building that would best serve his needs. It had the right elevation and the right angle that should give him an excellent shot. He was able to get access to the roof to check it out. He hid his sniper's rifle case under an old pallet. All that was left was the wait, the kill shot and then the getaway.

He then took another walk around the area to locate the best place to park his getaway car and to examine the event tents that were in their final stage of preparation. He was impressed with the size of the display tent. It made it clear to him that it was to be a significant event.

He had planned his escape so that it would not involve flying. He figured that he needed to make his way out in a low-key way. He planned on driving out in a used car. Buying a used car was the next thing he needed to do. Once he had the vehicle, he would return to the waterfront park and drive the escape route. He did not want to leave anything to chance. He always worked from a well thought out and choreographed plan.

Alex watched Brenda, Annie's Cincinnati art store partner, as she supervised moving the paintings from the third-floor museum to the air-conditioned tent down at the river front.

Alex had enjoyed housing the art because not only did it erase the memory of the museum with its forty-some human skulls, but it allowed her to have Trey and his family, and the rest of the team enjoy walking through the museum at their leisure.

She had held a house warming party where they had walked through the museum and had each selected the painting they desired. They had all declined the forty per cent discount in favor of having the discount go to her charity. She had shared that fact with Annie who said that she would bring a special surprise for each of those who purchased a picture early and gave the forty percent to the charity.

Alex let her know that her DEA friend in Chicago and the Head of the IRS in Washington had both purchased a painting.

Alex watched as the last picture was boxed and then carried the three flights to the front door and then the additional steps down to the street. She and Brenda followed the truck down to the River Front parking lot. Once there Alex spent her time focused on looking over the area and ensuring that the refreshment stand that was being set up would have the mix of refreshments she had ordered.

She then went back to the exhibit tent and stepped in from a hot muggy July day into the cool air-conditioning where Brenda was making sure that the art pedestals were stable and that the temperature and humidity was controlled as she desired.

The event was to begin that afternoon and would run over the weekend.

Annie, Brian, Linda, Lorrie, Kekoa, Anela and Brian's parents had all arrived at Lunken airport on Brian's private jet. They all proceeded to check in to the hotel before walking over to the park.

Annie had the special paintings that she had brought as gifts carefully loaded into the private limo that had driven out to the plane. She was eager to see the display that she knew was being set up.

Ten paintings had already been sold, and the show had yet to officially begin. She knew that her parents planned to buy at least one. She went down the list of friends that had said they wanted to buy one of her paintings and she counted at least another ten. This made her smile as she realized the number of friends she had counted. These were people that had befriended her since Alex had rescued her from the woods of Pennsylvania.

Lorenzo walked into the hotel, and he would have been surprised had he known the artist that was to be featured because he got on the elevator with that person with folks that he figured knew each other well as he went to his fourth-floor room. He felt prepared and was planning to stay in for the rest of the day and then be on the roof early the next morning. He would move his car to be in as close proximity to the parking exit as possible so that once he got his shot off, he would immediately be on his way out of the city.

Alex was just coming out of the art display area to the front packaging and cashier area when she saw Annie and all the rest approaching with a series of boxed cartons that she was sure contained additional paintings.

She and Annie exchanged hugs, and she then hugged everyone else. This was the first time she had met Kekoa and Anela. She had heard about the escapades that Brian and Kekoa had experienced and was aware that they were to be in court for at least the coming week to attend the trial of the wayward billionaire that they had been responsible for having captured.

She had spent a lot of time coaching Brian and was aware that he had duplicated her feat of shooting out the target's bullseye while being blind folded. She was also impressed with his astounding success at becoming super rich before he turned forty.

Brian was not sure what Annie's and Alex's fund-raising goals might be but he and Kekoa had agreed that they would really put the event in the not to be forgotten category by donating five million dollars.

This they figured was a pittance as compared to more than a billion dollars that the current case they were in Cincinnati to participate in would put into their bank account.

Alex led the way into the art display area. She had the extra pedestals put up for the pictures that Annie had brought as bonuses for every one of her friends. The pictures were Scapes of the locations that were associated with the locations that each person had close to their homes. She had sent Annie several pictures for the people that Annie knew. These were scapes that she associated with those friends.

For Johnnie she had sent a scape of what Johnnie saw looking out of the bushes of Hyde Park. This was an early scape before Johnnie had become her cyber analyst.

For Mary, Johnnie's significant other, she had a scape of her walking down the street in Philadelphia. That was the day she and Johnnie had first met Mary.

For her parents she had a scape of the lane leading up to the home she had grown up in.

She had the scape of Dexter on his yacht, the Golden Goose, with the barge she had set on fire lighting up the sky behind him.

She had sent in a scape of the capture of a killer in the Mississippi forest that Sheriff Wiggins had led.

She also had the scape of the Chief as he arrived at the scene where she and the team had essentially destroyed the building of a team of gunmen that had made the mistake of trying to resist arrest.

The surprise was when she watched the last painting being placed on a stand. It was her, standing in her bicycle-riding clothes, which made the ripples of her six pack stand out, made her legs look slender and long and her biking shoes still on her feet seemed to be short high heels. She remembered this scene well since she had survived an assassination attempt that took place in front of the public library.

She laughed and said that it was a great painting, but it was not a Scape.

Annie smiled and said that it was an Alex Scape and that if she looked closely at Matt in the background, she would see that he had a great smile on his face.

Alex laughed and gave Annie a hug.

2 The Shots that Should Have

L orenzo was up early as he had planned. The stars were still twinkling overhead as he walked across the square to the elevator that would take him down to sub level four. The beads of sweat on his forehead made it clear to him that it was going to be a very warm humid day. He hoped that he would be able to find a shady spot on the roof that he would be lying on.

He moved his car from the basement parking area to street parking near the exit to the River Front Park. He walked along the old rail tracks and then crossed through the pine trees and after checking that no one was around he climbed up on the roof of what he had realized was the park's maintenance building. The sun was just rising, and the day was just beginning to heat up, but he already could feel the humidity climbing. He pulled the bill of his cap down. He hoped that the opportunity for a good shot would be available quickly because as he looked around the roof he was going to be totally exposed to the rising sun. He stood the old wooden pallet that had been abandoned on the roof on edge so that a shadow was created in the area that he was going to be lying. He was trying to keep the black surface of the roof as cool as he possibly could. He rolled out his exercise mat that acted like an insulator.

He once again sighted through the scope to make certain he had the position that he wanted. He then lay down to wait. He would have liked to go for a walk, but he did not want to risk being seen climbing up or down from the roof. He accepted the waiting because it was a very common part of his job. He lay down, put his hat over his eyes, and took a nap.

He came awake to the music from a band warming up. He looked over the edge of the roof and saw that people were arriving and staking out their spots on the grassy hill in front of the band stand structure. He saw that many of them had beach umbrellas up. He wished he could have one where he was.

He saw that the concession stand was already doing good business handing out water, soft drinks, coffee, and rolls. He was able to read the menu sign and was impressed that everything was free of charge. He chuckled to himself as he got the urge to go down and get coffee and a roll.

He read the sign in front of the larger tent that invited everyone in for a free showing of *Annie L. Scots*, many Scapes scenes and it added that on exit each person could select a miniature picture of the Scape scene that they liked best.

The second thing that caught his eye was the donation station for an organization called "Young Women's Helping Hands" that offered a second Scape picture for a donation of any amount. He wondered how any persons associated with the scene below had earned Adriano's ire. It was not something that bothered him, but it did make him wonder because these seemed to be people that he would have wanted to have back in Sicily.

He finally spotted his target as she walked out to look down to where the first band was now playing. He waited until she turned around. He was just pulling very slowly on the trigger when suddenly she was pushed from behind into the tent. He managed to pull his finger off the trigger. He waited for just a second then decided that he had somehow been discovered and decided that it was time to abandon his assassination attempt and make his way to his car slowly but as fast as possible and leave the area. He would try again on another day from another location.

Trey had been following his normal routine when he and Alex were out in public. He was always slightly behind and on one side and at the ready. He was about to ask her if she wanted something to drink when he spotted the laser spot on her back. His reflexes took over and he pushed her as hard as he could into the tent and followed her in. He had expected to get hit but nothing happened.

Alex was surprised at the strength of the push that hurled her through the entrance flap and caused her to stumble and fall just short of hitting the first painting pedestal. She jumped up and reflexively pulled her weapon. Trey put up his hands up. Alex looked around to see if they had scared anyone and she put her weapon away. He told her about the laser beam. They both cautiously lifted the entrance flap and walked out along the side that was covered. There was only one close by building. They decided to check it out. Both of them would have preferred to have their weapons at the ready but that would have scared the people still arriving for the concert.

They circled around back of what they realized was the park maintenance building and cautiously approached the steel ladder going to the roof. Trey pointed at it and indicated that he was going up and that she should take a few steps back to provide him cover. Once he got to the top of the ladder, he cautiously looked over it and then wave her to come up.

Alex went up and they walked over to where a sniper's rifle and ammunition had been abandoned.

Alex called in to the dispatch center and asked that an investigative team come to investigate the scene of an attempted assassination. She gave the location and instructed those coming to the scene to refrain from using sirens or flashing lights.

She and Trey climbed down from the roof and stood by waiting.

Johnnie had been out by the concession stand flying Gunjfor taking pictures of the crowd when he observed Trey pushing Alex into the tent and following her in. He immediately took Gunjfor up and turned it slowly around and caught someone on the roof of the nearest building crawling to the fire escape in the back. He took Gunjfor swooping in for a close up but had to pull up to avoid the pine trees. From a higher vantage point, he spotted the person that had left the roof get into a car in the parking lot. He flew Gunjfor toward that location. He was able to get the direction that the car was heading and figured that a quick call to central might get a unit to cut him off and apprehend the person trying to get away.

He brought Gunjfor down and then walked to where he had seen Alex and Trey going.

They were just coming down from the roof when he got there.

Alex looked at him and asked if by chance he had been able to get anything with Gunjfor.

Johnnie smiled, shook his head, and said that he had the backside of the shooter and the back side of the getaway car, but he did not have much else but behinds of some person and that person's car. The licensed plate had a grey cover that hid the license plate.

Alex asked to see what Johnnie had captured. As she watched the video, she said that she wanted to get the information to the lab so that the photo analysts could do an in-depth detailed analysis. She said that the shoes, the shirt, and pants might all hold a clue as to who that person might be. She pointed to the license plate that had a grey cover that seemed make the license plate unreadable but perhaps the analysist might be able to see through it. The rear of the car had no auto make emblems, so she figured the shooter was a professional.

Johnnie got on line and sent the footage to the lab. Then he said that he was going back to filming the event.

Alex thanked Trey for literally having her back and gave him a hug.

Trey nodded and said that it was not often that he got the opportunity to shove her around. He then said that he was ready to enjoy the rest of the day with Nolan and Lesley.

Alex asked where they were.

Trey said that when he shoved her into the tent they were walking and looking at the Scape paintings. He added that Lesley had observed what had happened and had guided Nolan to the back of the tent. He figured he would have to explain the situation to them.

Alex shook her head and commented that she had no idea why she was on someone's hit list.

Trey laughed and replied that she had left a trail of bodies, people in prison and destroyed gunships and burned down coal barges that left a huge number of potential people mad enough that they might think about trying to do her in.

Alex said that she agreed that there was a long trail but that he was exaggerating the number of people left alive to try to get revenge.

Trey agreed and said that no one came to mind.

Alex said that it was similar to the Scape scene Annie had captured of what she called the Alex Scape painting that was featured as the first painting when a person entered the display tent. That was a case where a racist had decided to kill her because her skin color offended him.

Lindsey was standing pointing to the picture of the Scape that featured their backyard. It was of Nolan, Linda, and Laurie on the swing set. This was a painting that she had purchased during Alex's private showing of Annie's Scapes when Alex had hosted a party for all her friends. She was thrilled to be able to get a painting of the time several years ago when the kids were younger. The three kids were now at least six or seven years older and no longer children but young adults.

She saw Alex fly in and sprawl on the floor and immediately jump up with her weapon pulled. She watched as Trey followed her in. Alex immediately put her weapon away and the two of them cautiously left the tent.

She guided Nolan to the back of the tent expecting gunfire but there was none. She continued guiding Nolan around to take in all the different Scapes that Annie had painted.

She was hesitant to leave the tent and engaged Annie in conversation.

Trey returned and saw that Lindsey was still in the tent. He walked over and asked if she was ready to go sit out on the lawn and listen to the music.

She asked what had happened.

Trey responded that nothing had happened and that was a good thing. He said that he would share more once he knew more.

Nolan laughed and said now he understood why he had been kept in the tent. He then added that he was ready for something to drink, something to snack on, and he wanted to listen to the bands that Linda and Lorie had chosen for the event.

Trey took Lindsey's hand and led the way out.

Brian had been in the tent watching Annie as she walked around and engaged the people looking at her paintings. He had observed Alex as she flew in and landed at the base of the first picture. He remained seated but was ready to act if necessary. He called to Kekoa who was out on the lawn with Anela and asked if there was anything strange going on. He listened as Kekoa replied that things were calm, and the only action was on the stage. Kekoa added that the two girls had done a great job in selecting the first opening group.

Brian had noticed Lindsey's reaction, so he walked over and talked to her and Nolan. He knew that Annie considered Lindsey a good friend and the two girls still argued in fun as to who got to marry Nolan.

It seemed like quite a while before Alex and Trey returned but it was clear to him that they had things in control.

He walked over to Annie and asked if he could get her anything.

Lorenzo made his way to the highway and drove north. He was keeping his speed just below the speed limit and staying to the right most lane. He was thinking about what he needed to do. He definitely needed to find a place to stay for the night. It needed to be an out of the way place where he could get something to eat and hopefully buy a different car. He needed to shed all connection with his stay in Cincinnati.

He hoped to circle back and get a second chance at what he had been hired to do.

He drove until a sign loaded with fast food places and another that highlighted a number of hotels caught his eye. He figured that it was time to get something to eat and then get a room for the night and get some sleep.

In the morning after a quick breakfast, he drove around the area and found a used car lot that seemed to have a good offering of cars for sale. He found a car that seemed to be in good shape, and he traded in his current vehicle for the car plus a thousand dollars more.

He knew that the dealer was getting a good deal and if he had been in Italy, he would have bargained for a better deal for himself. He decided that he would rather get a different car and leave a happy dealer versus one that felt pressured to make the exchange.

He did not want to be remembered.

He called in to Adriano and let him know what had happened. He shared that he was returning to Cincinnati to finish the job, but he needed another sniper's rifle.

Adriano was surprised by the call but pleased that Lorenzo was planning to finish the job. He let Lorenzo know where he could pick up another sniper's rifle. He asked when he should expect the news of the targets demise.

Lorenzo replied that he was going to spend the day deciding on a new location for his next assassination attempt. He wanted a location that gave him a great shot and an easy escape. The location would depend on his targets movement.

He spent the next couple of days observing his target's morning and evening transit to and from work. She had a route down the steep hill from her home to a transit area where she crossed the highway and then rode past an apartment building where she was joined by an older bicycler who then took the lead.

The route down to the apartment building was consistent but the route from there to the police station varied randomly on each of his observations.

He decided that the best place for the shot was as she came down the steep hill and crossed on the road over the highway.

He then spent time identifying the best location that would give him a good shot and an easy get away. He decided that the best location was as she got to the bottom of the hill and was getting ready to cross over the US 71 highway.

He found a way to take the service elevator to the roof. There he found a good spot and set everything up.

On Tuesday morning Alex departed from her house and rode slowly down the steep hill that took her to the point where she crossed over US 71 to get into the downtown. She loved where her house was located and the great view it provided but the way to work was a challenge and she was currently replacing her bicycle brake pads once a week because she had to engage them almost continuously to get safely down the hill.

She was crossing the bridge when a careless driver put her so close to the wall that she had to brake and push herself off the wall to keep from going over the side. As she did so the head tube of the bike shattered. As she went over her handle bar she rolled and drew her weapon. She came up behind a car stopped for the red light. She looked up at the buildings on the other side. She saw a glint. She moved immediately to her right and heard the bullet hit the cement behind her. She took three shots. One at the glint and two on either side of the glint. At the range and the upward angle, she was shooting she was not sure she had chosen the correct angle.

The stop light turned green, and she jogged along with the cars as they made the left turn at the light. She then ran across the intersection and to the base of the building. She stopped at the entrance and called in a shot fired, and an officer needing backup and gave the address. The sirens and the flashing lights of the approaching police cars were visible in less than two minutes.

Alex explained the situation and that the shooter had been on the roof, but she was not sure where he might be at the moment.

She watched as the Chief accompanied by Trey and Johnnie got out of his car and came over to her.

She pointed to where her bike was laying at the side by the wall of the road and said that was where she had first encountered being shot at and that there was another point about fifteen feet in front of that where the second bullet hit the wall.

The Chief called one of the police officers and asked him to tape of the area along the bridge that was part of the crime scene but to keep traffic flowing.

He then asked if she was OK.

Alex nodded and replied that she was going to have a few sore spots from having rolled over her handle bar, but her helmet and pads had saved her.

Johnnie had launched Gunjfor and made her fly to the top of the building. He then showed everyone where the shooter happened to be. The picture showed a large hole in the back of a person's head.

Gunjfor had arrived just as a squad of officers came across the roof with their guns drawn. One of them waved to the camera and gave a thumbs up as he pointed to the body lying face down.

Johnnie kept Gunjfor hovering until Dr Rogers arrived and gave his thumbs up while his team took pictures before he turned the dead shooter over.

He then loudly commented that only a person who shot out bull's eyes blindfolded could do the kind of shooting with the kind of results that he was seeing.

Alex said that it was time she got a ride into work and walked towards the Chief's car.

He stopped her and threw his keys to her and said that when the site was totally in control, he would re-turn to the office, and they should discuss the case. He wanted to find out who was behind the current attempts on her life.

3 The Ground Hog's Paradox

*A*lex entered the station's ladies changing area, got out of her bicycle riding clothes, and sat down for a moment. She kept thinking about how similar the latest attempt on her life was to the day she had survived being shot off her bike as she bicycled into work a couple of years ago. It seemed too similar to be targeted in almost the same way. Then she had slowed down to avoid a hole in the street. That slight fraction of time altered the trajectory of the bullet meant for her head and instead it hit her backpack and ruined the computer that it carried. She had shot and killed the person doing the shooting and the person driving the light blue pickup with the gunman in the back. They died, she survived. But survival had been followed by a longer period of finding out the why and who wanted to take that pre-emptive action against her. Pre-emptive action that she later learned was driven by the color of her skin.

That fact had affected her more than she had been prepared for. She was used to obvious discrimination because of the color of her skin but to have someone try to kill her made the study of the time of Martin Luther King mean so much more to her than it had when she was in school.

This time a rude driver had caused her to brake and try not to be thrown over the overpass to the street below. That slight momentary slow down meant her bicycle was hit.

She had to roll over her handle bars in a very similar way as she did on the first occasion and her subsequent actions had allowed her to kill the sniper trying to kill her. Now she was wondering whether it was a pre-emptive or reactive action that the assassination attempt was based on.

After a moment, she walked out to the bull pen area where Bill and Trevor were sitting talking to Trey and Johnnie.

Bill looked at her and asked if she was OK.

Trevor smiled and added that he knew she was OK and went on to ask if she knew who was after her.

Alex shook her head and said that she thought she would name what had happened to her as "the ground hog's paradox" because it felt like she was living a previous experience over again.

She felt that some person had decided that she should be killed. It was most likely some person who she did not know but held some grudge against her. She added that she hoped that the why would become clear.

She pointed at Trey and thanked him for saving her the first time on Saturday morning.

She added that she would now like to thank the rude driver of the car that almost pushed her over the guard rail to the street below. That moment had caused the sniper to miss.

The two assassination attempts clearly meant that somebody wanted to kill her and like the time a couple of years ago, she had no idea where to begin with tracking down the person behind the current situation.

Bill asked her to remind him how the team had identified the person responsible for the first shooting.

Alex was quiet for a moment and then shook her head. She commented that it was more or less pure luck. She had spotted a stripe on a car with the same color of paint as that of the pickup used in the shooting. The owner of the car had given her the location of where she had recently bought the car and two amazing detectives, Bill, and Trevor, had identified the shooter.

Trevor laughed and then added that they had all almost met their end except for the fact that Cincinnati's Black Annie Oakley had single handedly repelled the that person who ruined a perfectly good fishing outing on lake Michigan.

The Chief walked in and said that he wanted everyone in his office in five and then went into his office. It was clear to the team that he was not in a good mood.

Alex said she was getting a cup of coffee and hoped that there was a bear claw left in the donut box.

Once they were all in the office the Chief looked around and asked if anyone could make any sense out of what had happened on Saturday and again this morning.

Alex said that it was a repeat of what had happened when a racist had decided that her skin color offended him. She felt this case was based on some offense that she was being held accountable for. She added that the two organizations that she had recently offended the most was the Mafia and the Gulf Cartel, but she had no clue if either of those organizations had a current personal vendetta against her or a contract out on her. She added it could just be a repeat of the first time based on the color of her skin.

Bill suggested they contact the "Angel on the hill" and ask her to find out if she had any idea if one of the Mexican cartels was involved.

Johnnie said he would contact her and ask.

Alex thanked Bill for the good idea. She said that instead of contacting her friend on the hill, they instead talk with Adolfo, her brother, who was in town. He and his wife had arrived on the weekend to attend Annie's art showing and to personally donate a large sum of money to her Open Hands charity. She was having dinner with them in the evening.

She added that if it was not one the cartels then it might be harder to figure out who in the Mafia might be responsible.

The Chief suggested that he talk with the Illinois lieutenant governor and ask her if she had any idea about a mafia connection.

Alex nodded and added that she was sure the mafia might blame her for the fact that the entire Chicago Mafia Leadership team had been killed even though she had been out fishing when it happened.

Matt and his EMT team had arrived at the shooting site with the fire trucks and had taken in the scene. He realized that the bike that was taped off in yellow tape at the side of the over pass was Alex's. He caught sight of Alex still in her riding clothes, catching a set of keys from the Chief and then getting into the Chief's car with Trey and driving away.

He knew that she was OK, so he relaxed and spent time talking to the police lieutenant in charge of the scene. He stayed clear of the Chief because it was obvious, he was steaming mad.

The police lieutenant describe the amazing shots that Alex had taken. All three shots had hit the sniper.

He and his team soon learned that the sniper was being examined by the coroner. He knew that Dr. Rogers would be giving Alex a hard time for over working him and his team. He marveled at the relationship Alex had with him. Alex hated the morgue and Dr. Rogers insisted that his reviews be done in the morgue. He would take his time, and he always had the corpse exposed and made sure to point out all the gruesome wounds. The smell of the morgue added to the discomfort that Alex felt.

She had shared with him that she often insisted that the Dr. come to her meetings as revenge. Matt had laughed and said that the Dr. had the upper hand in that situation since he always ended up with a cup of coffee and a donut when he came to her meetings, whereas she ended up nauseous.

He and the team had nothing to do for a few moments so they agreed to go to the police station so that he could touch base with Alex.

Alex was just leading the team to the huddle room when she saw Matt and his team walking in.

Matt smiled commented that he and his team were too late to save her at the crime scene, so they figured to come down and see if there were any donuts left in the coffee area.

Alex reached up and gave him a hug and said he and his team could have anything in the coffee area, but she and her team were going to go in and figure out how to handle this ground hogs day case.

Matt nodded and said he understood and that he was happy to see her taking the lead to figure out what was going on.

Alex reminded him that they had a dinner appointment with Adolfo and his wife and then turned and headed for the huddle room.

When they sat down Johnnie confessed that he had contacted Adolfo and asked him about any Cartel vendettas against her. He apologized about doing so but added that he and Adolfo had been exchanging texts since his arrival in Cincinnati because they had become fairly close since the time, they had collaborated on the Votive Candles case.

Alex replied that no apology was needed and asked what Adolfo's response had been.

Johnnie replied that Adolfo said he was ninety-nine percent sure that there was no cartel involvement but that he would check and verify his belief.

Alex nodded and said if that was the case, they needed to figure out the Mafia connection.

The Chief walked in and shared that he had just finished talking with the Illinois Lieutenant Governor who was surprised that her star employee had faced two attempted assassinations. He added that he had let her know that the employee they were talking about was his and not hers.

She volunteered that she had recently been informed of the aggressive nature of the new Chicago mafia boss by the Chicago Chief of Police. It seemed that this boss, Adriano Barbieri, had imported a significant number of folks from Sicily and was challenging the Gulf cartel for more control of the Chicago drug distribution market.

Alex asked if they had talked about her status as a special agent working for Jane being reinstated.

The Chief smiled and said that Jane had offered to reactivate her and Trey's status of working for her on special assignment but that this time the two of them would have to take a promotion and a pay raise.

Alex nodded and said that then she was set and ready to go. She added that she would appreciate Johnnie, Bill and Trevor being available to support her if things mushroomed.

The Chief smiled and said that her support was in place to be used as needed. He then looked at her and asked if her time in Chicago included a fishing trip for her team and smiled and said that he was on her team.

Alex laughed, shook her head, and then looked around and said that as soon as she figured out the timing of her assignment, she would schedule another fishing trip that included everyone in the office and their significant others.

Johnnie said they should all give a Marine "hurrah" for their upcoming fishing trip since he was sure Alex would soon solve the mystery of the ground hog's paradox.

Alex was sure that anyone outside of the office was wondering about the "hurrahs" that shook the walls.

Alex looked at Trey and asked if he was ready to go to Chicago to get a first-hand look at what might be going on.

She looked at Johnnie and asked him to dig into the new Mafia leader's actions, bank accounts and to get any other personal information he could. She wanted to be armed with as much information as possible.

Johnny smiled and said he was having his own ground hog's paradox because this was exactly what she had asked him to do several times before.

Trevor laughed and said that he too was having one, but it was about being left out and lonely, something that always brought tears to his eyes.

Alex smiled and replied that she would brush any tears from his eyes when he got that lonely.

The Chief once again knew that these two teams had a very close working relationship that spoke to Alex's ability to pull them all together.

4 The Windy City

*A*s the early morning flight to Chicago took a swing out over the lake as it made its approach Alex looked down at Lake Michigan's blue waters, pointed out the window that she could see her favorite fishing spot.

Trey leaned over to look out the window and jokingly said he too could see the red x that marked the fishing spot.

Alex looked at him and asked if he knew that Lake Michigan was the only one of the five Great Lakes of North America that was located entirely within the United States.

Trey shook his head and said until she had just told him he had never thought about it.

She went on to say that Lake Michigan had the longest north to south stretch of all the Great Lakes. This gave the region around it a very diverse climate, which allowed and supported the wide variety of plant and animal species in the area. She said the lake boasted a variety of natural habitats, including tall grass prairies, wide savannas, and the world's largest freshwater sand dunes.

The lake had fascinated her all her life and she continued to be amazed at how each time she returned home she learned something new and once again fell in love with the area.

She said that Chicago was home to some of the world's most iconic buildings. She said that this time she wanted to visit the Frank Lloyd Wright Home and Studio. And if they had time, they should also go to the Museum of Contemporary Art including the Sears Tower.

Trey said that he loved the Chicago-style hot dogs and the Chicago-style deep dish pizza and that they would have to take time to enjoy that. The rest of what she had planned would most likely be new to him.

The plane turned and the long coast line north toward Evaston came into view. Alex pointed out and said that she could see the buildings at North Western University where her father taught and where she had gone to school. She smiled and said that it felt good to be coming home but the reason for her return was eating at her.

Alex commented that when she grew up, she was taught that looking at the lake was always to look to the East. If she kept that in mind, she would always be able to navigate the north and south that had built up and flourished at its shore.

The plane was on its final approach as she commented how much she loved Lake Michigan. She shared the fact that her summers would have been incomplete without dips in the lake and fishing with her father. She added that the winters would have been a lot more manageable were it not for Lake Michigan's unforgiving cold freezing winds.

She and Trey had traveled light and pulled their suit cases along behind them and went out past the security area. She was surprised to see her father standing waiting for them. After giving him a hug she asked why he had come to pick them up.

He laughed and said it was the only way to bring her jag to her so she could enjoy it every moment she was home. He asked to pull her suit case but led the way when Alex refused.

She was happy to be able to drive the car that was her prize possession. She had not taken it to Cincinnati because it seemed that every vehicle or car, she drove there ended up with bullet holes in them or ended up ablaze to become a melted deformed cinder. Since she had started driving the departments oldest car it seemed that no one wanted to shoot at her.

On the drive home she looked over at Trey and asked if he knew that Chicago was founded by a Black trapper, Jean Baptiste Point du Sable Chicago's first permanent settler in 1779, a trapper and merchant credited with building the trading post that evolved into Chicago. She added that he hailed from Haiti and settled into what is now Chicago with his Ptawatomi wife, Kittihawa.

Her father added that Jean was honored in Chicago by having the Jean Baptiste Point DuSable Lake Shore Drive, DuSable Bridge on Michigan Avenue, and the DuSable Museum of African American History all named after him. He pointed out that he taught this in his philosophy classes, and it always surprises most of his students.

Trey looked back and said that it surprised him because he had never been taught that fact in any of his history classes.

Alex chose to take the surface streets instead of the highway. She preferred to enjoy her drive along the lake and through the universities along the way. It took her back a few years to when she had been going to Northwestern.

The driveway leading to the house seemed to have again grown thicker and the view of the house was like looking through a tunnel. It brought back so many good memories that she felt on the verge of tears.

Some distance south along the Lake Michigan shore line; Adriano was just getting into his office. He walked over to the window as he held his fresh cup of coffee and looked out over the beach area to the calm early morning lake.

He had received that startling news that his assassin had been killed. Apparently, he had been shot by the person he had been sent to assassinate. That seemed impossible and it made him wonder about the capability of the Black female detective.

He had his hands full dealing with the Mexican cartel competition.

He was upset about what he had thought to be an easy elimination of the person that had caused the Mafia to have a huge setback was turning out not to be as easy as he had thought it would be. He hoped to figure out some way to deal with his personal irritation.

He planned to discuss this situation with his inner group of the leadership team to see if they had any ideas.

Rose-Anne came out and gave Alex a long hug and said that she had talked with Jane about the reason for the trip and was about to apologize for her involvement in the original Mafia situation but stopped when Alex put her finger on her lips. She remembered Alex's instruction not to apologize unless she was the instigator.

She instead turned and gave Trevor a hug and said they should all go into the house. She added that she had nothing planned for lunch, but she was planning to cook a rib steak for each of them for dinner.

Alex said that a late dinner would be good because she planned to take two bikes with her down to Chicago's lakeshore bike path and bike into the downtown area, around the downtown and perhaps take in a museum or two as part of her surveillance of the situation.

Her father said he would get the bike rack mounted and the bikes ready for action and went out to the garage.

Alex thanked him and said that they would get lunch along the way because Trey wanted to enjoy either a Chicago hot dog or a Chicago deep dish pizza.

Trey said that sounded great as long as she did not plan to ride the entire eighteen miles of the bike path that ran along the shore.

Alex replied that she was planning to ride the Lakefront Trail closer to the downtown that connected to many of Chicago's most popular parks and beaches. This would facilitate doing the ride in just several hours versus in days.

She said that she had heard from a friend that the GLS café that was alongside the Lakefront bike trail was great and had a simple but good menu.

Trey said that as soon as he put his suitcase in his room and changed into his cycling outfit, he would be ready to go.

Alex said that she would be ready to go in about ten minutes.

Adriano was at the same time discussing with his leadership team what should be done about what had happened in Cincinnati. He was personally fuming about the situation.

Almost unanimously his team said that he should just drop the issue and focus on Chicago because they had their hands full with multiple small gangs that kept fighting with each other but also the fight for control of the drug market that needed their attention. They pointed out that they had had strong competition on a more dangerous level with the Gulf cartel, who were well organized and well-armed.

Adriano thanked them for their honest and direct view point and said he would consider their advice.

On the drive to the parking spot she had in mind, Alex shared the fact that Chicago's motto "urbs in horto" or city in a garden adopted in the 1830's alluded to the city's large, impressive, and historic park system. She planned to see much of it on the ride.

She said that of special interest to her favorite partner was the fact that in 1943, Ike Sewell invented Chicago deep dish pizza at his restaurant Pizzeria Uno, where it was still served to this day.

She added that they would bicycle through the area known as the Loop that followed the elevated "L" train tracks. She said that she felt that this area would give them a firsthand look at the drug traffic. She had no idea who controlled the drugs in this area but in her mind, it would provide a street level look at what was going on.

As they rode their bikes along the loop, she pointed out Jeanne Gang's Vista Tower that at the time it was built was the world tallest structure to be designed by a woman. She had graduated from the University of Illinois in Champaign-Urbana and later became a professor at the Harvard School of architecture. Alex added that she had found out that Jeanne's award-winning work had redefined Chicago's skyline.

Other of Jeanne's work in Chicago included the Nature Boardwalk at Lincoln Park Zoo and two boathouses along the Chicago River.

The bike ride would take them close to the DuSable Museum of African American History where she planned to stop for a quick walk through.

Trey said that it sounded great to him but he wanted to make sure that the restaurant stop was one of the first so he could recover from having to keep up with her but also, he figured that by then both of them would need to take a break.

The ride along the "L" seemed to be a series of staged drug exchanges that were clearly obvious and seemed to be happening at about every other alley way as they rode the loop.

They then headed toward the DuSable Museum of African American History and continued to see the proliferation of the drug distribution.

Once they were in the museum Alex focused on enjoying what was being shared. She had purchased a personal tour that provided a tour guide.

She learned about:

The Chicago resident Gwendolyn Brooks who became the first African American woman to win a Pulitzer Prize in 1950 for her book Annie Allen.

Senator Carol Moseley Braun, the country's first female African American U.S. senator who was elected in 1992.

She learned that though born in New York, Michael Jordan became synonymous with Chicago as he lead the Chicago Bulls to six National Basketball Association championships and earning the NBA's Most Valuable Player Award six times.

Clarinetist, composer, and band leader Benny Goodman, aka "The King of Swing," was born in Chicago.

Legendary contemporary jazz pianist, composer, and on-air jazz host Ramsey Lewis was currently a Chicago native.

And she was remined that Barack Obama, was a Chicagoan who was elected the 44th President of the United States to become the first African American to serve in the office.

She felt the trip to the museum had been well worth her time and the tour had lasted twice as long as she had planned because she had lost track of the time as she listened to her tour guide.

She thanked her for the tour and gave her a generous tip.

Trey commented that almost everything that they had seen and talked about was new to him and he wanted to bring Lindsey and Nolan to take a tour of the museum.

Alex was pleased with Trey's reaction because she had been a little apprehensive about what his reaction might be.

Just a few blocks away Adriano had just received a call from his Cincinnati informant that Alex Evercrest had taken a flight to Chicago. He was immediately concerned about that situation and wondered if she had somehow figured out that the mafia was connected to the assassination attempts.

He decided to tap into his Chicago network to see if he could find out where she might be staying.

Had he known that he, his home life, his bank accounts, and his criminal actions were all being analyzed he would have been even more worried.

312

5 Discovery

*A*s they rode their bikes back to where the car was parked Alex looked to the west and took in the Chicago skyline that was a black silhouette against the yellow-red tinged rays of the setting sun. A strong breeze from the right was delivering a cooling chill that provided imputes to quickly get to the car.

Trey commented that the lake seemed determined to blow him off the trail and that he was ready to get back to the house and enjoy a cup of hot tea.

Johnnie had spent the day hacking his way through a variety of firewalls as he pursued information on Adriano. He was surprised at the ease with which he got through the Mafia firewall. The information that he was able to extract was a great road map of the drug distribution network that was operated in Chicago. He was sure that Alex would be able to work with Harold Zimmerman, the DEA leader, to make a significant impact in reducing the drug flow in Chicago. He knew that Alex and Harold had close relationship that went back several years.

He had traced Adriano's Mafia history back to Sicily and had learned of his disciplined and rather hard-edged rise up the mafia hierarchy. Johnnie recognized that he approached his assignments with a thoroughness and intensity that left his competitors standing at the sidelines. It was clear that he had caught the eye of the mafia heads.

When the Chicago mafia organization was wiped out, Adriano was the one that was identified to reestablish the Chicago branch. Johnnie found an e mail that stated the expectation that he was to expand the Chicago market and to negotiate with the Mexican cartels to supply the drugs but to remove the Cartel organization presence from Chicago. He figured that this last expectation would be extremely hard to negotiate and might very well lead to a gangland war.

He then tracked the way the money was managed. He traced the money that was brought in by the street drug distributors and stayed locally. He traced the money that was paid to various organizations for various drugs, and he traced the money that made its way to the offshore accounts.

Johnnie was surprised at how many different groups produced a variety of drugs locally. Many of the names of these drugs were totally new to him and he had to do some research to learn what effect each had.

He was surprised that anyone would ingest such devastating and harmful substances that produced some sort of short term high, or hallucination followed by a long-term negative impact on almost every organ in the body.

His conclusion from what he was able to learn was that the drug business was very lucrative and that its customers were willing to pay whatever price was set at. The only thing that kept the situation under control was the competition between various distributors of the drugs.

Johnnie concluded that illicit drug making, and distribution was very similar to the legal drug making and distribution system.

He organized all that information and sent it to the rest of the team.

Alex was glad to be back at her Jag. After getting their bicycles secured in the bike rack, she got in and put up the top. Without the lake wind, the car was comfortable and actually felt warm. On the drive back to the house, Trey told her of the information that Johnnie had gathered about the current Mafia leader and his organization.

The thing that stood out to Alex was that Adriano, as she now thought of him, was a person that liked everything to comply with his will and that those who did not meet his wish were either pushed aside or eliminated. She felt that he was the type of person who would send an assassin to Cincinnati to eliminate a person that he felt had done something detrimental to the Mafia organization.

She was at a loss how she was going to prove such a connection and if she established the connection how she would handle that situation. It seemed to her the story of the chicken and the egg; which came first?

Adriano was incensed by the failure of his assassin and agitated further by the fact that the person responsible for killing him was in the Chicago area. He was pushed farther along his line of anger by the fact that his leadership team had suggested they not deal with this single individual whose jurisdiction was in Ohio. They had suggested that they all focus on the Chicago distribution area. He felt ignored and he did not like the feeling.

He had listened to their view point but was not inclined to follow the advice they were giving him.

He instead called in two of his field enforcers and gave them the order to go to the address in Evanston and eliminate everyone that resided there. The elimination order stressed that it was to happen that evening around the normal dinner time. They were to go in kill everyone that was in the house. They were to take a picture of each individual so that he had proof that the black detective was indeed among the dead.

After they left his office, he spent a few moments thinking through the time it would take. He then left for a walk along the beach before going home.

As he walked slowly kicking at a broken stick that had washed up on the beach, he wondered what the local police in Evanston would do about the carnage they would walk into when they were called to the scene. Since the killings would be done in the house, he hoped there would be a multiple day delay before they were discovered.

He would have loved to be there to witness the carnage. He turned and walked back to where his black limo and driver were waiting to take him home.

Ray and Baily were both friends from their days in the growing up on Chicago's south side. They had been basketball stars in high school and then they worked together in a fast-food kitchen cooking fry's, burgers and making chili. Every day after work they looked for a pickup basketball game. It was during one of the games that they were approached about getting into distributing drugs. When they found out how much money they could make it was a no-brainer. They jumped at the chance and went enthusiastically giving what they were doing no second thoughts.

Then one day they were pounced on by four members of an opposition gang. It took them more than a month to recover from the beating and they each had scars from stab wounds and Ray had a long scar across one cheek.

They decided that they would get even. After buying two, three fifty sevens and several hundred rounds of ammunition from the back of a grey van, they went out on the hunt for their attackers. Their approach was to find one of the attackers and without any warning shoot that person in the head. Their revenge was swift with no fanfare and kept as low key as possible. Low key meant that the police had no clue what was going on. Their drug supplier must have known because he asked them if they wanted to move up to being enforcers.

They jumped at the opportunity when they found out what an enforcer could make for occasionally doing more than threatening a store owner or whacking some person about to remind them not to cheat on the protection money they were to cough up.

Their actions and effective way of running the protection business soon got them promoted to reporting directly to the Mafia leadership team. This meant a different more violent level of enforcement. They both realized that they like what they were doing.

They had been out doing their job when the entire Mafia leadership team had been wiped out.

Adriano had kept them as his enforcers when he came to Chicago to take the Mafia reigns.

He had personally called them into his office. They both were overcome as they stood and listened to what he wanted them to do. He made it clear that they would receive a significant bonus for a successful hit job. He asked them if they were ready for this next step up on the enforcer scale. They had both answered that they were ready to do whatever they were asked to do.

The up-front sum of money promised blew their minds. The amount promised for a successful job was three times as much.

They looked at each other and smiled. They both knew they were going to be rich.

They were surprised to be given an address and told to go into the home and kill everyone. They were to leave no finger prints, no bullet casings, no evidence that could be used to trace the killings. It was to be an in and an immediate out job. They were to use the car that was waiting for them in the parking garage and when the they were done the car was to be returned and they were to leave the building, walked at least six blocks into the city and take a cab home to where they lived.

They stopped at the basement armory where there was a huge array of untraceable weapons to select the weapons, they felt would be most effective for the job. They were in awe of the variety that they could choose from.

They were really impressed with the bore of the four-gauge shotgun. They could put their finger into the barrel. When they saw the size of the brass shells and the shiny slug casings, they immediately picked it. They figured they would be unstoppable with such weapons in their hands.

They were now driving to a location where they would be stepping into the really big league of carrying out their role. They joked about how they would be able to walk in and blow anyone that was there in two with the weapons they had picked. They were both impressed as they drove through what seemed to be a tunnel with a huge home at the other end.

They parked and walked up to the door and Bailey stepped up and kicked the door expecting it to buckle and cave in. Instead, he almost fell down and hurt himself. His leg ached from the kick he had delivered.

Ray pulled him back and fired his shotgun. They both expected the door to explode and shatter as they stepped forward. They both ran into a solid closed door.

Alex was sitting with everyone else out by the pool as they were just finishing dinner when the racket at the front door occurred.

Her father laughed and said that whoever was trying to break in had just tested the door he had made.

Alex signaled Trey to follow her, and she rushed through the kitchen to the garage and went to the door that opened out toward the front door of the house.

She quietly said that she would take the kneeling position and that Trey should take the high position.

She then opened the door and yelled out to the two men standing at the front door to throw down their weapons and surrender. She was just about to say they were under arrest when both men turned toward her. She saw the weapons they had in their hands and fired two shots. Both shot guns went off and blew out a huge section of the front flower bed.

Trey had simultaneously fired his weapon.

Ray heard a female telling him to throw down his weapon and figured he would blow her away. He was turning to do so when the world went black.

Alex rushed out ready to fire again but realized that between her and Trey each of the two gunmen were twice dead.

She looked around to see if there was anyone else involved and rushed out to the car to verify that there was no one there. She also noted that there did not seem to be any law enforcement on the way in.

She called 911 to report a shooting and gave the address. She then went to the front door and rang the doorbell. Her father peeked through the crack as he opened the door.

He opened the door and pointed to the flattened slug that was imbedded in the wood. He then pointed to the hinge area where the edge of a half inch steel plate was visible.

Alex asked when he had the door installed.

Her father laughed and said that he had decided to build a special door after her last visit when she had sent a burning coal barge to the bottom of Lake Michigan. He had figured that with a daughter that took on drug pushers, drug cartels and the Mafia he needed to do something to keep his home safe.

Alex gave him a hug and thanked him for being proactive. She then asked that he go back to the pool area and assure his significant other that everything was in control.

She went out to where the car was parked, put her weapon on the hood and asked Trey to do the same. She then walked over to the flower bed situated between the front door and the garage and sat down. She wondered where the slug that had plowed through the flower bed and up rooted the three rose bushes would be found.

She would see that the rose bushes were put back into their original locations.

She watched as three police cars came up the lane toward them.

She was already thinking what her response should be for an obvious Mafia hit job.

She quietly asked Trey who he thought would be able to activate such a response to their presence in Chicago.

Trey had been thinking about the same thing. He was certain that only the top Mafia leader could possibly have the resources and the means to put a hit so quickly into motion.

Alex then said that she thought that it was the Mafia leader himself and that she wanted to immediately act to hit back. She said that she was going to see if Harold and the DEA would take immediate action. She said that she was also going to see if Johnnie could defang the serpent by locking him out of all access to his bank accounts.

Harold had just finished dinner and was getting ready to sit down and do some reading when Alex called him. He was amazed at what she told had just happened. He asked what she wanted him to do. He readily agreed to raid the Mafia leader's home. He would have an arrest and search warrant in his hands before midnight and he and his team and a sufficient number backup would raid the luxury apartment before sunrise.

He heard the sirens and asked that he be put in contact with whomever was in charge of the arriving police.

Alex said she was putting the phone down with the guns so she would not be accidently shot.

The arriving police all exited their cars with guns drawn and rushed forward.

Both she and Trey held up their open hands and identified themselves as police officers that worked for the Lieutenant Governor.

Alex was relieved when the person that seemed to be in charge had all the officers put away their weapons.

He came forward and looked at her and Trey's badges and asked what had happened.

Alex pointed to the phone next to her weapon and said that the area DEA leader wanted to have a word with him and was waiting on the phone.

She stepped back and watched as the conversation took place.

It was clear to her that Harold was exerting his influence by the way the officer was shaking his head in agreement.

He hung up and came over to her and said that her reputation was well known but that he had never expected to meet her. He said that he had watched the burning barrage for hours until it sunk and not long after he had been on the investigating team when a shooter had tried to kill her when she had family and friends out fishing.

Alex took his offered hand, shook it, and thanked him for being one of the brave doing his job.

He suggested that she go in and relax while his men processed the scene. He pointed at the two guns on the hood of the car and asked if they were the weapons used to shoot the two men on the ground.

Alex nodded and said that they were and that she need to arrange for replacement weapons because her case was only on its first day.

She led the way back into the house and went out to the pool area where her mother and father were sitting.

She smiled and said that she had forgotten what had been on the menu for desert.

Rose-Anne laughed and said that she had forgotten about desert. She then said that it was lemon meringue and a scoop of lemon ice cream on the side.

Alex said she would love a nice sized slice, and she would get a cup of iced tea to accompany it. She asked Trey if he wanted some iced tea.

Trey loved the way that Alex was able to step away from a harrowing experience and flow into what seemed like a very normal mode.

He knew why he was so devoted to his work partner. She not only was unbelievably brave, but she was unbelievably a people person who exuded a warmth that capture those around her.

Alex returned with two ice teas each with a lemon wedge on the edge of the glass.

She sat down and said she needed to call Johnnie and ask him to arrange it so Adriano would be unable to get to any of his money.

Johnnie was not surprised to get a call from Alex. He was very surprised when she shared what had just happened. He said he would be able to quickly change all the passwords to all the accounts that Adriano and the mafia headquarters had. He let her know that everything would happen in less than a half hour since he had already hacked into all the banks, and it would only be a matter of changing the passwords.

Alex thanked him and said that he had earned another tray of cookies.

She looked at Trey and said that it was great to be supported by the best.

Trey smiled and said that he was only second best because he could not shoot out the gun target's bullseye blind folded.

Alex laughed and said that she noticed that all his shots counted when they need to.

6 Smoking Gun

*A*driano arrived at his apartment building and thanked the driver, walked over to the elevator, got on and press the button for his floor. He looked at himself in the polished stainless steel of the elevator wall and felt pleased with the tall, slender, thin faced man with black eyes, distinctive cheek, what he thought was a strong chin, a well tapered nose and black hair that was combed back on the sides and back across the top.

The door opened and he step out into an entry foyer. His one bedroom, three thousand square foot apartment took up two thirds of the floor and was situated to the lake side of the floor he was on. There was a small fifteen hundred square one bedroom apartment to his right currently occupied by a rich widow that had live there since the building opened.

He was in the second year of a ten-year lease. He opened the door with the Ap on his phone and walked into the bright white twenty-foot white entry area with white walls that ran one third of the way toward the lake. To his left was a miniature statue of the thinker, that he had imported from Italy. It was highlighted by a spot light located at the top of the ten-foot ceiling.

The lighting of the foyer was an indirect light reflected off the ceiling from two light strips located about eight feet off the floor and hidden behind an angled shield.

He always felt as if he was home when he entered. The apartment had the smell he associated with it being new. He made sure that his cleaner kept it smelling that way.

Once in he hung his light jacket in an old closet that he had also brought from Italy that felt out of place but that anchored him to the feeling of his Sicilian roots he walked to the first hallway to his right and as he turned to go to his bedroom, he put his wallet in the alcove that he had built into the wall. This was where there was a key hanging that was for his antique Italian convertible sports car that was parked in the apartment's basement area.

He hung up his key ring with the keys to his office and an assortment of keys that he used at work or elsewhere on a second hook.

As he walked toward his bedroom door, the kitchen was to his left and to his right was the area he considered his morning and evening personal relaxation area. It was where he read the paper in the morning and in the evening, he sat and watched the news and then watched two of his favorite early evening shows.

The kitchen to his left had a great view of the lake and when he did cook, he enjoyed the fact that the arrangement allowed him to look out to the lake while he was standing behind the stove. The area to the front of the kitchen was where he sat to enjoy a cup of coffee or tea and just take in the activity out on the lake or the people walking along the beach.

The bedroom was in the middle of the next section of the apartment. To the right was a large walk-in closet that took up one third of the width and there was a grand master bathroom that took up two thirds of the width of that section of the apartment.

The master bathroom featured a glass enclosed shower, a jacuzzi, a two-sink counter with a mirror that ran its length. He seldom used the Jacuzzi and was thinking about having it replaced with a powered swimming lane.

He changed into his exercise closes and walked out of the second door of his bedroom into the exercise area where there was a treadmill on the left, a stationary bike in the middle and a free weight area to the right. The front of the area was open to the lake side of the apartment so as he exercised, he again had a great view out across the lake.

The entire lake side of the apartment was surrounded by a floor to ceiling glass wall that went from the entry foyer around to the lake front and then back to the entrance of the exercise area.

The front of the apartment was an area that pulled you in and made you feel that you would be pulled out into the void beyond the glass. There were no curtains but there were sections that could be moved out to break up the feeling of being at risk of falling. He never used the panels except when he entertained a large group of people.

Once a month he would host his top leadership and their families and then he would have the panels positioned so that everyone could feel comfortable.

This was his treadmill exercise day and as he walked, he was thinking about the past weekend when he had driven in his convertible.

He always enjoyed getting the car ready to go out. He kept it in a dehumidified bubble that lifted directly up toward the ceiling. He would check the oil and other fluids and then turn on the engine. Next, he would make sure the tires were at the right pressure. He would clean the wind shield and the mirrors. Then he would put down the cover and wipe off the leather seats with a leather treatment.

He would then put away all the cleaning gear. He was then ready and drove slowly out of the garage.

He mostly drove the smaller highways and always stayed exactly at or just below the speed limit. He was not going to stress the car, and he did not want to get a traffic ticket. It amazed him that he was constantly getting honked at and given the finger of some irritated driver that would speed by.

He had gone out to a nature sanctuary where he liked to hike and fish. When using his car and going fishing, he always fished catch and release because he was not going to carry any fish in the car.

As he slowed down his pace on the treadmill, he looked at his phone to see what time it was. He had expected a call from his two enforcers before he had started, and he was now angry that they had not followed his instructions.

He had made them stand in his office and repeat his personal number until they could do it from memory because he did not want them to write it down or put it on their phone. He wondered if they could possibly have forgotten.

The apartment bell rang, and he looked at the security screen to see who it might be. He saw that it was his Chinese dinner being delivered. He instructed the person delivering it to put it on the stand to the side of the door. He had paid and given a good tip via that Ap that he had so that he did not have to open the door to some stranger. He waited until the person got on the elevator and then went out and brought the meal in.

He chose to sit at the table in front of the kitchen so he could enjoy the view of the lake.

The more he thought about his two assassins the angrier he got. He decided to put them aside and focus on relaxing and enjoying the view.

After cleaning up from dinner he decided to take a long shower and get a good night's sleep.

Harold had activated his team, contacted the judge to get both an arrest warrant and a search warrant.

He was now on the phone with Johnnie who was in Cincinnati. They were discussing how to get into the apartment where Adriano lived. Johnnie said that he would turn off the security system and when they got to the floor where Adriano resided, he would open the apartment door lock, and they could enter cautiously. He would also control the lighting.

The only sensitive part would be to go into the bedroom and arrest Adriano. Johnnie added that hopefully, he did not sleep with a loaded gun under his pillow.

Harold got Alex on the line and asked if she wanted to be part of the raid.

She responded that she would love to be present on the phone but not in person. She said that she preferred to be sipping on a hot cup of tea and listening in.

He agreed to have one of his team members to call her so that could happen.

Trey commented that he would be on line with Alex.

Mary-Anne asked what time the raid was going to take place.

Alex let her know that it would be four in the morning.

Mary-Anne walked out of the kitchen and returned shortly carrying a table top speaker phone that she said she used when having a conference and said that she would fix an early morning breakfast of rolls, toast and whatever else they might desire.

She said that the phone would be on mute, and they could pretend that they were listening to an old-time thriller being performed on the radio.

Alex laughed and said that she was not sure about the thriller part and hoped it would be rather dull.

She connect her phone to the speaker phone and made sure everything was on mute.

Then she suggested they all get some sleep and come down bright and early.

Marge was given the duty of connecting with Alex. She laughed and asked if she could drop her phone in the event that she had to pull her weapon to defend herself.

Harold shook his head and joked that she needed to keep Alex involved since she was a better shot.

He then said that it was time to get the team to the apartment building and set up in the basement parking area. He had Johnnie on the line and when they arrived at the apartment building, he asked Johnnie to open up the entrance gate and was surprised that almost immediately after asking the gate went up.

The team got out and he made sure the each was wearing their Kevlar outfits. He made sure everything was ready. He had put in his ear buds so that he could listen to Johnnie but keep everything as quiet as possible. He then went to the elevator and was once again surprised when it opened as he approached it. He heard Johnnie say that he had the way prepared.

When the door opened on the thirtieth, the lights dimmed, and Johnnie said that he had disabled the security system, and the apartment door was unlocked.

The team entered and the lights came up to a low level.

Johnnie described the way to the bedroom and added the bedroom door was unlocked and as far as he could tell the lights were off.

Harold had one of the team kneel to the side of the door and push it open. He stepped in and to the side. Johnnie turned the lights to a very low level.

The team entered and surrounded the bed.

Adriano remained sound asleep with an eye cover over his eyes.

Harold quietly asked Johnnie to turn the lights fully on throughout the entire apartment.

When the lights were on, he loudly called out for Adriano to raise his hands because he was under arrest

Adriano ripped his eye cover off and sat up right in bed. It was obvious that he was confused.

Harold then repeated his request that Adriano raise his hands because he was under arrest for the attempted murder of a law enforcement officer.

Adriano said he had no idea what he was being accused of. He asked if the entry to his apartment was legal.

Harold handed him the search warrant and the arrest warrant.

Harold instructed him to get dressed and he would be sure to explain the situation as he was taken to a holding cell until he could stand before a judge.

Adriano made the mistake of using the line, "do you know who you are dealing with."

The entire team laughed and said that indeed they did, and they figured scum came in all shapes and sizes.

Mary-Anne had been making toast and listening in. She yawned and commented that she should have slept in with Russel who had declined to get up early to be part of the raid.

Alex thanked Harold's team for taking her along and that she was signing off.

She later called Harold and got brought up to date to how he was handling the operation, and that the main mafia office was cordoned off and an investigative team was going through it tooth and nail. They had already found the gun storage area where a huge arsenal of weapons were stored and had linked the ammunition there to the ammunition used by the two gunmen at her home.

They had the smoking gun, and it would be useful, but he said that the best weapon that would most likely to send Adriano to prison was as old as what had been used in the age of prohibition. It was the tax evasion information that Johnnie had guided the team to.

7 Introduction

*A*lex and Trey were talking about the fact that they were about to hit the twenty-four-hour mark of how long they had been in Chicago but that it seemed more like a month.

Trey shook his head and said that he thought that their world had gone into hyperdrive, and it was hard to fathom what had happened. He looked at Alex and commented that he really admired how she had immediately launched a counter attack to the unbelievable attack they had survived.

He then said that he also appreciated the   fact that her father had realized he had a dangerous daughter and had built a four-gauge shotgun, slug proof door that had given them a chance to take the two assassins down.

Alex laughed and said that they should give her dad an award for that door. She wished she had been around to see how he handled making the door. She said that she wondered what he had to do to reinforce the frame to hold the door.

They arrived at the apartment building and were guided to the area where Adriano's prize antique Italian sports car was parked. Alex walked over and looked at the dark plastic bubble and asked if she could see how it work. She took a series of pictures as the officer in charge pressed a button that caused the plastic cover to be lifted up. Alex took another series of pictures. She asked if the cover was custom made or if it was a specific brand name.

The officer pointed to a small emblem on the control panel. Alex walked over, read "Covers for Lovers.com," and took a picture of it. She said that she thought that her Jag should have something similar.

Trey laughed and said that the cover would most likely cost more than the Jag. Besides, she had a father that was constantly making certain that her Jag was in super shape.

Alex nodded and said that he was probably right, but she was going to check it out anyway. She then pointed to the Jag and said it was time to go and greet Adriano at his new residence.

When they arrived at the police headquarters where Harold had said Adriano was being held until his arraignment, after both showed their credentials, they were guided into the parking area.

Harold was standing up on the walkway waiting for them. He had two individuals standing with him that were in very formal-looking black suits, and both sported very nice leather brief cases. The only difference between the two was that the person that was a sandy blond had a light brown brief case and the one with black hair had a black briefcase.

Harold introduce brown briefcase as Andy Weller who was the IRS lawyer and black briefcase as Lenord Maxwell who was a criminal lawyer and a partner in the Maxwell Family Law Practice.

Alex greeted both of them and introduced herself and Trey as special agents currently working for the Illinois Lieutenant governor.

Harold said that he had arranged that they got to see and talk with Adriano before he called his lawyer. He had been made aware that Adriano had a lawyer that he insisted he get to call.

Alex stopped and asked that she be given ten minutes before she met with Adriano. She pulled Trey aside and said that she needed to talk with Johnnie because she had figured out a way to move Adriano into a tighter net.

She dialed Johnnie and asked him if he could do what Kekoa had done with the billionaire bank accounts.

Johnnie said he understood her request and he would immediately make a few key changes that would handle her immediate need and then he would contact Kekoa and take some lessons from him and organize everything the way that Kekoa had organized the material for the IRS.

Alex thanked him and then rejoined Harold. She let Andy know that he would get all the details that would let him track the money, get to the banks and to the accounts where the money was held. These banks would be in the US and offshore.

He would have that information by the time that Adriano was brought to court to be charged for money laundering and failure to pay taxes.

Andy asked how she could possibly do that in the next twenty-four hours.

Alex smiled and responded because she had a wizard whose magic supported her.

Harold asked who should take the lead when they met with Adriano.

She looked at Lenord, smile and said that he had the tougher case, and she was counting on he and his law firm to pile on and put Adriano in prison for the attempted murder of two law officers. She added that he might be acquainted with her mother who would be quite willing to help his law firm.

Lenord nodded and said that he was quiet familiar with her mother's reputation and would be sure to reach out to her.

Alex then said that she would appreciate taking the lead.

They were led to a meeting room where they were asked to sit on one side of the room. A moment later, Adriano, wearing an orange coverall and wearing white sneakers was led in. His handcuffs were connected to a ring on the table.

It was clear that he was upset and asked why he had not been allowed to call his lawyer.

Alex smiled and replied because she first wanted to introduce herself. She added that she had come to Chicago with peaceful intensions but had instead faced a chilling greeting colder than the wind from the lake on a cold winter's day.

She added that she was the person that he had tried to have assassinated three times. She then pointed to Leonard Maxwell and said that he would charge him with the attempted murder of two police officers. She added that those charges would keep him in court for at least five years followed by life in prison unless he were given the death penalty.

She went on to introduce Andy Weller the Chicago region IRS leader, who would charge him with money laundering and failure to pay taxes. Given scope of the number of bank accounts he managed, the result would be least thirty years in prison.

Finally, you have met Harold Zimmerman who with his team woke you up bright and early this morning and brought you to enjoy your orange outfit and she added that she was sure a very healthy morning meal. She then stated that the DEA would bringing charges of possessing illegal weapons. This would be the least of the charges but one that carried a fifteen-year penalty.

The final person who she introduced was Trey as the person who always had her back, and she pointed out that he had no one that was going to come forward to have his back. She added that his organization will tell you to be a good boy and face the music.

Now that I have made all the introductions let me tell you that you had better let your organization know that the Chicago Mafia is without its top leader and that you will be out of circulation for most of the rest of your lifetime.

Adriano looked at Alex and almost shouted that she had no idea how powerful he was and how soon he would be out and this time he would not fail.

Alex nodded and as she stood to leave, she said that he could now have his one phone call. She turned and everyone left with her.

After leaving the room Harold looked at her and said that was the most satisfying meeting that he had ever attended.

Andy thanked her for doing what she had just done. He was now really looking forward to getting the information that would make sure that Adriano was kept in jail for the entire time the case went on.

Lenord asked if her mother was as tough a nut as she was.

Alex smiled and replied that she was the softy as compared to her mother.

Lenord said that the first meeting he was planning to have after getting everyone in his practice up to speed was to meet with her mother.

Alex then invited the three go out on a weekend fishing trip that she was hosting. She looked at Harold and made sure he understood that it was he, his team, and all significant others.

On the way to the car, Trey said he was ready for his nap. Alex agreed and asked if later he wanted to go with her to the harbor and arrange for a weekend excursion on the Golden Goose. She also wanted to swing by the Pizzeria and arrange to have the event catered.

Trey said that sounded like a good plan otherwise he would spend the day in bed and not be able to sleep that night.

Alex said that after the previous night she figured she would have no trouble sleeping.

As she looked ahead to the house and saw that it was clear. The crime scene had been cleaned up and the bodies were gone, and the blood had been washed away. The roses were back where they had originally been. The only thing that remained visible was a shiny spot in the middle of the front door where the slug from the four-gauge slug had hit.

Alex parked in the garage and commented that her Jag had a very nice place to sit while she was away and that the cover over like the one Adriano had over his convertible was an over kill.

She walked back to the front door and put her finger in the hole that the slug had made. It was the only imperfection in an otherwise beautiful front door. She now took notice of the heavy-duty cement frame that supported the door. She stepped back and took a picture of it.

She wondered how much the door had cost her father.

Dexter was lounging behind the counter glad that it was a slow Thursday. He looked up, smiled, walked around the counter, and gave Alex a hug. He asked when she was going to host another of her famous fishing trips.

Alex laughed and said that was the reason she had come to him. She asked if Saturday would be possible.

Dexter said that the Golden Goose was ready to go out any time Alex wanted her to do so. He asked how many people would be going out so he could get everything ready.

She stopped to count and then replied that there would be twenty-five people.

He asked about children.

Alex smiled and said it would be the same three young people who were now no longer children.

She then shared some of the details of what had happened the previous day at her parents' home. She showed him the picture of the door that she credited with saving all of them. She added that her father had built the door after the two fishing trips that she had taken out on the lake. He told her that those outings had caused him to anticipate that his daughter might attract someone that might want to break in.

She said she had a picture of her father pointing to something and the picture of the door with the shiny spot where the slug had hit. She wondered if he might know someone who could merge the two picture, print it, and frame it.

Dexter nodded and said that he could sent the pictures to the person who mounted the fish for his guests, and he was sure that in a day he could get it delivered and have it on the Golden Goose.

Alex thanked him. Then she added that she wanted to connect him with her mother's pizzeria and let him arrange the catering and food for the fishing outing. Lunch was to be out on the lake, but dinner would be at her house, and he was invited to come as well.

She realized that she needed to call the two people she worked for and give them a first-hand report of what had transpired in the last twenty-four hours. It was to her a twenty-four-hour period that seem more like twenty-four months.

She drove to the Evercrest Pizzeria and walked in to greet her first police boss, Jason Shepard, who was now running the pizza shop.

He stopped what he was doing and came out from behind the counter to give her a hug. He asked what she was up to.

She said that if he came out fishing, he would get the scoop on what had happened in the last twenty-four hours.

He laughed and said that he would love to go fishing as long as a gun battle was not part of the trip.

Alex smiled and said that she did not think that would happen, but gun battles seemed to follow her footsteps.

She asked if she could have a plain cheese pizza with extra cheese.

8 Sent to the Closet

*A*driano could hardly contain himself as he watched the Black witch head out the door. He now had one goal in mind and that was to get released and have every person he had at his disposal assigned to eliminate her.

He made the phone call to his lawyer. He was confident that he would be able to manipulate the system and get him out on bail.

He made sure that it was understood that a substantial bonus on top of the normal fees was to be had.

The discussion of the charges led his lawyer to comment that they were not in a very good position. There were at least four major charges and depending on how the IRS split the cases it might be as many as ten separate charges.

He went on to say that the most damming charges that would keep him from getting bail were the three assassination attempts of a police officer.

Adriano was not pleased with what he was told. He needed to get out so he could leverage the people in his organization.

After his lawyer left, Adriano decided that there should be a fourth assassination attempt. He had a person on the police swat team that was a sniper and who was on his payroll. She had impressed him the day he had interviewed her. She had been on the payroll of his predecessor. Since his arrival he had continued to pay her five thousand a month to stand by and be available when needed. He figured that it was now the time that she was needed.

He was able to activate her by communicating through one of his field lieutenants who gave her the information needed for her to carry out the assassination.

This time he hoped that the assassin would succeed.

When Olivia received the order, she at first panicked. Then she realized that she had the opportunity to come out of the cold. She had been under cover for most of her police career. She wanted to get back to a normal life. She talked it over with her contact that worked in the Lieutenant Governor's office and got support for getting herself killed.

She would then be transferred to another police district and get back to having a real life. She was still young enough to have children and planned to do so with or without a significant other.

Her world was about to change for the better.

Jane shook her head as she thought about the situation. She had an undercover policewoman working for her that was supposed to off a special investigator that also reported to her who was going to kill the policewoman.

She had yet to hear from Alex, her special investigator. She had talked to Harold, her friend in the DEA and knew what had transpired the night before and the follow-up apprehension of the Chicago Mafia leader.

As if she had willed a call from her special investigator, Alex was at the other end of the line when she answered her next call.

Alex shared the fact that she was late in calling but it seemed that events had transpired so fast that she had trouble keeping up.

Jane let her know that she had talked to Harold and knew the details where he was directly involved but he only knew second hand what had happened at Alex's parents' the house.

Alex gave her an update about what had happened and the fact that she and Trey had killed the two men sent to kill them.

Jane then explained the situation that had come up because Adriano had ordered another assassination. She shared the fact that she had an undercover sniper on the swat team that also worked for the Mafia. She had received orders to shoot and kill Alex.

Alex asked how they should handle this new situation.

Jane said that her undercover agent wanted to get killed so she could return to a normal life.

Alex suggested that an attempt at the pier, or one out on the water as the Golden Goose went out as two potential spots. From a small boat out on the water, the person in the boat could get hit, fall over board and disappear below the water.

Jane said that the small boat scene offered the best way for it to take place. She would have her team set up the situation. The only other thing that needed to happen was that the scene be captured, and that it all seemed real.

Alex said that she would handle making it all seem real and getting it captured so it would make the evening news.

After hanging up she called the Chief and brought him up to date.

The Chief said that Johnnie had been giving everyone in Cincinnati a running commentary of what had gone on, so they were all up to date and everyone was eager to go fishing.

Alex did not tell him about another assassination attempt.

Alex said that breakfast would be available on board the Golden Goose bright and early and that it would leave harbor on time at eight.

The Chief said that they would all be there.

Alex spent the evening getting her props ready. Both her and Trey's issued weapons were being held in evidence, so she had cleaned and prepared her personal pistol that she used for target practice. She went out in the garage and loaded some bullets and put wax heads on them.

She selected one of her older blouses and cut a small hole in the middle of her chest then she used a piece of tape to hold the hole closed. She modified her Kevlar vest so that she could wear it under her blouse and were the hole in the blouse was located she positioned a flattened bullet by using two-sided tape to hold it in place.

The only person she shared what she was doing was Trey. He would film everything that was happening. Then when she was hit and knelt down, he was to pull the flattened bullet off the vest and hold it up for everyone to see. The two of them would take the dingy out to where the shooters boat was located and when they got there, they would signal back that the shooter was dead.

Then they would standby as a police boat came speeding out to take control of the scene. He should film the dead body being pulled out of the water and then stop filming.

She had sent Jane a text saying that her killer was to stand to take her shot and then when Alex raised her gun and fired twice, she was to fall backward into the water and stay behind the boat. She let Jane know that she had arranged for some local police friends to come out by boat and pull the body of the shooter from the water and zip her into a body bag.

After she got off the call, Trey commented that he would drive to the airport on Friday afternoon to pick up Lindsey and Nolan and bring them back to the house.

Alex suggested that she hire her personal cabby to meet them and drive them up.

Trey said that that felt like a great relief. He was still trying to recover from their Wednesday right and then their early morning participation in the arrest which was followed by going to the jail where Adriano was being held.

Alex suggested they relax by the pool and watch her mother busily making various snacks for the early evening get together.

Rose-Anne marveled that her daughter and Trey seemed so relaxed after having been involved in an assassination attempt and then having the Mafia boss arrested.

She had been contacted by the firm that was to prosecute the case against the Mafia boss and had agreed to meet with them after the week end.

Alex had let her know that one of the partners of the firm would be going fishing with them. She had laughed and said that her daughter was setting things up for her and thanked her.

Alex shook her head and said that setting her up had never crossed her mind. Harold was the person who had brought in that specific law firm. She pointed out that the local IRS had also been pulled in by Harold and he would also be going out with them.

She then reminded her that everyone going out would be coming to dinner after the fishing trip.

Rose-Anne said that one of the main dishes would be the fish that was caught but she also had Jason were working with a local caterer to have lobster tail, spare ribs, rib eye, prime rib, and a variety of sides such as butter milk biscuits, creamed spinach, delicata squash and twice baked sweet potatoes catered in.

Alex asked what she had in mind for desert.

Rose-Anne said that she had several deserts in mind such as, Baked Peaches, Strawberry Tart, Espresso Martini Ice Cream without the Martini, Chocolate Covered Strawberries, and a variety of ice cream flavors. She was leaving it up to the caterers based on what was available locally.

Alex said that it would be hard for her to control herself when it came to the deserts, and it would cost her hours on the treadmill.

Lindsey arrived from the airport and Anni came with her. Nolan, Linda, and Laurie ran to her and gave her a hug. Brian and Kekoa, and Anela had all flown up on the same flight.

Brian commented that he had never seen anyone that was as fast as she was at arresting the person who had tried to have her killed.

Alex was pleased to see them all and said they should gather around the pool area. She said that in a few moments her mother's Pizzeria would deliver several variety of pizzas and a wide variety of snacks such as bruschetta, meatballs, buffalo wings, honey BBQ wings, plain and spicy onion rings, zucchini fries, antipasto salad and garlic bread.

She pointed to the pool side refrigerator and said that it was loaded with a variety of soft drinks.

The chatter and laughter filled that pool side area. The food arrived and everyone dug in and continued the evening celebration.

About nine thirty, Alex suggested that those that were staying should make sure they were ready for bed and those that needed to get to the hotel should do so because it was going to be an early morning.

She said that she was calling it a day and going up to her room so she would be ready the next day.

Trey commented that he was still trying to get over the hours his work partner made him work and he was going to go up to his room as well.

Lindsey could see that Trey and Alex both looked exhausted, and she signaled Nolan that it was time to say goodnight.

Annie signaled to Brian that it was time for them to go to the hotel.

The evening ended and the cleaning crew from the pizzeria went into action and less than an hour later it would have been hard to believe that a major gathering had broken up.

Rose-Anne thanked Jason for having arranged for the food and the help in such a short time. She remined him that he was to come out fishing.

Back in her apartment Olivia was getting ready to get some sleep as well. She had driven out to where she was to be fishing and had rented a boat at the marina. She had been instructed to rent the boat from a small concern that was across the harbor from where the Golden Goose was tied off. She was impressed with the beauty of the yacht and wished she were going out on it instead of the boat she was to die on.

She cleaned her sniper's rifle and put it in its carrying case and then in the trunk of her car.

It took her forever to get to sleep, and it seemed that her alarm woke her up immediately afterwards.

The drive to the marina in the dark seemed an appropriate setting. She kept going over the upcoming shooting that would free her to live a normal life.

She had made sure she had no live ammo and that the one shot she would take was a wax head cap.

She knew that her actions had to be believable.

Everyone needed to believe she was dead.

338

9 Another Sniper's Death

*A*lex was up by five getting ready for what she hoped would be a believable performance of getting shot and of killing a would-be assassin. She had modified her Kevlar pullover so that it was short sleeve and hidden under her blouse that had the strategic hole at the center of her breast. She made sure that everything was as it should be then she drove to the boat harbor. Before going out to the Golden Goose she met with the local police team that would come out to pick up the body of the supposedly dead undercover policewoman who had been asked by Adriano to kill her. Alex thought through the very complicated and delicate performance that she and the person doing the assassination were undertaking. It had to be good enough to convince what would most likely be at least a local news cast audience.

After having agreed on the pickup teams actions and her actions, she walked out to the Golden Goose and put her personal items on board and then walked up to the bait house. She saw the lights come on just as she reached the end of the pier. She walked in and said good morning to Dexter who was just getting ready to carry a bait bucket and a bait box out to the Golden Goose.

He asked why she was so early.

She said that she had come to make sure that everything was ready on such short notice and that the group had grown by a few people.

Dexter nodded and said that he could handle a dozen more if necessary.

Alex replied that it would perhaps be only a couple.

She followed as he carried the bait bucket and picked up two more poles.

Once on board, he turned on the engine.

He asked if she would like a couple of pancakes for breakfast.

Alex smiled and said that she would love a couple and if possible two over easy eggs on top and a ton of syrup.

She was sitting out on the deck as the sun rose in a splendor of red, orange, and yellow splashing along the bottom of the few cumulus clouds that were floating slowly across the lake towards her. She saw her father park the large conversion van next to her Jag.

She laughed as everyone inside seemed to come out like clowns in a circus who come out of a tiny car in a continuous stream that seems to go on forever. She counted nine people in total. Then another van arrived and the Chief, his wife, Bill, his wife, Trever, his wife, Johnnie, and Mary all got out.

Seventeen people were all talking and laughing as they walked down the pier. She knew that Harold and his wife, and his team members and their spouses had yet to arrive, and they would add another eight people. It came to her that she had invited the lawyer and the IRS agents and that added four more. She then saw Jason and his wife arrive. That meant that if she counted herself and Dexter there would be thirty-three people on board.

She checked with Dexter who said that it would be crowded but that it would be no problem, and he had plenty of food coming and that there would be two caterers going out with them as well.

Alex thought through the performance that she had coming up and decided that she should take one of the rear fishing spots so that most of the people were behind her as the Golden Goose left the harbor.

After everyone was on board and had time to grab a breakfast box and find a place where they would fish Dexter declared that it was time to cast off.

She had a fishing box that held her gun next to her and had her pole leaning against the back deck rail as Dexter pulled away from the pier and headed out to the lake.

Alex saw the boat with the would-be assassin sitting exactly where she figured it would be. She looked back and saw the pick-up team putting their thirty-foot police boat into the water. It was now almost time for the spot light to be on her and she hoped that her performance would be believable.

She stood acting as if she were preparing her pole. She glanced around and saw that Trey was in position with his phone in hand.

She had just turned back when she saw the would-be assassin stand up and raise her rifle. Alex counted one and then fell to her knees, pulled her blouse so that the hole would appear. She opened her fishing box, pulled out her weapon, stood up, aimed, and shot three times. She watched as the shooter dropped her weapon into the boat and fell backwards into the water.

Trey rushed up, as if to check on her and she pulled a flattened slug from the hole in her blouse and handed it to him. She noted that Trey had his camera filming the entire time. She knew that she would later praise his focus on capturing the scene.

She took note that Dexter had stopped the Golden Goose.

She jumped up and said that they needed to get to the boat to make sure the shooter was dead. She rushed to where the Golden Goose's dingy was secured, dropped it into the water and she and Trey jumped in. They sped toward the dingy as she made a loud call for backup. It was a call that went nowhere and was done so it was heard by Trey's recording.

They got to the fishing boat, took a picture of the inside of the boat where the sniper's rifle lay and then took a picture of the shooter lying face down in the water with a dark circle of blood encircling it.

Then the sirens of the police boat caused them to pan the camera around to an oncoming boat speeding toward them. Alex put her hand with her gun in it up in the air as the spotlight on the boat focused on her. She made a production of putting the gun down. And shouting out that she was police.

The boat slowed and pulled along the other side of the fishing boat and with a pole pulled the "body" to its side. Two of the officers pulled the body out of the water. They made sure that the body had its back to the camera as it was pulled on board and then placed in a body bag. Only the zipping action was visible.

They then came around and had Alex put her gun in an evidence bag. And made a point of verifying her and Trey's badge ids.

When asked where she was going to be so they could follow up with her and return her weapon, she pointed to the Golden Goose and said that she was on the way to go fishing for most of the day.

They asked if she would come to the station once she was back and she agreed.

Trey quit recording the scene at that point and they returned to the Golden Goose.

The Chief watched the entire event and as Alex and Trey were returning, he felt like going to the back rail and clapping for one of the best performances that he had ever watched. He hoped that it was a good enough performance and be as good as what Alex wanted.

Alex wanted to ask someone if it were good enough but there would not be a second take it was good enough or it was a bust. She told Trey to release it to the news networks.

She went in and changed out of her blouse and put on a T shirt that boasted that she had caught the big fish. This was the T shirt that she had bought to celebrate her and Matt's relationship.

Dexter guided the Golden Goose out to where he normally went and then put it adrift out where the fishing was usually excellent.

It was hard for Alex to concentrate on fishing. After catching one nice trout she put her pole away. She filled a plate with vegetables snacks, got herself a large-iced tea and sat down at the table in the middle of the deck.

She wished that Matt had been able to come up for the weekend, but his team had been short of people, and at the last moment he ended up staying in Cincinnati.

The Chief came and sat down with her and congratulated her on her excellent shooting. He added that it was very lucky that she had worn her Kevlar protection to go fishing.

Alex knew that she had not fooled the Chief and that he was letting her know. She replied that after three assassination attempts on her she figured that she should be extra cautious. She then added that she would have to bring him up to speed on all the details when they had a chance to talk in private.

The Chief nodded and said that he would make himself available as soon as possible. He was wondering why he had been left out of the loop.

Trey came over to the table and said that three local news stations were sending their crews to interview her when they returned to the Harbor.

Alex groaned and said that she would try to enjoy the rest of the time out fishing so that she had enough energy to face the questioning she would be taking.

The Chief suggested that he and Harold get between her and the newscasters and field the questions.

Alex smiled and said that if he were Johnnie, she would make him two trays of cookies.

Johnnie had been fishing close by and had heard the exchange and said she should not be giving away his trays of cookies which he felt he had earned on this assignment.

Alex laughed and replied that when she got back to Cincinnati, she would just cook up a storm and bake a dozen trays of cookies.

The Chief got up and walked over to where Harold was fishing. He got his agreement to face the media and then went to get a brat. He had figured out that Alex needed everyone on board to believe the staged scene was real and the less everyone knew the more likely it would be believed.

Alex decided that the seat at the kitchen area table would be more comfortable. She was happy to see that the condiments and extra boxes of food had been put on the table and that no one was sitting where she wanted to sit. She slid in and was soon asleep.

The crew on the police boat turned to return to the harbor. Olivia got up and thanked them for getting her out of the freezing cold water. One of the crew laughed and said that the cold water helped to preserve dead bodies. He handed her a blanket and asked if they had come fast enough.

She said that yes, they had, and she was happy about the prospect of coming in from the cold.

He said that he would be glad to help her in her transition back to a normal life and would be happy to take her out to dinner whenever she was ready.

Olivia smiled and said that she would be happy to accept his invitation once she was free to do so. She was already happy about her return to the normal world. She spent the afternoon at a local pizzeria chatting with her new friend.

She received instructions to report for work at a police station in Waukegan. She was to leave her car where she had parked it and go by bus to her new apartment. Once again, she felt alive.

Alex came awake when the vibration of the engine of the Golden Goose let her know that Dexter was taking her back to the harbor.

She walked back out onto the deck. Her mother came over to her and asked how her nap had been.

The news crews at the head of the pier had each positioned their cameramen and interviewers and were ready to focus on the Black detective. The stations had done the initial investigations and knew that she was a top Cincinnati detective that was on special assignment with the office of the Illinois Lieutenant Governor.

They geared up their repertoire as the yacht approached the pier.

Alex waited as everyone disembarked. She was making it a point to be among the last to get off.

The Chief took the lead and walked toward the maze of the news crews. He knew exactly how to handle the situation.

Alex had been in similar situations and knew that the Chief and Harold would do the lead in. She would step forward, introduce Trey, and then answer about a dozen questions after which the Chief would step forward and close the interviewing down.

It went exactly as she figured it would.

Everyone else had left. The Chief and Harold went to where Harold's team was waiting.

She and Trey went to her Jag and then drove back to the house together. She complemented him on being an excellent cameraman.

Trey laughed and said he had a lot of practice doing selfies with Nolan and Lindsey.

He asked if she thought that the video was good enough to pull off their subterfuge.

Alex nodded and said that she hoped for Olivia's sake it was.

On his trip to the cafeteria, Adriano saw the news cast of the assassination attempt and the news interview. He was in disbelief as he absentmindedly poked at his meat loaf and mashed potato. She had survived four attempts and had killed three of the people that he had assigned to assassinate her. He was sure she had orchestrated his arrest and set up the charges he faced.

He figured it was time to see if he could bribe his way out of his current predicament. He also planned to seek help from his bosses back in Italy.

His lawyers successfully delayed the addition of a third charge of attempting to kill an officer of the law. He was informed that the charge would likely be added when the details of the incident were presented to the judge.

Adriano received additional bad news when his Italian bosses told him that he should face the charges and when it was clear what his fate was to be they would get back to him about his options.

For the first time in his career, he came to realize that he had lost control of the situation around him. He now realized that he should have listened to his leadership team about leaving the Cincinnati detective alone.

He was further dismayed when his second in his Chicago leadership team was promoted to run the Chicago organization.

It was then that he realized what it felt to be at the bottom of the barrel. The fact that he was still alive was the only bright spot in his very disturbed mind.

Alex and Trey arrived at the house to find everyone out by the pool enjoying each other's stories about the fish that they caught or the one that had gotten away.

They were both surrounded and had to answer a ton of question about what had happened. Her mother came to the rescue and said that she needed Alex in the kitchen for a moment.

Alex followed her mother and when they got to the kitchen her mother said that she was just a front for the Chief and the DEA, who were waiting in the library.

Alex thanked her and took a glass of iced tea and walked back to the library.

The Chief greeted her, held up a golf trophy, and presented her with the best actress of the year award.

Harold clapped said that the award would also be enriched with an around the world tour.

Alex smiled and admitted that it had been a staged shooting in order to give a long-time undercover operative the opportunity to come out of the cold. This operative, who was now turning thirty-five, had been undercover as a sniper assassin for the mafia for seven years. For the first time, she had been activated by the Mafia chief to perform an assassination. She needed her dying to be as real as possible.

The Chief smiled and said that he was proud of her and that he felt that she had pulled it off. He had watched the news reports and felt that the footage that Trey had shot, and released anonymously, had done the job.

Alex smiled and said that the only thing that it had cost her was the loss of an old blouse and the fact that she would have to buy a replacement for the top half of her Kevlar suit. She added that she was currently weaponless because her officially assigned weapon and her personal weapon were both being held as evidence.

The Chief laughed and said that since she had quit being issued new cars that had all been destroyed by her attackers, he now had money in his budget to replace her weapons. He said she should put in her order for a new weapon.

Alex gave him a hug and whispered that the one she had in mind would only cost a few thousand.

10 Unseen Spirit

*A*driano's time in his cell seemed endless. He had never spent so much time doing absolutely nothing. He paced around in his cell but that only seemed to make things worse. Once a day he was taken out to a fenced in courtyard and allowed an hour to walk around or do whatever pleased him. He usually walked, did a few pushups, squats, knee bends and sit ups on the well-worn bench that was in the courtyard. He realized that he had lost track of the number of days that he had been in confinement. He felt certain that it was beyond the legal time, and he was going to have his lawyer put in an objection about the amount of time.

His lawyer had let him know that the time was not excessive. She had also been surprised that the IRS had a very detailed accounting of the money flow, the amounts and how they were moved through specific banks to launder the money. She also became aware about how many of the details she was unfamiliar with. She had reviewed everything with various lawyers in the firm and they each privately said that her client's goose was cooked.

She kept that fact from Adriano because she knew it would infuriate him, and he would want her to take actions that were illegal.

After a week of waiting, Adriano was ready for any action, getting taken to court seemed to release his negative feelings. He had been allowed to dress in one of his expensive Italian black suits and he was wearing one of his impeccable polished pairs of black shoes. Except for being handcuffed, he felt human once again.

Two policemen escorted him into the courtroom. He looked around and was surprised to see that Alex Evercrest was not there. He had figured she would be present at the prosecution table or sitting behind it, but she was clearly not in the room.

He took another look.

His surprise affected him mentally because he had been so sure she would be there to gloat at his predicament. She was not there but he felt her presence. He did not believe in spirits but in this case, he was sure that her spirit was present and that it might even be laughing at him. He now thought of her as a shadow fighter.

He sat down with his lawyer and took in the other people in the courtroom. His second in command who had been promoted to take his place was not there but two of his leadership team were sitting in the back. This made sense to him since it would be a bad idea for the new mafia chief to be present at the trial.

The judge entered and all rose and waited for his order to be seated.

The judge turned to the prosecution and asked him what the charges against the defendant were.

The prosecution rose and detailed the charge of tax evasion and money laundering and sat down.

This was a surprise to the defense. The judge knew what he was walking into the room to preside over.

The defense had been prepared to declare innocence to the charge of attempted murder. She had been aware of the charge of money laundering and tax evasion but was surprised that it was the charge that the prosecution had decided to prosecute first. She had been sure that the more serious crime would be first.

She rose and let the judge know that her client was pleading not guilty to the charges.

She knew that he was guilty as sin, but her job was to defend him, and she hoped that she could somehow guide the trial so that she could get the minimum for those charges.

She knew that she would have her hands full during jury selection trying to identify jurors that would be amiable to the idea of not paying taxes. It would be harder to select them based on the millions of dollars involved in the money laundering scheme. It would be cheating on taxes versus on moving millions of illegally gained money to make it look as if it were legal.

She wished she had gone to work for a law firm that was not so closely connected to the Mafia. The firm was always skirting the illegal side but stayed just inside the legal part of the laws that they were dealing with.

She now wondered when and how the sledge hammer of the charges for attempted murder would hit. It was clear to her that the prosecution strategy was to prosecute the case that could quickly move forward and be resolved and then bring up the more complicated case.

She wondered how long she had while the prosecution hunted down bank accounts and where and when money had been moved in order for it to prove the money laundering part of the trial.

She was to be surprised by the fact that it would take less than a month.

Alex had returned to Cincinnati. She, Trey, Bill, Trevor, Johnnie, and the Chief were all sitting in a team room watching the opening session.

Johnnie had tapped into the courts video cameras and was moving from view to view that gave the rather dry proceedings some life. He was also providing some humorous dialogue about what Adriano was thinking.

It was clear by the dialogue in the room that everyone was enjoying the session.

They all would have been surprised at the accuracy of Johnnies' dialogue about the fact that Alex was not present as Adriano walked in and looked around several times.

Alex laughed and said that she had taken Brian's and Kekoa's advice to give the spot light to the IRS and the court lawyers and fade from the scene. She added that she had decided that she needed time to bake the cookies she had promised because she knew she would be held accountable to deliver the cookies as promised.

Johnnie held up one of her cookies and replied that it was great that they got to see the kickoff of the trial while enjoying some of those cookies.

Alex nodded and said that she hoped that replacing Adriano would end the pointless revenge attitude that he had exhibited.

The Chief added that he could now focus on what Cincinnati needed from his detectives.

Bill added that he too was ready to focus on the issues the area faced.

Trevor shook his head and said that he hoped whatever they were assigned would in the future once again get them an invite to go fishing. He had never been big on fishing until the several experiences of going fishing with Alex where not only did he always catch a fish, but he got to witness the star detective demonstrate her unbelievable markswomanship.

The Chief laughed and said he agreed and said that he believed Trevor had just coined a new word.

Johnnie focused in on the defense lawyer and commented that it was clear that she was surprised by the charge of money laundering and tax evasion being brought up first.

And that the charge of attempting to kill an officer of the law would be brought up at a later time.

He put the words, "Whoa, what is happening here. I was ready to plead not guilty to attempted murder. I know my client is guilty as sin of money laundering and not paying his taxes," into the defense lawyer's mouth.

That brought a chuckle from everyone in the room.

The judge then ruled that the case would move to the next stage. He stated that the requested bail was denied and because he thought that Adriano posed a flight risk his passport was to be seized.

The judge also said that he was having Adriano sent to a Federal Bureau of Prisons detention facility where he would be held throughout his trial and then after his trial if found guilty, he might be sent to some other facility. He added that his waiting time in prison would count as time served.

The entire proceeding took less than a half hour.

Adriano walked out in a state of shocked at the speed at which the proceeding had taken place and he was dismayed when he realized that he would be taken back to a prison where he would reside throughout his trial. It did not matter that his time would count to any sentence that might be imposed.

He had come to realize that time in a cell and the brief time out in a fenced in outdoor area made him feel like he was a chicken in a hen house. It was not a roam free environment and the thought that most chicken as they aged were made into chicken soup.

Nothing had gone the way he had expected it to go.

Once again, he experienced the strange feeling that he had engaged a person who had strange powers. Powers that he had never faced before in his lifetime. He looked around expecting to see that person and shook his head as he was told to change into the orange jump suit.

She had become a shadow fighter that had handedly defeated him. A shadow fighter that he would dwell on wondering how she had pulled it all off. A shadow fighter that had anticipated his every move.

Alex meanwhile asked the Chief where he wanted to have lunch.

The Chief pointed to Johnnie and said that he would go to any place recommended by the departments food expert.

Trevor commented that he wanted a river scene so he could once again observe Johnnie watching logs floating down the Ohio.

Johnnie smiled and named a newly opened restaurant that claimed a great view of the river and the best food in the city. He added that good food always accompanied a good view of the river.

Alex commented that she expected him to pay since he would soon be getting a rich reward from the IRS for having turned in the information that was the basis for their case.

The Chief said he would have to look into who would get the money since Johnnie was on his payroll.

Alex nodded and made the comment that the Chief could certainly challenge that but highlighted the fact that he was walking on egg shells since Johnnie's action might be considered illegal.

The Chief replied that he would focus on lunch and that he knew of no illegal actions being taken by any of his detectives or their supports.

Alex laughed and suggested that they get to lunch so they could all watch Johnnie watching logs float down river.

After arriving, getting their drinks, and putting in their orders. They discussed the court proceedings until the food arrived at the table. They were all sitting at a table that had a great view of the River.

Johnnie had order a T-bone steak and a baked potato. When the food had all been placed in front of him, he did look out on the river. He suddenly stood up and pointed and said that he saw a body entangled in the limbs of the tree floating by.

Trevor was about to make a smart remark about it when he stood, pointed, and said that he saw the body too.

The Chief made a call and before the log went out of view, they saw a police boat speeding toward it.

Alex looked at the team and suggested they focus on enjoying their meal because Johnnie had most likely just identified their next assignment.

Johnnie said that he was going to enjoy his steak and not look at the river for the rest of the time they were at lunch.

Little did anyone at the table know how right Alex was in her prediction. It would take the Cincinnati team up the river to crimes committed for several generations that had been occurring from Steubenville down the Ohio river to Marietta. These crimes were illegal but very profitable and had been happening for at least one hundred years.

The End of the Shadow Fighter

352

Moonshine

1 The Hooch and the Fortune

Hillary, her feet hanging over the edge of the cliff watched the black waters of the river below as the sky slowly changed to a mix of orange, yellow and pink. The sun seemed determined to drive the dark of the early morning back to where night hid from the day. The striking red color of the ferns along the cliff to her left and the layers of greyish blue along the mountain ridges out to the far horizon mesmerized her. She was taking a break from her morning hike that she had added to her regular visits to the stills that she owned and had hired still operators to operate.

She had spent the last few years acquiring and partnering with still operators across most of the state.

She enjoyed many an early morning hike as she was doing at the moment. Just as often it was an evening trip where she watched the sunset. It was a business that she had never dreamt that she would be running. She now considered herself the "Hooch Shine Mama."

She credited her grandmother and her own partying life to having gotten her into her current business.

Her grandmother had always talked about her "Appalachian culture." The culture was actually rooted in their Scottish roots, which went back to the sixteen hundreds Scotland. She was fascinated by her family history. It was one rooted in maintain their personal independence.

She was in her final year at junior college when her grandmother died and left her two million dollars. She was surprised by the amount and that her grandmother who had live a long life had been able to accumulate so much money.

The money represented a branch in the road that took her life in an entirely new direction. The inheritance made her question what she wanted to do. She had applied to several colleges but knew she had no real desire to pursue that path. She was an outdoor mountain girl.

Moonshine

The question of what she wanted to do drove her to the edge of sanity. She needed to find something other than working in an office.

Then one night at a friend's party she was introduced to a young man, Crayton Taylor. It was not a romantic attraction. She was mesmerized when he got a little drunk and told her about what he did to make a living.

He handed her an open quart jar filled with a clear liquid that had a faint tangy, pungent, malty, smell with a hint of alfalfa. She wondered whether it was tequila. Before tasting it, she asked what it was.

He proudly said that it was the hooch that was the icing on the money he made. He pushed the bottle toward her mouth and told her to take a sip.

She took a small sip and realized that he was talking about moonshine.

The smooth way it warmed her throat as it went down, followed by the warming of her stomach made her want another sip. She took another small sip and complemented him on how good it tasted and how smooth it was.

He smiled and said that it was a family recipe that each generation had worked on improving. He claimed he was the fourth generation of moonshiners and that his hooch had taken the taste up a notch.

He took another sip and handed the jar back to her.

She remembered laughing and joking as they passed the moonshine back and forth.

The next morning, he woke up in her bed and asked her how he had gotten there.

She smiled, told him that the two of them had finished the quart of his moonshine and she that she had barely been able to help him to her apartment. She asked him if he wanted to go out for breakfast.

He said that he would love to, but he needed to go up the mountain and get his still into action and then he needed to get to his day job.

She asked if after breakfast she could go along and be of help.

He nodded and said that if she could stay at the still, she could make sure that the temperature on the still did not go too high. He suggested that she bring a cooler with lunch and some drinks.

He drove his pickup to a where a small single lane road left the highway. He drove for about a mile and parked well into the brush. He then walked over to a narrow path that made its way through the brush. The trail looked more like a deer trail than a hiking trail. He carried her red metal cased cooler as if it were a feather and led the way up.

She was challenged by the slope up the mountain as she followed behind his almost jogging pace. He kept looking behind to make sure she was keeping up. He explained that he was late and needed to make it back to work in about forty-five minutes.

They were probably half way up to the top of the mountainside when he turned off the trail and led the way through a thick stand of trees.

Suddenly ahead of them was a rather large depression surrounded by rock and in the middle was a forest green elongated building that was about a highway lane wide. As they got closer, she could see through its horizontal boards and see three bright polished copper tanks.

She breathed in and seemed to both smell and taste the sweet, spicy, and fruity aroma as she walked in the door.

He led her in and proudly pointed to the three polished round copper structures that to her looked like large thermos bottles. The middle thermos was the largest. The first one was next in size and the final thermos, whose output went to a fifty-gallon drum, was the smallest.

He explained that the still was a fifty-gallon, ten foot high still and that the thump keg and worm box made the entire structure fourteen feet long.

He pointed to a pipe that was bringing in water to cool the distillate at the last stage. He said that the water from the spring at the outer edge of the depression was one of the secrets of the great taste of the hooch.

He handed her a small glass and asked her to taste it.

She was surprised that it had a unique flavor that most waters lacked. She wondered what chemical was dissolved in it.

He said that this was the day that he was kicking off the actual distillations cycle that would extend out for about three weeks and during that time would, if everything were kept in control, produce fifty gallons of pure hooch.

He looked at her and asked whether she could stay and monitor the temperatures and make sure the gas burner stayed on and that the cooling water pump would stay on.

Hillary had nothing planned and said she would.

He pointed to the cot that was against one wall and said that she could take a nap if she needed one.

He added that there was a great view of the valley when the trail reached the top of the ridge, and she might enjoy the hike there. He smiled and added that the black berries along the way were all getting ripe and might make the hike even more enjoyable. He told her to also look for the few gooseberry bushes along the way. They were golden in color and pure joy in taste.

He said he had to go and disappeared.

She watched the still operate for about an hour and realized that it seemed to be doing whatever it was supposed to. Everything was stable and there was nothing for her to do.

She decided that the hike up the trail was a good idea. She was constantly stopping to pick blackberries. The dark blackberries had a tart bordering on sweet and tangy flavor, while unripe berries were on the sour or bitter side. She only found one bush of goose berries, but they were truly pure joy to taste.

She got to the top and sat down on a boulder set a few feet back from the edge of a cliff that ended below in the jumble of jagged pieces of what had once been the face of the cliff.

She decided to call Crayton and ask a few questions about running the still.

She asked the cost of the materials that he put into the still.

He said that he normally spent about five hundred dollars for the grain that he put in.

She asked how much he sold a quart for.

He responded that for a quart he was currently getting fifteen dollars.

She did the math in her head and figured that each batch was worth three thousand dollars, so the margin was twenty-five hundred dollars.

That would be thirty-six thousand dollars a year.

She asked him how long the production season ran.

He let her know that he had extended it from the beginning of May to the end of October and he managed to get seven batches done during that time.

He added that he was working on shortening the time to make each batch to two weeks by preparing the mash ferment in a separate container. He said that approach would double his production.

She shook her head when she realized that he was currently making only eighteen thousand dollars for his efforts, and he was risking getting arrested, facing up to five years in prison and being fined ten thousand dollars.

She went back to the still and found a pencil and paper and spent the rest of the day figuring out how many stills were needed to make the risk an attractive choice.

The page she had scribbled on was totally covered when she decided that she would needed to control sixty stills to make it a worthwhile venture. When she factored in his doubling of his current production it dropped down to a more reasonable thirty stills. That was still a big number.

She wondered whether there were that many stills in existence and if not if there were that many locations available to put them.

She looked at the still in front of her and realized that there was enough space in the current building to put in two more stills.

That would reduce the locations from thirty down to ten or fifteen separate locations.

She could envision operating that many.

She then wondered how difficult it would be to get the amount of materials for three stills up and put in place. She also wondered if she could find the operators for all the stills.

She figured her best bet was to recruit existing moonshiners and see what kind of deal she could arrange with them. If the sites used by the moonshiners was big enough, she could triple their operations.

She figured they would be making three times as more money would attract most of them.

She knew that she was taking a branch in the road that she had never dreamt of. It was a branch that had a high risk, but it also had a high reward. It was certainly not a traditional line of work. She laughed and thought that she would label it as a career in mountain side hiking, hooch making and fun.

Not much later she proposed expanding Crayton's operation. He said he liked the idea. He would be able to quit his current line cooking job and spend his entire time running three stills.

He asked how they would split the money they made. She suggested that for the first year after the additional two stills were on line, he get one hundred percent of what they sold. Then his take would drop to seventy percent. She pointed out that it would be almost twice as much as his current income counting his day job and running his one still.

He said that sounded like a great deal for him but what about her?

Hillary said that she hoped that he would help her make similar deals with enough other moonshiners so that she could get enough from each still that she would make a small fortune.

He nodded and said that he knew of about six other people running stills, but he figured he could ask around and get more names. He was not sure if they would all be interested but he figured if she expanded their businesses, they would likely take her up on a similar deal to his.

It took her only three years to expand her moonshine business to the point that she was partners with eighteen operators that in total operated fifty-one stills.

She was shy of the sixty stills that she had at one time estimated she would need when she had done her first calculations, but it put her close enough that she figured that it was time for her to recoup her investment before going any farther.

She smiled as she looked in the mirror, realized that she had taken that other branch in the road and that she was happy about her choice.

2 Dam Right

Samuel stood on the grated metal walkway of the dam looking into the clear water that seemed to go down to a deep black depth. He could see fish eating the gear algae growing off the walls of the dam. The water of the Ohio was still clear, but Samuel knew that even this high up the river, the pollution whether visible of not was already in the river.

The Pittsburg buildings and factories were spewing their waste all along its banks.

As a dam lock gate operator, he also saw how the tugs seemed to treat the river as their garbage disposal container. He often envisioned not opening up the lock for one of the polluting tugs and making them pay a fine. It was a fantasy that he knew would never happen.

He had grown up boating, swimming in and fishing in the Ohio. His family owned a cottage on its bank and had a pier that ran a short distance out. This was where during the warm weather months they kept their ski boat and the fishing boat that was his father's pride and joy.

He still went out almost every weekend fishing with his dad.

Skiing was still high on his list, but his dad had more or less turned the black twenty-five-foot ski boat with its two one hundred horsepower outboard engines over to him.

It was usually he and his friends that did the skiing almost every weekend of the summer. He usually held a grill out on the pier.

They would ski off the end of the pier. He was a good enough skier that he could take off from the pier, ski up the river and on the return, he would let go close enough that he would ski in toward the side ladder and get on it before the water got above his knees.

It was his way of showing off to the young women that were watching.

He knew that he was fortunate to be living the good life.

His job as a lock operator was rather boring except when a barge was coming through the lock. At this stage in the river, most tugs were only pushing a couple of barges. His lock could only handle three at a time. This meant any ambitious tug operators choosing to push more than three barges needed to make more than one trip through the lock. The process of going through was time-consuming and most operators chose not to do so.

He and his friends often spent Friday nights at Mallard's Bar and Dance Club in downtown Weirton. The normal routine was to meet for dinner, sit and drink beer, and then dance the night away.

He lived within walking distance which allowed him leeway in how much he drank.

It was during one of these nights where a friend of his introduced him to Hillary. He enjoyed the evening chatting and dancing with her.

He was disappointed when she turned him down when he invited her to his apartment but perked up when she said she would love watching a barge go through the lock.

It was during her visit to watch a barge go through that she invited him to come down and party with her in Wheeling.

He accepted and the weekend he went to Wheeling and enjoying a great night dancing she invited him to her apartment.

Since then, he had been in Wheeling about once a month.

So far, he could not figure out how she made her living, but he learned that she traveled throughout West Virginia checking on her business investments. He was really curious what type of investments one could make in the state that would have you traveling around to check on it. He figured it had to be property and that she was some sort of realtor.

He wanted to go to the next level with her, but it was clear that she was not ready for anything like that, so he focused on his job and periodically going to Wheeling.

He knew that he was living the good life and that she seemed to be the last piece to that puzzle, but she seemed to be just out of reach his.

Hillary indeed was not ready. She liked Sam and enjoyed spending time with him, but she had similar relationships with at least a half dozen other very handsome and virile young men.

Sam was the oldest of those and the one that seemed the most stable and held the most promise, but she knew that she wanted to do much more before she settled down and settling down was at the bottom of the list.

She pushed forward and focused intensely on the expansion of her business.

She found that it took time to befriend the still operators. Many seemed to be from the shy and recluse side of the social spectrum. In each case she spent time to get to know them where they operated their still. She partied with each of them and learned who their friends were.

Several of her prospects were true loners and she spent significant time just getting to the point where they would sit with her at the bar and share a drink with her. She was often more successful asking if they would take her hunting.

When she was introduced to them at a bar, getting to their stills was often even more of a challenge.

The challenge multiplied when she got into proposing the expansion of their moonshine business. She lost that challenge to two of them but the rest, once they understood her proposal, accepted. Later when they realized how much more money, they were making they thanked her for being patient with them.

Some of the still operators ended up in her apartment but most did not. She had straight business relationship with most of them.

She spent more than two years and most of her inheritance expanding her still kingdom and making each still almost three times as productive as they had previously been.

She had to drastically sharpen her marketing and distribution capability in order to move the increased moonshine volume that each still was producing. She moved more volume by decreasing the unit cost of each jar of moonshine, and she was smart enough to decrease the quantity in each jar by a few ounces.

She also had to get the people running her stills to be more productive.

She coached them on how to time their three stills so that the work was balanced.

She made a point setting up a schedule of bringing up the materials for the still so that the work was distributed throughout the week or month.

The same was true for bottling and then distributing the moonshine.

She made sure that she watched the futures market to get the best price on corn and the other ingredients and set up a central distribution hub where all her still operators picked up their supplies.

Her ability to organize her supply chain, the production and distribution system was an example of supply chain management that would have ranked among the best in the country but of course she could not share what she was doing. Had Ford been alive and known what she was doing he would have been proud of her and named her his star pupil.

She did all this on a minimum of sleep and a minimum of partying.

It took its toll.

One morning as she brushed her hair and looked in the mirror, she saw a white streak of hair on the left side of her head. She held that strand of white out and looked at it for at least ten minutes.

Then she laughed because she realized that her business was finally producing the cash flow that she had calculated that day, just a few years past, when she had figured what it would take for her to build her moonshine empire.

It had cost her but now she was in control of a business that was churning out the cash that was rushing into her money well. It was as if it was being pumped in by a powerful water pump. In the next year she would recoup her more than two million dollars of investment and then in the following year she would more than triple the money that she had started out with.

Life could return back closer to normal. She could take time to enjoy some parties with her friends.

Layton had been one of the still operators who had taken the deal to expand his moonshine making operation. The increase in his income meant he could quit being a common laborer and enjoy some of the other pleasures such as chasing some skirts and partying on the weekends.

As his still operation tripled in volume, he realized that he was working harder than when he ran only one still and worked as a general laborer. After a year he came to the conclusion that what he was making was not enough and that he was going to demand a bigger share than he was currently getting. He figured he was in a great position to do so.

Hillary was surprised when Layton, the operator that she recognized as the least capable, producing the least and least trustworthy demanded a bigger share of the take. She knew that was not going to happen.

She explained to him that he was getting the biggest portion of the money that his three stills were producing and that he had the same deal she had with every other still operator. She shared that every one of those operators had let her know that they felt it was a great deal and were very happy about it.

Layton listened and negatively shook his head and said he didn't believe what she was telling him. He figured she was getting most of the money being raked in on the moonshine he was operating.

Hillary took him through the books that she kept on his still operation. She explained the arrangement, drew it out on paper so she could show how the finances were managed and the fact that his still was actually making slightly less than most of the others.

Layton got angry and accused her of trying to confuse him and that he was going to bring in the DEA and share what he knew about her operation if he didn't get a better percentage.

Hillary decided that she needed to meet his demand, until she could figure a way to get rid of him.

It was as if he had read her mind, he pulled out a pistol, that she recognized as a thirty-eight or something similar, and threatened to shoot her if she didn't double what she was currently paying him.

She recognized the danger she was in, nodded and said that she would write him a check for the money.

He said he did not want a check but wanted cash and that the two of them should go to the bank and get it.

She put her check book away and said that they should go down to her car and go to the bank. On the way down the path, she waited until the trail took a sharp turn and then grabbed his gun hand and turned it upward and under his chin.

Layton was surprised by the move and inadvertently pulled the trigger and killed himself.

Hillary was shocked by what had happened. She looked around to make sure no one was on the trail or in the woods. She pulled Layton's body back into the brush. She was thinking hard about what she needed to do.

She needed to get rid of the body and she needed to get someone to run the still.

Two people came to mind.

Crayton, her first and best still operator, had his stills only fifty miles away. She would offer him the opportunity to more than double his income if he ran both operations. She figured he would be willing since it would put him into a much better financial position. He was one of the still operators that she had come to trust.

Getting rid of the body was a little more of a sensitive issue. She thought about burying him somewhere on the mountain side but figured it might be too easily discovered by hunters or dug up by animals.

She decided to call Samuel to see if he might help her figure out what to do.

Samuel listened to Hillary explain what had happened. He said that he knew how to handle the situation and that they should do it that night.

He told her to meet him at the bottom of the trail. He would bring his pickup to where the trail came out of the forest. He would go up with her and bring the body in the back and then take the body to the Ohio river, weigh it down and dump it down stream of the dam where he worked. He figured the body would sink to the bottom and decay. It would never be discovered.

Hillary thanked him. She led him to Layton's body, followed his pickup to the dam, and watched as the body totally wrapped with a heavy-duty link chain was dumped into the river. She noted that Samuel threw the gun into the river as well.

She then followed Samuel to his favorite bar where they spent the evening dancing and having a few brews.

That night was the first time she went to his apartment.

It was also the first night of a long rain storm that set a new record for rainfall in a single week. By the middle of that drenching the Ohio river level rose to the point that for the first time since he had been hired, he had to open the gates to the dam's flood overflow passage.

The flow of the water was so high that trees and a ton of debris washed down river.

Hillary had gone to the river and stood almost a block back from the banks of the river and wondered where Layton's body might end up.

3 The Body in the Tree

*T*he river was a churning brown water with small branches and a generous amount of trash swirling along as it seemed to be rushing to somewhere important. Dr. Rogers took in the scene and wondered in what kind of shape the body would be in.

The hearse pulled up to where several police cars with their lights flashing were pulled over and directing traffic at the point where the tree with the body in its branches had been tied off. He directed the driver to park the van as close to the riverbank as possible.

Getting the body out of the tree was a little more of a challenge than had been anticipated. The body was wrapped in a heavy chain, and it had been skewered by one of the tree limbs. The limb entered the body just above the groin area and exited out the left shoulder.

As he looked at the situation it was clear to him that when he examined the body, he would find out that it had been dead before being wrapped in the chain and dumped into the river.

He was sure that the chain was the reason the body and the tree had remained together.

He had one of the firefighters cut the limb so that his team could take the limb and the body to the morgue. He watched as the firefighters cut the limb with a chainsaw. He was impressed with the balance the firefighter displayed as he handled the chainsaw. Then it was a balancing act getting the body and limb into a boat to bring it to shore.

His team struggled to get the body and limb into a body bag so they could transport the two to the morgue. They had to get the firefighter to cut another two feet of limb off to make it happen.

He looked around and counted six police, six firefighter and his team and shook his head as he thought about the fact that one body had used so many resources. The weary tax payer would wonder where their taxes were being used.

The team carried the body bag into the morgue and put it on the first table. After removing the black plastic bag, they stood around the body skewered by the tree limb wondering what to do first.

The consensus was that they should first take the chain off.

He made sure that pictures were taken so they could keep track of their unusual cadaver. This was one of the first times he had a person wrapped in chain and also skewered by a tree limb.

The lock on the chain proved to be a challenge but he found a diamond coated blade that slowly cut through the three-quarter inch lock.

The chain was also three-quarter inches thick and when put on the scale registered three hundred pounds. The weight of the chain was a clear indication that the body would never have surface on its own and the only reason it had been found was that the tree had skewered the body. The fact that the chain had no corrosion meant that the body had only recently been thrown into the river.

He also noted that the body's ears and nose had been nibbled on but were still mostly in tack. He estimated that the body had only been in the water a few days.

Once the chain was off, the team worked to get the limb extracted.

They had the limb on one examine table, the body on the other and they put the chain on the third table.

The clothes were removed so the body could be examined.

He did not expect to find much water in the lungs and did not. He figured the body had been thrown in after the person was dead.

The organs in the body cavity were torn and damaged by the tree branch but there was nothing else of significance except that the liver gave proof that the individual was drinking excessively. He was not surprised to find the traces of alcohol in the blood.

When he cut into the skull, he found the bullet and then found that it had entered through the roof of the individuals mouth. He thought that this was an unusual way to shoot someone.

He finally examined the clothes. The well-worn boots had pebbles lodged in the thick hard rubber treads. He put the pebbles into a bowl and asked one of the team to see if they might help in getting the location of where the body had started its trip down the river.

The belt buckle was unique in that it was a brass depiction of a black bear. He looked for a trade name and found a hand etched signature on the back side of the buckle.

He figured that Alex would be able track down the person who had made the buckle.

The thick flame-resistant, unlined, button-front work shirt that was thick enough to serve as a jacket in cool weather. It seemed to indicate a person who worked out in the elements.

The well-worn dungaree work pants were made of a heavy cotton denim. The cargo pockets were empty except for a few coins in one pocket a comb in another. The articulated knee area indicated that the person very likely was a construction worker.

The surprise was the round package of chewing tobacco that claimed to be the best in all of West Virginia that was in the right pocket.

He figured that might prove to be the best clue but that could mean the body had traveled some five hundred miles downriver.

The river had been running high and was moving at about twenty miles an hour, so the body had to be in the water for at least twenty-five hours.

To him it meant that the body had spent a great deal of time cycling from under water back to above the water as the tree rotated during its rapid journey.

He draped a cover over the lower part of the body and called to let Alex know that he was ready to share his initial findings.

Alex and the team had returned from lunch and had gathered in the huddle room and discussed Johnnie's spotting a body in a tree.

Trevor said that he thought the body had what looked like a chain round it.

Johnnie agreed and said that would indicate that they would be dealing with a murder.

Alex was about to agree when she received Dr. Rogers call.

She asked who wanted to go to the morgue with her.

On the way she stopped by the Chief's office and asked him if he wanted to go as well.

She noted that everyone was following her.

Dr. Rogers greeted them and then went over to the table. He began with the cause of death. He pointed out that the bullet had gone up through the roof of the mouth into the brain. The bullet was from a thirty-eight-caliber revolver. The area round the bullet entry indicated that the barrel of the gun had been held tightly to the bottom of the chin.

He said that if the body had been found without a chain wrapped around it, he would have been ruling it a suicide.

He skipped the part of the report about the body and went over to where the clothes were neatly arranged.

He pointed to three shallow plastic containers holding several pebbles in each. He said that his team had identified the pebbles as Augite, blue Kyanite, and yellow-green Epidote and that the most probable county to find this combination was in Wetzel County West Virginia.

He then picked up the snuff container and said that it also pointed to West Virginia and that the particular brand had been manufactured in Monongalia County.

Alex nodded and asked if there was any other useful information.

Dr. Rogers nodded and picked up a palm-sized brass belt buckle and pointed to the engraved signature of the person who had made it. He added that he was trying to see if the belt leather could be traced.

He pointed to the clothes and commented that the brand names had been removed so he was not sure if they held any clues as to the individual on the table, but the style of the shirt and pants indicated that the person might be a construction worker.

The boots were new and still had the shoe store's name located in New Martinsville, West Virginia

Alex thanked him on doing a great job in locating where the body had most likely come from. She said that now it was her teams turn to make the most of it.

She smiled and said that she was inviting him to participate tomorrow morning in the planning meeting that they would hold.

He nodded and thanked her for the invite.

Alex led the team out of the morgue. Once outside of the morgue she took several deep breaths.

Trey laughed and complimented her on having survived Dr. Roger's intentionally slow and deliberate presentation.

Alex nodded and said that she bet he generated that putrid odor just to get to her.

The Chief laughed and said that it had always smelled that way. He added that her reaction to it was the only chink in her armor that he knew of. He suggested that they briefly meet in his office before the team went to the huddle room to plan how to solve the case.

Alex agreed and said that though the body had been found in Ohio, they would need to get the authorities in West Virginia to allow them to investigate the case there.

Once in the Chief's office they sat down. The Chief said that he would contact the authorities in West Virginia and get their support lined up.

He asked Alex how she was thinking of utilizing the team.

Alex replied that at the moment she was not sure and that the team needed to discuss what they had learned and decide how to split up the investigation so they could make short work of it. She added that they had learned the most likely location of where the killing had taken place but had no clue as to the exact time and why it had taken place.

Trevor chuckled and said that the why was because someone had not liked the guy.

Alex shook her head and said it was time to go home but first thing in the morning they would work through how they would solve the case.

The Chief looked at the clock and said that by the same time tomorrow he should have been able to define how they would work with the authorities in West Virginia.

Alex led the way out. She and Johnnie headed to the locker room to change into their biking clothes.

As the two bicycled on the way to Johnnie's apartment, they chatted on their headsets about the fact that she most often walked her bike most of the way back to her house that was located halfway up Mt Adams because it was almost impossible for her to bike up the steep streets to her house.

Johnnie agreed that he would never be able to bike those streets.

The next morning, she met Johnnie at the door to his apartment building, and they rode back to the station together.

She was ready to dig into their new case.

Trey was already at his desk, and he said that Bill and Trevor had the box of donuts with them.

Alex took a minute to get a cup of coffee and then went into the huddle room.

Trevor pointed to a bear claw in the donut box and added that he was sure she would need that to guide them in figuring out how to solve a cold murder case that had not been reported by anyone in West Virginia.

Alex smiled and thanked him for the bear claw and critical advice.

Trevor nodded and replied that he was happy to share his wisdom.

Alex asked if he had any advice on how the team should approach the investigation.

Trevor nodded and said that they should split up the investigation. He wanted to find out who had made the belt buckle and if that person remembered the victim.

He figured that he and Bill could also see who might have remembered selling him the snuff.

Alex said that would work, she and Trey would follow up on the boots and the stones found in the boots.

Johnnie spoke up and said that he would check all the missing person's reports to see if there were any filed that might match the description of the person down in the morgue.

Alex added that they should plan in staying in Wheeling and reserve five rooms at one of the top end hotel chains. She looked over to Johnnie and asked him to pick the hotel and book five good rooms.

Johnnie nodded and said that he would also make some dinner reservations and restaurants with good views of the river

Alex laughed and said that would be fine as long as he sat with his back to the river since she did not want him finding any more bodies.

4 West Virginia

*T*he rays of the late afternoon sun made water of the river below seem to be a thread of gold weaving through the dark green of the trees lining its banks. Hillary loved sitting on the lip of the cliff and absorbing the beauty that embraced her.

She had spent the last few weeks worrying about whether Layton's disappearance would be missed and reported. She had no way of knowing if someone kept track of him. She did not know much about his family or his personal life.

She had met him at a Weirton night club and when she found out that he ran a still she had befriended him and not long after had successfully recruited him. He had been one of her reluctant converts that had been attracted by making more money and being able to quit his job as a laborer.

It became clear to her that he had not expected the increase in the work load of running three stills. He was making significantly more money, but the work load was what put him off.

He had expressed his belief that he should make more money. He had threatened to expose the operation to the DEA and then pulled a gun on her demanding they go to the bank and get cash versus accepting a check. She knew that it was time to get him out of the operation. She was not sure how, but she was sure that she was not going to give him any more money if she could help it.

The result of her attempt to take his gun away from him as they walked the path down the mountain side shocked her. Having a dead body to get rid of was not something she knew how to handle. She had reached out to the one person she trusted to share her predicament with.

Samuel had not even blinked an eye when he learned how it had happened.

He had asked if being a still owner was what she traveled across the stated doing.

She had admitted to him that she had a few stills that she owed. She had not admitted to running more than sixty stills in twenty locations across the state.

She wished that she could put the worry about Layton behind her, but it kept nagging at her.

She continued to make her rounds to make sure that the still operating partners were doing well and continued to be satisfied with their share of the business. With out exception she verified that the deal she had given them was one that they each felt good about.

She guided them to improve their yield and to adjust their prices so that they were competitive with the rest of the hard liquor market. This meant most of them saw an increase in money in their pockets.

She on the other hand focused on getting bargain prices on the grain they needed. She also guided her top still operators in introducing different flavors into their moonshine.

It seemed that everything had settled down.

Then she was watching the morning news up date and learned about a body being found in Cincinnati. As she watched the news piece, she realized that Layton's body had been recovered. She wondered if they would be able to trace him back to where he had been dumped into the river.

She was surprised at how fast the body had made it down to that location. She remembered well the torrential rain that had caused Samuel to open the dams float gates to let the water flow through. That rain must have been the cause of Layton getting so far down river in such a short amount of time.

She once again became concerned about her exposure. She decided that she would prepare herself to disappear in the mountains. She selected the most remote of the still locations and arranged to stay there when the time came to disappear.

She returned to her favorite mountain top spot and sat enjoying the sunset.

Back in Cincinnati, Johnnie was searching through missing persons reports looking for any linkage to the body they had in the morgue. He came up with three reports that might be for that person. One was in a county at the very eastern part of the state. One more or less in the middle and one in Weirton, West Virginia. He had no way to determine which report was the one that was linked to the body.

The missing report in the eastern part of the state talked about a person that was a truck driver. The second one described the person as having left to get a six pack that had not returned.

He zeroed on the one closest to the Ohio river. That missing person's report had been turned in by a Mrs. Lindi Harris for a Layton Harris who had not shown up for her birthday party and had not returned her calls.

He shared this with the team.

Alex said that now they would be able to focus on verifying if Layton was the person in the morgue.

She said it was time they made their way to West Virginia. She commented that the plan to stay in Wheeling put them in the vicinity of where they would be doing their investigation.

Bill asked whether they should each drive in their separate cars.

Alex said that because her car was one of the oldest in the lot she was going to see if she, Trey, and Johnnie could take the departments police van. If not, she would call ahead and make reservations for a car in Wheeling.

The Chief suggested renting a car in Wheeling because the police van was reserved to transport some prisoners to their prison locations.

He gave her the names of the Sheriff in Wheeling that she should contact when she got there.

As she walked out of the chief's office, she figured that she had several hours to spend sitting in the back of Bill and Trevor's car.

She walked to the huddle room and suggested that they all drive in Bill and Trevor's car.

Trevor smiled and said that he would sit in back and let long legged Trey have the front seat. He added that would allow him time to chat with his favorite lead detective.

Alex smiled and said that she looked forward to their five-hour chat.

She asked Johnnie if he could rent a nice sized car or pickup in Wheeling

It turned out that Trevor kept up the chat for most of the way. He went back to several cases where they had survived because they worked together so well. He conjectured that this might again be one where because of their close team work they would be having each other's back.

Alex listened and made a few comments, but she was thinking ahead at what they needed to do to get a break in the case.

Johnnie sensed Alex's mood and engaged in Trevor's conversation. He pulled Trey and Bill into the conversation and acted as the bridge that linked all the conversations together.

Alex knew that she had to get the local Sheriff to support the team. She was sure there would be some defensive posturing by the Sheriff, and she was trying to figure out how to get around that.

When they arrived in Wheeling, she asked Bill to stop at the first candy or gift store that he saw. He stopped in a small strip mall that had a candy store next to an Ace hardware store. She went in and bought ten bags of Lady Godiva, Ghirardelli mixed chocolates and Jelly beans. She came out with thirty bags of candy.

Trevor asked who she was planning to kill with sugar highs.

Alex smiled and handed him a bag of jelly beans and replied that she would start with him. She then asked what type of candy each person wanted.

Trevor asked what she was going to do with all of the rest of the candy in the bag.

She smiled and said she was going to buy cooperation.

Trey looked back and said not to doubt her effectiveness in using the candy approach.

Trevor shook his head and said he had experienced her ability to use chocolate to get whatever she wanted.

She then said it was time to go to the hotel and check in.

She suggested that after they checked in, they all go together to meet with the local sheriff and his team.

She called ahead and agreed to the meeting with the local sheriff to be at his office

Bill pulled into an empty parking spot in front of the Sheriff's office building.

Alex led the way in to the front reception desk. She identified herself and the rest of the team.

The receptionist asked if they were armed and said the weapons would need to be checked in. After they had done that she said that they would be taken to the meeting area.

Their guide was a young lady that was introduced as a new hire.

Alex and the team followed her to the elevators and went up to the second floor and were led into a large meeting room that looked out the front of the building. She could see the car they had come in.

She took a seat at one end of a very large table that had ten seats on each side and three on each end.

She watched as four people entered the room. It was clear to her that the sheriff had pulled in some additional branches of the law enforcement in the area.

She introduced herself and said that each of her team would introduce themselves. She then went up to each of those entering the meeting room, handed them a bag of chocolate and said that she hoped to sweeten the meeting a little.

The Sheriff introduced himself as Stanley and the lead detective in his office as Daily. He then introduced the head of the West Virginia State Police as Talus and the US Marshall that had jurisdiction in most of the state as Walter.

He smiled and added he had contacted his good friend in Loveland and gotten the scoop on what he was about to face. He held up the bag of chocolate and said that his good friend had warned him about the fact that he was about to be bribed and that he should just go along and enjoy the ride.

Alex smiled and said that she hoped that she and her team would be able to follow the leads they had gotten from a person that they had determined had been reported as missing in Weirton by a Mrs. Lindi Harris. She went on and said that she thought that the body back in the Cincinnati Police Station morgue was that of Layton Harris and that he was murdered somewhere in the Wheeling area.

Stanley shook his head and went on to say that his good friend in Loveland had also warned him about the speed with which she would be working the case. His friend had recounted the case of a young girl that had been missing for fifteen years and that she had come in and in less than two weeks had found that young girl, not far away from where they were, up in the Finger Lake region of Pennsylvania.

Alex smiled and said that was one of the better cases that she and the team had solved. She pointed at Johnnie as her magician and said that his ability to mine the information from the internet was what made the difference in that case and many other cases that she and the team worked on.

Stanley nodded and asked if Johnnie had found the missing person's report because he had not received his copy yet. He looked at the other three people that he had introduced and asked if any of them was aware of that missing person's report.

All of them said that they were not.

Alex nodded and said that she would have copies printed out if Johnnie could connect his computer and get access to a printer.

She then turned the focus back to what she was wanting to do and described what each of them would do.

She said that what the team was out to find people that knew Layton and what he did that might have gotten him killed.

She and her partner, Trey, were going to follow up on the boots and the stones that were in the soles of the boots. She added that they had the names of the stones from the soles of the boots and had a general idea where they might be found but she needed to get that location more focused so that she didn't spend months trying to find it.

She then held up the belt buckle, the belt and the can of snuff and said that Bill and Travis were going to try to find out where the buckle was purchase and what stores might sell the snuff that was a specialty of the area.

Talus picked up the belt buckle and said that he thought he might be able to take them to a flea market that usually only operated on Saturday and Sunday where they might be able to find the person whose name was engraved on the back. He laughed and said the snuff was sold in almost any grocery or gas station and using it in an attempt to get connected to Layton might be a life time effort.

Trevor thanked him for the heads up and said that though West Virginia was beautiful he preferred keeping the time in to a few days.

Alex said that she agreed with Trevor and that she was keen on moving fast so those involved in the murder would not have time to make their escape.

Sheriff Stanley pointed to Daily and said that he would be available to work directly with her and Trey and get them to where they wanted to go and make sure that folks understood that they were legitimate.

He then verified that Talus was available to help Bill and Trevor.

He then smiled and asked if they could take a brief break and enjoy the refreshments that had been brought in. He added that he had made sure that there were a couple of bear claw rolls as part of the sweets that had been brough in.

Alex could not have wanted a better outcome from the meeting. She would have to thank Evin, her Loveland sheriff friend for having opened the West Virginia door wide for her.

5 Connections

*A*s Crayton got into the pickup, the bark of the huge, gnarled limb of the centuries old oak, pushed by the wind gusts of the oncoming storm brushing lightly across the roof sounded like the squeal of a baby mouse. He turned the key and the engine popped and then began to run smoothly. It had taken him a day to get from his still to the one Layton had been running.

He wondered what had happened to Layton, but he liked the fact that by agreeing to run a second set of stills his income had doubled. He had found the title to the truck in the glove compartment. He drove straight to the county courthouse and had the title transferred to himself. He planned to use the pickup to get all the supplies for both stills from the central grain distribution depot. He would deliver the materials for his original stills and then drive the pickup to his new stills.

Setting up six stills to operate so they would each produce fifty gallons per month gave him a little bit of a math problem.

He followed Hillary's suggestion of increasing the price of the moonshine to match the increase of the price of regular hard liquor.

He really liked the feel of making enough money that he was actually able to save a significant amount. It was the first time in his life that he felt like he was getting ahead. It was hard work, but he felt that it was worth it, and he knew enough about the cost of the raw materials to know that Hillary had given him a good deal. She had warned him that she would soon need to reduce his take to make up for the inflation she was seeing in the cost of corn and other raw materials, but he felt that she would be fair.

He again wondered how she had convinced Layton to give up his business and figured that he would stay away from that subject since he sensed that the change had not been on a voluntary or friendly basis.

Moonshine

At one of his Saturday night outings, he heard the rumor that some investigators were asking around about Layton and what he did for a living. This had him asking his own questions. He was now sure that Layton had somehow met with a fate from which you did not recover. It was hard for him to picture Hillary being the person who would off one of the still operators, so he wondered what had happened. He could easily see Layton losing his temper and doing something stupid.

The next time he walked the path up to Layton's three stills he carefully looked for anything that seemed unusual or out of place. As he was approaching a sharp bend in the path, he notice broken branches on some bushes at the side of the path.

He didn't think of himself as a tracker, but it seemed clear to him that someone was pulled into the bushes. He examined the ground and realized that the crusty area of soil was likely to be where blood had soaked into it. He backout and examined the path and found a similar area. It was hard for him to visualize what had happened, but he figured that he had found the spot where Layton had met his end.

He knew that Hillary did not have an enforcer, and he didn't think she normally carried a weapon unless she was hunting and then she carried a rifle.

He knew that she instead worked to ensure that the still operator got a fair shake. She had spent a great deal of time educating him, so that he understood the entire flow from the purchase of materials to the cost of running the stills and the cost of the distribution of the moonshine. He had never spent time to understand all the costs and when he finally got that understanding he understood why she had insisted that he operate three stills and that he shorten the distillation time to the two weeks he had been testing. It had been an eye-opening moment for him.

He came to the conclusion that Layton had threatened her in some fashion, and he had underestimated her. He knew that Layton always bragged that he was a great shot and would take out any one coming after him at his still location. He figured that Layton had threatened Hillary and had misjudged her capability.

Crayton decided to go to Weirton to one of the night clubs that he knew Layton had often frequented. He spent the time buying folks some drinks and sharing some of his moonshine that he had brought with him. He found out that Layton had boasted that he was about to be making more money and would soon hold a party for all of them.

He knew then that his theory of what happened on the trail was the one that most likely had taken place. He was not sure exactly how it happened, but Layton had met his end at Hillary's hands.

He wondered how Hillary got Layton off the mountain side.

But he knew that it had to have been at the time she had come to him and asked him to take over running the three stills. When he got to the stills, they were all operating in parallel and would all produce their fifty gallons within a day of each other.

He then found out that they had not been properly loaded and would produce less than the fifty gallons. It was a very sloppily run operation. He recognized that Layton could easily have increased the amount of money he was making by almost twenty percent. He decided to shut down two of the stills and restart them to get them operating so that they operated in the right sequence.

He hoped that whatever happened would not affect him.

That was a hope that would soon be challenged.

Talus suggested that he meet Bill and Travis at the flea market parking lot on Saturday morning.

Bill and Travis arrived at the market as it was just getting set up.

Talus arrived and led the way to one square where the overhead canvas had just been set up and three tables had been arranged in a U shape under it. The person there said that it would take him a few moments to get his goods out and they should come back in about fifteen minutes.

Trevor pulled out the belt buckle and ask if it was one of his.

The person shook his head and said that it was not one of his but if they walked down about three booth spaces they would be at the place where the person who had made that buckle was located. He smiled and said that his buckles were of higher quality, and they should come back and see his display.

Bill said he would make a point of coming by to look.

As they walked on, he said he was curious about the comparison because he thought the belt buckle that they were carrying was very good.

The vendor at the booth they went to was in the process of arranging her display of necklaces, bracelets, rings and at one end belt buckles.

Trevor ask her whether she recognized the belt buckle he was holding.

She took it, turned it over and pointed the engraved signature.

She nodded and said that it was one of hers. She walked over to the end of the table where eight more buckles were on display. She said that the buckle he had was in the middle of the pack as far as quality. She pointed to one and said that currently it was the best one because not only did it have a more intricate design, but it had two small black opals as the eyes of the bear.

She said that if anyone of them was interested in a belt buckle, she would consider giving a ten percent discount for a cash purchase.

Travis picked up the belt buckle of the with the bear and the opals for eyes and asked how much she wanted for it.

She smiled and said that she would let it go for one hundred eighty-dollar cash or two hundred if it was a credit card.

Travis took out his credit card.

She asked Bill for the belt buckle he had shown her and as she held it, she said that she seemed to recall that she had sold the one in her hands to a local that often walked through the flea market. She recalled that he had paid sixty dollars for it.

Bill thanked her for the information and asked if she knew the name of the person who had purchased the buckle.

She shook her head and said that the only thing she remembered about him was that he had a pint jar that had a tangy, pungent odor that she connected to moonshine. She smiled and said that she often bought some moonshine from the booth that featured every kind of alcohol that was on the market, so she was familiar with its smell.

As Trevor was paying for the belt buckle, he was buying, he asked where the booth that sold the moonshine was located.

She said that it was usually located at the very center of the flea market.

Bill thanked her for the information.

He went back to first booth they had started and looked over the belt buckles. He decided that the belt buckles there were not as intricate or detailed as the one at the booth they had just left.

He looked at Travis and congratulated him on buying the best that was currently on display.

He then said they should go to the booth selling the liquor and see if that vendor could recall Layton being around.

After walking around and figuring out where the center of the flea market was, they found the tent with a display of almost every hard liquor on the market. One half of one table featured a wide variety of moonshine. Most of it was clearly labeled and had tax stamps on the bottle label. But on one end were a series of quart bottles that had black sharpy handwritten labels and a price.

Bill showed the vendor a picture of Layton and asked if he knew him.

The vendor asked who the three of them were and why they were asking about him.

Daily introduced himself, showed his badge, and said that Layton had died, and they were trying to figure out how that had happened.

The vendor nodded and said that he had often purchased his supply of local moonshine from Layton. He said that Layton did business with him on cash basis and supplied him with a good quality of moonshine.

Trevor asked if he had any of the moonshine that Layton had sold to him.

The vendor walked to where the moonshine was located and pointed to six bottles. He pointed to the display of the Moonshine and said that he tried to have a supply from across the state and as often as possible he tried to get ones that had labels showing that the taxes had been paid.

Daily commented that they were not interested in the details of his business but interested in what he might know about Layton.

Trevor said that he would like to buy the six bottles of the moonshine that Layton had supplied.

The vendor grabbed a heavy-duty paper bag and six smaller paper bags and put each jar of moonshine into the smaller paper bag and all six into the larger bag that had handles. He said that he would give a ten percent discount, and the price would be fifty-four dollars.

Trevor paid him in cash and took the bag.

Bill asked the vendor if he had any idea where Layton's still might be located.

The vendor laughed and said that yes, he knew the still was located somewhere in the mountains.

Trevor then asked the vendor if he recalled anything that might help in figuring out how Layton had died.

The vendor thought for a moment and said that Layton was something of a smart-alecky type of guy and that he also had a quick temper. He had seen him have a couple of run-ins with some other guys his age and knew that he carried a gun. He added that he personally had never had any issues with him.

Trevor thanked him and said that it was time they get on their way.

The three of them returned to the parking lot where Bill thanked Talus for his help.

Trevor offered Talus a jar of moonshine as a reward for giving up part of his weekend.

Talus laughed and said that he liked how the Cincinnati detective unit operated and took the moonshine.

A few blocks away, Alex and Trey walked into the camping outfitting store where Layton's boots were purchased. They casually walked around and looked over the boots and the various camping equipment.

A pair of boots that were duplicates to the ones that Layton had on when he was pulled from the river were on display with a red sales tag that highlighted a thirty percent discount. The pair on the shelf also had a pair of socks that were the same as Layton had on.

Alex pointed out to Trey that they had found a clean set of boots and socks that except for the size were duplicates of what Layton wore.

A clerk came over and asked if he could be of help.

Alex held out the boots and asked how many pairs of the boots he had sold. He said that the boots sold OK, but they were on the expensive side for the local population. He figured he had sold about one pair per month since they had started to feature it.

She showed the him a picture of Layton and asked if he remembered selling a pair to him.

He looked at the picture and said the he had sold him a pair and that was when he first threw in a pair of socks as part of the bargaining that went on. He said that the reason he remembered him was the fact that it turned out to be a cash deal and the guy had pulled out a roll of money and had made a big show of peeling the bills from it.

At the time he had marveled that someone would spend time rolling the money up so neatly and carry such large lump. He noticed that the guy wore a dockers style pants that the store carried, and he kept the roll on the left side.

He said that another reason he remembered the guy was his snide attitude. He seemed to want to be insulting.

The clerk looked at the picture and asked if the person in the picture was dead.

Alex let him know that the person was, and his name was Leyton. She held out the stones that had been found in the tread of Layton's boots and asked the clerk if he knew where the stones might be located.

The clerk said that the picture showed him the way he had wanted to see Leyton the day he had sold him the boots. It was great to make the sale, but he was mad the rest of the day.

He looked at the stones in the bag Alex had given him and said that he had recently picked that type of stones out of the treads of his hiking boots. The trail he had been on was directly east from the store and ran up the mountain to a lookout where he and his girlfriend had stopped, had lunch, and enjoyed the view. They had both removed the pebbles before going into his home because he had recently paid a small fortune to have the floor sanded and varnished.

He walked over to a table that had a large map of the area showing all the terrain and hiking trails that were within a fifty-mile area and pointed to the trail he had been on.

Alex asked if she could take a picture of the map and when she got his, "Sure" she took a picture of the area.

She didn't need anything, but she asked if he sold the map, and he said that the map was only five fifty and it had detailed notes about several of the more popular trails.

She then asked if he had the docker style pants that he had described.

He led her over to where the clothing was on display and asked her waist measure and pant length size that she normal bought. He went through the folded stack of pants and pulled out a tan pair and handed it to her. He said that he most likely had it in camouflage and dark green as well.

Alex looked around and saw the fitting room sign. She went in and tried the pants on.

She came back out and said that she would buy the it.

The clerk smiled and said that she was the kind of customer he liked. He took the pair to the checkout counter and asked if there was anything else she might want.

Alex looked over at Trey and Johnnie and asked them if there was anything that had caught their eye.

Trey nodded and said that if she was planning on going for a hike, they should buy two of the thermal jugs that were displayed on the counter.

Alex looked at Johnnie who shook his head and said that he had nothing to add.

The clerk smiled and said that he could give them a ten per cent discount on the jugs and he would throw in a bottle of their choice of soft drinks with each thermal jug.

Alex smiled and said that he had sold her and said she would take three jugs.

She asked if a credit card would work.

The clerk chuckled and commented that he had expected her to take out a roll of money to pay but was able to handle a credit card.

She thanked him for the information that he had provided.

She was walking out when the clerk said that he had just remembered one more thing.

She turned and stopped.

The clerk said that just two weeks ago he and his girlfriend went out on a Friday night to Lily's Bar because it was a pitcher of beer, all the wings one could eat and dance special that featured a local group that they liked.

He had noticed the guy in the picture sitting at the bar drinking and hitting on the waitress who seemed to be irritated by him doing so.

After getting the location to Lily's and thanking him for that information, Alex led the way out to the car.

She commented that the shoe leather approach had just yielded a ton of information.

6 Mountain Trail

*T*he grey of the sky, the cool in the air, the rustle of turning maple leaves caused Hillary to think of the fact that her business cycle would soon come to an end. She had been working on how to extend moonshine production to be a year-round effort. She was sure that she could make it happen, and she planned to start first by convincing Crayton to do it first.

She was walking up the trail to the still when she got a call from Ali, the local moonshine distributor at the flea market to let her know that he had just sold five bottles of Layton's moonshine.

A red flag went up in her mind.

She was just getting to the still where she was checking on the batches that Crayton had brewing. She had talked with him and had agreed to verify that the three batches were proceeding smoothly. He had asked for her help in getting the six stills synchronized. He said that Layton had his three stills all running in parallel and that he needed to get his three and the stills there all synchronized so that the six stills were each completing the batches in sequence.

Her reaction to the call was to go up the trail to where she could sit on the edge of a cliff. She sat there and cleaned the rifle she had started to carry. She had bought it and a three-fifty-seven after the incident with Layton. She had spent the last couple of weeks practicing at the gun range and target practicing from where she was now sitting with her feet over the edge of the cliff. She realized that she was actually quite good at shooting. This had boosted her confidence.

It had taken her some time to overcome the effect that Layton had on her. She had been surprised at his aggressive actions and more surprised at the accidental way she killed him.

But she felt that she was now back in control.

Had she known who was hiking up the trail that she had just walked up a few moments before she would not have been so confident.

Trey drove by the parked car and went up the road a few hundred yards and pulled into the trees out of sight.

He got out and looked around to see if there was any one around. He then grabbed his back pack and joined Alex who had her back pack over her shoulder.

Johnnie was close behind both of them.

Alex made sure there was no one in the car parked at the base of the trail. She then took a picture of the license plate and then went over to the trail. This was the third trail that they had gone to, and she hoped it was the one that they were looking for.

As she led the way she would periodically reach down and pick up a hand full of pebbles. She was pleased to finally see that it was the mix that they had been looking for. She showed the handful of pebbles to Trey and Johnnie and said that they were going to hike up the trail and see if they could find the still.

Trey moved up to the front and led the way. He, like Alex and Johnnie, were all wearing their Kevlar vests and were armed as well.

He was briskly hiking along when Alex told him to stop.

She pointed to her nose and put her finger to her lips.

She then slowly turned around for a three sixty turn and then pointed into the woods that her nose pointed to. She pulled out her weapon and led the way into the forest.

About a hundred yards later she stopped and pointed to a well camouflaged building. There was a thin plume of what looked like steam coming from three separate chimneys. She was surprised at the size of the building and the fact that three chimney indicated that there were three stills operating.

She signaled for Trey to go to the right and Johnnie to go to the left. She went straight forward toward the building.

She got to the door and waited for the two to move her way and then she knelt down and pushed the door open and rolled in.

Trey stepped in and to his right and Jonnie pushed the door fully opened and went to the left.

Alex moved immediately ahead and stepped between the two tall copper containers that were twice her height.

Johnnie continued to his left and around the left most container.

Trey went around the right end.

There was no one in the room.

They walked around the perimeter and commented at how beautiful the shiny copper vessels looked. It was clear that everything was operating in a preset automatic cycle.

Alex took in the cot, the stacked supplies, and the barrels at the end of the line that were slowly being filled.

She spent time looking at the personal things that she could find. It seemed that the place had recently been cleaned. She walked over to a standard-looking trash can and found that it was nearly full of some clothes and other personal belongings. She decided that they should take everything that was in the trashcan as evidence.

She pulled the plastic draw strings tight and had Trey lift it out. She then put in a new black plastic bag into the trash can.

Johnnie commented that the person who was running the place would know that someone had taken the contents.

Alex agreed but said that the contents most likely were those that had belonged to Layton and it might help them in getting some additional clues as to what had gone on before he had been killed.

After taking one more look around, she decided that they should leave.

Hillary sat on the ridge, took several shots with her scoped rifle, cleaned it, and then ate a sandwich. She decided it was time to get back down the mountain and go to the next still and see how that operator was doing. She figured that before the day was over, she would be able to visit two more of the still sites.

She got up and went down the trail. She went past the point where the still was. She was focused on finishing her day's visit cycle.

Alex got back to the trail and put the black bag out of site in the bushes. She then pointed up the trail and said they should go up to see if the person running the still might have gone somewhere in that direction.

Once again Trey took the lead.

When they reached the crest, Alex pointed to the spot where just moments before Hillary had been sitting and pointed to a piece of lettuce that was at the edge of the cliff. She walked over and looked around.

She asked Johnnie what he thought.

Johnnie looked closely at the site and said that somebody had recently been sitting and having a sandwich. He said that he smelled gun powder, and it reminded him of the after effects of when someone shot a high-powered rifle. It was weaker than the smell of the fifty caliber that he had used in Vietnam but still rather strong.

Alex asked Trey the same question and got a similar answer. He added that the odor was exactly what he was used to when he had been a sniper.

She nodded and said that they would need to be super cautious as they pursued the person who had off'd Layton because they might be dealing with a professional. A professional who had at least one kill under their belt.

Far down the trail, Hillary reached her car, got in, made a U turn, and drove away.

She had no clue that she had just walked down the trail past the still where three people looking for her where examining the operation. She reached her car, made the U turn to leave and in doing so missed seeing the car parked off the road ahead of where she had parked.

When Alex came to the bottom of the trail, she immediately knew that somehow the person who had been sitting up at the top of the trail had managed to get down the trail without being seen.

She commented that they must have been inside the still building and missed the person that came down from above.

Trey commented that either that person had just been lucky in their timing or had chosen not to engage them. In either case they should think of that person being very good at evading a confrontation and being an expert in what they did.

He threw the black trash bag into the trunk and got into the driver's seat.

Alex called Bill and Trevor and suggested they meet for lunch. Once she got the name of the restaurant, she said that it was time they drove back to Wheeling and enjoyed lunch where Johnnie could watch the logs floating down the Ohio.

Johnnie laughed and said that for the time being he had sworn off watching floating logs.

Bill and Trevor were waiting in the parking lot when they arrived. They felt good at having learned a ton about the person people called "Layton the horrible."

Trevor comment that he had given Layton that monicker because of what they had learned about him.

Trevor let her know that Talus had been a great guide and had helped them quite a bit. Talus had left them after letting them know that he had a grill out planned with his family and would see them on Monday.

She suggested they go in get a table with a good view of the river, put in their order and then spend some time sharing what each of them had learned.

After they had been seated, put in their order, and had their drinks brought to them, she suggested they share what they had learned.

She was pleased as Bill described their visit to the flea market and their talk with the lady that had made the belt buckle. She asked what Bill was going to do with the six quarts of moonshine he had bought.

Trevor smiled and answered that it was evidence that each of them could take home and safeguard. He said that there were only five jars left because he did not have a bag of candy to give Talus, so he had given him a quart of moonshine.

Alex chuckled and said that since she did not consume any alcoholic beverage her bottle was going to be gifted to the Chief. She added that in the future she was going to make sure they all went out with enough bags of candy.

Trey described their visit to the outfitters store where they got an insight to Layton's character. He added that they had also been able to find out the bar where Layton frequented. They had gone there and found out that he was tolerated but not liked by the bartender nor the waitresses.

Alex shared the fact that the clerk at the outfitters store had helped them find the trail where the rocks found in the treads of Layton's boots came from. They had hiked up the trail and located the still and had retrieved a fifty-gallon barrel of trash that they would be sorting through to retrieve whatever they thought might be evidence.

Trevor suggested that they take the bag back to Cincinnati and let their coroner and his team sort through the bag.

Alex smiled and said that was a great idea that would give her the chance to tweak Dr. Roger's nose.

She said that they had made progress much faster than she had expected and they should probably check out of the hotel and drive back to Cincinnati. She added that they would get back in the early evening. It would be a long day, but everyone would be able to go and sleep in their own bed.

There was total agreement as they all got up and walked out to the van. The energy level of the team had gone up at the thought of sleeping in their own beds. None of them were expecting what was ahead.

7 Back Tracking and Pursuit

Hillary thought of friends as a social electromagnet connection that when working provided a vibrant flow of unseen connecting energy. This belief was reinforced when she got a call from a longtime friend that worked in the sheriff's office that a black detective and some other detectives with her were looking into Layton's death. She asked her friend if she could have a picture of the detectives and was pleased to learn that her friend was in the process of writing an article highlighting the cooperation of the Sheriff's department and the Cincinnati detectives.

She casually asked where they were staying and got the name of the hotel.

As she was walking in, she went past five people walking out and realized that she had just walked past the person she had come to see firsthand. She waited a moment and then walked out and spotted them getting into a dark grey sedan. She took in the Ohio, "the heart of it all" plates as she walked to her car.

She was glad that she had her car packed to make the rounds of the stills, so it was a no brainer to decide to follow them. Once they got on US 70 it was rather easy to follow them. She stayed back two to three cars and followed them as they exited onto US 71 and headed toward Cincinnati. When they exited into the downtown area it became a little trickier. She lost them and pulled into an empty surface parking lot and thought about what she should do next.

She decided that she would have to work backward from the police station. She was not sure where her target lived but hoped that it was downtown somewhere. She would rent a reasonably priced hotel room in the downtown area. Her goal was to back track her intended target to somewhere where a clean shot at her could be had.

The next morning, she was at the station when she spotted her target arrive by bicycle accompanied by the Blackman that had been with her the day before. She did not want to try a shot near the station, so she planned to back track where they were coming from. She walked to the corner where she had seen them come from. She got her car and found a place around the corner where she could park. She planned to watch for the two of them the following morning.

She figured she would go for breakfast and then go enjoy the Cincinnati water front park.

When she parked in one of the garages, she was walking past an area filled with a variety of electric scooter boards but after trying them she figured she was good enough to enjoy them. She chose instead to use an electric scooter that she could stand on and control the speed with controls mounted on the handle bars.

She spent the day going from one end of the water front path to the farthest distance and then returning. As she looked out on the river she wondered where Layton had been found. What amazed her was how far he had traveled in such a short time. She recalled Samuel telling her that the rain that arrived the day after they had dumped Layton into the river set a record high and he had to open the dam to let the water go downstream to prevent flooding people's homes up stream. He commented that the water had damaged the pier that his father had going out into the Ohio.

The next morning, she was in place and was able to spot where her target turned and came north toward her.

She went to the point where the street turned to her left. There was a statue of William Harrison and after driving two blocks she took in a statue of James Garfield. Just across the street was the main library. She decided that she would see what she could find at the library to take up her day. She chuckled as she thought that she was learning more about Cincinnati than she had never imagined she would.

As she walked into the library, she saw a Mexican restaurant that she decided she would try out for lunch. There was also a steak place at the heart of the downtown that she had in mind for dinner.

She spent the day checking out what she could find out about the person she was planning to kill.

When she engaged one of the librarians and asked if there was any information about a black Cincinnati detective, she was given a link to a series of news reports that were available on line. She sat down on one of the computers and spent the rest of the morning learning about Alex Evercrest's prolific and very successful career.

It was hard for her to accept that she had targeted such a potentially dangerous adversary. She concluded that she would need to make sure she did not miss.

Alex returned from Wheeling and arranged with Dr. Rogers that she had returned with a large amount of evidence that he and his team would need to go through and examine. She loved the expression on his face when he realized that she was handing him a fifty-gallon trash can liner bag full of trash.

She said that she would need to have his report by the following afternoon team meeting.

She left the bag on the floor and took the elevator up to the first floor.

She went back to the team meeting and thanked Bill and Trevor for having suggested having Dr. Rogers and his team search the bag for evidence that might help the case.

That evening as they rode home, Johnnie mentioned that for the last few rides to work and back to his apartment he felt that they were being watched.

As soon as he mentioned it, she had her radar on high. She became super attentive trying to sense a watcher. Nothing she saw gave credence to what Johnnie had said he felt but the feeling did not go away.

The next day on the ride down to the bridge over Highway 71 she looked up at the building that just a few weeks ago had been used by the assassin Lorenzo Ciraulo who had tried to kill her. She was shocked as she looked up and she saw the twinkle of the sun hitting the lens of what she was sure was a scope on a high-powered rifle.

A plain white sided panel truck was making a last-minute left turn to go across the bridge ahead of her. She surged forward on her bike and caught the trucks back corner door hinge and let it pull her across. She was waiting for the rifle to come into view and when it did, she fired left-handed in hopes that she would hit yet another sniper trying to kill her.

She also decided that in the future she was going to find several more alternated routes to get to work. The current route would always be a great location to shoot at someone crossing the bridge.

Hillary felt the pain in her left shoulder as Alex's shot found its target. She almost dropped her rifle over the edge of the building.

She pulled a sweat towel from her carrying case and tried to stop the flow of blood. As she grimaced in pain, she took the scope off her rifle, gathered her things, and left the roof. She took the elevator to the second floor, got off and as fast as she could, she made her way to the garage, got in her car, and drove out and took the road that led to the Interstate.

She was out of the building in less than three minutes.

Alex had pulled herself totally behind the panel truck and once it had made the left turn, she released her grip, slowed down, and pulled into the alley and called in a shot fired. It was repeat of the last time. She heard the sirens but this time the Chief, Trey and Johnnie got to her location first.

She pointed to the building and said that she was not sure about the shooter. She added that this time she had only shot once because of how the situation had unfolded.

The Chief walked to where the first police cars were located. He gave them instruction and told them not to contaminate the site.

Trey came over to her and asked if she was alright.

Alex nodded and said that she needed to find more than one way to get from her house to work.

Johnnie immediately launched Gunjfor and was now displaying what he saw on the roof. He was hovering a few feet above the surface of the roof. There was blood on the roof. He flew Gunjfor over to the roof access door where there was a bloody hand print on the door.

As the first policeman exited the door Johnnie warned him that the outer door handle was part of the crime scene evidence, and that the elevator might also have bloody finger prints on the floor selection buttons.

Dr. Silvers came out from behind the policeman. He instructed his team to photograph the door handle and to go back to the elevators and examine them.

Alex suggested they go to the parking garage and see if they could find the location where the getaway car might have been parked.

Bill and Trevor had arrived, and they suggested that they begin from the point where the elevators came down to the lowest level and then determine which elevator had been used and work from there to the exit of the garage.

Alex said that sounded like a great idea and she led them to steps on the outside of the building that led to the parking garage exit. She pointed to a parking spot that was three parking spots up from the exit there where blood spots that had not yet dried.

Bill put a coin at each blood spot on his way up to the elevator while Trevor called in their findings to the Chief.

Less than two minutes later four policemen came rushing in the exit of the garage.

By this time Bill was at the elevator and said that he didn't think the elevator had been used to come down to this level.

He opened the door to the stair well and shouted out that there was blood on the stair well railing and that he and Trevor were going up.

Workers were arriving and two of the officers were reduced to guiding cars around the yellow taped area that ran from the entrance to the elevator area at the top of the entrance ramp.

Alex called to him to stop. She looked at Johnnie and asked him if he could fly Gunjfor up the stairwell.

Johnnie rushed to where Bill was standing and holding the door open.

Trevor smiled and looked at Alex and said he might be ready to sip on some of the moonshine they had brought back with them.

Johnnie had set up the Gunjfor's display on the steps. They were all following the bloody hand prints as he flew her up the two flights between floors. When they reached the second floor, Johnnie called in his findings, and which elevator should have blood in it and a finger print on the two button.

Alex smiled as she heard Dr. Silvers confirm the information and that he was on the way down with the elevator.

Hillary had stopped at her car long enough to take additional action to stop the bleeding. It was hard for her to believe that she was the one that was working to stay alive. She wondered how much blood she had lost. She was trying to figure out where she should go so that she could tend to her wound in a more permanent way. She had to find a place close by, but she had no clue how she might be able to check into a hotel without exposing herself.

She went on line and found a motel where she could check in and pay on line and the key would be left in the door for her. No other check-in was necessary.

She did that and once she got there and was in the room, she made sure the door was locked. She put the one chair in the room under the door handle so no one could surprise her. She took out her first aid kit and with some Vaseline and gauze she sealed the wound. It was extremely hard to do the area where the bullet had exited but once she managed to get that done, she was exhausted. She figured she would save taking a shower until morning.

The next morning, she managed take a quick shower and keep her right shoulder dry. She was starving and wanted to leave the area, but she knew that she had another problem to deal with first. She knew that a West Virginia plate would most likely earn her getting pulled over. She needed a different set of license plates.

She put her luggage and emergency kit in the trunk and took out a screw driver and a pair of pliers.

She struggled to get her front and back plates off. She was right-handed and used that hand to break the license plate screws loose but the pain forced her to revert to using her left hand to get the screws totally off.

Holding the two plates, she walked along the side of the motel building and along the back to where a car was sitting in the dark grey of the early morning. She struggled to get the screws to the back plates loose but managed to fight through the pain and finally do so.

She put one of her plates on the back and walked around to the front and almost broke down and cried out of joy when she saw that there was no front plate.

She rushed back to her car, put on the new plate, threw the screw driver and pliers back in the tool box and her front plate into the trunk.

She drove to the nearest fast-food drive through and ordered two sausage egg biscuits and a cup of coffee.

She would have loved to have stopped and gone some place where she could hold up for a couple of days, but she figured she had to get back home. She had to decide where in the mountains she was going to spend the next few weeks until she was sure that she had escaped.

8 Finger Prints

*T*he darkness holds many mysteries. The darkness inside the chambers where numerous corpses have lain are more mysterious than most. One can imagine the ghosts of all past chamber occupant harmonizing to their moans or their screams.

As Dr. Rogers and his team sorted through the pile of trash, they joked that they could hear Layton Harris laughing. The team connected a shirt, comb, tooth brush some finger prints to Layton.

They all laughed when Dr. Rogers held up a pair of gray, soiled boxer underwear and pounded on the door to Layton's chamber and shouted out that he should stop laughing. He then held one hand over his ear and said the laughter had stopped but that a freight train was now rumbling through his head. He then slumped slowly to one knee.

The team were all silent when he jumped up and threw the underwear to where the rest of the evidence was piled and shouted that they were done for the day.

They also learned that he ate a lot of junk food. They agreed that he would probably have died at a young age based on the junk food that was also in the black bag.

At that mornings shooting crime scene they recovered blood samples and three clear finger prints.

He had all the information but the on lined search using the finger prints had not turned up the person who had made the bloody finger prints on the roof door, on the elevator floor selection button and multiple times on the hand rail that went from the second floor to the parking garage exit area. He had more finger prints than usual but not who they belonged to.

He sent the finger prints to Johnnie explaining the situation.

He then took his paper reports and went to the huddle room where Alex was running a meeting with everyone in the case that was involved.

Johnnie let Alex know that he had just received the finger prints that had not come up on any of the police data bases. He said he was going to see if any of the police stations might have fingerprints on record that had not been entered on the state or national police data bases.

Dr. Rogers walked into the meeting and said that he had two reports.

He handed the first report to Alex saying that he was sure that the one she was most interested in was the garbage report. He added that it was fortunate that Layton had been shot and killed because it had saved him from dying slowly from eating junk food.

He held up the second report and said that it was the report where Alex had for once missed killing the assailant. He smiled, asked her if she was maintaining her shooting range practice schedule or if she were going soft on those who tried to kill her.

He handed her the report and then pointed to the donut box and asked if there were any donuts left.

Alex laughed and said that she appreciated his concern about her maintaining her shooting skills and added that she had left a stale donut for him.

He picked out a glazed cake donut and thanked Bill for getting him his favorite.

Trevor, using his whiny voice, said that actually he had just picked up his personal choice and now he would end up having to eat some other donut.

Dr. Rogers held out the glazed donut to Trevor and said he could have it.

Trevor shook his head and replied he was not sure whether his hands had been on a dead body or going through the trash bag and he preferred to get his own from the box.

The Chief had come in the huddle room and added that he hoped the good doctor had not polluted the rest of the donuts.

Dr. Rogers chuckled and thanked Trevor for the donut, added that the team seemed to be a little tense and he figured he would go back to the morgue where the bodies did not give him a hard time to enjoy the donut and a cup of tea.

The Chief looked around and asked if they had a lead on the shooter.

Alex was getting ready to hand the Chief the report that Dr. Rogers had given her, when Johnnie said "bingo."

He said he had a hit on the data bank in the town of Moundsville, West Virginia and the finger prints belonged to a Hillary Beavers, thirty-two years of age. She had been brought in for being forty miles over the speed limit as she raced her car through the mountains. He pulled up her picture and put it on the big screen.

Trevor said that he had seen her as they were walking out of the hotel on the day they were leaving.

Alex nodded and said that she had seen her too. She then looked around and asked if the team was ready to visit the area in that part of West Virginia again.

Trey said that this time he was going to check out one of the swat teams sniper rifles. He said that if they were going to have to hunt their target down in the mountains, they might be doing some long-distance dueling.

The Chief said that he would check on the availability of the departments transport van so the team could be better prepared.

Trevor commented that he would need to tune up his banjo so he could strum it while Bill accompanied him as they walked along the mountain trails.

Alex smiled and said that she appreciated his desire to use his banjo, but she preferred that they not scare the animals as they hiked the mountain trails.

She suggested that they spent the next couple of days getting ready. She suggested they all take their drones out and practice flying them since they would most likely need them to find Hillary in the mountains of West Virginia. She knew Johnnie didn't need practice but suggested he coach them on refreshing and improving their capabilities.

Johnnie smiled and said that he doubted he would be able to help her after her first flight since she had super drone flying capability, but he was sure he could help Trevor since the last time he had run his drone into a tree.

"Hey, I was chasing a motor bike through the woods and getting fired on," Trevor complained.

The Chief said he would come out and practice but then the team could take his drone as an extra in case they needed it.

Alex then said that after the practice she wanted to spend some time finding some new routes to come to work so that she would not be so predictable coming down from her home.

She also wanted to spend time on the firing range shooting Trey's sniper rifle. This, she noted, would take them into the weekend so they should plan on leaving on Monday.

Hillary made it back to West Virginia and went to her apartment and got ready to go to a still that she owned in the mountains outside of Barrackville.

She planned to take enough of her things so she could stay away for several months. It was difficult for her to get everything done that she needed to do but she worked through the pain. She packed her things in eight different backpacks so that she could carry what she needed up the mountain. She realized that she would need to make several trips, and she would only be able to use one back pack strap on her good left shoulder.

She also knew that she would have to practice using her left shoulder to fire her rifle.

She concluded that being wounded sucked.

She told her landlord that she was having a mover pack her things and take them to Weirton. She hoped that would throw off whoever might be looking for her. She indeed hired a mover but the few things she owned would be put in storage.

She knew that she still had to make the rounds checking on the operation of her stills. It was the only way she could collect her money and make sure that her still operators were doing their jobs. She decided to make Barrackville her new center of operation. She would open a bank account there so she would have a bank close by to deposit her money before moving it off shore. She moved her money off shore on a weekly basis so that she could keep the amounts low, but she usually moved more than twenty thousand each month.

She figured that she would never be found. She planned to keep a low profile and after a few months she was sure that the search would end. The moonshine business was one that stayed in the shadows, and she was planning to stay even deeper in those shadows.

Alex enjoyed getting back into flying her drone. She regained her ability to fly it with her eyes closed and when they all went out to the firing range for practice, she once again was able to hit the target's bull's eye ninety percent of the time. She was actually looking forward to flying her drone in the mountains.

She quickly got use to the snipers rifle that Trey had selected. She was able to take out the bull's eye every time she went through five shots.

Trey complimented her on her ability and commented that she would have made a good partner in Iraq.

She nodded and said that she preferred the work they were doing together.

On Friday Trey invited everyone to his house for a cook out. He said that he wanted to show off his new back yard. He added that he had removed all the young kids play equipment and had put in a large hot tub that he had surrounded with a trellis that had grape vines growing on them. He had paved in an area leading up to the hot tub where he had a new grill installed and where there was a beautiful heavy glazed wooden table made out of walnut. He said the table cost almost as much as the hot tub.

Alex asked when he had the time to make such a dramatic change.

Trey replied that he didn't have the time, but that Lindsey had convinced him to let her manage getting the change done. He added that Nolan had volunteered to help and had been the one that had found the table.

Alex said that she was looking forward to coming over on Sunday.

When she and Matt arrived, Nolan came out to greet them. Alex was amazed at how much he had grown in just a month. He was almost as tall as Matt and a good head taller than her.

Nolan led them in and then gave them a tour of the new back yard.

He lead him to a ground level, eight seat jacuzzi that had arm rests that had bottle holders in each arm and two sets of steps to make it convenient for its users to walk into the pool.

He said that the jacuzzi pool was great, but he went over to the table and ran his hand across the thick glazed table surface. He said that it was almost as great as the door to her Maui home.

Alex ran her hand the length of the table and said that it was marvelous, and the walnut grain gave it an intensity similar to the door.

She put her ear to the table surface and said that she could hear the rich woody bass notes.

She reach out and stroked a long blond streak that seemed to be shooting out from a knot and said that the walnut tree had produced its own blackhole that had a gamma ray's burst that went halfway along the table.

She added that the two long benches seemed to be made out of the same branch or at least the grain seemed to be the same.

Nolan said that she had it right. The benches were made from one branch cut length wise

He then added that her description of the table captured how he felt. He came over and gave her a hug.

Alex went into the kitchen where Lindsey was finishing making a mixed salad and complemented her on the transformation of the back yard.

Lindsey thanked her but she said that Nolan had been the key player in getting it done. He had worked with the contractor that had put in the hot tub. That contractor had linked him with a friend that made furniture. That was how Nolan had found the table. He fell in love with the table and had been willing to spend his own savings to buy it. She had told him that his savings was for college and that she was going to make his dad pay for the table since it was his fault to be working so much.

Alex nodded and said that it had been a series of back-to-back cases, but it was not Trey that was causing that to happen.

Lindsey smiled, nodded, and added that everything was OK. She was just relating how she had communicated with her ever-growing and smarter son.

Alex said that she was amazed how tall he had grown.

Lindsey replied that he was now taller than she.

Alex sighed and said that it seemed like only yesterday she had been pushing him on the swing set that was now replaced with a jacuzzi.

In a more serious tone Lindsey thanked Alex for continuing to go to AA. Having Trey go with her had changed her life and had changed his as well. He no longer woke up in the middle of the night thinking he was in some battle in Iraq.

Alex nodded and said that those sessions had changed her as well.

She said that the whole team was still attending a group session with their phycologist once a month as well. That session had helped the whole team get over the many gun battles they had been in, and it had also brought them very much closer and together.

Lindsey went over to Alex and gave her a hug. She said that from day one when they first met at the river front, she had recognized the fact that they were going to be very good friends.

Alex hugged her back and said that it was so, and she could not be happier about it.

9 Where in West Virginia is Hillary

It was five in the morning. It was dark in the parking lot. It was hard to see the black van from the door. Recognizing a dark figure walking toward you from across the parking lot was an impossibility.

Matt had backed their black van out onto the street one block above the street that was their home address. Their back yard was level with the street to the back of their home. He was driving Alex to work. He drove slowly down the steep roads to the Cincinnati downtown level. On the way they picked up Johnnie. He dropped them both off in the dark of the morning at the side of the police station.

Alex gave him a hug and kiss and wished him a good day.

She put her suitcase into the van then she went in to get her drone. As she returned with it, Bill and Trevor stopped by the van to put their things into the van. They too had to go retrieve their drones. Bill came out with two. He said that Chief was sending his along as a spare.

Trey drove in and after he retrieved his drone it was time to depart.

Bill and Trevor flipped to see who would drive first.

Bill was the loser. He got in and headed towards Columbus.

By the time they turned to head toward Wheeling, the sunrise ahead was a brilliant yellow, with a bright red band across the eastern sky that turned the scattered clouds a brilliant pink. Alex commented on the seeming depth to the sunrise and its beauty. She suggested that when they came to a breakfast place they stop.

After breakfast, Trevor took over the driving.

Alex, Trey, and Johnnie were in back looking over the map of West Virginia and guessing were a good location to put a still would be.

Johnnie suggested that having a still operation near a town where the moonshine could be sold would seem to be the kind of location that a still operator would want.

Trey pointed out that it had to be a location where the operator could bring in the needed supplies on a regular basis while at the same time not getting caught doing so.

Alex said that it would work best if the supplies were dropped off at night and then the supplies carried to the still after that.

Trevor announced their arrival to Wheeling and suggested they stop for lunch before heading to the Sheriff's office.

Alex agreed and said that she would give his office a call and let him know they were back and would be in after lunch to touch base.

Hillary was aware of West Virginia's position as the forty ninth poorest state and its ranking as the unhappiest state, but she could think of no better place to live.

It had hundreds maybe thousands of mountain like steep hills and numerous clear sweet water springs and a wealth of parks and nature preserves.

She grew up happy and grew up in love with the land around her.

She had selected her new center of operation based on its unique lay out. The stills were located in a small volcano like cavity about halfway up the mountain. She thought of it as a deep pock mark on the face of mother earth. It was surrounded by a dense stand of pine trees that hid it. The three stills were outside with only a heavy-duty tarp over them. There were two over hangs on each side of the path that came back to the stills. One side had been closed in and made into a living area. The other side, which was a little larger, was where the supplies to run the still were kept. She had some of the materials moved and rearranged and put up a cot and brought in a chair that she could use. She was planning ahead in case she needed to disappear.

The unique feature of the location was the sweet water spring that started from that point and ran down the mountain side.

It was the water used to run the still and the moonshine it produced was the best that was produced from any location.

For her main residence she rented a house that was only a block off of Buffalo Creek road where she planned to stay most of the time when she was not making her routine checks on her stills.

After lunch, the Alex's team went to the Sheriff's office. Alex led the way in and stopped at the Sheriff's support's desk. She greeted her, handed her a bag of chocolate candy, and asked her to let the sheriff know that they had arrived.

A few moments later they were all led to the conference room where sheriff Williams and his lead detective, Daly, were waiting for them.

Alex said good morning and gave each a bag of chocolate.

Sheriff William thanked her for the candy and asked what brought she and the team back to Wheeling.

Alex said they had come to arrest a Hillary Beavers for attempted murder and fleeing the scene.

Sheriff William asked how she could be so sure of who she was after.

Alex recounted the event surrounding the shooting and the multiple finger prints that had identified Hillary. She figured that Hillary was either hired to kill her, or she was the person who had killed Layton Harris and was trying to stop the investigation.

Sheriff William nodded and asked where she expected to find Ms. Beavers.

Johnnie said that they had an address in Wheeling.

Detective Daly said that he would go out with them to the address and help in the arrest.

The Sheriff William said that he would honor the agreement that he had made with her boss to let her make the arrest and take her back to Ohio.

Alex thanked him and said she hoped to be lucky enough to make the arrest that day.

Detective Daily said they should see how lucky she was and suggested he lead the way.

Alex had the team get their protective gear on before going to the address.

Daily said that he was impressed with the precaution they were taking. He said he would let them take the lead because his protective gear would make it almost impossible for him to walk.

Alex nodded and said she would take the lead.

When they got to the address and knocked on the door, the woman that opened the door was holding a baby. She was surprised and said that she and her husband had moved in just two days before and her house was a mess.

Alex asked if she owned the home and learned that it was rented. She asked if she knew where the previous renter had moved.

The woman said that the landlord had said that his renter hand moved to Weirton.

Alex thanked her and wished her a good day.

She turned and led the way back to the van.

She asked Johnnie to look up the owner of the house so they could find out which mover was hired to move Hillary.

Johnnie took about three minutes and gave Alex the number.

Detective Daily commented how great it was to have someone who was so versatile on the computer.

Alex smiled and said that she called Johnnie the wizard or her magician.

She then called the owner, identified herself, and asked which mover had been used.

Once she had the name of the mover, she asked Johnnie to look up the address. She suggested they go to the address and get the information first hand.

When they got to the moving company, Detective Daily took the lead, and introduced Alex and the team. He asked about the move.

The owner of the company asked his support to look up that move and let him know where it had been delivered.

He looked at the order and said that the two people that had worked that move were on the lot getting ready for a move in the morning.

He had his support call them in.

They came in, looked around and were quiet.

When they were asked about the move, they looked at each other and the older one said that they had been paid to lie about having moved it to Weirton, but he did not want any trouble with the law. He said the load had been put in the company's storage area waiting for a future delivery location. He had logged in that information as required by the company.

The owner thanked him for keeping things legal and said he could go.

He asked his support for the location of the pod or pods from that move.

Alex and team followed the owner out into a large warehouse where stacks of semi-truck trailer containers were located.

The moving company owner pointed out two containers that were stacked one above the other. He asked if he should have the seal broken and get the two containers opened.

Alex shook her head and said that at this time she did not need to look inside.

She looked at Detective Daily and asked him to mark them as evidence to be held until further notice.

The moving owner asked if paying rent was part of the evidence holding package.

Alex asked whether rent had already been paid and if so, for how long.

Once they were back inside the owner found out that the rent had been paid for six months.

Alex handed him a bag of candy and said that if it took longer than six months, she would make sure that he got paid.

He smiled, thanked her, and said that she had just made his day.

Once they were back at the van, she asked Detective Daily where to the south he figured was a good place to go to get out of sight or to hide.

He said that he really had no clue. He added that if he were trying to get lost in West Virginia he could go to almost any small town and become invisible. He thought for a moment and said that he would most likely find some place in the middle of the state.

Alex thanked him and suggested that the team get checked in and spend the evening deciding where they should begin the hunt.

After having checked in, Johnnie went to the restaurant across the street where the team was to meet. He set his computer up and decided to follow the money. He hacked into the local banks until he found the one that had Hillary's account. He was able to get the routing number of the bank to which most of the money had been transferred. It was a bank in Barrackville, West Virginia.

He then began to look at topographical maps around that area.

Alex and Trey walked together to the restaurant discussing how they were going find a person hiding in a state like West Virginia.

When she saw Johnnie's smile, she was immediately sure that he had made some sort of significand discovery.

Johnnie turned his computer so that Alex could see where he pointed. He said that he had followed the money and had found the area where their quarry was most likely located.

Alex smiled and said that at least he had taken the team to the haystack where the needle was hidden.

She asked him how far he had followed the money.

Johnnie said that he had noted some other banks that were not in state, but he had not pursued those accounts. He figured that he would do that in his spare time.

Alex asked if he had narrowed where in the haystack, they should begin their search.

Johnnie nodded and said that the town was located just west at the base of a mountain range that would be where to hunt.

Alex gave him a hug and said that he had just earned another tray of her cookies.

Trevor and Bill had just sat down. Trevor asked what Johnnie had earned cookies for.

Alex smiled and said that Johnnie had just told her where in West Virginia he would be driving in the morning.

10 Eyes in the Sky

The deep throbbing from her right shoulder bullet wound was slowly giving way to just a dull reminder of an even greater pain. The half dozen slow hikes required to get the stills she visited were in their own way therapeutic. She had kept in good shape, which she figured was a part of her feeling better but at the same time dealing with the pain had taught her a lesson in humility as she realized that her whole life was on the dark shadow side of the law.

As she pulled into the garage of the grey single-family two-story home with its spacious front porch, large living room bay windows and the fenced in back yard she wondered what her life would be like if she had chosen to marry Samuel. She might be laughing and chasing kids through the back yard.

She laughed as she turned off the car and chose to focus on the hot shower that she was eager to take.

She went in and headed straight to the shower. She looked into the mirror and saw that bullet scar was totally healed, and the scab had fallen off and left just a round pink spot where the bullet had entered. The hot shower was just what she needed.

It was dinner time. She had no intension of cooking. She decided that it was time to relax and enjoy the evening. As she drove to the bar and grill that she had in mind, she spotted a large black van that had Police written on the side. She drove slowly around the block so she could look at it again. This time she saw the word Cincinnati written in smaller gold letters.

She decided that getting out of town was more important than a casual dinner and celebrating the healing of her wound.

She turned around and drove back to her house and loaded up the stuff she had decided she would take with her if she had to run. It was not much since she had stored most of the stuff she wanted up at the still. She was still focused on figuring out how they had found her.

Moonshine

She was driving to the still when suddenly she decided that she should instead go to the still that Layton had originally run and that was now run by Clayton. It was a much more comfortable building, and the terrain was more appealing. She especially liked the spot on the trail that went farther up the mountain above the still where she enjoyed sitting and watching the sun rise in the early morning. She figured she might as well enjoy her time while she hid out.

Her gas gauge was almost on empty, so she decided to fill up. She automatically flipped her credit card onto the pump sensor and then gave out a groan as she realized what she had done. She was not too concerned because she was heading a couple hundred miles away, but she told herself to be more careful about using her credit card.

Not far away, Alex and the team were sitting and enjoying their desert and discussing how they would approach their hike in the mountains in the morning.

Johnnie, who had been sitting quietly working away on his computer suddenly said that he had movement.

Travis smiled and said that he heard a Johnnie but saw no movement.

Johnnie shook his head and said that he had been checking on Hillary's money movement when suddenly a credit card charge came in. He said that from what he could tell it was from a gas station just north of Barrackville.

Alex asked to see it on the map. She then said that it seemed that somehow Hillary had found out that they were after her and she was heading north.

Bill asked if they should get in the van and pursue her.

Alex looked again at the map and said that she was going to count on Hillary following old habits and that she would go to the still that was directly north of them. It was the still that she and Trey had previously visited.

She said they should get a good night's sleep, leave early in the morning, drive to that location and hike up to the still.

Hillary drove at the speed limit until she got to the small road that led to where she usually left her car when she went up to the still. She decided to park the car heading back the way she had come because that allowed her to park out of sight in the thick brush. The gravel in the path up the mountain side reflected the moon light and seemed to her to have a magic glow. The brush and forest to each side seemed to be the black cloak of a sinister demon. She smiled at what was passing through her mind and concentrated on not stumbling over any loose stones. It was once again clear to her why she had decided to hide at this still.

She reached the point in the trail where she needed to go through the thick brush back toward the still. It always amazed her that the brush never seemed to get thinner. She had mentioned this to Crayton who let her know that he watered and fertilized them because he wanted them to be thick and impenetrable.

She entered the building and in the dim light she could see that Crayton was sleeping in the cot. She decided that it would be safer for her to gently wake him.

He looked up at her and said that she was a little early and rolled over.

She decided to unroll her sleeping bag and get a few winks until he decided to get up.

Back in Barrackville Alex got up about the time that Hillary was laying down. She and the team had decided that an early morning drive up to the still was the best approach. She was the first to the van and got her things ready. She decided to wear both her Kevlar pants and jacket. She put those on and then pulled on a light jogging outfit. The rest of the team showed up and went through a similar preparation.

Trevar had come out with five bags of carry out breakfasts that he had been given by the desk clerk. He said that he wondered what the coffee would taste like, but he would settle for the caffeine.

Trey volunteered to drive and hopped into the driver's seat and asked everyone to put on their seat belts.

Johnnie took one of the very back seats and asked to be awakened when they got to where they were going.

Alex decided to follow Johnnie's example and almost immediately fell asleep.

Trey smiled as he looked around and realized that he was the only one awake. There were no cars on the road. The miles faded away and before he knew it, he was turning off on the small mountain road that he had been up once before. He drove the van to where he had parked before and pulled it off the road into the forest as far as he could.

He took a bite from his cold grilled cheese sandwich and a sip of his coffee. He had made good time, and the sun was yet to rise. He leaned back in his seat and closed his eyes.

Alex came awake when the van stopped moving. She reached into the cooler by her seat and took out an apple, tapped Trey on the shoulder, and asked him if he wanted it.

Trey was happy to take the apple since the cold grilled cheese was less than appealing.

Bill, who was sitting in the front passengers seat asked how many apples Alex might have.

Alex said that she had a couple for each of them and she had a couple of oranges for each of them as well.

Trevor thanked her for saving all of them.

Johnnie agreed and said that he would fix her breakfast at his place for a week.

Alex said that she had thought about this before they had left Cincinnati and had stocked up on the apples and oranges because she figured they would last a few days in her cooler.

She said that it was time they hiked up to the still.

Up at the still, Hillary and Clayton had just finished having an over easy egg and some toast. She had let him know that she was planning to stay for a few days. He told her he would be leaving to go to his own still. He said that he had the money for his last three sales at both places there because he had not been expecting to see her here.

Hillary said that she would be over in the next few days, and they could settle that business then.

She said that she was going up the trail to enjoy the early morning from her favorite spot.

As Hillary was hiking farther up the trail, Alex and team were just beginning their hike to the still.

Alex stopped at almost the same spot that Hillary had entered into the brush, but Alex was using her nose to find the still.

She led the way back into the brush and when the still came into site she signaled for silence. She pointed Bill and Trevor to the left. She pointed for Johnnie to stay on the trail leading to the still. She then signaled to Trey to go to the right.

They all met at the far side at the door leading into the building. Once again, Alex assigned each side of the door that each of them would go to.

She then quietly opened the door and followed Trey in to the right and Bill and Trevor entered in and went to the left.

The room was well lit and there was a person standing with his back to them scraping some plates clean into a bucket.

Alex saw that he had a gun holstered on the small of his back. She chose to quietly tell him he was under arrest and to raise his open hands over his head.

Alex saw his hesitation and said that he would die if he tried for his gun.

Crayton was surprised that someone had been able to come up behind him. He thought back at how good he felt at oiling the squeaky door hinges and getting them to be silent. He now appreciate the Japanese anti-ninja nightingale floor designs that he thought were a little over the top until this moment.

He raised his hands as instructed.

Alex asked where the second person happened to be.

He replied that there was no second person.

Alex looked at him. Then pointed at the two plates, two sets of coffee mugs and two sets of table ware and asked again.

Crayton took in the situation and figured that it was useless to deny that a second person had been there. He admitted that there had been a second person, but he was not sure where that person happened to be.

Alex looked around and decided to handcuff him to one of the pipes between two of the vessels. She asked him his name and learned that it was Crayton. She told him that she was not interested in his personal business and did not have the authority to arrest him for brewing moonshine unless he was not paying the taxes for the moonshine he produced. If he cooperated, she was inclined to release him, but she would report his operation once she got back to the local sheriff's office.

She asked Johnnie to stay and guard him. Johnnie nodded and said that he would.

Once Alex had left, Johnnie pointed to Crayton and said if he moved, he would get one between the eyes.

Johnnie took Gunjfor out of her case and armed her. Once he had her ready, he made sure that he had a clear image from her camera and then launched her and took her out of the door. He took her vertically up and out of the trees. He flew her up and got oriented to the trail below and flew her near the tree tops and took her up the trail.

Crayton knew that if he tried, he would probably fail to break loose. He could see the computer screen, so he watched in fascination as the old Black man expertly flew his drone along the tree tops that went up the mountain side.

Alex came to the trail and said that they should go carefully toward the top and said that she expected Hillary to be somewhere ahead.

Suddenly Trey took a step back and knelt. The echo of a shot followed. He said that he had been hit.

Alex put her drone on idle as she jumped over to check on Trey.

She heard Trevor and Bill both firing their weapons.

She realized that all of them were in the open and fully exposed to anyone trying to shoot them.

She suddenly heard distant gun fire and the scream of someone that had been hit.

She knew of only one person that was not with the team that would have been good enough to get behind Hillary and have taken action.

She jumped up and ran full speed up the trail. She expected to get hit but she wanted to get as close as possible to be able to get her shot off.

Bill and Trevor both followed.

Trey got up and hobbled up the trail.

Alex got to the bend in the trail from where the shot had been fired and as she sped around, she saw that Hillary had dropped her rifle and had limped backwards holding her leg and trying to stop the bleeding. She was about to fall off the cliff.

Hillary was looking into the barrel of a gun that was on a drone. She was trying desperately to stop the bleeding from the thigh of her leg. Then she realized that she was about to get arrested. She took a defensive step backward. Her foot was over the edge of the cliff. She realized that she was about to fall off and tried to lean back toward the ledge.

Alex jumped forward and grabbed Hillary by the wrist and fell to the ground trying to pull her back away from the edge. She realized that Hillary's weight was going to pull both of them over the edge. Suddenly she felt her legs pinned down. She held as tight as she could to Hillary's wrist, but she realized she would not be able to pull Hillary back up nor hold her for long. As she was about to lose her grip, two hands reached around her and grabbed Hillary by her arm and pulled her back to the top.

Alex rolled over and accepted Trevor's helping hands.

She thanked him for saving her.

He smiled and said that it was his pleasure.

She looked over where Trey had taken off his light wind break and was using it as a tourniquet to stop the blood flowing from Hillary's leg.

She looked at Gunjfor and gave a thumbs up. She said that he should land Gunjfor, and she would bring her back. She took the weapon from its holder and put it into an evidence bag.

She then called Sheriff Williams and requested his support.

It took more than thirty minutes before the sirens of the approaching help could be heard.

She walked over to where Trey was leaning against the rock wall and asked how he was feeling.

He shook his head and said that he had always wondered how when she had been hit at close range, had been able to stand, return fire, and kill the person who was no more than thirty feet from her.

He had been hit at about fifty yards and found it hard to breath. At that time, he had watched her pick up two kids and carry them for about a hundred yards before putting them down. He said that it was hard for him to get up and come up the trail.

Alex smiled and said that for her it was always about the amount of adrenaline that her body pumped out. She said that he was probably a low stress guy that pumped out less adrenaline.

She gave him a hug and said that she had watched him put the tourniquet on Hillary and promised to recommend him to Matt as a backup for his team.

He laughed and said that blood made him squeamish, and he might faint at some to the rescues that Matt made.

Hillary thanked him for helping her and said she was sorry for how everything had unfolded.

Alex shook her head and said that she had repeatedly tried to kill her and that the only thing she was most likely sorry about was that she had been caught.

She added that she was going to make sure that whatever judge and jury she stood before would know the details of how she murdered Layton, had attempted to kill her, and had shot her partner. She added the fact that based on the money flow that she had been able to document there would also be money laundering that would be added onto the other charges.

Alex looked at Hillary and told her that she was lucky to be living in a state that had abolished the death penalty and if she had been arrested in Ohio, she would be facing the death penalty.

The EMT's strapped Hillary down on the flat board and took her down the trail. The lead EMT looked around and complemented whoever had put on the torniquet for doing a good job and if that person needed a job, he had one on his team.

Alex looked at Trey who was smiling about the comment.

Trevor commented that they would need to treat Trey with kid gloves because now he had an alternate profession that he could pursue. He held out his wind breaker and asked if Trey was cold. Then he held out his hand to help Trey to his feet.

Alex led the way and carried Gunjfor back to the still and handed her to Johnnie and let him know that he had saved the team and the life of the person who he had shot.

She looked over at Crayton and said that she was going to let him go but she wanted his home address in case his testimony was needed.

He asked her why she was letting him go.

She pointed at Trevor and said because he tells me you make some very smooth and good tasting moonshine.

Crayton wrote down his home address and said he was throwing in his phone number as well. He pointed to a dozen jars of Moonshine and said that it was the first draw, it was smooth as silk, and they were welcome to all of it.

He then turned, walked out the door and seemed to disappear into the woods.

Alex said she was walking down the trail with Trey, and they would all gather at the van.

11 Suicide by Alex

*T*he walk back to the van gave everyone a chance to decompress. The sheriff and his team gathered around them and complimented them on having captured Hillary and of having saved her life as well. He asked if there had been any other weapon fired during the incident.

Alex said that no one else had fired a weapon. She said that only two shots had been fired. One by Hillary and one by Johnnie. She smiled and said that it was one of the few times that so few shots had been fired.

He said that he had the weapon that had been fired and that he just needed each of their accounts of the incident, but he could do that later and said that they were free to go on their way.

Shortly after that the team drove back to the hotel in Wheeling. They spent the early evening in the hot tub were Trey enjoyed letting one of the water jets surge against the spot on his chest where the bullet had hit. He commented that in the past he had watched Alex being hit and had never thought about how she seemed to bounce back almost immediately.

Alex laughed and replied that she had seen Trey hit so many times that all of his protection gear had been stripped from him and he had been able to go dancing the following day, so he had no reason to sob about being hit once.

Trevor laughed and said that Alex had been hit so many times in the butt in that same shoot out that she was talking about that he was surprised she had been able to sit down the next day.

Bill added that they had all survived multiple times with nothing more than a few aches because they took care of each other. He said that this time it was their IT genius or was it wizard who had provided the fire power that had made the difference.

Johnnie laughed and said that he was back at the still drinking that smooth moonshine and enjoying flying Gunjfor for fun when he spotted Hillary shooting at his friends. He said that his control finger accidently caused him to pull the trigger because he would never have thought of shooting someone from behind.

Bill asked when Johnnie had started to drink again.

Trey laughed and said that they should stop making him laugh because it hurt. He asked where they were going to go for dinner.

Alex suggested they walk across the street. She said that Sheriff Williams and Daily wanted to get their incident reports. They wanted to get everything organized for the prosecutors.

That evening the Sheriff said that it was too bad that the still was to be destroyed. It was a beautiful set up and the equipment was polished and in such a great shape.

Alex suggested that he keep the still in operation and make it a tourist attraction. She figured that it could become a duel money maker. It could make moonshine, and it would collect money from the tourist trade. She said that it could be a feature part of mountain hikes sponsored by local hike guides.

She smiled and said that she had the name and address of a very good operator that the Sheriff could hire to run the still. She did not tell him how she happened to have the number of a still operator.

Daily said that sounded like a great idea and getting an operator hired immediately was important since the still was in full operation.

The next day, on the way back to Cincinnati Alex invited everyone to celebrate the transformation of her back yard into something similar to what Trey had done. She gave everyone the date that was three weeks out.

The next day, Hillary was charged with the murder of Layton Harris, attempted murder of a police officer, money laundering and failure to pay tax. The prosecutor had a report that provided great detail about each charge.

Hillary's lawyer reviewed the charges and the details and let her know that she faced life in prison and that if she were found guilty on all the charges the best situation would be if she were able to get paroled for good behavior in thirty years.

Alex and Trey were both able to testify remotely and they followed the case on line.

The trial went on for two weeks and the sentencing was to be done during the third week.

Alex knew that the conversion of the backyard had been transformational. She walked slowly down the four steps of her porch and stepped into the backyard.

There was no lawn. Except for the flower beds the entire yard was paved with a mix of sandstone, bluestone, and a mix of other flat stones to form an irregular mix of colors. It had all been sealed with a clear coating. She walked around the rose garden along the entire outer edge of the yard.

She stood at the edge of the an eight-person, light green jacuzzi tub that sat down in the ground. She adjusted the sun cover over it and admired and thought about enjoying it both in the summer and winter since it had an electric heater to heat the water.

She turned and looked to her left of the back porch where a stainless-steel grill stood. To the right was a glazed walnut grained picnic table that Nolan had helped her select.

She went and sat on the smooth white cap of the round flower bed with a two-foot-high stone wall that was of darker stone. She put her hand up and cradled a bunch of Scuppernong grapes.

The center bed was designed to become a greenhouse during the winter months to ensure the grape vines would survive.

All the beds had an automatic water sprinkler system.

She and Matt had worked on the yard design together and they both agreed that tending to the flowers and the grapes was the extent of the yard work either of them wanted to do. Their three-tiered front yard was so steep that they had it being cared for by a gardener they had hired.

They were very happy with the way they had improved their new home.

Meanwhile Hillary sitting in a West Virginia prison awaiting sentencing, thought about life in prison. She thought about her times hiking and wandering in the mountains she loved. She came to the conclusion that she would have preferred to have fallen off the cliff rather than being saved. She thought about it and came up with another solution. A solution that she needed to escape to.

For the sentencing hearing she had been allowed to dress in one of her black pant suits. As she was getting ready to be led into court, she dashed to a side door that went directly out of the court house, ran across the street, then turned up an alley and went into the office building there. She walked casually across the entrance foyer.

She waited a moment until the metro stopped out front, went out and got on. She rode the bus and got off within a block of her bank. She went in, identified herself and withdrew close to ten thousand dollars.

She then walked to a nearby used car lot and paid cash for a car.

She went to a gun shop where in the past she had purchased multiple weapons and bought a used thirty-eight.

She then drove across the river into Ohio. She knew where she was going and what she was going to do.

She chose to drive on the smaller highways. It made the trip to Cincinnati a little longer, but she was not in any hurry because what she planned would take place in the morning or on some subsequent morning. She was not in a hurry because she knew it was to be her final drive.

Sheriff Williams had been sitting in court waiting for the sentencing proceedings to begin when he learned that Hillary had escaped. He left the courtroom and called in to his office and dispatched his deputies to see if they could catch her.

His men kept reporting in that they seemed to be one step behind her, and they thought that she had crossed into Ohio.

He decided to give Alex a call to give her a heads up.

Alex got his call and was surprised that Hillary had escaped. She asked about the situation and learned that she was being held by the State Police because he was one of the witnesses in the trial.

She decided that she would need to be extra cautious until Hillary was captured.

Hillary knew where Alex lived. She drove into Cincinnati and up to her street. As she drove slowly by, she took in the bike rack that was in the parking spot at the foot of the steps coming down from the house.

She knew what she would do.

The following morning, she parked one block above the street Alex lived on and walked to the corner on Alex's street and waited. The sun was just rising, and the rays of the sun was striking the taller downtown buildings. She absorbed all and took a deep breath. She knew her time was about to end.

Alex was glad that Friday was at hand, the yard party was to be on the next afternoon. She had an art display in her third-floor art gallery that had paintings from many of the area artists and about a half a dozen that Annie had asked her to display as well.

She and Matt had joked that Sunday would be their recovery day.

She was thinking about the weekend as she came down the three flights to the street. She had her bike chained to the bike rack that she had put into her on the street parking spot. As she stepped onto the side walk, she heard someone call he name.

She turned and saw Hillary pointing a gun at her.

As she stepped to the side, got to one knee, and drew her gun, Hillary fired twice.

Alex returned fire. It was over. She had fired three times, and she was sure that Hillary was dead. She called in the shooting as she walked up to where Hillary lay. She saw a tag on the trigger guard of the weapon with the words, "Thank You."

Alex shook her head when she realized that Hillary had shot at her not trying to hit her but having her return fire. It was suicide by Alex.

The Chief and Trey arrived together and took in the scene.

They both walked the crime scene and came back to where Alex was sitting on the steps up to the house.

The Chief asked who had shot first.

Alex said that Hillary had fired twice before she had returned fire.

The Chief said that Hillary was either a really a bad shot, or she was not trying to hit who she was shooting at.

Alex nodded and said that she was calling it suicide by Alex she handed the chief Hillary's thank you note.

The Chief shook his head and put his hand on Alex's shoulder and said that she should take it as a compliment from the person that had chosen her for her shooting skills.

Trey put his hand on her shoulder and said that he agreed with the Chief. He added that Hillary had decided that she was not going to spend life in prison.

Alex nodded and said that she was going to take her bike and go riding for the day and let her feelings about what had just happened process itself out of her mind.

Trey said that he would like to join her. He pointed at the other bike in the bike rack and asked if Matt would mind if he rode it.

Alex said that Matt had been on call, out all week with his team and the bike needed to be ridden.

The Chief wished them a good ride and said he was looking forward to the grill out and eager to see what she had done with her backyard.

The End of Moonshine

422

Grief's Trajectory

1 Ultimate Betrayal

Dale took a sip of his beer and gave a toast. Life was good. The love of his life had married him. He had been hired to work at by a local contractor. He had good friends to celebrate with. What more could a guy want?

He was out with his two best friends enjoying a day in the park. His beloved Cynthia had not felt well and stayed home. Home was a house they had just rented and moved into. They were still in the middle of unpacking the few boxes that they had. Their living room was empty. They owned a bed, a chest of drawers, a kitchen table and an old couch given to them by his parents. It was not much but they did not care.

They had each other.

Cynthia was the most important thing in his life.

He, Bobby, and Guy were enjoying day in the park. They had a table, and a grill stand where the red-hot charcoal was roasting some brats and sausages.

The beer was cold. The day was warm.

He looked past the newly planted young ten-foot-high maples surrounding the picnic area to the towering predominance of a single huge old oak wrapped by its cloak of dark green leaves as it dominated the hill and the host of red, yellow, and pink wild flowers seemly paying homage to it. The white puffy clouds in added a lofty touch of greatness and seemed to be embracing it.

The world was as it should be.

He watched a group of white boys arrive in a large flatbed truck. They stopped at the next grill, and all jumped off and then reached back and helped themselves from a cooler to some beer.

A short time later one of the group demanded that the three of them give up their table.

He figured that they were looking for a fight because no more than twenty feet away was the table that belonged with their grill.

He told Guy and Bobby not to engage. He turned so that he was looking at the large Oak tree in the middle of the field in hopes that nothing would happen.

When he felt a hand on his shoulder pull him around, he knew it had not worked. He hit the guy as hard as he could with his beer bottle, ducked and kicked him on the side of his knee and to took him down.

He was hit on his back with what he knew as a baseball bat because he heard the attacker shout out, "Home run."

He fell to the ground and heel kicked the second guy under his chin. He was sure the kick had taken him down.

He lost count of how many times he got hit. The fight ended when a group of folks from some of the other tables around broke up the fight.

He was about as busted up as he had ever been. He was on the verge of passing out.

Guy suggested they get home and get him fixed up.

Bobby threw water on the grill, grabbed their stuff, threw it into the back of the pickup, and jumped into the bed.

Guy said he would drive.

He got into the passenger's seat and that was the last he remembered.

He started to come too as he was being dragged across the grass. He looked up and realized that Guy was dragging him. He started to relax and then something hit him across the sided of his head and the world went black.

He came awake one more time as the rope around his neck tightened and he could no longer breath.

He looked down and was shocked that he was looking at the person that had been his lifelong friend. They had grown up playing together.

Then the world went black.

The lush dark green oak leaves touched by the morning dew rustled quietly in the morning breeze. The gnarled branches of the ancient more than one hundred-year-old oak tree limbs spread out some one hundred feet in diameter and reached up just as high up into the sky.

Its prominent lone location at the top of the knoll made it the strongest oak tree of the forest around it. It heralded its dominance and strength. It had been compelled to battle for its existence from the wind, rain, winter storms and the blazing sun.

Guy had watched it grow for more than fifty years as he battled his mind over his ultimate betrayal of his friend.

He wished he could embrace the righteousness the oak symbolized. For him it emphasized that it would never let him forget the one most immoral event in his life that for more than fifty years had haunted him.

He and the oak had mutually embraced that moment for all those years.

The oak had flourished and grown more than fifty feet in heigh and diameter.

He had killed his best friend in hopes of taking his place in his Dale's wife's side.

She had refused his proposal of marriage three times. Then he had learned she was pregnant with Dale's child.

That day his soul had shriveled, and he wished he could have died. Each year his soul had taken one more step into the grey of despair and regret.

He sat on the Oak bench made from a limb that had fallen from the tree. He had taken the fallen limb to the lumber yard and asked Bobby to make it into a bench and then he had donated it to the park. It had a brass plaque that commemorated his old friend that had been hung from a limb of the oak tree.

He often came to watch the sunrise and to remember. To remember   To remember.

To remember so that he could go back to his farm and for another day do the work that would allow him to live the life that he had lived for fifty years. It had been fifty years on his own. It had been a lonely fifty years. He thought of it as his hell on earth.

He had watched as Cynthia had also lived alone but he saw her with her daughter and saw the bright light that the two seemed to exude.

All around him he listened to the forest humming with life. The birds in the oak tree's canopy chirped and sang their sweet mating songs. They were singing about life. About a life of that was warm and natural.

He watched the sunrise breaking through the cracks in the greyish white clouds in the sky. The sun highlighted the hiking path out beyond the tree. The path was lined with wild flowers, ripe blackberries and occasionally a bush of luscious gooseberries.

To him it was a path that symbolized a way to a glorious future. A future that he had destroyed and buried for himself. A future that was now behind him and the short future ahead of him scared him because of what he figured was in store for him.

The path went through a forest that hummed with life. He had walked it often to revitalize his soul. A soul that had one very dark malevolent moment that had darkened out the entirety of the rest. It was a darkness that colored what he saw, made sweet wing taste bitter, and made a wonderful and gracious Strauss waltz flat. He walked a path that was frozen in time and frozen by the repulsive action that he had taken.

The oak drew his gaze back to the limb as if it wanted to remind him of that moment that though more than fifty years in the past needed to be put back to front and center so that he would never forget. The oak was trying to protect the world from the evil it had unwillingly been a part of. It would do so each time he returned to sit on the bench.

He had lived long. He had lived much longer than he had ever thought he would. Diamonds are made under pressure but the diamond that he had become had a major flaw that made it worthless. It would never be shared with another soul.

He looked at the acorns hanging in the tree and realized that it had soon to be small oaks sleeping in each. He had no acorns. There would be no replacement for him. He did not have acorns to drop, and he felt it was better that way. His was not a seed to pass on.

He was not sure whether there was a way for his soul to be embraced by the angels in white or whether it would be embraced by the angels in black. He did not deserve the first and he feared the embrace of the second.

What he was sure of was that a large egregious act had a life of its own and did not shrink with time but seemed instead to grow roots and anchor its self into one's very soul. These were roots with thorns that gave pain with every thought.

He knew that his sitting in penitence and embracing the righteousness of the oak was not enough. He knew that his donations to the food bank and to several charities were not enough. He knew that there was nothing he could do to undo his past actions. He knew that he would take his damaged soul to the grave with him.

There were now fewer days ahead for him. He was contemplating how he wanted to handle what he saw as his march to judgement. It was a march that held little hope. It was a march he could not avoid nor one that he desired to. It had been a long, lonely life that but for one decisive moment could have been avoided.

He had spent many an hour riding on his tractor, milking his cows, or sheering his sheep and thinking about what he had done and what he should do. But it did not seem to matter the amount of time that he had contemplated. He always came to the same conclusion that there was no righting the wrong he had committed.

2 Resilience

Cynthia ran her fingers along the engraved head stone. These were loving fingers that had memorized each of the letters. She had been tracing the engraving of those four letters on the plain head stone for more than fifty years. They were fifty years of longing and an ache in her heart that never left her. She would come to the grave each week and share what she and their daughter had been doing each week. She had shared every birth day, every holiday, and every school event with Dale. She let him know that she had a good job and had been able to save and help their child, their daughter go through college. She had let him know about their daughter's marriage to a lawyer in Cincinnati. The stories about each grandchild, two girls and two boys went on for just as long as the stories about their daughter. Each of the grand children had done well. They had all married and were about to bless her world with great grandchildren.

She told him about the good years, but she also told him about her frustration about not being able to solve the mystery of his death. She had not been able to get his case thoroughly investigated. She had been stonewalled by the local police who said that there were no credible leads. She was sure they were just stonewalling her.

She was a black woman challenging a totally white establishment. She was sure that she had been discounted.

She had asked about the fight that had occurred with the group of the young white men but was told that every one of the group had a solid alibi.

The coroner said that that strangulation was the cause of death but there was not any other evidence that pointed to a specific individual.

Now on her seventy seventh birthday, as she listened to the news, a ray of hope stood in front of the cameras answering questions in a news conference about her need to shoot a person who had attacked her. The person was a young Black female detective. This was a person who was in control, stood proud and was not cowed by the world around her.

Cynthia watched the news, and she knew what she needed to do. Destiny was calling her to act. She needed to go to Cincinnati.

After the grilling from the news crews about the shooting in front of her home, Alex got on her bike and along with Trey had ridden down to the water front. She set a fast pace along the water front. She needed to get over the fact that the person that she had brought to trial had come to her place and purposely shot at her to commit suicide. After an hour of hard riding, she and Trey had returned.

After securing the bikes, Trey said it was time for him to go home.

Alex went up to the house and was pleased to find that Matt was sitting and reading while he waited for her.

He looked up and said that he had heard that it had been a rough day.

She gave him a hug and kiss and asked what he wanted for dinner.

He smiled and said that he had prepared dinner and led the way into the kitchen where he had a candle burning and the boxes of the Thai dinner that he had ordered in.

Alex laughed and said that she was sure she was going to enjoy his cooking and sat down and put some rice on her plate and put a helping of Mongolian beef, several spoonful of mixed vegetables and then put soy sauce over the whole thing.

She related the events of the morning and what a negative effect it had on her.

She suggested an early bed time which Matt said would be great since he was exhausted from a nonstop day.

The next morning, she fixed breakfast and reminded him that the caterers for the big yard celebration would be there at ten to get everything set up.

Their friends arrived throughout the afternoon and soon the backyard was full.

All the friends were present, and a special surprise was the arrival of Annie, Brian, Linda, and Lorie who had flown in from Hawaii. Their arrival topped off the event.

Alex loved that fact that Annie had done such a thing. Annie said that a good friend was worth more than any painting she had ever painted. She then presented her painting of the transformed backyard.

Alex was surprised by the painting and asked who had sent her a picture of the yard.

Annie pointed to Matt and said he was the guilty one.

Alex said she was taking it up to her art gallery on the third floor and putting it in a place of honor. She announced that anyone wanting to see her current display of art and awards were welcome to go up to the art gallery and she would give a tour.

Everyone followed and after putting the gift painting on the very first stand she took everyone through the gallery that she had populated mostly with the works of new local artists.

Throughout the rest of the afternoon, the food flowed as if being attacked by a stream of locust attacking a wheat field.

The drinks were consumed as if they were the main course.

The celebration was an outstanding success.

The afternoon backyard party went well past sunset and into the evening.

Alex had arranged for the caterers to do the cleanup on Sunday and had scheduled the house keeper to come in on Monday.

Sunday she and Matt went for a bike ride starting on the water front and going out along the Loveland trail. She had arranged to have lunch with Sheriff Evin and his wife.

It was a great reunion where she shared the fact that Annie was doing quite well.

After lunch they had ridden back.

Matt left for work at four on Monday morning and left her sleeping.

She got up feeling energized. She spent thirty minutes running on her treadmill then she grabbed a cup of coffee but figured she would make a bear claw her breakfast when she got to work.

She rode her bike down to the stop light and automatically looked up to the roof where the two shooters of the previous attempts on her life had chosen as the best place to get their shots. She had arranged for a plexiglass barrier to be put across the entire front of the roof in order to prevent a third attempt.

She nonetheless reflexively looked up to make sure that there was no shooter.

She rode on and met with Johnnie at his apartment building and then they rode the rest of the way in together.

Alex walked into the bull pen and when she looked at Trey, Bill, Travis she knew that something was up. She walked over to where Trey was sitting and accepted the half of a bear claw that he held out to her.

She looked over at Bill and Trevor and asked what was up.

Trevor smiled and said that a little old lady had walked into the Chief's office, and the Chief had closed the door and the shades.

They all knew that when he did that something of importance was taking place and that he was not to be disturbed.

They were all wondering what that little old lady was telling the Chief and whether it was their next case.

Alex sat down, took a bite of her bear claw, and sipped on her coffee. She knew that if the Chief was serious about what he heard he would soon call her in and perhaps everyone else in.

Trevor nodded toward the door as it slowly opened and said that it was her turn, and she should make sure that no major gunfire accompanied the case that the gentle looking old lady might get them into.

Alex smiled and replied that she seldom had control about the amount of gunfire a case involved but she would keep his advice in mind.

She walked into the Chief's office and was introduced to Ms. Cynthia Hammer who stood up and shook her hand and let her know that she was counting on her to solve a fifty-year-old crime.

Alex smiled and replied that it seemed a long time to wait to report a crime.

Cynthia nodded and said that she had waited until she could find a person that was good enough to solve a crime that had never been properly handled and certainly not solved. She pointed at Alex and said that she was the reason she had come to Cincinnati to report the murder of her husband.

Alex listened to Cynthia tell her the story of losing her husband only weeks after their marriage and before he knew of her pregnancy. It was a tale that grabbed at her heart. The fact that the family had prospered over the years was the bright side. The fact that Cynthia had endured a lifetime of heart ache was the shadow and the heart ache.

Alex asked if the autopsy and investigation had shed any light on what had happened.

Cynthia said that the coroner had listed the cause of death as strangulation. The investigation ended a few days later and because at the time she could not afford to pay for the burial, Dale was buried a day later in a pauper's grave in a simple wooden coffin with only a wooden head stone. As soon as she could afford it, she had purchased a granite head stone to replace the wooden one that had been place on his grave.

She had tears in her eyes as she shared the story. She said that she always felt bad about Dale's burial but over the years came to realize that the burial had little to do with those that lived on. She had focused on using the little money she had to raise their daughter.

She knew where to visit him and had done so every weekend for over fifty years. She had kept his grave well taken care of and had flowers growing there for him. She smile and added that she had done it also for herself. Visiting him let her shed that tensions of the week and look forward to the coming one. She added that when their daughter was young, she often went with her to visit her father's grave.

She then once again pointed to Alex and said that she wanted her to reopen the case and solve it.

Alex looked at the Chief and asked him what he had in mind.

The Chief looked at her and said he wanted her to take a look and see if there was anything that might change the situation.

Alex thought for a moment.

She asked Cynthia if the men she suspected were still alive.

Cynthia thought for a moment and said that three of the six were alive and the one she suspected was among them. She added that the sheriff and coroner were long gone.

Alex then asked if Cynthia would authorize having Dale exhumed.

Cynthia asked it that would be necessary.

Alex nodded and said that the technology had changed dramatically, and the dead had a new voice with which to share their story.

Cynthia nodded and agreed to the exhumation, but she wanted to have assurance that everything be done with full respect. She added that she never had the curtesy of having been able to see Dale before he was buried and had always held the picture of him at their wedding in her mind. She planned to continue to hold that picture in mind and did not want to see him as a skeleton.

Alex assured her that Dale would be handled with due respect.

She looked at the Chief and asked if the Cincinnati police morgue could be used so that she could have the control to honor her commitment.

The Chief nodded and said he would let Dr. Rogers know.

Alex got up and asked Cynthia if she could walk with her to the lobby. On the way she learned that Cynthia's granddaughter, Hadly, had driven her to Cincinnati and was driving her back home after they did some shopping and went to lunch.

Alex smiled and suggested they try one of the restaurants that gave them a good view of the river.

Alex returned to the team, looked at Trevor and let him know that she thought there would be no fireworks, but they would need to work on time travel so that they could go back fifty some years to solve a murder.

3 The Sweet Birds Sing

*A*bout every three months for the last fifty years, the two of them had visited Dale's grave. Dale was buried in the paupers area of the graveyard that seldom got any attention or mowing so they would bring their weed eaters and cut the grass on his grave and several of the adjacent graves. The would weed the border of flowers that Cynthia had planted.

Bobby commented that he had forgotten most of the details to how Dale had ended up getting hung. All he could remember was riding in the back of the pickup truck trying to recover from getting the beating of his life.

He couldn't remember how many white boys there had been, but he remembered they were in the process of getting beat badly when the other picnickers had broken up the fight and the park rangers had told all of them to leave the park.

Guy repeated a lie that he had now mouthed for more than fifty years about Dale having dropped his wallet during the fight and the two of them having gone back. That was after he was dropped off at his house. When they returned to the picnic area there was no one around so they stopped.

He and Dale got out to look for the wallet. That was when the white boys had returned and one of them grabbed Dale as the two of them ran for the pickup. He had made it to the pickup and drove away from the five that were chasing him with clubs. He drove away but turned around and returned planning to use the pickup as a weapon. When he got back, he saw Dale hanging from the tree. He then drove to the rangers station and reported the hanging.

The rangers had called in the police and Dale's body was taken down from the tree and put in the coroners hearse and no one ever saw Dale's body after that.

Bobby nodded and said that maybe if he had gone back with the two of them things might have turned out differently.

Guy had heard this almost as many times as he had lied about what had happened.

He felt like telling him the truth, but he also feared what the truth held in store for him.

Usually after getting done at Dale's grave, they would drive out to the tree where Dale had been hung.

Once again, he would sit with the thoughts that had haunted him throughout his life time. He wondered what thoughts Bobby had.

He had asked once only to learn that Bobbie's thoughts were focused on enjoying the beauty of the giant Oak, listening to the birds sweet singing and the taking in the beautiful land all around.

He realized that Bobbie's life was in the light and his was in the dark shadow of his thoughts.

He never asked again but Bobbie often shared how much he enjoyed their visits and the beauty of the surroundings that he said was the embrace of their best friend Dale. He always made the point of saying that Dale had a place in heaven and was enjoy the radiant light, the warmth of heaven and the joy of peace they all were sure to find there.

He agreed that the tree stood in the glory of the sun and sky but for him it stood in the dark of night and even the stars refused to provide light. For him it was the place where he stood in the dark, but it was a place that he came almost every weekend. He was compelled by his deed to face it as a means of penitence.

He listened to the chirping of the birds and thought about why he had killed his best friend. He realized it was jealousy. He had wanted Cynthia and when the priest asked if there was any objections at speak now or forever hold their piece, he had almost objected. His heart had ached when the minister had uttered the words, "speak now or forever hold your peace." That day he had held his peace, but his jealousy had risen every time he saw how happy Dale was.

He came to the conclusion if Dale was not around, he would have a chance to capture Cynthia's heart.

The fight with the group of the white boys provided a situation that pulled him in, and he took advantage of it. He killed his best friend. And he knew that at the last moment Dale had realized who was killing him.

He waited a few weeks after Dale's burial, and he then began to court Cynthia.

He figured that he had what it took, and his family was the most affluent of the three guy's families.

She was kind but made it clear that she wanted him as a friend but that she did not have a romantic interest in him or anyone else.

He actually proposed to her three times but got turned down each time.

A few weeks later the fact that she was pregnant became apparent.

He wondered if Dale had known that he was to become a father.

That fact hit him hard.

Since he was living on and working on his father's farm, he would bring Cynthia milk, butter, eggs and a variety of the meat that he and his father butchered. He made sure that she had enough for her and later for her and her daughter.

His father had many friends at church, and he got his father to have Cynthia hired by the town's only black lawyer.

Life got into a fifty yearlong routine.

Alex asked Johnnie to dig into the case and see what he could find out about Cynthia's friends and the people at the time that Dale had been killed. She asked that he look into the six white men, the two black friends and the officials that were part of the investigation.

She went to see Dr. Rogers and explained the case to him and the fact that she was getting exhumation orders for Dale Hammer that was buried in a grave outside of Hamilton county. She said that she wanted him to examine the body and see what it might reveal that was not on the coroner's report of fifty years ago.

Dr. Rogers said that he would be willing to do the examination but figured that there probably not be much to work with. He ask what the condition of the burial had been.

Alex said that she had no clue since she had not visited the grave site. She asked if he wanted to go with her to see it and supervise the exhumation.

He said that he would wait until she had made contact with the county and cemetery officials and had arranged for the exhumation then he and his team would get involved.

Alex returned to her desk and asked Trey if he was ready to go to Wayland along the Scioto river.

Johnnie spoke up and said he wanted to go as well. He said that his interest was to see Ohio's back country. He added that he had done a quick check of the population of the area and found that Wayland was a small town of a few thousand and that there were six hundred people of color living there.

Trey got into the car, turned on the GPS, and said that it was about a two-hour drive and asked how long they would be staying there.

Alex said that on this trip she only wanted to drive around and see the place. She wanted to go to Cynthia's home, Dale's grave, and the town hall.

She asked if Johnnie could line up the phone numbers of the sheriff, the coroner for the area and the person who ran the cemetery.

She handed Johnnie a list of people that Cynthia considered close friends, long time coworkers and the men she considered to be the ones involved in killing Dale.

Johnnie said he would do it as they drove out to Wayland as long as his connection to the internet held.

They arrived right at lunch time. Alex pointed to a restaurant that advertised the best tenderloin sandwich in all of Ohio. She wondered who had verified that claim and said they should make sure the sign was true.

She called Cynthia and let her know that she was in town and planning to go to Dale's grave.

Cynthia asked to go along.

After lunch they picked Cynthia up. She then directed them out to the cemetery and led the way to the grave.

Alex commented that it must have rained recently because the ground was extremely soaked.

Cynthia said that the area where paupers were buried was more like a marsh when it rained. She pointed to a square piece of stone that was by Dale's grave and said that was where she sat when she came out to the grave. She said that she had to find flowers that grew in a wet environment. She said that she had thought about moving Dale's grave but until recently had not wanted to do it. But when she had agreed to getting him exhumed, she had purchased a plot at another cemetery for her and Dale, and she planned to have him reburied there. They would have adjacent graves.

Alex asked who kept the area around his grave mowed because the rest of the graves were over grown.

She took down the names of the two people that Cynthia said were Dale's friends and had been her close friends ever since the hanging incident.

Cynthia ran her fingers over the letter of Dale's name and explained to him that the person who was going to find his killers had come to see him, and he should send her a message.

Alex did not believe in ghosts, but Cynthia's actions had sent a shiver down her back.

She asked what Dale's two close friends were doing now.

Cynthia said that Bobby was now retired. He had worked most of his life at the local lumber yard and was now doing volunteer work.

She said that Guy was now running the farm that he had inherited from his father. She smiled and said that Guy had more or less fed her and her daughter for several years after Dale had been killed. He had provide the basic food that she at the time could not afford. To this day whenever they got together, he would give her some sort of food gift. He had become known locally for his generosity to the food bank and at the church for his food donations.

After they were on the way back to Cincinnati, Alex asked Johnnie to dig deep into each individual that had been involved in what had happened to Dale.

She shared the fact that she wanted to interview each individual and wanted to know their weaknesses.

She also wanted to contact current officials who needed to sign off on doing the exhumation. She decided that Dr. Rogers should be the person to arrange it.

Alex spent the rest of the week discussing how to approach the case with the rest of the team.

Travis seemed to be the one who, through his joking, actually helped her the most.

She decided that her focus should be on doing individual interviews and figuring out how she would know the truth to the words she heard.

She asked the Chief's support to set up the interviews but specified the order of the interviews. They were to be done in Wayland and should be at a place that those to be interviewed would be most comfortable.

She wanted to interview the three remaining white men first and then Dale's two best friends.

She met with Dr. Rogers and got him to agree to arrange the exhumation, the transport of Dale to his lab and then the autopsy of the remains. She shared the fact that Dale's wife was arranging the reburial to a new grave.

He said that she should arrange to have the new casket sent to the morgue and he would arranged for the mortuary to place the skeleton in that casket, and they would transport the casket back to Wayland for the reburial rites.

He looked at her and asked what she was expecting him to find when he examined the remains.

Alex shook her head and said she was not sure. He should look at the coroner's report that was on record and see if there was any thing missing.

Dr. Rogers repeated what he had said earlier that fifty years would erase most of what a body had to tell him.

Alex said she understood but she had the feeling that there was something about the case that did not make sense, and she needed to make sure each element of the case got closely and impartially examined.

She returned to her desk and found the appointment schedule for the interviews. She had three individual appointments on Tuesday and a combined appointment with the three on Wednesday. Then she had two appointments on Thursday with a combined appointment that afternoon.

A short time later she got a call from Dr. Rogers letting her know that the exhumation would be on Monday afternoon. He planned his examination on the following two days. The reburial could be as soon as the coming Friday as long as the new casket was available.

Alex called Cynthia to let her know about Dale's journey.

Cynthia said that she would plan to have Dale buried at his new resting place on the coming Sunday.

4 Resurrection

*T*here had been heavy rain over the weekend. The sun's early morning rays reflected off the water running through the tall grass as it made its way across the cut area around Dale's grave. It looked more like the grave had been placed in the middle of stream than just a low area. A board had been placed to redirect most of the water around the area where the orange backhoe was positioned but enough water ran toward the grave that the dirt that was dug up was replaced by water.

Dr. Rogers stood up above the area where the exhumation digging was taking place. He watched as the digging was stopped. He learned a moment later that water was running in and filling up the hole as it was being excavated. The digging had stopped so that a water pump could be brought to the site. He thought about what was about to happen and then he instructed his team to set up their transport system so they could put the casket into the largest body bag they had. He wanted the casket to be immersed in the water it had been sitting in for the last fifty years.

He had the team get some buckets ready so they could reemerge the casket as soon as they had it in the body bag and loaded in the van.

Alex listened to his instructions and asked what he was worried about.

Dr. Rogers explained that he was worried that exposure to air would accelerate the deterioration of the skeleton and make it impossible to learn anything. He said as a bone was exposed to air it had to be dried so that it remained stable.

Even with the pump running and sending a steady stream of water out of a fifty-foot-long hose the digging was slow. Getting the casket lifted was the next challenge. The person that went into the hole to put the lifting straps around the casket was wearing chest high waders and struggled to get the straps down and under the casket. He finally accomplished that task, and the casket was slowly lifted out.

The surprise for everyone was that the wooden casket was in a very good condition.

Dr. Rogers' team commented that it was made out of cedarwood that looked almost as if it had just been cut. They pulled the black body bag up around the casket and strapped it over the top, put it in the van, and then filled the bag with the water from the hole that had been dug. They closed the back doors and left for Cincinnati.

Alex wished them a safe trip back.

She then walked back to where Trey had been sitting on a tombstone and asked if he was ready to check into the hotel. They had the rest of the day ahead of them.

Alex suggested they go out to where the fight had taken place and to the tree where Dale had been hung.

Trey agreed that it would be a good idea. He suggested that after breakfast they should plan on having a picnic at the park and plan to spend some time there. He said it would get them ready for the three interviews they had the next day.

The drive out to the park was on a two-lane road with wide white gravel shoulders that wound between the high oak, maple and pine covered hills. The broad old oaks seemed to push away equally large old maples. Those two species in turn seemed to be fighting back equally old and many times taller but fewer in number of pine trees. The few cedars seemed to be hunkered down trying to get as much sunlight at the other trees allowed to get by them.

As they turned off the highway a six-foot high and ten-foot-wide dark brown wooden entrance sign welcomed them in large yellow letters to Scioto Park "where the heart is embraced in beauty." They followed the signs that led them to the picnic area.

From the description that Cynthia had shared Alex said that it still had the same number of picnic spots as it had fifty years before. She was sure that the stand of intertwined maples were the same trees that had been young saplings when the hanging took place.

Trey commented that the bright white cement platforms, new grills, and picnic tables attested to a recent update.

They were there a little early for lunch and decided to hike out to what, after seeing all the trees as they drove out, they now recognized was very large old Oak tree.

As Alex hiked across the grass covered ground that slowly went uphill toward the ever-growing vision of the oak blocking the sky she commented on its size and majesty.

Tray pointed to the bench that faced the tree and commented on the beauty of the grain and fact that it was in such great condition. He walked over and read the sign.

Alex walked up and read the dates Dale Hammer 1947-1966. She commented that someone that cared for Dale must have donated the bench. She noted that it was made of oak as she sat and looked at the tree. She took out one of the archaic pictures that Johnnie had retrieved from an old newspaper photo that showed the Dale's body hanging from the limb.

She pointed to a limb that she said still stood out as the limb off of which Dale had been found hanging.

She wondered out loud how much the oak had grown in fifty years. She figured from its appearance that it must have been significant.

She pointed to a trail on the other side of the grass clearing located almost directly in front of the bench and said they should see where it went.

More than an hour later she led the way back to the picnic area.

She anchored the table cloth with the picture of hot dogs with ketchup on one side, mustered on the other and pickle slices all embraced by a brown capped bun, down with four rocks that she had picked up from the ground. The table cloth was only half the size of the table that was obviously designed for large family gatherings.

She took out the two Cobb salads and the two bottles of iced tea.

Trey took the lid off the salad and looked at the strip of what he figured consisted of turkey chunks bordered by small tomatoes cut into quarters on one side and small squares of cucumber on the other. Then there was a row of sliced onions paired with a row small pieces of cauliflower. On the side with the tomatoes was a row of chopped eggs that had a row of chopped bacon paired with garbanzo beans.

He said that it was almost too beautiful to eat and asked her how long it had taken her to prepare it.

She held up the stainless-steel flatware and the two containers with blue cheese and said that she had contributed what she was holding, and the rest was prepared by one of her favorite small family restaurants on Price Hill.

Trey took his set of flat ware, said that in that case he was at ease at digging in and enjoying lunch.

Alex asked for his thoughts about the case so far.

He thought for a moment and replied that once again she had been handed a case that was different than any before it. He added that when he was sitting on the tombstone waiting for the coffin to be dug up, he came to the conclusion that the two ends of the circle that made up the case did not meet each other but passed close by and ended up joining some other circle.

Alex shook her head and asked what made him describe it that way.

He said that he didn't know but even their hike to the tree and up the path had reinforced the dichotomy that seemed to be present. Dale seemed to have been a great, kind, and caring individual but he was hanged by someone that had never been identified. He personally wanted to believe that the police and coroner had done their best to solve the case. He had some doubts because of the race issue but he still felt that something was missing, and they had to find that missing element.

Alex took a sip of her tea and said that she too had the feeling that something was missing.

She then said that she hoped that either they had to find something that the police had missed fifty years ago, or Dr. Rogers and his team would need to provide something new that the coroner had missed.

She looked at the sun making its way toward the western horizon and said they should get back to the hotel. She asked about dinner and was glad that Trey said that he would most likely skip it because they were having a late lunch and the salad had been very filling.

On the drive back to Wayland Alex once again took note of the size of the oak trees and realized that the largest one stood by itself, and it was the one that was at the focus point of the case.

She got a call from Dr. Rogers saying that the team had just spent the day removing Dale from his coffin and were in the process of making sure that he remained in stable condition but the team all agreed that his coffin was one of a kind and that it was a beautiful work of art. He added that it was clear that it had been made of pieces of cedar scrap wood, but it had been done with such skill that a true piece of art had been created. He said that he was calling to see if she would authorize having the coffin treated in such a fashion that would maintain its integrity. She thought for a minute and decided to risk having to pay for it personally. She figured it was worth the risk and told him to make sure the coffin got treated the same way that Dale was being treated.

Trey had been listening and said that he bet that the coffin would be quite valuable. He wondered if the art world took coffins in to its fold.

Alex gave a laugh and said that if he was suggesting she put it in her art museum he was barking up the wrong tree.

Trey shook his head and said that what he was suggesting was to see if there was anyone in the market for a coffin as a piece of art work.

Alex thought for a moment and said that as soon as she could get a picture of the coffin in its finished condition she would check with Annie and her art studio partner.

She then said that it would also depend on Cynthia approving such a move. She would check with her about what her intent was as far as reburying Dale. Alex remembered Cynthia had mentioned moving him to a new grave, in a cemetery where the two of them would be side by side but she did not remember if a new coffin was a part of that move.

On return to her hotel room, she took out the five folders she had prepared for the upcoming interview sessions.

She opened the three folders that were for the three interviews that she and Trey would hold the next day.

The first was for Willard Anison now retired from a steel mill that was situated along the Ohio River. He was the biggest and the toughest looking of the three persons remaining alive. He had married, had three children all of whom were still alive and all that had three children who were now adults. He and his wife had retired and moved back to Wayland to the home his parents had left him. He was now a volunteer with the police department and rode through the neighborhoods to make sure everything was quiet.

She again wondered if a person who had participated in hanging an innocent person because of his color would live a life so involved in community.

She wondered how the interview would go. She was to meet at his home at ten in the morning.

The second was Jason Applewood retired as a fire fighter from the Columbus, Ohio fire department. He had many commendations for his bravery and had one for daring to go into a fire to rescue two children. She noted that the children were black.

He had also retired back to a family home in Wayland. He had one daughter that had never had children but who had followed him in his career and was already headed to be as decorated as her father. Alex had been informed that the daughter would be at the interview.

She was to meet him at his home at one in the afternoon.

The third person Olson Lumber was still working at local library and was the director. He had gone on to college, had returned to Wayland, to his first and last job in the library.

He had three children, each of whom had married and had in turn had two children each. These children were either married or about to get married. He had the most educated children and grandchildren, and the family boasted of having a dozen BS degrees and three MS degrees. Alex was sure he most likely had the most educated family in Wayland.

She was to meet him at his home at four in the afternoon.

She shook her head and wondered how the interviews would go. The profiles she had in her mind of each pointed to people that had lived normal, good lives and all three seemed to be rock solid individuals.

She came back to Trey's comment about the strings at the end of the circle did not meet but seemed to go off in different directions.

The other three that had been involved in the fight with Dale had died consecutively one per year three years ago. The information that Johnnie had gathered on them added to her doubts about any of the six being responsible for Dale's death.

She recalled Trey's comment that the two ends of the case's circle seemed to miss each other and went off in separate directions.

She decided that the best action she could take was to go down to the hotel's small gym and get on the treadmill. She felt she needed the run for her body, and she needed a hand from above for he mind.

5 Three Interviews

*T*he sun breaking over horizon highlighted the dark green leaves of the young oak standing just twenty-five feet outside of the window. Alex watched a robin improving the nest that she had made in the crook of three limbs near the top of the six-inch diameter twenty-foot-high tree. She realized that she was into comparing oak tree sizes. She smiled as she realized that on every case there was some item that caught her attention and throughout that case it would always pop into her mind. She knew that for this case it was to be the size of Oak trees.

Trey asked what she was smiling about.

She pointed at the tree and asked him what he saw. He replied a small oak with a bird building a nest at the top. He smiled and asked if she was now into oak tree sizes for the rest of the case. He then went on and said that it was better than where the next body was to be found that she had gotten into during the Sins of the Daughter case.

Alex said that she agreed that trees were much better.

She then asked if he was ready for the interviews.

He smiled and said that he had read the work up that she had prepared. He hoped that the interviews did not raise the passions they had experienced during the Skull Collector case.

Alex shook her head and said that she expected the opposite. She was not sure what to expect but even before the interviews she felt they were on the wrong path and that his comment about the two ends of the circle not meeting stood out in her mind.

She added that Johnnie was the one that had gathered all the information. He had commented that other than a couple of traffic tickets and some late fees on their bank accounts he had come up empty handed on digging for dirt on all six of the men. She said that Johnnie had also spent time examining everything that had been saved to the computer system about Dale's case and there was nothing to incriminate any of them.

She was about to pay for breakfast when she got a call from Dr. Rogers.

He said that he wanted to give her a call before she started her interviews because he had determine the cause of Dale's death and it had nothing to do with the hanging. He said that he had started by examining the neck bones and the skull. The neck had not been broken and there was no indication of the damage that would have occurred when a person is hung and struggles in his death throes. Then when he examined the head, he found a unique depression that when he examined it closely turned out to have a faint outline of dimples in the flat of the depression.

He said that he had engaged his team in identifying what might have made the dimples. He said that the youngest of his team had excitedly shared that he owned the weapon that would fit the bill.

After the rest of the team threatened him for holding out, he said that he was sure it was a drywall hammer that they should be looking for.

Alex asked what led to that conclusion.

Dr. Rogers said that drywall hammers had dimples on the flat surface, the helped plant the nail and made dimples around the nail that then the putty would fill and allow a smooth cover over the nail.

Alex thanked him for the information and said that he had added one more question to her list of questions.

She looked at Trey and said that one of the problems they would have was that after fifty years would they be able to find the drywall hammer.

She called Johnnie to ask him to check if any of the six people she was to interview had been drywall installers at any time.

Johnnie replied that he did not have to spend any time doing that because he had put every job that every person that she was going to interview into the information that he had given her. He added that did not mean that they might not own a drywall hammer because he owned one and he was not a drywall installer.

She thought for a moment and asked him to get Dr. Rogers to give him a picture of the pattern in the depression and then to enhance it to what would be found on the actual hammer.

She looked at Trey and said that she wanted him to pay close attention to the reaction of each person when she asked about the drywall hammer.

Trey shook his head and said that the case had taken its first step in a new direction, and the end of the circle was now seeking the connection. He said that he would indeed be keeping an eye out for a reaction to the question. He said that they had time enough to walk to the river viewing platform at the end of the parking lot before it was time to drive to their first interview.

Willard thanked his wife for the great breakfast. He said that she was welcome to sit through the interview that he was going to have with some detective from Cincinnati in a short while. Her response surprised him. She asked him if he knew who this detective happened to be. He shook his head and said that he had no idea. She said that she had seen her on the news and had been impressed by her demeaner and the way she presented herself, so she had gone to the library and had looked her up and found out that she was a detective that had solved every case that she had been on. She dug until she got to the person that she was after.

He smiled and told her she could relax because he was innocent of doing what the person she was after had done. He had been in the fight that was at that time blamed for the killing but he and every one of his friends had been cleared.

A year later the two of them had met and now fifty years later if this detective was as good as she thought he would find out who had killed that kid so long ago.

He accepted his wife's hug and said that they should have some cookies, coffee, and anything else she wanted to serve ready because he was planning to be a good host.

Alex and Trey parked their car on the street. The side walk was trimmed in petite veronica flowers with vivid magenta blooms. Alex led the way along the walk trimmed in marigold flowers that appeared almost appeared to be bright yellow blinking lights guiding the way to the steps up to the veranda that cross in the front of the house and turned at each corner and continued on each side. She pointed at the Veranda and commented that it appeared to have recently been added to the house.

Trey asked why she thought it had been recently added. She pointed to the steps and the cement footings below the veranda and said they were white and that was a new feature to poured cement.

She walked up to the front door and stopped to appreciate the three-foot-high oval opaque glass in its center and the large brass lever handle door knob. She commented on the fine walnut grain of the door itself.

She looked at Trey and said that just the walk from the car to where they stood on the veranda convinced her that pointed to Willard Anison not being a person of interest unless he owned a fifty-year-old dry wall hammer.

She rang the doorbell and stood to the side. She smiled as she saw Trey step to the other side of the door. She realized they were following their normal habit of never standing directly in front of an entry door.

When Willard opened the door Alex realized that he was as tall as Trey and twice as wide. She was glad that he smiled, invited them in, and asked them to follow him into the family room.

He pointed to the living room that had the entry closed by a painters drop cloth and said that he was in the process of renovating it.

He pointed to the couch, and several easy chairs.

Alex complemented him on how rich the veranda made the home look. She then asked who had chosen the flowers that created such a powerful street presence.

Alex turned as a smiling, slender, elegant silver grey-haired woman carried in a tray of cookies and introduced herself as Alice and said the choice of flowers were hers, and Willard was the one that had built the veranda.

Alex walked over, waited a moment to allow Alice to put the tray down and then shook hands with Alice and said that the yellow marigolds felt like guiding lights and that the white of the veranda seemed to be the pearly gates to heaven.

Willard laughed and said that he would consider painting the veranda some other color because he did not want anyone to think they were entering the pearly gates.

Trey shook his head and said that perhaps a better description happened to be the entrance to Shangri-la.

Alice laughed and said that the interview had really taken a very different flavor than what she had anticipated. She had planned to stay away from it but after the initial interchange she had changed her mind. She asked what everyone wanted to drink and said that once she returned, she would sit in and listen.

Alex accepted a glass of iced tea and when Alice was seated, she asked Willard if he owned a drywall hammer.

Willard shook his head and smiled and said that now he was agreeing with his wife that the interview had a very different flavor than he had anticipated. He said that indeed he did, and it was in the living room. If she wanted to see it, he would go and get it and he could also prove that it was his because he still had the receipt for it, the dry wall and drywall putty that he had purchased as part of the living room project.

Trey picked up a cookie and said that maybe later before they left Alex might want to try the hammer out.

Alex smiled and shook her head and said that they could all relax because she had asked the most incriminating question first and Willard had passed the test.

She then said that what she was interested in was his detailed account of a fight that he and five of his buddies had been in some fifty years ago. She asked permission to record his story.

Willard smiled, shook his head, and said she could record all she wanted and that she would be recording one of the more stupid things that he had done in his life. The fact that it linked him to someone who had committed murder had bothered him for fifty some years.

Alex listened to how he and his six buddies had instigated a fight with three black men about the same age as that of he and his six buddies. They had been drinking all afternoon and one of them had thrown an empty bottle at the three. One of the three black men picked up the bottle and threw it back and hit Harry in the chest. That started the fight. It was six against three and at first, he and his buddies took a beating, but their size and numbers soon had them beating the three to a pulp. They were stopped by three family picnic groups and then told to leave by the park rangers that had arrived as part of their normal tour. He was driving and he saw the three black men get into to their pickup and also heading out.

He and his buddies went to their normal drinking spot along the river and finished the night bragging to each other about what great fighters they were.

It was only a few days later that he had been pulled in and questioned about the hanging. He was able to show that none of them had been involved. He figured that the cops would find out who had done it and jail the guilty individual.

He shook his head and said that now, so many years later, it all seemed unreal. He pulled his hair back and to show a light scar and said that the person that had been hung was the one he had fought with and that he had broken a beer bottle across the side of his head. He said that on almost every morning the scar reminded him about his stupidity.

Alex smiled and said that everyone had their own stupidity that they live with, and he should not let something that happened fifty years ago affect him.

Willard nodded and asked what someone as young as she was could have done.

She looked at him and asked how old he and his buddies had been.

He simply said touche.

Alex looked over at Alice and thanked her for the refreshments.

Alice shook her head and said that the interview was the first time she heard the entire story of the fight so she should be the one saying thanks. She came over and gave Alex a hug and said she expected to soon watch her standing in front of the news cameras describing how she had solved the case.

Trey shook hands all around and said he had one more question.

Everyone went silent in anticipation.

He smiled and asked for a recommendation of where to grab lunch.

Trey drove to the recommended lunch spot.

On the way Alex commented on the fact that their next two interviews they would probably just listen to different perspectives or versions of the story they had just listened to.

Trey asked why she thought that would happen.

Alex smiled and said that she thought that because the three had remained close friends for fifty years and good friends let each other know what is happening. She went on to say that it probably did not matter. What they should now be listening for were any slight differences to what had happened or differences that don't line up.

She then added that one of the three who had died might be the killer or we are looking for an unknown killer.

They both settled for the lunch special of Swedish meatballs in a thick creamy, velvety sauce served over egg noodles.

Alex commented that the food was very good but so far every meal seemed focused on making her run on the treadmill longer.

Trey commented that the lunch was as good as Willard said that it would be but now it would be very hard to stay awake through the next interview.

Alex said that they had time for a thirty-minute walk.

While they were walking, Jason and Willard were on the phone. Jason had his phone on speaker mode, and his daughter Susan was also learning about Willard's interview.

Jason smiled and said that he was glad it was not a witch hunt. Susan said that she would put her bat away and instead offer lemonade or iced tea. She said that it would be much easier to let the two detectives in.

Alex walked up to the double wide wood frame and glass front door and rang the doorbell.

The person that answered was about half the size of Willard. He introduced himself and shook Alex's and Trevor's hand and said that their reputations had already reached his house. He invited them in and turned and led them to the living room.

He introduced his daughter Susan who shook hands and asked Alex how her favorite Swedish meat ball dish had tasted.

Alex smiled and said that lunch was delicious, but it meant that she would need to run a couple of extra miles on the treadmill.

She then said that she imagined that her interview script had also been shared.

Jason said that it was a small town where everything made it around and she was big news.

Alex smiled and said that he then should know the answer to her first question.

He smiled and said that indeed he owned a dry wall hammer, but it was in Susan's house in Columbus, and it was only a couple of years old.

Alex took a moment to highlight his awards for his spectacular firefighting career.

Then she congratulated Susan for being the youngest woman firefighter to be awarded so many awards recognizing her bravery.

She smiled and said that what she really wanted to hear was his version of the fight that had occurred the day that Dale was found hanged.

Jason nodded and said that was a day that had followed him for his whole life. He said that all of his friends thought that and whenever it came up one of the group would bring up a different subject. They all agreed that they had been stupid, drunk, and probably a racist group. At that time stupid and mean but they had not killed anyone.

Alex listened as the story followed the lines that she had heard in the morning. There were a few slightly different viewpoints, but it was basically a duplicate of the story that had been told in the morning.

She looked over at Trey and asked if he had any questions.

Trey shook his head and said that they needed to go to the library to interview Mr. Lumber.

Jason chuckled and said that it was strange to hear his old pal who everyone call four by four referred to as Mr. Lumber. He was the only one who wore glasses and who had been smart enough to breeze through college and get his master's degree. He was not only the smartest but always the kindest.

Alex smiled and said that she would keep that in mind and not be too mean to him.

Susan chuckled and said that she would not report the rude nature of the interview she and her dad had just endured. She came over to Alex and gave her a hug and said that she hoped that the case got solved and closed. It would be a reward that everyone associated with that fight would appreciate.

Jason nodded and agreed that finding the person responsible would lift a weight from everyone's chest.

Alex said that she hoped that soon she would be able to lift that weight. She then led the way out.

Trey commented that he doubted the story that they were about to hear from Olson Lumber, Mr. Four-by-Four was going to be much different from the two they had heard.

Alex agreed and she added that it made the interviews on the next day very dicey.

She suggested stopping at the local ice cream shop and getting prepared by having a sundae or a smoothie.

Trey said that sounded like a great idea.

They arrived at the library a few minutes early and walked in to a wide-open area that had a check out desk on the left side and card filed cabinets to the right. Straight ahead of the entrance door was a wide area of book filled dark brown shelves.

Alex was impressed that such a small town would have such a nice library. She asked the person at the checkout desk to let Mr. Lumber to know that Alex Evercrest had arrived.

Olson had been part of the local grapevine phone calls and knew about the first question being about a drywall hammer. He figured that question was being asked because it was the murder weapon. He was not a do it yourselfer in anything beyond changing lightbulbs. He wondered if any of his deceased buddies had taken that secret to their graves. He didn't think so and if the was the case, then the blame for the murder took a very strange shift. He wondered if the young detective that was here to question him had any idea about what that shift implied.

He rose and checked that he had the refreshments set up in the meeting room and then walked out to the main part of the library. He was surprised at that two people he saw standing in wait. The person he knew would be Alex was petite, very good looking and seemed to exude being an athlete versus a detective. The person with her was a good two heads taller, buff looking and someone who one should avoid getting into a fight with.

He walked over and greeted them. He learned that the tall one was called Trey. He asked that they call him Olson but if they wanted to be like all of his remaining friends, they could call him Four-by or Four-by-Four.

Alex laughed and said that she preferred Olson.

He guided them to the meeting room, pointed to the refreshments that consisted of cut fruit and vegetables and some dip and said that he figured that by this time of day they had consumed more snacks then they normally would have. He said that besides the coffee and tea that was visible there was also a variety of soft drinks in the small refrigerator.

He then sat down and folded his hands in front of him on the table. He said that he did not own a dry wall hammer and never had because his ability to do home repair or home improvement was limited to signing a check to someone who knew how to do that kind of work.

Alex nodded and said that she was a certified profiler, and her assessment had placed him as highly educated, thoughtful, and quiet but very influential with the friends he was surrounded with. He was also thorough in what he did and did not like loose ends. She asked it that was a good description.

He nodded and said that she was investigating a loose end that had bothered him since the fight in the park some fifty years ago. He regretted that fight for all these years.

He was just as guilty of the start of that fight as the rest of his buddies but when it got underway, he realized that they might kill the three black men they were attacking. Several times he had kept one of his buddies from stomping the three who ended up on the ground.

He was later teased by his buddies, but they had all eventually thanked him for keeping them from killing one of the three. For a while he was called noodles by his buddies for being soft. But he knew that on that day he had done the right thing.

The remaining question for him was if not one of the group, then who? He said that the only other people that had been there were three family groups that had helped break up the fight and the two rangers who had ordered both his buddies and the three black men to leave the park.

The situation left few alternatives and the those seemed very unlikely.

Alex said that indeed the alternatives were unlikely. She said that the only thing that had changed from that time was the advances in science and the tools that the coroners worked with.

Olson nodded and said that the technology all around them including for the library had leaped forward at an astonishing rate.

He asked if there was anything else he could help her with.

Alex thought for a minute and asked if Bobby Tripperly or Guy Parrelly were active members of the library.

Olson thought for a minute and said that he would check on both names, but he was aware that Guy was active in the "Read to Succeed" program that he sponsored. He came in to tutor the young kids aged six to fifteen that would come to reading sessions.

Alex asked if she could get a record of the books either of them had checked out.

He tapped a message on his phone and a few moments later one of the librarians brought several printed pages and said that the record only went back two year. The computer system would go back close to ten years but before that time the files had all been paper and she was not sure if they still existed.

Alex accepted the papers and said that if she needed more, she would come back with a specific request.

She stood up, shook hands, smiled, and said that she just could not envision calling him anything but Mr. Lumber.

He laughed and said that he had never taken to anything but being called by his given name. He then said that everyone was getting together for a pot luck dinner at his house that evening to celebrate what they were calling interview day, and he was extending the invitation to the two of them.

Alex smiled and said that she was sure it would be a great dinner but since she worried about the optics of attending a social event with potentially guilty people she graciously declined.

Olson agreed and then recommended that they eat at Marlenes's because Tuesday nights was when she prepared the all you can eat prime rib roast with a variety of sides. The team had considered going there to celebrate but had decided that their conversations should be kept private in case one of them confessed to the crime.

As they were walking out, Trey laughed and said that he was sure that before the night was out those attending the dinner would know if they had taken the Olson's recommendation.

Alex nodded and said that the two of them were like two goldfish in a fishbowl.

6 The Tour

*A*lex and Trey drove back to the hotel in silence. They both had agreed that it had been a good day, and they felt that the interviews excluded the three men they had interviewed as the killers.

They knew that the next day they would be interviewing and digging into the stories of the two people that were known as Dale's best friends.

These interviews would be a little more sensitive since the two made less sense as being the killers.

Alex said she was going to run on the tread mill, do a few hundred pushups and hit her head against the wall for fifteen minutes to clear her head and then take a shower before they went out to dinner.

Trey laughed and said that he would join her in the gym if they both could fit in it at the same time, but he would skip the wall head banging. He then held up two fingers and said, "and then there were two."

Alex nodded and said that it did not make sense. They were best of friends.

After their work outs and shower they went to Marlene's Bar and Grill for dinner as recommended by Olson.

They found a parking spot about a half a block away. As they walked toward the entrance, the lime green paint peeling from the brick and flickering florescent Marlene sign made Alex feel that the place was going to be empty and abandoned. When she walked in, she was surprised to be told that there was only one table for two available or two seats at a table where a family of eight were sitting.

She chose the table for two.

The hostess pointed to the person wearing a chef's hat and who was brandishing a wicked looking twelve-inch-long stainless-steel knife and said that was Marlene the best chef in the city.

Alex remembered Olson saying the same thing.

The hostess let them know that once they had their drink order in, they were welcome to go and get whatever they wanted, and they could eat all they wanted as long as their plates were empty each time.

Alex looked around and tried to get a count of the number of people. There were a lot. She stopped trying and decided that she would focus on eating. After giving the waitress her drink order of iced tea, she got up and armed herself with a plate and approached Marlene who pointed her knife at her and said she was pleased to have the famous Cincinnati detective come to her place.

Alex shook her head, smiled, and said that there was no way to hide in Wayland.

Marlene nodded and said that was the way small towns worked, and she would let Olson know that his recommendation had been followed.

She pointed to two set of rib racks. One was red toward the center, and the other was only pink and closer to medium rare. She asked how many ribs and from which rack.

Alex pointed to the rack with the red meat toward the center.

Marlene said that was the choice that she would make for herself as well and said that Alex should come back as often as she wanted.

Trey got a similar engagement, but he chose the rack with a pink center.

They each took helpings of roast potatoes with gravy, some of Marlene's "Dripping" Yorkshire pudding, grilled cauliflower, carrots, and a cabbage salad.

Alex said that she was coming back for carrot cake and vanilla ice cream for dessert.

Trey said that he was going for the Crème Brûlée.

A few moments after they were back at the table and had taken a few bites Marlene came over to their table and asked how everything tasted. Then she asked if she could have her picture taken with the two of them.

Alex said that it would be an honor and asked for a copy of the picture.

Before she left Marlene smiled and said that they could have whatever she wanted for dinner free if they identified who had hung that poor man fifty years ago.

The next morning Alex decided to run for a couple of miles and to skip breakfast. She felt that the previous day had put pounds on her.

The morning interview was going to be with Bobby Tripperly who had spent almost his entire working career in a local lumber yard and had risen from a yard helper to being the lumber yard manager. The records Alex had prepared painted him as a person who had focused his effort in raising his family and otherwise had been pretty much a loner. He had recently resigned from working at the lumber yard but remained active in his church. She found it hard to imagine him killing Dale.

He had agreed to a nine in the morning interview time and had asked if his wife could be present for the interview.

Alex had said that having his wife was actually preferable.

On arrival to the Bobby's house Alex commented to Trey on how much the home mirrored Willard Anison's home.

The flowers along the entrance walk were red instead of yellow, the veranda did not circle around the house but appeared to have recently been painted and was a tan instead of white and the door had an intricate grained solid oak wood design.

She rang the doorbell and stood to the side.

The door was opened by a slender grey-haired woman who welcomed them and introduced herself as Mable. She stepped out and shook Alex's hand and said that Cynthia had commented at how confident she felt that the Dale's case would finally be solved. She shook Trey's hand and said that he was as handsome as Cynthia had said he was.

Alex followed Mable into the living room.

Bobby entered and shook hands and said that he hoped that he could shed some light on what had happened so many years ago, but he doubted that he could add anything new. He had told the police everything that he knew at that time. He said that after fifty years he was not sure he would remember many of the details

Alex asked if he owned a dry wall hammer.

Mable laughed and said that he not only owned a drywall hammer but owned about every type of tool that one could imagine. She said that the three tool boxes that her Bobby owned took up the second car space in the garage.

Alex asked if she could see the dry wall hammer.

Bobby led the way through the kitchen to the detached two car garage situated to the back of the house.

He pointed to the three tool chests that were about four foot high and had what looked like a blond hardwood top. He said that he had bought some of the tools but most of them had been given to him by the owner of the lumber yard as rewards for doing good work.

He pulled open the drawer that had each hammer laying in its cutout holding area. He picked up his drywall hammer and said that it was one that he had personally purchased when he did some of the drywall work in the kitchen.

Mable said that project ended up being finished by one of the local contractors after Bobby realized that he was a great lumber yard manager but not a very good do it yourselfer. She said the tools were very valuable and she had suggested selling all the tools and using the money to take a vacation to the Bahamas. She figured that there would be two benefits. One would be the vacation; the second would be a space to park their second car.

Alex took a picture of the dry wall hammers head and sent it to Johnnie and Dr. Rogers. It looked too new to be the one they were looking for, but she wanted confirmation.

She thanked Bobby for showing her the hammer.

He asked about the significance of the hammer.

She said that by the end of the week she would be able to share how it played into the investigation.

His question was one that helped her relax for the rest of the interview.

They all returned to the living room.

Mable said that she had some coffee, and some freshly baked, still warm chocolate chip pecan cookies and suggested they prepare themselves for the story heard by family and friends many times over the years.

Bobby began the story at the point that he, Dale and Guy had decided to enjoy a grill out in the park. This was a change from their normal spot along the Scioto river. They picked up a case of Miller High Life because it was the "Champagne of Beers," and they wanted to celebrate Dale's three months of being married. Cynthia had fixed the picnic basket with some baked sweet potatoes and a bowl of cold slaw. The main course was to be hot dogs and brats.

He said that at the last moment Cynthia had told them she was not feeling well, and they should go without her. Dale drove his old pickup truck to the park, and they picked a table that was located near a grill stand.

They has grilled the dogs and brats and had just finished eating when a truck loaded with a bunch of white boys stopped at the next spot. The table for that grill spot was about twenty feet away but they demanded that we give up our table.

Dale pointed to their table and said they should carry it over to where their grill was located.

One of the white guys said that they preferred the table we had.

Dale made some smart comment, something like over "his dead body."

One of the guys in the white group threw a bottle that almost hit Dale.

Dale picked it up, threw it like a football, and hit the person who had thrown the bottle.

The six white guys rushed the three of us and for a few moments we held our own, but we were getting hit by three of them at a time. It wasn't long before we were on the ground and getting pounded.

One of the group actually tried to stop the fight but he mostly ignored by the rest. They were saved by three family groups that rushed over to stop the fight. The women seemed to be more effective than their husbands because they stepped in between the guys beating us.

About the time the fight was ending two park rangers drove in and put an end to it by ordering both the white boys and us to leave the park.

It took us a few moments to clean up. I remember we gave about half of our case of beer, the extra hot dogs, and brats we had to one of the women that had saved us.

Dale was the most beat up of the three of us. I got into the back of the truck where I could lay down. Guy drove to my parents' house, this house, where I was living at the time. I got out and Guy drove off.

I learned later that Dale had lost his wallet, and they had returned to the park to find it. While they were there they were attacked by the same group. Guy was knocked out and when he came to, he saw Dale hanging from the Oak tree in the middle of the field.

The police investigated the hanging but cleared the six guys of the hanging.

Alex asked him which one of the six was responsible for the hanging.

He shook his head and said that most likely all six of them were guilty. He said that whenever any one of them came to the lumber yard he made sure that he was somewhere else, so he did not have to deal with them.

Alex asked about the bench that she had seen out at the oak tree that was commemorated to Dale.

Bobby nodded and said that Guy had brought the limb into the lumberyard and asked for it to be sawed in two lengthwise and have the bench ends made of the same limb. I spent almost a week getting that done and assembled. I had it delivered to the place where it sits today. Guy had the cement base poured by a local cement company ready to receive it. My guys bolted it down,

It has been in place for almost forty years. Guy and I have periodically sanded and varnished it to keep it in good condition.

He and I have gone out there at least once a month, rain or shine and sat there to honor Dale's memory.

Alex thanked Bobby for sharing his memory of the incident and said that when she solved the case, she would be sure to update him.

She got up to leave when Mable said that there was one important fact that had been left out.

She said that the reason that Cynthia had felt ill was that she was pregnant and had morning sickness. She had been planning to tell Dale but thought she would wait until he returned from partying with his friends. Cynthia's daughter grew up, had a family and her children had family.

Cynthia was now a great grandmother and was soon to take the next step up to great-great grandmother. So, Dale did live on through his daughter.

Alex thanked Mable for remembering to mention that part of the story.

On the way to the car, Trey said, "and then there was one."

Alex nodded and said that was indeed the case. She commented that they had a death not by hanging that had been made to look like a hanging, but they had no weapon to link the killer to the murder.

Trey suggested having lunch at Marlene's, he was thinking about a salad and figured that she would have a robust selection.

Alex agreed and said that she was thinking about a salad as well.

It turned out that Marlene's was almost as popular at lunch as it was for dinner.

She came over to their table and said that she was glad to see them. She smiled and said that now that they were friends, they should call her Marly since that was what all her friends called her.

When she found out what they had in mind for lunch she recommended the salad that she had named after herself, Marly's BEC salad. She smiled and said that it had tender beef, two eggs, cucumber, avocado, and mixed greens. She said that it went very well with a large, iced tea.

Alex said that it sounded great, but she already knew that she wanted only half of what she would be served.

Trey asked if the two of them could share one salad because they had one more important interview to do that afternoon and he had to stay awake for it.

Marlene asked who they were interviewing.

Alex let her know they would be going out to Guy Parrelly's farm.

Marlene said, "Wow it really is a small world. I buy most of my beef, get my milk and butter, buy both chicken, ducks, and turkeys from him. In the summer and fall I buy tomatoes, carrots, cabbage, and a variety of other vegetables from him."

Alex asked how long she had done business with him.

Marly thought for a moment and replied that it was close to thirty years, probably a year after she opened the restaurant. He was really good about extending credit to her in the early years. He had always been polite but very private.

Alex thanked her for the information.

After lunch, she decided to drive. The drive out to the farm passed through oak, maple, and pine forests on each side of the highway.

Then suddenly before them was a wide-open field that had a white wooden fence that went along the highway as far as the eye could see and back to the right where it crested the hill and disappeared.

Alex wondered how long it took to put in the fence and how long it took when it had to be painted.

The large two-story red brick farm house with its green topped roof had four second story windows above a wide veranda along the front that covered the four first floor six-foot-high windows dominated the top of the hill. It stood to the left of a white two-story barn that had a gothic arched green roof that matched the house. It had a rectangular extension with multiple windows that provided the much-needed light for the milk cows that could be seen grazing on the hill leading up to the barn.

There were several smaller structures that were all painted white and appeared to have corrugated tin roofs.

Trey commented that the place seemed to be kept in perfect condition.

Alex agreed that and said that Guy Parrelly must spend a great deal of time making sure everything was in great condition. He must also work every day if his farm was as productive as Marly had described.

Trey nodded and said that he was impressed with what he so far saw of the farm. He wondered how many acres made up the farm.

Alex drove slowly up the gravel road and pointed out that not only was the grass on each side of the drive mowed but each fence post had the weeds trimmed around them as well.

As she got close to the house, she saw someone sitting on a swing on the veranda.

She parked and got out and led the way up the steps. The person sitting stood up and met her at the top of the steps.

Guy had watched the car drive slowly up towards the house. He looked at his watch and took note that this Alex Evercrest was right on time. From her reputation he had expected nothing less.

When he had been asked to be interviewed by her, he had wondered if he should do it.

He had decided that it would not hurt.

He stood up and walked over and greeted her. He was surprised to stand almost two heads higher than her. "Small but mighty," went through his mind. Her white partner was almost as tall as he, but broader at the shoulders. He was definitely a tough guy and almost as big as Willard Anison who had beat the devil out of him.

He said they should call him Guy.

Alex thanked him for taking the time to share what had happened when Dale Hammer had been hanged.

Guy nodded and thanked her for looking into the case but said that after fifty years it was going to be hard to change the situation.

Alex nodded and said that she agreed that it would indeed be tough.

She then commented about how organized and neat the farm appeared. She wondered how he managed to keep it all looking so crisp and neat.

Guy smiled and said that he worked about eight to ten hours a day and always had the next improvement identified or the work for the day laid out. He was single and had every moment of the day to do work.

He asked if she wanted a tour of the place.

Alex said that she would love to get a tour.

Guy suggested they choose a cold soda to take with them. He said that he had some of his favorites in the cooler that he had brought out to the porch. He opened the cooler that had orange crush, strawberry crush, grape, root beer, and cream soda and asked what they might want.

Alex selected a strawberry crush, and Trey took an orange crush. Guy chose a root beer.

Alex followed Guy to the end of the of the house where he had a light green four-person golf cart with a roof top, brown leather seats, what looked like a black crash front bumper and a black square box on the back.

He commented that they were the first to ride in it. It was a reconditioned cart that he had bought less than six months ago. He said that the one he really liked had white seats, but he figured that the brown seats made more sense to have since it was going to be used on the farm. He said that he had cleaned it up for their visit in case they wanted a tour. He said that it had replaced an old 1960 pickup that he was in the process of restoring.

Alex commented that the cart looked brand-new.

Guy said that the part of the cart that got the most abuse was the box on the back where he carried his tools.

He said that he would begin the tour by driving around the outer property fence and that would take about thirty minutes. Then they could take a walking tour of the barn and finally finish back on the porch.

Alex said sounded like a good plan.

As they drove out past the large barn and what she took as the smaller chicken or poultry barn, she saw the object she most wanted to get a closer look at, but she decided to take the tour first.

Guy commented that he had put in the wooden perimeter fence the year that his father had passed away. He had probably painted the fence at least once every ten years and had just finished doing so. He pointed to the barn and said that he had painted it just last year and he had painted the veranda at the same time.

Alex asked what made the roof of the barn and the house green.

Guy said that his father had splurged on both roofs, and they were copper sheets that had turned green due to corrosion. He said that his father had gotten a deal on the sheeting when he was a young teenager and the two of them had spent a summer putting the sheets down and soldering them together. He held out his hand and pointed to burn marks that he said he had suffered from all the hours soldering.

He pointed to the gutters on the house and said that the gutters were made from the same copper sheets.

He then drove through the field and pointed out the milk cows and the cattle that would be slaughter. He pointed out that he had more milk cows than beef cattle and only raised enough of the cattle that so he could harvest about ten head each season.

Once they were back to the house he asked if he should continue the tour in the barn and the chicken house or if they should refresh their drinks and do the interview on the porch.

Alex suggested that they do the interview and then she thought that a tour of the barn would be interesting.

7 Final Interview

As Alex listened to Guy share his memory of the fight the house shadow seemed to slowly engulf the car and creep down the lane. The description of the fight was similar to what she had heard four times before. The drive to drop off Bobby was as had been described but then the story went in a direction that was new to her. She had heard Bobby's version, but Guy's version had more detail about the six persons that did not fit with what she had heard so far.

Her training as a profiler kicked in and she was sure she was listening to a lie. There seemed to be too much detail. She went into what she considered her poker playing face.

Trey was watching Alex and knew that something was off. He was now on full alert.

Alex thanked Guy for sharing his memories of that fateful day when he lost his best friend.

Guy nodded and said that even after all these years it was still painful. Painful he thought and still too vivid.

Alex said that a quick tour of the barns be great and then she and Trey would be on their way.

She wanted to get back to the chicken barn and the axe or perhaps the dry wall hammer that she had seen buried high in the light pole there.

As they walked toward the barn, she asked if Guy owned a drywall hammer.

He shook his head and said that he did not know what a drywall hammer was or looked like.

As they entered the barn Alex saw a lock on a door leading into what seemed to be a storage area.

She asked about it.

Guy said that he kept his seed supply there. He said that his seeds were the most valuable things that he owned.

He then pointed to the milking machines and said that they were probably as valuable but could not be carried off as easily.

Alex suspected that there was more than seed in the locked away it the storage area.

Trey loosened the strap on his holster. He knew that his partner had her defenses up. He was now more vigilant than ever. Something was off. He felt like he was once again on patrol in Iraq expecting the unexpected.

Alex listened as Guy explained how each morning, he milked the cows and then late each evening some of them got milked again.

She asked him about the poultry and what type of care they required.

He led the way there and as they approached the chicken shed and was about to enter, he heard Alex ask if he would show her the drywall hammer that was stuck on the pole.

He looked up and realized for the first time that the tool that he had thought of as an axe to chop off chicken heads was in fact a drywall hammer.

He realized that she had played him. He did not know how she knew about this particular tool, the thing that he had hit Dale with, but she somehow did. She must have seen it when they drove past it earlier and she had waited until he told his story before asking about it.

She had played him.

His anger soared and he was ready to kill just like his jealously had driven him to kill Dale.

He reached up and pulled the drywall hammer down and spun around with the intend of killing her.

Alex had taken a step back as Guy reached up for the drywall hammer. She anticipated his spin and as he came around, she was about to shoot the hammer out of his hand when the sound of three shots rang out and Guy went down.

She rushed to him and watched as he smiled and said that at last, he would get to see Dale and say he was sorry. Then he passed away.

Alex took a picture of the flat side of the hammer and sent it to Johnnie and Dr. Rogers.

She called Dr. Rogers and said she needed as quick of response as possible.

She then called the local sheriff and reported the shooting.

Trey asked if he had been too quick to shoot.

Alex shook her head and said that he had done everything exactly as he should have and had kept her from trying to disarm guy and possibly getting herself chopped up.

In less than five minutes Dr. Rogers gave her a call letting her know that she had found the murder weapon.

She then walked back to the barn and went to the room that was locked. She picked the lock and put the lock on a nearby two by four on the barn wall. She then opened the door and walked in.

She put in a call to Johnnie and asked him to get the Chief to get her a search warrant for all the buildings on the farm of a Guy Parrelly.

On the wall in front of her was a large picture of the hanging scene. On the shelf below the picture was the rope with which Dale had been hung. On the same shelf was a picture of Cynthia inscribed with *"My True Love."*

As she watched the flashing lights coming up the farm drive, she had a flash back to the time she had shot and killed four thugs who had almost beaten Trey to death. This time he had done the shooting to keep her safe.

Her phone rang and she knew the Chief was calling.

She answered and said that she could use his help by talking to the Sheriff that was arriving with a small army of helpers.

The Sheriff came up to her and asked whether she was cleared to take the action that she had taken.

Alex handed him her phone explaining that her boss was on line and wanted to speak with him.

She listened as the sheriff repeatedly said, "got it," "got it"

He smiled, handed her phone back and said that she had a boss that had her back. He then asked where the shooting had taken place.

Alex led the way back to where Guy was laying.

The coroner and his helper took pictures.

The Sheriff asked who had done the shooting.

Trey said that he was the one and was ready to turn his weapon in as evidence and held his gun by two fingers and dropped into an evidence bag that a deputy held out.

The Sheriff said that the last shooting in his jurisdiction had been more than five years before but that one did not involve a fatality.

Alex pointed to the dry wall hammer and said that Guy was about to try to kill her when her partner had taken his three shots.

She then said that the drywall hammer was the weapon that had killed Dale Hammer more than fifty years ago. So, it was now evidence in a murder case and an attempted murder case.

She asked if she could have it as evidence for the murder of Dale Hammer.

The Sheriff smiled and said that she had solved a murder that had haunted the community for a long time and since her boss had asked for his cooperation, he was going to follow her suggestions on how to handle both cases.

Alex smiled and said that she appreciated the cooperation. She was going to spend some time writing up her report and would request that a lawyer get assigned to the case that would charge Guy Parrelly. She admitted that she did not know what that might look like and she would follow the lawyers lead.

She pointed at Trey and said that it was his fault that they had a dead person who needed to be charged for two crimes with the same weapon. She figured a live one would have made it messier and taken longer but it would have been something that she could have handled much easier than the current situation.

Trey put up his hands and said that he was guilty of having her back and keeping her from getting chopped up or whacked on the side of her head.

The Sheriff laughed and asked how long they had been working together.

Trey smiled and replied that they had worked together long enough to know that they always had each other's back, but he was a few saves behind.

Alex asked if she could leave because she wanted to deliver the news of Guys death to two people that he had been close to. She wanted to do it before they heard the news from someone else.

The Sheriff nodded and said that she should hurry because news traveled fast in Wayland.

Alex thanked him and let him know that she would come to his office the next day to share her initial report and pick up the drywall hammer.

470

8 Realization

*A*lex called ahead to Cynthia and arranged to meet with her.

Trey had asked to drive so she was sitting and watching the countryside wiz by the window. She was thinking about the cows and other animals on the farm. She wondered if Bobby had any farming skills, if not, he might know who to call to arrange for someone to temporarily take care of the farm.

She wondered if Matt wanted to become a farmer. He had grown up in rural Mississippi.

She shook her head and knew that the outcome of the case was bothering her.

She had solved the case but somehow it left a very hollow feeling in her.

Trey looked at her and said that he felt bad about the shooting, but she looked like she had lost her best friend.

Alex shook her head and said she was thinking about who would take care of the animals on the farm.

Trey laughed and shook his head as he slowed down as they arrived at the Wayland city border. He said that he should have known that she would be thinking about something serious.

Alex looked over at him and said that the welfare of the cows and other animals on the farm was serious and needed to be resolved in the next couple of hours.

Trey suggested that she call the sheriff and have him arrange for someone to take care of the farm animals.

Alex said that was a great suggestion. She made the call and got confirmation that the Sheriff had someone in mind and would make the arrangements.

Alex let him know that she would be back on the farm in the morning to take pictures as part of her report.

The Sheriff said that he would have one of his deputies spend the night on the farm and he would be back to meet her in the morning when she came to the farm.

He let her know that the coroner had left with Guy's body and was on the way to the morgue. He asked who would be making the arrangements for the burial.

Alex said that she would see to the arrangements after she had a chance to talk with his friends.

Trey parked in front of Cynthia's house and asked if Alex was ready.

Alex took a deep breath and said that she was, but she wanted to make sure that he did not take the blame for Guy's death.

"You know she is going to ask how he died," Trey replied.

Alex nodded and said that if she asked how he had died they should say he was shot as he tried to hit her with the same weapon, he had killed Dale with.

Trey smiled and said that might work but he had no qualms about being the one that got pointed at for shooting him.

Alex led the way in and rang the doorbell.

Cynthia opened the door, and she invited them in. She went into the kitchen and pulled out two chairs and asked what they would like to drink.

Alex said that a glass of ice water would be great.

Trey said that he would take the same.

Cynthia poured three glasses of ice water, put them down on the table and sat down.

She then said that there had been five interviews, three of white men and two of black men. She then asked if any of the white men were guilty?

Alex shook her head and said that they were not.

Cynthia cupped her hands around her glass and bowed her head and asked if any of the two men that she considered her friends were guilty.

Alex was silent for a moment before she answered. Then she said that yes one of them was and she had solid proof.

Cynthia shook her head, looked up and said that she did not think that it was Bobby.

Alex said that it was not Bobby.

Cynthia had tears in her eyes as she said that only a month after Dale had been buried, Guy had come to her and let her know that he had feelings for her and would step up and take care of her if she agreed that they should date and then perhaps get married.

She said that at that time she said it was too early but a week later he came back and said that he had an engagement ring he would like her to have.

She had thanked him but declined.

When he returned a third time, she let him know that she had no intentions of marrying anyone and that she was pregnant.

Guy never approached her again about marriage but for years he made sure she had all the food she could possibly need and even to this day he always made sure she got a turkey for thanks giving, a duck for Christmas and every week he delivered milk, eggs, and butter.

She asked if he was under arrest for Dale's murder.

Alex was silent for a moment.

Trey said that Guy had attacked Alex with the same weapon used to kill Dale.

Cynthia looked across the table at both of them and said she did not want to know the details but if she got the gist, what he was trying to tell her was that Guy was dead.

Alex nodded. She explained that the examination of Dale's skeleton showed that he did not die of the hanging but was dead when he was hoisted up on the noose. The coroner said the cause of death was getting hit on the side of his skull by a dry wall hammer. The imprint on the on his skull was very clear and had a specific pattern.

Cynthia shook her head and said that it was probably the hammer Dale had just purchased because he had been hired to work on a big job to hang drywall but was required to have his own tools.

She went on to share the fact that on the day the three went to the park she had morning sickness and had chosen to stay home. Perhaps if she had gone Dale might still be alive.

Alex said perhaps but she had done the reasonable thing. There should be no "what ifs" associated with the decision she made more than fifty years ago. She had heard through the grapevine that she would soon be celebrating being a great-great grandmother. So, the next time she met with Dale, she would be able to share what fifty years had blessed her with.

Cynthia reached across the table and put her hand on Alex's and said that she had delivered what she had promised. It was different than what she had expected but now the loop was closed.

She then said that she wanted her to be present at Dale's reburial to the grave site where, when her time came, she would also be buried. She said that she had just arranged for it to happen Sunday one week out.

She then said that she was planning a celebration of life for Dale and for the joy of having been blessed by having fallen in love with him and having loved him all her life.

Alex said that she was looking forward to being there and was her better half invited.

Cynthia said that she could bring as many people as she desired.

Alex looked at Trey and asked if he was planning to come. He said that he would not miss it.

Cynthia said that she would see if Bobby would handle Guy's burial. She did not plan to attend but she knew that Guy had no family and even the worst sinner should leave this world with some sort of dignity.

Alex agreed and said that she was going to spend the following day wrapping up some loose ends and then she would be returning to Cincinnati.

Cynthia smiled and said that her grapevine had let her know that the two of them had found the best restaurant in town and had eaten at Marlene's twice.

Alex nodded and said that it was costing her hours on the treadmill trying to keep the pounds off, but she was planning to go to dinner there again.

Cynthia nodded and suggested that she try the oxtail that Marlene braised, and fire roasted and that took her three days to prepare. She usually offered it on Friday's but might have it ready on a Thursday. Make sure you also ask for the sweet fried plantains she finished.

If that is not available my second suggestion is the classic prime rib that she crusts with salt, cracked black pepper and sprinkles with rosemary. She saves the dripping to make a pan gravy that is heaven over mashed potatoes.

Alex laughed and said that either one would have her running at least two extra hours, but she would see what Marlene had available.

On the way-out Trey complemented Alex on how she had handled the situation.

Alex nodded and said that Cynthia had made it easy by the attitude she had displayed. It seemed that once it was clear that Guy was the killer all the behaviors that he had displayed took on a new meaning for to her. She added that she hoped Cynthia's daughter was available for a long phone conversation.

Trey suggested they go eat first and then go to the hotel for their workout or not.

Alex said that dinner sounded good, but a workout would be early in the next morning.

Marlene waved at them as they walked in. She walked over and said that she was ready to pay up with her free meal.

Alex shook her head and said that had not crossed her mind but braised and fire roasted oxtail with sweet fried plantains as a side would really be great.

Marlene smiled and said that she would make an exception and serve it one day early just because she had not only solved the case but had eliminated a court trial.

Trey said that he would take whatever Alex was having.

Alex said that a surprise side salad would be great and to drink she would go with iced tea.

Marlene said she had a bottle of Champaign that she would be glad to pop the cork on.

Alex smiled and shook her head and said she could only do it if it was alcohol free.

Marlene nodded and said that she had plenty of alcohol-free beer and only a couple of bottles wine. She added that sticking with the tea was probably the best choice.

She looked at Trey who said he would stick with the iced tea as well.

Alex looked at Trey and commented that they had missed their AA class on Tuesday.

Trey nodded and said that there was a meeting every night and they would just have to go to the next one that was available when they got back to Cincinnati.

The next morning Alex was on the treadmill for a solid hour running as fast as she could. She wished she was on her treadmill that gave her a view of the river and a slice of downtown Cincinnati instead of a room with no windows and a view of a yellow wall with a crack across it.

She had thought about the situation and decided that she needed to search the house to see if she could find a will that Guy might have written.

Trey came in and said that he was going to do a little bit of running and a few sit-ups but would be ready to get underway in about forty-five minutes.

Alex said that worked for her and she only wanted a cup of coffee.

She said that they needed to see if they could find a will.

Trey said that he hoped they found one since it would make it clear what Guy wanted. Trey commented that he hoped that Guy had been as organized with what he wanted to have done with his property as he was with making sure his property was in good shape.

After going through all the paperwork that was in Guy's very organized office Alex threw up her hands and said that she was about to give up. She walked out on the veranda and as she walked to the edge facing the barn a thought came to her.

She went down the steps and walked to the barn and went into the small room to the right of the barn entrance door. She looked again at Cynthia's picture and realized that it rested on top of an elongated stand. She lifted the picture and picked up the box and opened it and neatly folded was a sealed envelope and a will.

She read the will but left the letter unopened and knew that she needed to meet with Cynthia one more time.

She went back to the house and let the officer in charge know that she had found the will and that she was going to deliver it so the person it was for could decide how to handle the farm.

She took a moment to take a picture of the will. She sent this to the Chief and to Johnnie.

Trey drove to Cynthia's home and parked.

Alex led the way in and when they got to the kitchen and were sitting around the table she placed the will and the unopened letter in front of Cynthia. She suggested reading the will first and the letter afterward.

Cynthia read the will that left her all of Guy worldly goods. She looked at Alex and asked if that meant the farm and also whatever he might have in the bank.

Alex nodded and said that Guy's death certificate would need to be presented to the county office to transfer the property and the same was true for the bank. Alex added that she should check to make sure that all bills were paid as well.

She then pointed at the letter and said that she should read it, but she did not have to say anything but the two of them would be there just in case.

Cynthia opened the envelope and took out a single page, with neat handwritten small script, letter that apologized for the most egregious act that had ruined the beauty of life for him and had taken the most treasured love from hers. He said that one crazy moment meant he was forever in hell. There was no way to make any of it up. The letter ended by wishing her the best.

Cynthia looked up and pushed the letter over to Alex and said that the letter should be part of the investigation report because it made clear that he was guilty.

Cynthia said that she was not planning to move to the farm, but she had a grandson that wanted to be a farmer, and she would see if he wanted to run her new farm.

The End of Grief's Trajectory

<u>The Magic Touch</u>

<u>1 The Office</u>

Chase looked out to the lake from the bedroom window. The early morning sun made the rippling surface of the lake throw up sparkles as if the lake was bubbling in golden waters. He looked across the bed at Amelia and was amazed that after so many years she still looked the same as when they had first met at the medical school. She had remained single and enjoyed the company of many wealthy men that she had met in Chicago where she lived. He and Amelia were into each other physically and were friends who over the years had continued to have periodic trysts. They never went to the same place twice and this time they were in the Finger Lakes area of Pennsylvania staying in a boutique hotel. They had been enjoying doing a little fishing, some hiking but mostly staying in and enjoying each other.

Today he would be going back to Cincinnati to his loving wife and two kids. He loved his kids. His wife was a great facilitator of their social life. They thought he was attending a dentist retreat focused on dental implant techniques.

He smiled as he thought about the fact that it was half right, he had talked business with Amelia who was one of his partners in his dental implant money "enhancement" program and he was a dentist at a retreat.

He thought back on how he had arrived at this point in his career. He had graduated from dental school, attended specialty training in doing implants, worked for a few years in someone else's practiced and then the opportunity to take over the practice of a retiring dentist surfaced.

Having his own practice was when he had started to make some decent money, but it had taken some innovative steps to start making good to great money. Amelia, who worked for an insurance company in the role of approving insurance reimbursements was one of the key players that had aided that transition.

Her handling of the claims from his office allowed him to make claims that were higher than the normal compensation and getting them consistently approved for reimbursement.

It was his tax season and after returning home from his "Dental Convention," Chase focused on getting the paperwork for his taxes prepared. He leaned back in his chair, turned his chair away from the computer and looked out the window. It was after ten in the evening, and the yard lighting illuminated the drive up the long hill from the road to the house. He could just make out the roses that at this time of night appeared as black blooms in the circular rose garden at the center of circular driveway.

The perimeter lighting on his putting green just to the left of the window made the flag planted in the hole seem to be signaling someone in the dark. His nearest neighbor was a least half a mile away and he smiled at his imagination.

He looked back to the computer screen directly in front of him. He hated tax season. He had chosen his tax year to end in June. This kept his tax preparer from being bogged down by the taxes of the common people and able to focus on his account only. He kept the information the accountant worked with simple and "clean."

He personally thought that the taxes were far too high, the deductions he was able to generate and to claim was never as much as he wanted them to be. He had no intentions of making large contributions to any charity to reduce his taxes. He wanted all the money he generated to go into his own pocket. He found it easier to adjust his income and to redirect his cash flow out of the country to make his taxes amount to what he felt it should be.

He was making sure all the numbers that he was submitting in his dental office's income and expense form was what his accountant asked for and that it all added up the way he desired.

His recent tryst with Amelia was listed in his computer as a business meeting to discuss the proper way to submit claim forms. He never let his accountant see any of the details of which he was unsure. He did not want an outsider to know too much.

He figured he should be pleased that his dental practice was making a fortune and even after taxes he was well into the top one percent of income in the country. This was only the reported money. What went offshore was almost ten times what his office cash flow amounted to.

As a dentist with a well populated practice, he would have made good money without doing much else, but he wanted more than just a good income. He wanted much more, and he had found a way of getting what he wanted.

Making a fortune was possible because he had two friends in the right places.

One supplying inexpensive implants and one supplying unquestioned expense approval.

Amelia had gone to work for an insurance company and was in charge of accepting insurance claims. She personally managed the claims from his practice. She didn't have to do anything illegal. She just had to authorize full payment for the claims his practice sent in. The expense claims always claimed the highest charges that he could make. He smiled when he thought about the fact that he had a good imagination and his patients all had special needs that cost a significant amount. They were never charged the amount that he claimed so they were not alarmed about the costs he claimed. They paid twenty percent of the bills they saw.

She had her Chicago social circle that included powerful people that ran the lucrative drug trade. He was not sure what her involvement was in that social circle and had no intensions of finding out. He made it a point not to meet her in Chicago. He did not need to get entangled in that trade or with the people she associated with. He was sure that she was providing some sort of service that was also enriching her.

He was happily married, had two kids, and lived in the most exclusive village just to the east of Cincinnati. His wife was from one of the areas old wealthy families. She provided the social connections that allowed him to rub shoulders with the area elite. She also handled the kids and made sure they were in the best schools. She seemed to be clueless as to his personal dealings and he made sure to keep it that way. What made it a good association was that she had her own wealth which kept them from having money issues.

Their kids were both ready to graduate from high school in the next two years. They were bound for college. He hoped they would get a scholarship, but they had agreed that they would make sure that the kids did not end up in debt because of the cost of tuition. Paying for their tuition was no issue and represented only a drip in the bucket of the money he was generating.

The second person that made his scheme work was one of his buddies, Paul, who he had met when he was going to school to specialize in dental implants. He had gone to work for a supplier of dental implants. He was the source of implants that cost a fraction of what the top-quality implants cost.

The implants he supplied were made of less expensive materials and were imported from Guatemala or they were rejects from manufactures of the top implant producers. In both cases he figured that they would last long enough that if they failed the failure could always be blamed on time and some inappropriate action by the person that had the implant.

He just needed the implants to be impossible to trace back to their source.

The billing paperwork Paul sent in for insurance reimbursement was ten times more than what they actually cost to purchase.

The three of them, Amelia, Paul, and he had agreed to split the money that they made equally. This had made all three of them wealthy, able to afford many luxuries and had bonded them together.

Every tax season he shared his accounting numbers with them. It was the one time of the year that they met in person. They would agree to the location, meet there and then spent a couple of days splurging and enjoying themselves. They would spend time enjoying drinks by the pool of some top end hotel, do a little gambling if that was available and partake of the top meals.

Amelia spent one night with each of them. She said she did so because they were sharing everything equally and she thought she should too.

It had been ten wonderful years of getting together. Ten years where each of their fortunes went up by millions of dollars.

This year they were to meet in Miami. He was looking forward to relaxing on the beach and taking in the view of all the young ladies strutting by.

He focused back on the numbers in the spreadsheet showing on the computer screen. He did not want some accountant finding any chinks in the way he inflated the cost of the implants. The paperwork he submitted always supported the numbers and there was nothing for the accountant to question.

Paul provided an invoice for the inflated cost of the implant. This kept his office accounts simple and clean. Even if someone reviewed the paperwork, there was nothing to find.

This also meant that Amelia did not have anything to hide as she evaluated the insurance claims his office submitted to her insurance company. The only thing she did was to accept the claim as submitted. Her participation meant that a smooth cash flow was maintained.

The money from the insurance company was clean. He split the money, so the overcharge went equally to each of the three offshore accounts in their names. They could each draw from them as needed to support the needs of the lifestyles each of them enjoyed. Each of them enjoyed a superior lifestyle based on the money that was generated.

The reimbursement to his office went into the office's bank account and it matched what the accountant submitted in the tax paperwork.

He ran through the numbers in the income and expense report one more time. It was lengthy but clean. His accountant would be able to use it to generate all the tax forms and determine the taxes he would pay.

The next day he went to the office to interview a new desk clerk. His business was growing thanks to the personal advertising that Luna, the person who ran the office, had started doing on her own. He liked the fact that she had taken that approach on her own. He chose to reward her by giving her another good raise. He figured having another office worker to whom he paid the minimum wage would most likely pay off within the year.

She would be the second hire in one year. His first hire, Ezra, seemed to be working out well. He was a hard worker and handled the orders for the implant materials very efficiently. Next to Luna, he was the one that seemed to work the hardest.

Just as she did every morning, Luna parked her car, took a minute to unhook her phone from the charger and then put it in her purse. She was always the first to arrive, unlock the office and turn on all the lights. She knew that this was not something she got paid to do but she did it out of years of habit.

Once she got to the reception desk, she turned on the two computers. One was for logging the patients in and the other was for scheduling appointments as the patient was leaving. She had ended up with two computers when Dr. Mazerly, the dentist that had owned the practice when she first started, had brought in the second one from his home when he had bought a new computer for himself. She was glad that it was a one Dr. office. She had worked for Dr. Mazerly until he retired and sold his practice to Dr. Thornfield. Dr. Thornfield had slowly increased the number of patients, and the number of dental assistants. Two computers finally started to make more sense.

He had hired Emma and Bella, dental hygienists who she suspected were lesbians, but she was not sure. She was sure that they had moved in together, went to lunch together and often held hands as they walked to their car. She knew each had their own car because they seemed to take turns driving. She figured that she should just ask them but that would take all the fun at wondering and watching. They did a great job, and patients liked them and that was all that mattered.

The most recent hire was Ezra Nightshade, a dental assistant that specialized in dental implants. He was a quiet individual that was very organized and efficient. Most of the time he ordered and organized the tooth implants, the ordering of the crowns and other implant materials. He was a serious individual who focused on doing a good job. He was focused on his work, kept everything organized and was helpful. She liked that.

She not only handled the patients, but at first, she had also managed any office improvements that Dr. Thornfield decided to make. She had almost quit because she felt overwhelmed. When she mentioned that to him, he apologized, gave her a raise, and said that she should hire a contractor to manage the details of the improvements, and she focus on managing the contractor.

Both the raise and how he then seemed to check with her with what he wanted to do with the office made her feel she had some say and had some control.

He had added the job of billing and payment to her role so at the end of each month she once again seemed to hit a limit.

She took it on herself to assign setting up appointments of the outgoing patients to each of the dental assistants. At first, they resisted but she showed them how it would actually work in their favor because they could do that as they were winding down while the patient was still in the dental chair.

Ezra was the newest of the group, but he had helped her often enough that she liked him the best. Whenever he was free, he would asked how he could help.

Emma and Bella would get together when they did not have a patient and chat with each other but seldom came to the front desk to see if there was something to do.

As the number of regular customers increased, her job started to overwhelm her once again. This time she went to Dr. Thornfield and suggested that they hire another front desk person.

After a half dozen interviews, she was able to make a hire recommendation, and he had hired that person.

Afterwards she felt that the office seemed to be running smoothly and that nothing more exciting was on the horizon.

<u>*2 The Victim*</u>

Darcy was kneeling working on her flower bed in front of her house. She had tried her hand at creating a colorful flower bed with a mix of flowers that would attract honeybees and hummingbirds. She felt great about the fact that she had been successful in attracting both. She was not sure she would win any awards for the design of the flower choices and arrangement, but she loved what she had accomplished.

She felt that her choices had added both color and made the flower bed seem to be an extension of a flowery meadow. She had a wide variety of flowers such as the lavender Bee Balm, the black eyed Susans, the blue borage which had a cucumber-like taste that she liked, the California poppies, the violet chives, the lavender Liatris that the bees seemed to love, the bright orange Marigold, and the purple, white, and yellow blooming pansy, the Lavendar which she used to cook into shortbread cookies.

She smiled as she thought about the fact that she visited her flower bed to get some of its rich rewards as much as the bees and the hummingbirds. It provided her a connection to nature that delighted her.

This morning, she was feeling the painful effect of having a new dental implant. She went into the house to look at it in the bathroom mirror.

She leaned in toward her the mirror. She pressed lightly with her index finger on the implant tooth that she had just recently had put in. It looked fine but something was not right. The pain was not too bad, but it was constant. She had arranged for an appointment later in the day to have it looked at. This was her second implant. The first one, which was a back molar, had given her no problem.

Her clear dark brown eyes looked at the wrinkle on each side of her mouth. She smiled and took in the few wrinkles due to the fact that she was always smiling.

"Who could complain about a smile wrinkle," she thought.

There were a few wrinkles on the corner of her eyes that also appeared with the smile, but she thought they gave her character.

She brushed back her long hair that was now almost all grey with a few strands of black hair that created random streaks. She had accepted the loss of her beautiful black hair and had refused to dye it. She was proud to accept age for what it was. It was what it was, and she was aging gracefully and painlessly except for her new front tooth.

She was pleased that her slim brown eyebrows were still the same color they had always been. She thought that they provided a contrast to her hair, and they enhanced her looks.

A makeup minimalist she seldom used lipstick, she felt that her light pink lips were the right contrast to her almond-colored skin. Her parents had both contributed to her olive skin color. Her mother was of southern Italian heritage, and her father had been of Spanish heritage.

They both had passed on just two years ago. She missed them dearly but felt that they had lived long, good lives. They had lived out their entire lives on the farm where she had grown up

She turned her head both ways and felt that for a fifty-one-year-old she was still attractive. Her husband always made her feel good when he complimented her on her good looks.

The only thing that was not in as great a shape as she wished were her teeth. On the farm the well water did not have the fluoride that city water had. She had few cavities, but she had several teeth that had deteriorated faster than she had wished.

She had whitened her teeth and felt that had made a big difference as well. She didn't spend money on makeup, but she had spent a small fortune on her teeth. She felt that keeping her teeth in good shape was critical to enjoying her later years.

She drove to the dentist to get her tooth looked at. When she got to the office, the time to get into the dentist chair came faster than she had thought it would.

Ironically, she always feared going to the dentist, but she always enjoyed the comfort of the dentist chair. It made her want to close her eyes and relax.

Dr. Thronfield entered, flashed his brilliant smile, and asked how she was feeling.

She put her finger on her tooth and explained the problem.

He nodded and said he would take a look at it.

He asked his assistant nurse to take a picture of the tooth. He then let her know he would be back shortly to have a look at the Xray.

The assistant, who she had never seen before, introduced himself as Ezra and said that he had been trained as an implant specialist. He asked her to bite down on the shield that would let the picture of her tooth be recorded.

She bit down on the gadget that he put in her mouth and closed her eyes. She heard a buzz and then she was asked to open her mouth.

A few moments later Dr. Thronfield returned and stood with his back to her as he looked at the picture of her tooth. He hummed and hawed a few times and then he turned to her and said that there wasn't anything obviously wrong with the implant. He said that he was going to prescribe a pain killer and said that the pain should subside in a few days.

She nodded but, in her mind, she was thinking that she should say that she actually didn't want the medicine and that the pain indicated to her that there was something wrong with the implant and his response was not what she had expected.

Before leaving the office, she stopped at the desk and made an appointment for two weeks out.

She had no plans to fill the prescription.

Instead, she called a friend and asked her if she had a dentist that she used and felt good enough about, to recommend him. When she got the name, she realized that it was a woman dentist. Once she had the name she called to see if she could get a second opinion about some pain, she was experiencing with a front tooth implant.

She got the appointment for that Friday.

By Friday she was ready. Ready to have the pain come to an end.

She was greeted by a young female dentist who introduced herself as, Dr. Whitlock. She inquired about the pain and then focused on looking at her teeth. After a few moments she asked if she could get a full picture of all of her teeth.

Darcy liked how thorough she was.

After the pictures were taken, she was asked to wait while Dr. Whitlock went to her office where she would take a close look at her entire mouth.

When she came back, she asked if the implant of the molar in the back had been done by a different dentist than the one who had done the front tooth.

Darcy said that it been done by a Dr. Goldens because it had to be done by a specialist. At that time, she had been a patient of Dr. Mazerly who had sold his practice to Dr. Thronfeld who had recently done the front tooth since he did both general dentistry and implants.

Dr. Whitlock asked if she ever had any adverse effects from the back implant.

She said that she had none.

Dr. Whitlock nodded and said that the material of the front tooth was different from that of the back, and she suspected that the only way to end the pain was to remove the implant and examine it.

She explained that the pain would most likely end immediately on its removal. She said that she would recommend removing it immediately while she as in the office. Then a few days later she could put in a new implant. The same crown could be reused.

Darcy thought for a moment and asked what Dr. Whitlock planned to do with the implant.

Dr. Whitlock said that she planned to send it to get it examined to see what it was made of.

Darcy decided that if the pain was going to end with the removal of the implant, she was ready to do it.

She asked what the procedure would cost and was told that it would be close to two thousand dollars.

She realized that would deplete her entire dental insurance allowance, but she figured it would be worth it if it solved the pain issue.

After the numbing, the extraction was painless. She walked out with a gap in her front teeth.

When she greeted her husband, he asked what had happened to her beautiful smile and what she was sad about.

She explained what had happened.

He said she had done the right thing but that next time she should let him know she was experiencing pain.

She said that she would.

She took it easy for the next week. The pain was gone so she felt that she had done the right thing.

On her next visit to Dr Whitlock's office, she got a new implant put in. It took less than thirty minutes to get the new implant. She learned that it would be three months to allow the implant to be solidly in place. That time was a month longer than Dr. Thronfield had taken.

Dr. Whitlock let her know that the crown was of a lower quality than ones she used but it would do for a short time. She recommended replacing it as well.

Darcy figured that she would let Dr. Whitlock order a new crown.

She commented that she was mad about the situation.

Dr. Whitlock nodded and said that she was also mad, but she was going to wait until she heard back from the expert at the lab she used before she did anything else. She suspected that the implant material was of inferior quality or not compatible with the human body.

Darcy thanked her and asked if she would take her on as a permanent patient.

That got a smile from Dr. Whitlock who said that she could use more patients and that when they went to the front desk, she would make sure that her receptionist put her on the office patient list.

After leaving the office, Darcy sat in her car thinking about the situation. She wondered if there was anything illegal about using inferior materials for implants.

She was sure that she wanted to take some sort of action. The least of the actions was to ask for a refund from Dr. Thronfield. The other action might be to sue him if he was using inferior implant materials. But she was not sure if that would be a good use of her time. She wondered if there were other people that had experienced something similar to her.

488

3 The Snitch

*T*he creek water rippling down over the smooth flattened water worn stones broadcast the rapid's joyous gurgling that Ezra had listened to all of his life. It was a melody that soothed his mind. It was the melody that reinforced his soul.

He had walked this path many times and had been enchanted by the willows bending down to touch their leaves into the clear waters of the stream. Today he watched as a swallow broke off from its sky flying antics to glide within inches of the water's surface and then dip its beak into the water before rising back to join its frolicking brethren in the sky.

Then his eyes found the finches that were holding onto the branches of the willow picking off what he figured were the aphids and other small insects feeding on the leaves.

He and nature seemed to harmonize.

The swallow had sent him the message of belonging to the group but taking your own action to get the water of life that you needed when you needed it.

The finch told him to hold tight to the branch you had and take action against what was within reach.

He sat down on the large round boulder as he always did every time he made this walk. He looked down into the water and spotted a large catfish slowly opening and closing its mouth as if it was taking slow deep breaths.

He took a slow deep breath of his own.

He put his arms around his knees as he thought about the predicament he faced. He knew what he needed to do, knew he would do it and when he did it, he would lose his job. What bothered him was that he had just started his new job and knew it was not going to look good when he tried to get another job after only a few months. It might not look good, but he knew that would be the way he would go.

He took a deep breath and absorbed the smell of the decomposing grasses at the water's edge, the odor of the pines on the hill sides and the smells of the cattle that pastured just beyond the bend coming down along the creek.

This was a bouquet of fragrances that he would never be able to describe to anyone. It had to be experienced sitting where he was. It was what had colored his young life and given him the perspective that the world was made up of the good, the beautiful and the odor of shit that when mixed together was what life was about. This interpretation had guided him in how he handled the life situations that he had so far experienced.

He figured he was still young enough to hold onto his dreams but to realize that dreams tended to change, and they often changed for the better.

He was still looking for love and hoped that someday he would meet the right person. She would need to be independent and be a strong person who was not looking to being kept.

His current issue was what he had stumbled upon at work. He was sure that the Xray he had taken of a patients front tooth implant was a picture of a black-market implant. He had compared it to the implant that was in her record for a back molar and there was a stark difference. There was no way Dr. Thronfield could have missed that fact when he examine the Xray. He was the one that had put it in and unless he was blind the difference in quality should have been apparent at that point.

He was sure there was something rotten in Denmark and that he did not want to be a part of it. How to handle the situation was what he was trying to think through.

He watched as a grey heron landed in the grassy low and marshy area just across from him. It stood frozen for a few moments then in a lightning move its beak went into the shallow water in front of it and came out with a minnow. With a slight flip of his head, it threw the minnow into the air and then swallowed it on its way down.

He figured his job was about to take the same path as the minnow. He was going to get eaten.

He looked down into the water at the catfish and watched as it too made a swift move and a minnow disappeared down its throat.

The lesson for him in both situations was that the little fish always got eaten.

He knew that at the moment he was a little fish.

He smiled as he realized that at the moment nature was not giving him any inspiration to do the right thing.

Then he thought about what he had personally experienced growing up and that he had put into practice for how he lived his life.

In high school he had stood up to the bully and had taken his beating, but he gave the fight his all. He had not won the fight, but the bully had never bothered him again. He was able to walk tall and proud for the rest of the school year.

Then more recently he had refused to participate with a group of dental students that were cheating on tests. They consistently outscored him but on the final test they were caught and kicked out of the program. They lost everything. His score was good enough. He passed, graduated, and got a job.

He had taken the action that each situation had warranted.

Now he would take the right actions, and his job would most likely evaporate, and he would once again be looking for a job.

There was one more hurdle that he faced before he was ready to act. He was not sure to whom he was going to report what he had learned. The boss was the one he was going to rat out and certainly not the one he was going to confront. He needed to determine who to report the situation to.

He turned to see a box turtle moving slowly along the path that he had been walking. He smiled and knew it was giving him the message that he should move slow and steady along the straight and narrow path that he had always walked.

He stood up and stretched his arms over his head and let out a loud shout of "Yes do whats right but do it smart."

He went home and that night as he was watching the news, he saw a young black female detective being questioned by a news crew about her most recent case where she solved a fifty-year-old killing.

It caught his attention because when she smiled, her bright white teeth seemed to be perfect. She exuded a self-confidence and an ease as she spoke that called out to him. He decided that she was the one that he should share his predicament with and ask her advice on how to proceed.

The next day when he got to work, he looked at his schedule and arranged to take a day off. He figured he would visit the detective and would also spend some time looking for his next job.

He called the police station and made an appointment to see her.

He then looked at the want ads for a dentist that might be looking for a dental assistant with a specialty in implants. That did not yield any leads.

On the morning that he was going to see the detective, he stopped at the grocery to get a few items that he needed. As he was getting ready to check out, he ran into Mrs. Barlowe. He asked her how her implant was feeling.

He was surprised when she told him that she had the tooth replaced by another dentist and the pain had immediately gone away. She shared that she also had her crown replaced with a higher quality one.

He asked whether she had the implant and the crown that had been remove. He found out that her new dentist was in the process of having the implant and crown examined.

He let her know that he was looking for a new job because he was on the way to talk to a detective to report what he thought might be an illegal action at his current job and he figured that he was about to get fired. He let her know that it was her implant that he was reporting.

Mrs. Barlowe let him know who her new dentist was and that she had just set up her practice and might be looking for help. She asked him to keep her informed about what he found out because she wanted to take some sort of action.

Once he got to the car, Ezra looked at the time and figured he would swing by to the dentist that Mrs. Barlowe had mentioned.

A short time later, when he walked into the office, he was surprised to see the reception desk empty. He waited a few moments. He heard some conversation just around the corner from the desk and walked back and excused himself.

There was one patient in the chair, and a very good-looking dentist in the examination chair and no one else.

He excused himself and said that he was trying to see a Dr. Whitlock about a job.

She looked at him, asked him to wait a few moments out in the lobby and she would soon be out to talk with him.

He watched as the patient came out to make his next appointment. He noted that Dr. Whitlock was now sitting in the receptionist's chair making the appointment.

He knew that this was a person he would like to know better.

Once the patient left, she turned to him. She apologized and let him know that the receptionist had called in sick, and she was short of dental assistants.

Ezra introduced himself and briefly explained his experience and training. He then said that he had come because he had met Mrs. Barlow who had an implant that had caused her pain. He noticed from the Xray that the implant appeared to be made of a different material from the other implant that she had. He suspected that it was of inferior quality. His training led him to believe that it was a black-market implant that was significantly cheaper than what the normal implant cost.

He asked why she had replaced the implant and what she had done with the implant that she removed.

She let him know that she had sent it off to her lab to get it examined.

He then explained that he was going to meet with the Cincinnati detective unit, specifically with Alex Evercrest to see if his boss's actions warranted investigation.

He added that after meeting with her he was going to return to his current job and quit because he was sure that what was going on in that practice was not ethical.

He was about to ask for a job when a patient walked in, and Dr. Whitlock asked if he could return after lunch.

He asked for her number, walked out to his car, and drove downtown.

On the way he kept thinking about the situation in Dr. Whitlock's office.

He found a parking spot in the garage across the street from the police station and entered into the reception area. He let the receptionist know that he had an appointment with detective Alex Evercrest.

A few moments later he saw her come in. He stood up to shake hands and realized that he was standing a head higher than she. She was accompanied by her partner that was a head taller than himself. After introducing himself and learning her partners name, he followed the two.

Alex guided the person who had identified himself as Ezra into one of the huddle rooms and asked him to share the reason that he wanted to speak to her.

After hearing what he had to say, she let him know that he was potentially on to something, but he was not the injured party and unless he had direct evidence to a crime being committed, he did not have a legal right to complain.

Ezra let her know that he had talked with a Mrs. Barlowe and that she had gone to another dentist that had taken out the implant put in by Dr. Thronfield and had sent it off to get it analyzed. She would soon know if it was a black-market product.

He shared that he was going back to that dentist when he left and would let her know about what he had learned.

He thanked Alex for her guidance and said that he would get the person who was the injured party to come with him next time.

After leaving the police station, he called Dr. Whitlock and asked if he could bring her something for lunch. He liked the fact that she accepted and that she let him know what she preferred from the Chinese carry out that was close to her office.

When he returned to the office, he volunteered to handle the front desk for the rest of the afternoon. He also asked if she would consider hiring him.

He was relieved that she said that she would indeed hire him, but she wanted him to stay at his present job until she had the results about the dental implant.

She went on to explain that if it was a black-market implant, it would add a lot of weight to any accusation that was to be made against Dr. Thronfield if more wronged dental patients were to complain.

She added that she would also bring it up to the State Dental Board as an ethical violation

Ezra agreed to stay on and while they waited for the lab results, he would dig into the transplants that had been done.

He stayed and handle the front desk for Dr. Whitlock for the rest of the afternoon.

During their lunch conversation he had learned that she was single and not dating.

He found it hard to get up the next morning and go in to work.

He was glad that it was Friday.

He called Dr. Whitlock toward the end of the day and asked if she had heard back from the lab.

Then he asked if she would be available for dinner.

4 The Situation

Zia first met Fiona when they both started working for Dr. Thornfield. In only a few days, as they got to know each other, she knew that she was in a complicated situation.

Fiona had married Jason, who had been her childhood friend. When they were young, they had always played house and pretended that they were a happily married couple that had a perfect home. During the year after marrying him she found out that he had a huge temper. They were about to celebrate their one-year anniversary. During that short time, she had witnessed him lose his temper and almost beat people to death. She was the one who always stepped in to stop the fight. Once he was sober, he seemed to return to the Jason she knew. She was questioning whether there was a way for her to back out of their marriage in a way that they could remain friends and not have him loose his temper. Based on what she had learned, she suspected that was not how it was going to work out.

Her ambivalence towards continuing her romantic relationship with Jason was at a height when she met Zia.

At work her relationship with Zia was on a course where the two of them wanted to live together. This was an awaking of what her sexual persona happened to be. She accepted the fact that she had a greater desire to be with Zia than with Jason. This in itself was a surprise to her. She had always felt that there was something missing but had never imagined she was gay. Now that she recognized that fact she felt a relief.

The issue came to a head by accident rather than by a plan. She and Zia were out to lunch when suddenly Jason was looming overhead and loudly accusing her of being a lesbian bitch. It was obvious that he had been drinking because he smelled of alcohol and was very angry. He pulled her out of her chair and slapped her. He was about to hit her with his fist when Zia suddenly gave out a shout and hit him on the side of his head with a swift flick of her fist.

This surprised and stunned Jason who threw her down and turned toward Zia who was less than half his weight and two thirds his size. She took one step back as he stepped forward. She gave out another yell, leaped in the air, and kicked him in the side of his ribs. He grunted and took another step toward Zia.

Zia took a step to the side and then leaped forward as if to embrace him but hit him in the throat with the knuckles of one hand and hit him in the eye with the knuckle of her other hand.

Jason went down gurgling and then fell flat on his face as he passed out.

A policewoman riding a bicycle stopped and asked what had happened.

Fiona explained that her husband had gotten mad, had hit her and Zia had defended her.

She was asked if she wanted to press assault charges.

Fiona declined to do so.

By this time Jason was sitting up and looking around. He was in shock since he had never lost a fight and losing it to a woman half his size was about as humiliating as it could possibly be. He stood up and asked if he could leave.

The policewoman warned him about starting fights and said that the next time he would be arrested.

That was the first day that Fiona had gone home with Zia. She was afraid to go home by herself and face Jason. She did not have Zia's martial arts training.

The next morning, she waited until she was sure that Jason was at work and then she went in, got all her clothes, the few other personal things that were hers and moved them into Zia's apartment.

Since that day she had lived with Zia. She had found a lawyer, had put in the divorce papers, and had them delivered by a courier.

Jason signed them exactly on what would have been their one-year anniversary and had them returned via mail.

She was happy to have it over.

At work, Luna, the nurse receptionist that ran the office, seemed curious about her and Zia's relationship but never said anything.

The two of them kept things low key.

The office was run out of two separate wings. Regular dentistry went on in the wing she and Zia worked in whereas specialty dentistry went on in the other wing where Ezra worked.

She was surprised at the volume of work that Dr. Thronfield managed to carry.

Things seemed to settled down to a consistent routine, then one day Zia stayed home because she was feeling under the weather.

She went into work and was able to cover the work. Then as she was walking out, she was grabbed from behind and as she was spun around a hard slap made her ears ring.

She had been taking Taekwondo lessons with Zia, and she put everything she knew into action. She surprised Jason but he was twice her size, and she was a Taekwondo novice. She held her own as she backed away from him, but she knew that she was losing and was likely to take a beating.

Ezra came out from work and saw what was going on. He gave out a shout and rushed toward the two. He was ready when the person attacking turned towards him. He hit him as hard as he could on the side of the chin and watched as the attacker staggered backward away from him. He was glad to see him turn and run for a pickup parked in the rear of the lot.

He checked to see if Fiona was alright and then pulled her between two cars as that pickup screeched around the end of the parked cars and came towards them. It did not stop but went charging out of the parking lot.

Fiona thanked Ezra for coming to her aid.

She drove to her apartment and was surprised to be greeted by a police officer as she came out of the elevator.

He asked her if she lived in apartment three fourteen.

Her heart skipped a beat as she said that she did.

He said that her roommate was alive but in intensive care and gave her the hospital that she was in.

Fiona started crying and leaned against the wall. She asked who had done it.

He said that he was not sure, and the fingerprints found on the small bat that was the weapon was not in the standard police records.

Fiona said she knew who had attacked Zia and she suggested that he check on Jason's car registration for fingerprints and also to check if a black pickup truck had been spotted at the time the attack took place.

She asked if she could leave and go to the hospital.

When she got to the hospital, she found out what room Zia was in and went to that floor and reception desk.

She was greeted by the doctor who introduced himself and said that Zia had come around and had asked if her roommate was alright. He led her into Zia's room. She had a large bandage around her head and was hooked up to with a maze of wires on her body.

Fiona held Zia's hand and said she was sorry.

Zia gave a weak smile and asked her if she was the one who had wacked her on the back of her head.

Fionna shook her head and said that she was sure that it was Jason who had done it.

Zia nodded and said that made a weird kind of sense and that he was too afraid of her to face her in a face-to-face fight. She said that she was going to take him on in a legal fight to make sure he ended up behind prison walls where he would find out that his bully behavior would do him no good.

Fionna didn't know what to say. She just held Zia's hand and gave it a squeeze. It was hard not to cry in anger as she looked at Zia's bandaged head. She was sure they had cut off her hair to fix the wound.

She received a call saying that the apartment had been cleared and was now available for her to use. When she asked about the risk, the officer said that a police car would park out front for the evening. They were currently searching for the attacker, but he was not at the address she had provided, and it looked like he had taken all of his possessions with him.

The landlord had let them know that the rent ended at the end of the month and no arrangements had been made to extent the rental.

As she returned to her apartment, Fionna saw the black and white parked out front. She went up to the apartment, prepared a bowl of fruit and took it down to the two men sitting in the car and thanked them for being there. She asked them how she would reach them if her ex showed up. They gave her a number to call and said that if she called that number they would be up within a minute. They said that he would not get past them.

She then went up, locked the door, and leaned a chair under the doorknob.

Jason was up on the roof of a nearby building and had watched the entire time. He had made sure neither he nor his pickup was visible from the air. He lay comfortably under a leaf covered limb of a large old maple tree that reached across the roof as if it was embracing it. It was a warm day, but he had a bottle of water and a bag of sandwiches. He had watched as the ambulance arrived and then shortly afterwards as a person who he figured was Zia was loaded into the back. He was glad it was not a hearse. He wanted her to wake up and go through the pain of recovery and maybe her mental capacity would be reduced. He figured she would think twice about messing with him if they met in the future.

He left the roof and went to the dental office where Fiona worked and planned to do the same to her when she got off work. He figured she would be easy to take down and beat to a pulp. When she came out after work, he grabbed her, spun her around, and slapped her. He was surprised at the fact that Fionna hit him back and then put up a fight that he was not expecting. She gave him a bloody nose, hit him on the side of the head, and was putting up a good fight until he hit her in the gut. Then just when he thought he would be able finish her off some tough-looking guy attacked him and knocked him back. He was going to return the attack when suddenly he got hit multiple times.

He decided it was time to get away. He turned and rushed back to his pickup. He drove toward the two in hopes of hitting both of them but they both stepped back between two cars. He drove by, shook his fist, gave them the finger, and drove out of the lot.

He returned to the roof near the apartment. He was looking through his binoculars when Fionna brought out what looked like a bowl of grapes and maybe some tangerines to the car where two cops were sitting.

He didn't care about the cops parked out front. He would go in the back, do her in, leave and the two would be out front enjoying their goodies.

He got off the roof, went to his pickup and took out a bat from the bed of the truck. He had decided to make sure that Fiona was put in a hearse, not the back of an ambulance. He walked to the back of the apartment to the door that he had made sure would be open and where he had disabled the cameras. He had a path to the apartment that was all a blind spot. He got to the apartment door, leaned back and then kicked the door with all his might. He was surprised that the latch did not shatter, and the door swing inward. He stepped back and kicked it again and it still did not move. He cursed his bad luck.

He decided it was time to get out of the building and disappear before the two cops showed up. He ran down the stairs to exit and ran out.

He heard the shout for him to stop. He ran around the corner as a shot rang out. He felt the burn across his shoulder but kept running. He made several turn between buildings as he ran and lost the police. He returned to his truck and took out his emergency kit and worked on the long path that the bullet had taken across his shoulder. It felt like a streak burned across his shoulder.

He was pissed. Somehow, Fiona had blocked the door and had been able to let the cops know he was trying to get in.

He was going to have to get away, but he would have to stay off the highway and get to wherever he planned to hide via the back streets.

His revenge would have to wait for another day, but he would have it and the next time he would kill both of them.

5 The Case

*A*fter listening to Ezra, Alex asked Johnnie to look into Dr. Thornfield's practice, where he got this implants and where the money went.

She then went to the Chief's office and let him know that she might be bringing in a new case.

He listened and said that if she had several people that had suffered from his dental practice, had obtained legal representation and that law firm asked for help, he would consider opening a case otherwise they should stay away.

Alex walked out of his office and went to her desk.

Trey asked her what she had on her mind. She said that she was going to lunch, and she planned to visit a dentist after lunch.

Trey smiled and asked whether her perfect teeth had a cavity.

She shook her head and said that she had a hunch that she wanted to check out.

After lunch Alex drove to the office of Dr. Whitlock. She asked the receptionist if there was a chance that she would be able to talk with the doctor. The receptionist looked at her badge and asked if this was official business.

Alex smiled and replied that in her line of work she was never sure what was official and what wasn't.

A few moments later she and Trey were led to an office in the very corner of the building.

After being asked by the doctor to call her Ava, Alex smiled and said that she had found a person with the same first letter, in her first name, that was shorter than hers.

Ava nodded and said that the only other thing that was short was her height, but it seemed both of them suffered the same fate.

Trey spoke up and said that physical height did not impact the shadow that his partner cast.

Ava smiled and asked how she could help.

Alex asked her about what she had learned about the implants she removed from a Mrs. Barlowe and had sent to the lab for analysis.

"So, Ezra shared that with you," I just got the report back. The lab found that the material that the implant was made of was of inferior quality. They suggested that it was a black-market product but had no idea what its source might be.

Alex asked if she knew if Ezra had found a new job.

Ava nodded and said that she had hired him but had asked him to stay on in his current job and do some digging to find out how many patients had received the inferior implants.

Alex shook her head and said that was a dangerous thing to do. If he had names he should quit and leave the office before he was discovered. She had a sleuth that could get into contact with the people on the list and determine the situation.

"That sounds like a great idea. I will call him and get him to quit and come over and work in my practice. Not only do I need someone with his skills, but I need to be able to sleep at night and not worry about him," Ava replied.

She then smiled and said that she was a fan of hers and had watched every news conference in which she had appeared. She went on to say that she would be super confident that something would come from her getting involved.

Alex thanked her for the recognition she was giving her but what she needed was a number of unhappy dental customers willing to put in complaints about the implants that they had received so that the case could be officially opened.

Ava replied that she had one person that was willing to go to court over the matter. She had paid over six thousand dollars for a fake tooth and inferior quality crown.

Alex said that one would be a start, and it would open the door but a couple more would bar the door open for a full investigation.

She got the name, phone number for the number the one victim, and thanked Ava for her help. She then reminded her to get Ezra out of the office where he was currently working.

Ava watched Alex walk out and immediately called Ezra and told him to send her all his information and then quit. She shared that she had just talked to Alex who was going to take up the case and had advised her to get him out of the other office.

That evening before Luna shut down her computer, Ezra stopped at her desk and said that he would not be returning to the office. He said that an emergency had come up in his family and he was going to take over running the farm and was not sure if he was ever going to come back.

She looked at him, nodded, said that it was shock, said she would miss him and hoped that he would do well on the farm. She asked where she should send his paycheck.

Ezra thanked her for her good wishes and told her to send the check to his bank as usual.

He got to his car and found it hard to relax. He drove out of the lot and went to the grocery store parking lot. From there he called Ava and let her know that he had quit and had all the information with him.

She suggested that he take it to the police station and turn it over to Alex Evercrest before he went home.

He agreed and said that a weird thing had happened and shared the fact that he had been in a fight with someone attacking one of the hygienists. The next day he had found out that the other hygienist was in intensive care in the hospital. He was sure that it had nothing to do with the office but had to do with their personal life. However, he was worried about some sort of revenge by the attacker.

Ava suggested that he come and stay at her house until that situation resolved itself.

He took her up on her offer and thanked her. He asked what he could bring for supper with him.

She gave him her Hopesome home address where she had just moved into a huge granite stone home with a copper roof that was nestled among huge oaks and maples. It was too much home for herself, but she had figured that at the least it was a good investment. It had an over the three-car garage living area that she hoped Ezra would be willing to live in. It would be great to have someone else there to keep things seemingly normal. Besides, she really enjoyed her conversations with him.

Alex was surprised when she came in to work the following morning and found the thumb drive with a note from Ezra saying that he had compiled the names and condition of every implant that Dr. Thronfield had done since he took over the practice from Dr. Mazerly.

She gave the thumb drive to Johnnie and asked him to organize the information so that as they dug into the case, they could trace the source of the implant, the flow of the money and the information about the patient.

Johnnie nodded and said he would set it up like every other investigation they had done.

She then called Ezra to thank him for being so efficient.

She was surprised when he shared the fact that what was on his mind had nothing to do with the fake implants that were being used.

He was concerned about Zia and Fiona, two hygienists, one that was in intensive care and the other who was attacked in the dental office parking lot. He said that he was staying at Dr. Whitlock's home because he was worried about the person who he fought with in the parking lot when he helped Fiona. He was most likely the person who had put Zia in the hospital. He said that he had learned she was hit with a small baseball bat on the back of her head.

Alex asked why he would attack Zia.

Ezra shared the fact that Fiona's ex had attacked her during lunch and Zia had knocked him out using her martial arts skills. It seems that he was able to break into her apartment and was able to hit her from behind.

Alex asked which hospital Zia was in and said that she would check in on the situation. Once she hung up, she looked at Trey and said that they were going to go to visit one of the hygienists that was in intensive care.

Trey shook his head and commented that they were going from simple dental care to intensive care in just one day. He asked what she expected the next step to be.

Trevor and Bill had been listening in. Trevor smiled and said that he had no clue what was going on, but Alex's next steps were always deadly for anyone that was in her way to solving a case. He asked what case they had been assigned to.

Alex smiled and said that the Chief had not assigned anyone to any case.

Trevor asked when she was going to let the Chief know about the case she was working.

Alex bowed her head, said she first had to figure out if there was one case or two and then who should be assigned to each.

Bill smiled said that he wanted the one that did not include any shooting.

Trey stood up and said that he hoped that neither case had any shooting associated with them, but he figured that he and Alex needed to get to the hospital to see how the two cases fit together.

When they arrived at the hospital, they used their police connection to get access to Zia.

Zia gave a brave attempt at a smile and said that she was just realizing that she had almost died. She asked if Jason had been captured.

Alex said that she had just learned about the attack on her and that she was not on the case looking for Jason and had only learned of the situation a short time ago from Ezra.

She asked to hear what she could remember about what had happened.

Zia shook her head slowly and said that she had been dozing on the couch waiting for Fiona to come home. She came awake to Jason shouting at her to wake up and then the world went blank.

The next thing she remembered was dialing 911 and telling someone that she needed help. Then she had come awake here. She added that was all she could recall.

Alex let her know that she was going to dig into the situation and would most likely get the case officially opened.

She wished Zia a quick recovery and said that she would be in contact with her and that she should not leave the hospital without giving her a call. She handed her one of her cards that had her number on it.

On the way to the car, she called the Chief and let him know that she wanted to meet with him about the Dental Scam case.

She then called Bill and asked him to get the police report about the attack on Zia. She let him know that she was coming in to talk with the Chief about it and about the case that she had Johnnie doing some preliminary work on.

She called Johnnie and asked him to organize whatever he had been able to dig up in the short time he had been working on the files that Ezra had given them because she was coming in and wanted to have the Chief officially designate it as a case.

She arrived at the station and walked briskly into the bullpen area. Johnnie held up a folder and said that he was ready. Bill held up a folder and said that he was ready.

Alex nodded and walked to the Chief's office and knocked. She went in and a moment later she waved for everyone to enter the office.

The Chief smiled and looked at the group and said he wondered how long it would take for Alex to demand that she be allowed to go after the crooked dentist.

Alex said that she was actually bringing two cases to him. Both were located in the same dental office but one was a con scheme of interesting proportions and the other was about love gone wrong.

The Chief shook his head and asked if anyone in the room was surprised that Alex would bring up such a twist to a case.

Travis said that he did not remember a case that was normal and did not have some unusual twist since Alex had joined the detective unit. Even the last case was not normal because though someone did die, Alex was not the one that did the shooting and that was really abnormal.

Alex thanked Travis for his thoughtful commentary, but she wanted to hear what Johnnie had to share and then she would introduce the second case and have Bill share what he had learned.

Johnnie said that the doctor had been running his scam for more than ten years. During that time, he had been able to generate almost one hundred million dollars that he sent to three different offshore bank accounts.

He did not have time to verify if taxes had been paid on that money, but he doubted that it had. He would be able to verify that angle once the case was opened and he had access to the tax records. He then pointed out that there were only eleven individuals that were no longer patients of Dr. Thronfield and might be convinced to testify against him. One patient was ready to testify against him but there had not been time to identify anyone else and have their position checked out.

Alex looked at the Chief and said that she was relatively confident that one or two more customers would be found to testify against the doctor. She then said that she wanted the case officially opened so the needed work could be done to put the good doctor and whomever was working with him away in prison.

She then asked Bill to share what he had time to learn about how the dental hygienist from that same office ended up in intensive care.

The Chief held up his hand and asked how the second case was connected to the first.

Alex replied that they were linked only because the person who had given them the inside information about the good doctor was also involved in the situation that involved a love triangle gone bad.

The Chief chuckled and said that he was glad that there at least was the thinnest of linkage.

Bill shared the fact that the dental hygienist that was in the hospital had been surprised by her attacker who hit her with a miniature oak baseball bat. She just barely survived but was now on the road to recovery. Her roommate had been the wife of the attacker but had divorced him and had moved in with Zia. The report stated that her ex had returned that same night to the apartment and tried to break, but a chair propped under the entry door handle prevented him from getting in.

There were two police officers parked out front. One got to the door in just under one minute. The second went around the back of the building, got a shot at the attacker, and managed to wound him but the attacker got away.

Dr. Rogers team was able to get enough of a blood sample to verify that it was Jason Gravely the ex-husband. There is a standing warrant out for his arrest that lists him as armed and dangerous.

Alex looked at the Chief and said that they could work it as one case or two cases, but they needed his blessing to take the cases on.

The Chief ask how she was thinking about the cases.

Alex said that she felt that Bill and Travis should handle the love triangle case. She smiled and added that she was sure that Travis would have a unique insight to love triangles gone wrong.

He laughed and replied that he had been involved in dozens of love triangles during his thirty-five years of marriage.

Travis commented that it was just like her to give him and Bill the case that put people in the hospital and was the most dangerous.

Alex laughed and said that she thought she had heard him earlier say he wanted the case that had some gunfire associated with it. She added that she was concerned that he would be disappointed about her inability to satisfy that desire, so she had given him one that at least had some bloodshed associated with it.

Bill shook his head and said that they should ignore his partners complaints and suggested they focus on the case at hand.

She then said that she and Trey would handle the dental scam case.

She added that Johnnie would be a resource for both cases.

The Chief looked around and asked if the split made sense.

Bill said that it did and that it seemed clear that there were at least three people in danger of the ex-husband.

Johnnie said that he was sure that even without any patients willing to testify, he would be able to provide information to their IRS friends that would put the doctor away for many years.

The Chief nodded and said that they had two cases to solve, and everyone should work together to get them solved. He looked around and said they should get out of his office and get to work.

6 The Arrests

Chase learned about Zia and was disturbed that personal issues might upset his dental practice and might cause it to get investigated. He called Fiona into his office, asked her what was going on and why he should not let both her and Zia go.

Fiona knew that both she and Zia needed their jobs. She pointed out that she was working overtime to make sure that no patient was ignored. She had worked with Luna to make some slight changes to the schedule to make sure she could handle the load on her own. She pointed out that the insurance was covering the hospitalization costs and that it would not interfere with providing the services the patients would request.

Chase thought about the situation for a moment and figured that the office could weather what was going on. He asked if the person who had attacked Zia had been arrested. When he found out that he had not, an alarm bell went off. He could not risk some crazy guy coming into the office and wreaking havoc. He would need to set up some sort of security. He would get Luna to arrange it.

Fiona left the office knowing that Dr. Thronfield would soon find out that the attacker was her ex and then he would fire both she and Zia. She did not know what they would do then. She hoped that by that time Zia was out of the hospital.

She experienced a real low in her self-confidence. It seemed that everything that could go wrong was going wrong.

Once the case was official, Alex arranged a meeting with Dr. Thronfield's accountant.

Johnnie had done a very detailed analysis of the money flow. He had learned that the money from the insurance company was sent to a specific bank from which the money flowed four ways. One sum flowed back to the dental office and the other money split three ways and went to three separate offshore accounts.

She put in a call to Joe Brown the Cincinnati region IRS leader, and asked to meet with him to share a potential case for him to manage.

When he understood the details of the case, he asked if it was illegal to use inferior dental implants.

Alex said that she was not sure about that, but she was sure that the Dr. had not paid taxes on millions of dollars that he had sent to offshore bank accounts and that was what she was going to arrest him on.

She, Trey, Johnnie, and Joe met at the accountants office and asked about Dr. Thronfield's tax records.

The accountant objected to sharing the records until Joe spoke up and said that he had the official IRS paperwork that authorized him to review the records to see if the income of the practice matched what had been submitted as the amount that taxes were paid on.

The records that were shared were in perfect order. Joe made the point that Dr. Thronfield was not to be told of his visit for at least a week. Any sooner and he would arrest him for conspiracy to defraud the government.

When they left the office, Joe verified that Johnnie was sure about the more than one hundred million that had gone offshore. He then said he would get authorization to seize the doctor's personal computers at home and at work as well as any paperwork that might be found at each location. He figured to do a simultaneous raid on the Dr.'s office and his home within a day.

He said that it was clear to him that the operation was sophisticated and most likely needed some outside help for it to work.

He pointed out that someone had to supply the inferior implants and to bill them as if they were top quality ones. He added that there might be someone on the other end from where the money would come. He added that from his experience twenty percent or so would come out of the victims pockets and the other eighty percent or so from the insurance company. So, the two victimized entities were the patients and the insurance company.

Alex said that she would hunt down the supplier of the implants. She would have Johnnie work out how the money came in and then went to the off shore accounts. He would share this with Joe and his people as a guide for them to gather the in-court materials.

Alex returned to the office and asked Johnnie to identify the outside people that might be involved in the Doctor's implant scam.

Johnnie tracked down the dental implant supplier and learned that it was a person named Paul Elsher. He did a deep dive into Paul's personal finances and his ability to obtain the implants.

He had been expecting to find the implants coming from Asia but instead he found out that the supplier was a small company in Belize. He dug into that business and found out that they produced the implants and shipped them out to various Latin American countries and to a Texas address where Paul lived.

Paul in turn, using a dummy organization, shipped the implants to Dr. Thornfield's office as top-quality implants and charged slightly more than what top quality implants cost on the market.

Alex knew that this information cleared the accountant of any complicity in the scheme. She called Joe and let him know of the situation.

Joe thanked her and said that he would have the Texas regional IRS folks made aware of the situation and get prepared to assist her when she was ready to make her arrest.

She asked Johnnie to check on the insurance reimbursement side to see how Dr. Thornfield could consistently get the reimbursement that he wanted to get.

Johnnie was able to identify an Amelia Lockwood that worked for an insurance company but was also registered as an independent agent that handled all the submittals from Dr. Thornfield's office. She had agreements with the handful of insurance companies that handled dental insurance and all of the claims from his office were personally handled by her.

Alex let the Chief know that once again she was going to be going to Chicago and needed his help in getting her Illinois authorization re-established. She was sure that Lieutenant Governor Jane Stradford would once again give her legal status in her state.

She added that in Texas they could use Randolf Task the IRS agent there to help her when she was investigating Paul Elsher.

Unknown to Alex, she was on a Chicago mafia watch list at the airport. The new mafia boss learned of her arrival shortly after her landing. He had her followed to see what or who she might be investigating. He saw it as a potential opportunity to settle an old score. She was held accountable for eliminating his predecessor and the one before him. He did not intend on getting eliminated. He instead planned take preemptive action and do the eliminating.

The tail that he had assigned to follow her let him know that she had gone to the IRS building and had stayed there for an hour and then she had gone to the location where she and an IRS agent had entered the building.

He knew the address. He had attended several parties there held by his central Chicago area leader at his long-time girlfriend's luxurious penthouse apartment. He had not only enjoyed the party, but he was taken by the lady that he later learned was part of an insurance scam that was paying for her lifestyle. He figured that she must have gotten herself into the spotlight and was being investigated.

He sent up a sniper to a building that provided a good position from which to take a shot with the order to shoot to kill the detective and anyone with her.

Alex and Trey got out of the car, followed Andy Weller, the IRS leader and one of his partners. Johnnie had been able to determine that Amelia worked from home, so they took the elevator to the penthouse floor and rang the doorbell. They were planning to arrest Amelia, seize her computer and all the paperwork associated with her work.

Amelia came to the door and was going to deny them entry until she was handed the legal paperwork authorizing their entry and the seizure of her records. She was shocked when her linkage to the money that she had in her offshore account was disclosed and she was asked if she had paid taxes on it.

She at first denied having the account but when she was handed a picture of her sitting and signing the paperwork when she established the account, she knew she was caught. She had opened the account more than ten years ago and she wondered how the pictures could have been acquired and asked about it.

Alex smiled and said that she had the ability to time travel and get whatever she needed.

Alex led the way into the apartment and suggested they sit down while the IRS team collected all the records in which they were interested.

While they were sitting and watching the computer systems and records being carried out, Alex asked Amelia how long she had known Dr. Thornfield and Paul Elsher.

Amelia smiled and asked how the connection between them had been made. She was sitting and thinking that she would love to make a call to her mafia beau and ask for help. She was smiling but she would love to shoot all three of the persons sitting with her. She had her own gun but there was no way of getting to it otherwise she might shoot them herself. When she was asked to stand up and then had handcuffs put on, the smile left her face, and she muttered that they would regret treating her in the manner of a common criminal.

Alex nodded and quietly replied that was what a person in her position was labeled but that she was innocent until proven guilty in a court of law.

Amelia listened as she was read her rights. She was then escorted out of her apartment. The ride down the thirty floors was silent.

They were walking toward the black sedan when suddenly Amelia and the agents were knocked down.

Alex was pushed and then something hit her on her left shoulder. Before she could react, she was lifted by Trey who carried her under his right arm and ran into the alleyway between two buildings. He put her down and asked if she was alright.

She smiled and said that except for the rough handling she felt OK. She put her hand on her shoulder and asked if there was any damage to her jacket or if there was any blood.

Trey nodded and said that she was going to need to replace the jacket because there was a long gash across the shoulder. There was no blood. He commented that the sniper had relied on technology that improved accuracy, but the laser beam made the shot visible. He had spotted the laser and had pushed everyone and then hauled her into cover.

A few moments later the area was a sea of flashing red and blue lights.

Amelia was surprised at what had happened, but she was pleased that her friends had taken action. She decided it was time for her to demand a lawyer and to have all communication with the IRS handled by him. She was also going to have him sue the IRS for the pain of her bloody knee that she had gotten when she was pulled down behind the car when the shot had been fired.

Alex identified herself and Trey as agents with the Illinois Lieutenant Governor's office working with the IRS on a major tax evasion case.

Trey pointed out the most likely building from which a sniper might have taken the shot that had hit his partner.

Alex's jacket and Kevlar jacket were put in an evidence bag.

An EMT took a look at her shoulder to verify that she did not have a flesh wound.

She figured that she would not even have a bruise from the glancing hit. She gave Trey a hug and thanked him for his quick action.

He smiled, said that he was suffering from a sprained shoulder and that she would need to lose a few pounds.

She knew that he was joking but she replied that she was a few pounds over her fighting weight otherwise she would challenge him to a fight.

She checked with the IRS folks and got agreement that they had the case. She reiterated that her team would provide the necessary information that would lead them to an airtight tax evasion case. She then let them know that she and her partner were off to the airport on their way to Texas.

As they were getting on the airplane, Trey asked when she was going after the person who had ordered the hit.

Alex shook her head and said that she was not sure, but she was focused on getting to San Antonio so that she could arrest the third person that was part of the trio that was hoodwinking honest dental customers.

On arrival in San Jose, they were met by Randolf Task the regional IRS agent. On the way to Paul Elsher's home Alex updated him on the approach she had taken to eliminate the scam of implanting inferior teeth as quickly as possible.

Randolf said that he liked leading with the tax angle and then following up with a civil case suing the doctor for the damages, suffering, and pain. He made the point that the three that were being arrested would be in prison and they would be easy to find.

Paul heard about the arrest of Amelia from her mafia friend. He had a small fortune of dental implants he wanted to capitalize on. He was in his garage hurriedly closing down his operation and getting all the implants ready to ship out. He figured that in a few days he would fly down to his favorite resort in Jamaica and stay there until he figured where in the world he would permanently settle down.

He heard his doorbell ring and froze. He was not expecting anyone. He opened the side door of his garage and looked out to four people who were standing outside of the front door. He picked up the double barrel shotgun he kept by the door. He stepped out and called out to them to leave his property.

He watched as the tallest of the four at the door stepped forward and held up some paperwork and said that it was a search warrant and that he should put down his shotgun.

He was just pulling back the triggers of the shotgun and lifting the barrel when he looked down at a spot on the white shirt that was turning red. He continued to pull the two triggers back and then a second spot appeared on the left side of his shirt. His finger pulled the shotgun's two triggers simultaneously and the shot gun fired into the ground, lifted him into the air and he flew back into the garage. The world went black.

Alex shook her head and said that he had been stupid, and she had done what she did so that he would not lift the barrel of the double-barreled shotgun up any farther.

Randolf said that he had never seen anyone shoot so fast and accurately. As he walked toward the garage, he used his gun to point to the foot deep hole the shotgun had blasted into the ground. His partner had preceded him and said that Paul was dead. He added, "two to the chest and one between the eyes."

Alex listened as Randolf called in the shooting. He signaled to the team that had arrived by van and told them to gather all the evidence and put it into the van before the local police arrived so they could leave and get home by dinner.

He walked over to where he saw Alex sitting and talking to her partner. He listened as they joked about the fact that she was ahead on the body count of taking out those who made the mistake of choosing to use their weapons versus their minds.

It was clear to him that the two shared a much more dangerous profession than he.

Alex looked up at Randolf and asked for his people to let her know that they were at the right address and that the person she had just shot was Paul Elsher.

He said that they were at the right address and the van that was backing into the driveway was getting ready to load a ton of fake implants into it. They would also take the computers and all paperwork that they found. He added that his team would be gone in less than three minutes, but he and his field partner would stay until the local police cleared all of them to leave. He let them know that he had called, talked with the local chief of police bringing him up to speed on the situation and had been assured that after any required evidence was collected, they would be allowed to leave but the chief wanted their incident reports in by the end of the following day.

Alex nodded and said that she would have it done by the time she ate desert that evening.

Randolph suggested they go to one of his favorite places for dinner where he would recommend something like Texas Quail, grilled sweet potatoes, stuffed mushrooms, apple slaw and pecan pie for desert. He added that they also had some of his favorite wines.

Alex said that she would take his suggestion and their conversation ended as the local police arrived.

She was now thinking about the steps she was planning to take with the remainder of the case.

7 Triangles Don't Always Close

*T*he hours she was keeping exhausted Fionna. Released from the hospital but still recovering, Zia needed help in getting around. Fionna would make sure Zia had a good breakfast, left a lunch to warm up and then prepared dinner when she got home. The hours added up and the fatigue crept in.

Jason was still on the loose and that worried both of them.

She purchased and installed a steel bar that went across the entrance door in hopes that would prevent Jason from breaking in. She still put a chair under the latch. She had also put a bar in the sliding door that went out to the apartment's small corner porch.

She took note that Dr. Thornfield had hired some security guards, and she made sure she arrived to work after they arrived and that she left work before they left. She made it a point of giving them a few pieces of candy each time she met them. Their presence meant that she could at least relax at work.

She had gotten to like Ezra for the fact that he always checked to see how she and Zia were doing. He almost always walked her to her car after work. It was clear to her that he was concerned about the situation.

Jason was working part time at two jobs. He arranged his time so that he could spend time on the roof of the building where he could see the apartment that Fionna and Zia lived. He had also found a place he could park and then walk to where he sat in the bushes and watched the dental office's parking lot. Once he realized that there were armed security guards he stopped sitting in the bushes. He then focused on getting ready to get into the apartment where he planned to kill both of them.

He figured the opportunity to get to both of them had to show itself in the near future. He would be ready and eliminate both of them at the same time. He now had a three-fifty-seven and his slugger baseball bat as the weapons he was planning to use. He planned to use the baseball bat to beat the two to death.

The three-fifty-seven was to shoot any police shooting at him when he made his getaway. He hoped to kill the two and leave the building unseen and then leave the state and go somewhere west.

He was very familiar with the sound of the bat hitting a hard ball. He was looking forward to the sound of the bat hitting Fiona solidly in the head. He imagined it would sound like a dry tree limb being broken when the wind ripped it from the tree. He smiled at the thought.

Fionna knew that Jason would fixate on getting even and would be watching her and Zia until an opportunity to attack them seemed to be to his advantage. She was always on full alert when she got home and had to get up to her apartment.

The one consistent activity that she and Zia had participated in was in their martial arts classes. They were both in the same Aikido and Taekwondo classes. Zia was about four belts above her, but she was making progress up the belt sequence faster than Zia. She was determined to hold her own the next time Jason attacked her. She figured that there would be a next time, and it would be when she least expected it.

The two of them returned from the session where she had just earned her first-degree black belt. They had celebrated with a T-bone steak dinner, a bake potato smothered in butter and sour cream and four grilled asparagus spears each. They toasted with a glass of a lovely Cabernet Sauvignon that had a hint of the flavor of blackcurrants, mixed with a pepper-like lingering after taste.

They sat down on the couch to read, enjoy their wine and chill.

Suddenly the door and door frame seemed to exploded inwards with pieces of it scattering all around the entry and the kitchen. The chair and the iron bar was meant to keep the door from falling in but the battering ram being used blew through it as if none of it was in its path.

They both threw their glass of wine at Jason as he entered swinging a ball bat. Zia went around the left side of the kitchen island. She went straight for Jason. What was left of the door and the door frame all fell into the apartment toward her.

She watched as Jason dropped the battering ram and took hold of his baseball bat. As he started his swing, she stepped in toward him but still felt the bat hit her ribs. She took hold of the bat with one hand and rolled in backward toward him and hit him in the face with an upward swing of her closed left fist. She realized that Zia had jumped on his back and was trying to twist his head. She pried the thumb of his right hand back and he let go of the bat. He had reached up with his left hand and was trying to pull Zia off his back by her hair. He suddenly pulled his right hand back away from her and hit her on the back of her head with his forehead.

His right hand reemerged with a very large handgun. She pushed back toward his chest and grabbed his right wrist with one hand and put her index finger in with his trigger finger. The first shot went almost straight downward along Jason's leg. He pulled his arm upward as he screamed in pain.

She pointed the gun toward the other side of the living room and kept pulling the trigger. The kick back caused the bullets to walk up the far wall until the gun was empty.

She knew that she was slowly succumbing to the pain in her ribs and that she was close to passing out. She gave a scream and hit him in the throat with all her might and then collapsed.

She felt Jason falling and stepped to the side as he went down with Zia still on his back.

She collapsed against the wall and passed out.

When she came to, she watched as Zia used one of their steak knives to cut a hole in Jason's throat and poke a large bubble tea straw into his windpipe.

The firing of the pistol must have been loud enough that one of the neighbors called 911. Just a few moments later the police arrived in mass.

The EMT's check Jason out and complemented Zia for having acted in time to save Jason's life. They stopped the bleeding from his leg wound and then they strapped him to a board and hauled him out. Then they checked her out and said that they thought she had two broken ribs. They carefully strapped her down, put her in the ambulance, and sent her off to the hospital.

She was not sure whether she passed out, but she came awake in the dark of the night wondering where she was, then she saw Zia sleeping in the chair next to the bed. Jason's attack and her and Zia's actions replayed itself. She reached out and took Zia's left hand in hers and went back to sleep.

When she woke up again Zia was gone, and a note said that she had gone into work and would cover for both of them. She knew that they were barely getting by from paycheck to paycheck and neither of them could afford to be out of work.

The library cart came to her room, and she selected a book to read.

Before she could get into it, an attending doctor came in and let her know that she had three broken ribs that had been totally broken from the rib cage and had fallen into her chest cavity. He let her know that it was a small miracle that she was alive.

The ribs were reattached by screws at the backbone end, and the other ends were attached at the sternum by wires to the ribs above and below them. They were now stable, and everything was held in place with a tight wrap that she would have to keep in place for several weeks. He prescribed some pain pills and let her know she should not drive for at least a month after being released from the hospital.

She was just getting ready to open her book when Alex Evercrest, her work partner, and a lawyer walked into her room.

After greetings she asked why Alex had come. She listened as Alex introduced John Williams, a lawyer that she had asked to be the prosecutor to represent both her and Zia in court and to prosecute Jason for premeditated attempted murder.

She, Trey, and John had visited the scene and had been amazed that someone had not died.

She learned that the three of them had already stopped by the apartment and taken pictures of the shattered door, the bullet holes in the far wall, and the rest of the mess that had been created during the fight.

She was surprised that they had also interviewed the neighbor that had called in the 911. She was asked to describe the fight.

Alex listened to the description of the door exploding inward and the fight that ensued. She was impressed with the actions that both Fiona and Zia had taken, especially Fiona's firing of the revolver until it was out of ammo. The bullet exit holes could be seen from the ground and were as large as a grapefruit.

John had pointed out the use of the battering ram and commented that the attack was definitely premeditated. He pointed at the bullet trail on the far wall and wondered just how it had been made. As he listened to the story, he knew that it was going to be a case where he would put the attacker away for at least thirty years and at most likely for life. He was aware that Jason would be questioned by the police once he could talk. He would remain handcuffed to his bed and guarded that entire time.

Jason awoke to find that he had his right wrist handcuffed to the bed. He used his left hand to feel the bandaged that was taped over his nose. He could feel several bandages on his head as well. His leg was elevated and when he removed the sheet over it, he saw that the bandage ran from just above his knee down to his ankle. He remembered the pain when Fiona had pulled the trigger the first time. He had pulled his arm upward and she had kept pulling the trigger. Then she had finished him with a flick of her wrist. He could tell that he was breathing through a tube in his throat. When he looked at his right hand, he could see that he had a broken thumb.

He wondered how he looked.

The nurse who came in held up a mirror and commented that from what she had learned he was lucky to be alive and that the women he had attacked had done a good job on him and then saved his life. She added that she hoped that he was feeling as bad as he looked. She handed him a cup and let him know that he was on a liquid diet and would be given smoothies or soups that he could drink through a straw.

She smiled and wished him a very painful day.

A few moments later several policemen entered and read him his rights and asked him to indicate that he understood what he had been told. They let him know that he was being held for attempted murder. They then turned and left.

He looked at the wall and wondered what was in store for him. He wondered how long he would end up in prison. All he knew was that what he had planned had blown up in his face. He had envisioned looking down at two dead women. He had never envisioned ending up in the hospital in such a battered condition.

At work, Zia had been able to handle the double schedule. She was exhausted and now knew how Fiona had felt a few weeks back.

Luna and Ezra had been great at helping to manage the patients so that she could handle the load. Ezra had prepped the patients and chatted with them until she was free from the person before them. She figured that both she and Fiona should reward his friendship in some way.

She felt the effects of the fight the night before and then sleeping in the hospital chair next to Fiona's bed. She wondered how Fiona's day had been. Fiona had been in surgery for several hours as the doctors reattached her ribs.

She had planned to go to the hospital during lunchtime but had fallen asleep.

She was just getting ready to leave work when a John Williams introduced himself and said that he was on the way back to his office but thought he would stop by to get her version of what happened the night before.

It took her about thirty minutes to share what she remembered had happened. She realized that the entire attack had taken less than four minutes but her telling took three times as long and the attack seemed to have been much longer. It was definitely something that had distracted her for the entire day.

She was relieved to learn that Jason would most likely end up in prison for thirty years and perhaps for life.

Once the interview was over, she decided to go straight to the hospital. She stopped and got two smoothies and two orders of onion rings. She knew these were both Fiona's and her comfort snacks and comfort was what they needed.

It was hard to look ahead, but she felt that once Jason was put away, she and Fiona could safely get on with a life she hoped would be filled with more sunshine than rain.

522

8 The Root of the Matter

*A*lex and Trey were in the Chief's office bringing him up to date with the status of the case. She explained how during the arrest in Chicago a sniper had attempted to kill her, but that Trey had saved her life by pushing her so that the bullet hit her vest and then he had carried her into the alleyway. He had also pushed Amelia Lockwood to safety, and she was suing because she scraped her knee.

The Chief asked if they had determined who had set up the sniper and was that connected with the case.

Alex shook her head and said that she thought the sniper had nothing to do with the case. She figured it was most likely connected with the two previous cases where the mafia heads were killed, and she was blamed for their deaths.

The Chief asked what should be done about the sniper attack.

Alex smiled and said that she planned to chat with the Mafia boss and show him how detrimental killing her would be, but she would wait until the dental case was closed.

The Chief shook his head then asked if he wanted to know what the chat would be about.

Alex said that he probably should stay in the dark about what she would show and tell the mafia head.

The Chief nodded, said he understood and then asked about what happened in San Antonio.

Trey spoke up and said that a two-barrel ten gauge shot gun being raised to shoot had happened. He described the person they were there to arrest coming out of the garage pulling back the two triggers of a double-barreled shot gun, and then starting to raise it. Both he and Alex shouted out twice to put the gun down. When he began to raise it, Alex shot him. Amazingly the blast of the two barrels launched the shooter back into the garage, but he was already dead as he pulled the trigger.

The Chief looked at Alex and asked if there was any other option.

Alex shook her head and said that she was actually a little slow with her reaction because he was able to pull the trigger and the hole blown into the ground was clearly large enough to have killed all four of them.

The fact that they had retrieved close to six hundred inferior quality dental implants and the information of where the implants were made at least verified that they had the right supplier.

She added that he was guilty of participating in the scam and unfortunately had thought he could get away with a deadly threat.

She then said that she was going with Joe, their IRS friend, to arrest Dr. Thronfield right after lunch. She added that the IRS case would close down the operation. She then informed the Chief that she had connected John and Hanna to the victims of his practice, and they would be filing civil cases for injuries. That would potentially mean financial restitution and a ruling of compensation for pain and suffering to the patients. Between the two trials, she figured that the doctor would be out of business and in prison for a long time.

The Chief nodded and asked about the side case that involved the two dental assistants at the same office. After listening to how that was turning out he said that it was amazing that all of that was going on in the same dental office.

Alex smiled, said that she agreed and added that the root of the matter had to do with "love gone wrong, and greed gone strong."

Ezra had participated in three inferior dental implants a day for more than three weeks as he waited for Dr. Thronfield to be arrested. He had talked several times to Ava about the situation, and she had coached him to document the situations but to wait until the doctor was arrested.

Toward the end of his wait, he learned that Fiona was in the hospital after Jason broke into her and Zia's apartment. He was relieved to learn from Zia that Fiona was going to recover and that the two of them had put Jason in intensive care where he was recovering but was under arrest and would be facing premeditated murder charges.

During lunch he went with Zia to visit Fiona in the hospital and took a bouquet of flowers to her. He then helped Zia to handle a double workload so that she would not get fired.

Alex led the way into the dental office. She showed her badge to the receptionist and asked to see Dr. Thronfield.

When Dr. Thronfield came out to talk to them, Joe showed him his IRS credentials and let him know that he was under arrest for tax evasion and read him his Miranda rights.

Ezra had watched as the doctor was arrested.

Luna shook her head and asked what she was going to do about the upcoming dental implants and the regular dental customers.

Ezra said that he would recommend contacting Dr. Ava Whitlock to take over the implant cases and ask her if she knew of a dentist that could handle the general dental care cases.

He talked to Alex and let her know that he had documented all the dental implant cases that Dr. Thronfield had done since he had started doing so at this office. He said that there were several cases where the patient had complications.

Alex thanked him for the information and let him know that a lawyer from the practice of Williams & Waverly would be in contact with him and would be requesting it.

Ezra called Dr. Whitlock and let her know about Dr. Thronfield's arrest. He let her know that he was going to have the receptionist, Luna, call her to arrange coverage for the office's dental patients. He then had Luna call. He listened as Dr. Whitlock agreed to see the implant patients and give them the choice to become her patients. He also listened as Dr. Whitlock gave Luna the name of general dentist to take on the other patients.

He felt a huge weight lift off his shoulders as the reality of not having to keep secret the scam that Dr. Thronfield had been practicing.

Luna was shocked by Dr. Thronfield arrest. She was shocked but not totally surprised. She had gotten the impression that Ezra knew the details about the arrest and asked him about it. As she heard the details, she came to realize that the implant part of the practice had been a scam from the time the office had transitioned to Dr. Thronfield's ownership. She had the details in her records and knew that the IRS was going to want to have all of it. She also realized that the practice was going to take a hit in the cash it would be generating.

She worked with Dr. Whitlock and got her to agree to keep the current staff paid in the short term and to see how the two offices could be managed as one.

She was pleased with Dr. Whitlock's request for a recommendation for a receptionist for a job at her office. She asked about the salary and was surprised that it would be more than she was making. She asked if she could apply for the job and was pleased to know that she could.

Dr. Whitlock was pleased to be picking up a significant number of new dental implant clients. She would offer all of them a free consultation as part of having them move into her practice. She figured that if she also hired Dr. Thronfield's current receptionist the merger of the patients into her current practice would be seamless.

She called a good friend that had graduated a year behind her and asked if she was interested in acquiring a going general dentistry practice. She did not know what the practice would cost to buy but she shared that the current dentist had been arrested for tax evasion, and he would most likely be sued for malpractice. It could be a fire sale.

Dr. Thronfield was in a state of shock as he was taken to the IRS office where he was grilled on the details of all the implants that had he had done. It was clear to him that his goose was cooked.

He had amassed almost one hundred million dollars that he held in two offshore accounts. He thought these accounts would be out of the reach of the IRS.

Somehow, they had the details to the accounts and the exact amount of money that he had in each. They even showed him signing the papers when he set up the accounts. He wondered how they had been able to get those.

Then they showed him a picture of Amelia in handcuffs and of Paul being put into a body bag. He lost it and said he was done talking and he wanted a lawyer to represent him. He needed to figure out the way forward. He asked if he was allowed to leave but was informed that he would be held at least until charged. He would be allowed to call the lawyer of his choice, or he would be assigned a lawyer if he so chose.

He called the office of his long-time lawyer and was referred to one of the partners who specialized in cases dealing with the IRS.

The next day he met with a Lutecia Underway. She asked him if his patients were given a choice in the quality of implants.

He shook his head and let her know that the patients were never aware of what was going on.

She let him know that she would look into the possibility of him being sued by former patients when they were informed about what he had done.

He asked why they would be informed. She explained that he was being taken to court because of tax evasion and the IRS might dig into how he had made so much money. They seemed to be very secure on the case that they had, and she would seek to get the details.

She let him know that he would be going to court the next day to hear the charges against him and then she would have enough information to determine what their next action should be.

He was returned to his cell and issued a change of clothes and led to a shower area where he was told to shower and change into clean clothes.

That evening his wife came to see him. She asked what he was being charged with. He made up a story about there being a misunderstanding and that he would be cleared of any wrongdoing.

He thanked her for bringing in a set of clean clothes for him to wear to court the next day.

She let him know that she would be there, but she was keeping the kids in school and away from the trial. She let him know that he had made the evening news, and the kids knew about his arrest and were wondering what he had done.

The next day he was led to court where his lawyer declared that he was pleading innocent to the charges of tax evasion and money laundering. He was denied bail when the prosecution highlighted that he was a flight risk. He had to give up his passport and would remain in custody during the trial.

After the court session, his lawyer let him know that her office had received a call from a lawyer representing a Dr. Ava Whitlock that was offering to buy his practice.

He thought about it for a moment and figured that selling the practice was most probably a good idea. He would not be able to stay in Cincinnati when the details that would undoubtedly come out during the trial became public. He put the price at two years of practice income as it appeared on the tax record.

Joe called Alex to let her know of the outcome at court and the fact that the detailed information that she had turned over to his team was being followed up on and he would have a very foolproof tax evasion and money laundering case against the doctor that would put him in prison for at least ten years. He said that he felt great about the case, but the good doctor would still have quite a sum of money after paying the taxes and the penalty associated with the delay in paying.

Alex shared the fact that she was working with Hanna Waverly to sue him for the pain and suffering of the patients he defrauded. He would be close to penniless when she got done with him.

Joe chuckled and said that she had made his day and that he would charge ahead with his case. He asked her what she would be doing now that she had closed the case.

Alex replied that she had some unfinished business in Chicago that she had to deal with before she was ready to go on to the next case.

528

9 Jason's Trial

Jason's day in court rolled around. He was still aching from his wounds, his nose was still bandaged, he was now breathing normally but could hardly talk and in general he felt miserable.

Zia and Fiona were sitting just behind the prosecution's table. They were holding hands. They had watched Jason being led in wearing an orange jump suit and then sitting down at the defense table. He still had a bandage over his nose that Fiona had broken and a bandage over one eye that Zia had scratched. He was charged with premeditated attempted murder and faced a minimum of thirty years to life in prison.

Their personal lives had yet to get into a regular routine. Fiona was still trying to get over her broken ribs and to not yet able to carry a full workload at the office. So far by early afternoon the pain in her ribs made it almost impossible for her to continue. She really appreciated the help that Ezra gave her by taking over for her.

The office went into a few days of turmoil when Dr. Thronfield was arrested. The fear was that the office would close, and they would all be jobless.

She became aware that Ezra had been doing more than being a dental assistant. He seemed to be the central person who had all the information of the scam that the doctor had been practicing. He also seemed to have the connection to another dentist who a short time later took over Dr. Thronfield's business. She had come to the office and interviewed all of them and asked them to continue working at what was now her office. She had let them know that she would not be the one who would do the regular dentistry, and that she was bringing in a friend who was a general dentistry practitioner who would eventually own and run the practice.

She let them know that Ezra would be moving to her office since his specialty was on the implant side of the practice which would be handled entirely out of her office.

Zia squeezed her hand as John Williams, leading the prosecution team stated that he planned to show beyond a shadow of doubt that Jason had planned to kill Fiona and had tried twice to break into her apartment to do so. The first time he had been thwarted by the fact that he could not break into the apartment, and he had to run since the police were at that point still providing protection.

But that on the second time he had come prepared with a battering ram. He pointed to the battering ram and said that it was evidence that he was putting in front of them so that they could realize that Jason had planned his attempt at killing both Fiona and her partner Zia.

He then pointed to the small bat that was laying with the handle on the battering ram. He then pointed to Zia and stated that it had been used against her in revenge and had put her in the hospital. Then he pointed at the large bat. He said that it had been used at the same time that the battering ram had been used to break into the apartment when he went in with the intent of killing both of them. He pointed at Fiona and stated that she was still recovering from three broken ribs that had to be pinned and wired back to the rib cage during surgery.

Zia was called to the stand first. She was asked when she had first encountered Jason. She explained the lunch scene where she had knocked Jason down. She was asked about the fact that she was a mere one hundred five pounds, and she had defeated Jason who was twice as large and twice her height. She shared that she was trained in Tae Kwon Do and Akido.

Then she was asked what happened a few days later.

She shared the fact that she had been sleeping on the couch and when she woke up, she was being beaten by something and the next thing she knew she was waking up in the emergency room at the hospital.

She had suffered a concussion and found out later that Jason had broken into the apartment and beaten her with a miniature baseball bat.

John held up the miniature baseball bat and asked her if that was the weapon.

She replied that it was.

He asked her how she could be sure.

She replied that her blood was found on the bat and Jasons fingerprints were also found on the small bat.

She was then asked about the next encounter with Jason.

She replied that happened when she and Fiona were sitting on the couch and reading. The door and door frame imploded inward and the chair that was propped under the door handle broke down. She had jumped on Jason's back while Fiona rushed at him from the front. She added that she could hear Fiona's ribs cracking like wood being broken over one's knee as the bat slammed into Fiona. She was surprised that Fiona was able to step into Jason, deliver a throat punch, and shatter his nose before collapsing. She was still on his back as he collapsed because his Adam's apple had been crushed and he could not breath.

She said that Fiona was laying against the wall when she took a knife and opened up Jason's airpipe and put a large straw into it so he could breath.

Then the place was overrun with police and EMT's.

She was asked what happened next.

She said that the EMT's took Jason out first and complemented her on keeping him alive.

Then they carefully put Fiona on a carrying board so she could not move and took her to the hospital.

She was the only one that got checked over and given a clean bill of health and then she spent several hours as the police took her statement and documented the damage to the apartment.

Fiona was then called to the stand. She was asked why Jason had attacked her the first time. She replied that she had filed for divorce, he had signed the divorce papers but then had wanted to rescind and demanded that she return to him. He slapped her and then Zia knocked him down. He was about to retaliated when a policewoman on a bicycle showed up and sent him on his way.

She was asked when he showed up again and she pointed to the battering ram and said when he came through the door with the battering ram in his hands.

She was then asked what happened next.

She said that she attacked from the front as Zia jumped on his back from the side. The pain from getting hit did not register until she had stepped in, hit him in the throat with her fist and then she had driven upward with the heel of her hand into his nose. After that, her world went blank, and she collapsed. She recovered shortly and watched Zia cut open Jason's throat. At first, she had thought Zia was killing him but then realized that she was providing him a way to breath.

The next thing she remembered was waking up in the recovery room with Zia holding her hand. She was told that she was lucky to be alive because the three ribs had broken loose and were floating on her lungs but had not punctured them or damaged the heart which was just above them. She learned from the doctors that the three ribs were screwed to where they joined the backbone and wired to the good ribs at the other end.

She was asked about the pain and responded that it still hurt her to breath, and she was still required to wear a tight wrap to hold the ribs in place.

Suddenly Jason stood up started to come around the defense table as he shouted that he hoped her ribs would hurt the rest of her life because she had ruined his.

Two policemen pulled him back by the arms and chained both his wrists to the table and his ankles to rings on the floor.

The Judge called for a recess until after lunch.

Alex got a call from John and was informed that the morning session had gone even better than he could have hoped because Jason tried to attack Fiona when she was testifying. They were on a break until after lunch. He was going to deliver is closing arguments and the defense then would have their chance to try and prove Jason's innocence to the charge of premeditated attempted murder.

He said that the jury should be able to reach a quick verdict.

After lunch, the defense said that they would not call any witnesses but that the jury should consider the fact that Jason had never been in trouble with the law and would not benefit from prison time but what he needed was counseling. They should consider finding him guilty of a spontaneous action that deserved some prison time but not as many years as the prosecution was asking.

The judge then called the trial to an end and instructed the jury to go to the deliberation room and determine the guilt or innocence of the accused.

Less than an hour later the jury returned with a guilty on all counts verdict.

Jason put his head down on the table and then began shouting that the two bitches had ruined his life. He tried to pull loose, and he kept shouting that he planned to kill them. He then began pounding his head on the table. He was restrained by two policemen.

The judge said that he was sentencing Jason to sixty years in a maximum-security prison. He would be eligible for parole for good behavior after thirty years.

He then declared the case closed.

10 A Friendly Discussion

*A*lex had spent several weeks thinking about how to handle the Chicago mafia boss who evidently had some sort of vendetta against her. She figured that a surprise visit to his office where she would reveal the extent to which she had the pulse of his business would go a long way to getting him to focus on his illicit business and not on her. She hoped that her ability to have information about his family in Sicily, his cash flow in Chicago and the fact the she could tell him about his offshore accounts would shock him.

She asked Johnnie to use his skills to detail the cash flow of the mafia business in Chicago.

Once he had that detailed, she asked him to located the base of operation in Chicago and find a way to get into the Mafia boss's office without letting anyone in his security group know.

Then she wanted to know all the personal history of him and his family and their financial situation in detail.

Johnnie joked with her that it was going to cost her multiple trays of her cookies for such a huge request.

It didn't take him long to follow the flow of the money. A large amount seemed to go in circles in the Chicago area to pay off his field workers and as bribes to various police officers.

A small percentage went out to Sicily into accounts owned by the Italian mafia dons.

Most of it made its way via several banks to three offshore accounts and then ended up being invested in the stock market where the laundered money made legal income. However, it was income that was not reported, and no taxes were paid on it. Johnnie knew that Alex would want a detailed documentation of those accounts.

Locating the Chicago mafia office was not difficult but figuring out how Alex and Trey could enter and go to Aldo Viscuso, the Mafia Chief's office undetected was much more of a challenge. He worked backwards from Aldo's corner office.

He found a freight elevator that was just thirty feet away from the office. The freight elevator went all the way down into the basement parking area and could be controlled by whomever was riding inside. It could go to the desired floor without stopping.

He then located an emergency fire door that entered the building at street level that was only thirty feet away from the elevator. He spent time researching and then checking out his ability to blind security cameras and open the emergency door without setting off any alarms.

He was then able to access the controls for the lock on Aldo's office door and the emergency call button that was at Aldo's desk.

There were two cameras in Aldo's office on each side of the room that panned the entire room.

Johnnie and the rest of the team spend almost a whole day watching what went on. They noted that Aldo spent much of his time on the phone with his various lieutenants checking on the field work of enforcement and collection. He also spent time with several financial managers checking on the money flow and the standing of the money collection from various businesses.

They all agreed that Aldo spent too much time sitting and conducting what seemed to be a relatively boring type of work.

Alex commented that if she met Aldo at a party, his white beard, swept back white hair and his bifocal gold rimmed glasses made him look like one of her college professors. She would take him to be a friendly, amiable person with whom she could spend hours talking philosophy. He did not have the dark, sun-tanned look of what she envisioned an Italian mafioso would have. She added that he certainly did not have the vindictive appearance she had envisioned based on her recent experience.

Johnnie then suggested that they walk through how she and Trey would go to Chicago, he was not sure how they could disappear when they left the airport and then approach the mafia offices.

Johnnie walked them up to the emergency door and then timed their actions from the moment they opened the door and walked to the freight elevators, rode it up to the top floor, walked to Aldo's empty office and took up their position.

He said that he would put visual do loops in the security cameras so that they could sit and relax until Aldo returned to his office. Then they would each stand in the two alcoves that had Greek statues in them. Aldo's security should give him an OK and he would enter and sit down.

Then Alex and Trey would both make their appearance. Aldo would most likely reach into his desk for his weapon, which would not be there but in Alex's hand.

She was to walk forward and offer it to him and explain that she was there to show him some magic. She would ask him to access his bank accounts and see if they had the right amounts in them. She then would show him a current account with zero dollars after she had done her magic. The first showing would be the current amount, and the second showing would be the accounts with zero dollars in them.

She would then ask him to look at his computer screen and she would show him pictures of all his relatives and bosses in Sicily and let him know that she had the ability to zero their bank accounts as well.

She would let him know that she had a life AP that monitored her heartbeat and if it stopped, all the bank accounts that he used and those of everyone he knew would go to zero dollars.

Johnnie pointed out that they would need to get the two guards that stood outside of the office to somehow be distracted so that a getaway could be executed.

Trevor suggested that the two guards be called into the office and be disarmed, Alex and Trey would then leave and lock the door so that no one could get out and the alarm to call for help would be kept disabled until Alex and Trey left the building and drove away.

They went through the entire scenario several times and fine-tuned each of the steps.

Alex called Harold Zimmerman of the Chicago area DEA and asked him if he would help her, and Trey leave the Airport unseen.

He laughed and asked if she would tell him why she wanted to leave unseen.

She gave him a quick explanation that caused him to readily agree if afterwards they could have a drink together so she could share the meeting with the Mafia chief with him.

She knew that he would take her to his aunts restaurant where they had done something similar before. She asked him if he was acquainted with Andy Weller, the regional IRS leader, and if so, she asked him to invite him to the luncheon because she would have a gift for him.

Harold said that they had done some business together and he would make sure that he would come to lunch with them.

He then let her know that he would meet her at the planes exit door and they would leave by the stairs that led to the ground.

Alex gave him the flight and the alias names she and Trey would be using to make the flight.

They left the next day on an early morning flight. Alex let Trey know that Johnnie had done a detailed search of the offshore bank accounts that she was planning to give to Andy Weller so he could arrest Aldo Viscuso on money laundering and tax evasion.

Trey laughed and said that he now understood why she was going to promise not to bother Aldo again if he would promise to stop trying to kill her. He would be in jail for money laundering.

Alex nodded and replied that he was not going to go Scot free after assigning a sniper to kill her.

Harold met them at the planes exit door and took them down to a black limousine and drove off. He introduced Tom, the driver who both of them had met before and said that they would drop them off outside of the mafia offices at the emergency entrance and then return to pick them up when Johnnie let them know that they were on the way down.

Both Alex and Trey had on earphones and were listening to Johnnie.

Johnnie let them know that the entire team including the Chief were sitting in the huddle room following along.

They entered the building and walked over to the freight elevator and the door opened. After pressing six, both of them stood facing the elevator door hoping that the rest of the trip up would go undetected.

Johnnie suddenly commented that he was watching two guards just outside of the freight elevator walking the hallway in what appeared to be a security check. He said he would open the elevator doors as soon as they left the floor.

A few moments later the door opened, and they walked over to Aldo's office and entered. Alex went first to Aldo's desk, opened the right desk drawer, and took out a really powerful handgun that had three hundred grain bullets. She took it out and put in her pocket. She commented that she had fired a gun just like that at the firing range and it had a similar impact as a forty-five. The range master had commented that it was likely the most powerful handgun on the market. She checked the other desk drawers for any additional weapons but found none.

They each took one of the comfortable well cushioned, black leather covered chairs and waited.

The wait was a little nerve wracking, but they were counting on Johnnie's ability to monitor the movement outside of the office and give them an early warning.

A few moments later, Johnnie let them know that it was time to get into the alcoves and out of sight.

The door opened and two bodyguards entered, looked around and declared that all was clear.

Aldo entered, thanked them, and told them to go to the break area and relax because he was planning to spend the rest of the day making calls and checking on how the operation was running.

Alex smiled as she realized that Aldo had solved the one stumbling blocks of the operation by letting his guards go to the break area.

She heard Johnnie telling her that the break area was on the first floor.

He then said that it was time for her to do her part.

She stepped out form the alcove and said that it was really great to finally meet the person who had tried to have her killed. She watched as Aldo reached into his desk.

She took out his weapon and asked if he were looking for it and pushed it across the desk at him.

He looked at it and shook his head. Then asked her how she had been able to enter and remain undetected.

She said that she had a magician that worked magic for her.

She then said that she wanted to show him some of the magic that she could work that might convince him to stop trying to kill her. She then took him through the process of having the money in his bank accounts disappear and reappear. She asked him to call the bank of his choice and go online with them to check the amount of money in an account of his choice.

Aldo did as requested and was talking with them when the amount went suddenly to zero and as Alex said, "put it back" it went back to its original amount. He looked at her and asked how she could do that.

She smiled and reminded him that she had a magician working for her.

She then let him know about her heart Ap that monitored the beat of her heart and if it were to stop all of his accounts would go to zero. She then asked him to look at his screen and said that she was going to talk to him about his family, both families. His biological ones and his business ones. She commented that she knew where they all lived, where they banked and how much money each of them had in their accounts. They too would find their accounts zeroed out if her heart Ap stopped.

She added that she had friends on both sides of the law that wielded as much power as he. They were all willing to come to her aid when necessary.

She leaned in toward him and said that if he promised never to have someone try to kill her, she would promised to leave him and all his family and friends alone. She stepped back and asked him if he could make that promise.

He asked her why she was willing to make such a deal.

She looked at him and replied that she did not wish to kill another mafia head and get into a lifelong fight with his bosses in Italy.

He smiled and said that made perfect sense to him. He said that if she managed to get out of the building alive, he would make that promise.

Alex nodded and thanked him and then walked out of the office. She dropped all the bullets from Aldo's pistol on the carpeted floor as she walked to the elevator.

Johnnie let her know that he was going to keep everything in lock down until the end of Aldo's workday or when his guards returned from the break area. He added the entire team had a cheer they wanted to give her, and he put them all on loud as they shout out, "Great Job."

She and Trey made it back down to the emergency exit and got into the car awaiting them.

They were both looking forward to a great and relaxing lunch.

11 And Then there was Jail

Harold led the way into his aunts restaurant and then went to the back private room. He pointed at the head of the table and said that was where Alex should sit.

He asked Trey to take a seat to her right.

He said that lunch was going to be a surprise.

Harold's team members all entered and sat around the table.

A few moments later Alex watched as Jane Stradford entered and sat at the other end of the table.

Andy Weller came in next and sat to her right side.

A few moments later, to her surprise, Chief Johnson, Bill, Trevor, and Johnnie all entered and sat along the sides of the table.

The final two people to enter the room were her mother and father.

She smiled as she realized that someone had arranged the lunch and that she was about to get roasted. She wondered how they had all been able to get to lunch to make it happen.

Harold said that they were all there to celebrate one of the most daring detectives that any of them had ever met.

Jane stood up and said that she had learned about Alex's mafia escapade from Chief Johnson and they both agreed that going into a mafia's boss headquarters without an army was as close to suicide as one could possibly get. And doing so and getting out alive was just short of a miracle. However, since they were all there to celebrate the accomplishment, it now looked like the work of a genius.

Alex gave a little laugh and replied that they were forgetting the fact that she had a magician that made it all seem simple, and they should be lauding him because he was the one that had made it possible. She was just the puppet whose strings he expertly helped to pull.

Trey nodded and said that without Johnnie's expertise neither of them would have dared to do what they had done. He went on to praise the work that Johnnie had done in identifying the three participants in the dental implant case and how he had helped track each of them down. He then highlighted how Johnnie had even had a finger in solving the love triangle case that had gone on in the dental office. Trey commented that Johnnie was truly a magician.

Alex walked over to where Johnnie was sitting and handed him the thumb drive. She said that she thought he should be the one that presented the airtight case of money laundering and tax evasion by a local mafia boss to the IRS.

She smiled and said that she had to keep her promise to that mafia boss of not taking any action against him but that did not mean that the IRS couldn't put him away for the next thirty years.

Lunch was served, toasts were made, and they were all chatting and enjoying the celebration when Johnnie said that he had arranged for John and Hanna to share the progress of the trials that were both in progress and Joe would share what the IRS was doing in the case against the dentist. He connect to a large video screen and Hanna said hello.

Hanna reported that James, who had attacked both Zia and Fiona, had received the maximum number of years in prison and would only be eligible for parole after forty years in prison with good conduct. She reported that he was led out of court screaming that he would get even, which indicated that his good behavior was starting out on the wrong foot.

John reported that Dr. Thronfield tried to make the point that there was nothing wrong with using alternative implants and that there was no law against it. When asked if he had informed his patients of the fact that he was using black market implants, he had replied that he did not need to do so. Six of his patients had testified that they had suffered from the inferior implants and had them removed by other dentists at own their personal cost and wanted restitution.

He shared that the jury had only taken an hour to return with a guilty verdict. The judge imposed a sentence of fifteen years and a financial penalty of three hundred thousand dollars.

Joe then came on and said that he was bringing charges of money laundering and not paying taxes against Dr. Thronfield that would most likely add another thirty years to his sentence.

He was also aware that a class action lawsuit had been filed against the doctor for thirty million dollars by all of the previous implant patients. He figured that by the time the government collected the delinquent taxes, and the implant patients collected their money the doctor would be broke. He said that he would have felt bad for the doctor's wife and children, but he learned that she was independently wealthy and would not suffer from the doctor's sins.

The Chief stood up, raised his glass, and said that all seemed to be ending on a high note on the right side of the law and on a low note on the other side of the law and that was all for which he could hope.

Jane gave an alternate toast saying that she only had star special investigators in her organization that always delivered superior results.

The Chief shook his head and reminded her that Alex was on his payroll full time and not hers.

They both clinked their glasses and sat down.

Rose-Anne stood up and said that she was told never to apologize for having gotten her daughter involved in an investigation of the Mafia and she had never done so.

However, every time Alex came home, she worried about her daughter and her daughter's work partner. Every time whether for vacation or for work, her daughter was either getting shot or shooting someone. This was the first time she had been home where she had done no shooting.

Russel stood up and said that he had built a special metal clad door that had served its purpose when the mafia had sent in two hit men to kill the family but who instead were killed by his daughter and her partner. Another time he had watched her have a dual with a mad racist where she got shot but still continued to pursue him. The racist only got away for a short duration until in another confrontation he met his fate at her hands. He smiled and said that his gentle lifelong fishing partner had matured into a gentle but deadly Cincinnati detective that always got her attacker.

Just as he finished, Matt walked into the room and asked if he was too late to have lunch.

Alex jumped up and ran to him, said that she was happy to see him and gave him a kiss. She asked if he had planned to stay and do some fishing.

He pointed to the door as Lindsey and Nolan walked in and said that he certainly had, and he figured that Trey would also enjoy a few days with a pole in his hands and helping Nolan with his pole.

Alex looked over at her father and asked him to arrange to take everyone out on the Golden Goose for another fishing trip to their favorite spot on the lake.

The End of the Magic Touch

The Nine Towers of Ku

1 The Nine Towers

*T*he pine forest seemed to surround the valley's splendorous red, yellow, and lavender wildflowers and encapsulate the nine towered castle like, tan brick mansion that was at the center. The mansion sat on a thousand-acre plot. The driveway to the house ran for close to a mile from a small local highway. The isolation of the place was why Liam had purchased the property. It was exactly what he needed to do the style of recruiting that he had in mind. He knew that this place would allow him to operate freely and effectively.

He had been given a free hand at how he carried out his assignment and did not have to report his actions to Laticia, his sympathetic, softhearted boss. Soft hearted except when it came to following the rules and the adherence to lawful protocol. She was too by the book for him so he kept her in the dark as much as he could.

Liam did not have any of that sensitivity. He was a patriot did what he needed to do to get things done. He did what he thought was good for the country.

He sat on the stone precipice and took in the nine towers where he had chained eighteen drug distributors. It had taken him close to a year to carry out the task of getting the top distributors from nine major cities, so some of his guests had been chained in the house for a year. He wished he could have moved faster but he had kept them well fed and encouraged them to exercise.

His goal was to either enroll them in the elimination of key international agents or to eliminate them and find the dealers from their regions that would. The choice was to work for him or die. He had abducted his victims first on the west coast, then the east coast and finally down the middle of the country.

He had seventeen young males of various heritage, color, social standing, and he had one very good looking but very obstinate young lady that he was going to enjoy whether she agreed to his demands or not. He smiled as he thought of her as the icing on the cake.

He had an additional top drug dealer from each coast and from St. Louis chained in the downstairs part of the house. They enjoyed the comfort of the main downstairs bedrooms that were located around the base of eight of the towers.

This day, he had packed a picnic lunch and had hiked to where he was sitting so that he could contemplate the action that he would be taking over the next few days. The seclusion of the house had given him the luxury of not having to hurry but now it was time to take action in a methodical and swift manner.

He knew that he would enjoy the action and did not care how his recruits chose their fate. They were probably not aware of the price of saying no but that was what made it so exhilarating for him. He knew and that knowledge seemed to glow in his mind and excite his entire body.

One choice gave him a recruit that he had bent to serve him. That choice was less appealing to him than a rebellious no, but it was the choice he needed to carry out his mission.

The other choice gave him the same enjoyable taste equivalent to a box of top-quality Danish chocolates melting in his mouth, when he pulled the trigger of his forty-five and blew their faces off as the bullet put into the back of their skull exited in the middle of their face taking the soft jelly of their brains with it. It so excited him that he often had to suppress ejaculation.

Even sex was less exciting than pulling the trigger and enjoying the pattern made on the floor or the far wall. He always stood for a few minutes to take in the splendor of the red and white splatter.

The field of wildflowers surrounding the mansion seemed to augment the colors that were floating in his mind as he contemplated the coming few days and played various scenes in his head.

He knew that he would have a fair number of defiant noes and that often the second person having seen the result of a no would readily say yes.

Each day he would take the yeses and put them on flights back to their home towns with the first set of instructions that they were to carry out. He figured it would take him three days to empty the nine towers.

He contemplated all yesses from the top distribution leaders. They most likely would hear the gunshots that followed the noes, and they were in their positions because they knew how to negotiate, were more interested in living and to have a chance to money, they would make than in being defiant.

Once his recruiting was done it would take him a day to clean the place and get it ready for the next cycle of recruits. The recruitment would end when he had a sufficient number of distributors following his orders. Once they were all in place, he would focus their distribution to get the drugs flowing to the foreign agents he would target.

The drugs would be both legitimate and illegitimate. He had doctors on his payroll that would provide him the legitimate drugs, and he would have his recruits deliver those drugs but with the desired modification that would make them deadly.

He planned to carry out the elimination of the foreign agents in a swift and deadly manner.

He finished his lunch and went back to the house.

He entered via the back door that led into a grand kitchen that featured a hooded six burner gas stove at the center. A massive refrigerator with a black exterior that matched the black marble that embraced the gas stove stood directly behind it. Stainless-Steel clad pots and pans of every design hung on the left side of the stove and a large set of nonstick utensils hung along the other side.

A set of twelve premier knives rested in their oak wood holder to the right of the stove. It was definitely a kitchen that had been designed for a chef.

He walked around the island to the refrigerator and helped himself to a beer. He gave a laugh as he thought about the fact that he had a huge supply of hot dogs and eggs but not much else. He fed boiled eggs and hot dogs to his captives. He also threw in an orange and apple per day for each of them. They did not go hungry, but they did not get meals prepared by a chef.

He grilled steaks, baked potatoes, and made salads for himself and his three most important recruits. He intended to gain their support both through coercion and also by feeding them well. He wanted them to understand that he was not trying to muscle them into submission. They would have the same choice to make as those chained in the rooms above them, but he did not expect to shoot any of them. He expected them to be smart enough not to say no.

He put the water on for the hot dogs, took out the buns and condiments that were designated to the eighteen upstairs guests and added an apple for each.

The upstairs always got served first. That way he could focus on doing a good job with the four downstairs meals.

For his three downstairs guests and himself, he had the steaks marinating. He would dry fry them and then melt blue cheese over them. He had mashed potatoes to go with them as well as a large helping of asparagus spears. He would also provide each of them with a glass of beer.

He ate by himself. He did not want to have any social connection with any of them.

The next morning, he distributed the boiled eggs and an orange to the upstairs guests.

He prepared two over easy eggs and a large sausage patty for the downstairs breakfast.

This was the day that he would ask the crucial question to each of those that he held captive. He smiled as he thought about the fact that he was going to go by a FIFO order for all the people he had been holding in his human inventory.

He went upstairs and removed the breakfast dishes from each of the tower rooms. Then he returned to the first room where he was holding Orson Ambrose and Sebastian Cassidy who were his Seattle captives. He addressed them by their full names and told them it was time for them to choose to serve him or not. He had them kneel and stood behind them.

He pulled out his forty-five and asked Orson whether he was willing to do as he would be instructed to do.

Orson told him he was a bastard and should go to hell.

Liam smiled and pulled the trigger and watched the mix of blood, brains, and hair spray across the room. He stood for a long time enjoying the sight. He knew what the answer he would get from Sebastian and wanted to enjoy the answer he had received from Orson.

He stepped behind Sebastian and asked the same question.

Sebastian shook his head up and down indicating that he would do as told.

Liam pushed a mop and bucket in front of him and told him to clean up the mess his partner had made. He then pointed to a body bag that he carried into the room and told him to put his buddy into it and to clean the room. He let him know that he would be released and get to go home that afternoon.

His next two captives were the two from L.A., Elisa Amos, and Mateo Garcia. He went through the same routine. He was surprised that Elisa and Mateo both agreed to follow his orders. He had expected Elisa to say no to his request and had been prepared to take her to the bedroom before shooting her. Instead, he felt somewhat relieved that she had said yes. He had come to like her. She had a survivor attitude. He figured she would do well when she got back to L.A.

He informed the two of them that they would be returning to LA that afternoon.

His San Diego two, Thiago Bandello and Osvaldo Comonte ended up being a repeat of the first two. He shot Thiago and after enjoying the moment, gave Osvaldo the job of cleaning up and putting his buddy in a body bag.

He went to the next set of rooms that held the six that he had abducted along the east coast. Riggs Melville made the mistake of saying no. His buddy, Rowan, was eager to say yes.

The two from New York were both agreeable to doing as they were told.

It turned out that the Miami two followed the no-yes pattern and Dante Cruz ended up in the body bag.

He then went from the two in New Orleans, the two in St. Louis and the two in Chicago and got all yeses. He wondered if the shots from his forty-five had been heard by all those saying yes. He decided in the future to use a silencer so that he could get an honest answer to his question.

He then went downstairs and had the three leaders kneel in front of him. He asked the L.A. leader whether he would work with him to take out some bad international spies. He got the agreement that he had expected.

He let him know that he would be driven to the airport with four young drug runners. Two of whom were from L.A., one from Seattle and one from San Diego. He suggested that they all chat and agree to work together. They would all have first class tickets to L.A.

He did the same with the Miami leader and let him know that he would be flying out with four of the young drug runners.

He asked Mylo for his answer and then let him know that he would be leaving the grounds with six young distributors who seemed eager to be back in the field.

Unknown to Liam, a trespasser hunting rabbits and squirrels had been sitting almost in the same spot where he had lunch the day before. This hunter had heard the shots and had called in the shootings. The hunter was asked if he was sure about the shooting and that he should come to the station to put in a formal report. The hunter thought about it and decided that he might get sued for trespassing and decided to go back to his car and go home.

548

<u>*2 The Occupants*</u>

*O*rson could not remember a time in his life that he was not mad. His father had beaten him regularly for the smallest of excuses. His mother was a junky who was seldom coherent. He was often left on his own to feed himself whatever he could prepare. He ate lots of canned soups, peanut butter and jelly and salami sandwiches. He ran away from home at the age of twelve and never looked back.

He found home at a soup kitchen that let him work for some food and sleep in one of their cots that was available for the homeless. Then the soup kitchen closed, he was out on the street making his way as best he could. Dumpster diving was his main source of food.

He watched the drug pushers distributing and periodically getting into gun fights amongst themselves. Then one day the gunfight was all around him and one of the pushers died in his arms. Before dying he learned where his supplier could be found, he was also handed a roll of money to give to that supplier. It was more money than he had ever had.

It lasted him almost six months.

Then he went looking for the drug supplier. It wasn't hard to find him, but it was hard to convince him that he could be a good distributor and trusted to bring the cash back to him. He was given a high school as his distribution territory and was soon bringing in more money than had ever been produced there. He was rewarded by being assigned the local university where he had the same success. His final step up was to the central downtown area where he was just getting started when he was snatched off the street and put in the back of a panel truck into a cage.

His captor was a large dark-haired, bearded guy with piercing black eyes who simply said that he was going to be given the opportunity of a lifetime.

The real outcome was that he spent almost a year chained in a room with another Seattle drug distributor.

Sebastian had first met Orson in the Seattle city center where they were both distributing their drugs. They had territories adjacent to each other and agreed to cooperate and help each other. It turned out they had similar family experiences, so they related well to each other. To have ended up in the same cage in the back of a panel truck had been a surprise to both of them.

Orson was the angriest about having been kidnapped. Sebastian was upset but figured it did no good to get angry he wanted to get even. He wondered why and wondered what the reason might be for the kidnapping.

It had been almost a year and the only thing that he had gleaned during that time was that their kidnapper wanted he and Orson to become subservient to him. He knew that there were at least four more captives. Two he had learned were from the L.A. area and two were from San Diego. Elisa was the only female in the group, and she was a person that he would never want to have mad at him. And she was really mad at her abductor.

Elisa was not mad she was furious and was determined to take revenge on the person who had thrown her into a cage like an animal and then had kept her chained for close to a year.

It was enough time that she had figured out how she would eventually repay her abductor. His size and capability would not prevent her from getting even. If he ever let her loose, she would wait until the moment he let his guard down. Then she would take him down and she would put him through much worse treatment that he was putting her through. She was no stranger to killing. She had buried both of her parents to repay them for their years of abuse. She had almost a year to examine various scenarios for her pay back and she kept adding tortures that she would inflict on him. If she managed to get him in her clutches, he would end his life blind, tongueless, earless and have no gentiles and he would be screaming as he died. Her pastime was visualizing each of the barbarous things she would do.

Mateo knew Elisa well and he knew not to get her mad. He had many a beer with her. He had been present when she was fondled by a drunk as they sat at the bar. She had gone into action and had hit the guy in the throat and then when he fell to the floor, she had kicked him in the side of his head and stomped on his face. The EMT's had put him on a board and taken him to a local hospital where he remained for more than a month.

Elisa had ignored the entire process and had returned to nursing her beer as if nothing had happened.

He was surprised to find the two of them in the same cage in the back of a truck. Later and for almost a year, they had shared the same common area where they were chained by their ankles to two rings in the floor. He had listened to her describe all the things she planned to do to their capture.

She had also warned him to agree to whatever conditions that they were given for their release. She said that saying no might be what got them killed.

Thiago had been walking along the broad walk enjoying the setting sun before going to distribute his wares when he felt a gun on his back and was told to walk into the parking lot where he was put into a cage in the back of a panel truck. He was surprised to see four other people in two other cages before the back doors were closed and everything went pitch black. He asked if he should start yelling. He heard a feminine voice advise him to keep quiet. He felt the truck moving and short time later it stopped. Not long after the back door opened, and a second person was put into the cage with him.

Osvaldo had been approached, shown a gun by the person standing in front of him and told that he should do as he was told or get shot. He figured he was being robbed and offered to give up the money he had. He had been told to keep it but to do as he was told. He had walked as directed to the back of a panel truck and had gotten in. He was put into a cage with a person who looked to be Mexican or from some Latin American area. He got in and said hi.

The doors were closed, and all was black and then the truck drove off. Several hours later the truck stopped, and the back doors were opened. Their abductor entered and introduced himself as a member of the CIA and let them know that they were being recruited and their cooperation would be the ticket for their release.

He then escorted them into the rest area bathroom and said that the next stop would be several hours away. He let them know that if they gave him any trouble, they would be left at the rest stop as a body for the police to find later. The ride lasted for two days and then they were taken into a house where they were separated two to a room and chained to rings that were in a central area between the two bedrooms. The central area was about ten by ten and had a table and two chairs.

A day after they had been chained, their capture came in with a cooler and said that it was a week's worth of food.

Osvaldo tried to figure out if he could get the chain off his ankle but realized that the clasp was held in place with a rod that had no key.

Riggs had just finished a bowl of fake lobster tail and spaghetti when a dark-haired guy sat down next to him and suggested that he accompany him out to the parking lot. He figured he was being robbed and wondered if he should try for his gun. But that idea was short lived, and he felt a gun pressed to his back and his thirty-eight lifted from the back of his pants. He was led to the back of a panel truck and told to get in. He took in the two other cages and figured that he was part of some drug distributor pick up scheme.

Not long after, the door opened again and a second person who he recognized as another distributor that he did not know personally but who had had seen on the street. He was put into the cage with him. He learned his name was Rowan.

Then there was a several-hour drive which had him wondering where they were going. A short time after the truck came to a stop, he found out from the person to be put into the next cage, Ezekiel, that they were in New York City. An eastern looking fellow was the next person put into the van. He introduced himself as Boaz and asked if anyone knew what was going on.

The drive that followed took them all the way down to Miami. It was a logistical nightmare of periodic stops at rest areas and eating take out from fast food restaurants. In Miami, the third cage was filled with a Dante Cruz and a Kenji Mochizuki. On the long drive that followed, the two of them shared the fact that they made most of their money during the spring break. They distributed so many drugs of every variety that the rest of the year seemed like vacation.

None of them had any clue where they were going but they all figured it had to be north. They talked and realized they were all drug distributors. All they had been told was that if they cooperated, they would live to do their country a big favor. The implied threat of saying no was very plain.

Dante and Kenji were the last to be taken from the panel truck and led into the house. Dante counted nine circular towers as he looked up at the house. He wondered who would build such a monstrosity. As he was being chained to the ring in the floor, he realized that he and Kenji would be sharing one of the towers. He wondered where in the country they were located.

The next day their kidnapper brought in a cooler and they were instructed to make the food last for the next week.

He listened to Kenji comment that his room had a bathroom and a shower. He made the point that it was a better place than the dive he had been living in, in Miami. He had to admit that he too had been living in a dive.

Ambrose was doing a booming business even though there was no parade currently underway in New Orleans. A large number of tourists were doing a crawl from bar to bar, and he was able to intercept them and almost do a continuous sell of his various drugs. He figured he was having one of his better evenings. Then a tall guy in a devil's mask stopped him and told him to walk with him. He was about to tell him where to go until he felt the gun poke him in the side. He was guided to a white panel truck and then put into a cage.

Not long after the back of the truck opened, and another person was put into the cage with him. For the few moments that there was light, he recognized his new cell partner was of Cajun origin.

In the dark, he introduced himself and learned that his new partner was Enzo Beaufoy. He asked who the guy in the devil's masked was.

Ambrose said he had no clue, but he had interrupted one of his better distribution nights.

Enzo agreed and said that he was losing lots of sales.

The ride lasted for a long time and when he was given a bag with a burger and fries, he was able to learn from the ad on the bag that they had arrived in St. Louis.

He learned that the two put into the next cage were Zyair Smith and Lev Gataki. Zyair was black and a native of East St. Louis and Lev said he was from Russia.

It was another long ride with two meal breaks and bathroom stops at rest areas. Ambrose kept the conversation going as they rode along and said that he thought they were going north.

His direction was verified by the address on one of the ads on their fast-food meal bags. It was collaborated when the next two persons were put into the third cell.

Braylon Corbyn said he was from the Chicago area where he had grown up. Mykel Holmes said his family was from England, but he had grown up on the south side.

It was a long ride but shorter than the day before until the truck stopped and Ambrose and Enzo were escorted into a place that looked like some sort of medieval castle. They were led up long stairs up to a room where they had ankle chains put on and were told that they would be there for a few days before they would need to make a very important decision. Ambrose figured the important decision would have only one correct answer. He was worried about the answer Enzo, who seemed to be offended by being kidnapped, might give.

554

3 Main Room Guests

*L*iam was relieved to have gathered the street dealers and have them in their chains. He was now faced with the last step of his recruiting plan. It was going to happen in rapid fashion, and he hoped it would be as clean as the previous effort had been. He anticipated that it could be more dangerous. It was not going to be as simple as walking up to them and putting a gun to their ribs. His next recruits were at the top of their organizations and were usually surrounded by bodyguards. He planned to follow his west coast, east coast, and middle of the country abduction pattern. He had picked up two of the lesser distributors in Chicago, but he was choosing to pick his middle of the country leader in St. Louis. He had no desire to directly engage the Chicago mafia. He needed street presence in Chicago but did not need to get involved with one of the more powerful drug organizations.

He reviewed his L.A. abduction plan. He knew the name and had studied Jack Ahearn, the person that was currently one of the top drug dealers in the city. He had one habit that was critical for the abduction and that was his every Thursday walk along the beach front boardwalk. He was dropped off at one end and had one guard stay there and he had another guard drive to a street that came to the beach at the other end of the walk and take up a position there.

Jack then would causally walk leisurely along the boardwalk with a cup of coffee in hand.

Liam parked the panel truck that he had rented at the very end of the parking lot near to where the second guard was waiting. There was about one hundred feet of beach that he would need to cross to get to the street where the second bodyguard parked his car.

He got out and opened the back of the van and walked out to the front and leaned casually against the front grill. The warmth from the radiator on his back gave him the feeling of being embraced. He looked down along the walk where he could see a rather old man sitting on a blanket in the shade of a palm tree. He could just make out a series of T shirt shops and a café.

There were numerous people bicycling along to the end and then most would turn around and go back the way they had come. He hoped that when Jack got to the end and got ready to make the walk back that there would be no bicyclists.

He was not sure why the walk was such an attraction, but he was glad that it was because it provided the least risky way to snatch this L.A. distributor. The key would be to hit the guard in the neck with his dart gun just as Jack turned to go back.

As Jack approached, Liam walked to the end of the walk. He shot the dart and watched as the bodyguard that was sitting on a vine covered wall of a condo fell back into the vine covered ground and disappeared. He almost burst out laughing when he saw what had happened, but he moved quickly to intercept Jack and then guide him to the van.

He was pleased that it was impossible to see the guard at the other end. He hoped that there would be a long delay until the drugged guard managed to get out of the bushes. He figured if that was the time frame, he and Jack would be sitting in their first-class seats on a flight back to Cincinnati.

He explained the situation to Jack and suggested that he cooperate, and he let him know that within a few day he would be back in L.A. unharmed.

Once back in the house, he got everything settled with Jack who did object to being chained and said that what he was being asked to do would be very financially attractive.

Liam pointed out that he was chained but he should relax and enjoy his accommodation that was first class, and he should consider it a couple-day vacation. It would be a chance for him let all concerns about the business evaporate.

He was then off to Miami where he hoped he would have as quiet of a kidnapping. He was informed that the drug leader, Mylo left his yacht every afternoon and walked to a bay side flower shop where he bought flowers for his wife and then returned to the yacht. Then he and two bodyguards walked to where his limo was parked and drove home.

Liam parked his rental van across a green lawn in an outer parking lot located on the land side entrance to the shopping area. He then walked over to where he waited near the flower shop. He watched as Mylo approached unescorted. He stepped a little behind and to his left and suggested that the two of them walk past the flower shop and continue across the lawn to the black van. He was pleased that Mylo took it all in stride. He asked if Liam knew who he was kidnapping.

Liam assured him that there was no mistake and that if he cooperated, he would be back in a couple of days.

It was a direct flight to Cincinnati that took a couple of hours. By dinner time Mylo was seated and talking to Jack as they each cut into their steaming roasted prime rib with mashed potatoes and roasted vegetables and compared notes as to their abduction. Liam offered them a glass of a private reserve Cabernet Sauvignon that they both accepted.

He figured he would have enjoyed sitting down with them, but he had to feed the eighteen chained folks upstairs and then get ready for his flight the next day to St. Louis. Getting ready meant laying out enough food for everyone for the next few days. He was at the point that he was eager to get this part of his setup over with. It was too much work to feed this many people.

He flew to St. Louis and once there drove his tan van to the neighborhood where the top distributor lived. This was going to be a kidnapping that was to take place on the driveway leading up to Harper Bardin's residence. Harper had the habit of being dropped off at the end of his driveway and then walking the thousand or so feet up the hill to the front door of his house. Harper had a beautiful wife and two daughters. He had guards at the house but none of them were out on the grounds.

Liam had found the blind spot of the security camera system and had positioned himself in the bushes along the driveway. He watched as Harper was dropped off and the car drove off. He waited until Harper walked up to where he was parallel to him and then quietly asked him to step his way peacefully or die on the driveway.

Harper looked at him and asked if he was ready to die himself because he was making a big mistake.

Liam nodded and asked him to refrain from making threats and to step into the bushes with him. He disarmed Harper and then led the way to the point in the fence where he had created an opening wide enough for them to step through. He led the way to the van and put Harper in the front seat and closed the door. It had the child proof switch activated so Harper could not open the door while he went around and got into the driver's seat.

He explained that he would be back in less than two days and that he should relax and enjoy the ride. He let Harper know that he was going to be meeting his equals from St. Louis and Miami and would have a chance to make deals that would connect his network to distributors to both the east and west coast of the country.

The trip back to Cincinnati was uneventful and soon after Harper was talking to the other two distributors and comparing notes. The three of them seemed to get along well.

Liam let all three know that after a dinner of grilled picanha, with a side of rice covered with feijoada, fried plantains and mushrooms, followed by a dessert of cherry cobbler, he would share what he would be asking them to help him with. He assured them that their participation would enrich all of them and for the time they were working with him they were assured that no law enforcement agencies would bother them.

They asked who he worked for. He said that would remain an unknown to them, but they should be assured that he had the support of his hierarchy that any deal he made with, and they accepted, would put them off limits from local law enforcement. He then explained that he wanted to focus their distribution efforts to some key individuals that he wanted to either deport, arrest, or eliminate. The three of them would be asked to be of help in all three of those efforts. The eliminate action would be by making sure that if the person was using, he or she would receive a dose of drugs that was potent enough to kill them.

Harper chuckled and said that seemed to be easy enough since that often happened anyway with his current customers.

Mylo nodded and added that he would need to recruit the specific field individuals that would be the deliverers of the drugs.

Liam said that he had eighteen young recruits that he was holding upstairs. Each of the three of them had two of their own and then there were four more from their coast that each of them would be instructing. He painted the picture of how the three of them would have representation along the coast where they were located or along the Mississippi river from New Orleans to Chicago. He pointed out that they would be able to quietly increase their distribution regions.

He handed them their first-class tickets back to their cities. He said that he would give them the tickets for those going home with them, but he needed to go upstairs and verify who that was going to be.

It took him less than thirty minutes to return and hand each of the tickets for those going with them. He gave four to L.A. to Jack, he gave four tickets to Mylo to Miami and then he handed six tickets to St. Louis to Harper.

He smiled and said that he should have used a silencer so that he would have gotten honest answers from everyone.

The three of them nodded and commented that they were all glad that they had said yes.

Liam hand them their keys to their locks and then a hacksaw. He asked that they follow him upstairs to where their field workers were chained and that unlike their keyed ankle clasps the ones upstairs had been keyless pins that needed to be cut.

He chuckled and said that it would be a chance for the three to be the humble servants to their workers. They should think of it as a biblical moment.

He had each group strip their beds and bring the linen down to the laundry area. He also had the four bodies carried and placed in a wagon that he had brought around with the tractor and parked by the back door in anticipation of having a few noes.

He had removed the cages from the panel truck and had put in bench seats that would hold all of them. He then drove them all to the airport.

Once he was back, he drove the tractor out into the woods where he had a backhoe to dig a deep grave into which he placed all the bodies.

He had one more series of recruiting to do before he was ready to focus on snagging the foreign operatives he was after.

560

4 The Request

*T*he last case had ended only a week ago and Alex had focused on the firing range, flying her drone, and riding her bicycle on street patrol. The entire team was taking her lead and doing similar things. Bill and Trevor chose to drive around versus ride bikes, but Trey and Johnnie accompanied her wherever she went. They always met for lunch at a place that Johnnie got to choose.

It was one of their quieter weeks that they had enjoyed for as long as anyone of them could remember. Trevor was the one that commented that he was worried that it was the quiet before a storm. Soon after he had uttered that phrase, the Chief called them all into his office.

The Chief shared with them that he had received a call from the Ohio State Deputy Attorney General for Law Enforcement, Cynthia O'Reily, asking if she could get Alex to examine a very unique, unusual, and concerning situation just outside of Logan, Ohio.

He pointed out that the departments reputation for solving cases had caught the eye of state law enforcement leaders and that went a long way in ensuring that they would get the budgetary funds the department needed. He suggested that they take the police van and all five of them drive to Logan and meet with the Highway patrol officer in charge of a home in the middle of the forest being guarded and sealed off as a crime scene.

On the way out to the van Trevor commented that he should not have mentioned the calm before the storm. Bill chuckled and said they had no clue what they were being asked to look at and Trevor had no clue about any storm. He hoped that they would be able to clear things up just by looking. He then added that he doubted it. He figured they had weathered many a storm together and would do so again.

Alex said that they should all go prepared for the worst and that meant they would wear their protective Kevlar outfits when they got there.

The drive to the Logan area took about two hours. Johnnie kept updating them and then as they got close, he gave Trevor the detailed directions on how to get to the house where they were to meet the Highway patrol who was handling the investigation.

The drive up the small gravel lane, through a dense forest of maples, oaks and smaller cedars seemed to be leading them back in time.

Bill commented that the location was very secluded.

Trevor stopped the van when the house came into view. He counted the circular turrets and when he reached nine, he commented that nine was connected biblically to the ninth Psalm that predicts the coming of the Antichrist. He went on to say that the number nine was also said to be ruled by the Planet Mars and he made the point that the orange brick should have been red to give the home good luck, so he figured bad luck was at hand. He then added that in Japanese the word for nine was "ku" which is similar in meaning to "pain or suffering" and therefore associated with bad luck.

Bill asked him how he knew so much about the number nine.

Trevor smiled and said that he was born on September the ninth in nineteen fifty-nine and so he had been fascinated with the number nine all of his life.

Alex smiled and said she was glad that there were no nines in her birth date and suggested they get up to the house to check whether the nine towers had anything with them getting called in.

The Highway patrol leader introduced himself as Clay and said that he had never investigated a situation that seemed quite as weird as what he had found in each of the towers of the house as well as in the downstairs living area. He led the way in and turned right into an area he said they were calling "the downstairs ring and chain area" where there were three chains with locking leg irons. He pointed to the anchor points out and said that the chains were long enough to allow whoever was locked in them to reach the bedrooms and the bathrooms.

He then led the way upstairs and said that there were two leg iron chains in each of the nine towers, but they did not have locks but rather had leg irons that were put on with pins that were hammered into the leg irons. He pointed to each of the rooms and said that each room had clean bed sheets and bedding as if they were to be used in the near future.

Alex asked how the Highway Patrol had been called in.

He said that a hunter had called some shootings in but had waited a day to report what he claimed was gun fire coming from the house. This hunter had waited a day to come in and give his report because he was concerned about being sued for trespassing, but he was so sure that there had been gunfire in the house and knowing that he had convinced himself to take a chance and make the report.

Alex asked to see each of the rooms. She walked to the doorway of each and looked in. Then she returned to the first and laid down outside of the door and looked across the floor. She did this for each of the rooms and then returned to the first one and did it again.

Clay asked Trey what his partner was doing. Trey replied that she was looking for differences between the rooms because if there had been gunfire that had killed someone then there would have been a clean up to remove the blood. She was looking to see if there were differences between the rooms.

Clay commented that he and his troops had not found any blood anywhere.

Alex stood up and said that she wanted a forensics specialist called in to closely examine towers number one, three, four and six because they had been cleaned more than the other tower rooms. She expected there to be some indication of blood in them.

Clay asked one of his officers to arrange for a team to come in and check out the towers for blood.

She then asked Trevor and Bill to go out and find a wagon or other transport that could move bodies to some sort of burial ground.

She asked Johnnie to launch Gunjfor and see if he could locate where the burial of any bodies might have occurred.

Clay asked what made her think there would be buried bodies anywhere in the vicinity.

Alex smiled and said that she had no idea if there would be any bodies, but it was likely if the person who had made the report had heard gunfire that there would be at least some bodies. And she said that she was betting on four bodies that were buried somewhere. The chains indicated that whoever had been on them were not there willingly.

Not long after, Bill called her and let her know that he and Trevor had found a tractor hooked to a wagon that could have been used to transport bodies.

Clay nodded and said that his men had found the tractor in the barn, but it was clean and had not raised any flags.

Bill had been listening and commented that it seemed that the wagon had been hosed off before being put into the barn.

Alex asked Bill and Trevor to see if they could find any tractor tire marks leaving from the rear of the house and going somewhere.

Johnnie called in a few moments later and said that he thought he had found a grave that had been recently dug and then camouflaged. He gave them all directions from the house and suggested that shovels be brought out.

Clay again asked how a grave could be found so easily.

Trey commented that the entire team had learned to identify graves in the forest in a case where they went along the entire US-Canadian border identifying them and Johnnie was the best among them in using his drone in finding them. He suggested they take several shovels.

Trevor called in again and said that they had also found a baby backhoe that he thought they should drive out to make the digging easier. He asked if any of Clay's people knew how to use it.

Clay left and returned a few moments later with one of his men who said he knew how to operate the baby backhoe. He also had three additional men with shovels.

He commented that the situation was getting worse than he had thought.

They all rode the wagon out to where Johnnie was standing in the woods.

Once the leaves and brush were cleared off, it was clear that there was what appeared to be a filled in grave.

The backhoe dug slowly down to a full six feet. Then it snagged a thick black plastic bag. The driver of the backhoe backed away from the hole and got out and suggested that someone with a shove get into the hole to clear the dirt off the bag.

Alex asked everyone to stop. She said that she would like the body removed and transported to Cincinnati where she would have it examined by Dr. Rogers. She asked if he could make that happen.

Clay said that he had been told to do whatever she asked so he would arrange for the transport.

Alex asked that he also expedite the detailed examination of the towers she had identified but that everything in the house get a new detailed examination with the knowledge that at least one murder had been committed.

She said that the team was going back to Cincinnati and do some research on the property, and anyone listed as the owners.

Bill was doing the driving and Trevor was doing the talking about the fact that they had only found one grave.

Alex answered her phone and put it on speaker mode when she learned it was a call from Clay. He had called to let her know that four bodies had been lifted out of the single grave.

The bodies had been loaded into a hearse and were on the way to Cincinnati. He had instructed the persons transporting the bodies to deliver them to the main downtown police station. She thanked him for the heads-up and for how fast he was able to make that happen.

He chuckled and said that he did not want to spend the night at the crime scene site but wanted to get home to his family and enjoy dinner.

After hanging up Alex called Dr. Rogers to let him know to have his team be ready to receive the four bodies.

She then called the Chief and brought him up to speed on what the team had found and that he should declare it as a murder case called "The Nine Towers of Ku."

The Chief laughed and said that he was very interested how she had come up with that name.

Alex replied that Trevor was to blame and that he should talk to him about the number nine and all of its meanings.

She let him know that in the morning she and the team would get him up to speed on everything they had found out so he could communicate back to Cynthia O'Reily and the rest of the state's hierarchy.

566

5 Autopsy Trail

*A*lex walked her bike across the walkway to downtown that went over the various interstate highways below it. She was thinking about the case that she felt had a very creepy feeling to it. Who would chain up twenty-one people in a house for some reason and then shoot four of them.

She hoped that Dr. Rogers would provide some sort of clue that would help unravel the mystery that spread like a blank landscape across her mind. Once off the walkway she got on her bike and headed to meet up with Johnnie. The two of them met every morning outside of her old apartment build where he was still living and rode in to the station together. They each wore a headset that allowed them to chat on the way in. This morning, they discussed the weird aspects of the case. They were both in agreement that they needed to get some clue from Dr. Rogers because so far, they had found a murder crime scene but had no clue as to who the criminal might be.

Johnnie commented that he was going to dig into the property ownership and see what he could find out about who owned it.

Once they arrived at the station, Alex changed into her work outfit of a black pant suit and jacket. She then stopped and got a cup of black coffee and walked out into the bull pen. She and Johnnie, as usual, were the first to get there.

Johnnie fired up his computer and commented that Dr. Rogers must have come in early because he had sent him the DNA of the four suspects and let him know that he also had dental imprints and hoped that they could be used as positive verification if the DNA didn't immediately identified the individuals.

Alex suggested that Johnnie begin his search with the DNA information while she went down to see the doctor. When she arrived, Dr. Rogers greeted her and pointed to the bodies that were laying on the examination tables. Each of them had their head covered. He said that there was not much of the face left but a gaping hole, but the mouth and jaw were almost left undisturbed. He said that he had found two forty-five slugs loose in the body bags. He wondered where the third and fourth slugs had ended up.

Alex asked about the condition of the slugs and learned that they were slightly disfigured but from his examination it was clear that the gun that had fired the bullet was within inches of the back of the head.

Dr. Rogers said that this meant that the slug only made a small hole going in but literally blew out the entire forehead as it came out. The shooting had been execution style with a slight downward angle. He postulated that the person being shot was kneeling and the person pulling the trigger was standing behind. From those two suppositions he figured the person doing the shooting was six foot to six foot two inches tall.

Alex asked if he might also have the shooter's skin complexion, hair, and eye color.

"Yes, I will send that up in my next report," Dr. Rogers jokingly answered.

Alex asked if he was willing to go to the crime scene and do a detailed examination where the shootings had taken place.

Dr. Rogers said that he and his team would welcome doing so. It would help him answer a lot of questions that was running through his mind.

Alex suggested that they make a day trip to the site where the shootings had taken place and that they leave later in the morning. She then returned to the bull pen where everyone was sitting and getting started. She accepted half of a bear claw from Trey and after taking a bite and a sip of coffee said that they should all meet in the huddle room right after she brought the Chief up to date on the case.

The Chief waved her to the chair in front of his desk and asked for her update.

The update was short, precise as she explained why she had asked him to label the case, "The nine towers of Ku." She explained that it appeared that up to twenty-one people had been chained in those towers and four had been shot and killed while still being chained.

The Chief shook his head and said that his best two teams were constantly getting involved in cases that stretched his imagination. He added that the department had benefitted financially from their efforts and managing the budget had gotten easier, especially after she had stopped having her police cars shot up, blown up or burned to a crisp..

Alex laughed and remined him that she had not been the one to blow up, set her car on fire or turn it into Swiss cheese. She reminded him that she had been the victim.

He smiled and said that all he knew was that it had cost him being able to hire another investigative team so that he could keep wheels under her.

She let him know that she and the team were heading back to the scene of the crime, and she had convinced Dr. Rogers to take his team to the site and do a thorough examination.

The examinations of the four rooms where Alex thought the shootings had occurred led Dr. Rogers team to find the third and fourth bullets lodged in the wall. They had gone unnoticed because one had lodged at the very center of a black-eyed Susan flower in the wall paper and the other wall was covered with an arrangement of various colored spots.

The bullets had enough blood on them that Dr. Rogers felt certain he would be able to determine which of the four bodies had met their end in each of the towers. He then commented that the cleanup in tower number one had not been thorough, and his team had found blood on the wall. They found that though the floor had been cleaned there was evidence of blood in all four towers that Alex had identified. He had his team also looking for any hairs, skin droppings or finger nail clippings that might provide DNA of the occupants of all the rooms. He commented that they would most likely be gathering evidence for the rest of the week.

Alex examined the contents of the refrigerator and noted that there seemed to be two different menus for the occupants, hot dogs, and steaks. Given the ratio of the food in the frig she speculated that those held up in the towers had survived on hot dogs and the three held in the main floor had dined on steaks and baked potatoes. This was an indication to her that the upstairs prisoners were of a lesser status than those held downstairs.

She glanced at the trash can and asked Trey to put on gloves and pick up the top cover to see what was inside. She pointed to a set of discarded gloves and said that Dr. Rogers would most likely be able to get finger prints from the inside surface.

She went into the living room and noted that the coffee table near the couches were glass topped. She glanced down through the glass and pointed to finger prints on the bottom surface of the glass. She put a crayon circle on the top side so that Dr. Rogers' team would easily find them.

She was becoming more confident that they would crack the case. She figured that the hunter had caused the investigation to begin before the perpetrator had been prepared, otherwise she was sure that the place would have been cleaned more thoroughly and that no clue would have been found.

She asked Johnnie to expand his search for signs of any absent drug dealing leaders.

She noted that the marks on the floors up stair indicated that those captives had been held longer than the three held downstairs where there were no wear marks on the rug or floor.

She then took a walk out to the barn where the tractor and baby backhoe were once again parked. She looked over both pieces of equipment and the wagon as well and commented that all three pieces looked rather new and not weather worn as farm equipment often did.

She added finding out when and where they had been purchased to the list of things that needed to be followed up on.

She pointed at the fifty-gallon gasoline drum that that was mounted on a stand. She wondered if the gasoline had been purchased by the barrel. That would mean that some gas station nearby would have noted a fifty-gallon sale. Buying gas for the two units might be another avenue that could help identify the person or persons that lived in the house.

She went back into the house and asked Dr. Rogers to be especially thorough in processing everything in the fourth downstairs bedroom. She added that she thought the person in charge of the entire operation had used it.

She asked Johnnie to locate a local pizza shop where she could order enough food for everyone working the crime scene.

Clay, the Highway patrol leader had quietly followed Alex around and had been impressed with her thorough search for evidence. He was amazed at the wide net she was throwing to identify the perpetrator and the fact that she believed it was just one individual. He had expected that several people would have been involved but it was now clear to him that the search was narrowing down to one person.

When he heard her getting ready to order pizza for everyone he spoke up and said that he knew of a great pizza shop in Logan and suggested using them. He would send a couple of his men in to bring the pizza back.

Alex thanked him and suggested that they get one pizza for every two persons at the site and enough drinks to match.

She then asked if there were any gas stations where a person might fill a fifty-gallon drum and not get noticed.

Clay shook his head and said that the site was only about forty miles from Columbus where there were numerous places to buy fifty gallons and not be noticed but that buying that much at any gas station closer to their location would be noticed.

Alex asked about places to buy the farm equipment and was pointed to two places that were withing a few miles of where they were.

He added that the gas could have been part of the sales deal since these places made sure that the purchaser would be able to run the equipment immediately. They would also try to set up refill services to sweeten the sale.

The pizza arrived and Alex led the tway to a large maple tree and spread out a blanked that she carried in the back of her car. During lunch she asked Bill and Trevor to check out the places that sold farm equipment. She asked Johnnie to continue his research into ownership of the property.

She was going to see if she could get finger prints that would allow them to close in on the person who had set up a very elaborate kidnapping scheme.

She was beginning to suspect that the amount of money that such venture took could only be funded by a well-financed organization, and she thought it was too complex for any of the drug runners to set up. She was suspecting one of the US government organizations.

Trevor commented that once again they were well outside the scope of a normal crime and into the netherworld of secret government organizations. He made the point that killing individuals was a step to the dark side and highlighted a person that might have gone rogue. It would be a very talented person who when they closed in could become violent. What made it worse it seemed that he had the money to do whatever he desired to do.

Johnnie nodded and said that he would see if he could find such an individual and when he did, he would cut them off from the ability to easily get to the cash. He said that if he had the finger prints that were probably in the gloves, he would be able to identify him.

Alex said that she would get Dr. Rogers to process the gloves immediately so that they could get to the perpetrator as quickly as possible.

6 Derailed

*T*he police cars flashing lights at the end of the driveway caused Liam to drive slowly by. He did not know exactly what the cars were doing there but he was sure that in meant that his house had been discovered. He drove on and parked the van out of sight in the forest near where he had buried the four that he had shot just a week ago. He carefully walked to where the grave was located and was surprised to find that it had been dug up. He stood looking down into the grave trying to think through what he had to do next.

He had six abductees from Texas and now he had no place to put them. He looked down into the grave and thought about his next step. He decided that it was time for him to move on and find a totally new place from which to operate.

He realized that it was a setback, but he still had the three main drug distribution regions under his control and eighty percent of the foreign operatives he was after resided in those locations.

He decided that he had to get rid of the six that he had in the van and move on.

He told himself that he hated to do it, but he would have to get rid of six that he had just driven up from Texas and that it wasn't fair to them, but it was not his fault that he had no place to house them. He thought about the deep ravine not far from where the van was parked. He would take them two at a time, off them and push them down into the ravine. He figured that they would probably not be found for months or maybe never. He moved the van close to the ravine and then two at a time he marched them to the edge and then shot them from behind. It was over in less than five minutes.

He was disappointed that he had not had the time to enjoy disposing of them. He looked around and found several dead limbs that he threw down into the ravine in hopes that the bodies would not be visible unless one was actually in the ravine.

Early on when he first purchased the property, he had tried entering and walking the ravine and found it almost impossible, so he figured that the bodies were there for a long duration.

He returned to the truck and thought about next steps. He had his weapons, his travel suitcase and access to his accounts. He could set up his headquarters wherever he desired. He would send in reports to his boss that things were going as planned and he would soon be apprehending the spies.

He decided to operate out of New Orleans since he liked the Cajun cuisine, and it was a partying city that catered to a great number of strangers. He would be able to operate there and never be noticed.

In Tennessee he stopped and got rid of the panel truck and bought a used tan sedan. He drove on and when he got to Mississippi, he traded cars again and chose a black Cadillac that he drove on to New Orleans. He knew a place near the river where he could rent a rather comfortable condo that was modest but comfortable and it would allow him to walk to the park along the river. He would be moving into his elimination of spies mode and would need the use of his computer more than anything else. He wanted a good view from his work desk, and he wanted to be near some good restaurants.

He looked around his third-floor room and sat down at the desk that was in the rounded corner of the room that overlooked the open area with a grey stone and brick circle where two walking streets crossed just below.

His two-bedroom condo was all on the same floor and went from the corner room, two rooms wide, to the other end of the condo. The entire condo was twenty-five hundred square feet in size. It had a central open area where the kitchen and eating area took up most of the space. The eating area faced the exterior and had a small terrace where one could sit and enjoy the outdoors.

He was glad that he had the funds to enjoy what many would have considered a luxury. He considered it essential to his wellbeing.

He went up on the roof and found a way to leave that took him over two roof tops and to a fire escape that led down into a secluded alleyway. This gave him confidence that he would not get trapped in his condo if he were to be confronted.

Because he had lost his computer at the house of nine turrets, he had to reestablish all of his computer network connections. Setting all of his connections back up was challenging and time consuming. He hoped that his computer that he had left behind would not be found but he was not too worried if it was found because it had so many layers of encryption that it would be impossible for anyone to get anything useful from it.

At the same time, he was getting re-established, Alex and the team were back at the crime scene. They had done their initial search of the nine turrets and were discussing what they might be missing.

Trey commented that they had not found any indication of what the purpose of having people chained and held captive meant or why it was done.

He commented that the place was too clean and that even though their involvement seemed to have disrupted what was going on they had not found any damming evidence other than the grave with four bodies. He wondered why the house seemed so sterile.

Bill said that he agreed. It seemed that a phantom had been running the place.

Trevor asked if he meant spook as in some secret government operative.

Alex said that could be one explanation and they should begin looking for convenient places to hide the damming evidence. She asked Trevor and Bill to check all vents in the bedroom used by whoever had run the place and then do it in every downstairs vent. She and Trey would hunt for a hiding place in the kitchen and downstairs dining room.

Not long after, Trey discovered a very thin lap top computer hidden on the top shelf of the pantry. It had bottles of spices stacked on top of it and was not visible. He only discovered it because he was standing on a footstool and methodically taking all the spices off the shelf.

He handed that computer down to Alex who had been going through the under the counter shelves searching through pots, pans, and a large number of lids.

She said that she would ask Johnnie to see if he could get into it and see what he could find.

Johnnie had been out on the grounds flying Gunjfor and looking around the property from the air. He had wandered out to the edge of the property and had discovered a rather deep crevasse and began to explore it.

He walked over to the edge of the crevasse but stepped back and sat down on a fallen log and took Gunjfor carefully down toward some limbs that seemed out of place relative to the rest of the crevasse that he could see.

Then he saw an arm and as he took Gunjfor closer he could make out a body. He was able to see another pair of shoes and knew that he had found at least two bodies. He brought Gunjfor back up and put her away. He called to let Alex know that he had found more bodies and that it was going to take some special effort to retrieve them.

He let her know that he was walking back to the house because he need to replace Gunjfor's batteries.

Alex walked up to where Dr. Rogers and his team were still processing the tower rooms and let him know that Johnnie had found more bodies.

She then let Clay know that there were bodies down in a ravine and that between he and Dr. Rogers they needed to decide how to proceed to get them out of the ravine.

The entire team was waiting when Johnnie returned. He put up his hands and said that he needed to replace Gunjfor's battery and put the one she had used to charge back up so she could be used to provide a closer view of the bodies he had found.

He then opened his computer and played back what he had seen in the ravine.

Clay commented that it would take a helicopter to lift the bodies out of the ravine.

Dr. Rogers added that he wanted his team to go down into the ravine to examine the bodies before anything was disturbed. He asked if Johnnie could get some shots of the entrance to the ravine so he could decide how his team would get to the bodies.

Johnnie led them to the ravine where he set up his computer on the fallen tree. He then launched Gunjfor and took her down to the entrance of the ravine and flew her up toward where the bodies were located.

Dr. Rogers shook his head and said it looked impossible to hike up to the place where the bodies were located and that it looked like his team would need to be lowered down from the helicopter.

Clay said that the chopper was on its way from Columbus and would be arriving in the next half hour.

Dr. Rogers led his team back to the house where they got into some protective gear and got ready to go down into the ravine. He made sure they had their cameras and field equipment so they could examine the bodies before moving them. He point out that it was a risky assignment and if any of them had any issues they should say something.

Meanwhile Alex let Johnnie know about the computer that Trey had found and that after the recovery of the bodies, she wanted him to see what he could learn by getting into the computer.

Johnnie smiled and said that he was moving up from cookies to riverside steak meals as a reward for the magic she wanted him to deliver.

Alex put on a sad face and asked if he was getting tired of her baking him cookies.

Johnnie shook his head and said that his request was in addition to the cookies. He said that he was just hungry because of all the hiking he had done so far, and he really wanted something different than more pizza.

Trevor spoke up and said that he and Bill were done searching for hiding places in the house and that they could make a lunch run and get whatever everyone wanted.

Alex suggested that they specifically get what each of them wanted. She added that she was going for a salad with a salmon topping.

Once everyone had made their selection Trevor and Bill asked Clay for the name of a restaurant that would have the menu that would match the choices made. They then called in the order and said that they would return with everyone's lunch.

The helicopter arrived as Bill drove out. He commented that he was glad to be making the lunch run and hoped that the bodies were out of the ravine by the time they got back.

Alex, Trey, Johnnie, and Dr. Rogers stood by the edge of the ravine as two members of Dr. Rogers team was lowered down to the bodies. Once down they let everyone know that there were more than two bodies and from what they could tell the ones they could see had been executed in the same manner as the ones they had dug up.

They said that it looked as if they had been shot and then dumped into the ravine because the areas where the bone were protruding did not have much blood from the broken bone areas. They suggested having the bodies lifted and taken to an examination area where a closer examination could be made.

During the preparation to lift the first body, the two down in the ravine were able to verify that there were six bodies to be lifted out.

Dr. Rogers asked Clay if one of his people could drive the morgues van as close to the ravine as possible and to let the helicopter pilot know where to take the bodies that were lifted out of the ravine. It took about forty-five minutes to lift the bodies out and get the Dr. Rogers two people out of the ravine.

Dr. Rogers had done a preliminary examination of the bodies as each got lifted from the ravine. When the last arrived, he reported that they had all been killed in the same manner as the four he had examined previously. They were all male in their early to mid-twenties and they had most likely been killed in the last two days. He added that he needed to get them back to his lab so he could do a more detailed analysis.

Bill and Travis drove in with lunch as Dr. Rogers and his team were getting ready to transport the bodies back to Cincinnati.

Since most of his team had ordered steak or something other than a sandwich, Dr. Rogers decided they should eat and then drive back to Cincinnati.

Johnnie meanwhile had tried getting into the computer that Trey had found and commented that it was password protected, it was going to be a challenge to get into it so he might need to do it once they got back to the office.

Alex shook her head and said that it seemed that the discovery of the bodies and the computer was redirecting the team's focus.

She talked with Clay and asked him to keep the area secured and monitored until she released it. She doubted that the killer would return but figured the area needed to be kept as a crime scene until it was fully processed.

She called the Chief and caught him up on what had happened and let him know that everyone from Cincinnati was on their way back. She commented that whomever they were after was a serious danger and a killer that seemed to kill without concern to doing so.

578

7 Tracking

Once back in the office, Alex watched over Johnnie's shoulder as he worked at getting into the computer. First, he had to get past the password needed to turn it on. He tried the normal approach to turning on the computer for a few moments but then he plugged in a thumb drive prior to restarting the computer so that the Password Re-format routine that he had coded would invade the memory of the computer as it powered up and let him put in the password that he had chosen.

Alex asked him what password he had chosen.

He laughed and said that it was her first name because she managed to open up all doors or obstacles that got in her way.

Trey had been sitting quietly but started laughing when he heard the exchange.

Once Johnnie had the computer open, he ran into the next barrier in that all the files were encrypted and required administrative permission to get in.

He opened up another one of his hacking routines that searched for the administrators name and when he had it, he then opened all files. It took him the rest of the day to work his way to the point that he was able to begin to browse through the information that was stored on the computer.

He decided to transfer the entire content of the laptop to one of the departments computers and make a copy for himself as well. He then turned off the laptop and closed it.

Bill came into the huddle room and said that he was not sure what was going on but three people acting like they were in control had been escorted into the Chief's office. He added that the lady leading the group appeared to be upset and on a mission. Since they were the only ones handling an unusual situation, he thought he would sound the alarm.

A few moments later, the Chief's support poked her head into the huddle room and said that the Chief wanted everyone in his office.

Alex said she would be right in. She turned to Johnnie and asked if he had what they wanted off the laptop. He said that he had a duplicate of everything including the operating system and every bit and byte that was on the computer. She nodded and said that was good and asked him to bring the lap top with him.

She called down to Dr. Rogers and asked him to copy all of his information about the bodies he had processed and put the information on a thumb drive for her. He was not to say anything about the thumb drive when they all came to the morgue.

He asked what was up.

She let him know that she thought the CIA, or some similar entity had just arrived and might be in the mood to shut down what the department was working on.

She led the team to the Chief's office and the five of them entered.

The Chief introduced Laticia, Thermon and Ralph as CIA agents that had come because the beacon from one of their laptops had triggered a signal that they had traced to the department. He asked Alex if she knew anything about that.

Alex said that the computer had been found at the site where nine bodies had been found. She added that so far, they had not had time to analyze the contents of the computer. She added that it was password protected.

Alex then asked why a CIA computer would be found at such a site.

Laticia replied that she was not able to provide a reason, but she wanted to get the computer back and wanted to know more about who the dead might be and how they had died.

Alex knew that she was about to lose both the computer and shortly be told that the dead bodies would be picked up by CIA representatives. She was anticipating being told to stop her investigation.

Laticia said that the deceased were most likely foreign spies that had been caught and resisted arrest and put up a fight of some sort.

Alex resisted sharing the facts that would refute such a situation.

When Laticia asked where the bodies were located, Alex replied that they were in the morgue getting processed.

Laticia looked at the Chief and said that all analysis of the bodies should come to a halt. She then said that she wanted to get a firsthand look at the bodies and then she would have them transferred to a morgue in the Capital for a more thorough analysis.

The Chief looked at Alex and saw the face he knew all too well. He knew that Alex had all she needed from the bodies and that she was not buying any of Laticia's condescending words. He wanted to laugh because he knew that whatever Alex was willing to give up was of no more use and that she had what was needed to solve her case. He led the way to the morgue.

When he entered the morgue, Dr. Rogers smiled and asked what all the people were doing coming into his lab.

Laticia introduced herself and said that she needed him to stop all work he was doing on the bodies, and she wanted all of his lab records that had to do with the bodies.

Dr. Rogers walked by Alex bumped into her and dropped the thumb-drive he had into her pocket and then walked over to his desk. He pointed to a box with ten files that had the information on the bodies and said that was all he had on the bodies. He added that he was just about to put it all into the departments computer but had been too busy to do so.

Laticia pointed to the box and asked Thermon to take it with him when they left.

She asked if she could see the bodies.

Dr. Rogers opened up four of the slide out morgue body holders and pulled the bodies out half way. He then lifted the cover over the first body to show the faceless individual.

Laticia seemed to take a step back and she collided with Johnnie who commented that the gun battle with the bad guys had not been fair.

It was clear she had not expected to see what she was looking at. She hesitated for a moment and asked what the cause of death had been.

Dr. Rogers shook his head and said that it was a forty-five bullet to the back of the head administered at a range of about two inches. Most likely when the individual was kneeling in front of the shooter.

It was clear that Laticia was surprised and that the story she had spouted about a gun battle did not fit the situation.

Johnnie, who had remained standing close to her, commented that it clearly had not been a fair fight. He quietly added that maybe it instead was an execution.

She asked about the other six deceased.

Dr. Rogers said that all of them had met the same fate in the same manner.

Laticia said that she would have the bodies transferred that afternoon and said that she had to get to the local office and make the arrangements. She looked at Thermon and Jason and said that it was time they got back to the office. She asked the Chief to guide them back to the entrance.

He nodded and looked at Alex and the rest of the group then asked them to meet him in his office.

She waited a moment until the Chief had left and then thanked Dr. Rogers for having been so efficient at his examination. She handed the thumb drive to Johnnie and told him to move the information to some system outside of the department and then erase the thumb drive. She also asked him to move the image of the CIA computer to an off-station computer as well.

Then she asked if he had gotten what he wanted by standing so close to Laticia.

Johnnie said that he would have all the information moved out of the department by the time they got to the Chief's office he just needed to borrow Dr. Rogers' computer for a few moments.

He sat down and connected to one of the many cloud accounts he had and transferred everything he had to an account he titled Nine Towers. He let Dr. Rogers know that when the computer beeped everything would be done and the thumb drive would be empty, and he could use it for another purpose.

He then looked at Alex and said that the team currently had no information about the lap top or the dead bodies in any official department computers.

Alex led the way back to the Chief's office.

The Chief asked what had taken them so long to reach the office.

Alex smiled and said that they were chatting with Dr. Rogers about what he had found out about the victims.

The Chief nodded. He knew that more than that had gone on and Alex was protecting him by being vague. He asked whether he should close the case as requested by Laticia.

Alex shook her head in the negative and said that the people that were murdered may had met their fate in the hands of a CIA operative, but as far as she was aware that did not give them the authority to commit murder for their convenience. She was sure what they had stumbled on had surprised Laticia and that as a good CIA boss she was going to protect the agency.

She asked that he delay closing the case for two weeks and if she and the team had not solved it by that time she would come in and ask him to shut it down for her.

He nodded and said that he would delay the closing, but the team should be careful in going after a rogue agent willing to kill ten young men to accomplish whatever he might be trying to do.

Alex agreed that they were most likely after an unstable individual and that she would make sure the team did everything by the book and did it safely.

She looked at the team and asked if they were all with her in continuing the search for the killer.

Trevor smiled and said that the case had just become more interesting, and he was eager to see how she was going to guide the team.

Bill added that ten bodies in the morgue were enough of a red of flag for him to wear his Kevlar outfit in its entirety for the rest of the time they worked on the case.

Johnnie said that he had picked off the telephone numbers of the three FBI agents and if they all wanted to listen in to the calls that he was sure would-be taking place they should all go with him to one of their favorite lunch places and participate with him in watching logs float down the river.

Trevor laughed and said that he had thought Johnnie had been standing so close to Laticia because he liked her perfume. He added that he might not want to look for logs going down the Ohio because the last time they had watched for that log he had found a dead body, and currently they had a case with all the dead bodies they needed.

584

8 Dissension in the Ranks

*L*aticia knew she had a problem and that Liam had gone off the deep end. He was on assignment to find and neutralize any foreign agents that he could identify that were operating inside the US. She was at the moment trying to get over the shock that he had executed ten men, and she had no reports from him about finding any foreign agents.

She knew that he had planned to gain influence and some sort of control via the drug distribution network but that was the extent of what she knew about what he was trying to do. She had no way of contacting him. For security reasons he had always been the one to initiate contact and this time there had been silence for almost a year. She had made up her mind that she needed to report the situation to her bosses.

She had to position Liam's removal in a way that would keep her and those around her from being damaged by his actions.

She had turned his laptop over to her IT support and asked them to get into it so she could find out what Liam was up to.

They had let her know that they were trying to figure a way that they could get in but so far, they had run into a solid brick wall and that they did not know how to penetrate that wall.

She was not happy about their lack of success but at least that over confident black detective back in Cincinnati would have had the same problem and would know even less than she did. She was glad that she had derailed that investigation.

She looked over to where Thermon and Jason were reviewing the reports on the autopsies and asked what they were finding out. They commented that four of the deceased had been killed at the same time and then buried in a single grave.

The other six had been lifted from a ravine and they had been killed within a few minutes of each other but at least a week later. That timing meant that the Cincinnati detective unit had already found the first four and were most likely at the scene when the other six had been executed.

Jason commented that it seemed that Liam had been returning to the house and when he somehow learned that the police were at the scene, he must have decided to get rid of the six. From what he could glean from the reports, the house at one time had held up to twenty-one prisoners on chains prior to the first four deceased getting shot.

He added that it seemed that some of the prisoners had been chained for almost year. Jason went on to say that Liam had come up with a diabolical approach.

She commented that Liam had mentioned getting control of some parts of the drug distribution network and then using drugs to catch the spies that he had been going after. She figured that the prisoners were most likely connected with the drug business. She asked if they might have an idea of how to locate Liam.

Thermon shook his head and said that the only thing he knew about Liam was that he liked upper end places to live, and he liked to enjoy the best cuisine. He chuckled and added that the two criteria narrowed the locations to around twenty-five cities and only a few thousand top end restaurants.

Jason added that Liam also liked to attend car races and horse races and that might get them down into the hundreds of places.

If Jason could have been in New Orleans, at America's third-oldest racetrack known locally as the Fair Grounds Racecourse & Slots and watching the race, he would have been within a few yards of Liam who had come out to enjoy the race and afterwards was planning to go to enjoy a dish of Crawfish Etouffee tips served over rice. He was planning to focus on the great taste and use French bread with a garlic butter spread to soak up all the great tasting juices.

He had begun his moves on both coasts and in New Orleans. He was behind in getting started in St. Louis and he had decided to stay totally out of Chicago for the near future.

He was currently focused on L.A. and on New York City where the highest concentration of spying activity was taking place.

He was satisfied with the progress he was making and planned to begin the elimination of the most active spies.

He had been surprised that the most prolific spy was almost seventy and was one of his CIA bosses. His location in Washington D.C. put him out of reach there but he knew that this boss vacationed just north of downtown Miami.

In one meeting he had listened to him boast of going out to where the waves had not yet started to rise and then swimming a mile each morning along the beach outside of his beachside home.

The fact that he was able to afford a beach side home should have been a signal to someone inside the CIA but evidently his position had somehow insulated him from that scrutiny.

He initially had thought about a way to spike his medication, but he instead zeroed in on drowning him. It would give him so much more pleasure to pull his big boss underwater and look into his eyes as he tried to take in his last breath but instead sucked in salt water and drowned.

He gave a call to a friend back in the office and asked her to find out when the vacation was to take place. When he got that information, he made reservations in Miami.

He arrived a day before the big boss's vacation and walked the beach area. He found a dive shop at one end and rented a full dive outfit with a double air tank pack. He went to where some boats were for rent and rented a boat and took it along the beach to where he planned to stage the drowning.

He figured he could anchor the boat, get in the water, and get into position where he could pull his big boss under and then return to the boat and leave before anyone knew anything had happened.

A day later in the early morning as the sun was just warming the air, he anchored his boat, got into the water, and swam to where he planned to drown the big boss.

He could see him approaching and positioned himself.

He was able to grab one ankle and then the second one and then pull him under. The struggle was more intense than he had expected, and he missed being able to pull him down to where he could look into the boss's eyes, but the drowning happened as otherwise planned.

He was back to his boat and gone before anyone noticed a floating body.

He was sitting having a late breakfast when he heard the morning news announcing the fact that a swimmer had been found drowned.

He had a few more days before he was planning to drive back to New Orleans to plan out his next move. On the last day before leaving, he sent a text to Laticia saying, "number one spy drowned." He figured that would trigger a very intensive investigation into the drowning and most likely a search for him as well. He left the phone he had used to make the call in Miami.

The drowning had electrified the department. There were several theories about how that had happened. The coroner that had done the autopsy had listed the cause of death as drowning. He had noted that there seemed to be slight bruise marks on one of the ankles.

Laticia knew immediately that Liam had made those bruise marks. She went to her boss and suggested that a very detailed look be taken into the big boss's actions to see if there was any indication that he might have been a deep mole. That led to an argument with her boss but in the end, she prevailed, and the analysis got underway.

She assigned Thermon and Jason to do that analysis and instructed them to evaluate every moment that their top boss had taken in the CIA and even to go back to his early school years.

It took them several weeks of digging but they found a pattern where meetings with a soviet counterpart went on in unrecorded meetings and that trips to Russia seemed to be lacking the details of the meetings held there. They were able to match the meetings and then actions that the Russian's took to information that had been leaked.

Jason swore when he and Thermon shared their information because Laticia made the comment that Liam had just earned a pass even thought he had killed nine people on his way to eliminating a spy within the ranks of the CIA. He shook his head and said that it did not make sense to him.

Laticia said she agreed but the single discovery meant that a huge security leak had been plugged and would never operate again.

Liam rented a car and drove back to New Orleans and started to focus on his next spy. This time he was zeroing in on a Seattle operative that was focused on disrupting a political election that could mean the control of the US senate. This operative appeared to be working for the Chinese. He really did not care which foreign country was behind the fake information that was being pushed. He was setting things up so that this individual ceased to exist. He hired a local detective to learn what the operatives habits were.

It turned out that the operative was a single, white male police officer in his mid-thirties that went to a karaoke bar, liked to sing, and drank continuously. He was doing his false messaging for the Chinese, and he was doing it because of the easy money he could make.

He arranged for Sebastian Cassidy, the distributor he had recruited and told him whose drink to spike with an overdose of Fentanyl but to make sure the overdose was just to the deadly side but not an overdone because he wanted it to look like a mistake by the person doing the drinking.

It turned out that Sebastian chose to spike several drinks and after having several spiked drinks as his target stood up to sing and took a drink, he collapsed as his heart failed.

When he learned of the death, he sent a message to Laticia, "number two, Karaoke bar, Seattle."

Laticia read the message and shared it with Jason and Thermon. She asked them to verify that the person who had died was indeed an operative that should have been targeted.

Jason commented that the two of them were doing nothing more than following dead bodies.

Thermon added that he wondered if any potential spy would be brought to trial or if dead bodies was now the normal way to handle potential spies.

9 Wisp of the Trail

*A*lex spent two days after the CIA folks left working with Johnnie as they tried to determine where to find the owner of the computer. Since they could not have the information officially, they were working in Johnnie's kitchen, enjoying tea and cookies as Johnnie went through hundreds of files trying to flesh out what the person that they now knew was a CIA spook named Liam was planning and why he had killed ten young men.

The information on the computer verified that the first of those chained in the towers were put there almost a year before the others were killed and it seemed that a new batch was added from the east coast three months after those from the west coast and the final group was from the center of the country along the Mississippi. They shared the nine cities, Seattle, L.A., San Diego, Boston, New York, Miami, Chicago, St. Louis, New Orleans with Trey, Trevor, and Bill.

From what they could learn the abductions were based on convenience not on any specific criteria. Apparently the four who had been shot had refused to agree to work for Liam.

Trey, Bill, and Trevor were figuring out the identity of the four bodies found in a common grave.

The finger prints turned out to be key in linking the body that Trey was trying to identify to an Orson Ambrose who had been reported missing in Seatle.

A short time later Bill had a similar breakthrough with identifying a Thiago Bandello associated with a missing person's report in San Diego.

Trevor commented that once again he had been given the hardest to locate identities.

Bill laughed and said it was just because he was slow, and he should just accept the fact that he was just not as good as he and Trey.

A day later, Trevor let out a whoop as he got a hit on a Boston missing person's report.

Bill had taken up the search for the fourth victim and got a hit from a missing person report in Miami.

They all met for lunch at a restaurant that Johnnie had randomly chosen to share what they knew.

Johnnie started out the sharing by saying that he had a surprise. He asked if anyone wanted to guess what it might be.

Alex said that her guess was that he and Mary were moving in together.

Johnnie smiled and said that was partially true and checked to see if there were any more guesses.

Trevor laughed and said that his guess was that Mary was pregnant.

Johnnie laughed and said that since she was only two years younger than his seventy-seven years such a thing would make it a miracle and much more than just a surprise.

He said that he was moving into a house in Mt. Adams that was only two blocks away from where Alex lived.

He added that he had been worried about Alex riding her bike alone into work each morning and now he would be able to ride the lead all the way from her house.

Alex added that it was great that he and Mary were moving close by but now she would have to worry not only about getting shot but about him falling off his bike on the way down the steep road to the city center. She asked when the house warming party would happen.

Johnnie said that Mary would be sending out invitations.

He then said that he had a theory about what was going to happen on their case. He said that he figured the cities had been selected because of the spies or operatives that might reside there. The people that had been abducted were drug pushers and three key leaders of the drug distribution business. The leaders were strategically located on the West, East, and Center of the country. Originally the command center was to have been in the nine-tower home in Ohio but that had now changed, and a new location would have been chosen.

That location was the current critical unknown. The second unknown was who the targets happened to be.

So far Laticia's phone linkage had not yielded anything useful. He commented that if she got any communication from Liam, the target of their search, his phone would get the virus that was in her phone, and they would be able to find him.

Alex added that what they needed now was to be patient and see what Johnnie could do. She asked for him to see if he could find the money connection that Liam might have. If they could get to that source, they might be able to pinpoint his location as well.

Trevor commented that once again they were relying on an old, worn out, Vietnam War veteran for a miracle.

Johnnie laughed and invited Trevor to ride with him and Alex along the Loveland Trail to see who was worn out.

Bill quietly said, "Touche."

Alex asked Johnnie to continue to see if he could find a money trail. She added that as soon as he found it, she wanted to cut it off and see if they could flush Liam out.

She said they should go back to the office and put in their appearance and let the Chief know the progress they had made in just two days.

A day later Trevor said he had an unusual situation where a person who drowned in Miami was identified as a CIA high level employee.

Johnnie checked and said that Laticia had a text on her phone that said, "number one spy drowned." He said that he would see if he could locate the phone that had called her.

Two days later, Trey commented that he had something suspicious in Seatle.

Johnnie checked Laticia's phone again and found the message, "number two, Karaoke bar, Seatle."

He then fired up his online phone location routine.

Alex commented that Liam was now going after the spies that he had been told to apprehend but his approach seemed to be to kill them. She wondered if that was the intent of the CIA. She added that the person drowned in Miami had been identified as a CIA employee. She asked Trevor to follow up and see if he could find out what role that employee played in the organization.

She went in to the Chief's office and shared what the team had learned and let him know that Liam might now be killing spies, but it was clear to her that he preferred killing people versus bringing them in for trial.

He agreed but added that he and the team were treading on thin ice and that the CIA was a formidable organization to be challenging. He added that they were five going up against an organization that had thousands that they could leverage.

Alex agreed but added that a serial killer in any organization was bad for the country. She added that once she had him in custody, she hoped to get him in front of a judge before the CIA could step in. Then the trial would make them share more details about his role.

When she came back to the huddle room, Johnnie let them know that he thought he had the Liam's location. He said that he had managed to locate him in New Orleans.

Alex looked at the team and asked if they were ready to go to New Orleans. She and Trey would leave immediately, and the rest of the team would drive the department van down so they would have a mode of transportation that carried all their gear.

She and Trey would travel light, rent a car, move into position, and wait to make any move until they all arrived. They would verify where Liam lived.

On landing in New Orleans, they rented rooms in the hotel that was within walking distance of the address that Johnnie had given them.

They then went for a walk to the location where Liam was located. There was a restaurant with outside seating where they decided to eat dinner. They relaxed at the table with a very expensive glass of Pellegrino with as slice of lemon.

Alex ordered Jambalaya that promised savory, local crab and shrimp, and vegetables mixed with rice and spices.

Trey was looking forward to his order of a crawfish, alligator combination Étouffée with roux baste onions, green peppers, and celery served over rice, with a seafood-gravy topping over it all.

They had just dug in when Alex quietly let Trey know that she was watching Liam apparently coming back from a grocery shopping trip.

They both watched as he entered the address that Johnnie had given them. Then as they watched they saw the lights on the corner top floor apartment come on.

Alex called Johnnie and congratulated him on having hit the nail on the head as to Liam's location. She asked where the three of them were in their journey. After learning that they were halfway to New Orleans and planned to make it there early in the morning Alex gave them the address of the hotel where she and Trey were staying. She added that she would rent three more rooms and expect to have breakfast with them. She suggested that each of them get some shut eye as they drove because she planned to arrest Liam the following morning.

Trevor had been listening and said that he had already gotten a three-hour nap, and he would take over the driving from Bill so he could get his nap in. He chuckled and said that Johnnie seemed to have a natural sleep habit and was always needing to be awakened when it was time to take a nature break so he figured he would be good and rested when they arrived.

Johnnie came back on and said that the conversation that went on between Bill and Trevor was so boring that it put him immediately to sleep.

Alex laughed and said she was glad they were having a good trip, and she was looking forward to them getting to New Orleans where she would treat them to a couple of excellent meals.

10 Runner

The following morning Alex and Trey came down to the hotel desk and learned that Trevor, Bill, and Johnnie had checked in at three in the morning and that they planned to be down at eight. She asked where there was a good breakfast restaurant and the clerk said that the hotel was where they could get the best breakfast but there was also a corner restaurant named Maggie's that was her favorite because they had the best eggs benedict with a side of boudin sausage.

When Bill, Trevor and Johnnie got down to the lobby, they all went to Maggie's and had breakfast. Alex decided that the eggs benedict were as good as the clerk had said and she asked everyone how their choices had tasted.

Trevor commented that his order of country fried steak and eggs had been great.

Johnnie nodded and said that his buttermilk pancakes with two eggs on top and two bacon strips were great.

Bill said that his grits with a pad of melted butter topped off with syrup had him ready for action.

Alex let them know that they were only two blocks away from where Liam had his apartment. She suggested that she and Trey go up to the apartment and that Bill and Travis stay outside at the corner in case there was another way out.

She asked Johnnie to monitor the street that was on the opposite corner from where Bill and Trevor were standing.

When Liam had decided to rent the corner apartment on the third floor of the building he had done so after he had found a second way out of it that let him go across several roof tops and then climb down a fire escape to the street. He figured that if he were surprised by someone or some group of people trying to corner him, he wanted to be able to make a fast getaway. He had also installed a small camera above the door so she could see who was standing on the other side.

In spite of all the preparation he was still surprised to hear a knock on his apartment door. He looked to see who was on the other side of the door. He did not recognize either, the rather young-looking black female or the tall tough looking male with her. He, however, knew the look of people that were in the police business and figured they were looking for him. He picked up his getaway bag, his laptop computer, pulled his thumb drive from his desk top computer and went up the spiral stairs to the roof exit. He had no intentions of getting himself arrested.

He had no idea who would be trying to do so or how they had found him. He figured it might even be the CIA trying to rein him in.

He ran across to the back side of the building, jumped the very narrow passage way that existed to the next building and ran to the very back end of that building and then climbed down the fire escape to the street below. He had his car in the ground floor of that building. He went to it and drove out. He was heading toward the Pontchartrain bridge with the intent of getting out of the state. As he drove, his only regret was that he had splurged on a wide screen computer display and a desk top computer that he had to leave behind. He, however, had his laptop that had all of his work files, so he was still in good shape to continue the elimination of the countries enemies.

A few moments after, Alex again knocked on the door and when there was no answer, she picked the lock and then followed Trey as he took the lead. They both had their guns drawn but put them away once they had confirmed that the apartment was empty.

She pointed to the spiral staircase and went up and out to the roof. She walked to the edge where she was able to look down between the buildings.

She and Trey returned back to the apartment where she called Johnnie and asked him come up to the apartment with Bill and Trevor.

She asked Trey to find a rope or something else to keep the roof door from being opened while they were in the apartment.

She walked over to where a cup of coffee was sitting at the computer desk and found that it was still warm. She figured that Liam had chosen to disappear rather than open the apartment door. She wondered if he would be back.

When Johnnie came in followed by Bill and Trevor, she asked him to see what he could find on the computer.

She asked Bill and Trevor to see if there was any other useful things that might be in the apartment.

Johnnie let her know that the desk top computer did not have any of the work files he had found on the laptop that they had recovered earlier so Liam must have used the desk top computer as a way to power the large, curved screen and used a thumb drive to keep all of his working files.

Bill returned and said that Liam was a very neat person who hung his pants on pant hangers in the closet and had his shirts hung next to them and that all the hangers were equally spaced. He added that there was a sock drawer, a T shirt drawer, and a underwear drawer and that there were six of each item which meant that Liam was wearing number seven of each item. There was only one pair of gym shoes in a gym bag, so he figured his every day shoes were on Liam's feet.

Trevor came into the front room and shared that Liam had two sets of bath towels and wash clothes. He used one of the latest six bladed razors and had a small bag of floss picks and had a rotating electric tooth brush.

Trey commented that the kitchen was well equipped, and that the refrigerator was well stocked. A steak had been marinated and looked like it was what was planned for lunch along with a baked potato. It appeared that the breakfast dishes were rinsed and placed in the dishwasher. The refrigerator freezer had a gallon of pineapple sherbert that had a few scoops taken from it. He finished by saying that Liam had a bowl of fruit that had a fuji apple, a large orange, a grape fruit, and a group of white grapes in it. It was clear to him that Liam was a healthy eater and ate well.

Alex thought for a moment and decided that they should find out what they could but the opportunity to capture Liam had evaporated. She asked Bill and Trevor to see what they could learn by going to the restaurants and bars within walking distance to see if they could learn any more about Liam's habits and tastes.

She suggested they pick one of the restaurants where they would want to have lunch.

She asked Johnnie how close he was to finding Liam's bank account and if there was the possibility to cut him off.

Johnnie let her know that he was still working through Liam's encrypted computer files and that it would take a few more days to get through them.

She then asked him to send a text to Laticia letting her know Liam's New Orleans address but to wait until the team was ready to leave because the CIA might have personnel in New Orleans, and she did not want to be anywhere close when they got to the apartment.

She looked at the time and realized that it was going to be a late lunch. She decided that an early evening flight back to Cincinnati would be in order. She took the time to make three reservations back on the only direct flight that left at five thirty in the afternoon local time. That meant six thirty Cincinnati time. She decided that a late lunch was appropriate and that a snack for dinner would most likely be had on the plane.

She let Johnnie know that she had made a reservation for him so that he could get a in full day's work getting into Liam's files the next day.

She suggested that the three of them that were flying back that day, check out of the hotel and that Bill and Trevor stay, have a nice evening out and then leave early the following day and drive back to Cincinnati.

Over lunch Trevor commented that the trip to New Orleans seemed to have been a bust and that Liam was a very cagy individual.

Bill added that he was but that now he was on the run and the chances for him to slip up was increasing. He added that they were certainly dealing with a very smart individual that most probably had a twisted mind and was very dangerous.

Once they were at the airport, Alex asked Johnnie if he was able to send Laticia the text message that gave Liam's name and his New Orleans address.

Johnnie replied that he could do it just before the plane left.

Alex had been right in delaying the message until she was leaving because when Laticia received the message, she immediately called her contact in New Orleans and had a team rush to the address. They found everything the way Alex had left it and there was no trace of her presence.

Meanwhile Alex arrived in Cincinnati and when she looked up the escalator going to baggage claim, she saw Matt waiting for her and she saw Lindsey and Nolan waiting for Trey.

She let Johnnie know that he should plan on riding with her, and Matt. They would drop him off at his Apartment.

Johnnie shook his head and said that Mary had moved into their new house and had let him know that he should go there. He added that he would be down to her house in the morning to continue working through Liam's files that they supposedly did not have.

Alex said that she would open the back gate to the yard, and he should plan on entering that way so he would not have to walk the three flights of stairs up from the street in front of her house. She added that she would make a trey of cookies in the morning to make sure he had the energy to break into the critical files that enabled them to cut Liam off from access to his money.

She added that they should plan on riding down to the station after lunch to bring the Chief up to date and be there when Bill and Trevor arrived.

11 The Power of Money

*L*aticia wondered why Liam had sent her his New Orleans address when it seemed he had hurriedly abandoned it. She had been told that a steak that had been marinated had been left in the refrigerator as if it was to be prepared that day and the apartment looked as if it had been abandoned in a hurry. She kept wondering what would have made him do that.

She put in a call to her Cincinnati contact to see if Alex Evercrest was there only to find out that she was seen getting to the police station on her bicycle at lunch time. As far as her contact knew she had not left Cincinnati. That at least satisfied her that the criminal case against Liam had been closed.

She was left wondering where Liam had gone.

At that moment Alex was talking to the Chief and letting him know about the team's failure to capture Liam in New Orleans, but they had flushed him, and he was on the run.

She pointed out to the Chief that she was close to cutting him off from his money and that would make him easier to catch.

She added that she figured he had most likely fled north to St. Louis since that was within a day's drive from New Orleans. She planned to work with Johnnie to locate him again with the hopes of capturing him on her second try.

The Chief asked what she was planning to charge him with when she apprehended him.

She replied that she would bring him in on four counts of murder and then she would work with the prosecutor on how to charge him for a second set of murders in hopes that she could get him charged separately for the six individuals he had killed and dumped into the ravine.

She then hoped to have his sentences be declared sequential. She said that her goal was to have him in prison for the rest of his life.

He reminded her that they were dealing with a CIA agent and that the organization would want to take control of Liam when he was in custody.

Alex said that she would work with John to have him identify a judge who would act quickly to charge Liam and set a court date so that it would be harder for the CIA to whisk him away.

She let him know that she planned to work from home with Johnnie and that she would have Bill and Trevor working from the office helping to find Liam.

The bike ride back to her house was usually the most challenging. She seldom made it all the way up the steep roads to where she lived. She most often ended up pushing her bike up the street for the last couple of blocks.

She got back just before lunch at the same time that Trey returned with some carry out Korean food. He had picked up three orders and figured there was enough variety that they could each have a little of each item and be full when they got done and there would most likely be enough for several more meals.

She helped carry the food up the three flights of steps to the house. As they got to the top she looked back down to where her bike was chained to the bike rack and commented that she loved the house but her almost vertical front yard was a challenge. She was glad that Matt had found a gardener willing to take care of it.

Trey said that the front yard was a challenge, but for him it was the fact that the person that they ended up calling the skull collector had used the third floor as his skull museum for the skulls he had harvested from the many young women he had killed.

Alex laughed and said that the third floor was why she had been able to afford to buy the house. The fact that it had made the news made the house almost impossible to sell. She had taken advantage of the opportunity and made a low-ball offer that the owner accepted. She added that since then she had converted the third floor into an art museum that she was slowly filling.

They were eating lunch when Johnnie shared that he had found that Liam had at least a half dozen bank accounts spread across the country. He had close to six million dollars to work with.

He added that her idea that he had gone to St. Louis seemed to be the right one because there was one account in St. Louis that used Lee Havers as the person on record with the bank. A check had been cashed for fifteen thousand dollars from a realtor and on the check the realtor had written that it was for a deposit on a long-term lease to a condo and it had an address on the check.

He suggested that after lunch they could all go on line with him, and they could check out the condo on the inside and the outside and get an idea of how to capture him. Meanwhile he would close all the other accounts he knew of but leave the local one open so that they would not tip Liam off.

Alex said that she wanted Bill and Travis to get themselves set up in the huddle room and they could all participate in scoping out their next attempt at capturing Liam. She commented that they needed to figure out his escape plan and path so they could set a proper trap.

Liam meanwhile was in St. Louis shopping for clothes to replace those that he had left behind in New Orleans when he had to make a hasty retreat. He had found the condo on line and had done some research about the area and learned that there was underground service through the long-established neighborhood. His research was rewarded by learning that there was one service tunnel directly under the building and there was an entrance to it in the basement. Additionally, each of the ground floor units had a set of steps down to the basement.

He had contacted the realtor and after the showing he had written him a check using his St. Louis bank. He had set up multiple identities across the countries to allow him the flexibility to disappear when necessary and the St. Louis bank was just one of several.

He was still trying to figure out who was after him. He wondered if one of the other government agencies had somehow gotten involved or if he was being hunted by his own people. It would be so ironic if they were the ones after him.

He had rented the condo because it was a nice place, but the real reason was that it was built over an old large underground utility tunnel system that was accessible from the condo's basement. He spent several days installing sound and visual sensors so he would have an underground alarm system. He did the same around the condo property. He chose to operate from his laptop versus setting up the elaborate screen system as he had done in New Orleans. He was bothered by the fact that he had to leave so quickly that he had left everything behind. He wondered if mold was growing on the steak he had prepared for a dry fry and had to abandon in the refrigerator.

Alex had followed the tour that Johnnie took them on but was bothered by the fact that it seemed that it would be too easy to capture Liam. She commented about the fact that his condo was at ground level and that the layout made capturing Liam a piece of cake. The place in New Orleans had the same feel but had been on the top floor.

She asked what made Liam choose this condo on the ground floor where capturing him seemed even easier.

Trey looked at the area surrounding the condo and noted that the condo was the newest structure in an area where the other buildings looked to be at least ninety years old. He noted that there were no power utility lines overhead. This meant that there must be an underground utility distribution system that most likely contained both power lines and sewer piping. He said that his bet was that Liam had done his research and had found that he could get access to that system from the condo that he had leased.

Alex asked Johnnie to see if he could get the drawings of the underground system.

It took Johnnie almost an hour before he let out a whoop and said that he had found the tunnel system that went under the condo building. Most of the tunnel system diagrams were in the process of being scanned into the cloud and the only parts of the tunnel system that had so far been moved into the cloud were the parts where the new construction builders paid to get it done. He pointed out that the tunnel system split three ways right at the edge of the Condo property and that there was an entrance to the tunnel from the basement of the condo. The condo had a set of stairs into the basement from all four ground floor units.

Trevor commented that in New Orleans Liam had cameras on all the approach points to his apartment. He bet that Liam would put cameras around the ground level of the condo and do the same in the tunnel system and most likely would have a strategic one in the basement.

Alex asked Johnnie if he could hack into the cameras that Liam had set up.

Johnnie said that if he could get near enough to the condo while Liam's computer was on, he would be able to, but he figured that it would take longer than normal to get through Liam's fire wall.

Bill asked if there was a chance that they could recruit one of the other condo residences to help them.

Alex said that was a good idea and asked if Johnnie could get the names and occupation of the other condo lessees.

Johnnie chuckled and said that it would cost her one oatmeal raison cookie per lessee.

It took him about an hour to go through the county property records to find out who occupied each of the units. It turned out that the unit directly above Liam's was occupied by a sixty-five-year-old DEA retiree named Chester Ramperil.

Alex decided to see if her Chicago DEA friend, Harold Zimmerman, might be able to help. She called Harold and explained the situation.

He chuckled when he understood the request. He said that picking on the CIA was even a risk for him, but he had followed her escapades long enough to know that she would most likely succeed. He warned her that afterwards, whoever her target's boss happened to be, that person might be as dangerous as the person she was going to capture.

He said that he did not know Chester, but he would give him a call and let him know that his help to capture a serial killer was needed. He was sure that Chester would be cooperative and would allow Johnnie to set up his computer in his condo.

Alex asked if by any chance he might have five people that would be available to help capture Liam because there were five escape routes and she had only four people to cover them.

Harold asked her to wait a moment. Then after a few moments he came back on and said that his team was looking forward to meeting her in St. Louis to give her a hand. He added that the fee would be that she treat he and his team to a celebration night out to enjoy St. Louis style barbecue ribs topped with the sweet brown sugar, molasses and tomato sauce that came with it.

Alex thanked him and said that she was planning to go there in a day and gave him the time and place for all of them to join up.

He said that he would see if he could recruit the St. Louis DEA group to join in and wondered if her budget could include them in the celebration.

She said that she would be pleased to include them.

12 Team Work

*H*arold let his boss know that he had volunteered to help arrest a wayward CIA agent for the murder of ten individuals and that he and his team would be going to St. Louis to do so. He added that he had contacted the DEA leader in St. Louis who had agreed to participate in the arrest.

His boss asked who he was supporting and when he heard the name he gave his approval.

Once he had clearance, he and his team caught a flight. He had arranged with his St. Louis area contact for them to provide transportation in St. Louis. He was pleased that together the two teams would field ten personnel.

He let Alex know the number of people that he had coming to back her up.

Alex was thankful that she had the kind of support that would allow her to cover all of Liam's the escape routes.

She had reserved first class seats for the entire Cincinnati team. Trevor had made a point that she was the best person that he and Bill could possibly be backing up. She nodded and said that she had even made sure they all had some of the best rooms in a five-star hotel.

Trevor smiled and asked if she would be taking them all out for dinner.

She added that she was hosting dinner for the Chicago DEA team that evening at a top barbeque restaurant that had been recommended by the local DEA leader who had agreed to provide five of his team as backup support the next day.

Trevor said he was looking forward to St. Louis style barbeque and then asked how she planned to deploy the DEA support members.

She said that she was going to have them take positions around the exterior and down in the utility tunnels. She, Trey, Harold, and one other of his team would be on the three steps leading down into the basement from the three first floor apartments.

Johnnie would be in the condo above Liam's condo with the retired DEA agent and he would take control of all camera's and put a visual loop in so that Liam would not be able to detect or hear anything.

She smiled and said that she had saved the best position for He and Bill, who would walk up to the front door and let Liam know that he was under arrest. She said that she expected Liam to bolt and head toward the tunnel where she and Trey would take the lead to arrest him, but she suggested that he and Bill stand to the side of the front door just in case that Liam decided to take a few parting shots.

She said that once the arrest was made, she and Trey would escort Liam and go directly to the airport and fly to Cincinnati.

She looked at Trevor and asked him that if he survived would he then host the DEA to another dinner to celebrate the successful operation.

Trevor smiled and said that he had been prepared to complain about being the one to have to knock on the condo door but that hosting a celebration dinner trumped that complaint and he would be pleased to host such an event.

Alex nodded and said that she hoped everything would go as planned.

The evening dinner with Harold and his team seemed to center around tales they shared of the cases that they had previously been in together with her and Trey. They all thanked her for her gift to them of their Kevlar protective gear that had saved several of them since they received them as a gift.

They were all shocked when they learned the details of the ten young men that Liam had executed. They were all appreciative of how Alex was planning to disperse them and planning for her team to be the first line of action. They added that they would act if Liam chose an alternative for his escape route.

Early the next morning they assembled and met with the St. Louis DEA team and reviewed the arrest support scenario. Alex let them know that Johnnie would be the one that needed to get everything set before they moved into position.

Liam had a calm night and had awakened early. He planned to review his next spy take down that would happen in Boston but figured it could wait until after breakfast. He had a mini waffle maker that he had picked up while shopping and planned to use it for the first time. He also had a small bottle of pure maple syrup that he had paid an outrageous price for and planned to use on the mini waffles that he would smother them with.

After preparing them and putting them on the table he poured himself a cup of coffee and enjoyed his breakfast. He cleaned all the dishes and put the waffle maker away. Then he went in and fired up his computer.

Johnnie had gone to the condo above Liam's and had introduced himself to Sam, the retired DEA agent who took him into the kitchen and got him set up at the table. The two of them enjoyed a cup of coffee and chatted as Johnnie prepared to hack into Liam's computer.

Sam shared the fact that he had looked up Alex on the internet and found a ton about her many successful cases. He asked if Johnnie was the miracle worker that she had praised in almost all of her interviews as the reason behind her successes.

Johnnie nodded and said that she over did it a bit, but she was always making sure that her team got credit for the cases they had worked on. He shared that she had taken him off the street and had guided him to be her "miracle" worker.

When Liam turned on his computer, Johnnie put up his hand and declared that he was going into action and needed to concentrate. He sent in his hack routine and established control of all the peripheral detection devices. He then set up a continuous visual and sound loop into the entire system. Once that was done, he called Alex and let her know that it was time for everyone to get into position.

She, Trey, and Harold each went to the three first floor condos that had steps into the basement and after showing them their badges got the owner's permission to go down the stairs. Two members of Harold's DEA team moved into position at the bottom of the ladder that went down into the utility tunnel. The rest of the DEA support got into position around the building.

Bill and Trevor approached the front door and rang the doorbell.

The ringing of the doorbell and the announcement that he was under arrest and that he should open the door caused him to put three bullets through the door and then to grab his getaway bag and run toward the stairs leading down into the basement. He had not been expecting anyone. He knew that it probably was whoever had been after him in New Orleans. As he made his retreat, he wondered how he had been located so quickly. His first priority was to vacate the condo and then he would figure out who had been able to track him. He went speedily down into the basement.

The call for him to stop and kneel caught him by surprise but he reflexively pulled his weapon, but it suddenly seemed to catch fire and fly out of his hand. He looked at his hand and realized that there was no gun there. He was stunned by its absence and amazed that his hand seemed to be burning and his trigger finger was obviously broken but there was no bleeding. He looked over to where a young black woman was standing up and walking toward him. She told him that he was under arrest and to kneel down with his hands behind his head.

A tall guy was coming at him from the other side and had hand cuffs out ready to put on him and was reciting his rights.

Liam decided that he would comply and worry about getting released at a later time. He said his finger was broken and an older black guy reached up and pulled on it and popped back into place. The pull made him cry out but afterwards the pain subside. He asked why he had not waited for a paramedic to do that.

The old black dude answered that serial killers did not get medical aid from professionals. He then taped the broken trigger finger to the middle finger.

Liam knew then that he was not being arrested by any local police but some organization that had been at the house of the nine towers. He wondered how they had gotten permission to arrest him in Missouri.

Alex let him know that they had a flight to catch and that he should cooperate, or she would personally see that he did not make it.

He looked at her and asked if her shot had been an accident.

She shook her head and said that it had been the exact shot that she had planned and that she had almost the same skill with a knife for close in quiet work and she showed him her small belt knife.

He understood the reference to a knife for quiet close in work and intuitively knew she would do as she had threatened.

He decided that for the moment doing as he was told was in his best interest.

Alex led the way to the waiting car and they all drove to the airport where she had Trey take off the handcuffs and they walked into the airport and up to the first-class counter.

Liam was surprised about having his handcuffs taken off and more surprised to be flying first-class. He decided once again to relax. The worst that had happened so far was having his index finger taped to his middle finger.

Once they arrived at the Cincinnati airport, they were met by a black police officer that introduced himself as Chief Johnson and then he was introduced to a blond female as the lawyer that was going to present the charges against him to the judge who would be deciding about the next steps in his trials.

He began to realize that things were moving fast enough that he was not going to be able to utilize his CIA connections to keep himself out of jail.

It was a short ride to downtown where he was guided into a small courtroom.

The judge convened court as soon as they were all in the court and the prosecution presented two separate murder cases and six money tax evasion cases. Two IRS lawyers were there to present the six-money tax evasion cases.

He looked over at the young black female that he had learned was Alex Evercrest and the lead in tracking him down and arranging for the rapid proceedings. To his surprise his tax evasion case was to be taken up the following day.

He was sure that the way things were going he would be convicted and get six sequential five-year sentences before his cases for murder would begin. He knew that his goose was cooked unless the CIA intervened and pulled strings to get his release.

He figured that his one call would need to be to Laticia to see if she could get a lawyer to get him released.

612

13 The Escape

*L*aticia was furious when she found out that the Cincinnati detective was the one that had found and then arrested Liam. She was even more incensed when she found out that Liam had been charged with tax evasion and was to be sentenced the next day. She was not prepared to intervene because she was not sure how to extradite him. She also had no idea of what she was going to report to her boss.

She put a call into the head of the Cincinnati police department and insisted that he have Alex Evercrest investigated and have both her and her boss fired for breaking their promise to cease and desist as she had insisted. She was politely told to F--- off and stay out of his department's murder investigation cases.

She slammed the phone down and paced back and forth trying to figure out how she was going to message this to her bosses.

She figured she was the one most likely to get sacrificed if Liam was convicted of the murders and sent to prison. She would either be fired or sent to some backwater assignment.

She continued fuming, continued her pacing, and finally decided that she should go to Cincinnati and meet with Liam and see if he had any ideas of how to get out of the charges he faced.

Liam was in his third day of being held and taken to court on a daily basis. Each time he went he returned to his holding cell more convinced that the CIA had abandoned him, and he began to plan his escape. His hand cuffs were always put on with his hands in front of him. He was then taken to the courthouse that was across the street. One of his guards walked ahead of him and one behind. They were both armed, but it was clear to him they were junior policemen with little experience since it was always protocol to cuff a person behind his back.

He would refrain from killing them, but he would most probably need to shoot both of them. He had watched into which pocket the lead guard put the handcuff keys. He figured that the next time he was taken to court he would make his break as they went up the steps to enter the building. He counted on the guards inexperience and the fact that he had befriended them.

The next morning for the third time, he was told that he was going to the court. So far, he had been charged for not paying taxes and money laundering on his first two trips and on the third he was charged with four counts of the killing of the four drug pushers who had told him that they would not follow his orders.

He figured he was about to be charged with six counts of murder on this fourth trip. He was still upset that Laticia had not intervened. He figured it was time to make his move.

As the lead policeman reached for the court house door he turned, hit the policeman behind him in the side of the head with his fists closed and then hit the one in front of him in the same manner. Both were down and he quickly took both of their weapons, got the keys out of the pocket of the front guard, took off the cuffs and then use them to lock the wrist of the front guard to the ankle of the rear guard. He took both of their phones and threw their shoulder mikes far enough away that the two could not get to them. They were coming around as he got to the bottom of the steps and went around the corner of the building, ran to the alley, and ran behind the building toward the river.

He used one of the phones to contact his Cincinnati contact and asked him to bring him two thousand dollars in a mix of smaller bills and a passable fake ID. He ran the few blocks to the edge of the park where a few moments later, he met the contact. He thanked him for the quick response and then walked to where he saw bicycles for rent.

He walked over to and rented one for three hours. He rode along the bike path until he was near the Lunken airport.

He needed to get out of town but in a manner that would not leave a trail. However, ironically he found out that the first flight out went to St. Louis. He thought about it and figured that going there would definitely throw his pursuers off.

They would be looking for someone going anywhere but there. He bought the ticket and then walked over to the small shop where he bought a small, wheeled suitcase into which he put some snacks and then proceeded to walk through the security where he smiled when they commented that he was traveling light.

He commented that it was only a day trip, and he would be back in the morning.

When he got to St. Louis, he decided that he would go back to his condo and see if it was still being watched. He had the taxi drop him off two blocks from his condo and after making sure there was no one watching he walked up to the back door and retrieved the key that he had hidden under a flagstone and went in. He quickly packed his suit case, found the money that he had taped to the back of the kitchen sink and then checked to see if the refrigerator still had the food that he had left there. He made himself a half dozen salami sandwiches and then left the way he had come in. He walked back to where he had been dropped off and called another cab. He now had more than twenty thousand dollars which would allow him to buy a used car and then slowly make his way toward San Diego. Once there he could use the young drug dealer as he needed and then make his way out of the country.

Sam was sitting on his back porch and watched as a rather handsome man walked across the lawn and approached the back of the condo. When he lifted the flagstone and retrieved a key, he was sure it was the downstairs neighbor who had been arrested just a few days ago.

He went in to the living room and picked up the card of the IT expert that had used his apartment the previous week and called him to let him know that the person who had been the focus of the arrest was back at his condo. He figured that it was too soon for that to be a legitimate situation.

Alex and Johnnie both got to their desks with their cups of coffee and commented that riding into work was always invigorating since it was a downhill ride almost all the way. A few moments later Trey walked in with his cup of coffee, said good morning, and sat down at his desk. Bill and Trevor followed a moment later. They both had cup of coffee in their hands and Trevor had the box of donuts and sweet rolls that had become their daily morning gift to the team.

Alex asked if everyone was planning to be in court for the fourth time that week. She expected that they would all want to be to there to hear the final charge of six counts of murder made against Liam.

They were in the middle of discussing what they planned on doing on the weekend when Trevor nodded toward the Chief's office.

Alex looked over to see Leticia knocking on the door. It was clear that she was ignoring everyone in the bull pen area.

She watched as she entered the Chief's office and then she heard the Chief raise his voice. A few moments later, Leticia exited and slammed the door behind her and left.

Alex smiled, looked into the donut box, and picked out one of the jelly filled rolls that the Chief liked, walked to his office, and knocked gently on the door. She went in and handed him the roll and asked how his morning was starting out.

He looked up and said that he hoped that Leticia was going to get taken down a few notches and sent to the back woods of the CIA assignments. He took a bite of the roll and a sip of his coffee and said that he was going to enjoy listening to Liam's fourth sentencing. He congratulated her on how she had worked with the IRS lawyers to get the money cases prosecuted first so that Liam would be behind bars when the longer murder cases would be tried.

Alex said that she had learned that from her Hawaiian lawyer friend whose targets were billionaires who he went after for not paying their legal taxes.

The Chief said that he planned to be in court to witness the last of the cases to be presented.

Alex said that she and the team were all going to walk to the court house and get the premier seats and invited him to walk along.

The Chief thanked her, but said he was going to drive down and get their just in time to listen to the indictment.

She went out and said that it was time for them to walk to the courthouse and get into their seats there.

They were the first there and sitting behind the prosecution's table where Hanna was arranging her papers. She had been the one that was taking the early lead in charging Liam with the murders he had committed.

The assigned defense attorney came in and was accompanied by Leticia who seemed to be giving him some sort of direction. It was clear that the attorney was irritated as he pointed to the seating on the observes side of the railing. He sat down, opened his briefcase, and arranged several folders on the table in front of him. He continued to ignore Leticia, who continued to talk to him.

The Chief entered and asked what the holdup happened to be.

Alex let him know that the court was waiting for Liam to be brought in.

The judge entered and after a moment he made the announcement that Liam had just escaped from his police escort and was on the run.

The Chief looked at the five of them and suggested that when they capture him again, they perhaps should shoot him and save them all some time.

Alex nodded and said that he was elusive and finding him again might be a significant challenge. She suggested they get back to the station and see what they would do next.

Once back in the office they all gathered in the huddle room. Alex suggested they review what they knew and see how they could figure out where Liam might have gone.

She asked Bill and Trevor to check on flights out, Trey to check on buses leaving the area and Johnnie to check on any hits on the banks and to make sure that the St. Louis account got closed.

She then went to the Chief's office to make sure that she still had authorization to catch Liam.

Leticia was shocked to hear that Liam had escaped. She was speechless and wondering what to do next. She decided that she would see if she could get the help of the local detective unit that had so far been the ones that seemed to be able follow and capture Liam. She hoped that she had not offended the local hierarchy too much and could make amends with some financial or other support arrangements.

She went to the police station and asked to speak to the Chief of Detectives.

14 Last Chase

*T*he Chief was explaining that the case was taking a huge chunk out of his budget, and he was getting pressure to reign in the expenditures when his support called in to say that Laticia from the CIA was trying to meet with him. He looked at Alex and told her to stay. He then said to bring Laticia in.

When Laticia came in Alex stood up and shook hands with her.

The Chief nodded and pointed to the table and they all sat down. He looked over and asked how he could be of help.

Laticia shook her head and said that she had come to apologize for her behavior and to see how she could help in bringing Liam back in. She went on to say that initially she had operated under the CIA norm of pulling all investigations into the CIA realm, but it had become clear to her that she had lost control over her operative and it was time for her to support the only organization that so far had been able to track him down and to capture him.

She commented that she knew how much effort and resources must have been put into finding him the first and second time.

Alex nodded and said that Liam was a very smart and dangerous adversary, but he was now cut off from most of the resources he had used in the past unless he somehow had access to other CIA operatives and financial resources. She added that her team had him cut off from his money and was fairly certain where he had human resources that he had positioned. But it was going to be harder for her team to find him because of their success at cutting him off from his finances.

The Chief brought the conversation back to Laticia's offer of support and told her that he had stretched his budget in bringing Liam in and now that he had escaped it would drain his budget significantly to get him back.

Laticia suggested that she foot the bill for the previous efforts and that she cover the bill for his recapture. She added that the only thing that she would want in return was to provide the defense lawyer for Liam. She added that the current one might be the one that she kept on, but she wanted him only to keep the fact that Liam was a CIA employee out of the courtroom and out of the news as much as possible. She was not going to contest the money laundering charge or the murder charges. She was only going to insist that no death penalty be imposed.

Alex said that neither of them would insist on that since it would be up to the jury to find him guilty and the Judge to impose the sentence. She said that she was very biased since Liam had mercilessly executed ten individuals and though she found it hard to support the death penalty in most cases his situation was an exception.

Laticia said that she had come to the conclusion he needed to be brought in and incarcerated because he had killed two spies instead of capturing and bringing them in for interrogation.

Alex nodded and added that one of those spies was at the very top of the CIA and could have provided a wealth of information on how he had managed to avoid detection.

Laticia looked at her and asked how she could possibly have that information.

Alex smiled and said that she had a magician on her team. She went on to say that she knew that Laticia had two wonderful girls that were attending Brown and MIT, doing well and a stay-at-home husband who had provided them great guidance. She looked at Laticia and said that though her Cincinnati team and her were from the sleepy city of Cincinnati they had great capability and solved the cases that her Chief assigned them.

Laticia shook her head and said that she was impressed and a little taken aback. She said that she was in fact the one that was looking for help, that her career was in jeopardy because of the fact that Liam had gone rogue, she had lost control, and she needed a magicians help to save her career.

Alex said that she and her team members would figure out how to recapture Liam and make sure that he would stand trial for what he had been charged. She welcomed Laticia to be part of the effort and when it came time for the recapture to provide additional personnel. Alex then invited her to meet the rest of the team and to be part of the planning session.

Alex led the way to the team's meeting room and signaled the rest of the team to follow. Once they were all in the room Alex asked Laticia to introduce herself and to share what she was going to contribute in the effort to recapture Liam.

Once Laticia had done that Alex asked that they go around the room and introduce themselves.

Trevor nodded and noted that Alex put him at point to deflect any bullets that might come her way, but it didn't seem fair that she was letting a new member buy her way onto the team.

There was a moment of silence as Laticia looked at Alex.

Bill broke the silence by commenting that his partner was always seeing his glass half full, and that Laticia was welcome to help recapture Liam.

Alex smiled and let Laticia know that she was experiencing what happened in every session when the team met.

She then asked what each of them had learned.

Bill said that there was no indication that Liam had left via the Cincinnati airport.

Trevor said that the only flight that had left from Lunken airport went to St. Louis.

Alex asked Trevor to see if anyone had purchased a single seat and paid cash.

Laticia commented that it did not seem to make sense for Liam to return there.

Alex nodded but added that the flight was at the right time.

Trey said that there had not been any bus tickets purchased during the time frame of the escape.

Johnnie added that no attempt to access any of the closed bank accounts had taken place.

Alex looked at the team and said that she was betting on the flight to St. Louis, but she wondered where Liam would have been able to get the money to buy the ticket.

Laticia held up her hand and said that she was going to check on something. After chatting with someone, she looked at the team and said that a local support operative had given Liam two thousand dollars in cash and a fake passport. He did not realize that Liam was on the lam.

Alex looked at the time and said that it was time to watch logs floating down the river.

Johnnie laughed and let Laticia know that it was time for lunch, and he was tasked with selecting the restaurant for lunch, but he would let her select since it was her first time with the team.

Laticia asked if there was a good barbecue rib place with a view of the river.

Johnnie nodded and said that they were going to one of his favorite places.

Everyone was taking off their plastic bibs after eating barbeque spare ribs when Johnnie's phone rang.

Trevor commented that he was either getting a call to pick up a gallon of milk and a loaf of bread from his significant other or a call from Liam to let him know where he was.

Laticia looked at Alex and asked her if Trevor was joking.

Trey laughed and said that he would not be surprised if Trevor was right because Johnnie was their case bellwether as well as their magician who always came up with some break but only after a good lunch.

Johnnie thanked the caller and looked around the table. He said that their second floor retired DEA agent who had helped them to capture Liam had called to let him know that Liam had returned to his condo, stayed for a few moments, and then left with a large suitcase and a shoulder bag.

Laticia looked at him and asked if he was kidding.

Johnnie shook his head and said that was Trevor's job. His was to find logs floating down the Ohio River.

Alex said that she and Trey were off to St. Louis for a quick trip to see what Liam had taken from the condo and to see if he had left any clues as to where he was going.

She asked Bill and Trevor to check flights out of St. Louis.

She asked Johnnie to check out used car sales within walking distance or just a few miles from the Condo.

She looked at Laticia and asked if she wanted to go to St. Louis.

Laticia asked what Alex hoped to find in St. Louis since Liam was sure to be gone.

Alex replied that she didn't have anything specific, but she wanted to know why Liam had returned to the condo and what he had left behind that might give her a clue.

Laticia said that she would welcome the chance to go.

When they got to the airport and Alex walked up to the first-class counter, Laticia asked if she was expected to pay for the first-class tickets.

Alex shook her head and said that she only expensed the cost of coach tickets, but she and Trey always traveled first class. The choice to join them was up to her.

Once they arrived in St. Louis, Alex arranged with the cab driver to take them to the condo and then asked him to wait for a short time and then take them back to the airport.

She led the way to the second-floor condo and knocked where the retired DEA agent lived.

Sam opened the door and invited them in. After greetings he led the way to his back porch and pointed out the stone where the key to the back door was hidden. Alex thanked him for having called in the fact that he had watched Liam getting into the condo.

She then led them all to the stone, lifted it, took the key, opened the back door, and entered. She asked that no one touch or move anything.

She asked Trey to check the bedroom to see if anything was missing. She then walked around the kitchen area. She saw a discarded manila envelope in the waste basket. It had two strips of tape across it as if it had been taped to something. She noted that each of the cabinets had a strip of yellow tape across the two opposing doors.

That was true for all the doors except the two under the kitchen sink. She looked in the trash and saw the crumpled ball of yellow tape. She knelt down and looked under the sink. She returned to the trash can and picked up a manila envelope with tape across it.

There was one drawer that also was missing the yellow tape. She pulled it open and found a box of plastic wrap, a box of aluminum foil and a box of wax paper.

She then looked in the refrigerator. She spotted the cotto salami container that only had two slices left in it and a small bottle of mayo. She looked in the trash container again and lifted out the bread wrapper that had a heal slice left in it.

Trey came into the kitchen and said that the clothes in the closet were gone. As he recalled Liam had exactly one week's worth of clothes hanging there. He would need to review the list of things in the bedroom, but he figured that a suitcase was also missing. He added that there were no toiletries in the bathroom.

Alex asked what they had learned.

Sam said that he had seen Liam leaving with a large suitcase, so it made sense that he had it full of his clothes and also had the things from the bathroom in it.

Alex added that he had something taped to the back of the sink that had been missed when the kitchen had been searched. She figured the envelope that was in the trash would have contained a significant amount of money and perhaps a passport or two. The fact that most of the salami and loaf of bread had been used meant that he had probably made a half a dozen sandwiches and wrapped them with plastic wrap.

Trey said that Liam seemed to center on the number seven and most likely he had made seven sandwiches.

Alex nodded and said that it was time to get back to the airport so they could catch the late afternoon flight back.

On the way back to the airport she put in a call to Johnnie and asked him to see if he could find if a used car had been sold for cash anywhere close to the condo. She then called the barbeque restaurant and arranged for them to have Sam enjoy a dinner on her.

Laticia asked how what she had learned was going to help her find Liam.

Alex smiled and said that she was betting on the fact that he had made enough sandwiches so he could travel and not have to stop except for gas.

She bet on the fact that he would be trying to get out of the country. He could go north or northwest and go for Canada. Or he could go south, southwest and go for Mexico and parts farther south.

She was betting on southwest and that he was headed for San Diego.

Once she got back to Cincinnati, she was going to arrange for the team to go there if she could get some sign that was where Liam was headed.

15 The End Point

*L*iam got out of the cab that had stopped in front of the hotel that had a flashing light advertising a thirty dollar a night stay. He paid the cabby cash and left a nice but forgettable tip.

He then pulled his suitcase toward the used car lot that was a block away. As he approached the lot he saw several large SUVs. He planned to sleep in the back on his drive west. He found one that had been outfitted with cushioned side benches that folded down into a bed. It had a bent back door that refused to open but it had a space between the two front bucket seats that would allow him to get easily into the back.

When he pointed out that the back doors would not open because they had been damaged, he was able to get two thousand taken off and was able to get the van for under five thousand dollars.

Before agreeing to buy it, he said that he wanted to drive it to make sure it was not burning oil or had any other road problems. When he was satisfied that it would make it to San Diego, he paid for the car in cash.

He knew that the drive would be long and tedious. He set the cruise control a couple miles under the speed limit and then listened to music as he drove mindlessly across the country. He stopped at almost every rest stop to do exactly that.

He was taking his time and figuring out where he was going to go and how he might continue operating. He considered himself flying blind. He had no phone, no computer, had no weapon and no way to get more cash other than what he had with him.

He had two passports for two of his entities.

The plan that slowly bubbled up was to get to San Diego. Contact the drug pusher who had agreed to follow his orders and obtain a weapon and then generate some more cash by robbing him when he had the most cash.

He was already facing the trials for his other murders so if he ended killing a few more people it didn't matter as long as he escaped.

He was also coming to the realization that he needed to get out of the country.

Johnnie was looking for a cash car sale from a used car lot in St. Louis somewhere in the vicinity of where Liam had his condo. He shook his head as he turned on his search routine. He had designed it to first identify a used car lot, then examine the sales of the lot and then identify the ones done in cash. He stopped after the first car lot and tuned his routine to eliminate that low ball cash sales figuring that those autos would not make a cross-country trip.

He also eliminated anything over twenty thousand dollars and then activated his routine. His routing identified four lots that met his criteria. He examined the automobiles that had been purchased and picked the used car lot where a large SUV was sold.

He called the lot, talked to the owner, and asked about the sale. He found out that the person making the purchase was a rather handsome white man most likely in his early forties who seemed to know something about cars. The lot owner said that he was also a good bargainer and had bargained the price down because the back doors were jammed shut due to damage that had happened when the SUV backed into some mailboxes. He shared the fact that the SUV had a temporary card board license tag labeled StL 1020.

Johnnie called the station and asked that they put out a BOLO to watch for but not engage a black SUV with bent rear doors.

He then realized that it was well past midnight and figured he would let Alex know the details on their ride into work in the morning.

Laticia had come to appreciate the talent she had observed as she participated in the effort to apprehend Liam. She wondered whether she could entice Alex to become a CIA operative. She figured that she would make the offer. The worse that could happen was to be turned down.

She was more concerned about capturing Liam and getting him into prison, so she could position him as an agent that had gone rogue and should spent the rest of his life in prison.

She admitted to herself that she would sleep better if he got the death penalty. It was a frightening thought to her to have him alive and possibly escape and seek revenge.

She had been the one that had encouraged him to become the invisible agent that could operate on the fringes of the law.

She had recognized his ability to operate in that invisible area. Early on he had been very successful at bringing in his query and turning them over for trial.

She should have pulled him after a few years but had been swayed by the fact that his actions had a positive effect on her promotions. She had missed the fact that in the last couple of years he had killed many of the people he was after.

She had been shocked by the ten that he was now going on trial for. In spite of that she had tried to help him get away with it by using his CIA status. It had not worked and now she was working to get him permanently put away.

Alex was tired when she got home from St. Louis. Matt met her as she came in the door and gave her a hug. He said that he had heard about the escape and her effort to get enough information to again hunt Liam down. He asked how she was feeling. She replied that she would love to bend an elbow with a glass filled with some good West Virginia hooch but was going to settle for a cup hot of green tea.

He chuckled and said that he had saved her some of her favorite Korean dishes and would love to join her with a cup of green tea.

Alex said that she would pass on a late dinner but would love to spend a few minutes sitting on the couch and just leaning on him.

The next morning when she woke up Matt was already gone. She got up, turned on the switch to the coffee machine and then went to brush her teeth and get ready to ride into work.

When she looked down the three flights to the street where her bike was chained, she saw Johnnie standing and waiting on her. She trotted carefully down the front steps and greeted him. She unchained her bike, checked that her brake pads still had enough life to make it down the hill and then followed Johnnie.

They both had their head set on and he was immediately up dating her on what he had found and done while she was making her round trip to St. Louis.

She was pleasantly surprised that he had been able to find the SUV that Liam had purchased and was pleased that he had issued the BOLO.

She said that she had a tray of cookies or brownies as a reward for his being so successful.

He replied that this time he wanted an apple or a strawberry-rhubarb pie.

Alex laughed and said that she thought his request was a great one and that she would bake several strawberry-rhubarb pies and give one to each of the team members.

When they arrived at the station and walked into the bull pen, she knew that something was up when Trevor said that he thought she should have the entire bear claw for herself.

She looked at the piece of paper that Bill was handing her. She looked at Trey and knew that it was break in the case.

She looked at the paper, gave Johnnie a hug, and said that he, as always, was the team's magician.

Trevor asked why Johnnie was getting the hug.

Alex said that though the BOLO gave her name as the person issuing it, Johnnie had been the one that had done it.

Johnnie smiled and said that he had use her name since he was not authorized to issue one.

Trevor shook his head and said that law breakers should get punished not rewarded with hugs.

Alex looked at the paper and said that the SUV had been spotted just east of Albuquerque. She asked Johnnie to call up the locations of the two cities that the two west coast victims came from. She pointed at Seatle and San Diego. She said that L.A. and San Diego were two likely cities that Liam was heading and most likely both of them.

She looked around and said that they should all plan to get to San Diego to intercept Liam before he crossed into Mexico.

Laticia came walking in and said good morning and asked why everyone had a smile on their face.

Alex suggested they all go into the meeting room where they could focus their energy on how to recapture Liam.

She said that she was betting that the drug dealer leader that Liam had recruited resided in L.A. and would be a person that Liam would seek out. Then afterwards, he would seek out the lone surviving recruit in San Diego. In both cases he would be seeking money, and weapons. She figured that money would be the primary focus since he was cut off from his normal access to cash.

She looked over to Johnnie and asked him to put a watch out to see if Liam tried to access any of his accounts.

Laticia asked how Johnnie could monitor whether Liam tried to access his accounts.

Alex replied that was why she called him a magician and that was all she would say about it.

Laticia nodded and said that she would like to offer Johnnie a position in her organization.

Johnnie gave a little laugh and asked her if she knew how to bake a strawberry-rhubarb pie.

Laticia shook her head and replied that she didn't know how to make one.

He replied that then she had no chance of getting him to leave the team he was on. He added that in Cincinnati he got cookies, brownies, pies and had a good salary and was very happy.

Laticia nodded and added that he was also on a super team. It was clear to her that she was in a room where everyone seemed to be in tune with each other. She wondered how a person created such a team.

629

16 San Diego

*A*s he drove along, Liam realized that he would be arriving to the L.A. area during the afternoon rush hour. He decided to stop at a campsite just outside of Palm Springs. He could spend the rest of the day relaxing and planning how to get back into the swing of things.

Once he had a parking spot in the campsite, he drove to a nearby shopping center and bought a phone for less than one hundred and fifty dollars. He had the phone activated and figured he could use it to connect with the local L.A. drug leader the next day to arrange a meeting with him on his walk along the beach. He then found a store where they had a laptop that was on sale for two hundred fifty dollars. He planned to spend time during the evening to check and see if he could get access to any of his bank accounts. If that worked, he would take out as much money as possible and get it transferred to a sleeper account he had in Mexico City.

On the way back to the campground he stocked up on some snacks. He spotted a steak house and decided to splurge and have a large T bone steak, a nice glass of wine and some decadent desert of some kind before going back to the campsite.

When he got back to the campsite, he tried each of his banks. He was surprised that he could not open any of his accounts. How that had been done was a surprise to him because each account had been set up under an alias. That meant that those six identities were compromised. Without the ability to withdraw money, he was essentially broke. He was down to few hundred dollars.

He spent a few minutes recalling the phone number of his L.A. drug dealer. He was surprised that he remembered it. He put it in his phone and then dialed the number. He was surprised when the dealer answered. He took the opportunity to set up a meeting with him along the board walk for the following day.

His goal was to get a loan of around twenty thousand dollars. He remembered a pawn shop where he figured he could get a cheap gun in case he needed one for the meeting.

He needed to get back on his feet so that he could set up a new operation. He decided his best bet was to get into Mexico and then figure out how to get to Brazil where he had some good connections and then finally disappear somewhere in Argentina.

It was apparent to him that some very sophisticated technology was being employed in those trying to capture him and he needed to lay low for a period of time.

Back in Cincinnati, Johnnie got excited when the monitors that he had set up to watch and see if Liam might try to get into his accounts. The monitors went off one bank after another. He let the team know what was happening and that he would soon have Liam's location. Each hit let him add more of his tracking routine until he had it installed into the computer Liam was using. Johnnie commented that Liam did not have any protection on the computer he was using so it had been easy to put his tracking routine into the computer without being flagged. He had the location where the computer was being used and said that he had one way of tracking that required the computer to be on line and a second way that required he and his computer to be within six football field's distance if the computer was off. He said that he would continue to keep his tracking routine operational at all times so that he could slowly locate where Liam happened to be.

Alex noted that Liam was in Palm Springs that was just outside of L.A., and said that the team needed to get there and then rent a van large enough to comfortably transport all of them.

Laticia had listened to Johnnie explain his capability and commented that the team had a better detection system with a fraction of the sophisticated equipment that she had at her disposal. She volunteered to provide the transportation and a driver when they got to L.A. She then said that she had access to a private jet that could take them all out to L.A. and could leave at any time Alex wanted to leave.

Bill spoke up and said that he could be ready to leave in an hour. He only needed time to pack enough clothes for a couple of days.

Everyone agreed that was sufficient time.

Alex said that would be great. She added that she figured that Liam would stop in L.A. before going south to San Diego so they would fly into L.A. and then plan on finding and following Liam as he traveled.

Liam spent the evening monitoring the news via his new computer. He was glad that his escape did not warrant national attention. He was unaware that such news had been suppressed to keep him from knowing that he was being tracked. The next morning, he drove to the beach walk where he would be meeting with Jack, the L.A. drug leader with whom he had an agreement.

He was aware that the agreement had been extracted under duress and that asking for money was not what he had wanted to do but he had done so and gotten agreement to a sum of twenty-five thousand dollars. He would have liked to get twice as much but settled for that amount. He would see how much he could get from his San Diego contact.

He arrived at the beach walk early and decided to get on line, monitor the news, and see if he was still invisible.

The flight from Cincinnati left from the Lunken airfield and the team slept all the way. Once on the ground in L.A. they drove to a remote hanger where they were met by Jason and Thermon, Laticia's two aid's and led to a large black conversion van. After loading the bags, they all got in.

Alex had saved the seat behind the driver for Johnnie who fired up his computer to begin his search for Liam.

Laticia asked where they should go.

Trevor said he wanted to see what kind of beaches L.A. had to offer.

Alex looked at the map that Johnnie had on his computer and said that they should drive north on highway one and then cross over to Vista del Mar and drive south along the coast to see if they could locate Liam.

Laticia asked why that route.

Alex said that it was the first circle that she had in mind and then they would expand outward if they struck out.

When they started their southward drive on Vista del Mar, Johnnie said that Liam had just come on line, and he would have the location in a few seconds. Johnnie located the street that led to the beach near Sante Monica Pier. He directed them to within two blocks of where the signal was originating. They pulled over and parked. Alex asked Trevor to casually walk to where the signal had originated and see if they had the right location. He should also identify the SUV and verify that it had a temporary tag.

Johnnie spoke up and said that the computer had been turned off and he was now locating the car via his computer-to-computer connection. He suggested that they wait a moment and then to casually walked by the SUV.

Trevor said that he was going to change into a short-sleeved shirt and shorts so he would look like he was headed for the beach.

Bill said that he would walk to the corner and standby in case anything transpired.

Trevor was gone for about five minutes and then returned to say that the SUV had bent back doors, had temporary tags, and gave the number on the tag. He let Johnnie know that he had sent the picture of the SUV and the tag to him.

Johnnie logged in the temporary tag and searched the St. Louis area to determine if it originated there. A few moments later he had the information and learned that the SUV had been purchased for sixteen hundred dollars that was paid in cash. It had been sold to a Lester Stock, and the signature was nothing more than a squiggle.

Laticia pointed out that Stock was part of Liam's last name, so she felt that they were nine-nine percent certain to have the right SUV.

Alex suggested that while they waited for Liam to come back, they should get some carryout so they would not have to stop once they were back on the road.

Jason pointed out that they had passed a fast-food restaurant a few blocks back and suggested they go there and order lunch. They were in line to place their order when Johnnie said that Liam was on the move.

Liam had watched as Jack walked along the broad walk toward him. He picked out the two bodyguards walking in parallel out in the parking lot. He decided to step into the door of a bungalow until Jack passed by and then he would step out on his left side. When Jack came by, he stepped out and thanked him for agreeing to loan him the twenty-five thousand. He let him know that he was aware of his two body guards walking in parallel in the parking lot.

Jack said that the last time he had been kidnapped and ended up chained to the floor of a house someplace in Ohio. He said that this time he wanted to make sure that it would not happen again.

Liam said that this time he was the one that needed the help, and he would make sure that the loan was repaid with interest either in cash or in a significant in flow of drugs. He took the envelope that he was handed and put it inside of his shirt. He then exited to his left between two houses and went around back to an alley. He looked back to make sure he was not followed. He came out to where his car was parked, got in and drove away.

Jack had thought about trying to capture Liam and chaining him in one of his warehouses and perhaps beating him as well but the walk along the beach had too many witnesses. He did not want to attract attention and figured that the money was insignificant. He had bargained it down from fifty thousand to the twenty-five that he had just given to Liam. He now knew that Liam was running from something. He hoped to find out that whoever was chasing him caught him and perhaps killed him.

He called Elisa to let her know that he thought Liam was headed to San Diego.

She said that she was headed there and hoped to be on hand when Liam tried to get money from Osvaldo.

He then alerted the Puget Sound contact, and the San Diego contact to be on the watch for Liam.

He was betting on San Diego and sent one of his men down with Elisa to give Osvaldo a heads up and a hand if needed.

He had been coaching Osvaldo who was now second in command in the San Diego drug distribution effort. Osvaldo's uncle was the number one and had welcomed getting connected with the L.A. organization since it helped him overcome some of the smaller local Mexican gangs that competed with him. The flexibility to float any extra drugs from one city to the other improved the distribution fluidity and made managing the cash flow easier. It was a win-win for the two organizations.

Johnnie was constantly giving an update on location and Jason, who was now doing the driving, was keeping up with Liam. He found it hard to keep the right distance behind so they would not be spotted but managed not to lose Liam as they drove south on the very busy interstate five. Jason was keeping track of Liam's car visually and followed him off the interstate to a large truck stop where Liam gassed up and then walked into the station to a Cheeky Fela fast food restaurant.

Alex suggested they gas up and go next door to the competing fast food and get a late lunch. Everybody was back in the van and were watching when Liam returned and got in his SUV.

Laticia asked when Alex planned to capture Liam.

Alex said that she hoped to utilize Laticia's San Diego team so they would have overwhelming superiority when she closed the trap. She hoped that wherever Liam chose to spend the night was conducive to his capture.

636

17 Payback

*O*svaldo received the call from Jack letting him know that Liam had stopped and received twenty-five thousand dollars of a fifty thousand dollars ask and that he was probably on his way to San Diego and might try to get more from him. He in turn let his uncle know of the situation. Osvaldo was hoping that he would be contacted. He had no intentions of giving Liam any money, but he had other plans for him.

His uncle slammed his hand on the desk where he was sitting and told him that Liam was going to pay for having killed his favorite nephew, Thiago. He described how he was going to shoot him through both knees, then his feet, then his shoulders and finally he would shoot him between his eyes.

He was silent for a moment then shook his head and described another scenario where he would first nail his feet to the floor and his hands to the wall before shooting nails from a nail gun all over his body and then finishing him off by shooting a nail through each eye to kill him. He nodded and said that he would use a nail gun. He made a call and gave instructions on how to prepare the warehouse for a special occasion.

The two of them were sitting in the warehouse office when Elisa and one of Jack's men arrived. They said they were there to make sure that Liam got what he deserved and that they were there to take part in whatever retribution that might be planned.

Liam got to San Diego and found a motel that had a vacancy sign flashing out front. He parked and went in and got a room. He had been working on remembering the phone number that he had listed for the one survivor from San Diego. When he recalled Osvaldo, the phone number popped into his mind. He could not remember Osvaldo's last name but that did not matter, what mattered was being able to call him and let him know that he wanted to meet, and that Osvaldo should bring fifty-thousand dollars with him.

Osvaldo was still in the warehouse office sharing a drink with everyone when he answered the call from Liam. He agreed to fork over fifty-thousand dollars, but that Liam needed to come to him since turning over that much cash was going to be a major effort.

Liam agreed but warned him that he would be armed and would not hesitate to shoot if it was a trap.

Osvaldo replied that he had learned his lesson and personally would not take any action against him.

Once the call was over, his Uncle laughed and said that Osvaldo should enjoy watching. Elisa said that she wanted to participate and fire the nail gun into Liam's private parts.

Johnnie had managed to keep track of Liam because he had hacked into the computer but other than location he had no other way of knowing what was going on. Suddenly he said that Liam was on the move. Everyone had been sitting debating whether they should get a room for the night, but Alex had decided that they should wait to make sure that Liam was staying in for the night.

Trevor gave her a hard time about missing his dinner time.

Alex reached into her bag and handed out an energy bar to everyone in the van.

Suddenly Thermon pointed to where Liam had parked and said that Liam was leaving the hotel. He started the van and followed.

They drove into a warehouse industrial area and watched as Liam pulled up to a warehouse door and honked. The door rolled up and open and once the SUV drove in it rolled back down.

Thermon parked on the street, and everyone got out. Alex reminded everyone to put on their Kevlar outfits including their gloves and head gear.

Laticia commented that her team had the standard bullet proof vests and that she was impressed with what the Cincinnati detective unit gave to its people.

Bill shook his head and said that their protective suits were gifted by Alex, and they had saved each one of them multiple times. They were all believers in their gear.

Alex noted that the warehouse was twenty bays long and that the car had entered in about the middle. She suggested that Bill and Trevor lead the way down the front and Thermon and Jason follow them. She, Trey, Johnnie, and Laticia would go down the back side and see if they could find a way in.

Trevor pointed out that there were regular entrance doors by each one of the roll up truck doors and that they would try the ones closest to where the SUV had entered.

Laticia commented that she had put in a call to the San Diego folks and had learned that the San Diego team had been prepared to join them the following day and that it would take them several hours to get to where they were currently located. She had told them to get prepared just in case she called for help.

Alex led the way around the back. She saw that the back was a duplicate of the front and figured that trucks could drive in one side get loaded or unloaded and then drive straight out the back. She counted the doors and pointed to the one she thought would be where the SUV would drive out.

Inside Osvaldo greeted Liam and said he was pleased to see him. He did not say why he was pleased until Liam was near him, and his uncle's men jumped out and put guns to Liam's head and disarmed him. Two of them literally picked him up by the arms and carried him into the room where his uncle was waiting for him with the automatic heavy duty nail gun.

Liam was pushed down into the chair and his uncle nailed his hands to the arm rest, then had his feet positioned and nailed them to the floor.

Liam screamed continuously as his hands were nailed to the chair, and his feet were nailed to the floor.

His uncle then explained that he was going to feed him as much money as he could stuff down his throat as he alternately continued to put nails in every part of his body.

He then handed Elisa the nail gun.

She asked if Liam remembered her.

He nodded his head and said that he hoped that she did not hold a grudge.

She laughed and said that she did not hold grudges but focused on getting even and then she shot a series of nails between Liam's legs.

Liam continued his screaming. It was hard for him to think. He needed to somehow get the nail gun to stop. His mouth was forced open, and a wad of bills were stuffed in.

Osvaldo stood to the side and commented that he was going to keep his promise and not take any action against him but his father and uncle of the person he had shot back in Ohio was going to keep shooting nails into him until he begged to die.

Alex was counting the doors as they walked along the back when she said she thought she heard someone screaming. She picked up the pace and when she got to the door that she figured was the right one, she tried to open it but found it locked. She took out her kit and after a few tries she managed to pick the lock.

It was dark inside and almost impossible to see anything. She led the way toward where the screams were coming from.

Trevor led the way along the front of the warehouse and opened the door nearest where the SUV had entered. Once inside he cautiously moved towards where it was parked. The four of them had heard the screams and had their weapons at the ready.

All was quiet as Johnnie led the way toward the location of where he instinctively knew the screams had originated.

He spotted movement on the other side of where the SUV was parked. He flashed his light, got a response, and knew that Trevor and Bill were approaching from the other side. There was a door lit by a small overhead light to his right.

They approached and Johnnie knelt down and tried the door that opened inward into a well-lit room that was empty except for Liam who was riddled by nails and most certainly dead since he had a nail through each eye.

Alex slowly approached Liam and realized that he had hundreds of nails in his body. There were four nails in his skull. He had a nail through each eye and one nail in each temple. She wondered which of the four nails had ended Liam's life.

A few moments before, one of Osvaldo's men had come in and said that there were eight people that had entered the warehouse and were coming toward where they were located. His uncle said that he was done and fired his last four nails and pointed to the exit to the roof and said that they should all go quietly and leave their trophy to be discovered by whoever was coming. He was sure it was not any of his competitors so it must be the law, and he did not need to have a run in with them over some worthless scum that was now dead. He added that he was feeling good, and that he was treating everyone to a round of drinks. They should all go and celebrate the passing of a person who did not deserve to live.

Laticia stopped when she got into the room. She placed a call to the San Diego team and said that she needed them to come and clean a site and make what they found disappear. She did not want the local law or the media to find out about the situation. She wanted it to be a very thorough job and that nothing should be written, and everything needed to be disappeared. She then detailed how to get to where they were located.

She looked at Alex and asked her what she planned to do.

Alex shook her head, replied that her case was closed, and she was ready to return to Cincinnati and formally write up the paperwork to close it.

She added that Liam had killed the wrong person when he had killed the individual from San Diego, and he had underestimated the type of revenge that would be implemented.

She then shared that she had been asked whether she thought Liam should get the death penalty and she had said that he certainly deserved it though she was usually against it. However, at that time, in her heart she felt he deserved it.

Seeing what had happened to him she figured that some being had agreed with her and had delivered a fate beyond what she could ever have imagined. The thing that bothered her was that she felt that how Liam had died was appropriate for the deaths that he had so negligently handed out.

Trevor shook his head and said that he felt the same way and it did not bother him.

Johnnie said. "A man reaps what he sows. The one who sows to please his sinful nature, from that nature will reap destruction. Let us not become weary in doing good, for at the proper time we will reap a harvest if we do not give up."

642

18 Case Closed

*A*lex was sitting with Tracy, her analyst, and sharing the fact that her lack of remorse for how the person who she was after had died was having a negative effect on her.

She commented that the case where she had hunted down and killed many of the members of several groups who kidnaped, raped, and then killed women had not affected her like this most recent case.

The case where she had hunted down a woman who had killed her mother and then had become a black widow that killed the men she had sex with had not affected her like this most recent case.

The case where she had had almost lost her partner and then had followed a trail of drug dealing bosses who she eliminated had not affected her like this most recent case.

Even the case where she was the target of a racist maniac who she ended up following into the woods of Mississippi killing had not affected her as much as this most recent case.

Tracy asked what made this current case so different.

Alex thought for a moment and commented that in the other cases she had to deal with the fact that she had killed multiple people or had been the target of killers trying to kill her.

She always tried to arrest the people she was after, but she never hesitated to shoot if they tried to kill her.

She said what was different in this case was that she felt no remorse for the fashion of death that the person she was after had suffered but instead that she thought that he got what he deserved.

She mentioned that Johnnie had quoted a biblical verse about reaping what one sows.

She not only agreed with it but wondered if it was enough and would there have been an even more cruel way to inflict death.

It was this last thought that bothered her.

Tracy asked what the perpetrator had done to make her think that.

Alex said that he had executed ten young men and dumped six of them in a ravine because he had decided they were useless baggage.

She thought for a moment and added that perhaps she had wanted him to face the jury, then listen to the guilty verdict and then spend the rest of his life behind bars thinking about the nature of his crime.

She looked to Tracy and said that he had suffered an agonizing and painful death, but she added that it had been over too fast and instead of regretting having killed the young men, the moments before his death was focused on his pain, it was focused on himself.

Tracy nodded and said that she found it admirable that what Alex was describing was not the need for revenge but the need for the guilty person to spend time contemplating the error of their ways.

She suggested that Alex share her perspective with the rest of the team. She let Alex know that the rest of the team had scheduled sessions with her so she might have another perspective once she had experienced those sessions but for the time being she suggested that Alex should not worry about the lack of remorse but focus on the good feelings she had about the friends around her.

Alex thanked Tracy and went back to where the team was sitting around their desks.

Travis looked at her and asked if her session with Tracy had done any good or was, she just as crazy as before.

Alex smiled and just replied, "I love you too" and sat down. She shook her head and said that as horrible as the sight had been of the way Liam had died, she had found it hard for her to feel sorry for him, but she felt angrier that he would not get to think about what he had done. She said that she felt he had gotten off easy.

Bill nodded and said that he understood her feelings and that for Liam it was over but for the team they would live knowing that ten families would wonder what had happened to their sons. He said he had similar feelings about Liam having gotten off easy.

Johnnie pointed to the Chief's office where Tracy was just closing the door and commented that whatever Alex had just shared with her had caused Tracy to meet with the Chief.

Not too long after Tracy left, the Chief signaled for all of them to come to his office.

After they were all seated at the table he asked if all the closing paperwork had been submitted. He asked each of them to give a quick summary of their perspective of the case. They all had very similar points about the case and how its closure had been very different than they had expected.

The Chief then said that he had a few additional pieces of information that he had to share. Each of the ten victims had been identified and their next of kin would be notified. The IRS had collected the taxes on the Liam's accounts. He added that the remainder of the money had been put into a fund that had been set up to help needy kids. He went on to share that a report from Laticia complemented all of them for the professionalism, skill, and bravery that they had shown in the field.

She recommend that each have the entry put into their records that the CIA thanked them for the help in neutralizing a roque CIA agent.

He went on to share that the department received compensation for the time and effort that the team had spent on the case as well.

He smiled and said that the department was extremely happy with the fact that the budget was back in balance, and he would be able to gainfully employ them on the next case.

He looked around the table and said that he felt so good about everything that he was inviting them to a Sunday grill out at his place.

The End of the Nine Towers of Ku

Abandoned

1 A Life Worth Escaping

Bento thought back over his life and realized that it had been one spent at the bottom of Brazilian society. His parents tried to give he and his eight brothers and sisters as good of a life as they could. Theirs was a hard life being servers of the wealthier. His mother was a maid to several families that were not necessarily rich, but they were well enough off to have a part time maid. His father was a laborer that was often unemployed and looked for day labor. They both worked hard to keep a roof over their head and keep everyone clothed and fed. They were firm but they never beat any of them.

He always figured their big mistake was having eight kids. He was the youngest. He got all the hand me downs in clothing. He was also often the one that got the least food when times were extra hard.

His tumbles with his brothers and sisters hardened him and he learned to get what he needed. He knew it had definitely shaped how he assessed those that he mixed with.

His schooling was spotty, but he did get through Ensino Médio, (secondary education). He was not a great student, and he did not like the school environment.

Then after getting out of school the reality of his situation hit him. No matter how hard he tried, he couldn't find a meaningful full-time job. To no avail he tried every means possible to land a job that paid well enough that he could move away from his parents and live on his own.

Then one of his school friends got him to become a "distributor" which was a fancy name for becoming a drug dealer.

Abandoned

It turned out he was very good at being a distributor and was soon making enough money that he was able to enjoy some of the things in life that he had always seen others enjoying such as a day on the beach, eating at a restaurant, even dating. This made him become even better at distributing.

He was soon rising in the ranks of the local drug ring. He was called in to meet with the two big bosses who congratulated him on his good sales and gave him a bigger territory to manage.

He was able to move into a much better neighborhood and into a decent apartment. Decent in that it was at least a step up from what he had been living in.

Not long after he met Janaina at a small local diner. He asked her out and soon they were dating on a regular basis. He was pleased that she was attracted to him. She had a knockout figure and her tanned white skin, black hair set her apart from other young women he had his eyes on.

It helped his ego that she said that he was the best-looking guy that she had ever thought of going out with. It was about a year later that he proposed.

His mother suggested he bring Janaina to dinner so that she and his dad could meet her.

That dinner turned out to be a catastrophe.

His mother was surprised and upset that Janaina was white. She let him know that she did not approve and didn't want mulatto or a pardos for a grandchild.

His father didn't say anything, but he did not come to his defense either.

It was clear that he was not going to get the approval of his parents, but he was not going to change his mind because they objected.

When he got married, his brothers and sisters attended his small wedding but neither of his parents showed up. Janaina had no relatives and there were only a few of her friends at the wedding. Almost all of the distributors that he managed were in attendance, which made him feel good since it showed him that he was doing a good job with them. He also realized that he truly was a drug dealer.

He was making enough that he could afford a small loft apartment, some new furniture and food was no longer an issue for him. It seemed that the two of them were headed into a good life.

Less than a year later, Janaina let him know that the was going to be a father.

This was good news, but it also bothered him.

Good news in that he wanted to be a father.

It bothered him that his child would someday find out that he was a drug dealer. He had become one of the top distributors and the big boss had put him in charge of several other distributors.

His job was to make sure that those working for him gave him the right amount of money and that they kept only the cut they had agreed to. He was very good at making sure that those working for him were "honest."

Since all the sales money came to him and he took it into the office, he was often in possession of more money than most people made in a year.

The day came when he rushed Janaina to the hospital and waited outside of the delivery room. They had spent many hours looking at baby names and had selected one for a boy and one for a girl. It would either be Afonso if a boy or Aurea if a girl.

The nurse who came out let him know that he had a beautiful baby girl and that he could see her through the window in the nursery. He stood looking through the glass and what he though was the best-looking baby in the nursery.

He waited until she as carried out and followed the nurse to the room Janaina was in. He gave her a hug and then held Aurea for the first time. He though his heart was going to break because he was so happy.

A few days later, Aurea came home with Janaina. A home that now had a happy but worried father. He decided that he had to find a better life for his family than the one he had grown up in. He dutifully saved as much money as he could while he looked around for a way to escape his current role managing half a dozen distributors.

He was aware that he couldn't just tell his bosses that he was getting out of the distribution business. He was at a level where he had seen what happened to those that cheated or tried to move to another organization. Those people were somewhere pushing up grass and flowers. They could neither quit nor change allegiances. He did not see a way that he could possibly escape his current situation.

He was watching the news about a shooting in Cincinnati, Ohio and listened as a black female detective was being asked about the fact that she had solved a fifteen-year-old cold case and had saved the person who was now a young woman that had two children by her kidnapper. The story seemed to spark and light a fire within him. He had no idea where Cincinnati was located other than in the US, but he now had a goal. He would leave Brazil and go to Cincinnati. He would go where a black woman was seen as a heroine.

He found out where Cincinnati was located. He then found out how much it would cost to get there. His goal to save the astronomical amount and to get visas took him much longer than he anticipated. The time turned into years and his role in the drug distribution business continued to flourish.

Aurea's sixth birthday was the catalyst that finally and very loudly fired the starting gun. During the party she said that she wanted to be just like him.

"Just like him." "Just like him." "Just like him." Kept going through his mind. He didn't want any of his children to ever be just like him at least not the person that he currently had become.

He got the tourist visas for the US. He then skipped the payment on his apartment and arranged with Janaina to leave the country. He was short on the amount of money to pay for the airline tickets, but he had an upcoming money collection round that would give him what he needed and enough money to live for a few months in the US.

He figured that the amount of money did not matter. If he took it his fate would be the same no matter the amount. He made his collection rounds and headed straight to the airport where Janaina and Aurea were waiting for him.

He was constantly looking out for anyone that might be looking for him.

He was a wreck by the time that they got on the plane. He knew that he would be hunted but once on the plane he was able to relax and when the plane finally took off, he felt that he had made his escape. He doubted that anyone would learn where he had gone, and he was going far enough away that he figured no one would be sent after him.

The plane laned in Miami where they went through customs before going on to Cincinnati on a regional flight.

He was surprised that they landed in Kentucky at the Cincinnati International Airport. He got a ride to the hotel that he had rented that was on the western side of the city. He rented a room with two beds, for two weeks. On the same day as his arrival, he walked across to the other side of eighth street and got two jobs. One was as a short order cook, and the other was managing the cash register at a gas station. He was surprised at how easy getting started was for him. He wondered about how long it would take to work his way up to some bigger, better paying jobs.

He asked Janaina to find as inexpensive an apartment to rent as possible and to get Aurea enrolled in school.

He was surprised at how quickly Janaina found a furnished two-bedroom apartment that was over a small restaurant in the downtown area. It was very basic and had mostly older furniture and appliances.

It was within walking distance to his two current jobs and the school where Aurea would go. This would allow him to continue working where he was until he could figure out how to get some better job or jobs.

He was impressed when Aurea took the school's entrance test and got placed one level above what he and Janaina expected. She had done so well that the principal commented that she was being placed one level above that was normal for her age, because her math and reading scores were so high that it was warranted. The principal also said that her verbal English skills were a little rough but good enough that she would have no problems.

Janaina was also very happy about everything. She had Aurea enrolled in school and she had talked herself into a part time job at the restaurant that was just below the apartment.

He was relieved that with their three incomes, they would be able to pay the rent, have enough money to buy food and be able to save for a rainy day. He figured that in a few months they would be in good financial shape.

The year flew by. There was little time for anything but work and more work. He made it a point that whenever he could the three of them did something together. They often went to the riverfront and enjoyed the free games that were available there and to have a picnic on the lawn.

On one occasion he splurged and rented a segway so that Aurea could experience riding it. They had a great time riding it together for a short time, but he was afraid that they might have a wreck.

During the summer they attended several free outdoor concerts where they sat on the hillside and enjoyed a picnic. Then during the winter, they made it to the ice-skating rink and all of them tried their luck on the ice.

Aurea was the one that seemed to be a natural. He and Janaina took off their skates and watched Aurea go around the rink. They held hands and smiled as they watched their beautiful daughter laughing and enjoying herself.

In the spring they walked across the Purple People's Bridge and when they got to the other side, he bought Aurea a bratwurst that they all ended up sharing.

He and Janaina agreed that their move to Cincinnati was the best decision they could have made.

Aurea spent almost all her extra hours at the main public library. Janaina had enrolled her in an after-school program that featured a variety of supervised activities. This allowed her to work at the restaurant while Aurea enjoyed herself in a safe environment.

It was a good year, and it seemed that life for him and his family was on an upward path.

He was standing at the grill flipping a series of burgers when the cashier said that there was a rather tough looking dude at the counter asking to talk to him. He walked out and almost fainted when he saw Cristiano standing on the other side of the counter. He knew that Christiano was the mean partner of the drug distribution ring in Sao Paulo and if he was in Cincinnati, it meant trouble. He almost turned and ran but instead he faced Cristiano as if he had no fear when in fact, he was about to wet himself.

Cristiano spoke to him in Portuguese and asked him if he had the money that he had taken from his operation.

If the situation hadn't been so serious Bento would have laughed. He had spent the money and there was no money other than the little he and Janaina had been saving. That amount was a far cry from the money he had taken from the drug business. He knew if Christiano had personally made the trip he was there to make a point and to make an example of what happened when someone crossed the organization.

Christiano shook his head and smiled as he said that if he got his money back, he would only kill him but if that didn't happen, he would take some of that payment from Janaina before he killed her.

He figured that there was no money, so he said that he was also planning to cut out his tongue and cut off his ears, take them back to Sao Paulo and hang them behind the bar with a sign that declared that thieves were always caught and rewarded for their actions.

He asked what Bento had to say while he still had a tongue.

Bento stood silently as he thought about what he had to do.

Christiano nodded and said that he would be waiting out in the parking lot and that Bento should make it easy on himself. If he came out to the parking lot, he would kill him before cutting out his tongue.

Bento nodded and put up his hand and then turned and went back into the kitchen area. He did not stop at the grill but headed straight out the back door. He ran all the way back to the apartment.

Janaina had just returned from school with Aurea. She was surprised to see him and when she understood that they had been found she was as afraid as he was. She knew that they had to make a run for it, and she knew that they had to find a safe place to leave Aurea.

She said that they needed to get out of the apartment, and they needed to get Aurea to a safe place.

He convinced her that they would be safe until the next day.

Janaina said that she knew where they had to take Aurea and they had to do it very early the next morning.

A few hours before sunrise they all left the apartment with all the food they could carry and with Aurea's clothes, the few toys she had and a family picture of the three of them together in the park. It all fit in a large black plastic bag.

Aurea was confused about what was happening. She kept asking why they were walking across town in the dark.

Janaina led the way and crossed on the walking bridge that led to Mt. Adams. She was taking her to the only place she felt that Aurea would be safe. She did not know how she was going to be able to leave her there by herself, but she knew that she had to leave her and that she and Bento needed to try to make their escape afterwards.

She stood and looked up the three long series of steps that led to the house. She took Aurea up and had her sit on the porch swing with all her things. She then gave her a hug and let her know that she was loved but she had to stay here where she would be safe.

Bento knelt down and gave her a hug and repeated the fact that she was loved. He handed her a large envelope and said that she should give it to the lady that would come out on the porch later in the morning.

He looked at Janaina and said she should stay.

Janaina shook her head and said that Christiano had come for her as well. Back in Brazil he had often threatened to have her when she was through with her lover. He would just find her later, so she was going as well.

They both descended the steep steps and walked back to the downtown area.

They asked each other where they should go. They came to the realization that there was no place to run to.

They decided to have breakfast at the restaurant where Janaina worked and wait for the inevitable.

They had just finished their breakfast when Christiano walked in. He looked around and asked if he could join them at their table. He smiled and asked if they were ready for a ride out to the countryside. He then asked where their lovely daughter was and when he got no answer he simply said "good" I have no interest in her.

He stood up and said they should follow him.

The owner came out and asked if everything was OK.

Janaina smiled, said that she appreciated his concern, but everything was fine as she gave him a hug and then followed Christiano out to the car.

The owner followed but stayed in the doorway. He took a picture of the license plate and stepped back inside. He figured he had enough of his own problems and didn't need to get involved in his employee's problems. He suspected that they were in the country illegally.

Christiano instructed her to sit in the back and let her know that he had a gun that would be aiming at Bento if she tried anything.

He then got on seventy-one, drove several exits past King's Island before exiting and driving through the farm country. Then at a sign that declared that the road was to be used by only authorized personnel, he turned and went into the forest. He hoped that it would not be used while he was having the graves dug and he was covering them up.

He stopped the car and instructed the two of them to get out and walk around to the front of the car. He screwed on a silencer as he walked around to meet them.

Janaina saw what he was doing and as fast as she could she ran towards him. She hoped to knock him down so that Bento could kill him.

Bento realized what she was doing and rushed after her.

Christiano barely had time to finish putting on the silencer before he was hit and knocked back a step by Janaina. He shook his head and said "muito ruim para você" and shot her between the eyes.

Bento thought he was going to get a chance at taking Christiano down when he felt the bullets hit him in the chest. He gave Christiano a finger and then the world went black.

Christiano shook his head when realized that he would need to dig the graves to bury the two. He had planned to have the two dig their own graves.

He put on his rubber gloves, cut off Bento's ears, his tongue and put them into a plastic bag between aluminum foil and sealed it. He dropped the bag into a US priority mail envelope that he would mail when he got to the airport.

He found a place where a natural dip in the land provided some initial depth and then he went to work. He decided that one grave would be sufficient. He put them both in, covered the grave, made sure there was a rock layer across the top and then put old leaves and some tree branches over all of it. He stepped back and decided that it would never be found.

Not far from the grave he found a large flat rock and put the gun under it. It was a gun that he had paid for in cash on the street and would never be traced to him even if it was found.

He then left but before reaching the highway, he threw the shovel into the ditch.

He felt justified and successful as he drove back to the airport.

A short time later, he drove into the car rental and a few moments after that he rode the shuttle back to the terminal. Once inside he dropped his envelope into the mailbox then walked up to the check-in counter. He was not flying directly back to Brazil but was flying west to visit the Grand Canyon and then walk out on the see through walkway that would give him a look down into the canyon. He also planned to visit Bryce canyon and enjoy a hike before flying to Mexico City where he would spend several days and then fly back to Sao Paulo.

He figured that he might as well mix some pleasure with business. The business had been quickly done and the pleasure, though brief was what he was on his way to do.

He looked forward to getting back to Sao Paulo and a relaxing time there. He hoped that the mail would get there before him.

2 The Package on the Porch

Matt was still out with the EMT team, but Alex figured he would be arriving shortly. She was ready to prepare breakfast and was waiting until he arrived. She had invited Johnnie to join them and afterwards they would take their normal ride into work.

She hoped that Matt had an easy night, but she knew that was seldom the case. He told her the time right after the closing of the bars usually was peak time for his team to make several runs from some accident to the nearest hospital.

The doorbell rang and she figured that Johnnie had arrived. She went to the door and opened it.

She was not surprised to see Johnnie, but he was holding a bulging black bag in one hand and had his other hand on the shoulder of a beautiful, auburn-haired young girl who looked to be frightened.

He commented that she had been sitting on the porch swing and said that her mother and father had dropped her off where she would be safe.

Alex knelt down and asked the young girl her name and learned that it was Aurea. She then asked Aurea why her parents had left her on the porch.

"Because they wanted me kept safe and you are the only one, they trusted to keep me safe," Aurea quietly replied. She gave the envelope she had in her hand to Alex and said that her mother said that it was for her.

Alex accepted the envelope looked in it expecting to find a note and was surprised that it did have a note, but it was also filled with one-hundred-dollar bills. She looked up at Johnnie and asked what was in the black bag.

He put it down, looked into it and replied that it looked like clothes and a few other odd and ends.

Alex asked Aurea to follow her and as she led the way to the kitchen she asked if Aurea would like to have some breakfast.

She had Johnnie put the bag down just outside of the kitchen door.

She handed the envelope to Johnnie and asked him to count the amount of money in it.

She offered Aurea some eggs, pancakes, and a lot of syrup.

That got a smile from Aurea.

Alex asked when her parents would be back to pick her up.

Johnnie chuckled and said that given what was in the bag and the money in the envelope he figured it might be a long time.

Alex was trying to figure out what to do when Matt walked in from the backyard.

He smiled and said that he wasn't expecting company for breakfast.

Alex gave him a hug and introduced Aurea who had been dropped off on their front porch for safe keeping.

Alex asked him to sit down, and she would get him his breakfast.

Matt sat down and started a conversation with Aurea.

Alex knew from past experience that kids normally liked Matt and Matt had a natural way of talking to them.

He first asked her for her mother's and father's name. He asked where she was from and learned that they had come from Sao Paulo. He learned that they had been in Cincinnati almost a year.

He soon knew what school she was attending and the names of her teachers. He learned that her favorite place was the library where she normally spent her after school time. She liked the River Front Park because there were free games. He found out the address where she and her parents lived.

Alex kept quiet as she wrote down what she was hearing.

Johnnie joined her and asked what she was planning to do about the situation.

She replied that she was going to take the day off to find out what was going on.

Johnnie offered to help and suggested that he call Mary and ask her to come over to watch Aurea while the two of them investigated the situation. He added that Matt needed to get to bed and get some rest since he had been out the entire night.

Alex thought for a minute and then said that if Mary didn't mind her help would be greatly appreciated.

Johnnie gave a little laugh and commented that Mary would most likely love to do it. He walked out into the backyard and made a call. A short time later he walked back in with Mary.

Matt finished his breakfast and thanked Aurea for sharing her time with him. He looked at Alex and asked if she had the situation covered and smiled when he saw her mouth a thank you to him. He nodded and said he was going to take a shower and then get a good night's sleep.

Aurea asked who was going to take her to school.

This was something that Alex had not thought about.

Mary sat down at the table and asked where she went to school. She said that she would take her and asked when she had to be there.

Mary looked at Alex and asked if she had the right idea of why she had been called.

Alex nodded and said that if Mary could accompany Aurea and find out her routine it would be a great help. She added that all expenses would be paid. She also asked if she could get one of the guest bedrooms ready for Aurea.

Johnnie pointed to the black bag and said that he figured everything that she had was in the bag.

Mary opened the black bag, looked into it, and let out a whistle. She reached in and took out a framed picture of Aurea and her parents. She handed it to Johnnie and said the picture might come in handy.

Alex walked out of the kitchen to the back porch and called the Chief. She informed him of the situation and let him know that she was going to treat the situation like a case, but she was going to take the day off to do so.

He said that she did not need to use her vacation and that he wanted her to come in and that he wanted Trey to join her in her investigation. He made the point that parents dropping off their child on a strangers porch was very unusual and he figured the situation merited handling it like an actual case that needed to be investigated.

She agreed to come into the office with Johnnie and to get things organized.

When she went back into the kitchen, Johnnie asked her if she planned to eat breakfast.

She shook her head and said that the two of them should plan to ride to work and figure out what the next step would be.

She went to the drawer in the kitchen and took out several hundred dollars and gave it to Mary and told her to use a taxi and spend whatever she needed but to get receipts because the situation might turn into an actual case.

Mary looked at the amount of money and shook her head and asked what she thought a taxi was going to cost.

Aurea asked if Alex was going to find her parents.

Alex sat down at the table and put her hands on Aurea's hands and said that she was going to do everything possible to find them but while she was looking Aurea would be staying in a room in the house and would be kept safe. She should plan on going to school, then to the library afterwards and that later they would all have dinner either at the house or at a restaurant.

She then said that she and Johnnie were leaving, and that Mary was going to make sure she got to school and afterwards to the library.

She looked at Mary and asked her to find out what she could from the teachers and the librarians.

She followed Johnnie down the front steps to where they had their bikes chained.

The two talked back and forth via their headsets on their ride down the hill to the police station.

Once there, Alex stopped to get her cup of coffee before heading over to her desk.

She knew she was in for a quiz when Trevor smiled and asked why she was late for work.

Trey handed her half of a bear claw, and she slowly took a bite before replying to Trevor.

Johnnie walked in with his coffee, looked into the donut box, and picked out a glazed cake donut.

She smiled and replied to Trevor's question that she had been looking for a suitable case that they could work on, and she was going to make sure he got the exciting end.

Trevor laughed and said that he had never figured out what end the dull part of any of her cases happened to be.

The Chief came over and suggested that she, Johnnie, and Trey accompany him into his office.

Bill laughed and said that it seemed that they were going to be left out.

The Chief looked over to him and said that he should be glad to be able to relax while he ate his donut and had his coffee.

Once in the office, the Chief asked Alex to the situation. He made the point that parents dropping kids off to a stranger for safe keeping was very unusual. He stated that he was going to treat it as a formal case that involved potential danger. He said that he had already informed his bosses and they all agreed that given the history of your cases it was warranted.

Alex shook her head and asked what they meant by the history of her cases.

He asked her how many times she had been shot and ended up in the hospital.

She nodded and said that it was more times than she cared to think about.

He handed her the folder that was labeled, "The package on the front porch case."

She read the label and laughed. She said that it was the most beautiful package that she had recently seen. It had dark brown eyes, auburn hair, and a honey-colored skin and it was well composed and polite. She knew she was from Brazil but had yet to follow up on that.

The Chief smiled and said that she should make sure that she did not get too attached to that beautiful package.

He asked her how she planned to proceed.

She said that the place she was going to start was the hole in the wall diner just a few blocks away. Then she was going to the Cincinnati Library and talk to some librarians and finally she was going to walk to where Aurea went to school and see if she could talk with Aurea's teachers. She said that by the late afternoon she hoped to figure out how she would proceed.

She added that she had Mary was looking after Aurea and probably talking to some of the same people.

The Chief then asked if she planned to leverage the rest of the team.

Alex smiled and said that she would love to as soon as she had something for them to do but at the moment, she was not sure what that might be.

He nodded and looked at Trey and simply said, "have her back."

Trey smiled and asked if he meant "hold her back."

The Chief laughed and said for him to do both.

Alex smiled, waved her case folder, and walked out of the office.

She walked over to where Bill and Trevor were sitting having their morning coffee and asked them if they wanted to come along and enjoy brunch at a small local restaurant.

Trevor nodded and said that he would love to but that she had to lead the way into the restaurant because he did not want to be asked along just to serve as a shield.

Bill gave Trevor a shove and said that the next time bullets flew he was going to stand behind him.

Alex led the team to the small restaurant. She and Johnnie had made it a point to try breakfast and lunch at almost all the downtown establishments. This particular one had been visited once but had never made it to their favorite list.

She walked in and was greeted by the same person who had served her before. She asked for a table for five.

He smiled and said that he was pleased that she had decided to come back. He asked her to be patient because his normal waitress was absent.

Alex put in her order for tea and a scone and once the orders were in, she asked where the waitress that was absent had gone.

The owner said that she and her husband had an early morning breakfast and as they were finishing a large rather rude man came in and spoke to them in a foreign language. Then the waitress got up gave him a hug and followed the man out to his car.

He said that he followed them out to door, and that he got a picture of the license plate. He pulled out his phone and pulled up the picture.

Johnnie took the phone and sent the picture to all of them. He looked over at Trevor and asked him to follow up on it.

Alex asked the proprietor what language the rude person had used.

He shook his head and said that it was not Spanish but seemed similar.

A few moments later, Trevor's phone buzzed. He kept saying, "yes, yes, OK," and then hung up.

He looked around and said that the car was a rental that had been rented at the airport.

Alex asked that he and Bill follow up and see if it was still out and if not see if they could find out to what airline the renter had gone to. She added that the car should be impounded so that forensics could go over it in detail and get fingerprints and DNA.

Trevor nodded and said that he was glad that so far, he and Bill got the easy end of the case.

Alex smiled and said that they should get going while the trail was hot and to make sure neither of them got shot.

Once they had left, she looked at Trey and Johnnie and said that she was beginning to think that they would not find Aurea's parents alive. She hoped that she was wrong but to have someone come to Cincinnati from Brazil to meet with them felt ominous to her.

She wondered what the two had been running from. She looked at Johnnie and asked if he could look them up on some database that would have their visa information. And if he could follow their names to wherever it might lead.

She was quiet for a moment then asked Trey whether she could bring Aurea to his grill out on Sunday.

Trey nodded and said that he had just gone through all the toys that Nolan had outgrown. He was planning to pass them on to friends or give away. He figured he had plenty that might interest Aurea but there would be no kids her age to play with at the grill out.

Alex smiled and said that Matt was coming along and would fill in.

She then suggested they go to the library and see what they could learn there.

Johnnie nodded, said that he still had many librarian friends that he was sure would have noticed Aurea and might have some information that might prove useful.

Several librarians knew Aurea and commented that she was a bright young girl that must have been related to Johnnie because she always made sure to attend the lectures that had refreshments provided.

That gave Johnnie a laugh. He added that no one as pretty as Aurea would be a relative of his.

He asked what other things that Aurea was into and learned that Aurea loved to do research on the internet and by research she was into researching famous individuals and the histories of various countries.

Trey asked if that was common for someone so young and learned that it was not and that was why it was being mentioned.

Alex asked about Aurea's parents and learned that Aurea's mother would sign her in and then leave for work. She would return on time to sign Aurea out and take her home. It was clear that the mother took very good care of her daughter and the two of them were close.

Alex thanked each of the librarians and then took a moment to summarize that they had learned that Aurea loved the treats she could get at the library, and she was into learning about the history of the world around her. She added that the treats would be attractive to any kid but Aurea arranged her time so she could enjoy one each day. She was also a serious young lady in that she was into studying history and famous people.

Back in the office, Johnnie focused on getting into the database that would have the visa information for Aurea's parents. He also ran the face recognition program against the news databases in Sao Paulo. It did not take long for him to find a couple of articles that had Bento's picture. Several times he was standing behind the ring leaders of a drug distribution ring that controlled most of Sao Paulo.

Once again Alex commented that she was feeling more and more like they would not find either Janaina or Bento alive. She wondered if either of the two ring leaders might be the one that had left the diner with the two.

She asked Johnnie to go back with a picture of the two and see if the diner's proprietor recognized either of them. She also asked him to send the pictures out to Bill and Trevor to see if any of the ticket agents recognized either of the two.

She led the way to the school that Aurea attended and once there she introduced herself and the fact that she was trying to find out what she could about Aurea's mother and father. She did not learn much but was asked to clarify the fact that Aurea was accompanied to school by a Mary Higgins, and she wanted confirmation that everything was legal and appropriate.

Alex assured her that Aurea was being looked after while she tried to locate her mother and father.

She was then able to talk to several of the teachers that had nothing but praise for Aurea, her behavior, and her high standing in all of her classes.

She unexpectedly felt sense of pride in the positive information she was learning about Aurea.

After returning to the office, she was sitting at her desk when Bill and Travis returned from the airport and said that they had struck pay dirt in that one of the ticket agents recalled one of the men in the pictures and called him a rude dude because he was upset that he couldn't get a first-class seat.

He was headed for the Grand Canyon and was traveling on a one-way ticket. The agent conjectured that he must be leaving from that airport on a ticket of some other airline but when he had asked about helping to make a good connection, he had been told to mind his own business.

Alex asked Trevor and Bill if they wanted to join in on an evening dinner at a restaurant of Johnnie's choice.

Both of them said that they had other plans for the evening.

Trey spoke up and said that he preferred to go home to dinner.

Matt was still out with his EMT team at dinner time, so Alex, Johnnie, Mary, and Aurea went to dinner at a restaurant that had a great view of the River Front Park's play area and the John A. Roebling Suspension Bridge that crossed the river to Covington.

Aurea was immediately drawn to the window and said that she saw a couple of places where she had played. She turned away from the window and then asked whether Alex had found her mother.

Alex said that she had not.

After ordering dinner, Alex shared the fact that everyone that she had talked to had said nice things about Aurea. She asked Aurea if she would like to go with her and Matt to a grill out at Trey's house.

Aurea asked if there would be any other kids there.

Alex shook her head and said that there would be no kids but plenty of toys, an outdoor swing set and plenty of great food.

Aurea nodded and said, "OK."

3 A Call of the Heart

*J*ohnnie continued tracking Christiano's travel but the trail was cold. Christiano left the country for Mexico City just ahead of when Johnnie found out where he was. Once out of the country, Johnnie knew that the final destination would be Sao Paulo. He let Alex know and then began to see how he could find a computer trail to him. Alex let everyone know that for the moment Christiano had successfully made his escape. She contacted her friend the "Angel on the Hill" and asked if any of the cartels were supplying drugs to Christiano and the distribution ring that he operated in Sao Paulo. It was not long before she learned that indeed a large amount of drugs went that way. She was not sure what she would do with that information, but it confirmed the drug connection. She would keep that in mind as she thought about how to get to him.

She asked Bill to get the mileage that the rental car was used after Christiano rented it. She discussed this with Trey and Johnnie and after deducting the mileage to and from downtown Cincinnati from the Airport there were about seventy to seventy-five unaccounted miles. She went forty miles up both interstate seventy-five and seventy-four and looked where she ended up. She tapped on the screen in the area where that mileage ended and said that she thought they would find the bodies somewhere off of highway seventy-four because it had the most forested area.

The problem as she saw it was that they would be hunting blind over a very large, wooded area. She asked if anyone had any ideas.

Johnnie raised his hand and said, "Vultures."

Trevor laughed and asked if he expected the bodies to be laying out in some field where the vultures would see them.

Johnnie shook his head and said that vultures had an acute sense of smell and would probably be able to get the scent even from a buried body. He added that they should pay attention to the vultures circling over the established cemeteries.

He suggested that they contact the forest service and see if they would check out specific areas below any circling vultures in the area that they suspected the bodies might be.

Alex laughed, said that it was a great idea and that she hoped that the forest service would think so as well since she would be asking them to look skyward to find circling vultures. She made several calls and got in touch with the service. She shared the case she was on and that a drug enforcer might have killed two individuals and buried them somewhere in a fairly large area and she had no other idea than to see if the vultures might be sensitive enough to smell the bodies that would be buried somewhere in the woods.

She agreed with the ranger that it was a long shot but did get his agreement to have his personnel keep an eye on the vultures and explore the ground beneath where they were circling.

He said he was only doing it because he had followed a couple of her cases and knew that she had solved some very weird ones. He said that if his folks found anything he would contact her, but she had to promise to highlight his organization for the help they might provide.

Alex laughed and said that she would be glad to give all the recognition to him and his organization. She added that she didn't need her department tagged with using vultures to solve their cases.

Trevor laughed and said that the team had use just about every other means to solve their cases and many of those other means had come about because of Johnnie. He pointed over to him and said the if vultures worked, he would personally buy him a lunch at any restaurant in town.

Alex went into the weekend having done all she could do. She didn't have much to show for her efforts but didn't know what else to do. This frustrated her and she planned to spend extra time on the treadmill.

She decided to focus her efforts on Aurea. That afternoon after school she asked Auria if she liked to bike ride.

Aurea said that she did but that she hadn't had a bike to ride since they had come to Cincinnati.

Alex said they should go to a bike shop and see if they had any bikes that would be Aurea's size.

During the short ride to the bike shop Alex asked Aurea to share some of her memories from Brazil.

Aurea said that she knew that she and her parents lived in Capão Redondo which she knew was a poor section of Sao Paulo. She added that though they were poor she got to attend school, and they often went to the beach in Santos. Her father had said that soon they would be moving to a better neighborhood but before that happened, he said they were instead coming to the US.

Since Alex knew that Bento had been part of a drug distribution gang, she figured that he had arranged his departure using the money that passed through his hands. Getting the money back or just getting rid of the person who took it was probably why Cristiano had come to Cincinnati.

She thought of the vultures and wondered how long a body had to decompose before the vultures would be able to get the scent.

They arrived at the bicycle shop and her favorite bike mechanic, Sam, greeted her. He asked if she had brought one of her bikes in and learned that she wanted to buy a bike.

He commented that she had three of his best bikes and wondered what she would do with a fourth.

Alex held Aurea in front of her and said that it was for her.

He nodded and said that he had several that would be just right for her and led them to the four bikes he had in mind.

Alex looked them over and said that the two that had multiple gears would most likely be the ones that would allow Aurea to keep up with her and Matt.

She asked Aurea which of the two bikes she liked best.

Aurea asked if she could really have one of them. She looked over one that was a vibrant pink and shook her head and said that it was too girlish. She asked if she could try out the black one.

Sam pushed the bike out the front door to the large parking lot in front of the store. He had Aurea straddle the bike and adjusted the seat to Aurea's height and leg length.

Aurea pushed off and expertly got on. She struggled with changing gears but soon got the hang of that. She rode around the lot several times.

Her laughter and bright smile was all that Alex needed. She let Sam know that he had made a sale.

Sam commented that Aurea seemed to be a natural. He put the bike on the rack on Alex's car and then led the way back into the store. He asked who Aurea was and why she was buying a bike for her.

Alex said that it was a complicated story but she was currently charged with taking care of Aurea and she wanted her to participate with her and Matt and some of the things she enjoyed so she was buying her a bike so she could do so.

Sam nodded and said that for that brief explanation he was giving her a ten percent discount.

Alex thanked him and said that it was almost time to bring her three bikes in for their annual tune up and parts replacement. She went ahead and scheduled that and then led the way out of the store.

Aurea walked to the back of the car and ran her hands along bike's fenders and asked if the bike was really to be her own.

Alex laughed and said that it was too small for her so, yes it was hers.

Alex asked if Aurea had any other outfits to go out riding.

Aurea said that she only had one set of pants to wear.

Alex said that she was going to take her shopping in a special place. She then drove to the Goodwill Store where she always went when she needed a new outfit. She always bought her work outfits there because of the very reasonable price that she normally was able to find.

Once they were inside and looking for some jeans and other suitable riding pants, Aurea commented that her mother had taken her to a store that was much smaller but that was very similar that had good prices on all the things in the store. She asked if this was the same kind of store.

Alex said that it was and that she came shopping whenever she needed a new outfit to wear to work.

Aurea said that she thought Alex was rich and wondered why she would shop at a store for poor people.

Alex replied that she was not rich, and the store was not just for poor people. She had a good job that she liked, and she had a nice home, but she felt like she was a person that managed her money so that she could also help others.

They left the store with several outfits for Aurea that made sure she would have enough play and school clothes.

Alex said that there was one more special place they needed to stop before they went back home.

She pulled into her favorite ice cream shop and led the way in.

She pointed to the board and said that every choice was a good choice, and Aurea should choose the flavors and suggested get only two scoops because the scoops were large.

Aurea looked at the board for a long time and said that there were too many choices.

Alex laughed and said that she agreed and that they would have to come back many times until they had tried them all.

Once they had their ice cream she led the way to a table in the corner.

She asked what else Aurea remembered about Brazil.

Aurea said that she remembered her grandmother who she knew was mad at her father because he had chosen to marry her mom. She had been kind the few times they had met but it was always for a short time. She also knew that her dad's last job paid more but it was not a nice job because she heard her grandmother arguing with him about it. After that she never saw her grandmother again.

Alex could image the grandmother realizing that her son was a drug dealer and getting mad about it. She wondered how that mother would feel when she learned that her son had been killed by the people that he had worked for when he had tried to escape that life.

Alex shook her head and told herself to stop jumping ahead of what she knew for sure. She had no bodies, so she had nothing but conjecture in her hands. She watched Aurea enjoying her ice cream. It had only been a couple of days, but she knew that she was already getting too close. It was not going to be easy to step back from what she was feeling if her mother and father were found alive.

She shook her head as the thought about relying on vultures to find Aurea's parents.

She and Aurea got back to the house a short time before Matt was to get home. The plan was to go for a bike ride before going out to dinner.

She would make sure that she adjusted her dinner reservations at the Riverside Inn to include Aurea. She was sure that the view and barbeque would be something that Aurea would enjoy.

Matt arrived home right on time and said that he had a bike ride's worth of energy left but that going to dinner would need to be via taxi.

He asked if Aurea fit on any of their bikes and smiled when Aurea said that she had a new one of her own.

He looked at Alex and asked if she had been to the bike shop and how many extra hours was, she going to make him work for that visit.

Aurea took his hand and asked if he was the one that had to pay and that she hoped that he did not have to work too long.

Matt knelt down, gave her a hug, said that he was just joking and that they should all get ready for a nice ride. Then later they would enjoy a nice dinner together.

Alex coached Aurea on the ride down the steep streets and said that going down was difficult because they had to use the brakes but coming back from the ride would be harder because they would all end up pushing their bikes back to the house.

The ride on the bike trail allowed Alex to talk to Matt. She asked him what he thought about having a daughter like Aurea.

Matt looked at her and asked if she was seriously contemplating taking Aurea in.

Alex nodded and said that there was something about the situation that seemed to be calling to her. She asked him again about Aurea.

Matt smiled and said that he liked her as well but that he was going to wait until the case was closed before giving his answer to the question. He did not want his heart in one place if Aurea's mother was found alive and things had to change.

Alex said that was fair because she had the same reservations.

She reminded him that in two weeks they would be going up to see her parents and that by that time he might have to give her an answer.

Matt laughed and said that he knew she always solved her cases in lightening fashion and that he would get himself ready for such an event. He smiled and said that it would be an easy decision.

The ride as always seemed to relax Alex and when they returned the way back up the hill was not as hard as she had made out and Aurea was able to pedal up much of the way.

Matt said that he was game to walk down to the restaurant, but he was sure that he did not want to walk back up to the house.

They all went to get a quick shower. Aurea commented that she knew she was living in rich person's home because she had her own shower.

Alex smiled and said that she had to share hers with Matt and he was really a big guy.

Matt laughed and said that he would make room in the shower any time she wanted to join him.

They left and walked down the hill with Aurea holding both of their hands as they walked along. She chattered all the way to the restaurant about how much fun the ride had been. Alex looked up at Matt who just smiled and shook his head.

They were seated with a great view of the river. Alex suggested sharing a slab of ribs but each of them should have their own baked potato with all the trimmings.

Aurea looked at both of them and said that she was beginning to think that they were really rich people who didn't know they were rich.

Alex nodded and answered that maybe she and Matt would need to rethink their status.

On the ride back from the restaurant Aurea fell asleep sitting between the two of them.

Alex instructed the taxi driver to drop them off on the street above the address she had given her. This allowed them to carry Aurea in via the back yard that was at that level.

They carried her to her bedroom that Mary had arranged. It seemed that Aurea had been using it for some time even though it had only been a few days.

After getting her into her bed, Alex led the way to their bedroom and said that she was going to get ready for bed and that she planned to sleep in late.

Matt gave a little laugh and asked if that meant getting up by seven in the morning.

When she awoke, Alex looked at the clock and saw that Matt had been right. It was only seven in the morning, and she was ready to get up.

She was in the kitchen getting things ready for breakfast when Aurea walked in and asked if there was something to eat.

Alex gave her a hug and said that after watching her eat the night before she didn't think she would need to eat for another week.

Aurea sat down at the table and put her head down on her arm and said that she could wait until later.

Alex asked if some warm oatmeal with golden raisins and honey drizzled on top and a cup of warm milk sounded like something she might want.

Aurea nodded her head.

Alex got her the oatmeal and microwaved a cup of milk to warm it up. She then sat down with her cup of coffee and a bowl of oatmeal. She peeled an orange and put the sections on a small plate at the center of the table.

Aurea was almost done eating when Matt walked in and said that he hoped that the two of them had left him a little bit for him to eat.

There was a knock on the back door.

Alex let Mary and Johnnie in.

Mary put a plate with a loaf of banana bread that she had already sliced in the middle of the table.

Alex thanked her as she got up and got the butter out. She buttered a slice and put it on a plate for Aurea.

She then did the same for herself. A warm wave of pleasure seemed to flow through her as she realized that she was totally into having Aurea at her table.

Later that evening, she, Matt, and Aurea sat in the family room reading. Aurea had brought home several books from the library. She was starting to read <u>The Adventures of Huckleberry Finn</u> by Mark Twain.

Alex poked Matt and pointed to the book Aurea had in her hands.

Matt only smiled, nodded, and quietly said that she was definitely reading above age level.

Aurea looked up at them and said that she was just an old person in disguise and flipped to the next page.

That got a chuckle from both of them.

It was only a few hours later when they arrived at Trey's house for the barbeque. Lesley gave Aurea a hug and said that she had invited a neighbor and his family to the barbeque, because they had a daughter the same age and the two of them could have the run of the back yard and tackle any of the games available in the basement.

She took Aurea by the hand and walked with her to the backyard where she introduced her to Pattie and suggested they use the swing set, or they could get whatever they wanted to eat or go to the basement and play any games they wanted to play.

Lesley came back onto the porch where Alex was sitting and commented that Aurea was the beauty that Trey had described.

Alex shared what Aurea was reading.

Lesley laughed and said that Alex was acting like a proud mother boasting about how smart her daughter happened to be. She asked whether Alex was getting prematurely serious about the situation.

Alex nodded and said that she probably was. She and Matt had talked about having kids, but she had been afraid of getting pregnant because of the number of times she had been shot. It had made her hesitate about having kids.

She added that she was sure that Aurea would need a home. There was no way that she would let her be placed in the foster care service and she had learned that though there was a grandmother in Brazil there had been little connection between her and Aurea. If it came to it she would figure out what it would take to get the grandmother to relinquish any claim to Aurea.

She said that as soon as she was sure that Aurea was an orphan she would put in the paperwork to be her legal guardian until she could work through the adoption process.

Lesley took hold of Alex's hands and said that she hoped that everything would work out as Alex was anticipating and added that she and Trey would be on hand to help.

Alex thanked her and said that she did not want to find out that Aurea's parents had been killed but things were looking that way.

671

Alex Evercrest Collection Two

4 Trip Home

Alex called home and let her mother know that on her and Matts visit they would have a surprise for her and that she would never be able to guess what the surprise might be.

Rose-Anne knew that her daughter was always into something and that she most often had no way to guess what that might be. She responded that as long as it did not involve thugs trying to shoot their way into the house as they had done on a previous visit, she was looking forward to any surprise that Alex might have. She asked how many other people would be coming with her because she had also been surprised when it seemed that she had invited everyone she knew to come over to the house for dinner.

Alex said that only one other person other than Matt would be coming. She added that going out fishing would be one of the activities that she wanted to do but otherwise sitting around the pool was as exciting as she wanted the visit to be. She asked if coming in the middle of the week would work. She was happy to get an OK.

Rose-Anne said that she was working from home and that any day during the week would work. She asked whether she should plan for a formal dinner or if anything that she had ready to eat would work.

Alex said that she should not cook a formal dinner and that anything for lunches and dinners would work. She wanted to take it easy and wanted to go out fishing at her favorite spot on the lake.

Visiting her mother a few days early allowed her to get out of the office before she went crazy. The case seemed not to be making any progress and that was really bothering her..

Matt had let her know that he would be off Wednesday and Thursday and that going to Evanston would work as long as he was back by late afternoon on Friday.

That fit exactly what Alex wanted. She figured that she would get Aurea out of school and the three of them could fly out early on Wednesday.

At work she was frustrated by the lack of progress, and she knew that she was driving everyone crazy trying to figure out what they could do next.

The rental car was in the impound lot where Bill and Travis had followed the thorough examination that had been done. They got fingerprints that matched both Janaina and Bento and a third set of prints that Johnnie was trying to track down on the Brazilian data base but figured it would match that of Cristiano.

Johnnie said that breaking into the Sao Paulo police data base had been easier than he had anticipated and that he would soon have Cristiano's prints verified. He said that he would see what else he could dig up on he had his partner.

Trevor had chosen to tone down his teasing because he sensed that this case had become very personal to Alex. He and the team had talked, and they all realized that Alex had gone way past the line of not getting personally involved. They all agreed that having Aurea live in her house was like baiting a mouse with cheese or any one of them with a free ticket to a ballgame. They were all in agreement that when they found Aurea's parents, they would not be alive but so far, they had no break in the case.

The Chief noted Alex's tense behavior. He noticed that the normal back and forth among the team was also absent. At home he talked to Mary-Anne about the situation and followed her advice to say nothing at work unless Alex broke out of her normal control mode. She said that saying nothing was probably the best he could do.

The Chief realized that until the bodies were found or Janaina and Bento turned up there was little that could be done.

Alex and Matt both admitted to each other that both of them had crossed the personal involvement line and that their trip to her parent's place would seal their desire to adopt Aurea. Both of them were finding it hard to wait the couple of days before the trip.

Unconsciously Aurea's curiosity about Alex's parents and where she had grown up provided the conversation that let Alex explain her younger years in a natural way. She shared the fact that she had gone out fishing with her father almost every weekend during the summer.

She had learned to cook and sew from her mother.

She shared the fact that in high school she had been an editor on the school newspaper, had been a cheer leader on the football team and had been elected student council president. Each of those points caused Aurea to ask a bunch of questions and the evenings were full of discussion.

Those discussions led Aurea to ask questions about Matt's early years and how he had met Alex. He said that he had grown up in Mississippi in a small town where his parents raised him and his brothers and sisters. He shared that his family had been very poor. He let her know that he had done very well as a football player. Football had gotten him a chance to become a marine and he had gone to the Navel Academy, graduated, and had then gone to Iraq where he was a sniper.

Aurea asked what a sniper did. He explained the concept but did not explain that he had earned several metals for his actions. Actions that had killed the enemy by shooting them at a very long range.

Aurea sat thinking about both Alex and Matt. She hoped that someday she could be as successful as the two of them seemed to be.

The day before the trip Alex walked from the office over to Aurea's school, let the principal know about the situation in trying to locate Aurea's missing parents and that Aurea would be missing school the rest of the week but if she could get her assignments, she would make sure that Aurea did her homework and not fall behind.

She was pleased that all the teachers involved gave her the homework assignments and when they learned that Alex was going to her mother's house and was taking Aurea, they said that seemed to be a good idea. They asked about Aurea's parents and said they understood that the two had been missing for several weeks and that did not seem to be a good sign.

Alex agreed that the situation was not good but said nothing more. She once again pictured vultures circling overhead.

Trey had walked over with her and on the way back he said that everyone in the office was on edge because of the fact that it was clear to them that she was well over the line of personal involvement but that they were all rooting for her.

She replied that she could not help it. She had fallen in love with Aurea. Having been around her for almost two weeks had been more than she could handle and until the case was solved, she was going to be a wreck. She said that she was leaving for the rest of the week to give everyone in the office a break and it would let her introduce Aurea to her parents and get their reaction.

Trey smiled and said that her parents would fall in love with Aurea just like he and Lindsey and everyone that had met her had. He added that now it was only a matter of time.

As they rode their bikes home, Johnnie commented on the fact that the team was rooting for her and hoped that when the case was over Aurea would end up being in the home where she was currently living.

Alex thanked him for the comment and said that this case had exposed a part of herself that she had not known existed.

Johnnie laughed and asked what that might be.

Alex confessed that she had wanted to start a family but had been afraid to get pregnant. She was afraid of being shot and having her baby get killed. She wanted a family but at the same time, she was selfish enough to want to keep doing what she was doing. It was one of the few situations that she had not known how to resolve.

Johnnie nodded and said that he understood the feeling of "dammed if you do and dammed if you don't." He said that had been his feelings the day he had flagged her down in front of the library. He said that the action he took at that time changed his life. He said that the actions she was taking was going to change her life and like his, her the change would be for the better.

Alex looked up from where she was locking the chain on her bike and thanked him for his words of wisdom.

He nodded and said that he was pushing his bike up to his house since he would be starting his ride in the morning from there. He wished her a good trip to see her mother.

That evening Alex gave Aurea a small suitcase to pack her things that she wanted to take for their two-day visit. She helped Aurea decide which outfits to wear and made sure she had her toothbrush and hair brush.

The two of them then went into the master bedroom where she packed her bag. They pushed both bags out to the back door.

Aurea asked why they were going to leave by the back door and Alex explained that the house really sat level to the street behind the house and the taxi would pick them up there.

Alex asked if a pizza sounded like a good choice for dinner.

Aurea said that she would love a pizza especially one that had lots of cheese on it.

The two of them went online and after a few moments they agreed on a large thin crust pizza with extra cheese and everything on it except hot peppers.

Alex said that while they waited, they should go to the third floor and walk through the art gallery together.

They had only got to discuss the paintings that had been done by Annie when the doorbell rang.

Alex followed Aurea down and told her not to open the door. Once she checked that it was pizza being delivered, she opened the door. She had already paid and given a tip, but she handed the delivery person another tip and said that it was for having climbed the stairs. That got a smile from her and a comment about why they would ever have built the house in such a fashion.

Alex carried the pizza into the kitchen and put it on the table where the two of them dug in.

Matt came home a few minutes later and joined them at the table. He was in time to eat almost half the pizza while it was still warm. He commented that it was one of the better pizza's he had eaten lately but he figured they could go to Alex's mother's Pizza shop and enjoy an even better one.

Aurea laughed and said that now she knew that Alex came from a rich family. Her mother owned a Pizza shop, and her father was professor.

Alex smiled and said that her mother was also a very successful lawyer in the Chicago area and the pizza shop was her hobby. And that yes, she admitted that she was from a very well-to-do family.

When they got to the airport and Alex led the way to the first-class line, Aurea pulled on Matt's hand and smiled and silently mouthed the word, "rich."

Alex went down the escalator and instead of walking to the far terminal she decided that she would ride the tram so that Aurea would be get to ride it.

Aurea said that the last time she had ridden on it was when she and her parents had arrived in Cincinnati.

Alex nodded but said nothing. It was a reminder to her that the reason she was going to Evanston was because she thought that Aurea's parents were dead.

She once again envisioned vultures flying in a circle high in the sky.

As she was walking past the shops going to the gate, she realized that Aurea did not have swimsuit. She led the way into one of the shops featuring swimsuits and asked the clerk if she had an appropriate swimsuit for Aurea.

The clerk took the two of them to one of the counters and pulled several styles out.

Alex asked Aurea which one she liked best.

Aurea looked over to where Matt was standing near the doorway and once again mouthed, "rich." She turned back to the counter and pick the one she liked the best. She and Alex went into the booth where she tried it on. She commented that the lady clerk had a good eye for size and said that it fit just fine.

Alex agreed and said that they would buy it and then they needed to hustle to the gate.

When they got on the plane, Alex asked which seat Aurea wanted to sit in and was not surprised that she wanted the window seat. She herself preferred the aisle seat and Matt had the aisle across from her.

The flight was uneventful.

The surprise came when the three of them were met by Harold Zimmerman at the exit of the plane. He said that he and his team was there to personally escort her and the surprise home for a celebration dinner that her mother was throwing.

Alex looked at his smug face and shook her head. She asked how he had found out about her arrival.

He said that he had officially been sent by the Illinois Lieutenant Governor to escort her, and he had no idea about anything that was going on.

Aurea boldly asked who he was and why he was escorting Alex.

Harold knelt down shook her hand and said because the Lieutenant Governor of the State of Illinois had heard that she was coming and decided that such a beautiful young lady deserved to be personally met and protected.

Aurea looked up at Matt and asked if everything was OK.

Matt nodded and said that Alex had quite a reputation and was a lifetime Illinois State Marshall of the highest rank and that the Lieutenant Governor was not only her boss but also her god mother.

Aurea nodded and said that she must be really old.

That got a laugh out of Harold who said that he would never repeat those words.

He led them down the outside steps and over to the van and introduced the rest of his team.

He asked if the luggage was in the back of the van. One of his team pointed to where two baggage handlers were looking for the baggage.

Alex took her wallet from her purse and handed some money to him and said to give it to the baggage handlers. She then got in, took a seat, and had Aurea take the one next to her. Matt took the one closest to the door and closed it.

The luggage was loaded in back and they all left the airport.

During the drive to her house, Alex asked who had shared her surprise with Jane. He said that Jane had learned the secret from someone in Cincinnati.

He added that Jane had somehow wrangled invitations to dinner that evening to Alex's mother's house for all of them but had not shared the secret only that it warranted a celebration. Jane was having the event catered by Rodolpho who ran her mother's pizzeria.

Alex laughed and said that the last few trips to Chicago had consistently been surprising events to her and this one seemed to be off on its own trajectory and she just planned to enjoy it.

Aurea had listened to the conversation. She took Matt's hand and asked what the surprise was going to be.

Matt shook his head back and forth and told her that in a few moments she would find out.

The van turned into the lane leading to Alex's parents' home. It stopped when the tunnel-like tree covering framed the house ahead.

Harold had Aurea stand and take a look.

Aurea asked if that was the house Alex had grown up in. She didn't wait for an answer but looked at Matt and once again said, "rich, but really rich."

The van drove up to the circular driveway and parked.

Rose-Anne and Russel came out of the house and walked briskly out to the van.

Harold and his team formed a greeting lane and Alex, Matt and Aurea were guided up the middle.

Harold announced the arrival of the famous Cincinnati detective, her husband, and the most beautiful surprise that he had ever seen, Aurea.

Rose-Anne went straight to Aurea and gave her a hug and said that she was really happy to have her at her house. She then gave Alex a hug and said that she had been repeatedly pleasantly surprised by what was happening on this visit. She said that Jane had refused to say anything about who Alex was bringing with her but that it would be the surprise of her life.

After giving Matt a hug, she took Aurea's hand, said that she was very happy to have her be the surprise and led all of them into the house.

Alex stopped and listened as her mother went through her lengthy description of the two circular staircases leading to the bedrooms on the second floor. Her mother pointed to the circular chandelier hanging above the circular black mahogany stand that featured a vase of fresh white flower. She then pointed into the spacious greeting room, then turned and pointed into a dining area. Alex then followed her mother and Aurea through the tunnel leading to the grand family room with the six-foot-high fireplace that had carvings of a group of dancing partiers in the floor directly in front of it.

Aurea looked at Alex and smiled and mouthed, "really, really, really rich."

Alex took Aurea's hand and said that she was going to show her the room she would have for the next couple of days. She signaled for Matt to follow her. She looked up the stairs and saw that their suitcases had been put at the top level. She went up and asked that they first all go to the room that she and Matt were staying in.

Once there she sat down on the floor with her back to the bed footboard and asked Aurea to sit down with her. She said that she had not expected to be met by Harold and his team, nor had she expected her godmother, who was also the Lieutenant Governor, to get involved. She had hoped for a quiet way of sharing both bad news and what she hoped was good news.

Aurea put her hand on hers and said that she thought the bad news was about her parents and she did not want to hear it. She had been counting the days and knew that more days the worse it was for her parents.

She had tears in her eyes when she asked about the good news.

Alex wiped the tears away and said that she hoped what she was going to share would be the good news and that was that she and Matt wanted to adopt her.

Aurea smiled and said that would be wonderful and leaned into Alex and gave her a hug. She did the same to Matt who was sitting to her other side.

She then stopped and asked about her grandmother and would she be a problem.

Alex said that she had plans to deal with her so that she would allow the adoption. She then suggested that they all change into poolside clothes and go downstairs and finish the tour by joining the party that would be going on there.

Aurea gave her a hug again and quietly said that Alex had grown up as a rich girl.

Alex nodded and said that she had always been parent rich and had never taken into account that she had also been rich in the other physical things.

Once out by pool side, Alex decided to enjoy the party. She watched as Aurea jumped into the pool and swam back and forth. She took in the conversation and realized that everyone was very much aware of her intension of adopting Aurea and thought it was a really good idea.

Dexter, the owner of the Golden Goose yacht, came over to her and asked if she wanted to go out fishing in the morning.

Alex said that she was indeed looking forward to it but that this time perhaps they should plan on going out at a reasonable hour that was more like eight or nine in the morning.

Dexter nodded and said that time would be fine and that everything would be ready. She should relax and just show up. He smiled and said that he hoped that the adoption would go smoothly.

Abandoned

5 The Golden Goose

When Jane arrived, she lavished praise on the idea of having Aurea in the family. She was dressed in red and wore a yellow rose near her left shoulder.

Alex thought about a long-ago time at a Christmas party when she was a few years older than Aurea when she had first noticed the looks her aunt drew for the very fashionable way of dressing. She smiled as she thought that Jane had retained all of that beauty.

She was well aware that Jane had been re-elected twice because not only did she do a superb job, but she also knew how to work the press and the public. She worked the celebration party and had everyone supporting a new family member.

It turned out that everyone that was at dinner was also planning to go out fishing on the Golden Goose.

The celebration went well into the evening, and Alex was exhausted by the time they went up to bed. She was glad that she had arranged for a late start to the fishing trip.

Alex knew that Dexter would not accept payment for the outing but as always, she would gift his favorite charity with the amount that he charged to rent the yacht. This was a quietly agreed-to-way that they had settled on when she had insisted that she pay for using the yacht. He still blamed himself because he had rented a fishing boat to an old college friend who then attacked and wounded Alex because of her skin color. After that he had declared that she could go out on the Golden Goose free whenever she wanted.

She could not accept that arrangement and finally settled on gifting one of his favorite charities.

In the morning after a leisurely early morning breakfast, Alex led the way into the garage and over to her shining black Jaguar. As always, her father had gotten it detailed as well as having its maintenance done before her arrival. She put the top down and asked Aurea to sit in the back and enjoy the ride to the fishing pier where the boat they were going out on was docked.

Aurea looked at the car and asked whose it was.

Alex said that it was hers. She said that her father had given it to her as a high school graduation gift. It was an old car when he had given it to her and said that now she could register it as an antique. She had kept it at home because until she had bought the house in Cincinnati, she had no place to park it.

Aurea walked around the car with her hands on it and said that she didn't want to say anything, but she did not know anyone who had received such a beautiful gift for a high school graduation.

The ride to the boat dock took only a few minutes and they were quiet minutes where the only sound was that of Aurea humming.

When Aurea saw the Golden Goose, she asked if that was the ship they were going to fish from and was that the one that Alex's father had taken her fishing on.

Alex pointed to where her father's boat that was tied to the pier and said that was the boat they had used.

Aurea nodded and said that made her feel better.

When everyone got on board, they all headed out to the spot where almost every weekend, when she was Aurea's age and to the present time, she and her father fished. She watched as this time her father helped Aurea bait her line and then taught her how to cast it out.

Her mother quietly asked how she felt.

Alex smiled and said that watching Aurea with her father brought back many happy memories and now the memories would have a new twist.

She asked her mother whether she would work up the adoption papers, select the court and judge to adjudicate it.

Her mother nodded and said that she would do it and treat it as one of her gratis cases.

That got a chuckle from Alex who said that she would be glad to pay her outrageous fees. She got a hug and heard her mother say that she was so happy that Alex was adopting Aurea.

They both looked over where Aurea was laughing as she pulled in a large lake trout. She was getting coaching from about four different people, but Alex's father was the one that was giving the helping hand and making sure that Aurea was letting the trout run but was slowly getting her to bring it in toward the boat.

Rodolfo came over and said that his boss had informed him that she wanted to have a special pizza for lunch the following day.

Alex said that she wanted him to surprise her and serve whatever pizza he thought would be the most interesting one he could think of, but she knew that Aurea liked extra cheese

He nodded and said that he was going to think very hard on that order. He then asked how many people were going to have lunch with her. She looked around and said that there would most likely only be five people in total.

He said that he would prepare two special pizzas.

Alex looked over to where her father was holding a large multi-speckled trout that was about two thirds as long as Aurea was tall. She rushed over and took several pictures. She then asked what Aurea wanted to do with the trout.

Aurea looked at it and asked if she could get it mounted and hung up in their family room back in Cincinnati.

Alex nodded and then heard Dexter say that he would arrange to get it done.

Aurea then asked if she could fish some more.

Matt said that she could but only if he got to help her this time.

Alex chose to stand on one side of Aurea while Matt helped her bait the line and then stepped away to let her cast it. The cast was not as far as Alex's father had cast the previous line, but it must have been to the right spot because almost immediately she had a strike and was fighting yet another fish. This time the trout was almost as large as the previous one, but it proved to be tougher to bring in. By the time she had it next to the boat and Matt had it in the scoop net it was clear that she was worn out.

Rose-Anne said that she would serve that trout for dinner that evening along with baked vegetables.

Alex led the way to where Dexter was grilling hamburgers, bratwurst, and sausages.

Aurea pointed to a hamburger and said that she wanted it on a bun with a tomato slice and lettuce.

Alex prepared the burger and asked what condiments Aurea wanted.

The choice was ketchup, and mayonnaise but no mustard.

They all sat down at the table under the canopy and sipped on their lemonade. Alex had chosen a bratwurst, and Matt had a hamburger with everything on it.

The fishing seemed to naturally taper off as everyone chose to have something to eat.

Alex saw Dexter cleaning the second trout that Aurea had caught and realized that she would not need to do it. She was already looking forward to how her Chef Mother would prepare it. She knew that it would be some wonderful creation that would taste like no other trout before it. She was sure her mother was already thinking through how to make the dinner special.

The loving way that both her mother and father were treating Aurea made her realize how much she had counted on their support and acceptance. She was now reassured that her own deep feelings about the situation had the support of the people she counted on most.

Dexter made sure everyone had their fishing lines in and were ready to go back to shore. He then guided the Golden Goose back to the pier and displayed his ability by the way he brought in and tied it off himself.

As they walked up the pier, Alex heard Aurea ask her father whether they could go out in his boat to go fishing. Her father nodded and asked if she wanted to go out early the following morning. Alex smiled and wondered if she should go along. She then heard Matt ask if he could go along. Alex decided that she should be a chauffeur but let her father and Matt go with Aurea.

Rose-Anne wondered how Alex was taking the attention that Aurea was getting from everyone. It was clear to her that Alex had transitioned into a loving mother. She hoped that the adoption would work out otherwise she knew Alex's heart would be broken.

She planned to have the paperwork ready before the three of them left.

The afternoon was spent by the pool where everyone relaxed, chatted, and watched as Aurea enjoyed the pool, just floating and paddling around from the sunny side of the pool to that part that was in the shade.

Rose-Anne decided that making the dinner special would entail her getting Aurea to help prepare it. She asked Aurea if she wanted to help her prepare Trout Almondine for dinner.

Alex smiled as Aurea said that she would love to. She decided to watch to see how Aurea would take to helping get everything prepared.

Her mother led the way into her kitchen where she put on her chef's toque and adjusted one and put it on Aurea's head. She then put on her apron and found a smaller one for Aurea. She had some small plastic gloves that were still too large for Aurea but would serve the purpose.

She then placed three trout on a cutting board and said that she was going to prepare two of them and that Aurea would prepare the one she caught..

Alex was using her phone to record each step of preparing the Trout Almondine.

Her mother steaked two of the trout and helped Aurea steak her trout.

She took time to show Aurea how to hold the knife and curl the fingertips of the hand holding the fish. She joked about the fact that finger tips would ruin the Almondine.

Then her mother chopped most of the onions but showed Aurea how to cut the onion in half and put the flat side down before slicing it and then chopping it.

She then had her chop a few of the onions.

She then salted and peppered the steaked fish on both sides.

The next step was to brown some almond flakes in a skillet and after removing the almonds from the frying pan, she put some olive oil in and let it get hot while she began to coat the steaked trout with flour.

Rose-Anne was going slow on purpose so that Aurea could keep up.

When the oil in the frying pan was, she carefully placed the trout skin down to get the presentation side a nice brown color. She explained this to Aurea and let her put a couple of slices of trout into the pan.

Aurea was engrossed by getting to do what Rose-Anne was showing her.

While the trout was browning, some potatoes and asparagus was prepared and put into the oven.

She then poured a glass of sherry into the frying pan and got the pan to flambe. The fire in the frying pan was a highlight of the preparation and a surprise to Aurea. As the flambe ended the fish were place on a serving tray.

Rose-Anne added some chopped onions and a cup of heavy cream into the frying pan and then she pinched in some salt and sprinkled black pepper over the contents of the large frying pan. She continued to have Aurea repeat each of her steps.

The final step was to chop some chives and mixed it with the sauce that remained after the fish were removed from the frying. She stirred it and added some more butter.

Then it was time to put the sauce over the fish that had been neatly arranged on the serving dish. The final step was to sprinkle on the roasted almonds and put two stems of chive across each fish steak.

Aurea was all smiles as she put on the chive on the fish.

The baked potatoes and asparagus were also ready and put on serving dishes.

Together they split the baked potatoes, put butter, chopped chives in the split, and put each potato in a separate dish. They put butter on the hot asparagus and put the asparagus and potatoes on the separate serving dishes.

Rose-Anne declared the dinner ready and said that they had to quickly set the dinner table out by the pool.

Once that was done, she and Aurea carried out the food and called everyone to dinner.

Everyone commented about the great dinner and how good the Trout Almondine tasted.

Aurea said that it was the first time she had been allowed to cook, and she thought it was better than fishing.

Alex smiled and said that she had enjoyed watching much more than fishing as well.

That evening she let her father know that she was going fishing with him as well. She did not plan to fish but she was going to go to take pictures of the fishing trip.

Her father said that he was glad she had decided to go along. He was sure they would all have a great time.

Her mother said that she had some things to do, and she would look forward to again having Aurea cook the evening dinner with her.

686

6 Fishing and Pizza

*A*lex and Aurea sat in back and Matt and her father were in front of the Jag as they drove in the early morning dark to the docks. Once they arrived, Matt and her father went to get the boat ready, and she and Aurea walked up to the bait shop to get the bait. The shop was very interesting to Aurea who looked at the variety of bait that was available.

She made the comment that the bait section smelled funny.

Dexter enjoyed showing the variety of bait that he had on hand and said that Aurea should try each kind to see which was the best bait. He said that somedays one type was better than another, but he had no clue what would work the best that day, so he said he was sending Aurea fishing with a little of each.

Aurea said that the only ones that bothered her were the wiggly grubs and the crickets. She thought the grubs were gross and she felt sorry for the crickets. She said the worms didn't bother her, but they were so big that they would be hard to put on the hook.

Dexter laughed and showed her a handful of smaller worms and put them in a box and gave them to her as well. When he offered her some minnows Aurea said that she couldn't have them put on the hook.

Alex led the way to the boat. It was still the moment in the morning when the sky was slowly going from a black to an early morning grey just before the sun finally won the battle and the sky went to a cloud covered light blue.

Once they were all in and underway out in the lake, her father asked Aurea if she would like to guide the boat.

She knelt on the seat and put her hands on the steering wheel.

Alex took pictures of her father standing behind Aurea ready to take over if necessary.

Once they got to their fishing spot and the engine was off. The poles were prepared, and her father cast the line in for Aurea.

Alex sat on the edge of the boat taking pictures. Aurea was in the front seat and Matt was fishing from the side. Her father was up with Aurea helping her, but he was soon back with her as he let Aurea fish on her own.

Aurea and Matt were both having good luck and it was not too long before they each had a couple. Aurea challenged Matt to a contest to see who would catch the most fish.

Alex watched as Aurea tried each of the bait. It turned out that the gross grubs were what the fish were biting on and soon Aurea was well into the lead with a large number of crappies, two trout and one bass.

It was clear that she was enjoying the crappies because they were biting, and they were easy for her to pull in. She seemed to pull in one after another in a steady stream.

Her father was cleaning them as she pulled them in and then he put them on ice. He commented that he would rather clean them while they were out on the lake then get back and have to stand at the cleaning station.

Matt said that he surrendered and put his pole away and cleaned the fish he had caught. He had chosen to focus on the bass and trout rather than the crappies.

Aurea finally said she was done and that she thought it was more fun to fish from the smaller boat.

Alex said she agreed and that she was glad that Aurea had caught enough for their dinner that evening.

Aurea smiled and said that she hoped she would be able to help prepare dinner that night.

They got back to the pier just before lunch.

Alex made a call to her mother and suggested they meet at the pizza shop.

Rodolpho greeted them and said that he would put the pizzas into the oven and then led them to a table that he had prepared. He pointed to the variety of drinks and said they should help themselves to whatever they might want.

Alex settled for iced tea. She looked around and noted that most of the tables were full. She was happy to see that her mother's Pizzeria was doing well.

Rodolpho had three pizzas brought to the table. He pointed to one that he said was a thin crust tavern style Chicago pizza with extra cheese and peperoni. The second one was a New York style made with a hand tossed thin crust and the third one was a West Coast pizza made the way the Caltech college students liked it. He smiled and said that he had chosen to make the three so that Aurea could get a taste of pizza across the country, but ones that were made in the best Pizzeria in the world.

Alex cut three smaller pieces and put it on one of the plates and handed it to Aurea. She then put the same size pieces on her plate before getting out of the way as everyone took a piece.

They were all chatting and enjoying lunch when a young woman excused herself and asked if she could get Alex's autograph.

Alex was surprised as she listened to the young lady explain that she was going to North Western because she had learned that was where Alex had gone. She said that she had read about her saving the young girl that had been missing for fifteen years. She was also aware of the coal barge she had sunk as she battled mafia hit men out in Lake Michigan.

Alex was a little taken aback but she nodded and said that she did not have a pen.

The young woman handed her a pen and a book by Professor Raymond Szymanski, "How to Profile a Killer."

Alex recognized the name of her favorite professor. He had taught her and the entire Cincinnati detective department using that book. She knew that the young lady was indeed influenced by her own academic career. She wrote, "Hope you do well, and I look forward to your success," and signed it.

She watched the young lady go back to where she was sitting with a young man. She looked over to her mother and said that she was a little surprised, but she figured that her admirer had come to the Pizzeria hoping to get that signature.

Aurea had listened to the exchange. She looked at Matt and said, "very rich and very famous."

After enjoying the pizza and complementing Rodolpho on the great pizza, they all returned to the house and went out by the pool and relaxed.

Alex sat reading and watched as Aurea swam or lay on a towel in the sun. She dozed off and when she awoke, she learned that Aurea was in the kitchen making a strawberry rhubarb pie and getting the crappies ready to be fried for dinner. She went into the kitchen in time to see Aurea putting the crisscross strips on the top of the pie. She then watched as her mother showed how to prepare the crappies with some salt and pepper seasoning. Her father had removed the scales but left the heads on in the style that her mother preferred.

Aurea asked about what would go best with the fish.

Alex listened as her mother suggested they have fresh mashed potatoes topped with butter and a serving of grilled cauliflower on the main plates and have a sliced tomato and olive oil salad on the side. Her mother made the point that the dinner would be simple but delicious and desert would be warm rhubarb pie with a scoop of vanilla ice cream.

Alex smiled as Aurea said that she couldn't wait until she tried the rhubarb pie because desert was always what she based how good a dinner had been. She added that she had never tasted rhubarb pie.

Alex had been reading the adoption papers her mother had given her when she dosed off sitting out by the pool. She knew this was a sign that Aurea had been accepted into the family. It was clear that she had made the right choice in coming home to get the slow case's slow progress out of her mind.

She dreaded returning to Cincinnati because she had talked to Johnnie and knew that no progress had been made.

Friday morning after breakfast, she drove the Jag to the airport. He father was along to take the Jag back home. They all hugged at the curb before the three of them went over to the check in counter.

The flight was short and uneventful. She saw that Matt was taking the opportunity to take a nap. Once back in Cincinnati they all got into the car and drove home.

Aurea had been quiet on the way home. When she got to the house she asked if her mom and dad had been found. She had tears in her eyes.

Alex felt a pang of sadness go through her. She had been so focused on her own feelings that she felt guilty about forgetting about Aurea's feelings. She gave her a hug and said that she would immediately let her know when she learned anything about her mom and dad. She knelt down and gave Aurea a hug.

Aurea nodded and said that she was expecting bad news, but she still wanted to know what had happened.

Alex said that she expected bad news too, but she wanted Aurea to know that she was loved and would always have a place with her and Matt.

Aurea nodded and added that she also now had a grandmother that would teach her how to cook and a grandfather that she could go fishing with.

Matt acted hurt and asked why she didn't want to go fishing with him.

That seemed to break the spell and Aurea laughed and said that they should go fishing every weekend.

Matt said that he knew a lake where they could go on the weekend. He then excused himself and said that he had to get ready to get to work.

There was a knock on the back door and Johnnie and Mary came in carrying a large casserole dish and a bowel with a mixed salad. They said that they had brought over a dinner offering and hoped that they could all figure out what to do on a Friday evening. They suggested finding a good old-fashioned movie and just chilling out on the couch.

While Mary and Aurea got the table set, Johnnie let Alex know that no progress had been made in locating Aurea's parents. He said that he had been able to get all the information needed for the Brazilian arrest. He added that he had all the firewalls hacked and the ability to get a video feed from the bar that Christiano used as his headquarters.

He then said that he had checked with the forest service officer and had his assurance that his team was watching the sky as they had been asked to.

Alex knew that it would be a long weekend for her. She decided to take a long bike ride with Aurea on Saturday morning and on Sunday afternoon Matt could take her fishing. The rest of the time would be spent out in the back yard or making sure that Aurea was ready to go back to school with all her homework done.

The weekend seemed to drag by. Alex was glad that Matt had offered to take Aurea fishing. They drove to Caesar Creek State Park where they rented a boat and went out fishing. The fishing was OK but nothing like what they had experienced out on Lake Michigan. They stopped fishing after catching several nice sized crappies.

Alex stopped at the cleaning station and gutted the fish while Matt drove with Aurea and found a table located under a covered area. He returned and picked her up and they set up the picnic table with the chicken, onion rings and cold slaw lunch they had picked up on the way.

It was good that they had chosen a table that was under roof because not long after they had started to eat the rain began and it was heavy enough that they could not see the lake. They were enjoying lunch, just chatting with each other, and watching the rain come down in buckets.

Aurea commented that the rain reminded her of the rain back in Brazil where she was allowed to run out in the rain and get totally soak. She smiled and said that it was like swimming, but she could walk, look up and open her mouth and take the water in.

Alex said that she could run out in the rain if she wanted to.

Aurea shook her head and said that the rain seemed to be too cold to have fun in it.

Alex agreed and said that she liked the sound of the rain hitting the roof while they were all able to stay dry. By the time they got done with what she thought of as their picnic dinner the rain had subsided, and she suggested they drive back home and, on the way, stop at their favorite ice cream shop and enjoy desert there before going home and getting ready for Monday.

7 The Circling Vultures

*A*lex and Johnnie rode in to work and Mary took Aurea to school. Alex had made sure that Aurea had all her homework done and had reviewed it. She was very pleased with Aurea's neat writing and how she clearly organized her homework. She had also made sure that Aurea was wearing one of her new outfits.

On her ride into the station, she was thinking on how she could somehow break the barrier that she faced in closing the case.

Johnnie could tell that Alex was focused on thinking about the case, so he purposely asked questions about her trip home and about how the fishing had been. He knew that they were currently depending on vultures to give all of them a break in the case. That worried him. He hoped he was right about the vultures supper sensitive smelling ability.

She and Johnnie were the first to arrive. Alex got herself a cup of coffee before going to her desk. They were usually the first and this morning it gave Alex a moment to think about how she needed to conduct herself. She knew that she had so far her personal behavior caused the team to be on edge.

She was having trouble figuring out what to do to break the case. She was anxious to make things happen but had no clue how she could make that happen. She knew she had to tone down her current behavior.

Trevor was getting on her nerve with his constant joking about the rate at which she was making progress, but she had to handle it better than she had done so far.

Johnnie had made significant progress in the information he was accumulating on Christiano that would make it easy to nail him if any bodies were ever found.

He had also done a complete work up on Aurea's grandmother who was now a widow for about a year. She was surviving on a pittance of a government allowance.

He said that it was harder to get specifics about her day-to-day life because she was not on the internet or any social media, but he had found her address.

Alex figured that the grandmother would be open to allowing her granddaughter to be adopted if there was something in it for her.

She contacted the Brazilian consulate and got the adoption paperwork required by the Brazilian government. She visited the consulates office and got help in properly filling it out. Her goal was to make sure that it was exactly what the Brazilian government required. When she was done, she knew that all that she would need would be the grandmother's signature and the signature of witness to that signature to make it official.

She planned to seek the signature by explaining the situation and she was prepared to offer the grandmother an income that would match the average income in Brazil in exchange for her signature on the adoption papers. She had already decided that she would feel better if the grandmother had the income, so she asked Johnnie to locate the nearest bank and to set up an account in the grandmother's name and put in seven thousand dollars.

She figured that having the account in place would make sure that she would walk out with the adoption paperwork signed.

A few moments after she sat down at her desk, Trey came in with his cup of coffee and asked how her trip home had gone.

Alex was about to share the highlights of the trip when Bill and Trevor walked in.

Trevor held out the box of donuts and said that salvation was on hand.

As he did on almost every morning, Trey took out a bear claw, broke it in half, and gave half to Alex.

She took a bite and a sip of coffee then said that she wanted to apologize for having driven the team to the edge and she wanted to thank whoever had leaked her desire to adopt Aurea to the Illinois Lieutenant Governor because that person had done her a great favor.

She added that she was going to do her best to stop driving them crazy.

Trevor looked at Bill and asked if he had made such a call.

Bill shook his head and said that Trevor knew full well that neither of them had done such a thing because the two of them had enjoyed their fishing trip to Lake Cumberland and having a picnic with their wives.

The Chief had come over for a donut and said that he had not called Jane or even talked to her for several months.

Johnnie shook his head and said that he was innocent.

Trey looked at Alex raised his hand and said that Lindsey had her back and insisted that he make the call. He had explained the situation in detail to Jane. She had let him know that she knew exactly how to handle the situation.

Alex went over to Trey and gave him a hug and thanked him. She then said that it was just what she had needed.

She then said that Aurea had a great time, and she finally recognized how deeply she had gotten into this case. Never before had she let herself let it be so personal but this time she could not control her feelings.

She added that she was still overwhelmed by her feelings, but her mother helped put everything into perspective. She pointed out that the situation seemed to point to the fact that Aurea was already an orphan. Also watching Aurea have a great time allowed her to accept the fact that her feelings were the right ones.

She then stopped talking and asked if there was anything new and took another sip of coffee as she watched everyone shake their heads in the negative.

The Chief told everyone to take it easy and perhaps go to the gun range and practice. He said that it always worked for him to go there to reduce his stress.

Alex said that she was going to take his advice. She was greeted by the range master who asked her if she wanted a blindfold to see if she could duplicate her previous achievement of shooting out the bullseye while blindfolded.

Alex smiled, shook her head, and replied that she wanted to relish repeatedly seeing the bullseye disappear and added that she wanted her gun barrel to turn red from repeat firing.

The range master asked what had her so worked up.

Trey was standing at the next firing station preparing to practice as well. He said that he should just watch Alex shoot and not get her started on what was bothering her.

Alex nodded and put on her hearing protection and then checked her weapon before raising it and firing.

She turned, sent out her target and began firing.

Trey stopped after he had used three targets and watched as Alex repeatedly pulled in her target and put out another one. She went through half a dozen targets as she played with putting patterns in them as well as shooting out the bullseye. She shot her initials into the last target, pulled it in, and put down her gun. Its barrel was not red hot, and she had gone through a box of bullets.

The range master picked up her used targets and laughed and said that he would see if he could give her a master marksman rating. He added that he hoped she would be able to solve whatever case she was on otherwise he would need to order extra ammunition for her to use.

This caused Alex to smile and say that she was sure that there would be no other case that would affect her the same way as the one that the team was currently facing.

She and Trey were standing at the cleaning station and cleaning their weapons when she said that she was ready to go searching through all the forests in Ohio to find the graves of Aurea's parents. She looked at him and asked if he thought they were dead or if they were in hiding.

Trey simply replied, "dead." He then said that it was time to get back to their desks and have another cup of coffee. He added that his practice had helped him and then watching her he realized how the case was affecting her.

When they got back to their desks, Johnnie suggested they walk to their favorite Thai restaurant and have lunch.

Everyone agreed that would be a great idea.

Once they were seated in the restaurant and had their orders in Alex made a point of asking Bill and Trevor how the fishing at Lake Cumberland had gone.

Trevor went into a long description of having to constantly duck as Bill cast his line and having to help Bill get his fish into the boat. His tale had everyone at the table chuckling and Bill defending himself.

Alex knew well enough that Trevor was doing his best to lighten the moment. He was a relentless teaser, but he was also a great fearless detective. He and Bill made a great pair.

They were just getting ready to leave when Alex's phone buzzed with the sound she had assigned to the Forest Service. She put up her hand, put her phone into speaker mode, put it on the table and everyone leaned in to listen. The ranger said that he had thought watching vultures was a crazy idea, then after a pause he added that it had worked and that he was standing at the site where they had found what seemed to be a grave.

He added that his team would never be able to see buzzards circling without going to check out what they were circling over.

He had called her as soon as it had been found and wondered what he should do next.

Everyone at the table all said, "finally," at the same time.

Alex asked him to block the area off and to keep his folks from wandering around because she wanted it treated like a crime scene. She would arrange for the coroner and his team to come out to the site and take over its management and dig up the graves. She then asked if he could give her the directions to the site.

He chuckled and said that his map addict on the team had written down the coordinates and he was texting them to her as they spoke.

She said that she wanted to reward his group not only with public recognition but also with a personal reward from her if the find turned out to be the graves of the two she was looking for.

The service officer was silent for a moment and then said that there was only one grave.

That gave Alex pause. She looked around the table to see the reaction. She was less sure about what had been found but she still planned to ask Dr. Rogers to take his team out and dig up the grave.

Trevor commented that they had the experience of finding two bodies in one grave and he was putting his bet on the fact that they would find two in that single grave.

She hung up and let Trey know that she was going to the morgue to get Dr. Rogers out to the site.

Trevor shook his head and laughed. He commented that now he would have to tell his friends that his team was using vultures to solve murder cases.

Alex nodded and replied that it was better than relying on him to give her a clue on what to do.

Bill laughed and added that except for Johnnie the rest of the team had been clueless from the start, and he was for giving Johnnie the choice of where to have the celebration and it would be on Trevor's dime.

Trevor did a little bow to Johnnie and complemented him on not only being Alex's magician but also a vulture whisper.

When she entered the lab, Dr. Rogers looked up from his desk and commented that if she was coming to the lab without him calling her it meant that she was going to ask him and his team to do something out of the ordinary and that probably meant extra work. He then asked what was up?

Alex explained the situation and asked him to take his team to the coordinates that had been given her by a forest ranger that had found a grave that might hold two bodies.

Dr. Rogers smiled and said that last time he and his team had gone out for her they had ended up processing more than sixteen bodies and going through an eight towered ten thousand square foot house looking for finger prints and bullets. He hoped that this time it would indeed be only two bodies.

Alex let him know that she was going to let the Chief know about what she was sure was a break in the case and she wanted to follow him to the location where the ranger was waiting for them.

Alex left the morgue and went up and informed the Chief. She knew that she had also stressed him when he commented that he hope this would let her close the case.

She and Trey walked out to their old police car, and she asked him to drive so she could make some calls.

Trey followed the van used by Dr. Rogers.

Dr. Rogers knew that this case seemed to be very personal for Alex and that solving it held some other implications that he was not aware of. He would tread lightly as he processed the bodies until he understood the situation.

He had his GPS coordinates set to the one given him by the forest service officer and was driving carefully through the country roads leading to the site. He realized that there were two cars following him and wondered who else was following.

His arrival was greeted by at least half a dozen forest rangers standing in front of a taped in area of the forest. He was glad that he had been using GPS because he would otherwise never have found the site.

He arranged to have his van driven near the grave site but asked that everyone stand back in case he found any footprints or tire tracks.

The ranger said that his team might have made many of the footprints when they were looking for the grave, but they had not driven any vehicles into the area.

The ranger walked with him to the spot where they thought was the grave.

Dr. Rogers had his team set everything up and he had one of them using a ground radar at the grave site so that they would have visual confirmation before removing the stones over the suspected grave. He wanted an initial scan, so his team had an estimate of the depth to the body.

The radar image showed more than two feet so he was sure that there would be two bodies and had his team prepare two carrying boards.

Alex stood back with the rest of the team. She asked why Bill and Trevor had come along.

Trevor laughed and said that the Chief had told them to have Trey's back in case they had to engage in any gun battles in the forest.

Bill shoulder bumped Trevor and made the point that the Chief had said nothing of the sort but the two of them were bored and figured that going on a drive to witness what the vultures had found was more interesting than sitting at their desks twiddling their fingers.

She pointed to where Dr. Rogers team was digging and said that she figured that it was indeed a grave.

Alex said that the four of them should examine the area around the grave to see if they could come up with any evidence that might be useful.

Trey pointed to several boot prints and put-up evidence markers. He went over to where the rangers were standing and verified that none of them had a similar looking boot heal.

Trevor and Bill said they would make a sweep between the trees near the grave. Bill picked up a thin flat rock and let out a whistle and pointed under the rock.

Trevor held out an evidence bag as Bill put on his gloves and lifted the rock to show a revolver with a silencer laying under the rock. He was about to pick it up, but Alex asked him to wait so that Dr. Rogers camera person could film the find.

Dr. Rogers walked over and looked at the revolver. He commented that he would take the gun in with the bodies that were being dug up and get the lab to process it for fingerprints and to match it to the bullets that he now figured he would find in the cadavers.

His team was lifting out the first body they had just dug up and getting it ready for transport. Alex saw that they had a second board ready for another body and felt fairly certain that Aurea's parents had been found. She asked if the first body was that of a woman.

Dr. Rogers put up his hand and said that everyone, but his team should stay back. He walked over to where the first body was strapped to a board and verified that it was a woman. He looked at Alex and said that it was very likely that they had found the husband and wife that she was looking for.

Alex said they should look for additional boot prints that matched the one found by Trey.

As the four of them worked their way closer to the grave they found several more boot prints. She had Trey get a plaster mix from their crime scene case.

He cast the boot prints that they found. The casts revealed that the heel on the right boot had a distinctive zig zag crack in it.

She took pictures of the casts and then turned them over to Dr. Rogers' team.

The second body was lifted out and prepared for transport.

Dr. Rogers verified that it was a male and said that he and the team would return to the station and do the detailed autopsy there.

Alex asked the rangers to keep the crime scene tape up and leave the grave open. She would let them know when everything could be turned back over to nature.

Johnnie had launched Gunjfor and was standing with the entire ranger unit. He was flying Gunjfor in a circle with the vultures and giving them a view from up high.

They were all laughing and saying that they now had a much better understanding of how lucky they all were to have vultures in the sky.

Alex, Trey, Bill, and Trevor all walked over and again complemented Johnnie on the fact that he had provided the means of cracking the case.

On the drive back to the station, Trey asked what she was planning to do about Aurea. She looked over at him and said that she was going to verify that Aurea wanted to live with her and Matt. She was hoping that would be the case.

He nodded and asked what Matt thought about her idea.

She said she would not have ever let her intentions leak the adoption idea with him if Matt had not already agreed to it.

Trey then asked if Aurea had any other family members that might be interested in raising her.

Alex let him know about the grandmother on the husband's side.

He then asked about the complications that might arise in working with the Brazilian government on her adoption.

Alex said that she had already gotten all the paperwork processed and now she planned to go to Brazil to get everything officially settled.

Trey looked over to her and said that he was looking forward to backing her up in Brazil.

She asked why he thought he would be going.

He looked at her and asked why she thought he wasn't going.

They arrived at the station and after parking the car they walked in together.

The Chief called them into his office and asked them to bring him up to date. He let them know that he had followed all the radio exchange that had occurred, but he wanted to get their perspective.

Alex recounted what Dr. Rogers, and his team had found and what she, Trey, Bill, and Trevor had found. She shared that Dr. Rogers, and his team had the bodies down in the morgue and were doing autopsies.

He asked her how she planned to close the case and what she was planning to do about Aurea when she closed the case.

Alex said that she was planning to charge Christiano with murder and was going to adopt Aurea.

The Chief apologized about laughing and said that once again she was able to surprise him. He asked how she was going reach into Brazil and arrest Christiano.

Alex shook her head and said that at the moment she was not sure, but she was planning to go to Brazil and before she left to go there, she would let him know.

He then asked about how she planned to adopt Aurea.

She reached into her purse and lifted out a folder and put it on his desk.

The Chief opened it and slowly leafed through the several pages in the folder. He said that they looked official, but they were in a language that he could not read.

Alex said that they were the adoption papers that she was going to get Aurea's grandmother to sign.

The Chief looked at her and said that he hoped she would be gentle with the grandmother.

Alex nodded and said that she would be kind, sympathetic, and generous but that she intended on leaving Brazil with a successful agreement to the adoption.

The Chief looked at Trey and said that if Alex had any intention of confronting Christiano, he wanted him to have her back. That meant that if there was any evidence that linked Christiano with the murders, Alex was not to go alone to Brazil.

Trey looked at Alex, then back to the Chief, nodded and said that he would have her back. She would not make the trip to Brazil alone. He would be with her even if he had to travel on his own dime.

The Chief shook his head and said that he was officially on the case and normal expenses would be paid by the department.

The Chief's phone rang. He put it on speaker mode, and they heard Dr. Rogers say that he was ready for the preliminary report, and they should come down to the morgue.

The Chief led the way out of his office. He called over to Bill, Trevor and Johnnie and said they should follow.

Dr. Rogers greeted them and pointed to the two bodies that were covered by white sheets. He said that they were both in their late twenties. The woman was white, and the male was brown and most likely of mixed parents. He said that he had run their DNA against the DNA that he had from some hair samples that Alex had provided. He added that there was a parental match.

He added that the two had been shot at close range and it appeared to him that the two might have tried to overcome their killer because of the way they were shot. He said that the gruesome part was that the ears of the male were cut off and his tongue seemed to have been ripped out. He said that his team might need to go back to the grave to see if they could find them.

There was a moment of silence, then Johnnie spoke up and said that he knew where the body parts could be found.

He asked to use Dr. Rogers' computer, sat down and a few moments later he was able to project a view of Cristiano pointing to a placard that had a tongue and two ears mounted on it with the words, "Here is what happens to those who try to leave our team," but the words were in Portuguese. Johnnie said that he had been able to get through the rather poor computer fire wall and get into the camera system used by the bar where the placard was hanging. He added that he had the address of the bar as well.

Dr. Rogers asked how Alex wanted him to proceed.

Alex asked him to finish doing a thorough autopsy. She would work with the Brazilian Consulate to have his work documented, authenticated and the information sent to the Sao Paulo Senior Delegado which she explained was the long name for Chief of Police.

She planned to go to Brazil retrieve the tongue and ears and have their DNA run to verify they belonged to Bento Carvalho that was currently laying on his embalming table. She hoped to also be able to find the boots that had been at the grave site and turn all the evidence all over to their counter parts in Brazil and have Christiano charged for murder.

She looked over to Trey and asked if he would take a picture of Bento with his missing ears and missing tongue.

Dr. Rogers shook his head and had one of his team take the pictures and send them to the team. He said that he was trying to keep the autopsy as uncontaminated as possible. He still had a few steps to get it all done and wanted to keep everyone away.

The Chief thanked Dr. Rogers and asked to be informed when the autopsy was complete. He then led the way back to his office. He looked around at everyone and commented that once again the team had unraveled a complex case, and it was getting a unique ending. He asked what Alex wanted to get out to the news.

Alex said that she had promised the Forest Ranger Chief a spotlight but that she wanted any news announcement to be held after she had Cristiano arrested.

She looked over at Trey and asked if he was willing to fly to Sao Paulo on the following day.

Trey nodded and said that he would need a visa stamp on his passport to be able get into the country.

Alex nodded added that she too needed a visa and said that she was sure they could get them from the Brazilian Consulate, especially if the Chief gave him a call and explained the situation.

She had extra energy when later she and Johnnie rode their bikes across downtown. They rode until the slope up the hill got to the point where it was easier to walk than to bike.

Johnnie asked if she had any idea of how Aurea was going to take the news of her parents death.

Alex shook her head negatively. She said that the hardest part of the day was still ahead of her. She was not sure how she should break the news.

Johnnie suggested that she let Mary deliver the really bad news and that she be the one that offered to have Aurea live with her.

Alex continued pushing her bike up the walkway and thought about Johnnie's suggestion. She was chaining her bike to the bike rack in front of her house when she finally answered him.

She asked if he thought Mary would be willing to do what he suggested.

Johnnie smiled and said that when Mary understood the situation, she would not only be willing but would want to. Mary would want Alex to share only the good news.

The two walked up the three sets of steps up to the porch and into the house.

8 Linkages

*I*n Brazil, Fernanda sat in her tiny three-room house. It was all that she could afford because she was getting by on the subsidy she got from social services.

The money that Bento had provided for a long time had run out and she got almost nothing from the rest of her children.

Until a year ago she and her husband had enough to cover their living expenses. Now she was at the point where she did not know what she would do in the coming months to survive.

She had spent her whole life cleaning people's homes or doing the same in some hotel, but she now had trouble standing for more than a short time.

When her husband was alive, and they were both working they always ended up having enough to raise their large family.

She thought about sitting out on the sidewalk and begging.

She was not sure that would work without her getting in trouble with some gang that would demand some of her money.

She wondered where Bento, his white wife and their mulatto daughter had gone. She had heard nothing, but she was sure that he was in hiding.

She knew that he had been distributing drugs, so she figured that he was hiding from the police.

She figured the fact that they had all disappeared meant that they were hiding so they could be together.

In Cincinnati, Aurea was expecting the worst news about her mother and father.

It had been more than two weeks.

She had followed the same routine of going to school and afterwards going to the library.

She always made sure to attend some lecture that had refreshments. The lectures were usually interesting but what she really enjoyed was the afternoon treat.

Afterwards she would cruise the internet and spend some time improving her English. She especially like to use the map feature that let her go to anywhere in the world and be able to walk the streets in some foreign city.

The librarians all helped her select books to read. Once they found out that she did not want kids' books but books by famous authors they got her into reading books like Mark Twain's Tom Sawyer.

The internet had allowed her to check about missing persons, and she learned that after forty-eight hours the missing person was most likely dead. Her parents were now missing for more than two weeks.

She liked Mary who was like a nanny to her but the person who she really admired was Alex. She treated her like an adult. She was kind and she was generous. They had gone out shopping and now she had a new bike, and she had several new outfits. She gone to her mother's house where she had gone fishing and got cooking lessons from Alex's mother.

She also liked Matt because he was fun to play with. She was learning how to play chess, they put together puzzles and he helped her do her homework. He seemed like a person who was fearless but was very gentle.

Getting her homework done was easy and even though she was the youngest in most of her classes she was at the head of most of her classes.

All three had gone out riding their bikes together. Her bike was amazing. It had six gears, hand brakes, front and rear suspension and it rode like a dream. Even the seat had its own suspension.

She wondered how much it had cost but was afraid to ask.

Alex had spent time with her and had explained how to check and replace the brake pads. She needed to do it often because she was constantly braking when going down the steep hills of Mt. Adams.

She had her own room that seemed like a small kingdom. Alex had told her that she was not rich but to her the house they lived in was amazing.

She had visited the third floor that had been turned into an art exhibit show room and was amazed to find various gorgeous paintings of local artists.

The ones that really stood out were the paintings by Annie Scots an artist that when she looked her up on the internet, she found out was very rich.

Annie had been saved by Alex after being a chained prisoner in the woods for fifteen years. She now lived in Hawaii where she had met her husband. She had two daughters, Linda, and Lorie, who had gone to college and were now working in the family business.

She wanted to have her mother back but as the days passed, she felt that something bad had happened.

She wondered what would happen to her if her mom and dad did not come back for her. She got on the internet and asked what happened to abandoned children.

She learned about child social services where orphaned or abandoned children were sent. She knew that she did not want that to happen to her.

She had wondered whether Alex and Matt might be able to keep her. She knew that she had a grandmother in Brazil, but her grandmother was old, and she had never been nice to her.

She did not want to go back to her grandmother or to Brazil.

She decided that she would have to wait until Alex found her mom and dad.

Alex had discussed her upcoming trip to Brazil with Matt. The two of them had agreed about going ahead with the adoption process if Aurea wanted that to happen.

Alex said that the two of them should sit down with Aurea and share the sad news about her parents. Then they would let her know that the two of them wanted to adopt her.

If Aurea had a positive response, then Alex, on her upcoming trip to Brazil would get the grandmother to sign the release that would allow the Brazilian adoption to take place. Once that was accomplished, they would also file the American adoption paperwork that her mother had prepared so that in the future the two of them would also have legal standing as parents in the US.

Getting the visas to go to Brazil was expedited but it took longer than Alex had anticipated because the visa was issued in New York.

The day before going to Brazil, Alex had Mary and Johnnie over for dinner.

After dinner, Mary led Aurea into the living room where they all sat down.

Mary led off by saying that she had sad news about her parents.

Aurea put up her hand and said that she knew the rest and didn't want to hear anything else.

Alex gave Aurea a hug and said that she was sorry about what had happened.

Aurea asked if she was going to be sent back to Brazil or have to go into the childcare system.

Alex asked if she wanted to go back to Brazil.

Aurea started crying and through her sobs, she said that she didn't want to, but she didn't want to go to child social services either.

Matt sat down next to her and asked if she would want to be adopted by him and Alex.

Aurea wiped away her tears and asked if that was possible.

Alex took out the adoption papers and showed her the Brazilian papers and gave her a chance to read them. Then she showed her the American adoption papers.

She said that she was going to Brazil and would get Aurea's grandmother to sign the papers. That would make Aurea her and Matt's daughter in Brazil. Once she got back, she and Matt would have a judge notarize the American adoption papers and they would become her legal parents in the US.

Aurea asked if she would lose her family name.

Alex asked what she wanted.

Aurea said that she would like to make her name Aurea Carvalho-Evercrest.

Alex wrote that down on the American adoption papers and said that would be the name on the American paperwork.

Aurea nodded and gave both Alex and Matt a hug.

She then asked where her parents would be buried.

Alex said that they would find a nearby cemetery when she returned, and they would arrange for a burial service.

The following morning after seeing Aurea off to school with Mary, Alex rode with Johnnie down to the office.

On the way he let her know that he was going to have her on camera when she went to the bar to arrest Cristiano.

He said that he was sure that everyone in the office would be watching and cheering her on.

The Chief briefly called her into the office and said that he had contacted his Sao Paulo equivalent and arranged for the arrest of Cristiano.

The two of them would be with the Brazilian team when the arrest was made. He smiled and said that he had done his best to ensure that she was the person making the arrest.

He commented that he had received assurances that you would have all the backup that was warranted for that risky operation.

The Chief said that the Brazilian Chief there was very interested in making an arrest and was very pleased with the forensic information that Dr. Rogers had sent down.

The arrest would be made by his officers when she confronted Cristiano. They would retrieve the tongue and ears and get them to the lab immediately and once confirmed they would lock Cristiano and his partner away for life.

Before they left the office the Chief once again cautioned them and told Trey to have her back.

Trevor made a smart-alecky remark to the effect that he knew Trey was a fearful guy and he would be glad to have her back, and Trey could stay safe at home with his family.

Alex smiled and gave him her standard reply, "I love you too," and walked out with Trey to the waiting cab.

The flight to Brazil was on a new plane and the first-class seats were the new lay down style that felt like real beds. Alex spent a few moments sharing her adoption plans with Trey and then said that she planned to sleep all the way so that she would have all the energy she would need to make sure she got her two agenda items accomplished.

They arrived in Sao Paulo in the early morning hour. She and Trey both put on their Kevlar jackets beneath their sports jackets before deplaning. They were greeted as they got off the plane and were escorted to an office where they met the local Chief and after a brief introduction, he introduced a lady police officer, Lara, who was a Brazilian version of Alex in stature.

It was clear to Alex that the choice had been to match the two of them when she shook hands with Lara and then was introduced to her partner, João who was that same size as Trey.

She liked the idea and was pleased that both of them spoke impeccable English.

Having no language barriers going into a dangerous situation made her feel much better.

Lara explained that her unit was taking the lead but there would be a small army of police that would back them up.

She and João would accompany Alex and Trey into the bar that was Cristiano and his partner's headquarters to make the arrest. They would be backed up internally by at least six additional police officers.

There would be some thirty police surrounding the area. She handed both of them weapons that she asked not be used unless a gun fight was initiated by Cristiano or his partner.

Lara smiled and commented that Alex's gun fighting reputation was known to all of them and she was sure that if anything happened, she would make a difference so she should feel free to use her weapon if needed.

She smiled again and repeated, "if needed."

Alex took off her jacket and put her weapon on and then put her jacket back on.

She said that she felt at home and now she also felt ready to enter the lion's den.

Lara nodded and said that João would drive them to the bar and hopefully by late that evening they would all be enjoying dinner at her favorite Churrascaria and toasting, the arrest success with a Caipirinha and having two top drug dealers in prison.

On the way Lara said that she had some protection vests in the trunk that they could use when they went into the bar.

Alex let her know that she and Trey already had their protection on.

Lara commented that she had not noticed it and wondered if it would hold up in a gun fight.

Alex nodded and said that both of them had survived multiple gunfights because of what they had on.

They arrived at the bar and were getting ready to enter. Alex noted that the external back-ups were all rushing into place and that everyone seemed to know what to do.

She was pleased with the arrangements that had been made.

It was clear that they had surprised everyone sitting inside.

Christiano and his partner were sitting at a table just in front of the bar. As soon as they realized it was a raid, they both dropped to the floor, drew their weapons, and began firing.

Alex drew her weapon and fired just as she was hit in the side by Cristiano. She stood her ground, and her shot hit him in between the eyes. She then turned and began to strategically shoot anyone that was firing a weapon. She knew that Trey was firing and doing the same.

The room had seemed to explode.

She shot the bartender as he raised a shotgun.

Trey was standing beside her, and they both emptied their weapons and took out someone each time they fired.

The room went quiet as fast as it had exploded into a storm of gunfire.

The number of police seemed to mushroom as the room went silent and the remaining members of Cristiano's gang that were still alive were hand cuffed and led away. There were several that were wounded and were being attended to.

Lara and João came over to them and commented that they had never seen two people that were so deadly.

Lara's eyes went wide when she noticed the bullet hole in Alex's jacket. She asked if she was OK.

Alex said that she was going to have a large bruise that would be painful for a few days but otherwise she would be fine.

She was sad to have lost another jacket but that was easily replaced.

She added that she planned to handle it like all the other times she had been hit. She hoped that taking some pain killer and time in the hot tub would be enough.

João pointed to a hole in Trey's jacket and asked what type of bullet proof vest the two were using because he was interested in getting something similar.

Trey commented that it was the type that had kept the two of them alive through multiple gun battles.

Lara walked over to where the EMT's were treating the wounded. She returned with two tubes of salve that she said would help ease the pain.

Back in Cincinnati the morning was just underway when the action began, the Chief, Dr. Rogers, Johnnie, Bill, and Trevor sat with their morning cups of coffee and their donuts as if they were going to the movies.

They viewed the entire situation from just before Alex and the police arrived.

They all gasped when Cristiano and his partner immediately started firing. It caught all of them by surprise, but they noticed the immediate reaction by Alex and Trey. They were firing before any of the Brazilian police had even drawn their weapons.

Then they watched the amazing, synchronized gun display that Alex and Trey put on.

The two seemed to be demonstrating a shooting dance routine.

The two of them took out all but two of the gunmen before any of the other police even began to fire.

The yelling and cheering in the conference room attracted the entire squad. They all came over to the conference room window to see what was happening.

Johnnie looked at the Chief and asked if he should play the gunfight scene again and got the nod to do so. The Chief invited everyone in and explained what had just happened.

The reaction of the rest of the department mirrored the reaction of the smaller group.

During the second viewing Johnnie commented that he thought both Alex and Trey had had been hit by the first two shots but had continued firing until their guns were empty.

Bill agreed and said that they would both be sitting in the hot tub that evening. He recalled having done that several time when all of them hand been hit.

The Chief said that he was treating everyone to lunch in celebration of what Alex and Trey had just done.

Lara came over and asked that Alex and Trey give her their weapons and act like they never had them. She explained that the weapons and any one that had used them would have to explain why they used them to the police internal affairs division. She and João would claim that they had used the weapons otherwise Alex and Trey would be stuck in Brazil for many days in some stuffy office.

Alex thanked her but Lara laughed.

She said that Alex's and Trey's shooting would make she and João famous for their ability to kill the two leading drug dealers in Sao Paulo and most of his inner circle.

They were likely to get promoted and get a raise.

Alex laughed and said that she was glad to help.

That evening at the Churrascaria Lara's Chief called for a toast to his two top gun slingers and their American partners. Alex raised her non-alcohol Caipirinha and joined the toast.

She said that she and Trey had a gift for their two partners. She handed Lara a package that had her Kevlar outfit in it and said that if it didn't fit, she would send down another one.

Trey did the same and gave a package to João.

He and Alex had agreed that not having to face the Brazilian equivalent of internal affairs made the gifts seem a pittance.

During the dinner, Alex asked Lara if she would accompany her the next day so that she could get some adoption papers signed.

Lara asked about the situation and commented that her boss had the ears and tongue of the person that Cristiano had killed and was having the DNA compared to that sent to him by Dr. Rogers.

She now understood why Alex had come down to make the arrest and she would take it as an honor to help her get the adoption papers signed.

Alex made an excuse to everyone at the celebration about needing to get ready for the next day and she and Trey left.

When they got back to the hotel, she said that she was going to sit in the hot tub.

Trey said that he would join her.

When they got to the tub it was clear that each of them was going to sport a significant bruise on the right side of their ribs.

The next morning, Lara and João met them and drove them to the address where Fernanda lived.

Alex had explained her goal and had asked Lara to come in with her.

Joao said they were in a neighborhood that having them stay to watch the car was a good idea.

Lara was dressed in basic black and looked like a partner to Alex. They knocked on the door and asked if they could enter. After a brief introduction, Alex, through Lara, shared that both Janaina and Bento were dead.

She then shared the fact she wanted to adopt Aurea.

It was clear to her that Fernanda did not want to take Aurea in, but she was sharp enough to bargain for something in exchange.

Alex made her first compensation offer on the low side and after a series of offers and counter offers, she hit the amount that she had Johnnie put into the bank branch that was closest to the address where Fernanda lived.

She had Fernanda sign the adoption paperwork and had Lara sign as a witness. She handed Fernanda the account booklet and let her know that a similar amount would be put in every month for the rest of her life.

Fernanda thanked her and wished her well. She felt a sense of relief to have enough to live on and not to have to raise another child.

She felt certain that Aurea would be much better off with the person who had spent the time to come to meet with her and was willing to give her money to adopt Aurea.

Lara walked out and complemented Alex on her bargaining skills and asked if she had gotten what she needed and the dollar amount that she had wanted to hit.

Alex gave Lara a hug and said that everything had come out as she wanted. She had gained a daughter and the amount she had agreed to was almost to the dollar what she had planned. Having Lara there to translate had made the meeting the success she needed.

Lara laughed and said that she had been worried that Alex would be out bargained but it had become clear to her by the way the bargaining went that Alex had the upper hand. She asked when had she set up the bank account and how had she done it from outside the country.

Alex said that she had a magician that she was able to leverage to get most things in the world done.

Trey was standing and listening to the exchange and said that Alex attacked everything in the same manner that she shot her weapon. She hit the bullseye every time.

Lara nodded and said that the preliminary autopsies indicated that the two of them had killed most of the shooters. Christiano and his partner had their bullets in them and the remaining bullets from their weapons had killed every person that they hit, and they had not doubled up on any of them.

The coroner had praised her and João for their exceptional marksmanship. He said that he was making sure his report would go to the top department leaders.

Lara went on to say that she and João were sure to get a lot of recognition, probably a pay raise and very likely a promotion for what had occurred during the gun battle.

Alex laughed and said that she hoped the two of them would indeed get promoted and if either of them decided to come to the states they should come to Cincinnati, and she would host them.

The next day, Alex and Trey were on their way back home.

9 Arrangements

On their return Alex immediately called John and asked him to contact her mother and arrange to proceed with the adoption. John said he knew the judge that he would recommend, would talk with Alex's mother, and arranged for it to happen. He said that he was so glad to be involved and thanked her.

Alex had another matter that affected Aurea that she had promised to take care of. She had returned with Bento's missing pieces which she took to Dr. Rogers.

He commented that he had watched the gun fight and that everyone had watched her, and Trey display their synchronized gunmanship. Even though he knew that the gunfight had been started by Christiano he said they seemed to have practiced that event and it looked as if they were firing and moving in rhythm.

He said that he also thought both of them had been hit but it appeared that neither had gotten any medical attention.

Alex admitted that both of them had been hit but their Kevlar jackets had protected them, and they did not want to get held up with follow up medical attention or face the Brazilian internal affairs division.

Dr. Rogers shook his head and added that the entire department had by now seen the shootout and she and Trey were both legends.

He added that the Chief had let him know that practice on the gun range had skyrocketed.

Alex asked Dr. Rogers about arranging the burial.

He suggested a mortuary she should use so that she could get arrangements made to handle the ceremony.

That evening she asked Aurea whether she wanted to have an open coffin ceremony.

Aurea shook her head and said no but she wanted the family picture that had the three of them standing together made big and have that be what was on display during the ceremony.

Alex was glad that was the choice.

She went to mortuary that had been recommended and made the arrangements.

The ceremony was held on the weekend and was attended by the entire team. It was a simple one and the trip to the cemetery was only a short few blocks away and everyone walked to the burial site. Alex had selected the site that was only a mile away from her house. She wanted to make it easy for Aurea to visit it if she desired to do so.

She was worried that Aurea was holding her grief in and asked her if she wanted to talk to anyone about her feelings. Aurea said that she had talked about how she felt with Mary and had been asked the same question. She said that she was sad and at the same time she was happy and that made her feel guilty.

Alex said she had just the person that would help her talk through those feelings. She said that what the two of them talked about would only be between them.

She arranged for the therapist that the whole team used and set up a time after school that Aurea could meet with her. She personally had gone and talked with her several times in the last few weeks and knew that she would help Aurea work through her feelings.

The next thing she happily focused her energy on was arranging the adoption. She sent out the invitation to family, friends, Aurea's teachers, and the librarians at the downtown library.

She, Matt, and Aurea walked down the aisle passed a packed gallery that had every person that she had invited present.

The Chief and Rose Anne, Bill and his wife, Trevor and his wife, Trey, Leslie, and Nolan, Annie, Brian, Linda and Laurie and Annie's parents, Kekoa Ikaika and his wife Anela Kamaka, Brian's parents, Brenda Langley, her art studio partner, Johnnie, and Mary, her mother and father.

Jane, the Illinois Lieutenant Governor.

Dexter, the owner of the Golden Goose.

Sandra Olsen, her one time police woman guard.

Harold Zimmerman and his Chicago DEA team, Andy Weller the Chicago IRS head, Joe Brown Cincinnati IRS leader, Randolf Task, the Texas IRS leader, James Kaizer, Sheriff of Wiggin Mississippi and his wife and kids.

Angelica, the Angel on the Hill and her brother and his wife.

Cais Leu her long time Vietnamese college friend, Evin Williams the Loveland Sheriff and his wife Irene, Brian Lexter the Cincinnati FBI bureau chief and his wife, were all sitting in the gallery.

The surprise was that all the teachers in Aurea's school and the librarians from the downtown public library were all in the gallery as well.

The gallery was packed and there was standing room only.

Alex had invited all of them to a celebration at the restaurant where a few years earlier Alex had shot and killed the thug that had come to kill Johnnie.

The owner of the restaurant was ecstatic about being chosen to host the celebration and made a special point of letting them all know that Alex was one of the persons that had made the restaurant so successful.

Alex smiled as she thought about the fact that she might have a few more people than she had estimated. She hoped the restaurant was up to it.

The three of them walked slowly down to the table where John and Hanna were waiting for them and sat at a table with the two of them to face the Judge's desk. When the court bailiff called the court to order, everyone in the court room stood up.

Judge Kimberly Nugent, the same judge who had presided in the "SLATE" case entered, sat down behind the bench, and in a very formal and serious tone asked the courtroom deputy to administer the oath to the three very lucky people sitting before her.

She had a big smile on her face as she asked the judicial clerk to read the adoption request.

None of this was actually necessary. They could have met in her office and had the paperwork signed, but she and John had decided to make it a formal court affair.

She then asked Aurea if she wanted to be the daughter of Alex and Matt. When she got a simple yes.

She asked why she would want that to happen.

Aurea stood and in a quiet but clear voice said that her parents had taken her to Alex's and Matt's house and told her that she had been brought there because they knew that Alex would keep her safe from the bad people that were after them.

They had faith that they were putting her on the porch of someone that they trusted.

Aurea looked at Alex and Matt and then went on to add that she had felt their love and wanted them to be her parents.

She was going to be able to keep her biological family name and add Evercrest at the end.

They had found a nearby cemetery and had made sure her biological parents received a proper burial.

She would miss her mother and father, but she knew that she was with the two people that she would be very happy to call mother and father.

She had tears running down her face as she finished her reply.

Alex and Matt, both gave her a hug.

The Judge Nugent smiled as she signed the paperwork, handed it to John, pronounced Alex and Matt the parents of Aurea and then slammed her gavel down and declared court dismissed.

There was a loud cheer as she came around from the judge's desk to the table where Alex and Matt were giving Aurea a hug and said that she was so happy that she had been the one given the privilege to make it all official.

Everyone in the court room came down from the gallery onto the main floor and gathered around giving hugs and congratulations.

Alex stood back from the crowd as she thought about the fact that she felt that she had been given the best wish that she could possibly have been granted.

Her mother gave her a hug and quietly said, "It's a little overwhelming "I know that it is not only what you wished would happen but as you can see everyone that knows you wanted to be here to see you get your wish."

Alex nodded and said that she was glad that there was time for all of them to walk to the park so she could have time to decompress.

The gathering at the restaurant was a huge success. The music in the background had been selected by Aurea, was upbeat featured violin, piano and viola pieces. This was in contrast to the more somber music that she had selected for her parents commemoration service. Alex noted the difference of the music selection between the two events and felt very good about it.

She was also impressed with Aurea's depth of musical expertise.

The celebration went well into the night and afterwards she, Matt, Aurea, Johnnie, and Mary all walked up the hill to Mt. Adams.

The next day there was a much smaller gathering at her house. Her parents were staying for a couple of days as were Annie, Brian, Linda, Laurie, Kekoa Ikaika, his wife Anela Kamaka and Brian's parents.

She had invited Annie's parents and Trey, Lesley, and Nolan as well for the backyard grill out.

Aurea confided to her that she was a little overwhelmed by the way everyone had congratulated her on getting the best parents that she possibly could have gotten.

Alex chuckled and said that she would remind her of that when they got into a disagreement. She said that she would just say, "the best parents ever."

The End of Abandoned

Northern Lights

1 Twelve Barrels

Grayson unhooked his oil line from the pipeline, came down the ladder with the capped oil line. He slipped the line into its tube mount on the frame above the oil barrels. He put the ladder alongside of the tube and strapped it in place. He made sure all twelve barrels had their fill and vent openings tightly secured. This was the exact process that he had practiced for the past ten years.

He took the oil from the pipeline, transported it to Valdez, and sold it to his contact, Miles Walker, who worked for an oil company but had his own side hustle buying oil from small oil producers.

He made two trips a week and sold twelve barrels each time. Miles provided him with twelve empty barrels and paid him sixty percent of the current market price for oil. He wondered where Miles got his empty barrels, but he never asked. He took them, filled them, and returned them.

For the last ten years since he had quit working on the pipeline as a welder he had made his living by tapping into the pipeline in several locations where he had installed the taps before he had quit working on the line. The taps were inconspicuous and did not show up on any of the pipeline drawings.

He was his own boss, had plenty of time off and was making around ninety grand a year. It took him about ten minutes per barrel or two hours to fill all twelve barrels. Thirty minutes to set up and the put away his line and ladder. And then there was the drive to Valdez that ate up sixteen hours each way three times a week. So, in total he spent about sixty working hours a week, made eighteen hundred dollars or around ninety grand a year. That put him at the top of the money-making ladder. He felt really good about that.

Often after one of his trips he would go out to celebrate another successful run by splurging on a nice dinner and enjoying a few drinks. That periodically included going out with the one of the few available women that resided in Valdez or Fairbanks.

At first he had just stayed at a bed and breakfast but then he had purchased a home. He spent about two thirds of his time at his house and during the summer weather he would walk around the track that surrounded the Valdez High School football field or go fishing in the harbor. He felt that he had successfully set himself up for life.

He was well known at the five hotels in Prudhoe Bay and Deadhorse where he had stayed if the weather kept him from making the trip back to Valdez. He hated to do it because it meant that he had to keep his truck running the whole time so he would not risk ruining his engine due to the cold.

He learned that timing the filling of his barrels and then getting on the road was a critical factor. He followed a strict routine and usually got home before bad weather kept him out.

Then one day he climbed the ladder to his oil tap line and found that someone had sealed it so that he could not open it. He could figure out how to open the valve safely without the risk of breaking the line and creating an oil spill. He decided that he needed to find out who had sealed the valve, and he needed to eliminate that individual or else his he faced the certainty of having to work for some company once again for a pittance. He felt that his future was at risk, and he was not going to accept that risk without a fight.

He found a high point where he had a good view of the above ground part of the pipeline. His taps were spread along the four hundred twenty miles that were above ground. The specific locations were determined by the fact that he could reach them with his ladder and have his truck close enough that his hose could reach all of the twelve barrels. That meant that most of his taps were closer to Prudhoe Bay area or in the few spots that were farther south. He had a few others that were harder to get to, so they were seldom used.

For several trips he would slowly drive along Dalton Highway and follow the pipeline. He was trying to find who might have discovered his taps. He was aware that each of the large oil companies had inspection teams that drove the pipeline to make sure that there were no leaks. That inspection happened every day and took in all four hundred twenty miles of the above ground pipe. His taps were on the opposite side of the pipe of where the inspectors drove so they could not be visually seen from the road. He was looking for someone who was looking from the tap side of the line.

It took him almost six months to finally see someone walking on that side of the pipe. He stopped his truck, took out his rifle and looked through the scope at the person. It was clear to him that he was an Inuit. They had fought for years to block the pipeline but had lost to the money handlers who had bought off the Inuit leaders as well as all the Alaskan politicians. The money had talked, and the pipeline went in.

He had no idea who this individual happened to be.

He watched as the individual stopped at a point where one of his taps was located. In this area he always filled the oil in the dark of night. He knew that he needed to take action because he could not afford to lose any more taps, especially taps in the easy to access areas.

He looked around to make sure there was no one on the road, or with in site and made his decision.

He looked through his scope put the cross hairs on the person's chest and pulled the trigger. It should have been a kill shot but his target had at the last moment bent over to pick something up from the ground and the shot had hit him, knocked him down but he saw the person crawl away.

He jumped off the truck and ran toward the pipeline. When he got there, he was surprised to find nothing.

He looked along the creek and again he saw nothing. He looked for a trail of blood and found nothing. He knew that he had not missed but he found nothing. He walked along the creek looking for any sign. He finally gave up and returned to his truck. He picked up the single casing from the back of the truck bed and put his rifle back on the rack and strapped it in. He drove about ten miles to where he had another tap, filled his oil barrels, and then drove on toward Valdez. He knew he had to return as soon as he could and set himself up to shoot anyone else that might show up.

Ignirtoq looked along the pipeline that he had walked multiple times from one end to the other. He had walked the many miles of exposed piping, and he had walked over the miles where the pipeline was buried. He understood that it was purposely built to have a zig-zag pattern in case of a significant earthquake. He had been a young boy when the plans to build the pipeline had been made public and had participated with his Inuit brethren that objected to having it built.

Money ended up winning. The state and federal government politicians were influenced by the desire for the oil money and succumbed to the allure of the tax income, the royalty income, and the promises of other improvements. The North Slope Borough representing the Inuit was allotted enough shares of stock that they were convinced to approve the pipeline and were now getting six hundred million a year in dividends and had become the wealthiest company in Alaska.

Ignirtoq had come to accept the pipeline and the fact that his people as well at the other indigenous people had also benefitted. He had taken advantage of the situation and had attended University of Alaska Fairbanks and had majored in forestry. He had stayed in the university to earn a graduate interdisciplinary degree that spanned across mechanical engineering, linguistics of the region, and tribal governance. His resume and his Inuit heritage made him an attractive hire to the oil companies.

He was hired by one of the big oil firms and went to work for them after his graduation. He had accepted the role as a technical inspector of the oil line and became familiar with every above and below ground mile of the line. He worked for more than ten years and rose to a mid-level manager.

His life in his community took on a political slant and he was elected a local tribal leader. He saved almost his entire income and when he quit the oil company to pursue other avenues, he knew that he had enough to live comfortably.

It was at this point that he got married to the young woman who he had met while at the university. They had only one child a son, Kaskae who after his wife died of lung cancer, he raised on his own. The two of them were close and they still lived together. They had hunted and fished together, and he had taught him all the ways of surviving in the Iñupiaq Region. He had shown him how to survive where the ground could not support large trees, and he had taken him to the mountains where the snow depth often would reach more than twenty feet. There he had taught him how to shuffle through the snow on large snowshoes and to build a shelter using the snow and then being able to sit inside where a large candle would provide enough heat to allow them to sit in, take off their coats and be comfortable in their thermal underwear.

All of this was going through his mind as he closed the opening to the crevasse at the edge of the stream. He needed time to assess how badly he was hurt, and he had to make sure that the person who had shot him could not find him. He had his own weapon, but he needed to recover before exiting and making his way back to his all-terrain snowmobile scooter that he had left not more than a mile away hidden in under some brush.

Kaskae had been expecting his father home. He knew that his father was most likely on one of his many inspection tours of the oil pipeline and perhaps had forgotten the time. If he had planned to be out for more than a day, he would have let everyone know. There was no word from him, and he did not show up to dinner.

He called his cousin Atiqtalik, who was a local forest ranger, to see if she had heard anything only to learn that she had not. She shared that his father had let her know that there was someone stealing oil from the pipeline. He didn't care about the thievery, but he was worried that the thief might create an oil spill.

Kaskae asked how anyone could possibly tap into the pipeline since it operated at a very high pressure.

Atiqtalik said that she had wondered the same thing and had asked his father who explained that the taps would have had to be put in during the construction of the pipeline and since they had not been noticed then they would have been put in by someone working during the construction of the pipeline and be installed in such a fashion that the tap would blend in with the other equipment that might be part of the various pipe joints.

She added that she and her team had been stumped and had reported the possibility of someone selling stolen oil. She had been informed that there were several sellers of small quantities of oil by the barrel that fit the profile but most of them did have their own small oil wells, and it would take some time to check them all out.

She said that she would get her unit to go along the pipeline and see what they could find.

A few days later she replied that she had found the all-terrain snowmobile hidden in the brush. She had left it in place just in case her uncle came back he would have it if he needed it.

Grayson returned to the area where he suspected the person he had shot should be. He again checked everywhere and after spending more time than he wished he decided to take his oil to Valdez. He had used up a full day in hopes of finding the person he had shot and who he knew he had hit. It puzzled him how that person could disappear in an area that had no place to hide.

He decided that he would next use one of the taps that was farther south and stay away from the area where this mysterious person had appeared. He continued to be worried about the fact that the person had somehow been able to identify the oil tap. It was well enough disguised that it had never been noticed by anyone inspecting the line. Whoever the person was they had to know a lot about the pipeline to have found the tap.

He decided that he would curtail his oil runs and return and focus his efforts on finding and eliminating anyone looking for the taps. He felt he had to protect his investment.

Ignirtoq assessed his wound and decided that it was superficial. He thought about the situation and decided that everyone needed to think he had been killed.

He needed to be dead so that he could get the person who he knew would solve the mystery of who was stealing the oil, and she would only come if he was thought of as dead. He had been impressed with her ability to solve cases that others failed to.

He sent his brother a cryptic message that he had been shot, was dying and that he should contact an Alex Evercrest, in Cincinnati, Ohio and see if she could be hired to solve who had killed him.

He figured it was a long shot, but he had enough food and water that he could last for several weeks, and he had a fishing line that he could throw into the stream below to catch a few trout.

Atiqtalik learned of the call that her father had received. She looked up the person who her uncle had called out by name and was impressed by what she learned. She wondered when her uncle had learned about her, but she decided she would make the call to see if she would take on the case. She decided to go through the official organization channels. She wanted to make sure that she got a positive response to getting this "Alex" involved in a case that was taking a very weird twist.

She had the tribal leaders to deal with. She was a forest ranger and not a criminal law enforcer. She wanted the help if she could get it.

She asked Kaskae if he had the money to pay for such a venture.

He said that he was on his father's bank account and there was more than enough money available if she thought involving a Qallunaat would do any good.

Atiqtalik laughed and said that the person she was getting involved was not a Qallunaat but was black.

That caught him by surprise. He asked why she was asking for her. She replied that she had a reputation for solving cases that no one else could and that his father had somehow zeroed in on her.

Kaskae said that if his father had specifically called this detective out then he had to support getting her to Alaska.

Grayson returned from Valdez to the location where he had made the shot that he knew had hit the person he had aimed for. He came prepared to stay and wait for his quarry to show himself. He did not plan to set up a camp, but he had a portable one-person hutch that he could sit comfortably in, stay warm and enjoy his coffee. He figured it was just like a hunting trip, but he was hunting a very specific two-legged game. He found a location where the hutch camouflage disappeared into the background.

He laughed as he thought about the well-known saying, "there is a woman behind every tree." It was a joke about the fact that there were so few women in this northern region and no trees that anyone could hide behind. In this case he was the shooter that was waiting behind those same trees.

He would wait until he either saw the person who had somehow hidden from him or saw his body hauled away.

2 A call out of the Blue

*T*he Chief listened to the person on the other end as she explained the reason that he should grant the request to have Alex help to solve a potential murder case that involved her grand uncle. The details seemed to be sketchy and not clear to him, and he was skeptical of taking the case on since it was in northern Alaska along the oil pipeline. He wondered whether Alex would even be interested in taking on such a case.

He asked the person on the phone to hold on for a moment. He went to the door and signaled Alex and Trey to come to his office.

They entered and he briefly explained the call and then put the call into speaker mode and let the caller know that he had called Alex and her partner into his office to listen to her request.

Atiqtalik introduced herself and shared the fact that she was a forest ranger in the northern part of Alaska and lived in Wiseman which was just east of Gates of the Arctic National Park and Preserve. She chuckled and asked if either of them had a clue where she was located.

Alex laughed and said that she certainly would need to look on the map of Alaska to have a clue. She went on to ask why she was being asked to investigate a potential murder.

Atiqtalik replied that her grand uncle had disappeared, but he had contacted his brother, her father and let him know that he had been shot but hoped to recover but if he did not return in a day or two that his brother should call in Alex Evercrest to find the person who had killed him.

Alex asked if her grand uncle's body had been found.

Atiqtalik was silent for a moment and then she said that it had not. She had found his all-terrain snow scooter hidden in low spot under some brush along the oil pipeline. She went on to explain that her grand uncle constantly patrolled the pipeline to ensure there were no leaks.

He had recently become convinced that someone was stealing oil from the pipeline, and he was trying to find out who and how that was being done. He was sure that such activity would lead to a major spill.

Alex looked at the Chief and asked if he had the funds to let her, and Trey do an initial investigation to determine if there was a case.

Atiqtalik spoke up and said that she was prepared to cover the cost of that initial investigation and any additional cost if Alex took up the case.

Alex said that the initial investigation would be having her, and her partner come to the location that was specified. So, the expenses would be to get there, get a hotel room, and then have some sort of transportation.

Atiqtalik replied that she would cover that but if it became a longer-term case, she was not sure how that would be handled.

Alex suggested that they should take it one step at a time.

Atiqtalik suggested they fly into Prospect Creek, and she would meet them there with her partner and take them to the hotel were they could stay.

After the call Alex looked over at the Chief and commented that this was very different than the start of some of the other cases.

He laughed and said that he no longer evaluated how her cases did or did not start. He agreed that it was different than being shot at on her bike ride into work, or having a child dropped off on her porch, but it was similar to getting a call from the Royal Canadian Mounted Police and asking her to help them on a case that turned out as a hunt for a serial killer black widow.

Alex looked at Trey and asked if he could leave the following day.

Trey nodded and said that he and Lindsey did not have any plans.

She let the Chief know that she was going to get his support associate to arrange the flight to Prospect Creek, Alaska.

The Chief laughed and asked what the population was at Prospect Creek happened to be and how large the plane taking her there was going to be.

Alex shook her head and said she had no idea how to answer either of his questions. She added that she knew that Fairbanks Alaska was ten percent the size of Cincinnati and that Fairbanks was around thirty thousand, so she figured that Prospect Creek was really small. She then added that they would most likely be flying in into Prospect Creek on a piper cub and both of them might have to peddled to provide the power for the plane.

She estimated that they would be gone for a week unless they actually had a case to open then she would talk with him to determine what to do next.

The Chief nodded and wished her a good trip.

She left the office and shared what had just happened with Johnnie, Bill, and Trevor.

Trevor looked at her and joked that she was probably using the trip as an excuse to go skiing and she was leaving those who were serious about doing actual work behind.

Alex said that as far as she knew she would be on some of the flattest terrain in Alaska and looking up at an eight-foot diameter oil pipeline. But if she found some good skiing she would make sure to give him a call.

She looked at Johnnie and let him know that she was riding home and that he was welcome to ride with her.

Trey said that he was going home as well and would pack for Alaska. He asked about the weather.

Bill said that it was the time of year when it would be very cold in the northern part of Alaska and long underwear would be appropriate.

On the ride home, Alex chatted with Johnnie and asked whether Mary might be able to spend a few more hours taking care of Aurea and making sure that Matt had some help in the evenings and early morning.

Johnnie replied that he was sure that Mary would be able to do that. He suggested that once they got to her house, she talk with Mary so that the two of them were clear on what was wanted.

She got home just before Mary and Aurea came home from school. They came in the back door because the two of them were still able to ride their bikes and the street behind the house was at the same level that they rode from the house to the school.

Aurea was surprised to have Alex home early and asked what was up.

Alex explained about the call and the trip she was going to make.

Aurea surprised everyone by commenting that Prudhoe Bay was the farthest north location in Alaska, it was where all the oil wells were located and that the coldest part of the year was just starting. She added that all of Alaska had less than half population of the greater Cincinnati area.

Alex complemented Aurea for knowing so much about Alaska.

Aurea said that was one of the places she had visited online. She was fascinated by the fact that the oil pipeline was so big and traveled across a great deal of the state to a location where ships and trucks could be loaded year-round to move the oil to market. She went on to explain that it represented about twenty percent of the oil produced by the United States.

Mary said that it was time for the two of them to go to the library to their first seminar and she wanted to get there early enough so the two of them did not miss out on any of the refreshments. She took Aurea the hand and said that their cab was waiting. She made sure Aurea had her homework with her so that it would get done before they came back for dinner.

Alex spent a few moments with Johnnie after the two of them left. She clarified that she was planning to get him involved if she needed any specific information.

Johnnie nodded and added that cookies were still the currency of choice for any specific requests that required his magic touch.

Alex laughed, went to the cupboard, and took out a container full of cookies and said that she was paying in advance because she didn't want to be stuck in ten feet of snow and not be able to get his help.

She then said that she had to get her things packed for the trip.

She packed both her thermal underwear, her full Kevlar suit and all the winter clothes she thought might come in handy. She managed to get all of it into one large hard-shelled suitcase. She had a second smaller case as a carryon for her computer and paperwork.

She had just finished when Matt came in, looked at the still open suitcase and commented that he was glad that he had come home before she ran away.

Alex laughed and said that she had just finished packing for a trip to the North Pole and planned to visit Santa and ask him personally for what she wanted for Christmas. She gave him a hug and then went down to the kitchen and said that she was going to start dinner.

She got him a snack and then let him know that she was going to Alaska to investigate a potential murder.

Matt listened and said that it sounded like a potentially dangerous investigation.

Alex nodded and said that she was going to be as safe as possible but as always, she would approach it as if someone was trying to shoot her.

Dinner was ready when Mary returned with Aurea from the library.

Mary excused herself and said that she and Johnnie had agreed to go to dinner and then take a walk around Hyde Park.

After dinner, the three of them spent a quiet evening chatting and reading in the family room.

Matt left to meet his EMT team at four in the morning. He quietly wished Alex a safe journey and went out to his team who had come by to pick him up.

Alex got up and made breakfast for her and Aurea.

Mary came in as the two of them were just finishing cleaning off the table and putting the dishes in the dishwasher.

Aurea gave Alex a hug and asked her to call and to send pictures.

Alex said that she would do that every day.

After Mary and Aurea left, Alex took her suitcases to the street in back, got into the cab and headed to the Airport.

She met Trey and the two of them went to the counter and checked in. They checked their luggage through to Fairbanks where they were to be met by Clay who would fly them on a Piper PA-18 Super Cub chartered by the U.S. Fish and Wildlife Service. He explained that Atiqtalik had arranged for him to fly the two of them to Bettles, which was a change to the where she had previously said would be the final destination.

He explained that the new location was closer to where they would be staying and would save them a lot of time.

He led them out to a white van and got their suitcases in the back and had them sit on the bench seats behind him. He drove out to the cub.

Alex noticed what to her were extremely large tires on such a small plane. She asked about the size of the tires.

He laughed and said that they were twenty six-inch Alaskan Bushwheels and cost close to two thousand dollars each. He used them because they were tough, and they let him land on almost any surface.

Alex looked at Trey and said that the planes were getting smaller, the tires were getting larger but at least they didn't have to peddle but would still be flying first class.

Clay smiled and said that he was pleased that she thought the flight would be first class and he assured her that she would not have to peddle. He pointed to a cooler with refreshment that they could enjoy on their first-class flight.

Alex was surprised at the smooth take off, the fact that the inside of the plane was not as loud as she had expected and that the view of the terrain was constantly changing from a thick dark green pine cover with a few broad leaf trees to a more rugged terrain where the trees diminished and by the time they reached Bettles both the number of trees and their size had both greatly diminished. In fact, it appeared as if the trees were huddling along various small streams and there were vast distanced between the huddling trees.

Clay brought the P18 cub to a smooth landing and guided it back to where two people were standing by a white SUV with blue and red flashing lights on the top and a green strip from the headlights running just below the side windows to the backlights.

Clay let them know that the one that looked like a forest ranger was Atiqtalik and the stout stocky guy was Kaskae her cousin. He added that Atiqtalik was the one that had made the arrangements with him. He was aware that Kaskae's father, Ignirtoq was missing, and that Alex had been asked to investigate his disappearance.

Alex asked why he said that Ignirtoq was missing.

Clay smiled and said that Ignirtoq was too stubborn to have been killed. He added that Ignirtoq was a master of the terrain, knew how to survive in the most terrible conditions of weather and through the most difficult of situations. Clay said that his money was on the fact that he had wanted her to come to Alaska to solve some problem that he had not been able to solve and that his death was the only way to get her to come.

Alex laughed and said that she was going to keep his words in mind as she evaluated the situation.

He brought the plane to a stop a short distance from the SUV.

Kaskae led the way to the plane and helped get the luggage out.

Atiqtalik greeted Alex and Trey and introduced Kaskae.

She thanked Clay who shook hands with both Alex and Trey. He added that he bet her a cup of coffee that he was right.

Alex nodded and said that she would add dinner to the bet and waved as he got back into the plane.

Atiqtalik asked Alex what Clay was betting about and that she should be careful when betting with him because he seemed to always win his bets.

Alex shared the fact that he had a theory about the situation that she had been asked to look into and that losing to him would be a win for all of them.

As they walked up to the SUV Alex commented that the SUV had the same kind of tires that Clay had on his plane.

Kaskae laughed and said that the way his cousin drove the tough Bushwheels were needed. He said that his old pickup had regular tires because he could not drive so much better than Atiqtalik and he could not afford such expensive tires.

Atiqtalik shook her head, laughed, and said that she actually worked and had to drive thousands of miles over some really tough terrain, and the tires were well worth what the forest service paid for them. She added that she was also a much better driver than Kaskae.

Alex listened to the two tease each other on the way to the cottage where they were to stay and knew that the two enjoyed the banter.

3 Out to the Pipeline

*A*tiqtalik again thanked Alex for her willingness to come out to help determine what had happened to her grand uncle. She smiled and said that she was taking both of them to a two-bedroom cabin that was used by visiting forest service members. She said that she had stocked it with some basic food goods so that they would not need to drive to one of the few places where a dinner could be ordered.

She admitted that it was also much less expensive for her to cover the costs. She had obtained permission from her superiors to use the cabin at no cost as long as when she was done' she made sure it was once again ready for use.

She asked whether that was acceptable to the two of them.

Alex said that it would make things easier and if it saved them time, she figured it was fine, especially since she knew that Trey was such a great cook.

Trey smiled, agreed, and added that he hoped that peanut butter and jelly was included in the supplies. And then he added that he hoped that Alex's snoring wouldn't keep him awake at night.

Atiqtalik laughed, commented that she was glad the two of them got along so well, then asked whether the two of them had come with some heavy-duty winter clothing.

Alex said that she had the heaviest winter clothing that she possessed and hoped that it would be adequate.

Kaskae added that if necessary, he could get additional clothing for her, but Trey was so much larger than most of the folks he knew but if necessary, they could make a trip to Prudhoe Bay where the store would carry goods for someone his size.

Trey commented that he thought he was well prepared but getting out for a day in the current weather would determine if the trip to Prudhoe Bay would be necessary.

The drive to the cabin took only a short time. The route went across some very open and sparsely covered areas then entered a more wooded location. The surrounding view was breath taking in its contrast to the parks Alex had been used to around Cincinnati where the various lush green full branched trees were many and large. The few pines in the valley seemed to stand in contrast to the mountains, the rocky terrain, and the vast expanse of sky. The rather large frozen snow-covered lake spoke very clearly to the cold that Atiqtalik had been talking about. It made Alex shiver just looking at it.

Alex commented about the vast valley, stoney bare mountains and the contrast to the parks she had visited.

Atiqtalik nodded and replied that the snow had come early, there was more currently on the ground than she had been expecting this early in the season, and she too knew how different the Gates of the Arctic National Park and Preserve was from all the parks in the lower forty-eight and even from the parks in the southern part of Alaska. She added that the desert based national parks were the opposites to the parks in the Arctic region.

A log cabin surrounded by pine trees with a thick layer of snow on the steeply pitched roof came into view. When they got ready to enter the log cabin, Atiqtalik shared the fact the cabin had been modernized and been remodeled. It operated on solar panels with a battery system that provided all the electrical power to run the lights, heated inside, and the water for showering. She added that showers needed to be short because the hot water heater was small.

The range used gas, and its gas tank was the small portable kind since it needed to be inside because tanks outside would have to be heated.

The hood over the stove vented along a flat vent that ran across the wall and left the cabin as a cold exhaust. That vent only ran when the stove was being used.

She pointed to the end of the cabin that was a glass wall from floor to ceiling and said that it was a triple layer, air filled window that withstood the arctic cold very well. Then she pointed to two side coverings that she said should be closed at night or when the weather got really cold. It then would provide the same or better insulation as the rest of the cabinets. She added that during the winter the cabin was heated no matter if it stood empty.

She then suggested that they use the paper plates since washing the dishes would consume a lot of the water that could otherwise be used for the shower.

She then led the way to the bedrooms and said that each room had purposely been built in its own enclosure so that each was entirely inside the cabin with no wall to the outside. And each had insulation as effective as the outside walls. The rooms were effectively acting very similar to an igloo and a person's heat would heat the room to a comfortable level.

She pointed to the thick down filled looking bed cover and said that it provided all the warmth a person needed, though she personally found it a little too warm.

Trey commented that the cabin certainly seemed to be extremely well built and had been specifically designed to handle the northern cold.

Kaskae said he had been impressed with the remodeling that the forest service had done. He added that he was trying to incorporate some of the things he had learned into his small home.

Atiqtalik suggested that they get situated and that in the morning she, Kaskae and her forest ranger partner would stop by around seven in the morning and they would go out to where Ignirtoq's snow scooter was located.

Once Atiqtalik and Kaskae had left, Alex suggested that they first call home since there was a four-hour difference in time zones and it would be getting late in Cincinnati. When she called, she found out that Matt was already out with his team, and Aurea was just getting ready for bed.

She shared the details of where she was staying and then listened as Aurea shared what she had learned about the area.

Alex said good night and then called Matt and let him know she had arrived safely. The call did not last long because he was on a run on the way to the hospital.

After her calls, Alex looked over what was available to prepare for dinner. She found that the most interesting thing was a cut of caribou that looked very much like a thick T-bone steak, some yellow beets, and some potatoes. She checked with Trey about that combination and then began preparation of dinner.

Trey was online talking with Lesley until dinner was ready.

After dinner they both said that they needed to get some rest so that they would be ready to go looking for Ignirtoq in the morning.

Trey gave a laugh and said he would wash the dishes, which was joke since it consisted of only the flatware and disposing of the paper plates.

Morning came much too quickly and once again Alex was in the kitchen area making a pot of coffee when Trey came in and said that he would fix breakfast and asked if two eggs some bacon and a couple of pieces of toast with jam would be sufficient.

After breakfast they heard a knock on the door and let Atiqtalik, Kaskae, and another ranger in.

Atiqtalik introduced her partner, John, and said that he was dropping off four snow scooters before he went out to check to make sure that everything in the park was as it should be.

She added that the four of them would be travelling to the pipeline on the snow scooters. She said that this would give Alex and Trey the opportunity to get some skill on them before they got to the pipeline.

As Trey and Alex got ready both she and Kaskae were checking on how the two of them were dressed for the cold. Both of them were congratulated on having on the right clothes and each of them were asked about the extra layer of a material that Atiqtalik was not familiar with.

Alex explained that the extra layer was a bullet proof vest and pants that each of them were wearing.

Atiqtalik said that she hoped that there would be no gun fire.

Alex smiled and said that she hoped for the same thing but if someone had killed her great uncle, she and Trey were operating with the expectation that there was someone out there that was armed and dangerous.

Kaskae said that he did not own any bullet proof vests.

Atiqtalik said that her vest was with her partner since she had been focused on searching for her grand uncle and had not thought about someone shooting at them.

By the time they reached the pipeline, Alex and Trey were both enjoying their scooters and had tried a variety of maneuvers that both Atiqtalik and Kaskae had demonstrated.

Grayson was sitting in his hunting blind enjoying his coffee as he had done for the last several days. He had parked his camouflaged snow mobile behind the blind. He had walked out halfway to the river bend and verified that his setup was virtually invisible to the casual observer.

He had found the hidden snow scooter and had figured out how the person he had shot had gotten to the area. He figured that if he had not killed him then that person would return to get the scooter. He then planned to finish the job and then haul the body some place far away.

He first heard and then saw the four approaching snow scooters. They headed directly to where the scooter was hidden in the slight depression in the ground, so Grayson figured they were associated with the person he had shot. In fact, one of them was dressed very much like the person he had shot.

He picked up his rifle and looked through the scope. He picked out the person that looked like they were associated with local law enforcement and might be armed. He was just pulling the trigger when one of the other persons in the group stepped suddenly forward and knocked his target down as he pulled the trigger.

At the same time as he felt the kick of his rifle, he felt the bullet hit him in in the chest. He could not believe that anyone with a handgun could have hit him and have done so with such a lightening reaction. He put his finger where the bullet had penetrated his thick jacket. His instinctive reaction had been to fall backwards off of his chair. He knew the only reason he was alive was because the jacket had been heavy enough to stop the bullet that had no power left to penetrate all the way to his chest.

He was still in shock from having been hit as he turned and crawled out to his two wheeled power scooter as two more bullets hit the ground behind him. He was not sticking around to duel with anyone that could shoot like he had just experienced.

Alex saw the laser beam target Atiatalik's back. She stepped forward, gave her a push and at the same time felt a bullet hit her in the side. She instinctively fired in the direction of where she felt the shot had come from. She heard Trey's two shots as she jumped on her snow scooter and went zipping toward where she had shot. She heard a second scooter and knew that Trey was right behind her. She could finally make out the camouflaged blind and saw a scooter throwing up a plume of snow far out on the horizon. It was well out of firing range.

She stopped at the blind and examined it and the surrounding. It was clear to her that whoever had been using the blind had done so for several days and was prepared for whomever showed up to retrieve the hidden snow mobile.

Both Atiqtalik and Kaskae had followed Alex and Trey up to the blind. Atiqtalik asked how Alix had known to push her. When she learned about the laser beam, she asked if Alex had been hit.

Alex put a finger into the hole in her coat and said that her bullet proof vest had stopped the bullet, but she was going to have a nasty bruise since it had been some sort of high-powered rifle. She figured the bullet was still somewhere in her clothes.

She then knelt down and let out a deep breath along the handle of the chair and was rewarded by several fingerprints. She took out her phone and took close up pictures. She did the same with the cup that she picked carefully up and again was rewarded with several fingerprints that she took pictures of.

She sent the pictures immediately to Johnnie with a message for him to identify who they belonged to.

Atiqtalik said that she had never seen anyone get fingerprints in that manner.

Trey laughed and said that neither had he, but he was not surprised by anything his partner did. She had destroyed a coal barge and a helicopter gunship, and she had only had a fishing pole when she took on the gunship.

Kaskae shook his head and said that now he knew why his father had insisted that Alex should be the one to come and solve his murder case.

Alex said that they should see if she could lose her bet to Clay who had bet that his father was still alive. She said it was time to either find a dead body or to call Ignirtoq back to life.

She looked from the blind down to the bend in the river.

She asked how Kaskae would call to his father in his native language if he were alive.

He said that he would call out "Atelihai, Uana, naluanmiutun, and let his father know that the person who shot him was on the run.

Alex thanked him and said that she was betting on Clay being right and she was going to walk along the riverbank and call out to Ignirtoq and see if she could get him to show himself.

She said they should all follow her.

She left he scooter by the blind and walked to the bend and in a loud voice she called out, "Atelihai, Uana, naluanmiutun, Alex and I am calling you to come out and let us know that you are alive. The person who shot you is on the run, and we need your help to pursue him." She repeated it several times and then she stood looking up and down along the river and repeated what she was saying several more times.

Suddenly a voice behind them quietly said that he was quite eager to help.

Alex turned and smiled and shook his hand. She added that she had just lost a bet to Clay, and she was very glad that she had.

Kaskae gave his father a hug and said that he had been very worried about him.

Atiqtalik said that he had cost her a small fortune to get Alex and her partner to come to Alaska.

Ignirtoq said that he had the money, but he knew that the only way to get Alex to come was to die.

Alex nodded and said that he had been right and now that she too had been shot, it had become an actual case, and she would be pursuing the person who had shot her. She added that she hoped that his knowledge of the north would make her hunt successful.

Ignirtoq's eyes got large, and he asked how badly she was wounded.

Atiqtalik let him know that Alex had taken the bullet meant for her when she had stepped forward and pushed her out of the way.

Alex said that she was going to use all the hot water in cabin when she showered and afterwards, she was going to put on some salve that would reduce the pain and finally she was going to need to lay down.

Ignirtoq asked if she did yoga and smiled when she replied that she did.

He suggested that she lay down in her bed and do the Savasana pose and let herself relax and go to sleep.

Alex smiled, nodded, and said that she would do as he suggested.

She then asked where he had been hiding.

Ignirtoq walked over to the riverbank's edge and pointed into the small cave like enclosure. He smiled and added that he had the Savasana pose and had reduced his breathing rate and spent much of the time sleeping.

She then said that she was going to go back to the cottage and that she would see them all for breakfast in the morning.

Once she and Trey had returned to the cottage, she said that she was going to take a few minutes to talk with Johnnie, the Chief, and to Matt. She commented that she had not anticipated an immediate gun battle, but she once again knew that she had spent her money well in buying the Kevlar outfits.

Trey asked if she was up for a BLT and a large glass of milk as a substitute for a larger meal.

Alex nodded and said that she would be ready for that after her shower.

738

4 In Pursuit

Grayson kept his snow mobile going full throttle as he sped away from the pipeline. He was still in shock that anyone could return fire so swiftly and accurately with only a handgun. He figured he needed to get out of the area as quickly as possible. He figured that he could get to Fairbanks by morning once there he would decide what to do next. He knew he needed to lay low. He wondered if he had left anything behind that might get him identified.

He counted on the fact the local rangers would not have any sophisticated way of figuring out who he was, but he had not been prepared to make a run for it. He decided that he should act like they knew who he was.

His best bet was to plan on a hunting vacation in Canada. He drove all night and made it to Valdez early in the morning. He called and arranged for a flight into Canada. Then packed his hunting duffel with all the equipment he needed, put his rifle in its carrying case, went to the bank and withdrew thirty thousand dollars and headed to the airport.

He would buy an all-terrain vehicle and get his hunting permit on arrival in Canada and then head for the woods. He was going to disappear for several weeks.

In Cincinnati, Johnnie was running the fingerprints that Alex had sent him. When he ran it against the Alaskan police data bases, he found that they belonged to a Grayson Gagnon who had a couple of speeding charges but otherwise did not have a record.

He sent the information to Alex.

Alex was pleased to get a quick hit on the prints. She called and talked with Johnnie and asked him to find out Grayson's address and all the information that he could find on him.

Ignirtoq arrived at the cottage for breakfast.

Alex shared what she had learned and said that she would soon know where his attacker lived and then she planned to go there and if he was still around, she would arrest him but if he was not there she would see if she could learn where he had gone and then pursue him.

Ignirtoq asked if he could accompany her and Trey.

Alex said that he could, but he could not participate in the capture.

They were still having breakfast when she got a call from Johnnie. He let her know that Grayson had a house in Valdez and gave her the address.

Alex asked if Ignirtoq knew how to contact Clay and arrange a flight to Valdez.

Ignirtoq said that he could. He used Alex's phone and placed a call to Clay and arranged for a flight from Bettles to Valdez for three people. He agreed to a flight at ten and that he would bring everything to the end of the runway flight parking area.

Alex smiled and said that he was welcome to come along but when they got to Grayson's address he would need to stay with the car when she and Trey approached the house.

Ignirtoq nodded and said that he would follow her lead in the hunt for Grayson, but he wanted to be on hand when they finally captured him.

He said that he wanted to arrange for a modern phone when they got to Valdez.

When they met Clay at the airport, Alex smiled and said that losing the bet to him was one of the best things that could have happened. She added that if things worked out, she would take him to dinner that evening at the place of his choice.

He smiled and said that his favorite place was right on the harbor, and he was looking forward to splurging on her dime. He looked over at Ignirtoq and thanked him for staying alive.

The flight down was uneventful but finding a rental car was almost impossible. They ended up settling for an old pickup truck that one of the people at the airport rented to them for cash and their promise to bring it back by morning.

Trey drove the pickup and followed his phone's map to the address. He drove by and they were able to see a large pickup in the back with a snowmobile in it. Trey parked a block away and he and Alex got out of the pickup, took off their heavy coats and put on a light jacket.

They then made their approach with their guns drawn and at the ready. Trey stood in the driveway where he could see both the front door and the pickup truck.

Alex approached the front door and called out that Grayson was under arrest and that he should come out with his hands up. She got no response. She knelt down to the side of the door and picked the lock and slowly opened and again shouted out her order. She then went in and slowly made her way through the house. It was empty.

She had Trey come in and help her with a quick search to see if there was anything that would give them a clue as to where Grayson might be going.

Trey found a series of hunting brochures that described hunting lodges in Canada. He also found a gun rack with several rifles and pistols in it. There was one empty rifle rack and one empty pistol holder.

Alex looked over the array of boxes of bullets and determined that the rifle that was missing was likely a 7 mm rifle.

She said it was time to get back to the airport to see if they could get more information about where in Canada Grayson had gone.

When they got back to the Airport, Clay was still there talking with some of the other pilots. He said that he would check to see if any of them had made a flight into Canada.

Not long after he returned and said that a Grayson Gagnon had purchased a one-way ticket for himself. He had declared two weapons that cleared customs in Canada. He had a large duffle bag, in which he carried all of his hunting equipment and a separate smaller duffle with his clothes. The pilot said that it was clear to him that Grayson was a skilled hunter and carried only the essentials.

Alex decided that she needed to make a few calls to her Canadian Mounted Police friends and arrange for their help.

She first put in a call to the Chief, apologized for calling so late. She then brought him up to date on the case. She let him know that she was in pursuit of the person who had shot her and also the person who she had come up to find. That person was alive and helping her to pursue the shooter.

She went on to let him know that she was going to contact the head of the Canadian Mounted Police and asked him to do the same.

The Chief agreed to make the call the first thing in the morning. He told her to be careful but to bring this Grayson person in or to do whatever she had to.

Alex then called Johnnie and apologized to him for the late hour, but she needed to make sure that he locked Grayson out of his bank account.

Johnnie let her know that he had already done so, and he saw that thirty thousand dollars had been withdrawn the day before.

Alex thanked him and after hanging up she said that it was time to pay off her gambling debts.

Clay said that he could show her the way to the restaurant. He said that he would make sure they got one of the tables with a great view of the harbor.

While they waited for the order, Alex called and made hotel arrangements. She said that she hoped to be able to fly into Canada late the following afternoon. She explained that she hoped to get the support of the Royal Canadian Mounted Police.

Ignirtoq asked how she had such a close connection with the top brass in that organization.

Alex explained that she and her team had solved a case that had stumped them and had their support in several battles along the US–Canada border.

Clay said that he was getting more impressed each time he flew her somewhere. He asked if she needed a regular bush pilot.

Alex laughed and said that after her call in the middle of his night, her boss most likely would like to hire him to fly her somewhere in Canada and leave her in the bushes.

Alex went to bed early that evening because she wanted to make the calls to Montreal which meant that she would need to get up at three in the morning since she wanted to talk with Reginald Sailor, Reg to her, the head of the <u>R</u>oyal <u>M</u>ounted <u>C</u>anadian <u>P</u>olice when he came into the office at eight.

She got through to him exactly when he came into the office. He was surprised to hear from her but said that it was a pleasant surprise and wondered what she might be calling about. When he heard what had happened and that she was wanting to get the support of the RCMP, he said that he would make a call to the regional leader and have his folks at her disposal.

He added that she should give the person she was pursuing a chance. He gave her the name of the regional commander but added that he doubted he would be greeting her personally since he was recovering from having his horse step on his foot.

Alex thanked him and said that she would be flying into Canada that morning and hoped to track down the person she was after and if she were lucky, she would have him in custody by the end of the day. She added that so far the person she was pursuing had been able to be just one step ahead of her.

The call had taken only a short time and Alex decided to get back under her blankets and see if she could get a couple hours of sleep.

She woke up a short time later and went down to the hotel's breakfast area. It turned out that breakfast could be ordered. After placing her order, she poured herself a cup of coffee and had taken the first sip when Trey came over to the table. Soon, Clay and Ignirtoq came over to the table.

Alex let them know about her call to the RCMP chief and the fact that they would be greeted by some of them when they landed in Chilliwack, Canada.

Clay said the flight would take several hours.

Grayson landed in Chilliwack, waited for his rifle to clear inspection, and then immediately looked for a snowmobile to buy. He wanted to get out into the forest and disappear. He found a used one that was the size that he wanted. He didn't bargain too hard because he wanted to buy it and disappear. He loaded his equipment on it and headed out into the forest.

He had purchased three hunting permits for deer, elk and for bear. He did not plan to use all three permits but he wanted to have a permit so he could shoot which ever animal crossed his path first.

A day later he shot a deer and quickly skinned, cut it up and disposed of what he did not want. He set up his camp about a mile from where he had downed the deer.

He had brought salt, pepper, some onions, garlic, and a cast iron frying pan with him. He prepared a boneless steak to fry, and he also cut some of the meat and skewered it and roasted it over the open fire. He sat enjoying his dinner.

He thought back over what he had just experienced. He was not sure who he might have engaged but he was sure who ever it was they were formidable enemies, and he needed to lay low until they tired of looking for him.

He heard but did not see a helicopter but decided to douse his fire just in case it was putting up a plume.

About the same time the helo was flying over where Grayson was camping, Clay was almost to Chilliwack. He taxied into the area where he was directed by the tower and commented that it seemed that a small army of red coated RCMP mounted on great looking horses were waiting to greet them. He brought his plane to a stop and turned off the engines.

Alex was the first to exit and was greeted by a young looking RCMP woman officer who introduced herself as staff sergeant Delia Tislen.

Alex shook hands with her and introduced Trey, Ignirtoq and Clay.

Delia said that she and her squad were to help in hunting down a fugitive that had entered into Canada to escape being caught. She said that she had a helicopter searching the area looking for any signs that might indicate where he might be hiding. She shook her head and said that there was a lot of forest to disappear into, and she hoped that her folks could find out where that fugitive might be.

She then looked at the suitcases and suggested that they go to the lodging that she had arranged and get situated. She asked if the three of them could ride horses.

Alex nodded and said that she would love that and that she would work on relieving her muscles after each day of riding.

Delia smiled and said that she had long ago learned to relax and just blend with the motion of her mount. She said that matching the rhythm was the secret to not having a butt or back ache.

Ignirtoq grunted and said that his old body would be the one that would be complaining the loudest about bouncing up and down in the saddle, but he was determined to keep up.

Delia said that she had arranged for a large trailer to be set up at a nearby campground where they could stay. This would simplify the logistics of getting out into the forest. She and her team would be staying in the same campground as well but would be at the edge of the campground where they could also keep their mounts. She commented that the campground owners were pleased to have the business since things had been slow.

Once they arrived at the trailer and had all their belongings put in the trailer Delia suggested they make sure all of them got along with their horses and afterwards they could catch dinner at a local Bistro.

Alex made friends with her blond maned female mount that towered over her by introducing herself as she gave her an apple. She scratched it behind its ears and spoke to her quietly. She then mounted her from the left side and settled comfortable into the saddle.

She watched as Trey expertly got on his mount that was at least a hand taller than her mount. She almost burst out laughing as she watched Ignirtoq being helped up into his saddle. He had trouble getting his foot into the stirrup and swinging his leg over the saddle. It was clear to her that he would be the one that would most likely be sore.

They went out for a short ride and then returned to the edge of the camp where the RCMP unit was camped.

Alex got off her mount and thanked her for the great ride and then began to loosen the saddle. She was relieved by a sergeant who took over and suggested that she go with his boss to have dinner and then get some shut eye.

The restaurant was just over a mile away and soon Alex had her order for an Elk steak in wine sauce in and was engaged in conversation with Delia. She learned that Delia and her team had all hastened to meet her and that the makeup of those that she had with her came from several locations in British Columbia. She was out of the British Columbia divisional headquarters located in Vancouver.

She and the rest had been waiting for most of the morning for her arrival at the request of Alex's RCMP friend and her bosses' boss. Delia asked how Alex had befriended the top Canadian RCMP leader.

Alex briefly explained the case that she termed "The Sins of the Daughter," to a wide-eyed Delia.

Delia commented the case had become a legend in the rank and file of the RCMP. She now understood the order to support and do whatever she was asked to do.

The dinner table went silent as they all dug into the food that had been brought out.

After dinner, Delia suggested that they take a car ride to see some of the scenic sights while they waited for any message that might indicate in which direction they should ride to investigate a potential sighting of a camp.

They spent a significant amount of time sightseeing and chatting as they waited for some sort of sighting that would give them a direction to go to investigate.

They had just returned and were getting ready for the evening when a call came in about the sighting of a plume of smoke. They got the coordinates and when they looked at the map Delia suggested they get an early start the next day and ride out to check on the person or persons that might be at that camp. She added that the chopper noticed that the plum they had seen disappeared almost immediately, so she figured that someone was trying to minimize the chances of being spotted,

After having doused his campfire, Grayson decided to move his camp south about a mile. He did not want to be surprised and figured that the move would ensure that he would continue to be left alone.

He went back along the trail that he had made and used a tree branch to eliminate the tracks his snowmobile had made.

He gave up the camouflage activities after doing about a quarter of the distance. He walked back to his snow mobile and set up a new camp. He figured he would cook his dinner and make a stew in his frying pan and heat it when he made a morning coffee. He would then not light a fire until late the next day.

He figured that he would go out and hunt for rabbits and other small game. That would give him something to do during the day. If he tired of hunting, he figured he would read one of the books he had brought with him.

He felt confident that he had made his getaway and figured that he was in a land where he could remain invisible for as long as he needed to.

5 Plume Coordinate

*T*he morning darkness had not yet given way to the slowly rising sun when Alex, Trey and Ignirtoq walked back to where the RCMP unit was camped.

Delia led them to the three horses they would ride.

Once again Alex first greeted her mount and spent a few moments giving her a half of an apple. She had given the other half for Trey to give to his mount. She then mounted and said that she was ready.

Delia asked if they had come prepared to spend the entire day out. She added that she had prepared some sandwiches and had water as well.

Alex nodded and said that she had made some sandwiches as well, but she was sure the three of them would welcome anything that Delia had to feed them.

The sun slowly crept across the forest, and the tall brown barked pines seemed to have a mystical life of their own as they swayed gently in the light breeze. Alex seemed to breath in the scent of the pine and feel a magical power surrounding her. The rhythm of the slow trot of her mount was calming. She thought about what might be ahead. She opened her jacket to ensure she had easy access to her weapon. She took off her right glove and rode with her right hand in her pocket.

Trey was also riding easy and noticed Alex getting ready. He followed her lead, opened his jacket, and removed his right glove.

Delia was focused on her map and had her team zeroing in on the coordinates that the chopper pilot had given her.

When they arrived at the coordinates Delia thought at first that a mistake had been made because there seemed to be nothing there, but Ignirtoq got down from his mount and examined the area and then said that whoever had camped there had tried to erase their presence. He then said they should follow him.

He walked slowly along but said that the track was rather easy to follow. They had gone along slowly until the point where the tracks of snow mobile were no longer covered.

Delia had three of her team ride three abreast in front and her, Alex and Trey rode behind them.

Alex asked whether the three in front had bullet proof protection.

Delia said that all of her team had protection. She asked about Alex, Trey, and Ignirtoq.

Ignirtoq spoke up and said that he did not have any protection.

Delia asked him to ride behind all of them.

Alex said that she and Trey had their protection on.

They had just finished that discussion when suddenly one of the lead officers seem to fall off the back of his horse and then the sound of gunfire reached their ears.

Alex kicked her mount and galloped forward as she fired her weapon toward the small target that she could barely make out. She was trying to get close enough where her accuracy would greatly increase.

She felt more then saw Trey riding parallel to her and also firing his weapon.

Grayson was just enjoying his morning coffee when he took a moment to scan the area from which he had come. He was amazed to see what he took as a small army of red coats. He knew that the RCMP was coming his way. He aimed, shot the middle rider, and saw him fall off his mount. Then he immediately ripped down his tent and threw everything he had into the carrying basket in the front of the snow mobile. He had just gunned the throttle when he felt a sting across his neck. He was shocked to have been hit. Then he felt two hits in the middle of his back and knew that he had to get away before the two riders shooting at him got any closer. He began a zig-zag course through the trees in hopes not only to put distance between him and the shooters but also to put trees in the way and block any clear shots.

During his zig zagging, he lost the tent and the chair that went with it. He saw his cast iron pan fly out and hit a tree.

He succeeded in slowly pulling away from the two charging horses.

He stopped looking back. He knew he had to get out of Canada and get across the border and into the US.

He was a US citizen, and he had his passport with him.

To be totally legal he needed to have his weapons go through customs, but he had no plans to visit any of the official crossing points.

He was going to cross over and keep going south until he ran out of snow.

Alex quickly realized that she and Trey were not going to catch up to Grayson. She stopped, dismounted, and began to walk her mount back the way they had ridden. She picked up the frying pan. A short time later Trey picked up the tent and chair. Neither of them were interested in the things for evidence.

They had all they needed to arrest Grayson what they needed was to capture him.

When they got back to where the camp had been, Alex spotted some blood in the snow. She knew that at least Grayson had been wounded.

She and Trey cleaned up the camp site and then proceeded to walk back toward where the RCMP group had gathered around the one that had been shot out of his saddle. He was still laying on the ground, but it was clear that he was not badly hurt because he was talking to Delia.

Ignirtoq asked if either of them had hit Grayson.

Alex said that she had but evidently not bad enough for him stop.

She asked how far they were from the US border.

Delia looked on her map and said that it was about ten miles south.

Alex asked where there was an official border crossing point and found out it was back in Vancouver.

She thought for a moment and said that she needed to cross where Grayson had crossed and asked if Delia could make the crossing official and if she would lend her the three horses. They would return the horses once they had secured an alternate mode of transportation.

Delia made several calls and got clearance to act as the border inspection agent. She rode to the border with the three of them and wished them well and asked that Alex keep in touch with her and let her know how the pursuit turned out.

After getting across the border Grayson went about ten miles to the south and then headed west. He wanted to ditch his snow mobile and get a car or pickup so that he could drive off and not be found.

He rode the thick snow along the side of highway five forty-two and headed west.

He was looking for any vehicle that might be for sale.

He was going through Maple Falls where he spotted a car in front of the post office with a for sale sign. He inquired in the post office and found out that one of the postmen had the car up for sale. He bargained for it and was able to negotiate getting the car and using the snow mobile as part of the payment.

He put all his things into the car and headed out.

Alex had followed the snow mobile tracks and was coming along not far behind. She spotted the snow mobile parked in front of the post office and stopped and inquired about it and learned of the car sale.

The person who had sold the car said that for him it was a great deal because the snow mobile was worth more than the car and he had been able to get one thousand dollars on top of it all.

Alex got the description of the car and the license plate number and the direction that Grayson had taken.

Alex asked if he knew of any other vehicle that was for sale and said that he had seen a pickup with a for sale sign only a few blocks away. He looked at the three horses and asked what she was planning to do with them.

Alex said she was hoping to find someone to take them back to Vancouver and return them to the Royal Canadian Mounted Police.

He said that he had just the person she should talk to and for the right price she could get his buddy who had a horse trailer to take the horses back.

Alex got that number and made the call and a few moments later a large six wheeled pickup pulling a four-stall horse trailer pulled into the post office parking lot.

The three of them watched as the horses were loaded.

Alex made the arrangements to get the horses back to Canada. She called Delia and got her in touch with the person bringing the horses back.

Ignirtoq shook his head, smiled, and commented that they had gotten the horses taken care of before they had their next ride.

Alex nodded and got directions to where the for-sale pickup was located. She led the way and the three of them walked to where the pickup was parked in front of a well-kept log home. She knocked on the door and was greeted by a young woman. When she asked about the truck, the woman called to someone inside that she called Sanders.

Sanders came to the door and Alex asked about the truck. He replied that he had bought it and then realized that it was a gas hog, and he could not afford to drive it the thirty miles each way to work. He said that it was a great pickup but just too expensive.

Alex asked him how much he wanted for it. He said that if she would take over the payments, he would be happy to let it go for what he had spent on it so far, which was five thousand dollars.

Alex agreed to the arrangement and asked for him to get online with her financial agent and arrange the money transfer.

She then called Johnnie and asked for him to make the transfer into Sander's bank account.

Trey had called the station, given them the description and the license plate number of the car that Grayson was driving and had a BOLO put out that described the driver as armed and dangerous. He asked that the location and direction should be noted but the car should not be stopped.

Ignirtoq asked the seller's wife if she could recommend a place where they could get a good meal.

She said that there were not too many places close by but there was a pizza place just a few miles to the west in Maple Falls.

Sander's shook hands all around and said that they had made his day, and he would be able to get a good night's sleep now that he had sold the truck.

Trey got into the driver's seat and turned the pickup on. He looked at the gas gauge and said that the first thing they needed to do was to stop at the gas station and fill up.

Ignitor said that after filling up they should go to a restaurant and get something to eat. He said that there were several restaurants just fifteen or twenty minutes to the west.

Alex contacted Bill and Trevor and asked them to monitor the response to the BOLO and asked them to contact her as soon as they figured out where Greyson might be headed.

They decided to stop for the night and get some rest.

Bill called to let Alex and Trey know that the Washington State highway patrol was tracking Grayson's car. He had been spotted going down Interstate Five and then a short time later he had taken Interstate Ninety and that currently he was stopped in Cle Elum at a hotel.

The highway patrol was going to put on a tracking device that would allow them to track the car from the air.

Alex decided that the three of them should drive on until they were close to where Grayson had stopped so they would be in position if there was an opportunity to capture him.

Grayson was exhausted from escaping from Canada and then driving most of the day. He knew that he needed a few hours' sleep, and he knew that he needed to get back to the forest where he could once again find a place to keep out of sight long enough to have the search for him die down.

He got about four hours of sleep and decided he needed to drive on. Three hours later he was in Spokane where he decided that it was time to change cars.

He found a used car dealer and negotiated a trade for a pickup truck that had off road tires. He planned to cross into Idaho and go into the Idaho Panhandle National Forest where he would set up camp.

He drove on to Post Falls where he located a camping supply store and purchased the equipment he needed, additional ammunition and a deer hunting permit. He stopped a local grocery and bought some salt, pepper, onion, and some potatoes. He planned to hunt to get his meat supply.

At the border, the Washington highway patrol escort handed off to the Idaho Highway Patrol who greeted Alex back into the state. One of the officers joked that she had to stop chasing the bad guys into their state.

Sheriff Walter Wigger came online and said that he had learned of her chase and planned to join her.

Alex joked back with both of them about the fact that the bad guys must think that Idaho provided safe haven to them.

Once again, the day ended before Alex was ready.

She accepted a dinner invitation from Sheriff Wigers and decided to try and relax.

She made several calls back to Cincinnati and after spending time talking to both Aurea and Matt, she was ready for dinner.

Sheriff Wigger let her know that the highway patrol helicopter had spotted what they were sure was Grayson's campsite and they and his men would move in the following morning and make the arrest.

Alex thanked him and focused her attention on the menu and what she wanted for dinner.

Grayson heard but did not see the helicopter, but its sound caused him to put everything into the back of his pickup and head out of the woods. He looked on his map and decided to head to Salt Lake City. He drove all night until he got to Pocatello where he got a room so that he could get a few hours of sleep before going on. His nightlong drive had given him time to think, and he had concluded that the hunt would only end when he killed his pursuers. He needed to devise some sort of trap where he could isolate the persons chasing him and then pick them off one at a time. He needed to find a place where he had the advantage of height and range.

Back in Cle Elum Alex got up for an early morning breakfast.

At breakfast Trey said that he wanted to purchase a rifle so that the next time they got a long range shot he would be able to respond. He said that he was looking to buy a 308 scoped rifle and a box of ammunition and asked if their budget would cover it.

Alex nodded and said that she was tired of shooting and hitting Grayson and not taking him down. She asked how much money he was talking about.

Trey shook his head and said he guessed somewhere between five hundred to a thousand dollars. He said that it depended on the exact model of rifle and the power of the scope.

Sheriff Wigger had come in at the tail of the conversation and said that he frequented a gun shop that had several 308s and a variety of scopes.

He would be pleased to take them there, but he suggested that they first go out to the coordinates that the chopper pilots had given them and that after the arrest buying the riffle might not be necessary.

Alex asked Trey if that sounded reasonable.

Trey nodded and said that he would wait and see. It they captured Grayson there would be no need for him to purchase the rifle.

Four highway patrol officers, Four of Sheriff Wigger's personnel and Alex and Trey left their vehicles about a mile from where the camp site was located. Ignirtoq followed behind them.

They spread out as they approached the campsite location and approached with their weapons at the ready.

Ignirtoq was keeping an eye on the truck tracks when he noticed a second set of tires that were leaving the area. He was wondering about them when they got to the campsite and found it empty. He said that he had followed tire tracks in, and he had spotted another set that might have been leaving but had not stopped to examine them.

He identified the spot where the pickup had parked and then he was able to identify the outward going tracks by the direction the tire treads pushed the dirt in the tracks.

This time he was in the lead as he followed the faint tracks back to the highway. When they reached it, they were about a half a mile from where all the squad cars had parked.

Ignirtoq pointed down the highway in the direction where the pickup had gone. He looked at Trey and said that it was time for him to go to the gun shop because the next time they caught up with Grayson they might once again be dueling at long range.

Sheriff Wigger said he would take them there. He said that if Grayson continued to stay on the main highways the highway patrol would spot him, and they would know where they needed to go. He added that at the local speed limit and the eight-hour head start they had to figure that he was somewhere five hundred miles away.

Alex found it hard to stay put but decided to do so until they could get the next location where Grayson might be. She went to the gun shop with Trey and watched him pick out the 308-sniper rifle and scope. Trey also selected a hard carrying case that had space for the rifle, scope and one box of ammunition.

He asked where he could site it in, and the Sheriff took them to a local gun range where Trey spent a short time sighting in the rifle. He had Alex take a few shots and then put everything into the carrying case and said that he was ready for their next encounter with Grayson.

6 High Ground

*I*t was almost noon when Grayson woke up. It took him a moment to get his bearings and to realize that he was in Pocatello in a hotel room. He was sure that his marathon drive had put him well away from his pursuers, but they had repeatedly been able to find him. He got up, showered, and then focused on where he planned to ambush the people pursuing him. He wanted a location that would ensure that he could see who was coming and where he would have a chance to eliminate all of those coming for him.

He was determined that whether it was one or a dozen he would be prepared to kill them all and he would have the tactical advantage that would let him.

After spending quite some time studying some detailed maps of the area, he found a small logging road that went out to one of the mountains to the east of the town. He decided to check that area out and see if he could find a location that gave him the advantage he was seeking.

He kept wondering how he had consistently been found. He had checked his truck, and all of his gear to make sure that somehow a tracking device had not been planted on it or on him.

Back in Cincinnati, Johnnie stayed online throughout the night and most of the morning tracking every cash transaction that had been made in a five-hundred-mile vicinity of where Alex was going. He skimmed over hundreds of cash transactions but none that were large enough or made sense in how it related to what Greyson might purchase. He was looking for a large gas purchase or a hotel stay and finally he found one at a hotel. He called Alex and gave her the name and address of the hotel.

Alex thanked Johnnie for providing her his magic touch and let him know that she was on the way there and that he should continue to see if he could get additional information on where Grayson might be.

Ignirtoq shook his head and said that he would hate to be the one running from her. He asked how this, "Johnnie" was able to figure out where Grayson had paid cash at a hotel.

Alex smiled and said that was the magic that Johnnie provided her with.

Ignirtoq asked if the magic was legal.

Alex said that she could not answer that without putting his life at risk for possessing such information.

He nodded and said that he understood and was glad that she had access to such magic.

They spent the day driving to Pocatello and late in the day they checked out the hotel that Grayson had used.

Alex showed that desk clerks a photo of Grayson and verified that it indeed was him. She asked if they had any idea where he might have gone and learned that he had asked about a scenic peak that he would be able to drive to.

One of the clerks volunteered that he had shown him several logging roads that went out to two of the major peaks to the forest in the east. He pulled out a map of the area and pointed them out.

Alex looked at the time and said that they would be able to take a quick look at each of the locations to see if any of the roads had been recently used.

Ignirtoq asked the clerks when it had rained last in the area and learned that just two days previously it had rained uncharacteristically heavy. He thanked them for that information and said that he was ready to go and look at the roads that had been pointed out.

Alex took the time to make three room reservations before leading the way out to the pickup.

They checked out the four roads. They found what Ignirtoq said were fresh tire tracks on the third road. The fourth road had no fresh tracks.

The sun was setting as they returned to the hotel.

They spotted Elly's Diner and decided to give it a try.

Once they were seated Alex looked at the menu and said she was going to order the nine-ounce slow-roasted prime rib served with Yukon gold mashed potatoes with gravy, the seasonal vegetables and sweet onion rings with a cup of Illy's famous clam chowder.

Trey said he was going for the flat iron steak grilled with steak seasoning topped with steak butter and served with a baked potato with gravy. He added that he was also having seasonal vegetables and onion rings.

Ignirtoq gave his order for the beer-battered golden wild Alaskan cod, panko coated deep-fried shrimp that came with tartar cocktail sauce and lemon.

He then asked about what there was for desert and found out that the choice that evening was for a fresh lemon meringue pie with either a scoop of vanilla or pineapple sherbet. He nodded and said he would go with the vanilla scoop.

Alex and Trey both spoke up and said they would add desert to their order. Alex took a scoop of vanilla whereas Trey chose the pineapple.

During the meal, Trey said that he wanted to stop at the local hardware store and buy a half inch thick piece of plexiglass to put across the front window of their truck. He reminded Alex of how she had been saved from a sniper shot during their Sins of the Daughter case.

Alex agreed that so far Grayson had been able to take a shot at them from a distance and had done so three times. He had shot Ignirtoq, then had shot her and the third time he had shot one of the RCMP riders that was in the lead. She figured that they should all want the plexiglass protection.

The next morning, they ended up going to three different shops before finding the plexiglass sheet that they were looking for. They ended up having to buy a full sheet and having it cut to the size that fit across the front window. They used the extra to have side window shields made. The plexiglass cost more than the rifle but Alex was determined to be able to take any long distant hit from Grayson and then get close enough to give Trey a chance at taking his shots.

She had the left-over piece cut so Trey could lay behind it and have some protection while he got his shots in.

She left the shop feeling that they were as well prepared as they could be.

They had breakfast and then went to the road that Ignirtoq had identified as the one that had the tire tracks indicating a pickup or a truck with similar tires.

Alex had chosen to drive. She had Ignirtoq holding the extra piece of plexiglass and Trey riding shotgun with his weapon pointed at the floor. She knew she was most likely sitting in the seat that would take fire.

Trey had chosen to buy a vest that had loops where he had put five cartridges. He wanted his hands free to handle his weapon and be able to quickly set up his firing position.

Alex looked over and said that he looked like a handsome movie star from one of the fugitive hunting movies.

Ignirtoq joined in and said that his sunglasses made him look more like a hired killer.

Trey looked at them and said that except that there were trees and grass, he felt like he was back in Iraq going into combat.

They had driven to the point where they could see a bend in the road and a cliff that had small pine trees and a variety of small bushes all trying to get a foot hold on the side the craggy stone face that towered high above them.

Alex slowed down to about ten miles an hour while she scoured the heights.

Ignirtoq commented that someone sitting on top would have a great tactical advantage.

Grayson was sitting on a stool watching for any incoming vehicle when a flash of sunlight exposed the incoming pickup.

He got down on the flat surface and set up his tripod holder and positioned his just purchased expensive 6.5 Creedmoor with a tactical strike scope.

He made himself comfortable, adjusted his scope and took aim at the driver of the pickup. He then slowly pulled the trigger and felt the confirming kick of the rifle on his shoulder pad.

He saw the bullet hit the windshield and watched as the glass shattered into thousands of pieces. He was shocked that the pickup driver was still in control and driving.

Alex felt the hit in the plexiglass and the blast of air that blew in some of the windshield glass as most of it bounced off the plexiglass. She saw a series of boulders ahead and aimed the pickup in that direction. It exposed the driver's door window and suddenly it too exploded as a second bullet hit. She put the brakes on and skidded sidewards as she turned the steering wheel to the left.

She watched as Trey rolled out behind the boulder and was immediately joined by Ignirtoq who had carried the plex shield out with him.

Trey position the shield between the boulders and set himself up with three bullets on the ground out to his right. He then adjusted the tripod legs to the height he desired and then waited until he saw the glint of the scope at the top of the cliff.

A bush near the top of the cliff gave him the windage and he judged the distance and estimated the drop his 308 would take, then an instant later he smoothly pulled the trigger.

Grayson shot at the driver two more times. He was sure the disappearance of that individual meant he had scored.

He was taking a look for the other individuals when suddenly a burning pain went down his back. He crawled back from the cliff's edge and knew he needed to make his escape before he passed out from the burning pain. He turned and was dragging his rifle back to the pickup when he was hit in the leg by a second bullet. He felt the warm blood running down his leg. He got to the pickup and threw his rifle into the passenger's side, used his belt to make a tourniquet for his left leg. He got into the pickup and took off. The back window of the pickup shattered as did the butt of his rifle. He first reaction was to curse the fact that he had just lost the use of a great piece of hardware. His second reaction was to start worrying about the blood that he saw in the seat around him and the pain that was radiating from his back wound. He wondered who had the skill to make such shots.

He drove out through the forest until he knew he had to stop and treat himself as much as he could. He needed to get away and find a place where he could hide and recover.

Alex cautiously sat up behind the steering wheel and scanned the cliff with the binoculars that she had purchased. Everything looked clear. She called for Ignirtoq and Trey to get back into the pickup so they could drive to the top of the cliff and see what damage Trey had caused.

Trey said that he figured he had gotten some sort of hit because the firing had stopped. He was just not sure how much damage he might have done.

The drive up took them about fifteen minutes.

Alex was disappointed to find that Grayson had once again escaped.

Ignirtoq got out and found the position from where the shooting had taken place. He pointed to the dark spots on the surface stones and loose dirt and said that Grayson had been hit at least once and had initially lost a lot of blood. He pointed to the spot where he said that Grayson had paused and to evidently stop the bleeding. He then walked over to where he said the pickup was parked and the turn marks made as Grayson drove his pickup away from the scene.

Ignirtoq followed the tracks to a point in the road and pointed out into the forest and said that the tracks headed due east down the mountain side. He said that he would follow the tracks through the forest. He added that he wanted to make sure they did not follow Grayson into some unseen ravine.

Alex saw a wide valley below ahead of them and Ignirtoq stopped and pointed eastward and said the tracks seemed to go out into the valley and probably into the forest ahead.

She shook her head and said that she was heading back to Pocatello, get new glass for the pickup and then get the highway patrol to locate Grayson once again or to find a hospital that had treated a gunshot wound. She asked Ignirtoq to get in and then she turned and drove back the way she had come.

Greyson stopped his pickup after crossing the wide valley. He looked behind him and saw no one following. He pulled down his pants and put some wadding into the bullet hole in the thigh of his leg to stop the bleeding. He took off his jacket and made sure the bleeding from the wound in his back had stopped.

He cleaned the blood from the front seat and decided to lay down in the back seat. He was able to lay on his stomach and get a brief rest.

Once back at the hotel, Alex contacted Johnnie and asked him to see if he could find where Grayson might be going.

She then called the Chief, updated him, and let him know that Grayson had once again escaped but she was sure that Trey had wounded him so they were looking for where he might be treated for a gunshot wound.

Her final work-related call was to Bill asking him to renew the BOLO and alert the Wyoming and Utah highway patrol to be on the lookout for an armed and dangerous person.

She then called Matt and let him know that she was still in pursuit. She let him know that she planned to get up early and talk with Aurea before she went to school.

Matt let her know that he loved her and wanted her back in Cincinnati unharmed and in one piece.

She then asked Trey and Ignirtoq if they were interested in a Chinese dinner and asked the desk clerk if there was a Chinese restaurant nearby. It was close enough that Alex suggested walking.

It was a cold but refreshing walk that helped relieve the stress that the afternoon had inflicted. They saw the restaurant when they were within a block and decided that they would order a variety of different menu items and then share.

After getting seated, Alex took on the role of placing the order. She looked down the menu and ordered an egg roll for each of them, an order of pot stickers, fried wonton, and salt and pepper calamari.

She then ordered mains of sweet and sour pork, sweet and sour shrimp, Beef with Sweet Pea Pods.

She asked Trey and Ignirtoq if they thought that was enough.

Ignirtoq smile and said that he was sure it was enough, but he also had his eye on the golden bread starter.

Trey laughed and said they should order the fortune cookies to see what their fortunes would look like.

After the order was in, Alex said that they were closing in on Grayson, but he was proving to be elusive and hard to capture. She said that now that he was wounded, they might be able to close in and finally make the arrest.

She added that they needed to go to get the windshield and driver's door window replaced before driving on.

She added that she hoped that by morning they would know where they were going.

In the morning Alex was surprised by a call from the front desk letting her know that her luggage had been delivered. It was a call that she had not expected and when she went to retrieve the luggage, she was surprised to see Clay standing with the luggage.

Clay said that he had been hired by Delia with instructions to get the luggage to Alex and to deliver a message that the horses were back in their stalls and had each been treated to an apple as a reward for their good service.

Alex gave him a hug and asked if he had time for breakfast before he headed back.

Clay said that he would love to have breakfast and that before he flew back, he was planning to sleep for most of the day because he planned to fly back to Fairbanks.

Trey and Ignirtoq came in and greeted Clay and thanked him for delivering their suitcases.

Alex led the way to the restaurant where they all ordered breakfast and chatted for a short time.

Trey broke the breakfast mood when he said it was time to find an auto glass replacement shop and ask for immediate service in replacing the windshield and side window.

Clay wished them luck in chasing Grayson down. He added that he was amazed that they had been able to track him down across a large part of Alaska, through Canada and now down four states in the lower forty-eight. He added that they needed to keep the state count down.

Alex got the auto glass shop to expedite the work by letting them know that they were after a dangerous armed fugitive that had shot out the windows during a gun battle. She watched as four technicians all worked on the pickup.

The shop had a small store where they sold a variety of equipment. She bought a tarp to wrap the luggage in and a cooler to carry some drinks and sandwiches.

Once the glass was replaced, she had the plexiglass on the inside flipped so that the spot where the bullet had hit was on the passenger side. She then asked the shop to fasten the plexiglass to the windshield.

She gave the four workers a good tip and then the three of them returned to the hotel.

Now that she had clothes she planned to shower and change before driving on.

When they got back to the hotel, she placed an order for some ham and cheese and salami and provolone sandwiches with condiments in small packages on the side. She made the point that she did not want soggy sandwiches.

After taking a shower and checking out, the three of them looked on the map and decided to drive south to Ogden hoping to hear from someone about where Greyson might be.

Greyson had driven all night and was exhausted. He knew he needed medical attention. But if he stopped at a large hospital, he was likely to get arrested.

He looked on the map and saw the Uintah and Ouray Reservation and figured that he could find a small local emergency care facility where he could get the help he needed and then escape somewhere to the east.

He drove past Ogden then caught interstate eighty-four and then he took highway forty and drove into the Indian reservation. He drove for several hours until he finally saw the sign for the Uintah and Ouray treatment center. He hobbled in and let the attending physician know that he had been accidently shot.

Once he was in the room with just the doctor and the nurse, he took the nurse hostage and told the doctor to fix the wound on his back first and then the wound in his leg.

He winced as the doctor worked on his back. He was told that he was still alive because the bullet had lodged by his tail bone. If it had exited, he would most likely have bled to death.

The doctor them looked at the wound in the thigh of his leg and said that he was lucky there as well because no major arteries had been hit. He then declared that he was done, and that Grayson should let his nurse go.

Grayson said that he was taking her with him but that in thirty minutes he would leave her unharmed at the side of the road as long as there were no police chasing him.

He hobbled out to the pickup guiding the nurse at his side. He got behind the wheel and when he looked at the gas gauge, he realized that he needed to stop to fill up.

He asked the nurse if she had a family and learned she had a seven-year-old daughter.

At the gas station as he was filling the tank he leaned in from the driver's side and told the nurse that he was going to let her stay at the gas station if she promised to wait thirty minutes before calling the police.

She promised that she would wait.

He looked at her and told her that if the police were to engage him before the thirty minutes he would return and shoot both she and the doctor.

He watched her shake her head up and down and swear that she would wait thirty minutes.

The nurse knew that she could wait thirty minutes, and this crazed man would still be driving for hours across the reservation. She figured he was toast and would be captured before he left the reservation. She went into the station and bought herself a soft drink, took it out, and sat down in the chair that was just outside of the door.

7 Finally

*A*lex was looking out at the wide valley that held a few trees but was mostly yellowing grass with a few interspersed bushes. It seemed to stretch all the way to the horizon in both directions. There were a few traces of snow, but it was clear that winter had not yet hit in this region. Her phone rang and she knew that either Bill or Trevor was calling her.

Trevor came on and let her know that the BOLO had been answered and that Grayson had received treatment from a doctor at a facility on the Uintah and Ouray Reservation and headed east out of Bridgeland after filling his gas tank. He had taken a nurse hostage but had released her at the gas station unharmed and told her to wait thirty minutes before calling in any authorities.

Alex thanked him for getting the information to her after work hours and added that for her it was still daylight, and she was going to go to the care facility to see what she could learn and then she and Trey would decide whether to pursue or wait until morning.

Trevor wished her good luck and said that he, Bill, and Johnnie were trying to make sure she had the latest information and any help that she might need. He asked if there was anything else she might need at the moment.

Alex said that she needed good luck.

After getting off with Trevor, she put in a call to the highway patrol and got an escort to the reservation. They were greeted at the border of the reservation by a unit that took over from the highway patrol. They said that they had tracked the pickup that they were after until it had left the reservation. They said that they had wanted to stop it but had adhered to the instructions that came with the BOLO.

Alex thanked them and asked to be taken to the facility where her fleeing fugitive had received treatment.

Once they arrived, they were led to a meeting room where the doctor and nurse were sitting. Alex introduced herself and explained that the person who they had treated was fleeing from her because he had shot her, the person sitting next to her and a Royal Canadian Mounted Police. She pointed at Trey and said that he was the one that had wounded the person they had treated.

The doctor shook his head and said that each of the two wounds could have been fatal had they just hit slightly differently but as it turned out the wounds were significant but had not proved to be fatal.

Trey nodded and said that he had tried his best, but the exchange of gunfire was at the maximum range of his weapon and except for the first shot the other three had been blind shots. He was surprised that he had hit his intended target twice.

As they were leaving the facility they got a call that let them know that Grayson was heading due south and had been spotted approaching Grand Junction and as far as the highway patrol could tell the pickup had not left the town.

Alex thanked them for the information and said that she was on the way.

Once they got to Grand Junction Alex wondered if Grayson was at some hotel or whether he had changed his mode of travel. She called Johnnie and asked him to see if he could figure out where Grayson happened to be.

It was an hour later that Johnnie called back and let her know that a one-way ticket to Fairbanks, Alaska had been purchased by a person calling himself G. Gay.

Alex thanked him went online and learned that it would take Grayson from fifteen to twenty hours to reach Fairbanks. She searched for a shorter flight and found one out of Denver that took only five hours. She called Alaska Airlines and was able to purchase three first class tickets.

She looked over at Trey and asked whether he could make the drive to Denver in two hours.

He smiled and said that she ought to arrange a highway patrol escort so that he would not get a speeding ticket.

Once they had their escort they made the journey about ten miles per hour over the speed limit. They had a lead and a tail escort that had their lights flashing and sirens wailing. It was a speedy journey.

Alex looked at Trey who was tapping his steering wheel to the rhythm of the flashing lights and humming the Marine hymn and knew that he was focused on getting to the Denver airport and to capturing Grayson.

Grayson was relieved not to be driving. He was exhausted. He figured that he could relax until he got back to Fairbanks. He could not believe that he had been hounded for the entire time he had left his house. He wished that he had never shot at that first nosy person because it had turned his life on its head. How he had been tracked still mystified him.

Alex thanked the men in the two highway patrol vehicles, she arranged for her pickup to be taken to the local impound lot where later she would have it handled. She then led the way into the airport.

She approached the first-class ticket counter and checked her luggage in and stood aside as Trey checked his luggage in. He then found out how to check his rifle in as well. He had to carry his weapon case to a special area to get it checked. The fact that he was a detective with the Cincinnati police helped expedite the process.

Ignirtoq put his one suitcase on the scale and took his first-class ticket and followed Trey over to where the sniper rifle was being checked in.

They were escorted by a security person and taken through security. Then they were led by a gate agent to the plane. They had just sat down when the pilot greeted everyone and let them know that in five hours they would be in Fairbanks.

Alex sat back and thought through the chase that they had been on and marveled at the fact that they were now closing a loop that she hoped would end at the Fairbanks airport.

She called Bill and asked him to arrange to have the local authorities in Fairbanks meet with her so they could arrange Grayson's arrest.

Bill chuckled and said that she should just have stayed in Alaska and waited for Grayson to return.

Alex said that she agreed except for the fact that Trey had to shoot him to get him to return to Alaska. She heard Trevor say that he thought that both of them were dead shots and wondered how they could have missed Grayson so many times.

Alex smiled and replied that she still loved him in spite of his stinging comments.

Grayson was on his second lay over waiting to continue his flight to Fairbanks. He found a store in the airport that had some pain pills and took several of them in hopes that the pain in his back would lessen. He found it uncomfortable to sit so he decided to walk around while he waited to continue his flight.

He rued the day when he had taken that first shot and missed killing the person checking out his oil line tap. The irony was that he had no idea who that person was nor any of the other persons chasing him except for the Royal Canadian Mounted Police. All strangers to him and all determined to catch him. He hoped that the U-turn that he was taking would throw them off his trail and he could get back to the country that he knew.

The flight from Denver to Fairbanks was smooth and the service on the way there was as expected. Alex relaxed knowing that she would arrive well ahead of Grayson and would be able to arrange for backup from the airport security.

She was surprised when she and Trey stepped from the plane were greeted by an airport security guard that introduced himself and said that he was to take them to the lounge to get any refreshments they might want and then later he would return to have them meet with the folks who were prepared to help her make the arrest.

Alex asked who had contacted airport security.

He replied that he thought it was her boss, Trevor Carter, who explained the situation that he had assigned you to fly in and make the arrest.

Trey laughed and said that yes, the boss was always making sure that Alex was kept in line and doing what he had told her.

Alex thanked the officer and said that she would enjoy the lounge until it was time to make the arrest. She asked that she have enough time to talk to all the folks to make sure the arrest was carried out with as little action as possible.

Once situated in the lounge she realized that there would be at least six hours of waiting. It was too late to call home, so she decided to take a walk around the airport and see what shops it had. She found one that had the Alaskan State flag on sale. She bought it for Aurea and added a bag of Ghirardelli chocolates to it.

Once back in the lounge, she asked Ignirtoq what he would be doing now that the chase was almost over.

Ignirtoq thought for a minute and then said that he was going to find every oil tap that had been installed and get them put on the drawings for the pipeline. He was then going to go fishing and try to get the thrill of the chase to die down so he could enjoy playing with his grand kids and have fun with all of his other relatives.

He asked her what she was planning to do.

Alex said that she was planning to enjoy spending time with her new daughter who she had recently adopted and hopefully get another invite to a grill out at Trey's home. She also planned on going on several long bike rides and get back into riding shape.

Trey said that he and his wife were trying to deal with having their only child away at college and having grill outs was one way that they dealt with that situation. He was sure to have a grill out in the next week or two.

Ignirtoq went back to the food line multiple times and commented that if he stayed much longer, he would need to join Alex on her bike rides.

The security officer came in and said that the team that would make the arrest was ready for her to talk to them. He guided them to an open area at the end of the passenger security clearance area where they were all standing.

She learned that the local police had sent a unit over to participate in the arrest and then transport that person to the detainment center until his arraignment.

Alex introduced herself, then introduced Trey and Ignirtoq. She gave a brief description of the long chase and of the various times they had exchanged gunfire with Grayson. She added that she wanted their support but that she and Trey would take the lead in making the arrest and only wanted them to get involved if Grayson put up some sort of resistance or was somehow armed.

She said that she was armed and would take any action that would be necessary, and they should keep their weapons in their holsters.

Alex asked what gate the plane would use to deplane and then led the way there. She positioned everyone in a large circle around the exit area and instructed them to make their presence known but to keep back unless she called them into action.

The plane pulled up into position and the jetway was slowly positioned. Alex watched the first-class passengers as they came out. It seemed to her that everything was moving in slow motion. She knew that her adrenaline had kicked in.

She stood out in the middle area and watched the passengers walking out. She finally saw Grayson limping out of the jetway and raised her hand as a signal that she saw him.

Trey positioned himself to Alex's left and was ready to act if Grayson put up any resistance.

She walked up to Grayson and quietly told him that he was under arrest and that he should kneel down and raise his hands.

Grayson thought about running and took a step away from the person in front of him and then realized that there was a second person with her and then he noticed all the blue uniformed security guards and police standing ready in case he tried to make a run for it.

He raised his hands and said that he could not kneel down because he was wounded.

Trey pulled Grayson's arms behind him, put handcuffs on him as he recited the Miranda rights.

Once Grayson was handcuffed, Alex asked the police to take him to wherever the holding area happened to be.

Alex thanked everyone for providing back up. Once they were at curbside, she checked with the Fairbanks police who said they would take Grayson to the Fairbanks Correctional Center while he waited for his arraignment appearance.

Alex thanked them and said that she planned on returning to Cincinnati and hoped to attend the arraignment by video.

The officer in charge said that he had attended several arraignments where witnesses from some far parts of Alaska had participated in that manner. He was certain that she as the arresting officer could do the same.

She looked at Trey and asked if he knew what time it was and if they should plan to get a hotel and get a few hours' sleep.

Trey shook his head and said that he had no clue, but they should decide what to do after finding out when they could catch a flight to Cincinnati.

Ignirtoq let them know it was six in the evening. He said that he was calling Clay to see when he could get a flight to Prospect Creek and then decide whether to get a room.

Alex went to the ticket counter and found that there was a flight leaving for Cincinnati at ten that evening and arriving in Cincinnati at ten in the morning the following day. She let out a groan, looked at Trey who mouthed "let's do it."

They purchased two seats in first class, checked their luggage, and then went to the lounge to wait for the flight.

Trey told Ignirtoq that he wanted him to have 308-sniper rifle and scope.

Ignirtoq said he couldn't accept such an expensive gift.

Trey said then he would sell it to him for a dollar.

Ignirtoq took out his wallet and extracted one dollar. He said that he understood the concept and he was very pleased to be able to buy a great hunting rifle. He took the case and said that he would take pictures of anything he shot with it.

Ignirtoq said that Clay would be meeting him in less than an hour. He wished them a safe journey and said that his time with them was memorable in many ways but that it had been an honor to have helped in the capture of Grayson.

Alex gave him a hug and told him that he had been a great help and that she would mention that in her report.

When the plane finally departed, and Alex was situated she was able to sleep for most of the flight to Cincinnati. Once in Cincinnati and she got to the escalator leading to luggage claim she looked up to see Trevor waving to her.

He and Bill gave her a hug and complemented her on catching the bad guy and not killing him.

Alex smiled and said that Trey had provided the initial pain that Grason needed and now she hoped that the prosecutor and judge would put him away for the rest of his life.

Bill said that they had orders to make sure she did not come into work. He shook Trey's hand and complemented him on his shooting and told him that he was to go home as well. He added that Travis was driving Alex's old car and would take him there.

Alex arrived home close to noon and decided that she would take it easy but that she was going to bake a large batch of cookies that she could give to Johnnie and the rest of the team.

She put the Alaskan Flag and the chocolate on the kitchen table and then prepared the cookie dough.

She had just placed two warm cookies and a glass of milk on the table when Aurea and Mary came in the back door.

Aurea rushed over to her and gave her a hug and said she knew that she would be home. She had done her homework at school so she would be able to go out riding.

Alex gave Mary a hug and thanked her for watching Aurea while she was gone.

Mary replied that it gave her something to do during the day and she loved doing it.

Matt called and said that he would be home for dinner and asked if he should bring home their favorite Korean mix of starters and main menu items.

Alex told him to bring home whatever came to him and that she and Aurea were going out for a bike ride and would be back for dinner.

8 One More Time

The next morning Alex followed Johnnie down the hill as they rode their bikes into work. They chatted over their headsets about the chase that Grayson had taken her and Trey on. Alex commented that it had been one of the more extended ones that she had experienced, and she was glad that it was over. They arrived at the station, and both took their bikes into the locker room and got into their daily work outfits.

Alex walked in with a cup of coffee and was pleased to see that Bill and Trevor were already there and had left the donut box on her desk. She took out a bear claw, cut it in half, and put one half on Trey's desk. A moment later he walked in and said that he felt like warmed over toast and hoped the bear claw and some coffee would put some energy back into his body.

The Chief walked in and came over and helped himself to a jelly roll. He congratulated all of them for having once again having worked together to solve their case.

Trevor nodded and said that "yes some of us had to do the grunt work and some of us got to do the exotic travel from Alaska through Canada and down the Rocky Mountains until they tired of the beauty and relaxation of it all and finally made an arrest. An arrest that did not have any gunfire associated with it," and in spite of that Bill and I still brought in donuts.

Alex laughed and said that the next time they should trade places and when he and Bill got back, she would buy the donuts.

Bill shook his head and said that he would rather not.

The Chief shook his head and said that he had real work to do and walked away toward his office.

Alex looked over at Trey and said that they should go to a huddle room and see if they could knock out the case report before lunch.

She and Trey were almost done with the report when her phone went off. It was the sound of a bear roaring and was the ring that she had assigned to Ignirtoq. She looked at the time and realized that it was only three in the morning in Alaska. She put the phone on speaker mode and said hello and asked why he was calling at three in the morning.

Ignirtoq said that he had just been notified by the police that Grayson had escaped. He added that he was going to be going on the hunt with a beautiful new 308-sniper rifle and scope that he had bought for a pittance from someone at the airport that had lost his mind and sold it to him for a dollar.

He went on to say that he was sure that she would soon learn of the escape and that she should wait until he had his chance to hunt Grayson down before she did anything.

He added that he and Clay had gone out to celebrate and they had not left Fairbanks so there was no way Grayson knew where he was. He on the other hand was pretty sure that Grayson would go to his house in Valdez and get whatever he needed to once again hide out.

Ignirtoq chuckled and said that Grayson was on his territory and would find it hard to hide. In the morning, he and Clay would fly to Valdez, and he would see if Grayson had made it to his house.

He ended the call by thanking the two of them for having given him lessons on how to hunt Grayson down.

Grayson found it absurdly easy to break out of the holding cell. He had found a hairpin and had decided to try his luck at picking the door lock. He had positioned himself so that the camera could not see what he was trying to do. He played with the lock for less than ten minutes when suddenly he heard it click, and the cell door was open. He saw that the camera in the hallway seemed to move to scan different parts and then repeat the cycle. He timed it so he walked away from his cell after the camera had scanned it. He walked slowly and steadily out of the holding area, out into the street and turned at the first corner. It was early in the morning, and the streets were bare. He knew that he needed to get out of Fairbanks as quickly as possible.

He figured his best chance was to get to Valdez and to his house so that he could restock with what he needed to hide out. He looked ahead and saw a maintenance truck parked outside and all-night café. It had its engine running to keep its engine from freezing.

He looked in the café and saw two men sitting at a table having a cup of coffee and chatting. He looked in the truck and was pleased to see a jacket and a brown Russian Ushanka hat. He walked around to the driver's side and put the truck into gear and eased it out into the street and drove slowly away.

Once he had gone past the café, he turned on the head lights and headed for the highway that would take him to Valdez. He drove at the speed limit but was worried about having the police after the stolen truck. He drove until he reached station twelve of the Alaskan pipeline and pulled into the parking lot and parked at the far corner of the parking lot. He was on familiar ground and knew that all the vehicles would remain running, and most would remain unlocked. It was just past the starting hour so he would have an entire shift's time. He walked out through the parking area and noticed that there were several black pickups that all looked the same. He picked the one that was parked next to a tall white van that obstructed the security camera, got in and slowly drove out of the lot.

At the gate he flashed his driver's license and drove slowly out. He smiled and waved at the gate guard and got on the highway. An hour and a half later he arrived in Valdez and stopped at Safeway, went in purchased a loaf of bread, mayo, a head of lettuce, tomatoes, a T-bone steak, a dozen eggs, fresh sausage, ground coffee and a quart of milk.

He drove slowly by the police station and finally arrived at his house. He pulled into the driveway and put the pickup in the garage. He took his groceries in and prepared himself a couple of fried eggs, several patties of sausage and buttered toast with strawberry jam. The fresh cup of coffee with cream and sugar rounded out the breakfast and made him feel like a freeman again.

He wished he could spend the night, but he figured that he needed to get the things that he needed and head out before the police came to check on what he was doing. He went to the box where he had stashed emergency cash and counted out what he had. He was down to his last fifteen thousand dollars.

He walked down to the house that had a car sitting out in the driveway with a for-sale sign and an asking price of three thousand dollars. After some bargaining, he got it for twenty-five hundred dollars and was able to keep the current license plates with the promise that he would get it changed that day.

He drove the car to his house, loaded everything that he thought he needed. This time he took most of his guns. His favorite of the lot was his Ruger American black bolt action that fired 7mm Remington Magnum bullets. He considered it the second-best rifle that he had owned and was sad that his favorite had been destroyed during the chase. That 308 had a greater range and more striking power but the 7mm had great accuracy and he figured that it would be his primary weapon as he once again headed out to disappear in the woods.

It never crossed his mind that in the lower forty-eight most people trying to hide headed into a big city to disappear whereas his desire to hide in the woods was a very Alaskan mentality.

Ignirtoq knew that he and Clay were at a slight disadvantage as compared to Alex because he did not have the resources to find where Grayson might have gone. However, he felt confident that one of the places he would go would be to his house in Valdez.

Clay flew into the airport and parked his plane. The two of them asked around to see if they could rent someone's car or pick up. One of Clay's acquaintances offered to lend him his pickup since he would be gone for a flight up to Prudhoe Bay. He asked that it be parked back where they got it.

Ignirtoq said that he was pleased to have the use of the pickup, but he wanted to pay the going rate for its use. He walked out to the dark blue, large pickup with a full back seat and full bed. It was a huge pickup. He asked Clay whether he was comfortable driving it.

Clay said that it put his pickup to shame, and he was going to enjoy driving this one. He drove it back to where he had his plane parked and they got the things that they wanted from the plane. He took his long rifle twenty-two that used a heavily loaded cartridge that gave it extra distance and put it on the floor behind the driver's seat.

Ignirtoq took out his rifle case and put it on the back seat. He said that he didn't think he needed it while they were in Valdez, but he wanted it close at hand just in case.

They drove to the home address that Alex had given him but parked a block down the street and Ignirtoq took out his 308 and Clay carried his twenty-two. The two of them walked back to the house. They knocked on the front door and got no answer. The two of them walked around the side of the house to the garage. They looked in through windows and saw a large black pickup. They tried the back door of the house but got no response.

Ignirtoq commented that they were a little late getting there and Grayson had already left. They were driving out when he noticed a car for sale sign laying on the curb of a house and decided to stop and ask about it.

The young woman that came to the door said that they had just missed buying a great low milage tan Ford sedan that her husband had let go for a great price just that morning.

Ignirtoq asked if the car had a license plate and was able to get the license plate number. He thanked the young woman and then drove to the local police station.

Once there he explained the situation and after the officer there had called the Fairbanks Police the Valdez police went out the Grayson's house.

Ignirtoq accompanied them and was able to get an idea of what Grayson was up to. He found the bread wrapper and other things in the kitchen that let him know that he had stocked up on food and was planning to go out into the woods.

He decided to stop at the local outfitter to see if Grayson had also purchased camping gear.

Once he found out the equipment that had been purchased, he knew that Grayson planned to go deep in the woods somewhere but he would need to be able to go in and out over time so he would need to be near some useable road. He studied the area map and zeroed in the area around the Glacier Lookout area. It provided road access and was out of the way. This would allow him to drive there and then hike into woods and set up camp.

He asked if Clay still wanted to accompany him.

Clay said that it beat the mindless hours of flying that he often did. However, he wanted to have a good breakfast, a solid lunch and a good night's sleep before heading out into the woods. He said that he needed to stop one more time at his plane and get his winter gear so that he wouldn't freeze to death in the woods.

Ignirtoq admitted that he too needed to get the right gear to go into the woods after Grayson.

They stopped at the City Diner to have breakfast. They agreed to get a carry out lunch and that they would stop at the grocery and buy the goods to have what they would need for a couple of days. They then drove to where Clay had parked his plane and got the other things they needed.

The drive out to Glacier Lookout took them about an hour. The distance was only about fifteen miles but for half the distance they were on a single lane snow covered road. It had been cleared but it had snowed, and the going was slow.

Ignirtoq had called ahead and arranged to get keys for two rooms at the Valdez Glacier Campground where they paid for the rooms and got instructions on how to use the room heaters.

Just before they arrived at lookout facility they spotted where a car had been driven into the woods. They did not stop but they were now sure that they had made the right choice.

Ignirtoq said that in the morning they would walk back and then go from tree to tree as he tracked Grayson to his campsite. He pointed out that they would need to be very careful because Grayson had been able to get in the first shots each time he had been confronted.

The next morning, they both had a hearty breakfast of pancakes, eggs, and ham. They then made themselves sandwiches and filled a large thermos with coffee.

Clay joked that they were carrying more food than anything else.

Ignirtoq nodded and said that he hoped that they would capture Grayson early in the day, but he did not want to get exhausted, cold, and hungry because they had not planned ahead.

When they got back to where the car was parked, they verified that the license plate number was in fact the one that was on the car he had purchased. Ignirtoq began a slow and cautious tracking of where Grayson had gone.

He moved along the trail that had been lightly covered by snow but was very clear to him. He kept looking ahead through his scope trying to make out where Grayson's camp might be. It was close to noon when he saw a wisp of smoke. He said that they should stop and get a bite to eat because they should take off their backpacks and get ready for action.

After lunch he moved from tree to tree and each time he looked ahead to where he had seen the wisp of smoke. Finally, Ignirtoq was able to make out the camp.

Grayson had selected relatively a place to get out of sight because he did not want to be caught out on the road. He had come up into the mountains as far as possible. He did not have the best car to negotiate the snowy roads or to think about going off road through the forest. He had done the best he could and driven up to one of the few very remote areas, driven the car off the single lane road and then covered it with snow so that it could not be spotted from up above. He then used a sled to pull all of his gear several miles into the forest. This time he had returned and spent time covering his tracks as best he could. He hoped that his path would be invisible from the sky.

He had brought a handful of books and planned to sit in his small tent where he could stay warm, read and to periodically make sure there was no one about.

Ignirtoq positioned his rifle across the fallen tree branch and took aim. He remembered Trey's instruction about the three-foot drop of the bullet at maximum range and about the effect of the wind. He took his first shot and saw a hole appear to the left of where Grayson was sitting. He quickly loaded the second cartridge, made he windage adjustment and fired again. This time he saw Grayson fall back into the tent.

Grayson was still trying to comprehend the action of the first bullet when he was hit in the chest and knocked from his chair.

Ignirtoq rushed forward to where he saw another fallen tree and got down behind it.

Clay was hiding behind a large boulder. He did not think that he could hit anything because he was so far from the camp, but he figured he might provide some misdirection, so he fired his weapon.

Grayson lay back for a moment and thanked the stars for having thought about buying a bullet proof vest. He recovered and crawled out of his tent and looked through his scope and saw the gunfire from behind the boulder. He estimated that the boulder was about four hundred feet away. He lined up his sights so that the next time that shooter exposed himself he would take him out.

Ignirtoq carefully sited in on where Grayson was laying behind the fire ring that he had made. He had his head, and his arms exposed. He knew that at this closer range the drop would only be about a foot. He did not want to get into a duel. He carefully took aim and was about to pull the trigger when Grayson rolled away from the fire ring and out into the open and fired his way.

The bullet hit a foot to his right, but he knew the next on would most likely hit him.

He was surprised when a bullet hit one of the fire ring stones and caused Grayson to once again roll away.

Clay waved to him from behind a tree that was at least ten yards closer than he was.

He ran forward and had just gotten behind a large pine when a bullet hit the tree.

The gun battle that he had hoped to avoid was happening. He thought about how to best handle the situation and could not think what that might be. He thought about everything that Trey had shared with him and remembered Trey saying that sometimes the most effective way was to expose oneself and take a hip shot and then laydown and quickly take the kill shot.

Ignirtoq shook his head and felt that he was about to die but it might be a quick way to end the duel. He jumped out and gave a loud yell and took his hip shot as he fell forward. He ejected and loaded in rapid succession. He felt the bullet when it grazed his shoulder, but his sight zeroed in and he took his shot.

Grayson had figured out that he had two people shooting at him but the one that seemed to have the superior fire power was the one he needed to focus on. He was surprised when that shooter jumped out into the open, fired from the hip and fell forwards into the show. It threw off his first reply shot. He had his bead on the shooter when suddenly the world went black.

Clay hesitated a moment, but he realized that Grayson was either dead or wounded so badly that he was lying face down in the snow. He rushed to where Ignirtoq was laying and turned him over. He was hit in his left shoulder but smiled and said that he had learned from a war hero on how to take out the enemy.

He said that they should verify that Grayson was dead and then call the Forest Service to get their help.

778

9 Alaskan Hero

*A*lex had been worried about Ignirtoq going after Grayson and had put out her feelers as to what was happening in Alaska. She got hold of Atiqtalik and Kaskae and asked them what they knew and then was more worried when both of them said that they had not heard anything. She called the head of the Fairbanks police and learned that Ignirtoq had gone to Grayson's house in Valdez and had found the stolen vehicle in the garage and had also identified an automobile that Grayson had purchased in his neighborhood.

She learned that Ignirtoq had engaged the Valdez police department and then had gone after Grayson based on where he might have gone. Alex doubted it was a random guess and figured that Ignirtoq had a good idea of where to look. She was relieved that Clay seemed to be going along. Clay, she felt would be the help that might make a difference.

She went into Friday worried about what was happening in Alaska.

Late Friday, Johnnie got a call that he knew would be a big relief to Alex. He agreed to work with Ignirtoq to make a video of the scenes of the chase and of the final confrontation. He said that he would need to let Alex know that the chase was over and that he was safe, but he would keep the rest as a surprise.

Ignirtoq said that he would call Alex and let her know how things had ended but he wanted the video to be a surprise.

Alex was indeed relieved when she heard Ignirtoq relate how he and Clay had worked together and had bested Grayson. He did not say more because he wanted to leave the details of the story to be part of the narrative for the video he was working on with Johnnie.

Alex focused her effort on closing the case. She asked Johnnie to move the money that Grayson had in his bank or invested, to a trust that would be used for the indigenous people in Alaska

She let Aurea know about the fund and asked her if she wanted to give it a name. Aurea thought about it and said that it should be called the Alaskan Black Gold Fund for Indigenous People, (ABGFIP). Alex let her know that she was going to be named as one of the executors of the fund along with Ignirtoq. Aurea asked what she would be doing as an executor. When she found out she said that would be a great project that she could write about. She added that she was going to study and write about the Inuit people.

Alex went into the weekend with mixed feelings. She and Trey had done their best to put Grayson behind bars but by escaping he had taken the situation to another level. He had been prepared to resist capture for a second time. This time his pursuers knew how to prepare for the encounter and had been able to track him down almost immediately.

It made her sad that someone could live a life so apart from the society they existed in. Grayson had done nothing for other people or the community that he lived in. She wanted Aurea to be exposed to helping others and enriching the society around her.

The weekend caused her to focus on Aurea, Matt, and herself. On Saturday she led them on a long bike ride along the Loveland trail. She ordered a lunch for the three of them from one of the small restaurants situated along the trail. They stopped and spent time enjoying a slow leisurely lunch of chicken, mashed potatoes, green beans, and a small mixed vegetable salad on the side.

She then led the way up the trail until she recognized the shop that served a variety of ice cream. They stopped there and each had two scoops of the ice cream of their choice.

The ride back to their house took the rest of the afternoon. Once back at the house the next important event was to select a restaurant that they all agreed on for dinner. Once that happened Aurea got to select the food that was to be delivered. Alex smiled and said that Aurea could order anything she wanted as long as she also ordered some onion rings.

After dinner, Alex spent an hour jogging on the treadmill before saying that she was turning in early so she could get a few extra hours of sleep.

The next day they arrived at Trey's house early and she took a seat on the porch and accepted a lemonade and a tray of vegetables with a Thousand Island with garlic dip.

She enjoyed the snack and watching Aurea playing chess with Matt. As she watched she realized that Aurea was a better player than she was and that she was challenging Matt. She was happy when Sarah the neighbor girl showed up and the two of them went off to play together in the basement.

She was surprised when Lesley asked her to come with her to her bedroom where she wanted to show her the new dress that Trey had picked out and see what she thought of it. The two of them walked up stairs and Lesley commented that Trey had let her know that during the fugitive chase he felt like he was back in combat, but it was different because he did not feel the stress that he had felt then.

Alex wasn't sure what was going on, but she knew that Lesley was acting a little out of character. It was when they came back on the porch and Alex saw the rest of the team sitting in front of a large TV screen that she realized that Lesley had taken her to the bedroom to get her out of the way.

Aurea was beaming and cried out that it was a surprise and that everyone in the family and all her close friends were online and ready to hear about the manhunt that she, Trey and Ignirtoq had been on and that Ignirtoq would be narrating a movie put together by he and Johnnie. She highlighted the Hawaii connection. Then the Chicago connection, the connection from Texas, the Alaska connection, and the Royal Canadian Mounted Police connection from Vancouver.

Everyone called out surprise in unison and then Ignirtoq came on, introduced himself and then he introduced the two main stars, Alex Evercrest and Trey McGregor. He showed the picture of his grandniece, Atiqtalik and his son Kaskae the two people he had to fool so they would pull in the greatest detective that lived in Cincinnati. He said that he had done this after he had been shot by Grayson Gagnon. He convinced his brother to call Atiqtalik and tell her that he had been fatally wounded and needed the best detective in the world to find out who had killed him. Atiqtalik had talked to Kaskae who was convinced that they were being conned by his father but if his father was determined to get this "Alex" person up to Alaska they might as well go along with him. The scene on the screen panned out on the bend of the river and took in the eight-foot diameter Alaska Oil pipeline. It then walked slowly up to where a snow bike was hidden under some brush.

He then had a picture of Alex looking at the camera and a picture of someone being kicked out of the way, Alex being hit by a bullet and then firing her weapon as she staggered backwards.

Alex chuckled and asked who her body double happened to be because the response shot was very slow.

Ignirtoq laughed and said that he had so many volunteers to appear in this movie that he was not sure who had played her role, and he apologized for not having anyone that was tall enough to fill in for Trey.

Audre shook her head and commented her mother had not told her about getting hit by a bullet.

He then showed the tent that had been knocked down when Grayson had hurriedly left on his snow mobile, and it showed Alex running after him firing her weapon.

The next scenes were of Clay's piper cub getting loaded with their luggage and all of them getting on. Then the landing in Canada and being greeted by Sergeant Major Delia Zennesky of the Royal Canadian Mounted Police. The video continued as they were taken to the trailer where they spent only one night before they rode out on horseback to hunt Grayson down.

The shot that took down one of the lead RCMP was the first time that Alex had seen it, and she was surprised by the fact that the lead rider had survived without any major wound. The next scene showed she and Trey urging their mounts in the chase after Grayson.

She laughed at both of their despondent faces when they rode back to the RCMP group.

It was also clear to her that Ignirtoq had improved on taking pictures because as they rode into the US, he was taking side shots as well as periodically getting some frontal shots. He got great shots of the pickup, interior. Shots of her and Trey and always the panoramic view of the country they were driving through. She wondered if Ignirtoq had a video early on during the chase.

Then the scenes were of getting the plexiglass shield put in and a few moments later it showed the shattering of the front and side windows. The video sound that was captured when the windshield seemed to explode seemed to amplify the scene. The next shots showed Trey preparing to take his four shots and the sound of and the smooth action of each of the shots. Then for a long moment there was silence and then her voice calling for them to get in the pickup so they could go to the top of the mountain to see how Trey had done.

The scene then panned on an empty campsite.

Ignirtoq had kept his camera running and a narrative of what he was seeing. It was the first time that Alex had heard it. She listened as he then gave a lesson on how to track the vehicle through the rough terrain. She looked around the porch, saw that everyone was glued to what was being shown and knew that everyone was enjoying the presentation.

The final scene was her and Trey arresting and having Grayson led away.

Then in bold letters the video displayed, "AND THEN HE GOT AWAY." "Time to refill your drinks and get popcorn."

The screen went black, but Ignirtoq's voice announced that he and Clay decided that they should see if they could end it all and prevent a replay of the first half of the video.

The video then began with Clay bargaining to use a friend's pickup that was outfitted for off-road hunting and going through the forest. Their drive to Grayson's home and their knocking on the front door, looking through the windows of the garage and seeing the stolen pickup and then approaching the back door and again getting no response. Clay could be heard asking how Grayson had left when the pickup was still in the garage.

The video continued and showed the car for sale sign as they drove out of the neighborhood. The conversation with the young housewife verified that Grayson had purchased a tan sedan that had been for sale.

Ignirtoq could be heard saying that Grayson would need to get some new camping gear because he had lost three sets during the chase. The next scene was in the camping outfitters and a discussion of the most nearby remote places to get deep in the forest. The old clerk took out a map and point out three different areas that he considered remote and hard to get into where the forest provided great cover.

The next three scenes were mini scenes of checking the roads into the three areas with cuts back to the map and showing where the roads went. One check panned on the entrance to a campground and then the road that went past it up the mountain to Matanuska Glacier State lookout point. Ignirtoq pointed to the car tracks and said that he bet that they would find Grayson when they went to where the road ended. The view of the snow covered surrounding with the green of the pines breaking the brilliant white of the snow reflecting the sun and the wind blowing the dry snow between the pine seemed to cast a spell that caused everyone to hold their breath.

Ignirtoq commented that he was going to continue taking pictures, but he was no longer going to talk because he knew that somewhere close ahead, he was sure that Grayson would be sitting in his tent or at a campfire. The camera caught Clay going from tree to tree and Ignirtoq doing the same.

Then the camera caught Grayson sitting in his tent, raising his rifle, and looking through the scope. The screen went blank, but the sound captured the sound of a bullet hitting something close to it and then the close at hand sound of a shot being fired. The sound of another rifle close to where Ignirtoq was located could be heard and then Clay shouting that he would provide cover, but he needed Ignirtoq to take Grayson out.

Ignirtoq could be heard saying he was going to take Trey's advice, step out, fire from the hip, and then fall to the ground and take the kill shot. The sequence was caught in sound and with Clay shouting that he would provide cover. Ignirtoq's two subsequent shots could be heard and then the camera came back on and Ignirtoq could be heard quietly saying that he thought that it had worked, and the shoulder wound didn't hurt too much.

After a moment, Ignirtoq stood up and the camera captured his slow, cautious walk toward the camp. Then Grayson's body was in the center of the screen, and a dark pool of blood could be seen in the snow.

The camera turned and took in the surrounding panoramic view. The next scene was of an approaching helicopter, its landing and the paramedics and police getting out of the helicopter.

Clay could be heard asking if Ignirtoq would be OK.

The camera seemed to change hands, and the scene was Ignirtoq being treated for a bullet wound in the shoulder and then getting air lifted out by helicopter.

The camera caught a flurry of police arriving up the trail.

Then it went blank and came on with the scene of Ignirtoq sitting in a hospital bed with Atiqtalik and Kaskae on each side of the bed.

Ignirtoq smiled and said that his lesson from Trey on how to take out the enemy had worked but Trey had failed to warn him that he could also get shot.

The video ended with, "The good guys won and lived happily ever after."

There were cheers from everyone listening and congratulations on effectively closing the case.

The Chief added if he got a copy of the video, he would not need a written closing report and added that he was now ready for the main barbeque course of Brats and Wursts.

The End of Northern Lights

End of Collection Two

Thank you for reading this far

Go to　　https://www.remwriter95.net/

For more of Ron Mueller's books

About the Author

Ronald E. Mueller

remwriter95@gmail.com

Ron grew up in what is now Flint River State Park in Southeast Iowa. The 170-year-old house Ron lived in is built into a hillside. It faces a 125-foot-high cliff towering over the little Flint River. The house and the land talked to him about; the passing of time, the struggle to conquer the land, the struggles people faced and the wonder of nature.

He climbed the cliffs, crawled into the caves, dove from the swimming rock, collected clams from the bottom of the pond, gigged and skinned frogs for their legs. He trapped muskrats for fur, hunted raccoon in the dead of night, and with only a stick hunted rabbits in the dead of winter.

His young life was outdoors, and nature tested him.

He walked to a one room stone schoolhouse uphill both ways. A stern but warm-hearted teacher, Mrs. Henry was instrumental in shaping his character as she shepherded him from the fourth to the eighth grade.

It was a great way to grow up.

Ron graduated from Burlington, High School, went to Vietnam in the Navy. He graduated from The University of South Florida with a master's degree in engineering, worked for thirty eight years for Procter and Gamble, traveled around the world thirty times.

He has remained happily married for more than fifty years. His daughter and his two sons are all successful and his three grandchildren have all graduated.

His wife has humored and supported him as he became a full time professional story teller.

His experiences inter-twined with snippets of fantasy lend themselves to the adventures he leads the reader through.

<u>Books and Stories by Ron Mueller</u>
<u>Fiction Series</u>
The Alex Evercrest Series
    The River Front
    The Girl on The Grill
    Missing
    Maggot
    Racist
    Votive Candles
    Windy City
    Country Road
    Pool of Blood
    Sins of the Daughter
    Body Parts
    The Skull Collector
    The Vanishing
    The Shadow Fighter
    Moonshine
    Grief's Trajectory
    The Magic Touch
    Nine Towers of Ku
    Abandoned
    Northern Lights
    New Direction
    A Family Affair
    Disruption
    The Saint Lebuinnus Church Murder
    Evercrest Collection One
    Evercrest Collection Two

<u>The Taelo Series</u>
Taelo: The Early Years
Taelo: The Golden Feather
Taelo: Journey of Discovery
Taelo: Dangerous Passage
Taelo: Condor Clan Slingers
Taelo: Circumvention
Taelo: The Journey of Sages
Taelo: Future Leaders Journey
Taelo: Collection

<u>A Taelo Story</u>
White Swan and Quiet Pheasant
The Child's Name
Floating Cloud
Quiet Rabbit
Busy Bee
Little Otter & Talking Wren
Broken Spear
Burley Bear & Meadow Flower

<u>Science Fiction</u>
The Savitar Series:
    Journey's End
    Savitar
    Confluence
    The Savitar Collection

Alex Evercrest Collection Two

Bram Nielson Series
  The Fold
  The Message
  Fold Wormhole
  Negative Fold
  Ripples in Time
  The Nielson Collection

Single Science Fiction Books
  Current Past and Future
  The Event
  The Door
  Viajante 7

A Brian Oneil Novel
  Hawaiian Phoenix
  Moon Curser
  Death Broker
  Brian O'Neil Collection

The Problem Solver Series
  Solutions
  Drug Lords
  Border Crosser
  The Problem Solver Collection

Imagination by Courtney Huynh and Chloe Parker

Characters in the Story

Alex	Cathy	Evercrest	Police Detective
Matthew	Timothy	Knolton	Alex's suitor
Rose-Anne	Germain	Evercrest	Alex's mother
Russel	Johnson	Evercrest	Alex's father
Helping Hands charity			Alex's nonprofit org
Trey		McGregor	Alex's Detective Partner
Lindsey		McGregor	Wife
Nolan		McGregor	Son
Johnnie		Smith	Old Viet Vet
Mary		Higgins	Johnnie's Phili "friend"
Bruce	Lincoln	Johnson	Cinci Chief of Detectives
Mary-Anne	Leslie	Johnson	Chiefs Wife
Bill	Hamilton	Danson	Detective
Travis	Bailey	Carter	Detective
Dr. Rogers			Coroner
Jane	Elousie	Stradford	Lieutenant Governor
Felix			proprietor at fishing dock
Golden Goose			Name of the Yacht
Sandra		Olson	Policewoman guard
Annie	Lorie	Scots	Missing girl
Linda		Annies	older daughter

Northern Lights

First	Middle	Last	Description
Lorie		Annies	second daughter
Harold		Zimmerman	Chicago DEA
James	Oscor	Kaizer	Sheriff of Wiggin
Abbie	Alisa	Bender	protect Alex married James
John	S.	Williams	Lawyer that was abused
Hanna		Waverly	John's mate
Angelica			Angel on the hill
Brian		Lexter	Cinci FBI Bureau Chief
Cais		Leu	Alex's Viet friend
Tracy		Hunter	Trey's Analyst

Body Parts

First	Middle	Last	Description
James		Westin	Surgeon -Plastic
Reston		San Clemente	Mafia head in Cincinnati
Dennis		Radly	Hit man
Sara		Laderly	Nurse - Fiancé to James
Zack			body parts worker
Brent			body parts worker
Joshua		Grant	Janitor
Luca		Bianchi	New bodyguard
Angelo		Ricci	New body handler
Dario		Rizzo	New body handler
Leyton		Riley	2nd dissection Dr.
Connie		Mandolin	Cleveland Chief's support
Samual		Jefferson	Black support in Cleveland
Michele		Sorento	LA Mafia boss
Daniela		Brickly	First victim of LA operation

Skull Collector

First	Middle	Last	Description
Levi	Aram	Misle	serial killer
Arthur		Milster	Sheriff
Reston		Sanclemente	Mafia head in Cincinnati
Dario		Rizzo	New body handler
Luca		Bianchi	New bodyguard
Angelo		Ricci	New body handler
Evin	Gerald	Williams	Sheriff of Loveland
Irene			Sheriff's wife
Jay		Heston	Chief of police in Cleveland
Heather		Preston	First victim
Linda		Preston	
Arnold		Preston	
Brian		Lexter	Cincinnati FBI Bureau Chief

The Vanishing

First	Middle	Last	Description
Lissa		Maliber	Mother of missing son
Jesse	T	Maliber	Lissa's son
April		Maliber	Lissa's Daughter
Rick			Bully Leader
Eli			Bully

Sylvester		Bully

The Shadow Fighter

Adriano		Chicago Mafia Boss
Lorenzo		Italian Sniper
Ray		Mafia gunmen
Baily		Mafia gunmen
Andy	Weller	IRS lawyer - Chicago
Lenord	Maxwell	Criminal lawyer - Chicago

Moonshine

Hillary		Moonshine queen
Crayton	Taylor	Moonshiner
Samuel		Dam Operator
Layton	Harris	Moonshiner who gets killed
Mrs. Lindi	Harris	
Stanley		West Virginia Sheriff
Dailey		
Talus		West Virginia State Police
Walter		US Marshall

Grief's Trajectory

Dale		Victim
Cynthia		Dale's Wife
Bobby		Dales Friend
Guy		Dales Friend and Killer

The Magic Touch

Chase	Thornfield	Dentist doing inferior implants
Amelia	Lockwood	Approves fact implant claims
Paul	Elsher	Supplier inferior implants & crov
Luna		Dental office supervisor
Ezera	Nightshade	Dental Hygienist recognizes scan
Dr. Mazerly		Previous owner of the practice
Zia		Dental Hygienist
Fiona		Dental Hygienist
Darcy	Barlowe	Patient that has a problem
Dr. Ava Whitlock		Dentist that Darcy second opinio
Jason	Gravely	Vindictive ex of Fiona
Joe	Brown	the Cincinnati region IRS leader
Randolf	Task	Texas IRS agent
Andy	Weller,	the Chicago IRS leader

The Nine Towers of Ku

Liam		CIA operative
Orson	Ambrose	Seattle captive
Sebastian	Cassidy	Seattle captive
Elisa	Amos	LA Captive
Mateo	Garcia	LA Captive
Thiago	Bandello	Sandiego Captive
Osvaldo	Comonte	Sandiego Captive

Riggs	Melville	Boston Captive
Rowan		Boston Captive
Ezekiel		New York Captive
Boaz		New York Captive
Dante	Cruz	Miami Captive
Kenji	Mochizuki	Miami Captive
Braylon	Corbyn	Chicago Captive
Mykel	Holmes	Chicago Captive
Zyair	Smith	St. Louis Captive
Lev	Gataki	St. Louis Captive
Ambrose		New Orleans Captive
Enzo	Beaufoy	New Orleans Captive
Jack	Ahearn	LA Leader Captive
Mylo		Miami Leader Captive
Harper	Bardin	New Orleans Leader Captive
Laticia		CIA Agent
Thermon		CIA Agent
Jason		CIA Agent

Abandoned

Bento	Carvalho	Father
Janaina	Carvalho	Mother
Aurea	Carvalho	Abandoned
Cristiano		
Fernanda	Carvalho	Grandmother
Lara		Woman Police officer Brazil
João		Male Police officer Brazil
Judge Kimberly	Nugent	

Northern Lights

Ignirtoq		Old Inuit who discovers some oil
Atiqtalik		Local Forest Ranger
Kaskae		Son of Ignirtoq
Grayson	Gagnon	Oil Thief
Myles	Walker	Buyer of the Oil
Clay		Bush Pilot
Reginald	Sailor	RCMP Chief
Delia	Tislen	RCMP field leader

https://www.remwriter95.net/

Published by: Around the World Publishing LLC.